DISNEY DESCENDANTS 2

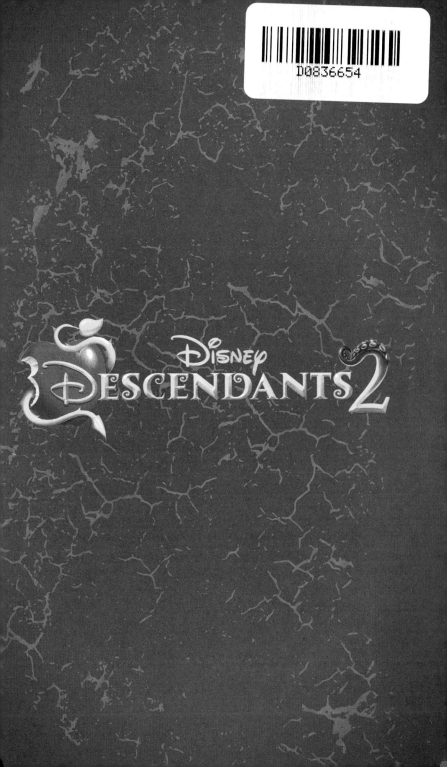

ALSO FROM JOE BOOKS

Disney Princess Comics Treasury
Disney Frozen Cinestory Comic
Disney Cinderella Cinestory Comic
Disney Descendants Wicked World Wish Granted Cinestory Comic
Disney Descendants Wicked World Cinestory Comic Volume Two
Disney Descendants Wicked World Cinestory Comic Volume Three
Disney Descendants Wicked World Cinestory Comic Volume Four
Disney Star vs the Forces of Evil Cinestory Comic
Disney Star vs the Forces of Evil: Deep Trouble Comics Collection
Disney Tangled Before Ever After Cinestory Comic
Disney Princess Comic Strips Collection Volume One
Disney Princess Comic Strips Collection Volume Two

CINESTORY COMIC

JOE BOOKS

Published simultaneously in the United States and Canada by Joe Books Ltd,
489 College Street, Suite 203, Toronto, ON M6G 1A5.

www.joebooks.com

First Joe Books edition: October 2017

Print ISBN: 978-1-77275-769-9

Joe Books™ is a trademark of Joe Books Ltd. Joe Books® and the
Joe Books logo are trademarks of Joe Books Ltd, registered in
various categories and countries. All rights reserved.

Library and Archives Canada Cataloguing in Publication
information is available upon request.

Printed and bound in Canada
1 3 5 7 9 10 8 6 4 2

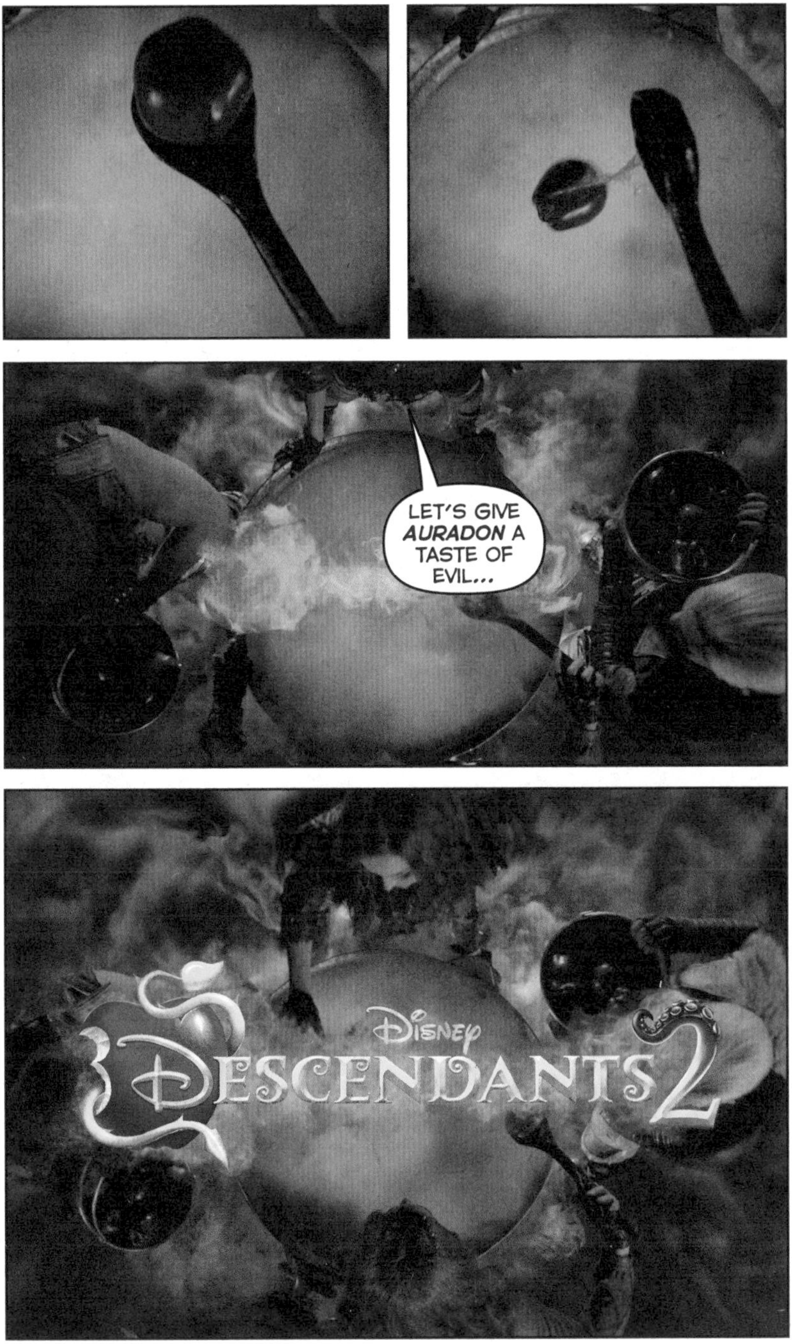
LET'S GIVE AURADON A TASTE OF EVIL...
DISNEY
DESCENDANTS 2

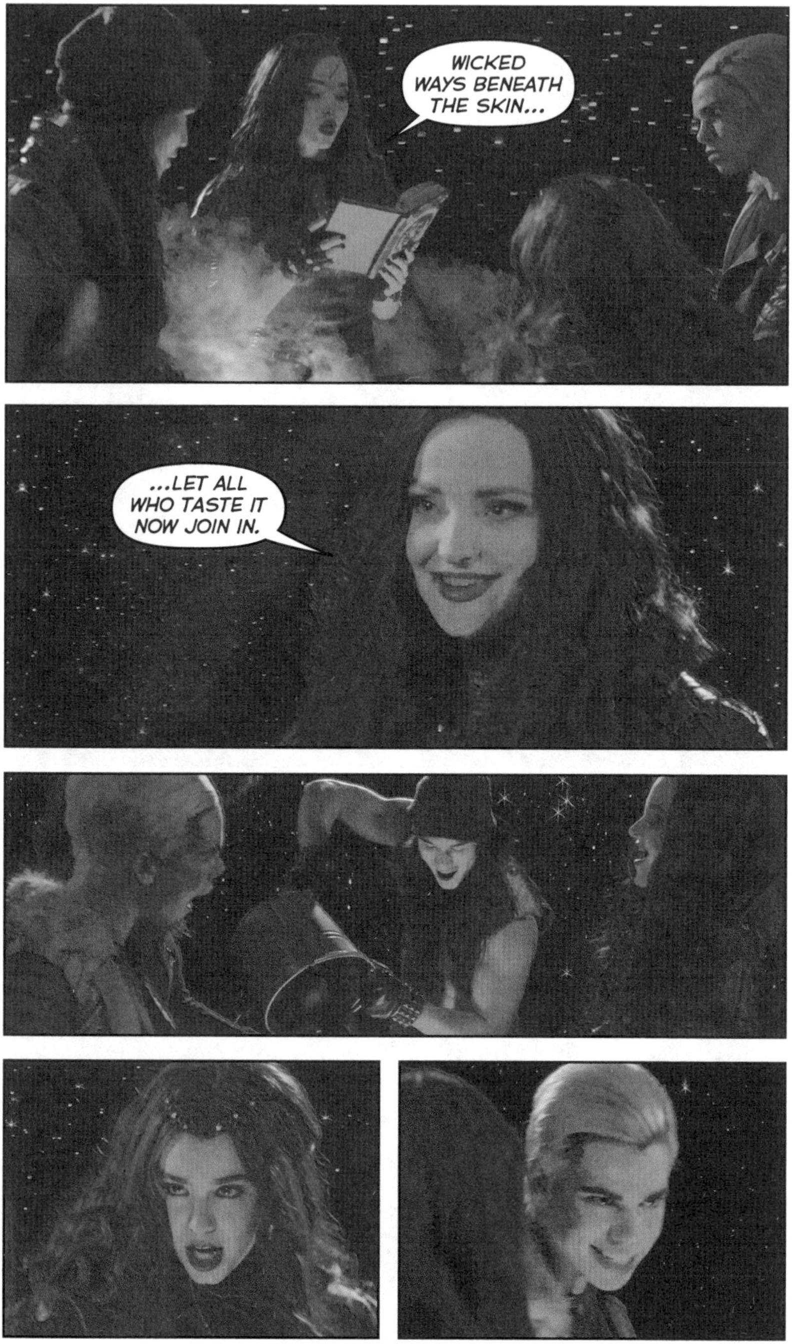
WICKED WAYS BENEATH THE SKIN...
...LET ALL WHO TASTE IT NOW JOIN IN.

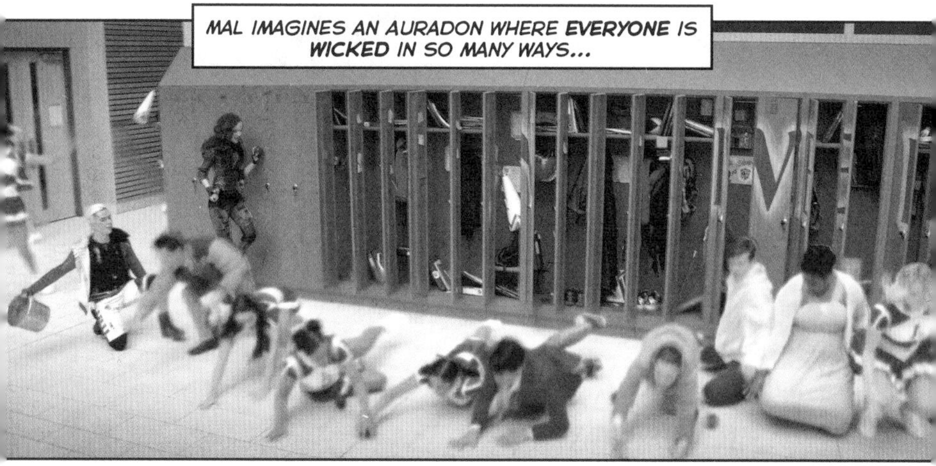
MAL IMAGINES AN AURADON WHERE **EVERYONE** IS **WICKED** IN SO MANY WAYS...

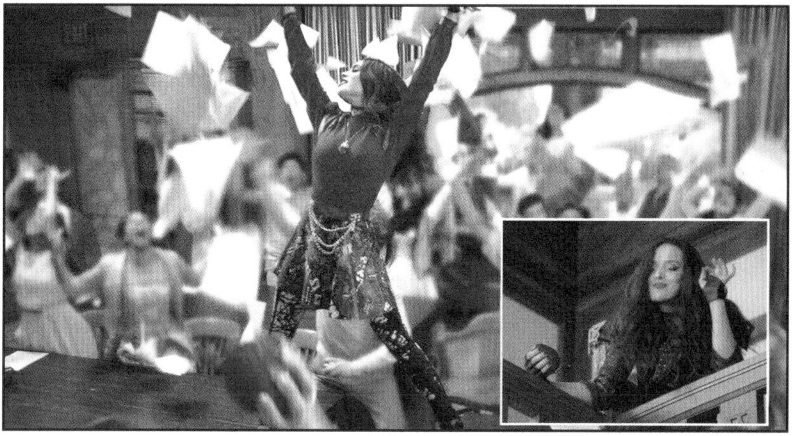

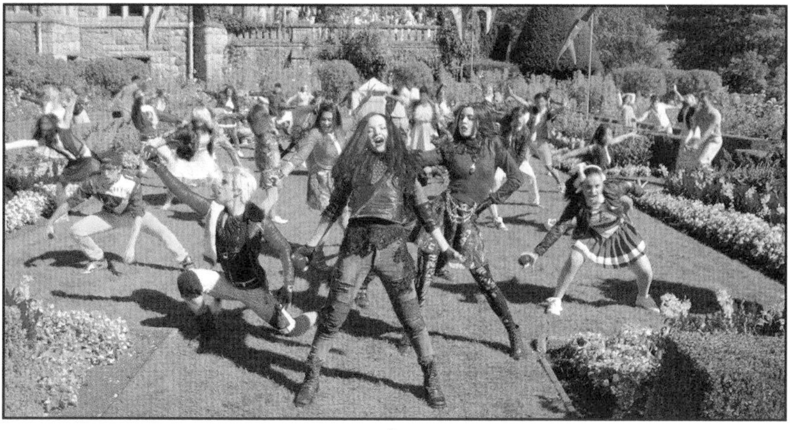

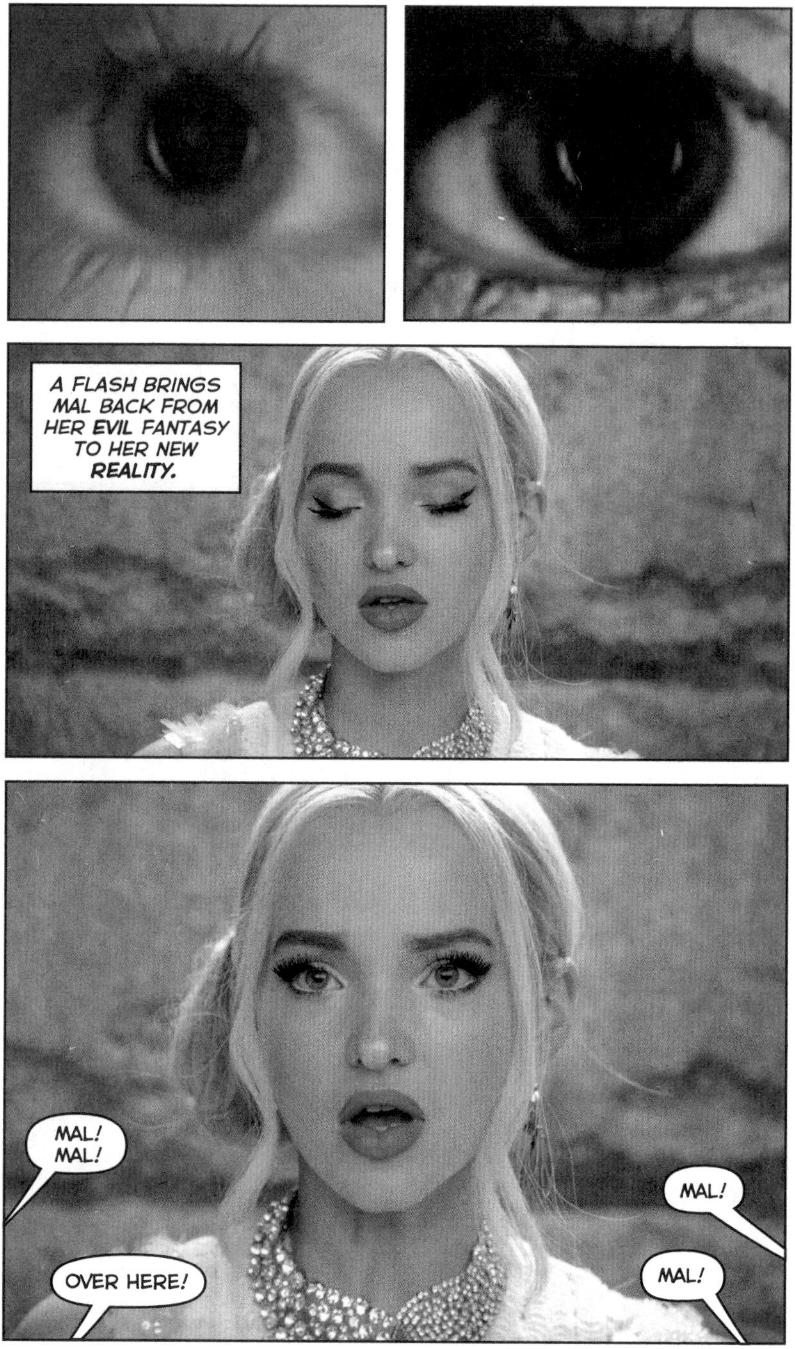
A FLASH BRINGS MAL BACK FROM HER EVIL FANTASY TO HER NEW REALITY.
MAL! MAL!
OVER HERE!
MAL!
MAL!

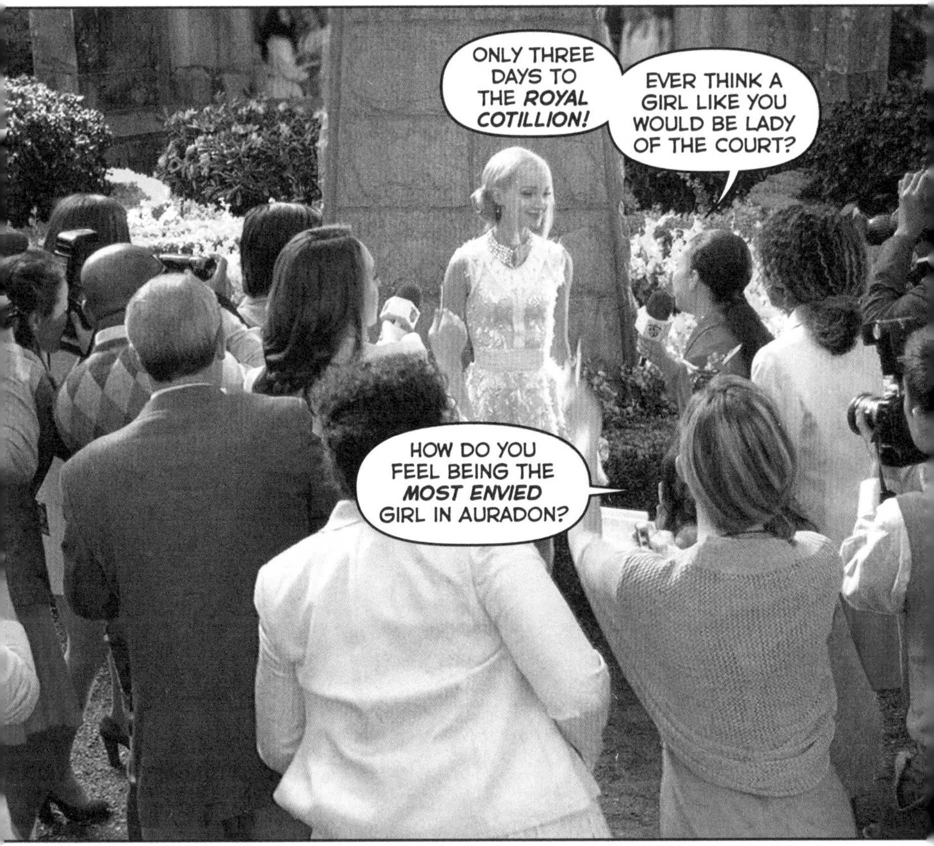
ONLY THREE DAYS TO THE *ROYAL COTILLION!*
EVER THINK A GIRL LIKE YOU WOULD BE LADY OF THE COURT?
HOW DO YOU FEEL BEING THE *MOST ENVIED* GIRL IN AURADON?

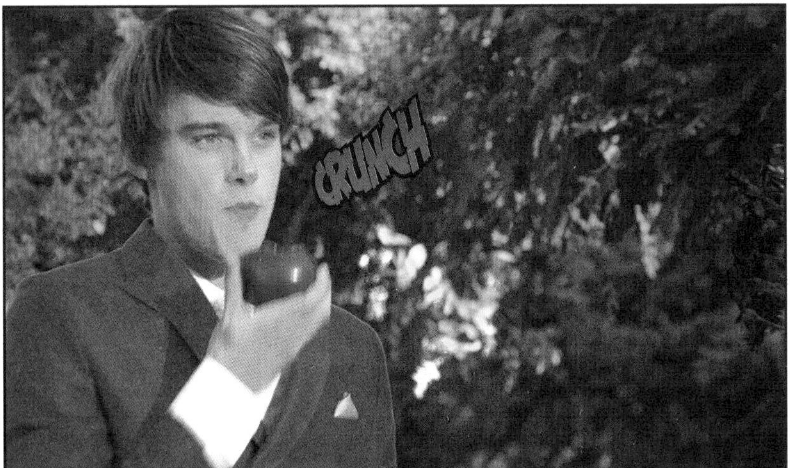
CRUNCH

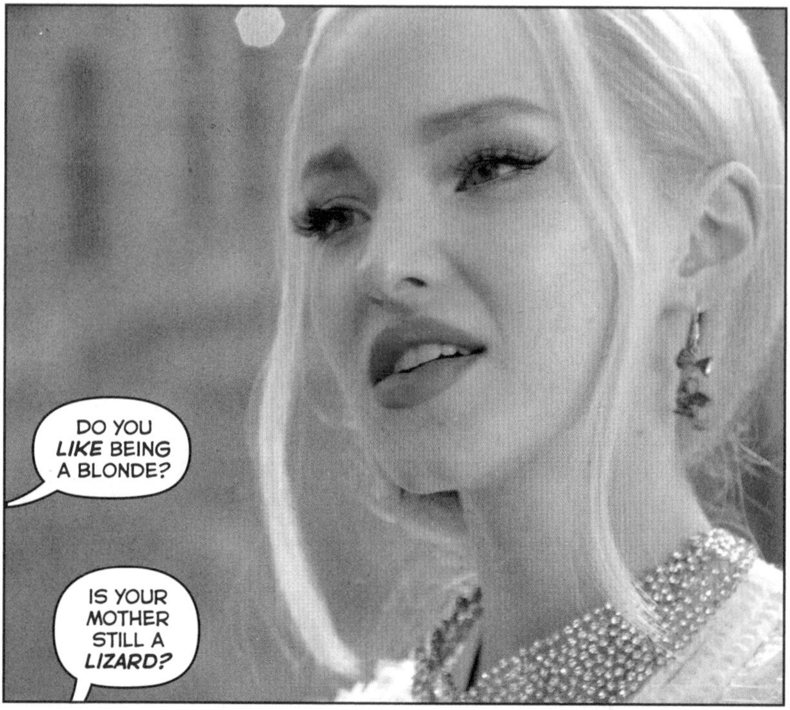
DO YOU *LIKE* BEING A BLONDE?
IS YOUR MOTHER STILL A *LIZARD?*

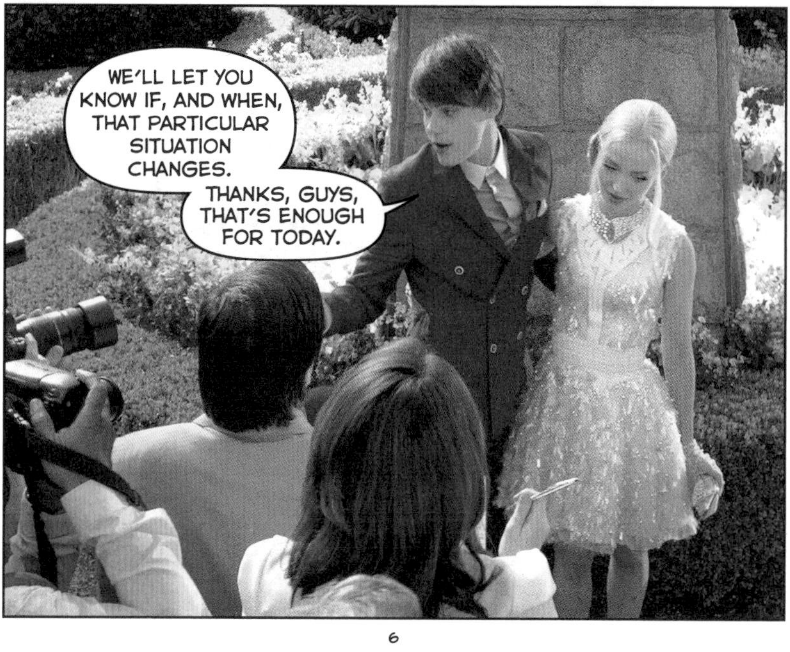
WE'LL LET YOU KNOW IF, AND WHEN, THAT PARTICULAR SITUATION CHANGES.
THANKS, GUYS, THAT'S ENOUGH FOR TODAY.

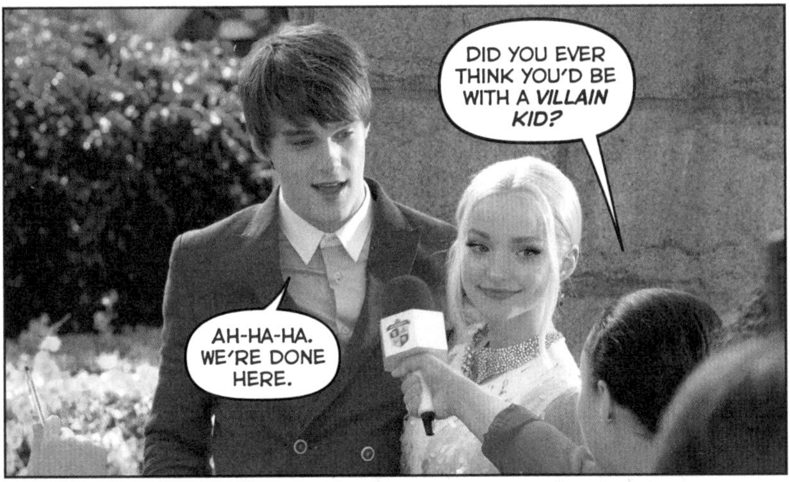
DID YOU EVER THINK YOU'D BE WITH A VILLAIN KID?
AH-HA-HA. WE'RE DONE HERE.

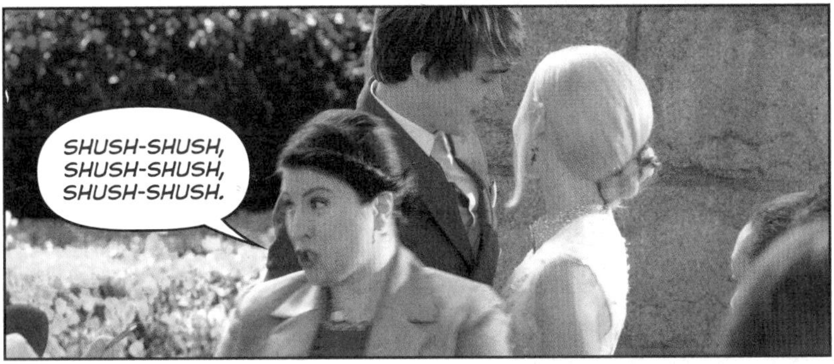
SHUSH-SHUSH, SHUSH-SHUSH, SHUSH-SHUSH.

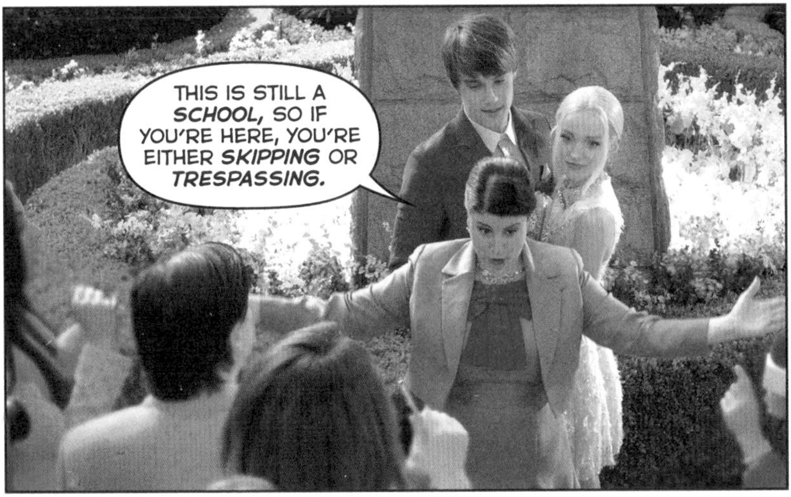
THIS IS STILL A SCHOOL, SO IF YOU'RE HERE, YOU'RE EITHER SKIPPING OR TRESPASSING.

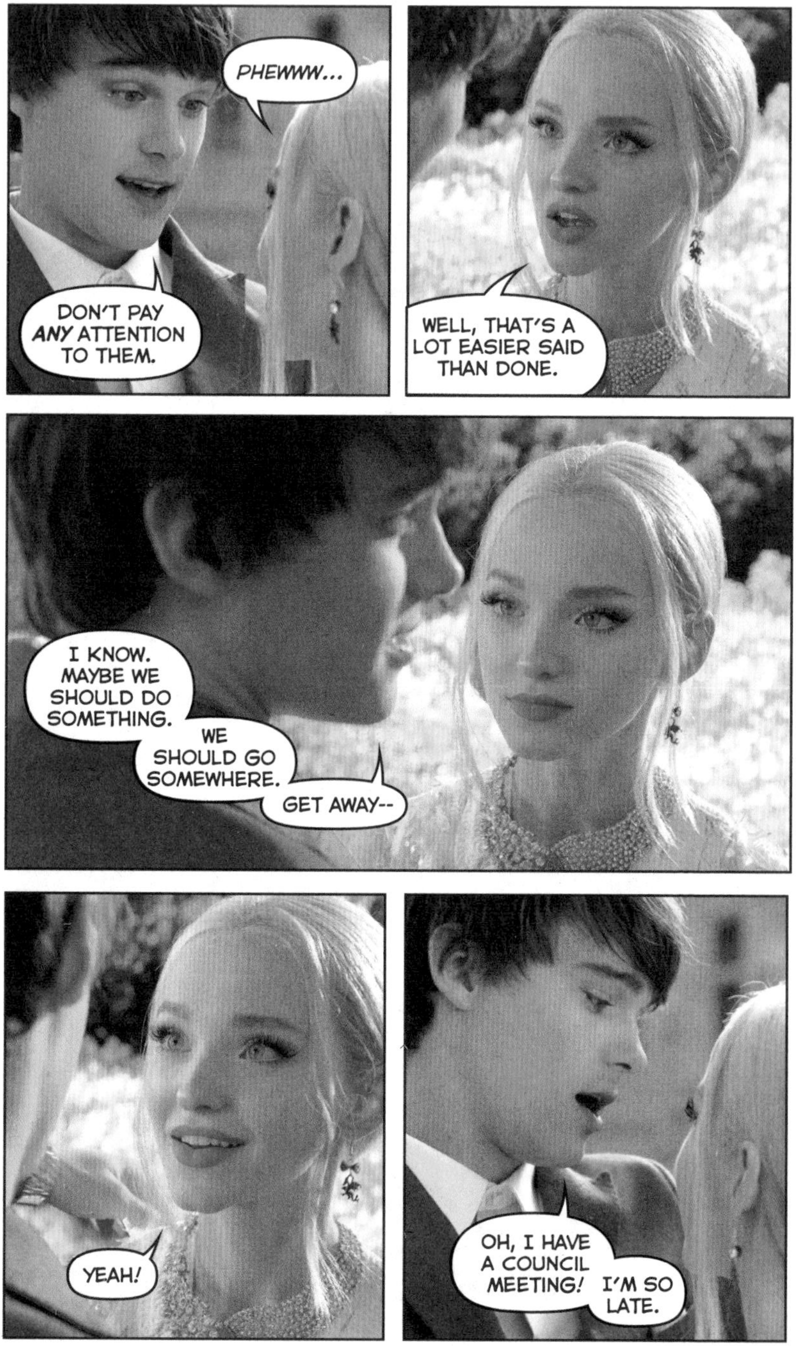
PHEWWW...
DON'T PAY *ANY* ATTENTION TO THEM.
WELL, THAT'S A LOT EASIER SAID THAN DONE.
I KNOW. MAYBE WE SHOULD DO SOMETHING.
WE SHOULD GO SOMEWHERE.
GET AWAY--
YEAH!
OH, I HAVE A COUNCIL MEETING!
I'M SO LATE.

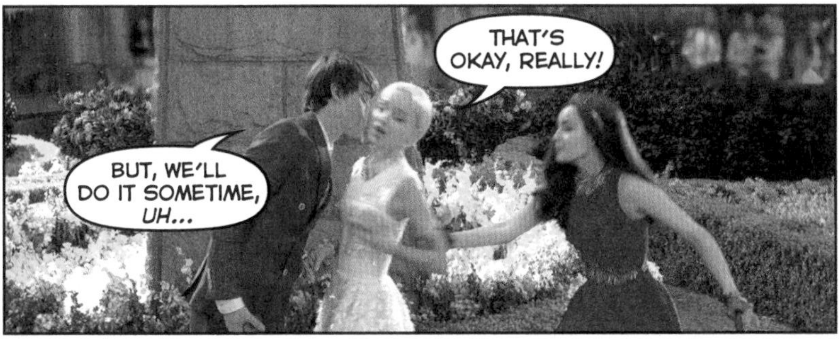
THAT'S OKAY, REALLY!
BUT, WE'LL DO IT SOMETIME, *UH...*

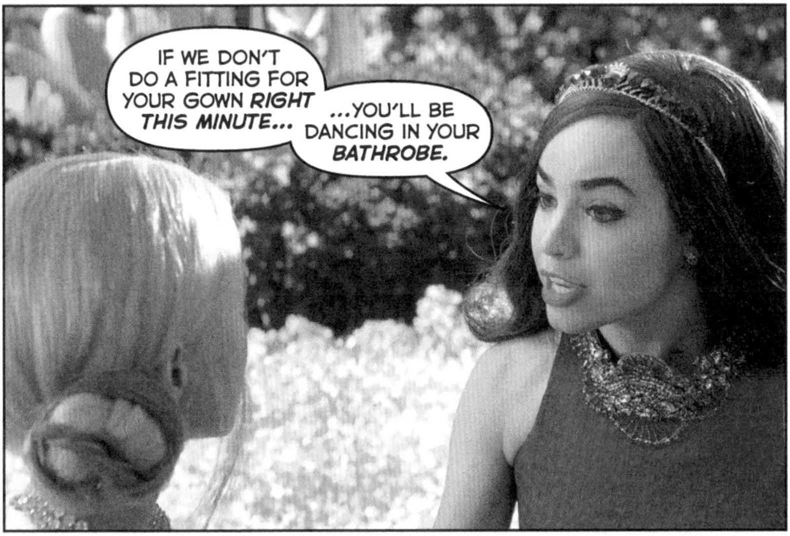
IF WE DON'T DO A FITTING FOR YOUR GOWN ***RIGHT THIS MINUTE...***
...YOU'LL BE DANCING IN YOUR ***BATHROBE.***

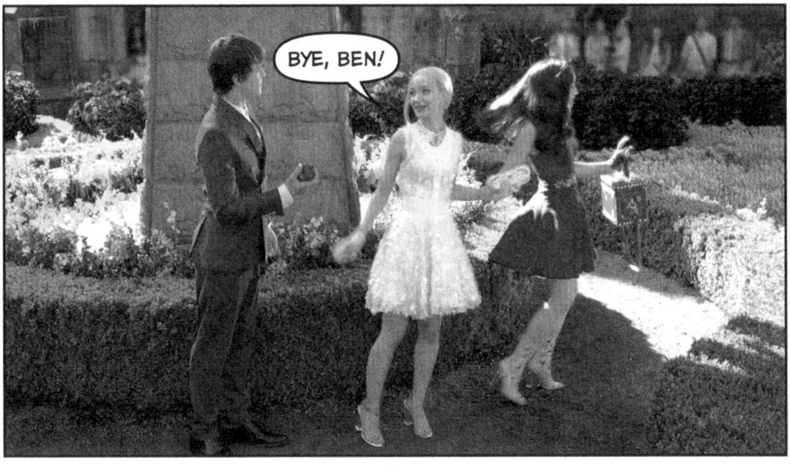
BYE, BEN!

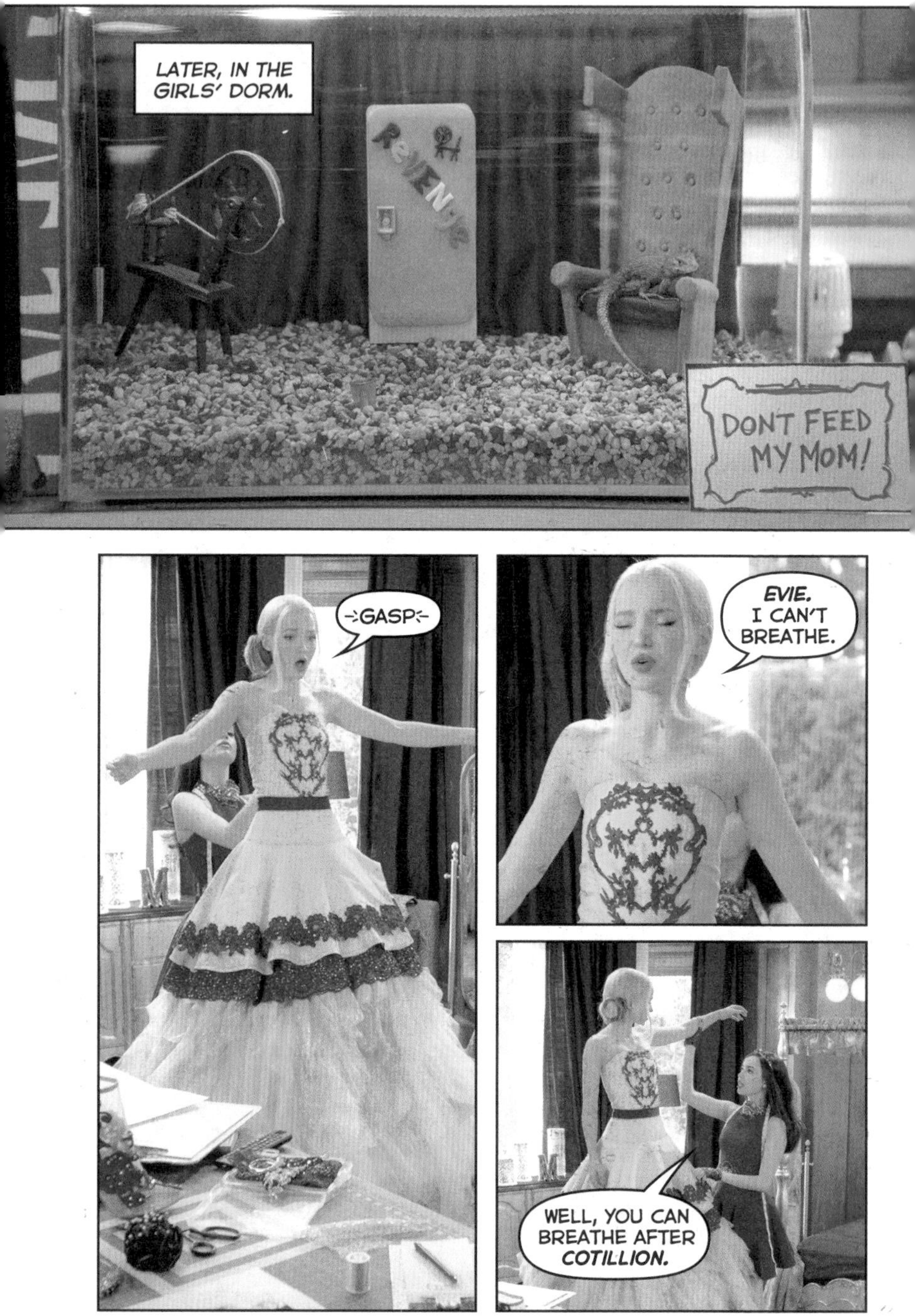
LATER, IN THE GIRLS' DORM.
DONT FEED MY MOM!
-GASP-
EVIE. I CAN'T BREATHE.
WELL, YOU CAN BREATHE AFTER COTILLION.

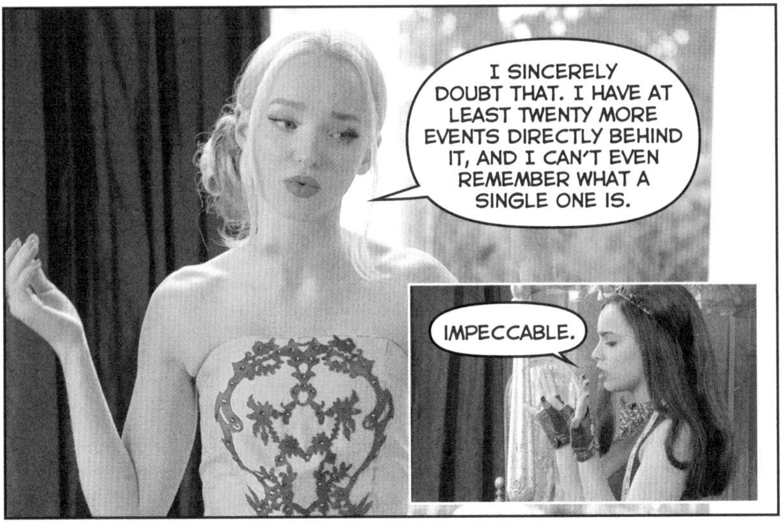
I SINCERELY DOUBT THAT. I HAVE AT LEAST TWENTY MORE EVENTS DIRECTLY BEHIND IT, AND I CAN'T EVEN REMEMBER WHAT A SINGLE ONE IS.
IMPECCABLE.

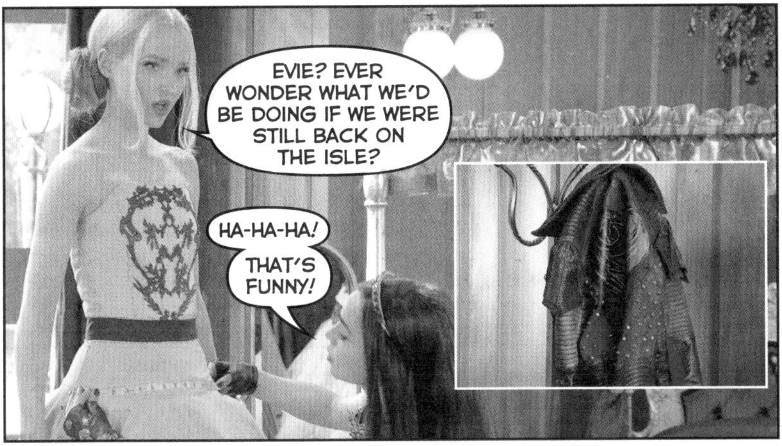
EVIE? EVER WONDER WHAT WE'D BE DOING IF WE WERE STILL BACK ON THE ISLE?
HA-HA-HA!
THAT'S FUNNY!

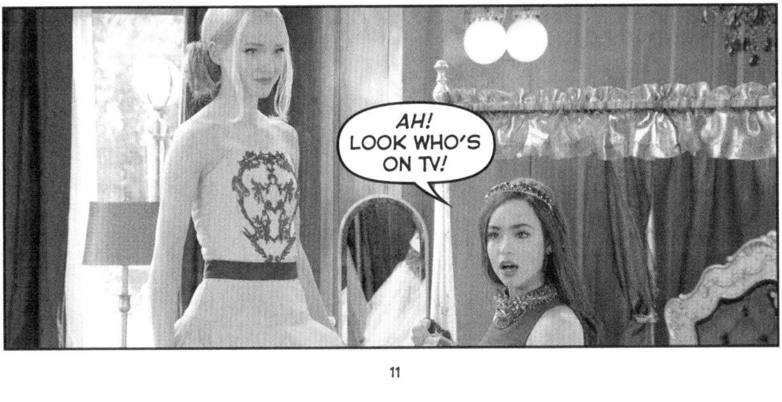
AH! LOOK WHO'S ON TV!

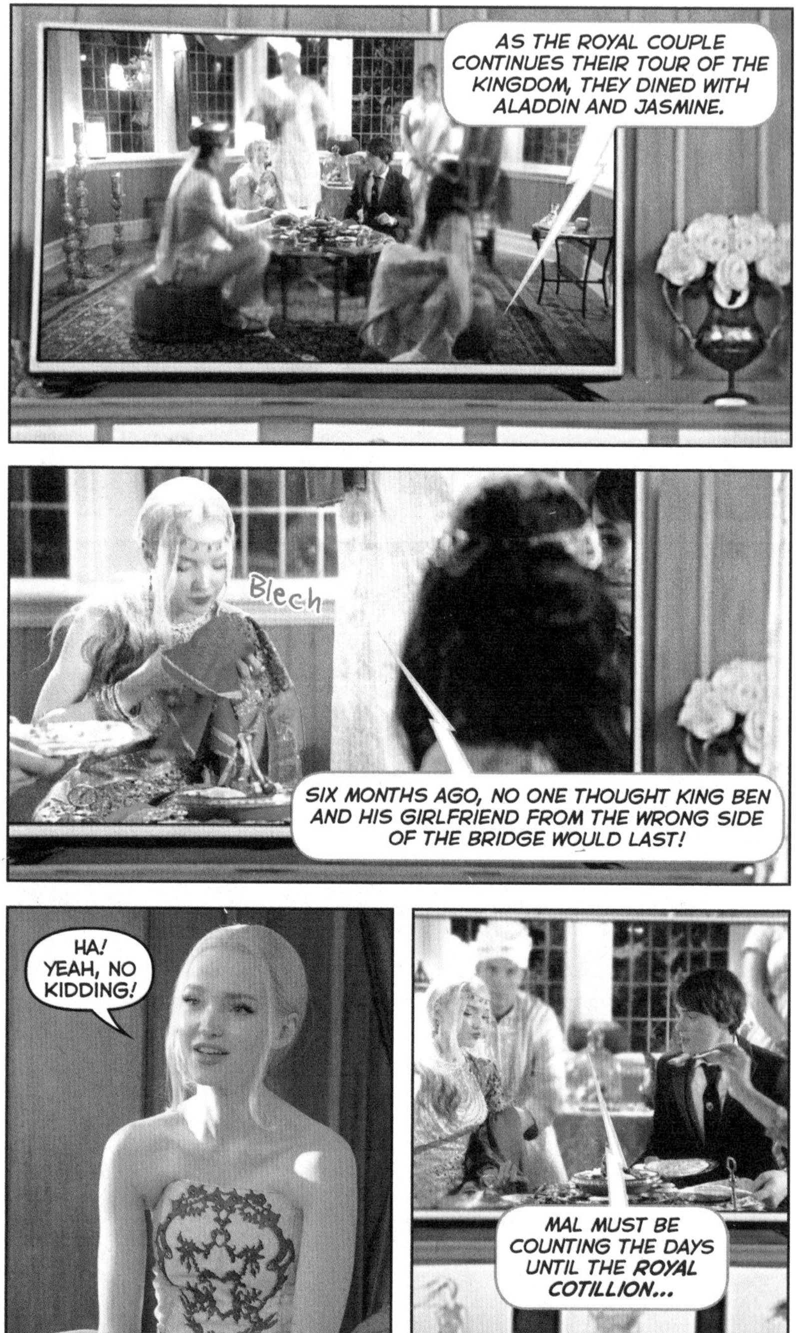
AS THE ROYAL COUPLE CONTINUES THEIR TOUR OF THE KINGDOM, THEY DINED WITH ALADDIN AND JASMINE.
Blech
SIX MONTHS AGO, NO ONE THOUGHT KING BEN AND HIS GIRLFRIEND FROM THE WRONG SIDE OF THE BRIDGE WOULD LAST!
HA! YEAH, NO KIDDING!
MAL MUST BE COUNTING THE DAYS UNTIL THE ROYAL COTILLION...

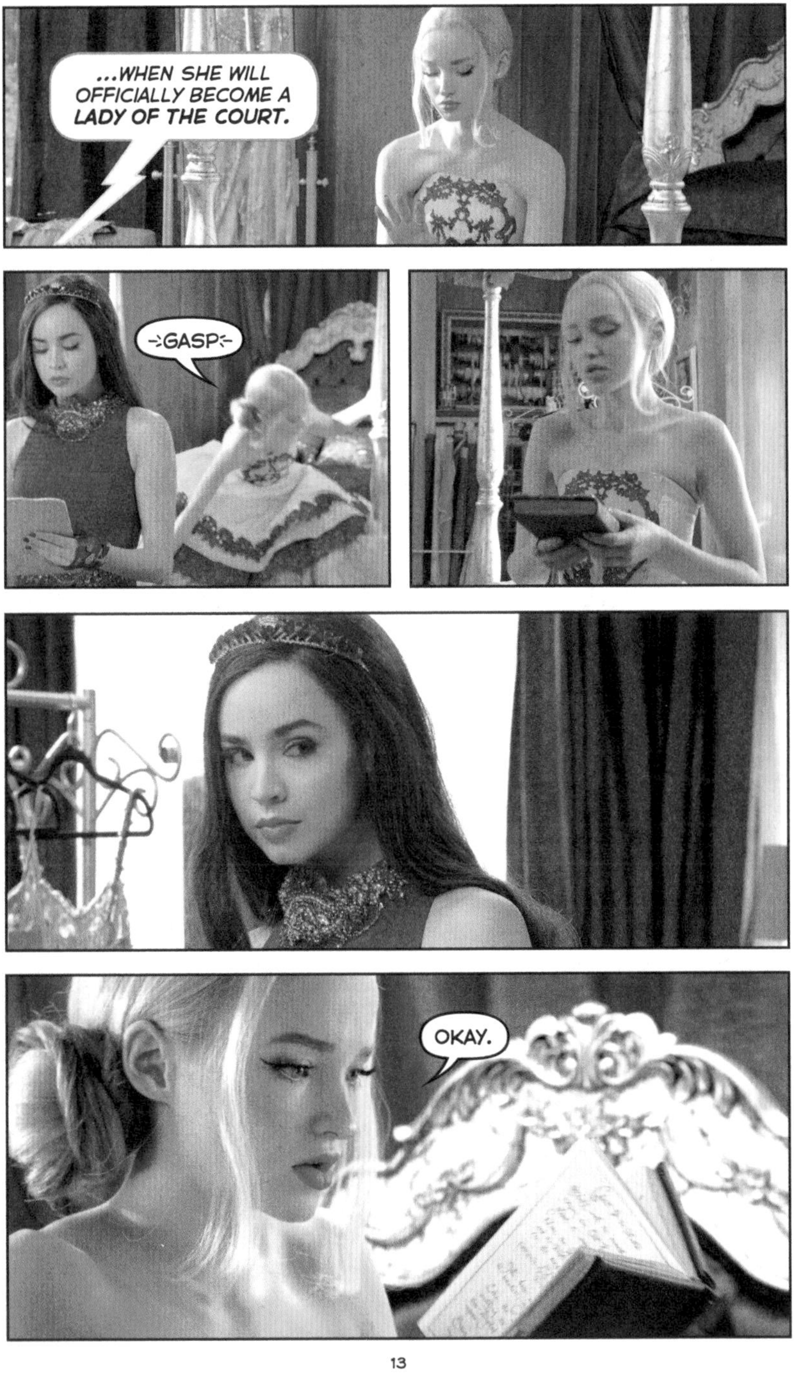
...WHEN SHE WILL OFFICIALLY BECOME A LADY OF THE COURT.
-GASP-
OKAY.

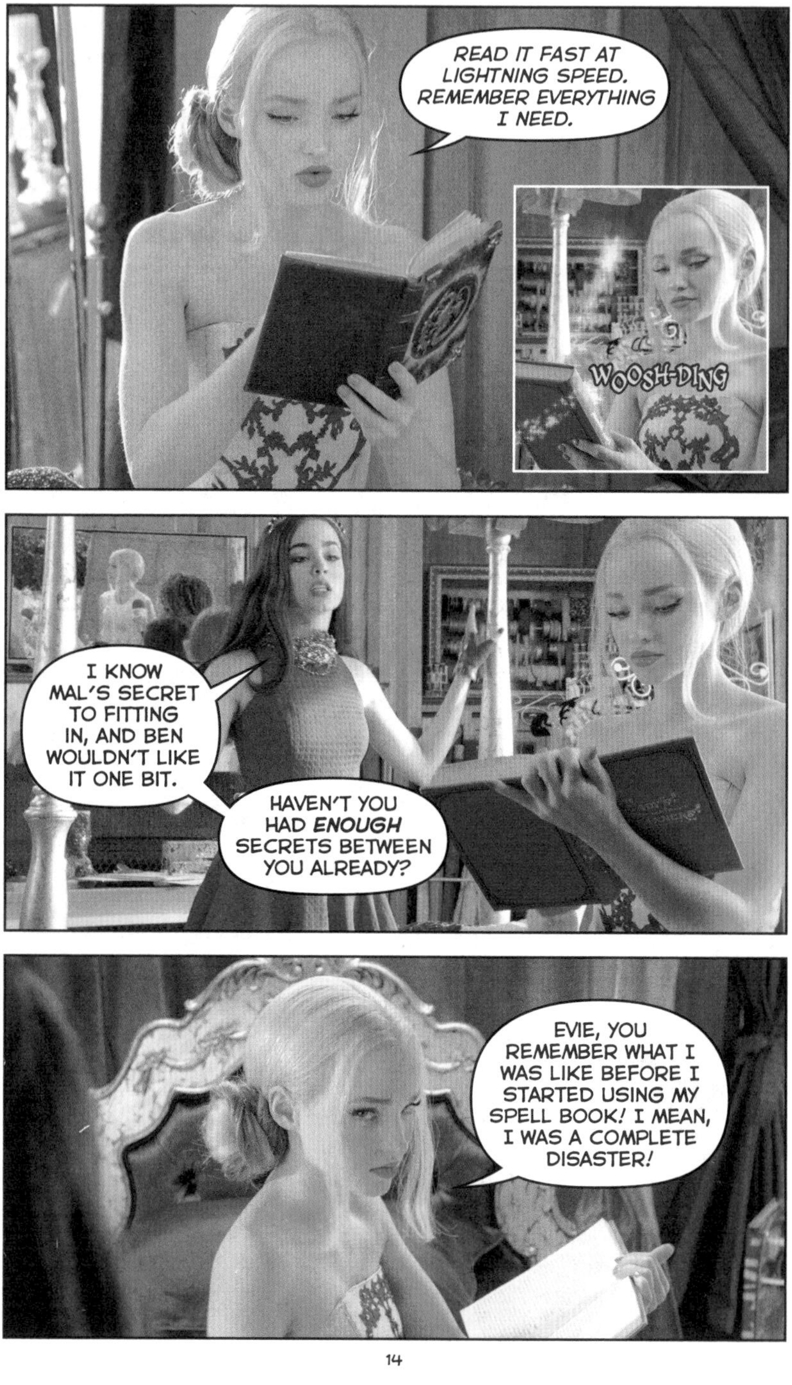
READ IT FAST AT LIGHTNING SPEED. REMEMBER EVERYTHING I NEED.
WOOSH-DING
I KNOW MAL'S SECRET TO FITTING IN, AND BEN WOULDN'T LIKE IT ONE BIT.
HAVEN'T YOU HAD ENOUGH SECRETS BETWEEN YOU ALREADY?
EVIE, YOU REMEMBER WHAT I WAS LIKE BEFORE I STARTED USING MY SPELL BOOK! I MEAN, I WAS A COMPLETE DISASTER!

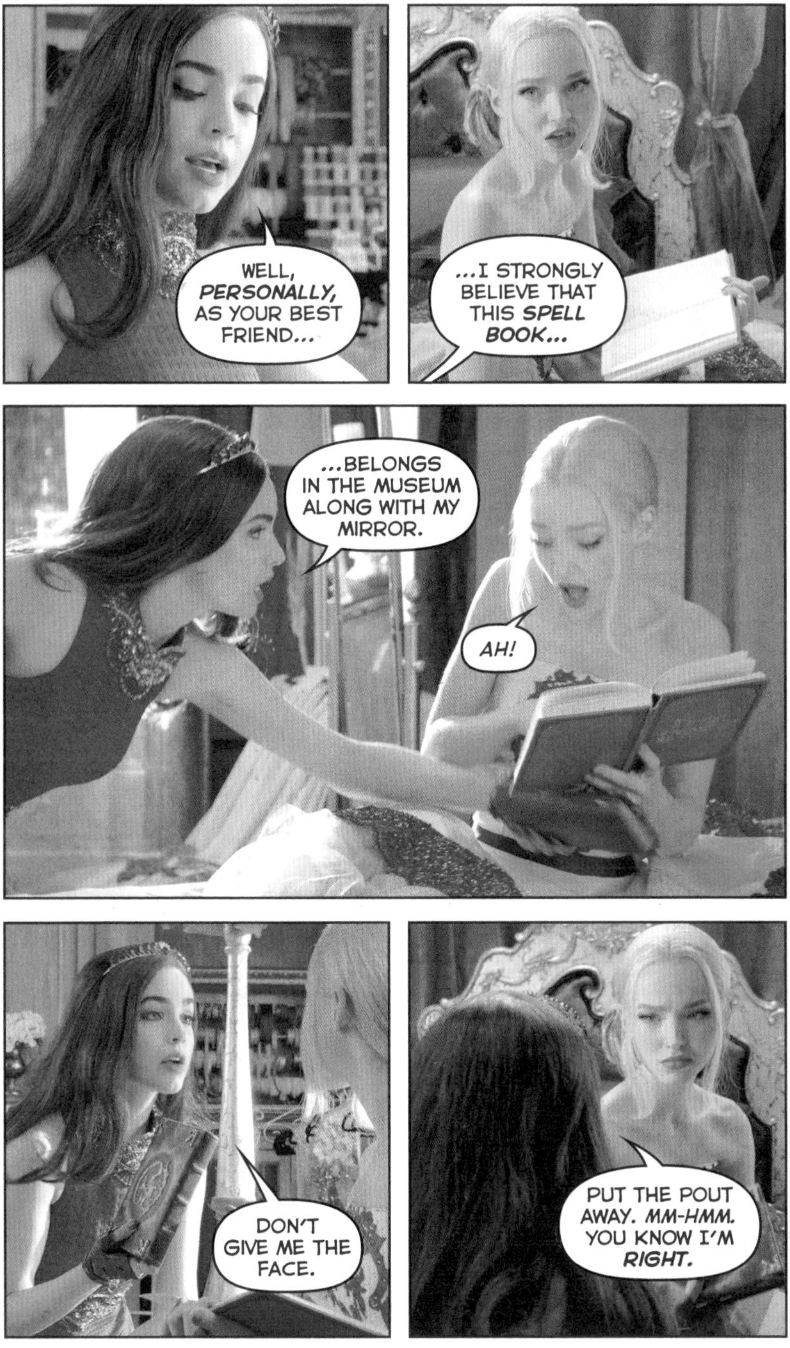
WELL, PERSONALLY, AS YOUR BEST FRIEND...
...I STRONGLY BELIEVE THAT THIS SPELL BOOK...
...BELONGS IN THE MUSEUM ALONG WITH MY MIRROR.
AH!
DON'T GIVE ME THE FACE.
PUT THE POUT AWAY. MM-HMM. YOU KNOW I'M RIGHT.

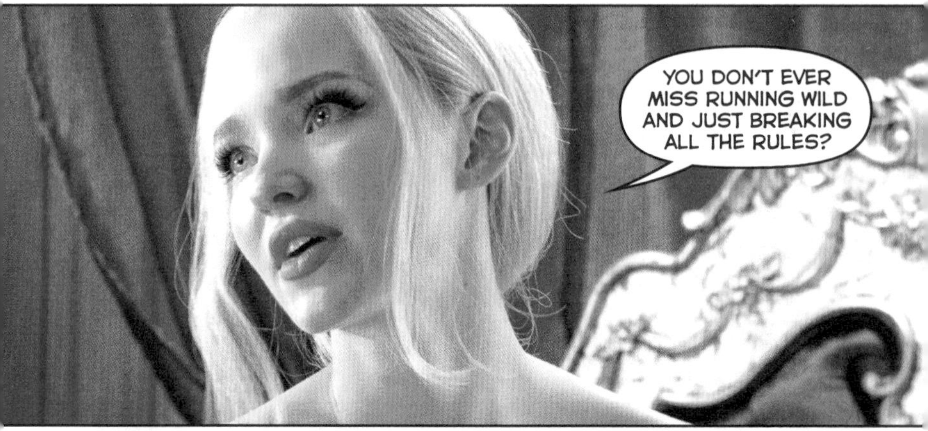
YOU DON'T EVER MISS RUNNING WILD AND JUST BREAKING ALL THE RULES?

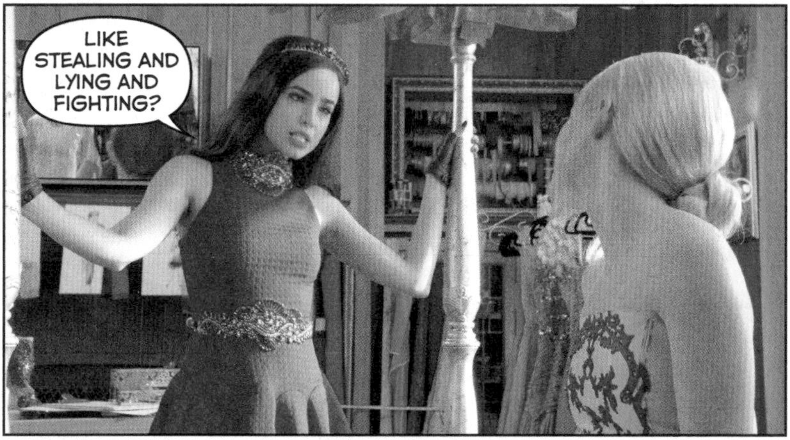
LIKE STEALING AND LYING AND FIGHTING?

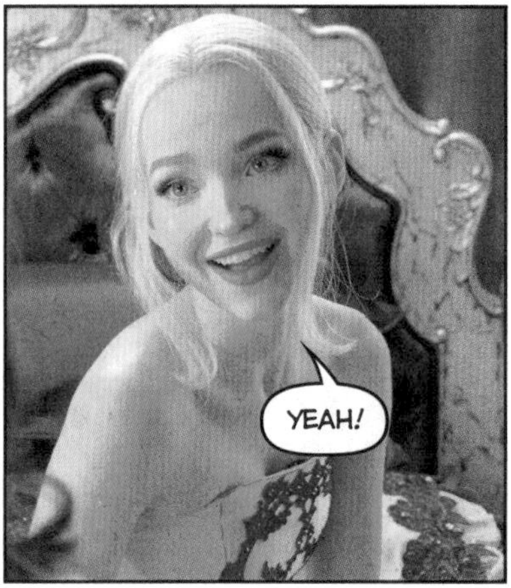
YEAH!

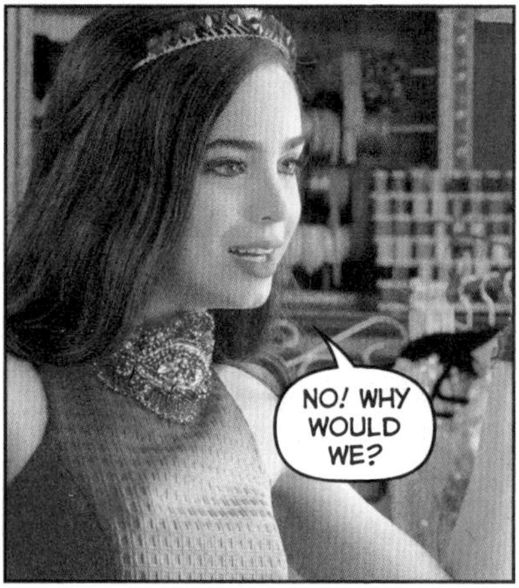
NO! WHY WOULD WE?

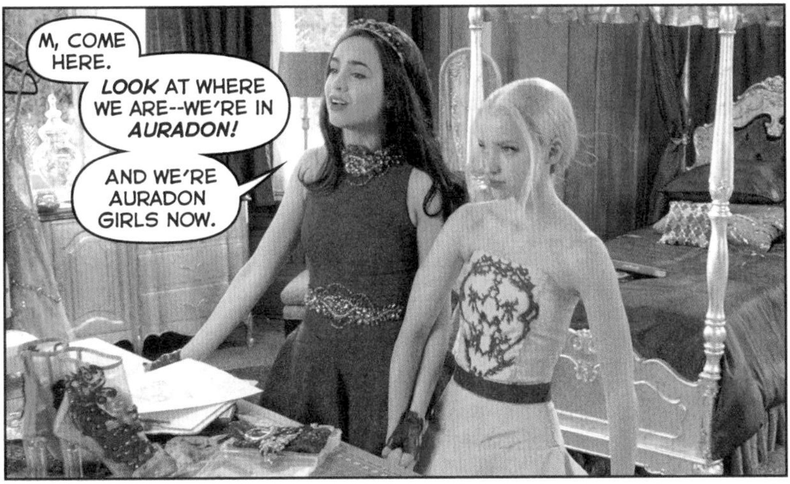
M, COME HERE.
LOOK AT WHERE WE ARE--WE'RE IN AURADON!
AND WE'RE AURADON GIRLS NOW.

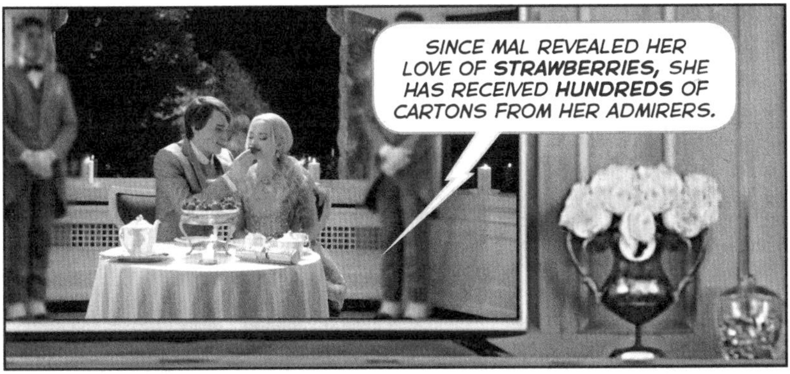
SINCE MAL REVEALED HER LOVE OF STRAWBERRIES, SHE HAS RECEIVED HUNDREDS OF CARTONS FROM HER ADMIRERS.

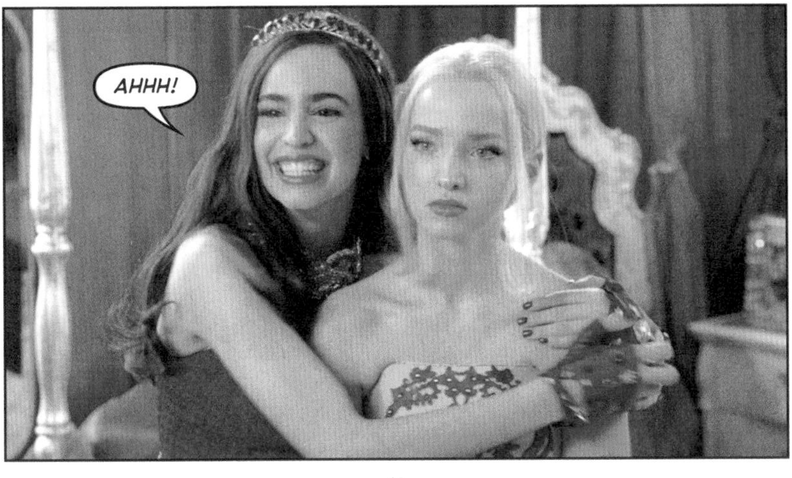
AHHH!

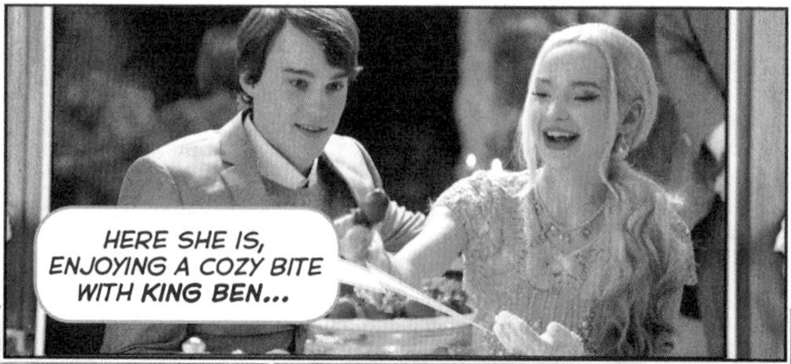
HERE SHE IS, ENJOYING A COZY BITE WITH KING BEN...

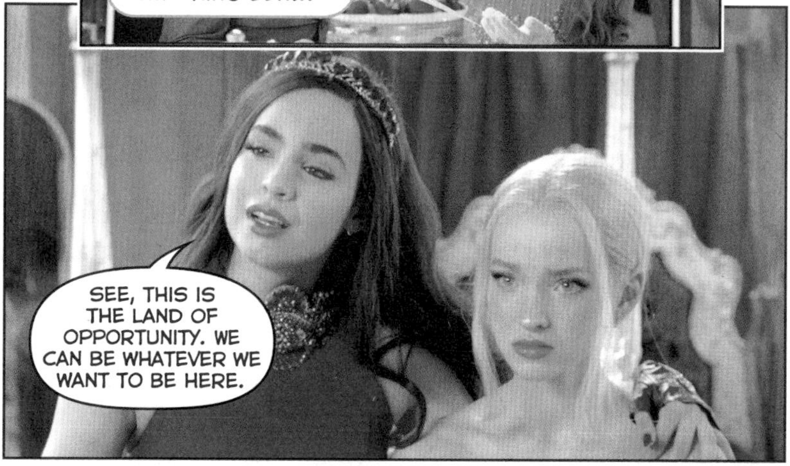
SEE, THIS IS THE LAND OF OPPORTUNITY. WE CAN BE WHATEVER WE WANT TO BE HERE.

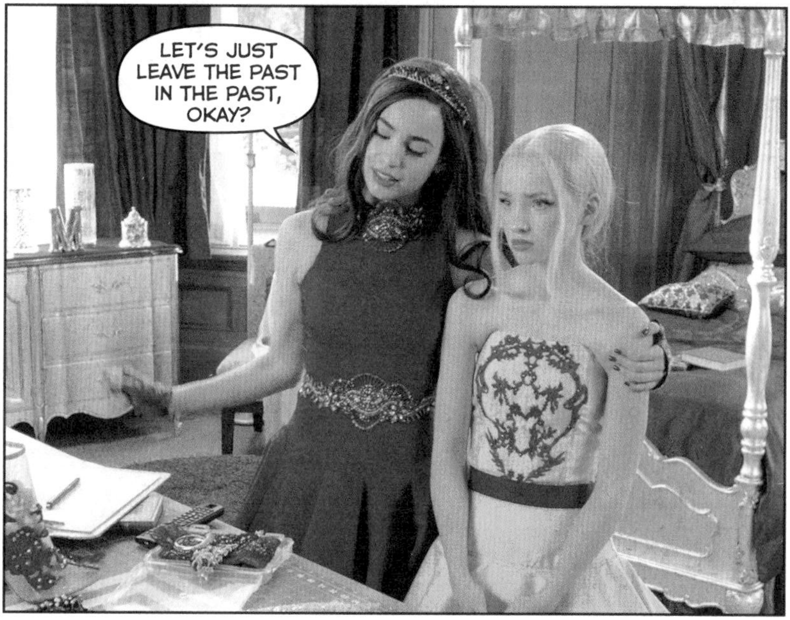
LET'S JUST LEAVE THE PAST IN THE PAST, OKAY?

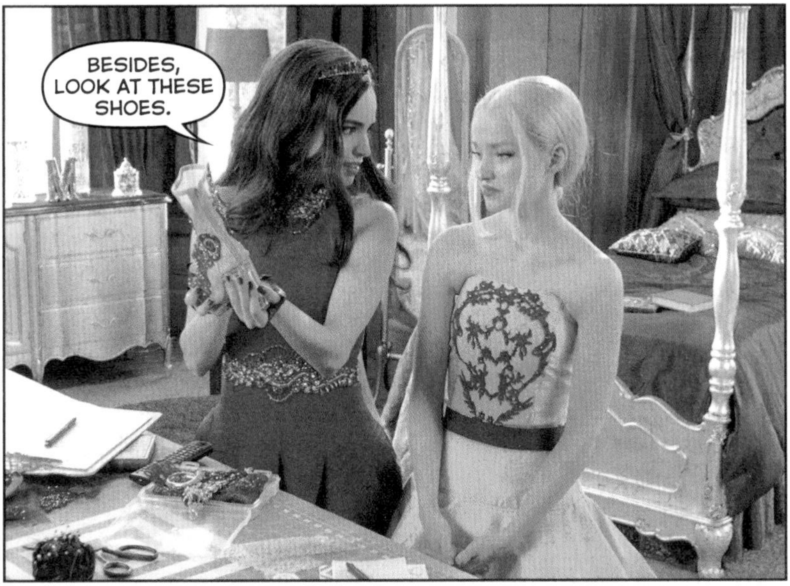
BESIDES, LOOK AT THESE SHOES.

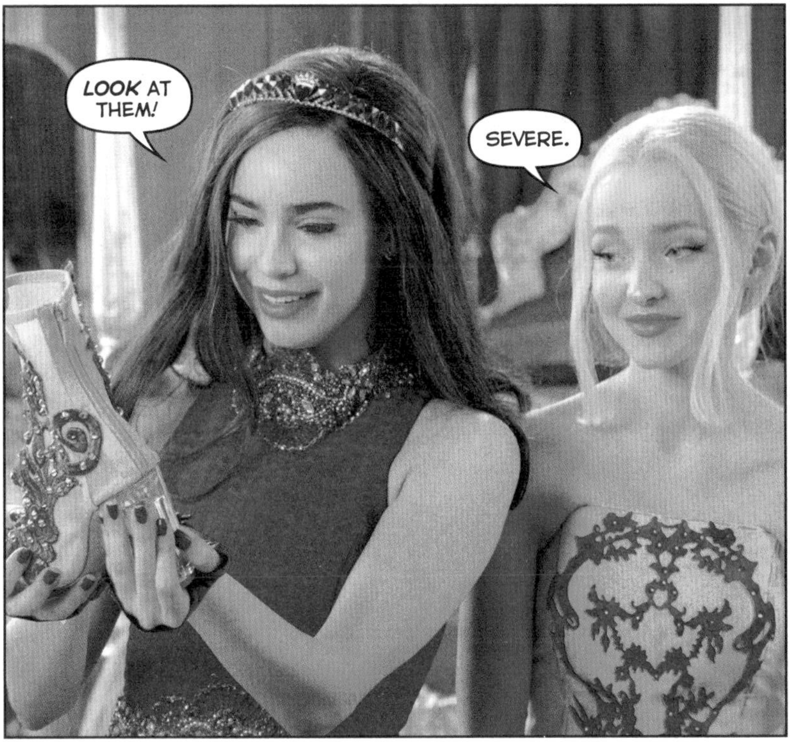
LOOK AT THEM!
SEVERE.

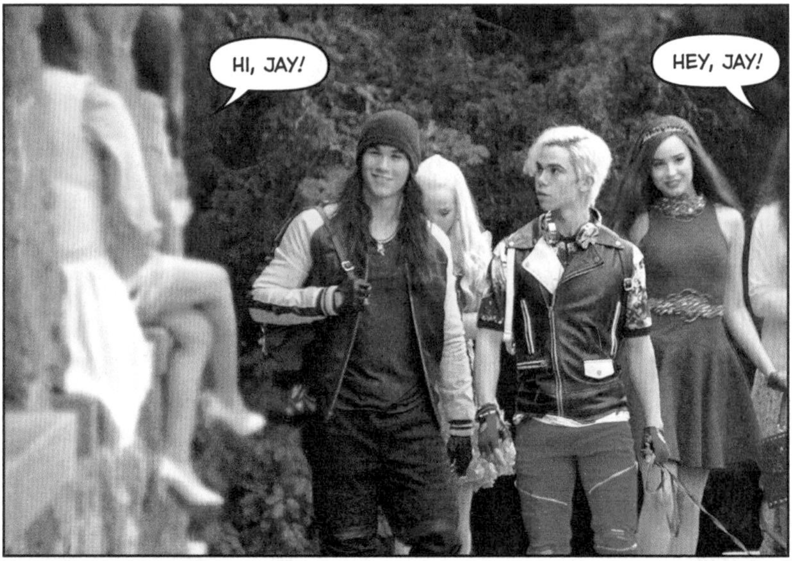
HI, JAY!
HEY, JAY!

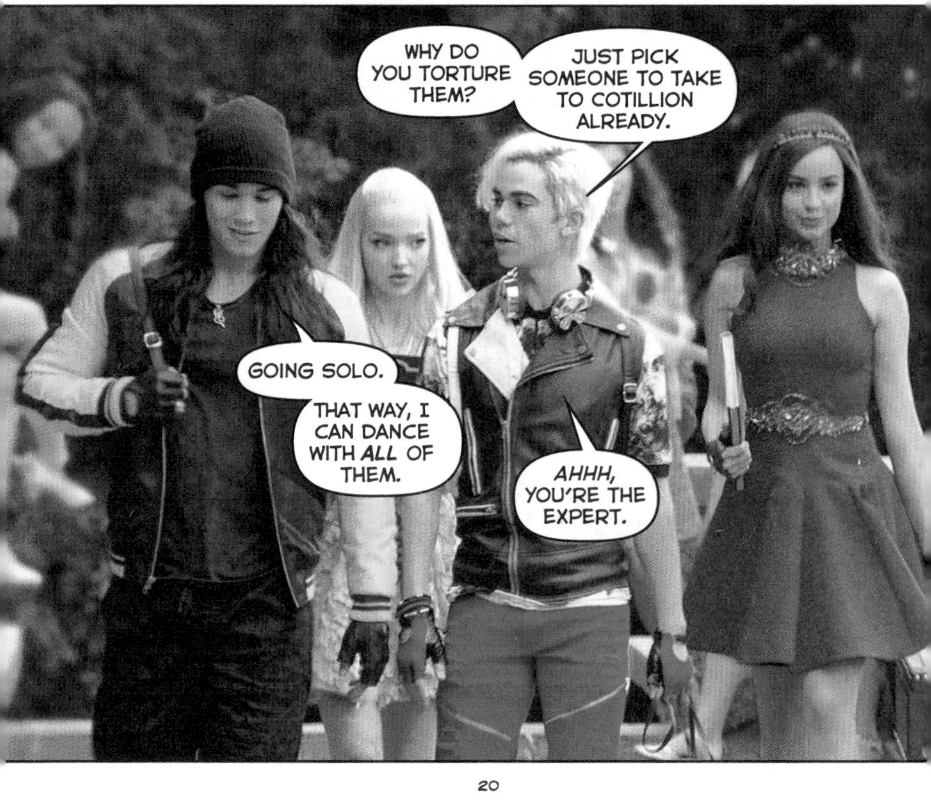
WHY DO YOU TORTURE THEM?
JUST PICK SOMEONE TO TAKE TO COTILLION ALREADY.
GOING SOLO.
THAT WAY, I CAN DANCE WITH *ALL* OF THEM.
AHHH, YOU'RE THE EXPERT.

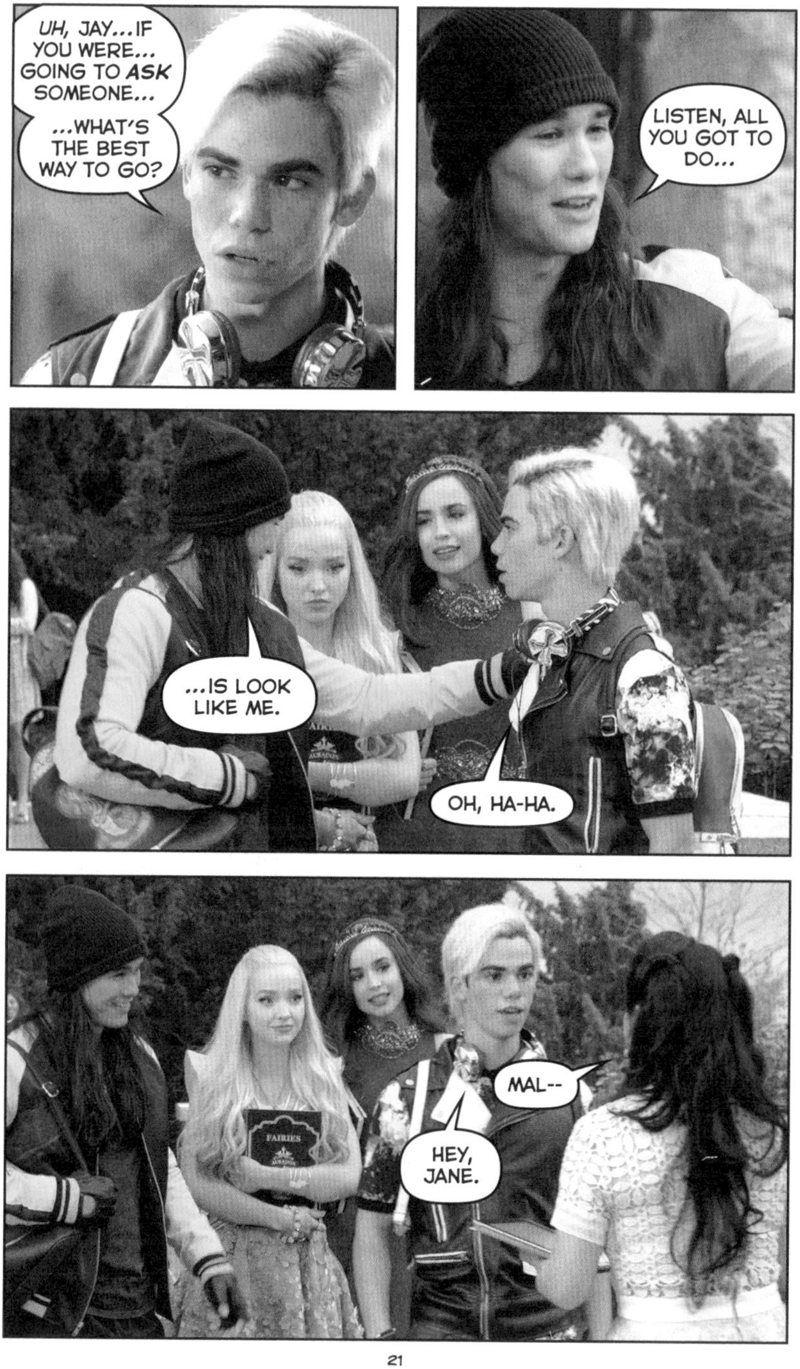
UH, JAY...IF YOU WERE... GOING TO ASK SOMEONE...
...WHAT'S THE BEST WAY TO GO?
LISTEN, ALL YOU GOT TO DO...
...IS LOOK LIKE ME.
OH, HA-HA.
MAL--
HEY, JANE.

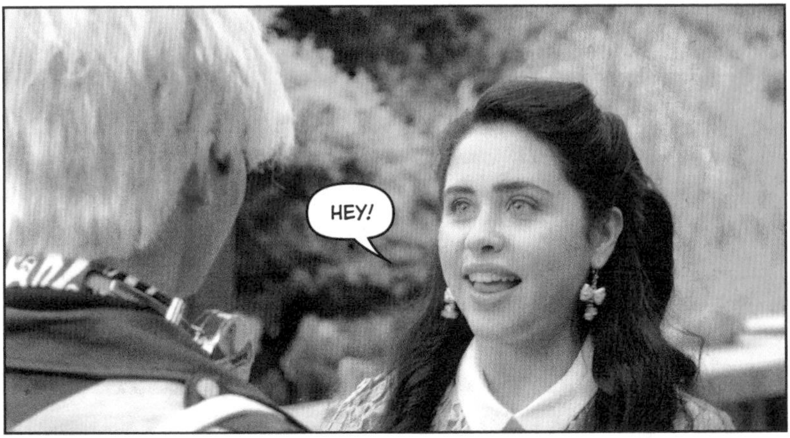
HEY!

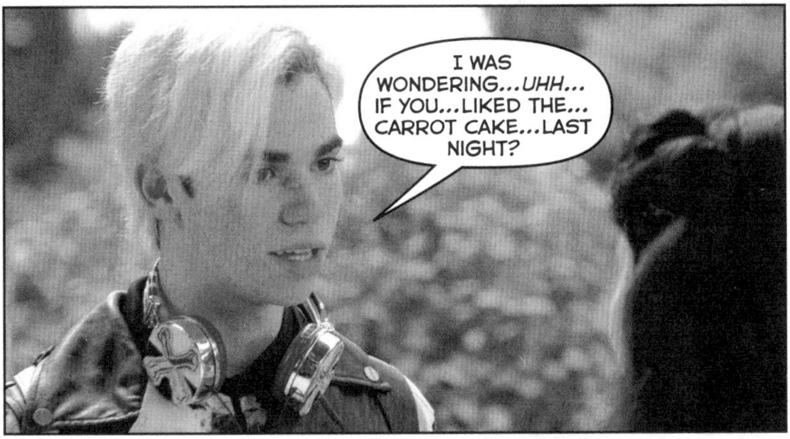
I WAS WONDERING...UHH... IF YOU...LIKED THE... CARROT CAKE...LAST NIGHT?

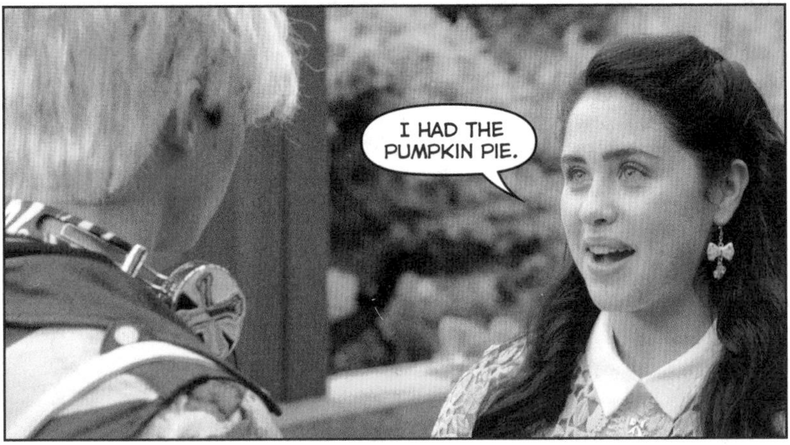
I HAD THE PUMPKIN PIE.

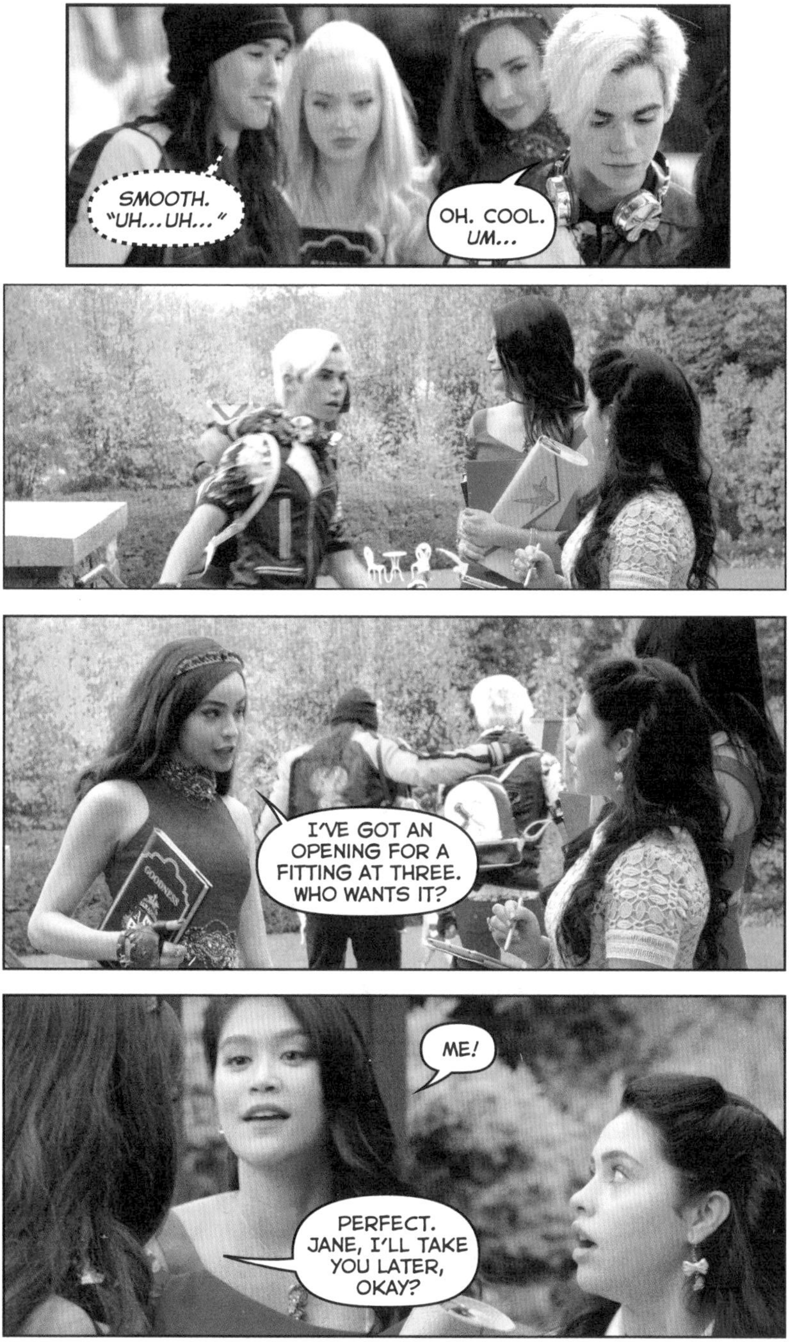
SMOOTH. "UH...UH..."
OH. COOL. UM...
I'VE GOT AN OPENING FOR A FITTING AT THREE. WHO WANTS IT?
ME!
PERFECT. JANE, I'LL TAKE YOU LATER, OKAY?

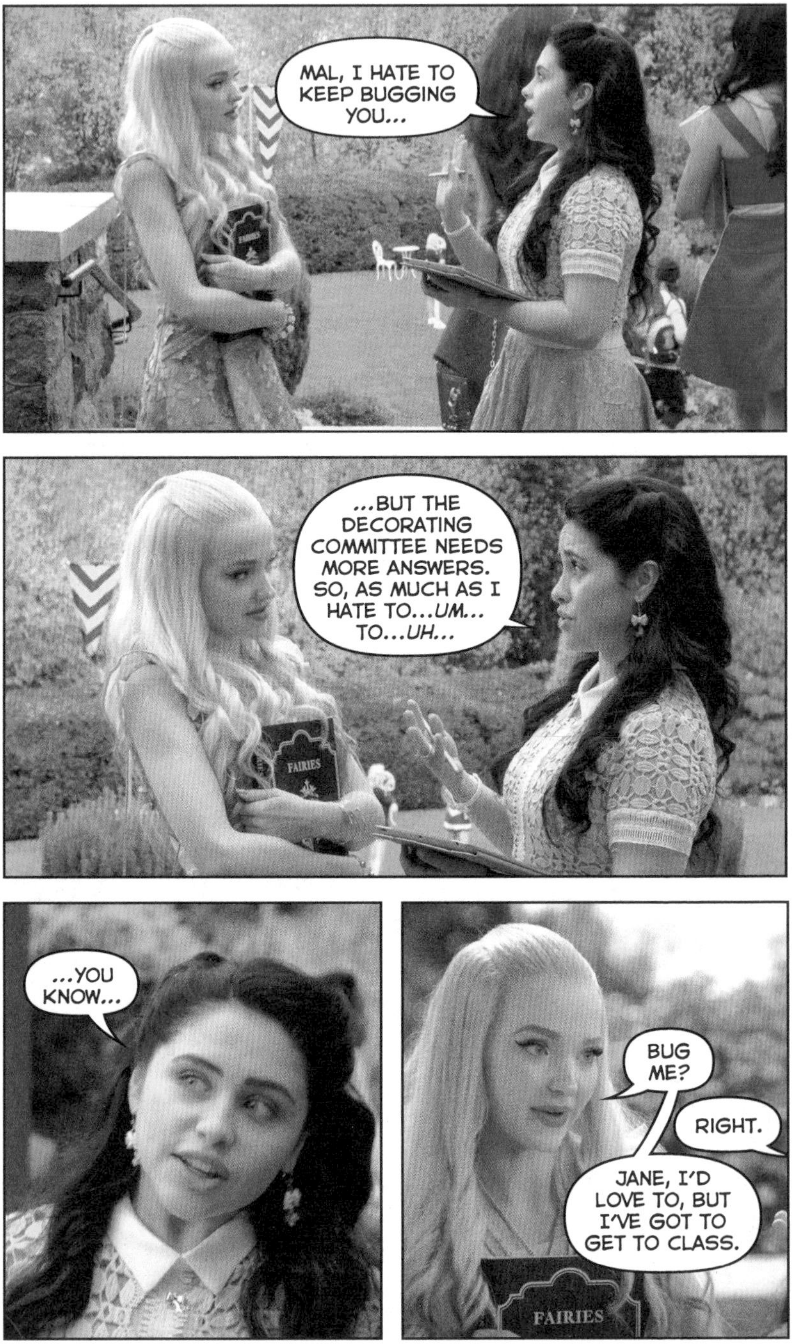
MAL, I HATE TO KEEP BUGGING YOU...
...BUT THE DECORATING COMMITTEE NEEDS MORE ANSWERS. SO, AS MUCH AS I HATE TO...UM... TO...UH...
FAIRIES
...YOU KNOW...
BUG ME?
RIGHT.
JANE, I'D LOVE TO, BUT I'VE GOT TO GET TO CLASS.
FAIRIES

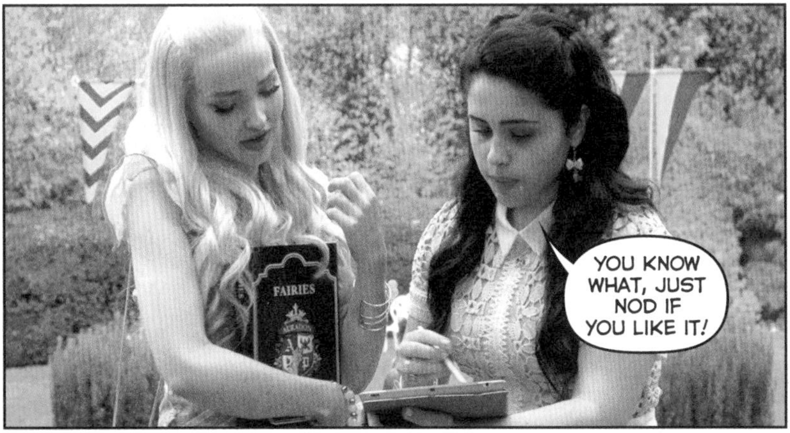
FAIRIES
YOU KNOW WHAT, JUST NOD IF YOU LIKE IT!

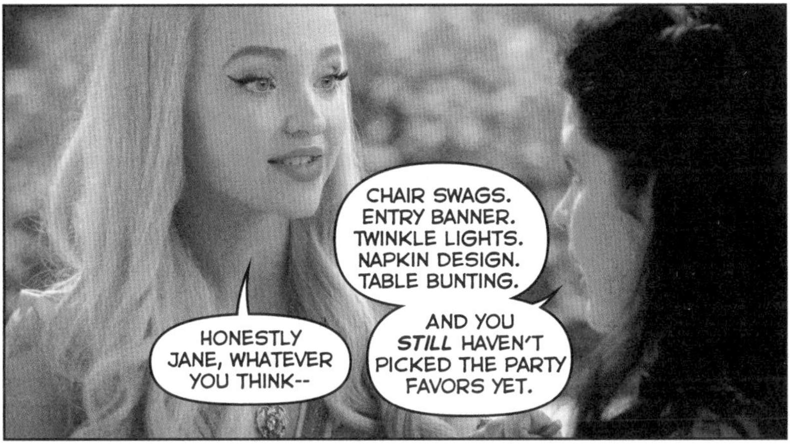
CHAIR SWAGS. ENTRY BANNER. TWINKLE LIGHTS. NAPKIN DESIGN. TABLE BUNTING.
AND YOU *STILL* HAVEN'T PICKED THE PARTY FAVORS YET.
HONESTLY JANE, WHATEVER YOU THINK--

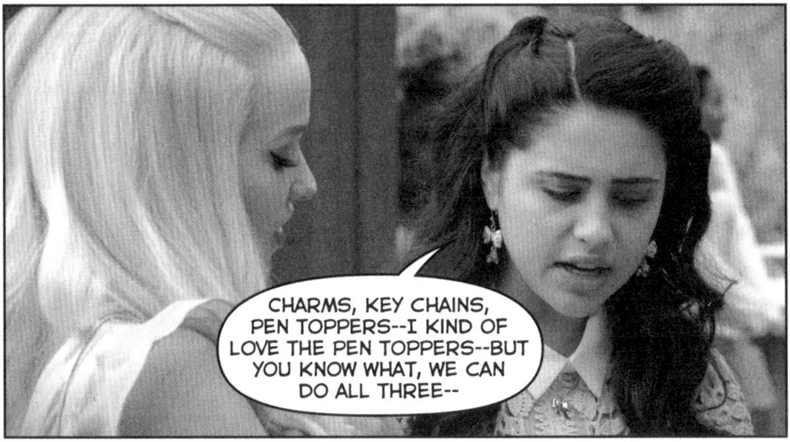
CHARMS, KEY CHAINS, PEN TOPPERS--I KIND OF LOVE THE PEN TOPPERS--BUT YOU KNOW WHAT, WE CAN DO ALL THREE--

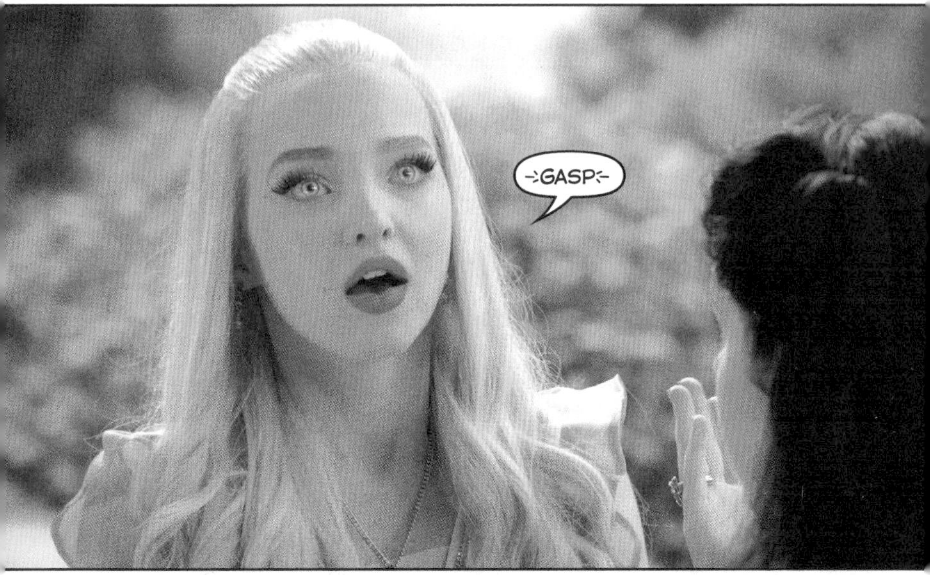
GASP

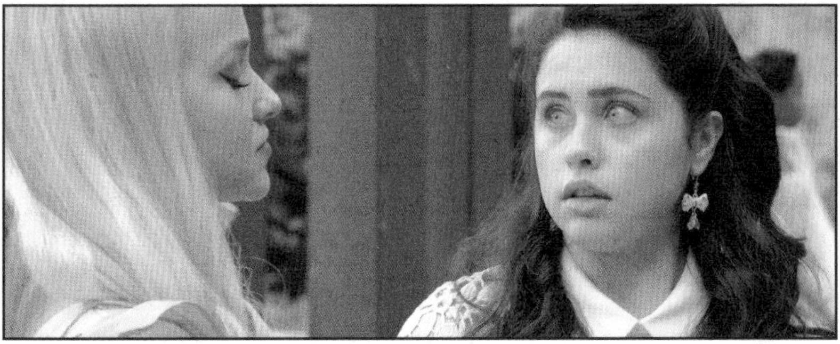

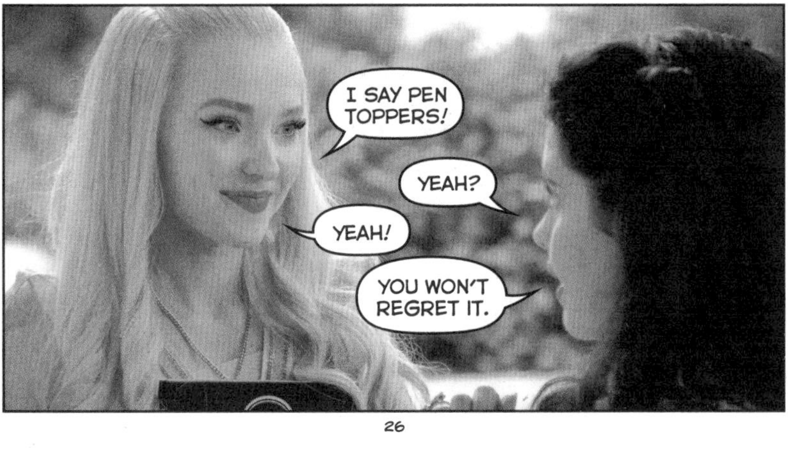
I SAY PEN TOPPERS!
YEAH?
YEAH!
YOU WON'T REGRET IT.

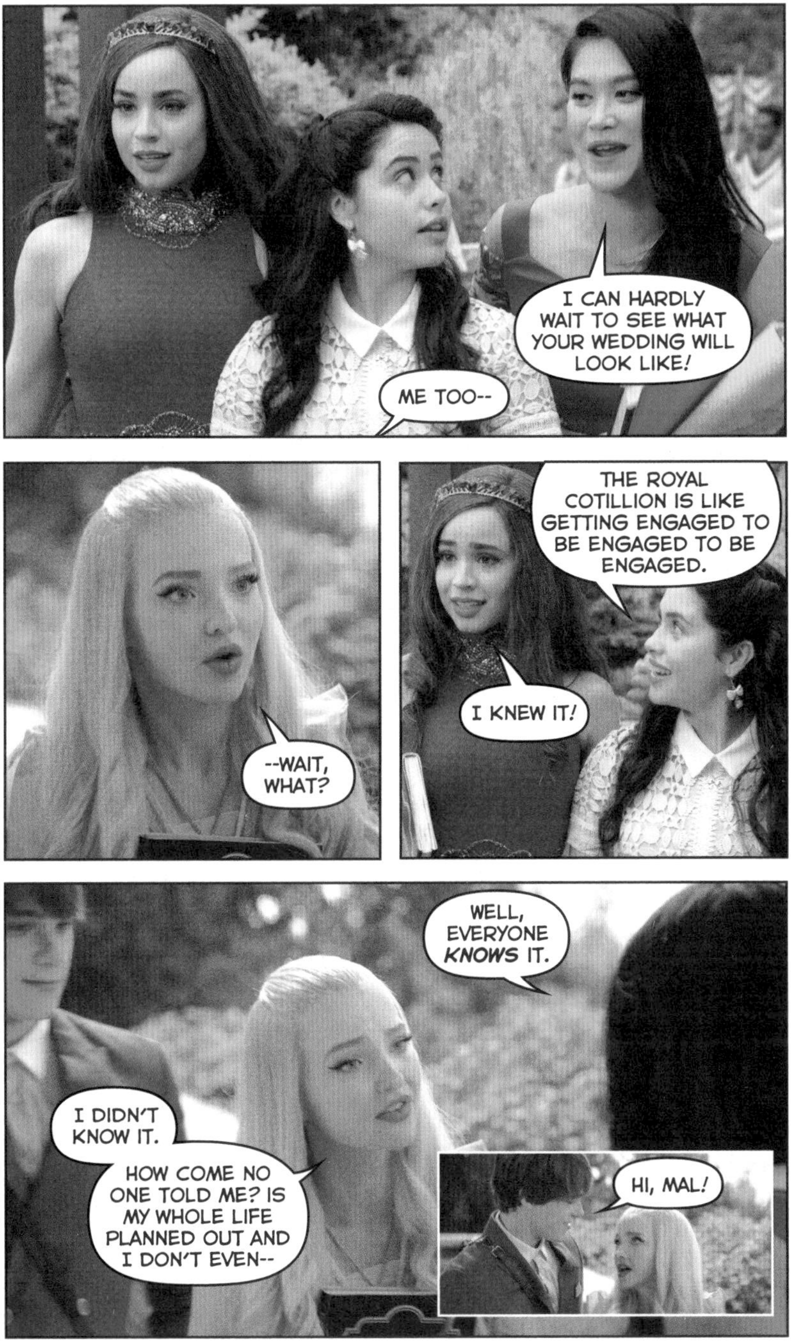
I CAN HARDLY WAIT TO SEE WHAT YOUR WEDDING WILL LOOK LIKE!
ME TOO--
--WAIT, WHAT?
THE ROYAL COTILLION IS LIKE GETTING ENGAGED TO BE ENGAGED TO BE ENGAGED.
I KNEW IT!
WELL, EVERYONE *KNOWS* IT.
I DIDN'T KNOW IT.
HOW COME NO ONE TOLD ME? IS MY WHOLE LIFE PLANNED OUT AND I DON'T EVEN--
HI, MAL!

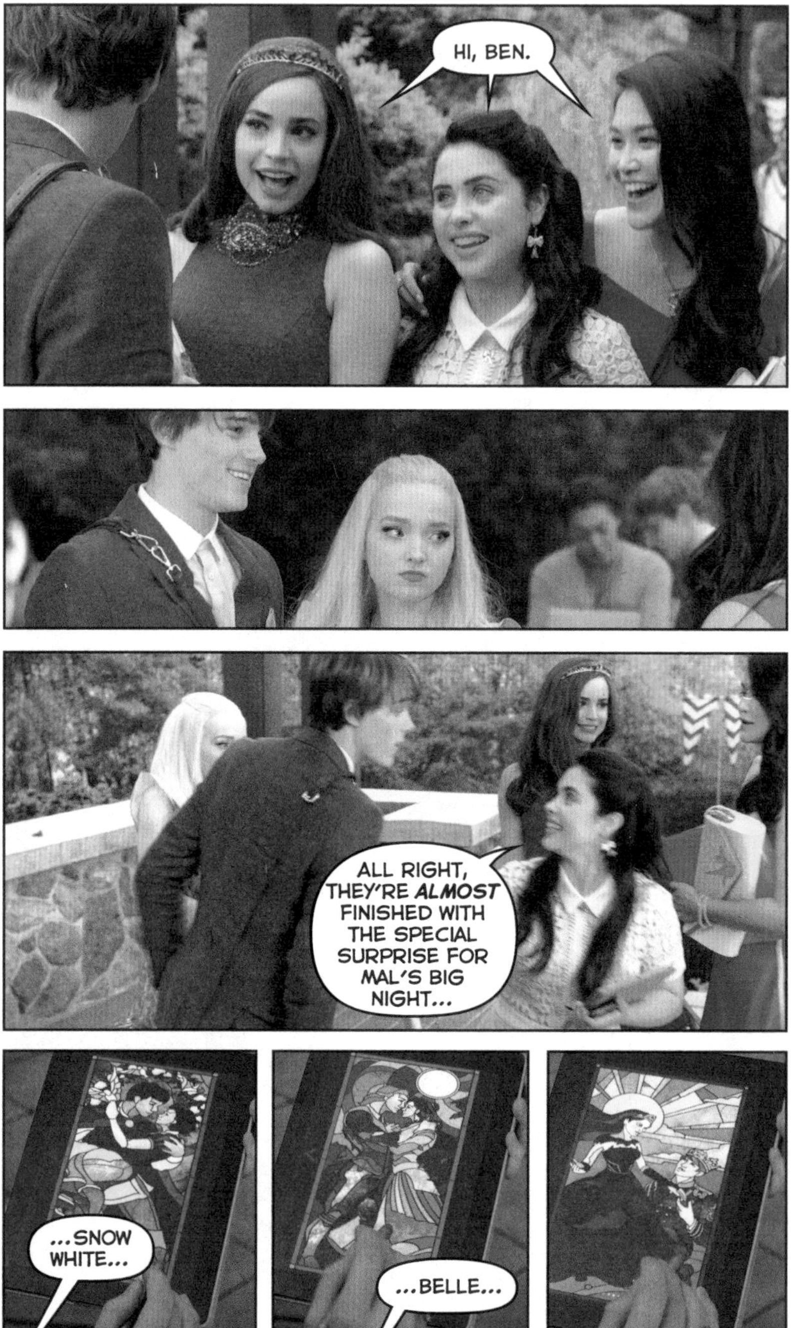
HI, BEN.
ALL RIGHT, THEY'RE *ALMOST* FINISHED WITH THE SPECIAL SURPRISE FOR MAL'S BIG NIGHT...
...SNOW WHITE...
...BELLE...

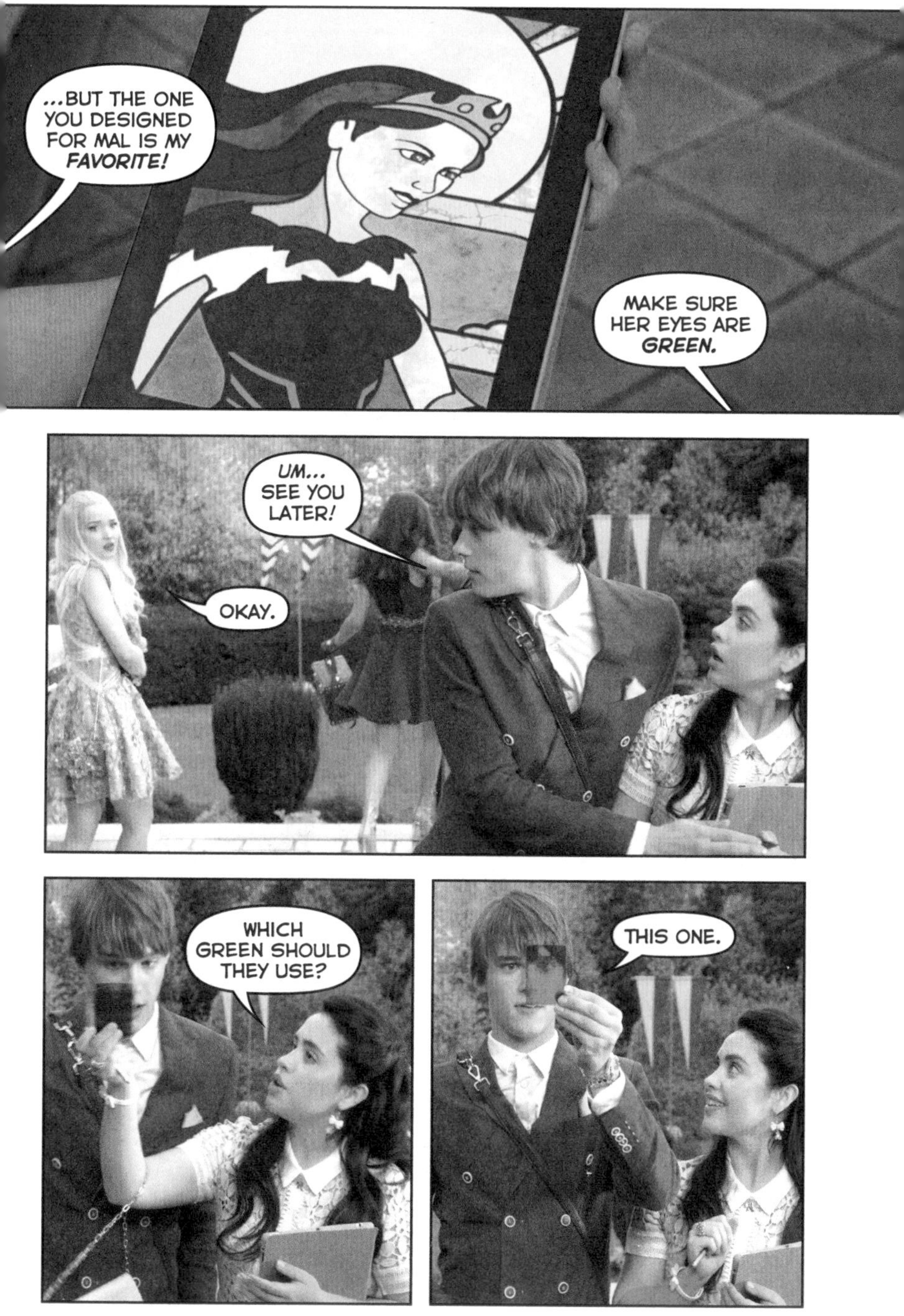
...BUT THE ONE YOU DESIGNED FOR MAL IS MY *FAVORITE!*
MAKE SURE HER EYES ARE *GREEN.*
UM... SEE YOU LATER!
OKAY.
WHICH GREEN SHOULD THEY USE?
THIS ONE.

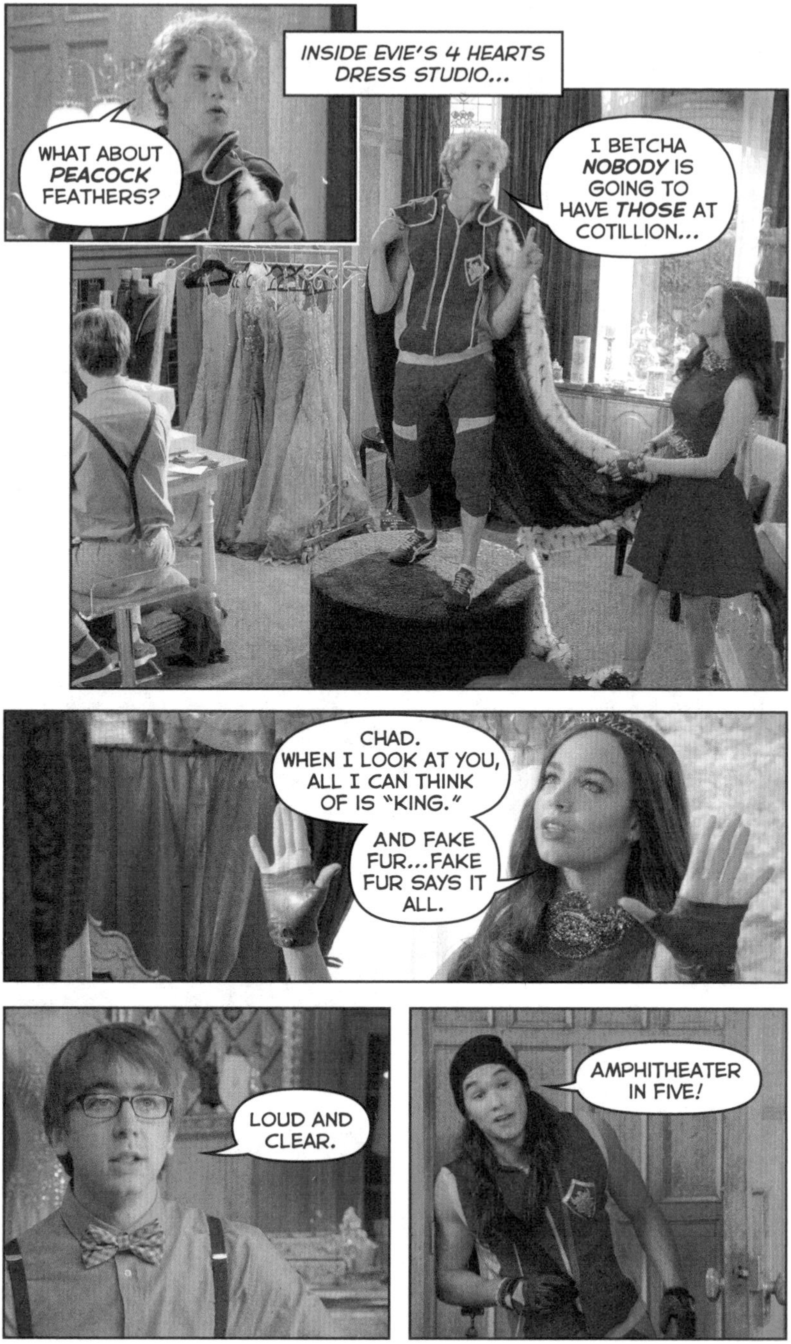
WHAT ABOUT PEACOCK FEATHERS?
INSIDE EVIE'S 4 HEARTS DRESS STUDIO...
I BETCHA NOBODY IS GOING TO HAVE THOSE AT COTILLION...
CHAD. WHEN I LOOK AT YOU, ALL I CAN THINK OF IS "KING."
AND FAKE FUR...FAKE FUR SAYS IT ALL.
LOUD AND CLEAR.
AMPHITHEATER IN FIVE!

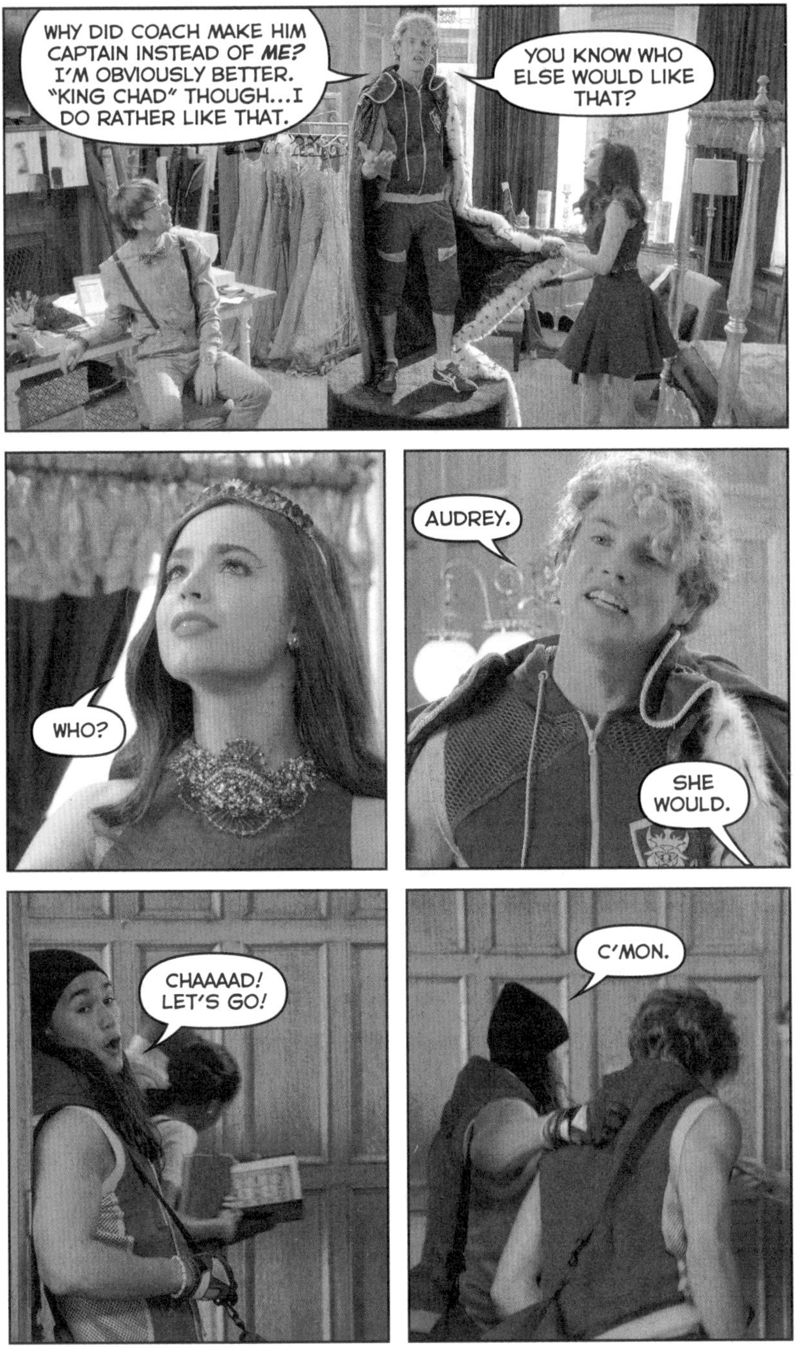
WHY DID COACH MAKE HIM CAPTAIN INSTEAD OF *ME?* I'M OBVIOUSLY BETTER. "KING CHAD" THOUGH...I DO RATHER LIKE THAT.
YOU KNOW WHO ELSE WOULD LIKE THAT?
WHO?
AUDREY.
SHE WOULD.
CHAAAAD! LET'S GO!
C'MON.

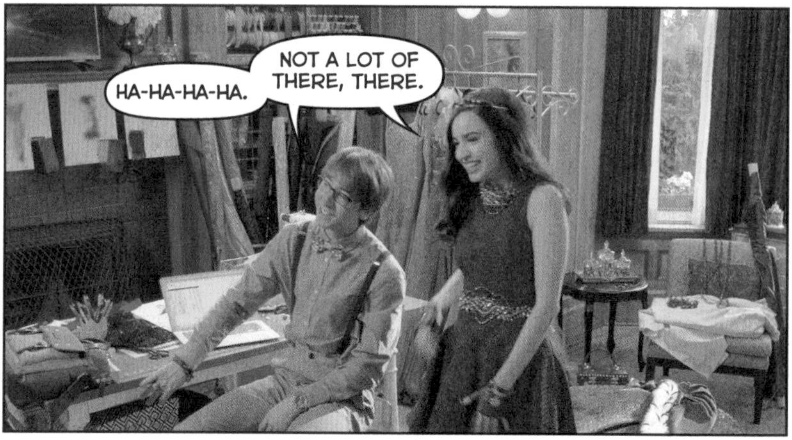
HA-HA-HA-HA.
NOT A LOT OF THERE, THERE.

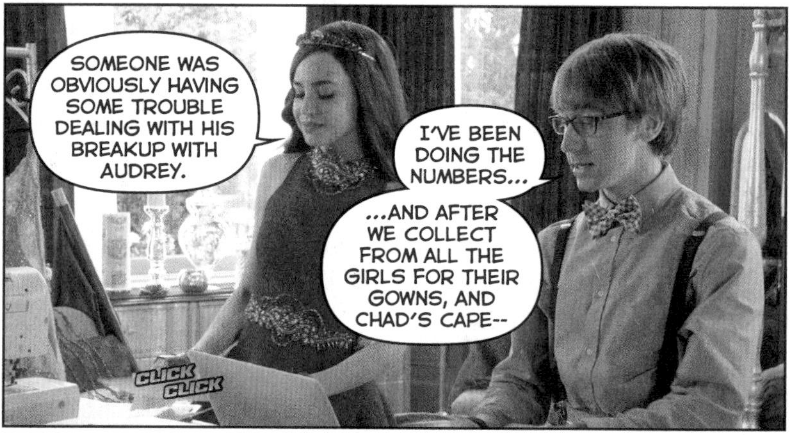
SOMEONE WAS OBVIOUSLY HAVING SOME TROUBLE DEALING WITH HIS BREAKUP WITH AUDREY.
I'VE BEEN DOING THE NUMBERS...
...AND AFTER WE COLLECT FROM ALL THE GIRLS FOR THEIR GOWNS, AND CHAD'S CAPE--
CLICK CLICK

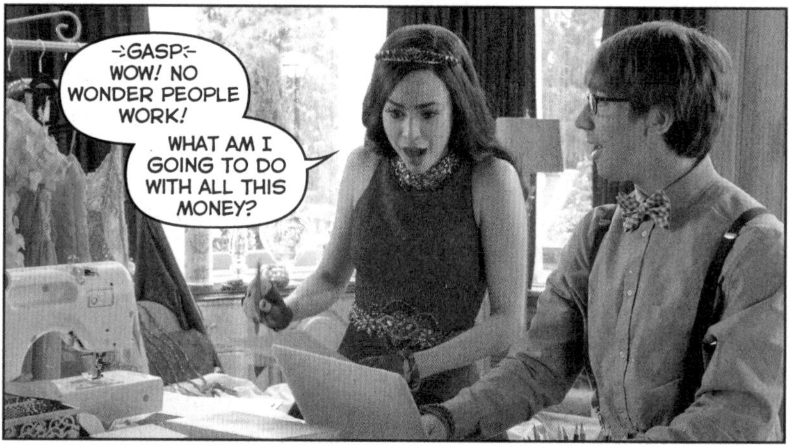
-GASP- WOW! NO WONDER PEOPLE WORK!
WHAT AM I GOING TO DO WITH ALL THIS MONEY?

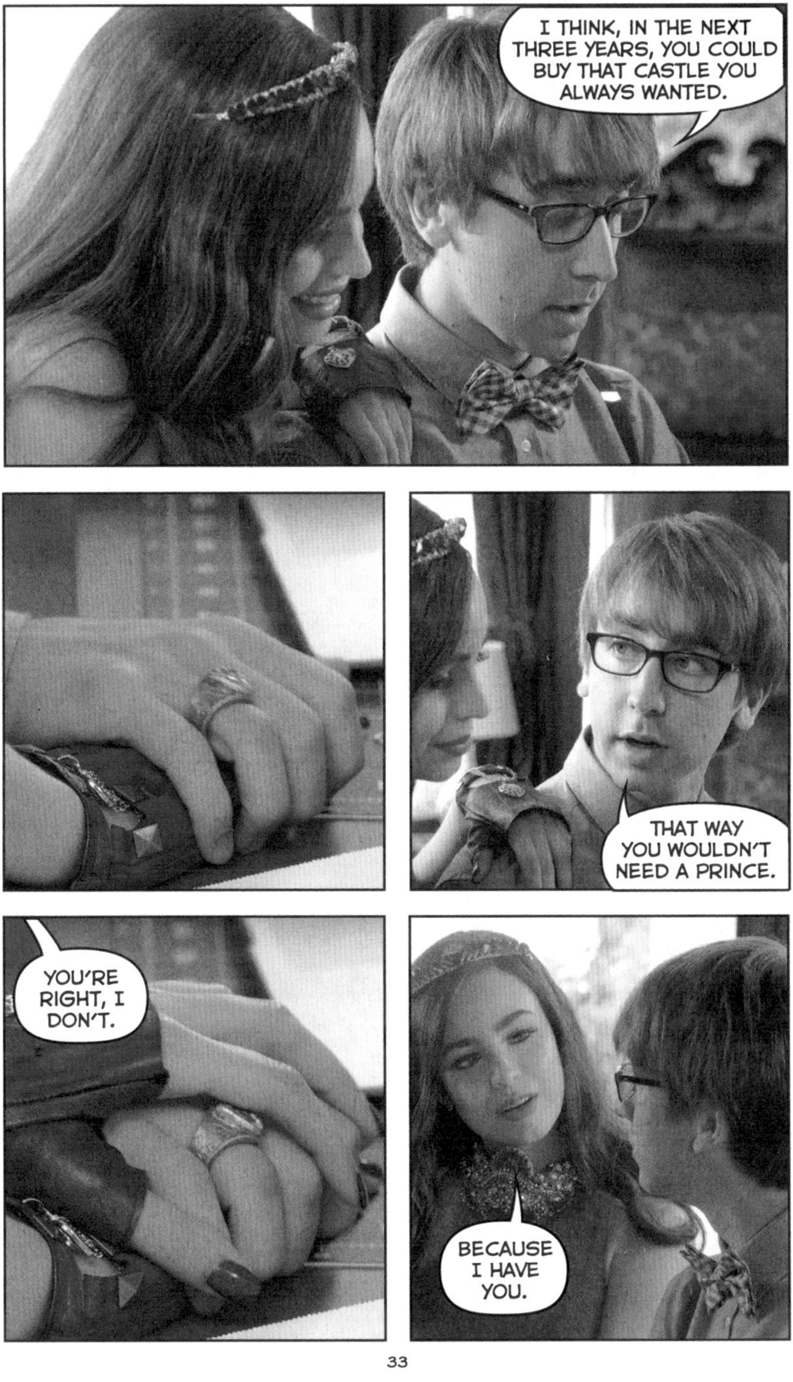
I THINK, IN THE NEXT THREE YEARS, YOU COULD BUY THAT CASTLE YOU ALWAYS WANTED.
THAT WAY YOU WOULDN'T NEED A PRINCE.
YOU'RE RIGHT, I DON'T.
BECAUSE I HAVE YOU.

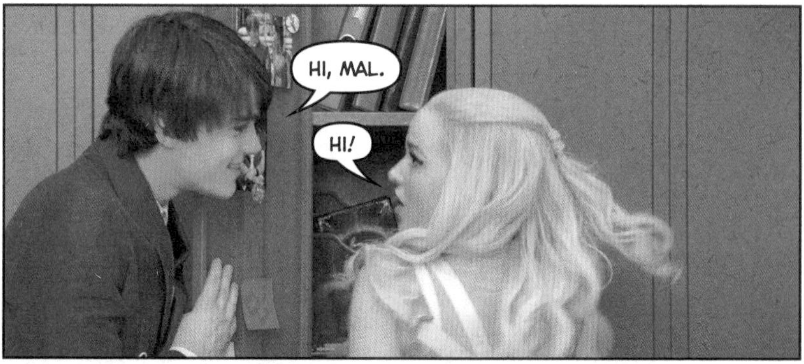
HI, MAL.
HI!

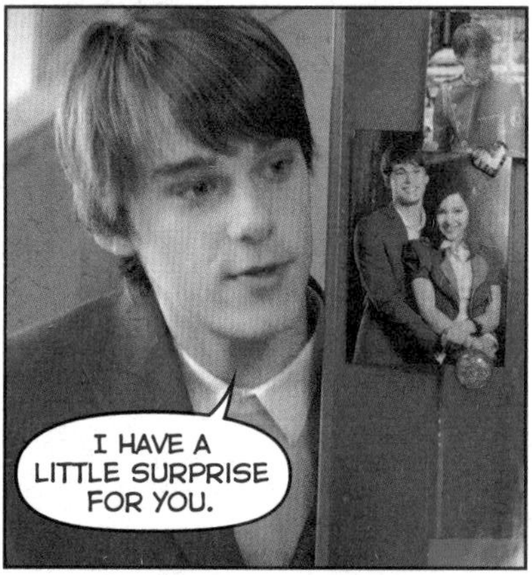
I HAVE A LITTLE SURPRISE FOR YOU.

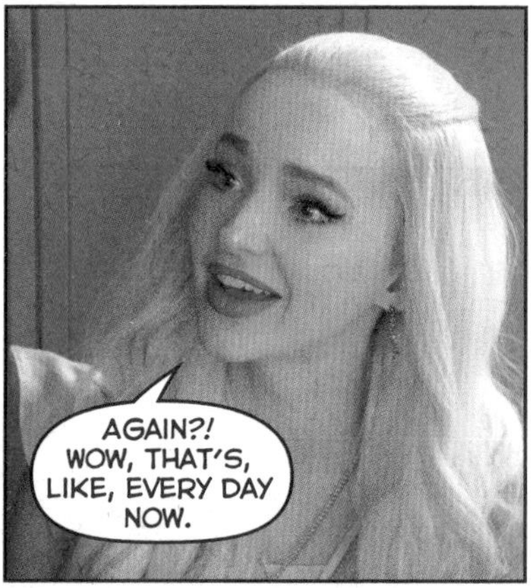
AGAIN?! WOW, THAT'S, LIKE, EVERY DAY NOW.

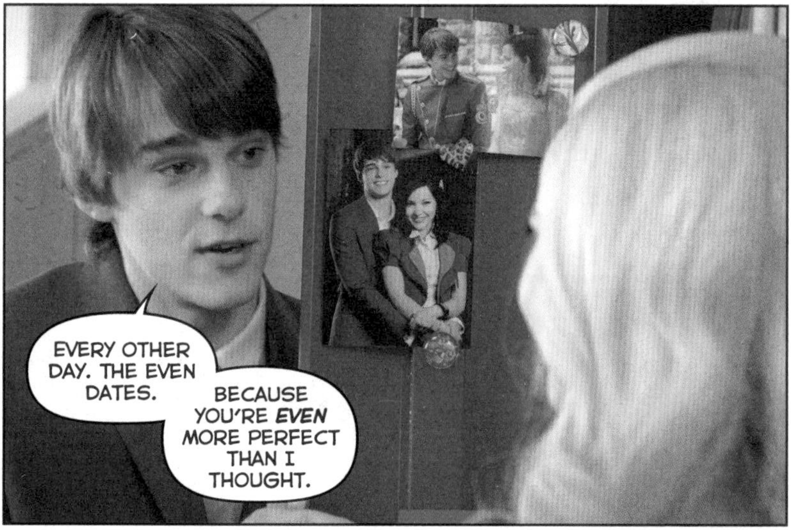
EVERY OTHER DAY. THE EVEN DATES.
BECAUSE YOU'RE *EVEN* MORE PERFECT THAN I THOUGHT.

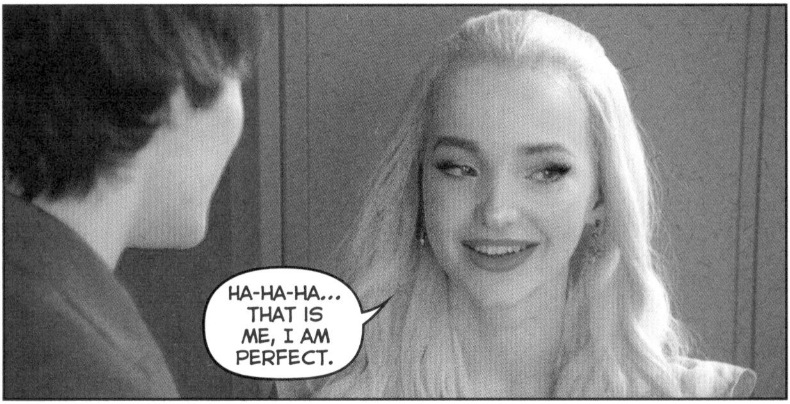
HA-HA-HA...
THAT IS ME, I AM PERFECT.

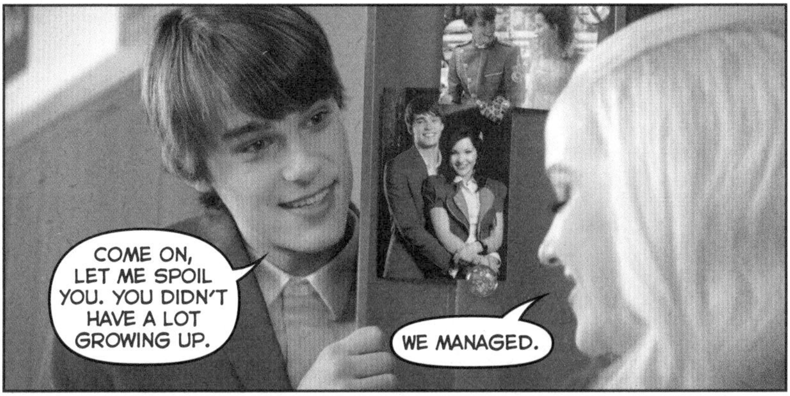
COME ON, LET ME SPOIL YOU. YOU DIDN'T HAVE A LOT GROWING UP.
WE MANAGED.

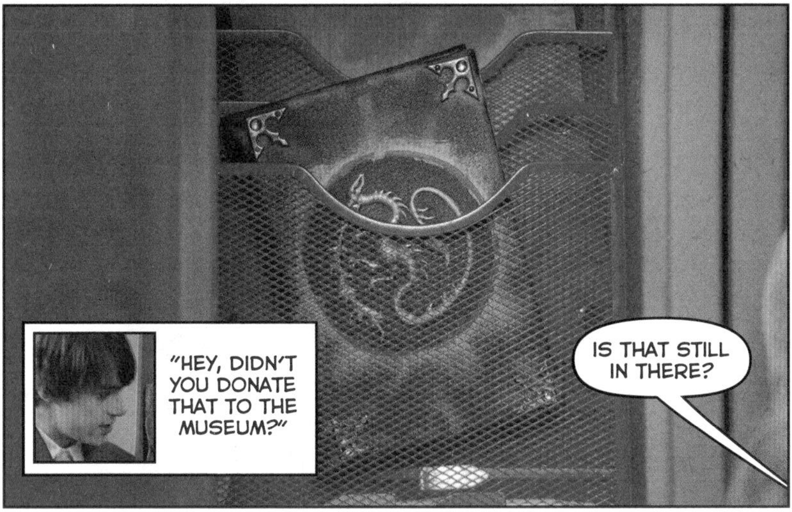
"HEY, DIDN'T YOU DONATE THAT TO THE MUSEUM?"
IS THAT STILL IN THERE?

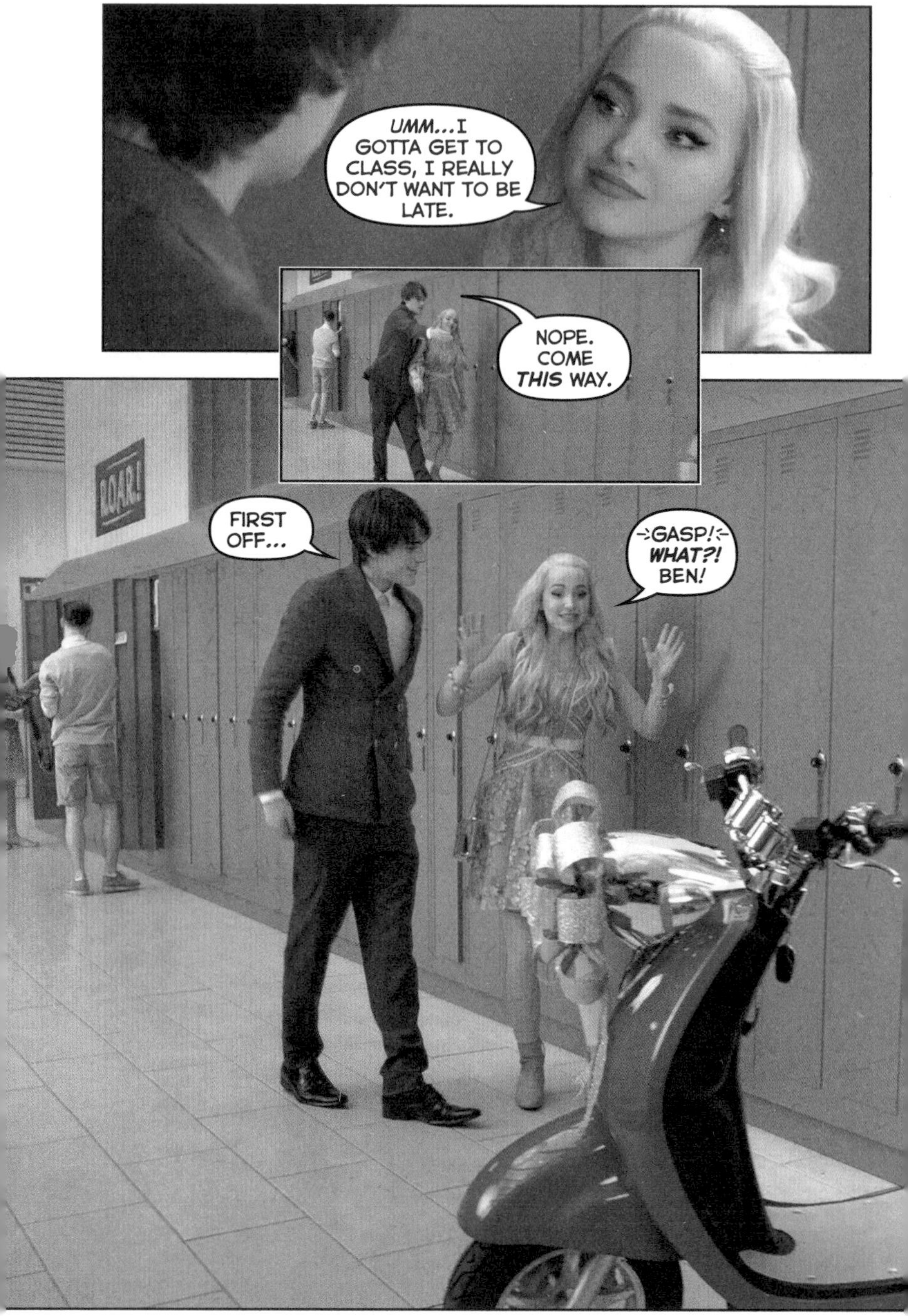
*UMM...*I GOTTA GET TO CLASS, I REALLY DON'T WANT TO BE LATE.
NOPE. COME *THIS* WAY.
FIRST OFF...
GASP! *WHAT?!* BEN!

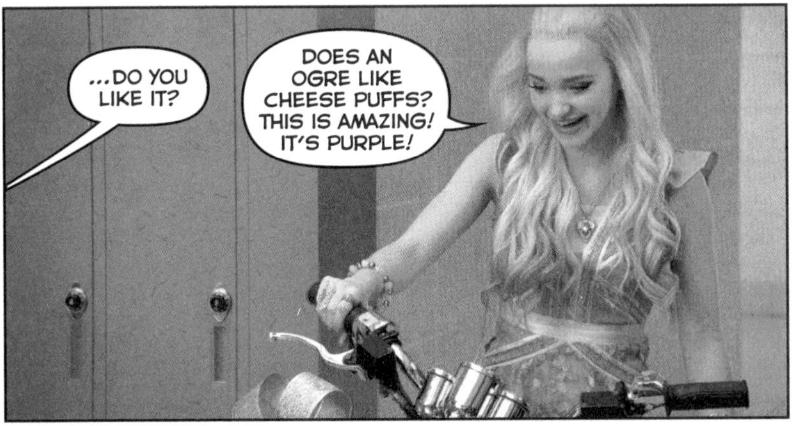
...DO YOU LIKE IT?
DOES AN OGRE LIKE CHEESE PUFFS? THIS IS AMAZING! IT'S PURPLE!

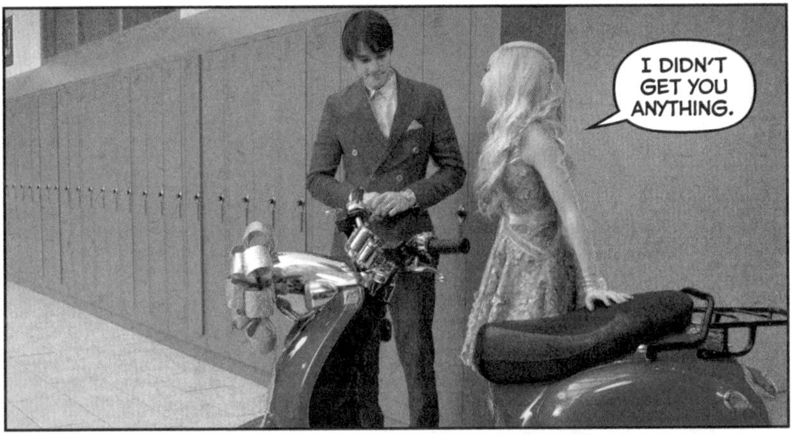
I DIDN'T GET YOU ANYTHING.

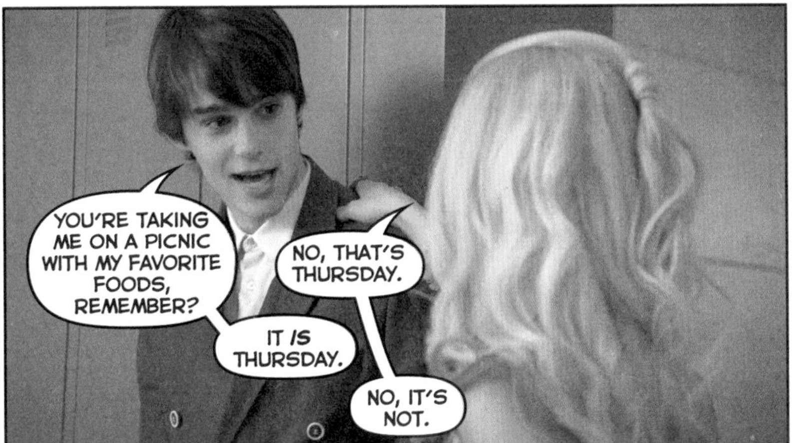
YOU'RE TAKING ME ON A PICNIC WITH MY FAVORITE FOODS, REMEMBER?
NO, THAT'S THURSDAY.
IT *IS* THURSDAY.
NO, IT'S NOT.

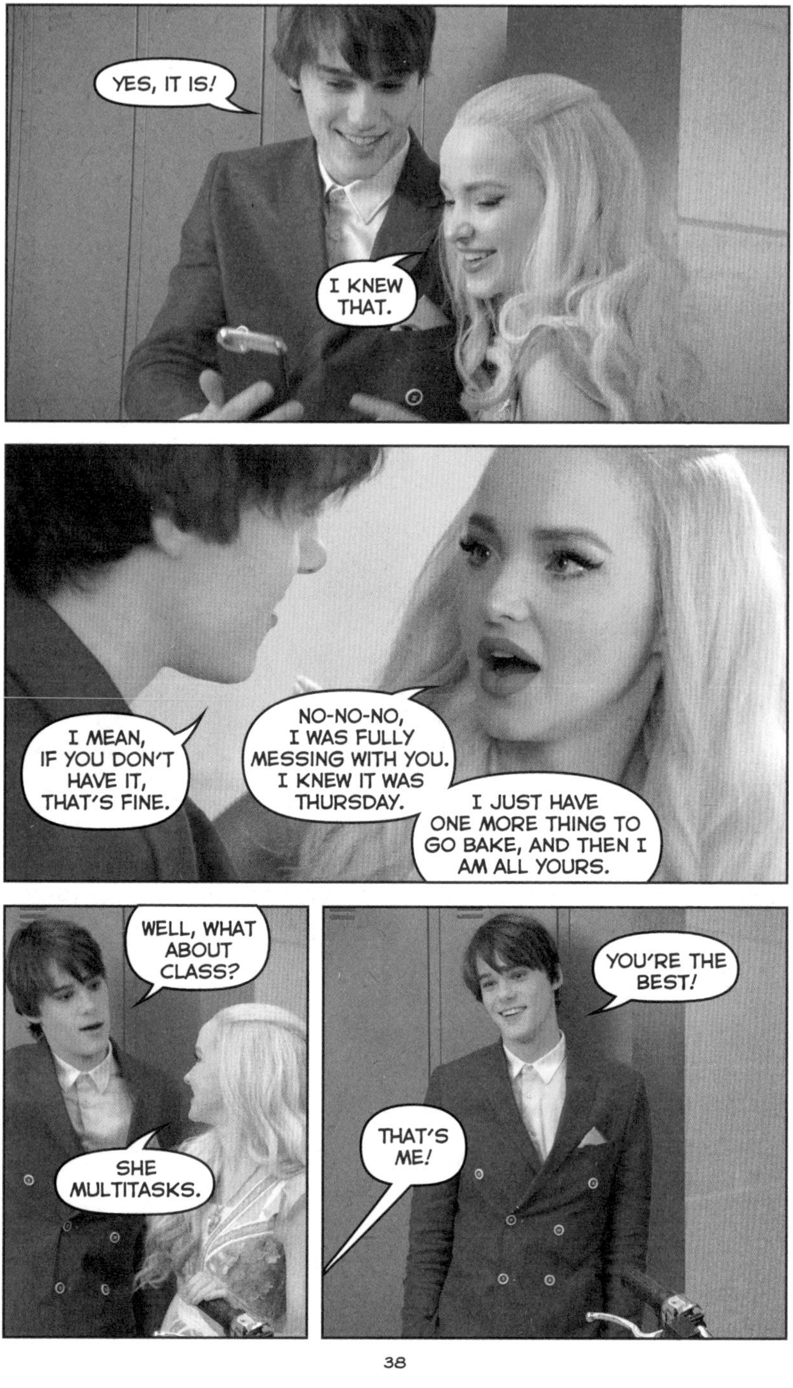
YES, IT IS!
I KNEW THAT.
I MEAN, IF YOU DON'T HAVE IT, THAT'S FINE.
NO-NO-NO, I WAS FULLY MESSING WITH YOU. I KNEW IT WAS THURSDAY.
I JUST HAVE ONE MORE THING TO GO BAKE, AND THEN I AM ALL YOURS.
WELL, WHAT ABOUT CLASS?
SHE MULTITASKS.
YOU'RE THE BEST!
THAT'S ME!

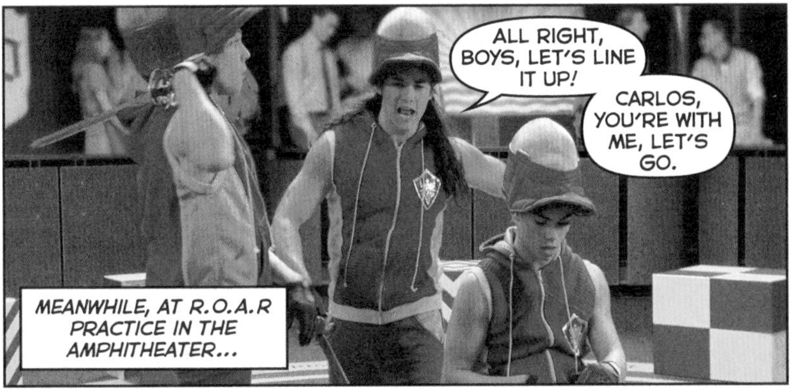
MEANWHILE, AT R.O.A.R PRACTICE IN THE AMPHITHEATER...
ALL RIGHT, BOYS, LET'S LINE IT UP!
CARLOS, YOU'RE WITH ME, LET'S GO.

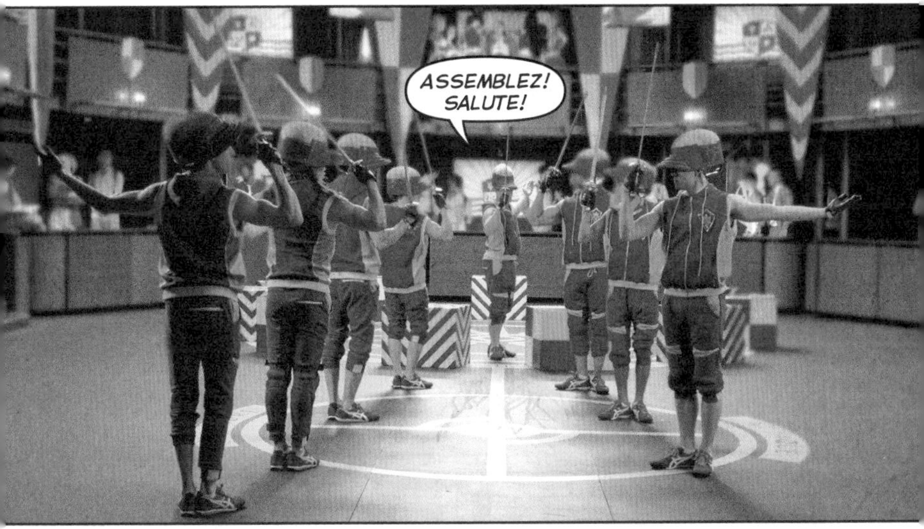
ASSEMBLEZ! SALUTE!

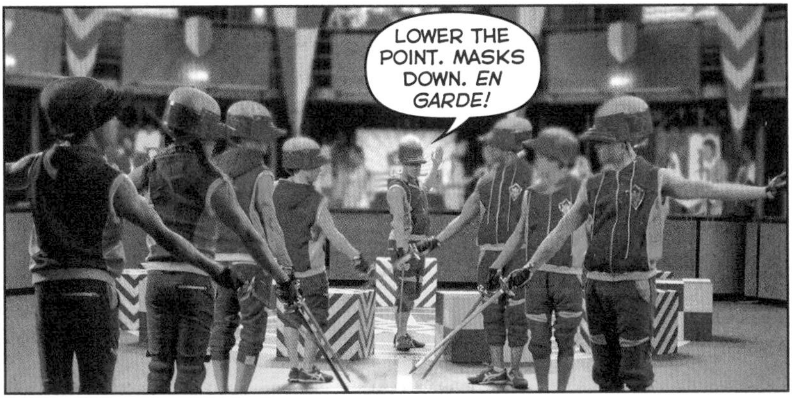
LOWER THE POINT. MASKS DOWN. EN GARDE!

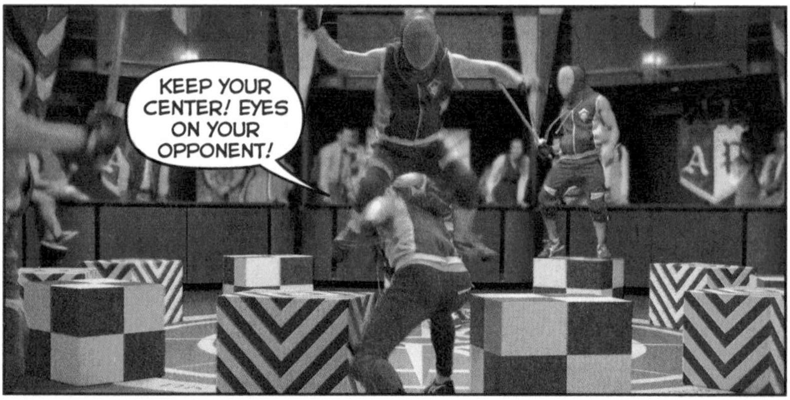
KEEP YOUR CENTER! EYES ON YOUR OPPONENT!

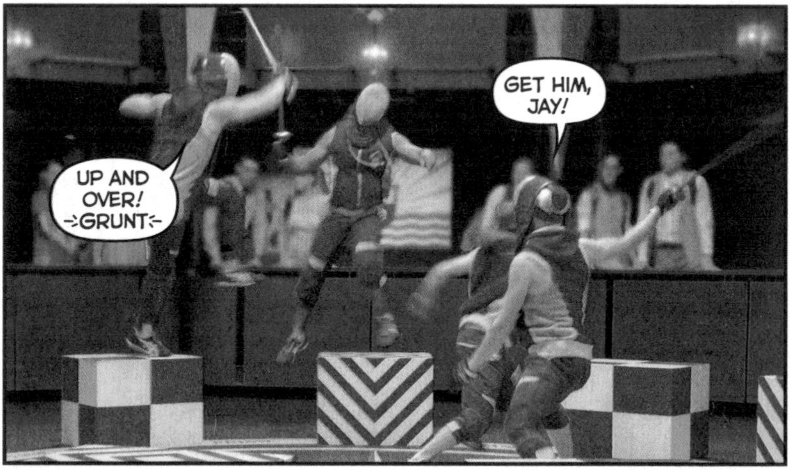
UP AND OVER! ~GRUNT~
GET HIM, JAY!

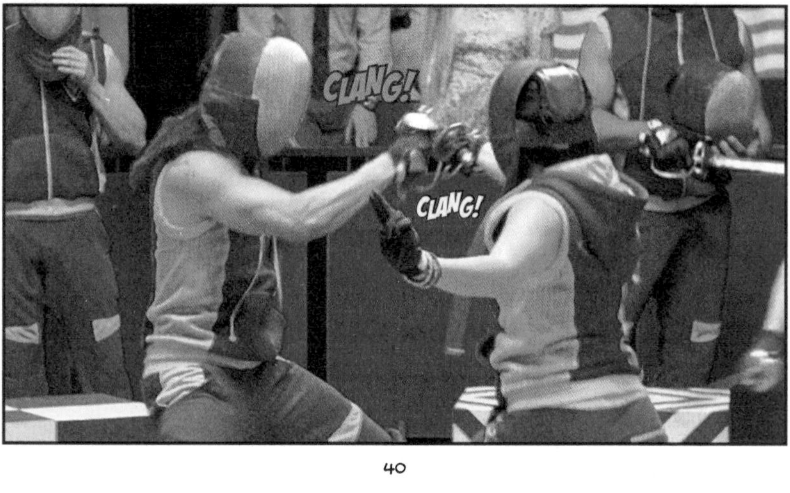
CLANG!
CLANG!

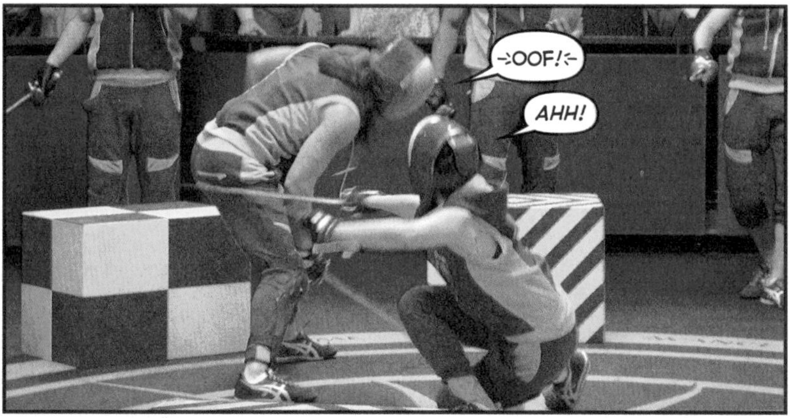
OOF!
AHH!
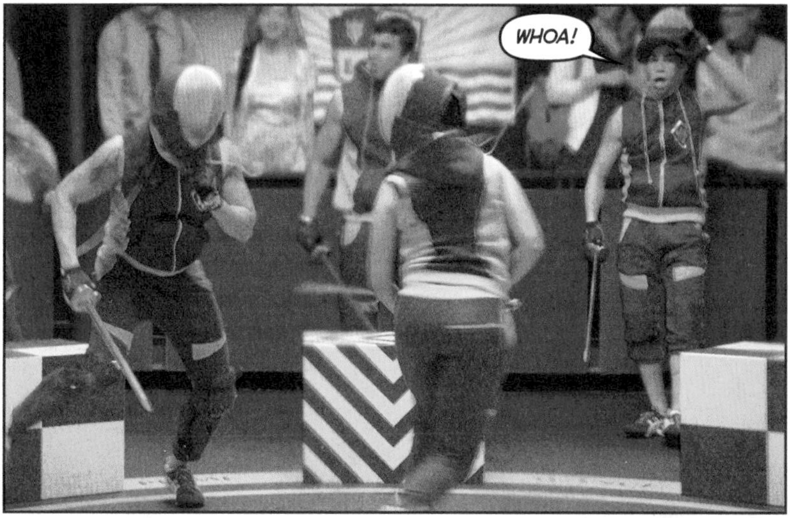
WHOA!
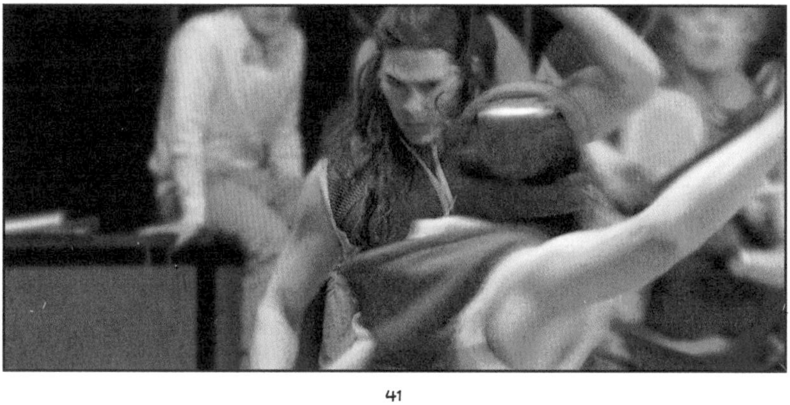

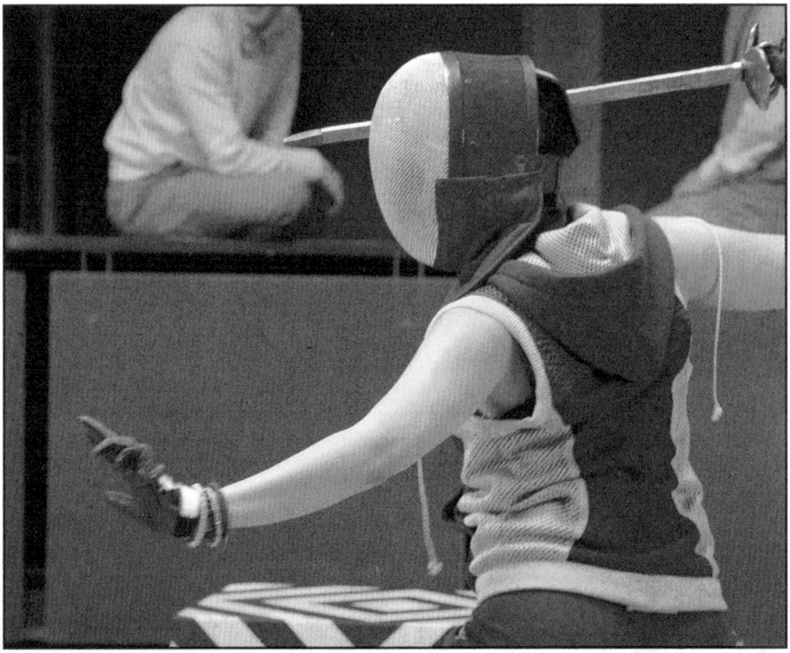

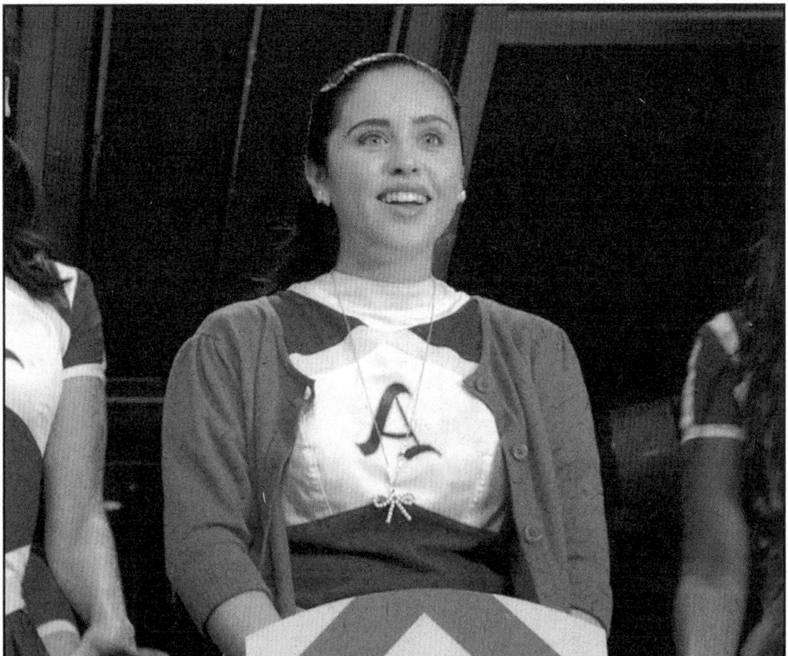

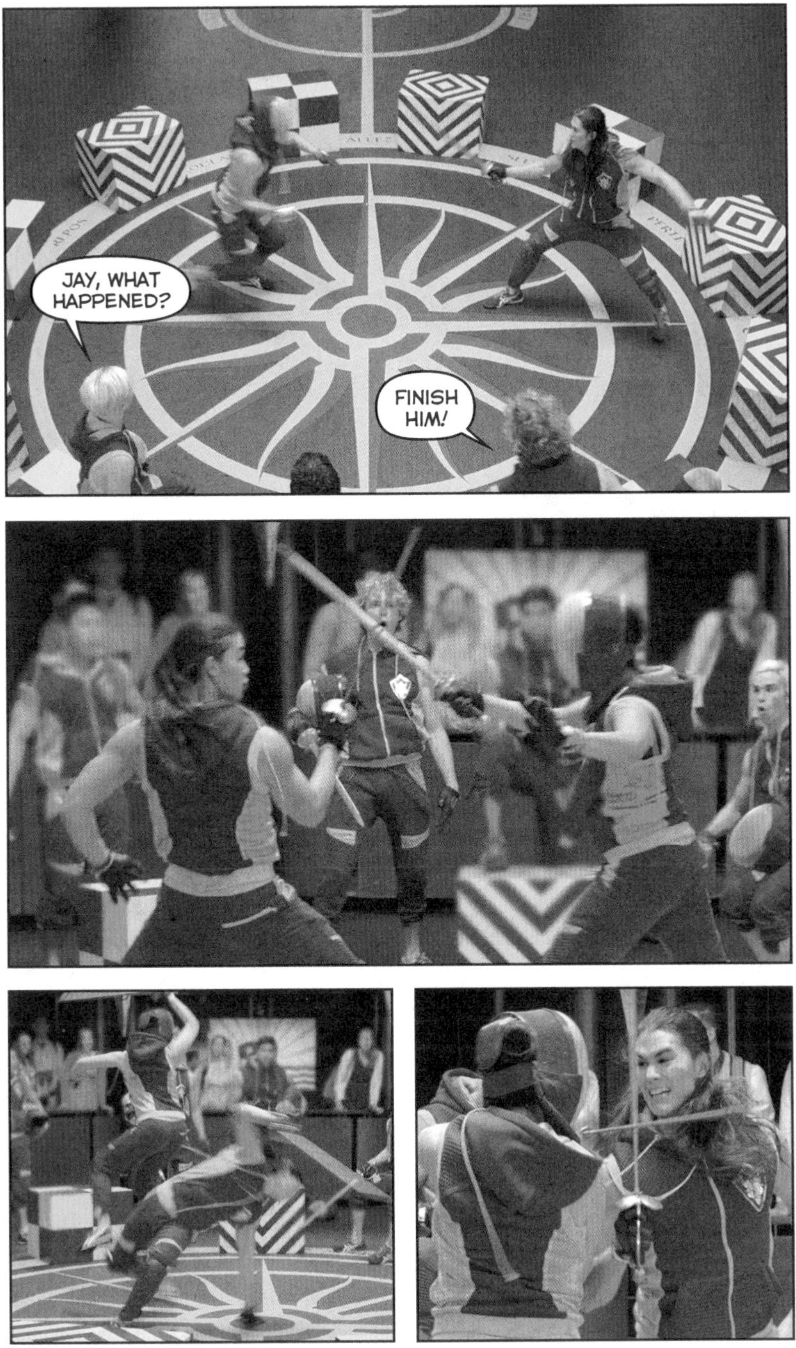
JAY, WHAT HAPPENED?
FINISH HIM!

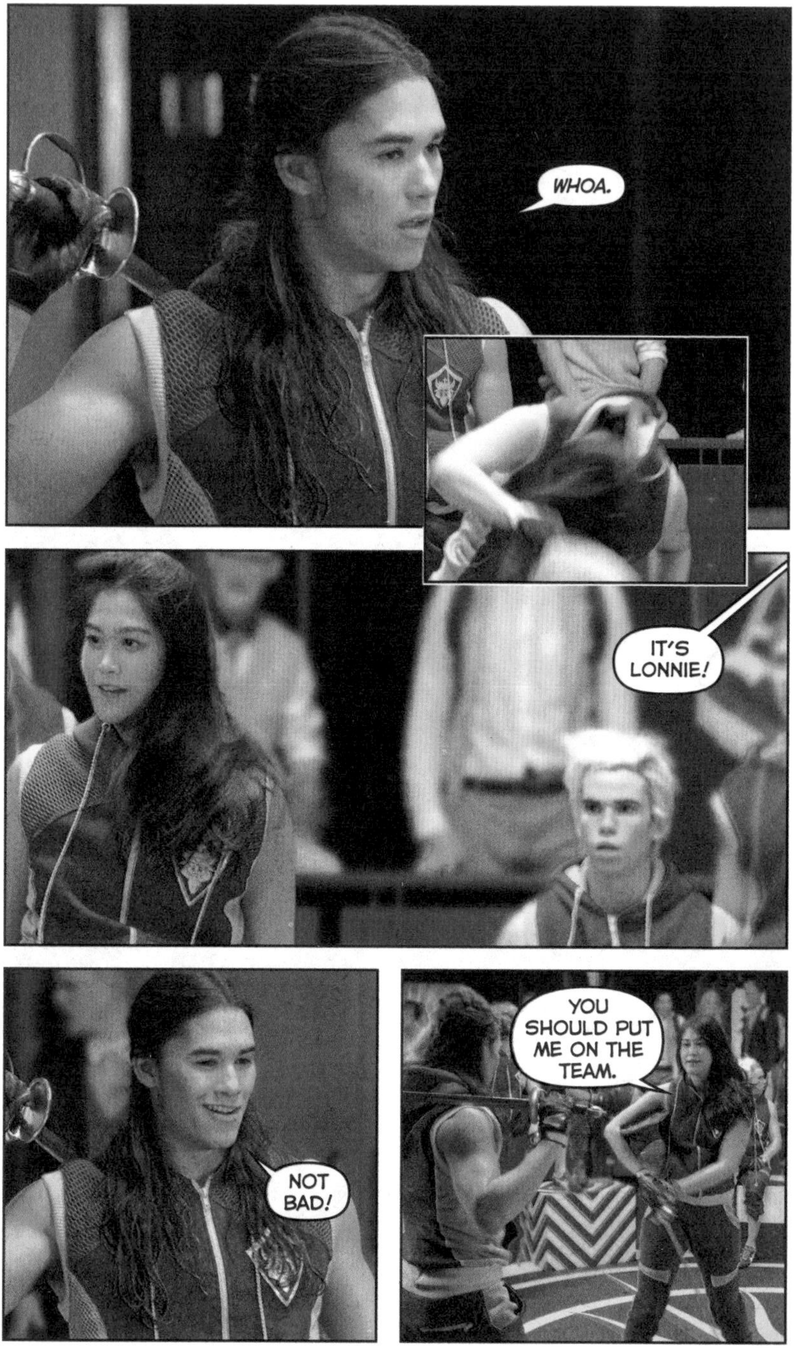
WHOA.
IT'S LONNIE!
NOT BAD!
YOU SHOULD PUT ME ON THE TEAM.

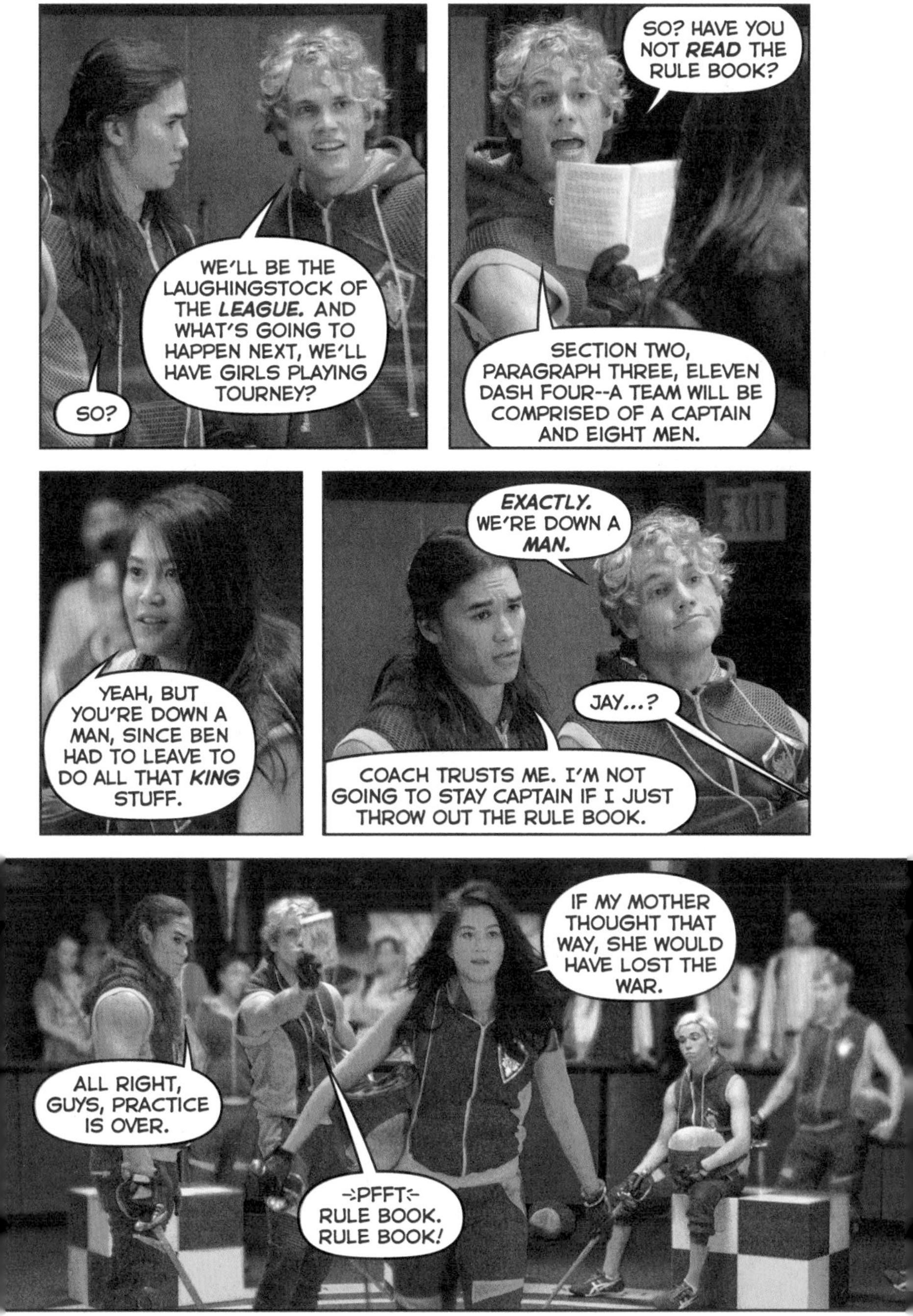
WE'LL BE THE LAUGHINGSTOCK OF THE *LEAGUE.* AND WHAT'S GOING TO HAPPEN NEXT, WE'LL HAVE GIRLS PLAYING TOURNEY?
SO?
SO? HAVE YOU NOT *READ* THE RULE BOOK?
SECTION TWO, PARAGRAPH THREE, ELEVEN DASH FOUR--A TEAM WILL BE COMPRISED OF A CAPTAIN AND EIGHT MEN.
YEAH, BUT YOU'RE DOWN A MAN, SINCE BEN HAD TO LEAVE TO DO ALL THAT *KING* STUFF.
EXACTLY. WE'RE DOWN A *MAN.*
JAY...?
COACH TRUSTS ME. I'M NOT GOING TO STAY CAPTAIN IF I JUST THROW OUT THE RULE BOOK.
IF MY MOTHER THOUGHT THAT WAY, SHE WOULD HAVE LOST THE WAR.
ALL RIGHT, GUYS, PRACTICE IS OVER.
PFFT RULE BOOK. RULE BOOK!

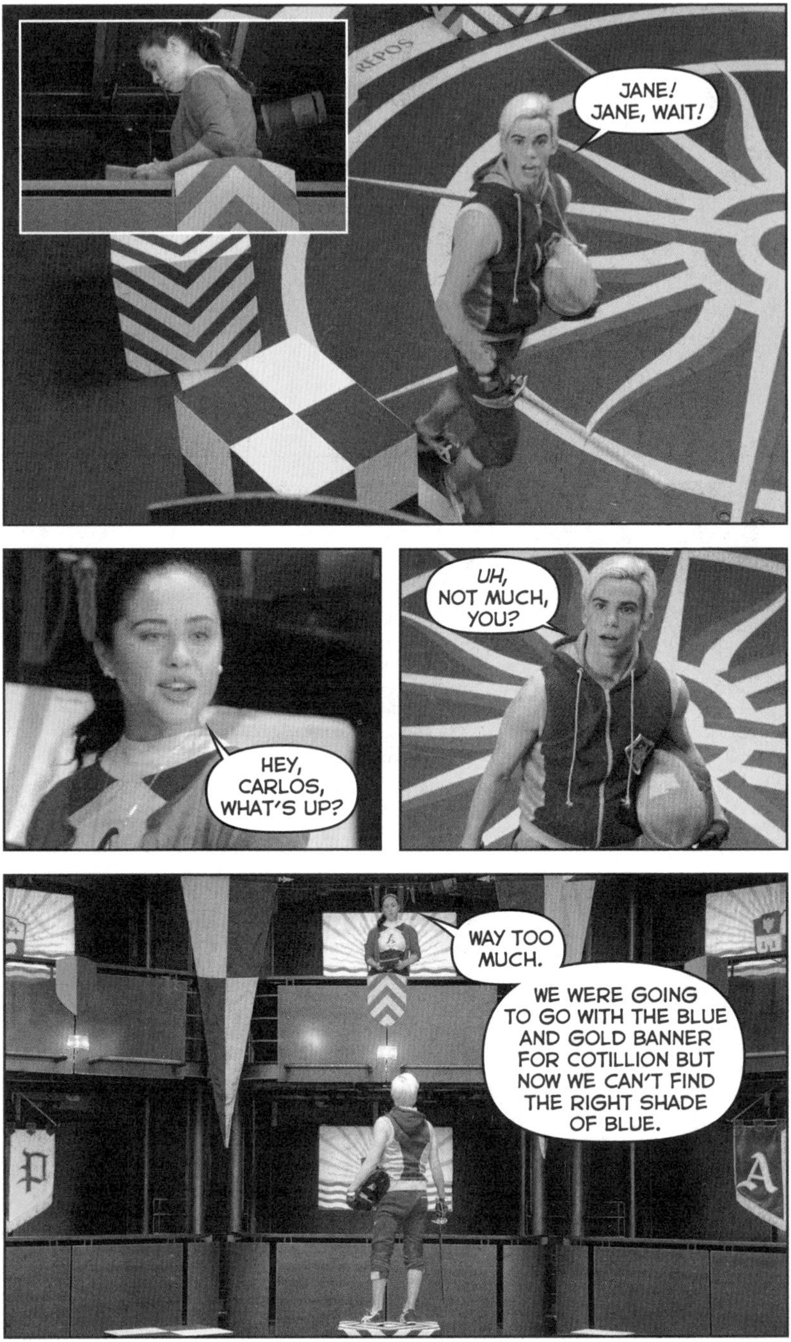
JANE! JANE, WAIT!
HEY, CARLOS, WHAT'S UP?
UH, NOT MUCH, YOU?
WAY TOO MUCH.
WE WERE GOING TO GO WITH THE BLUE AND GOLD BANNER FOR COTILLION BUT NOW WE CAN'T FIND THE RIGHT SHADE OF BLUE.

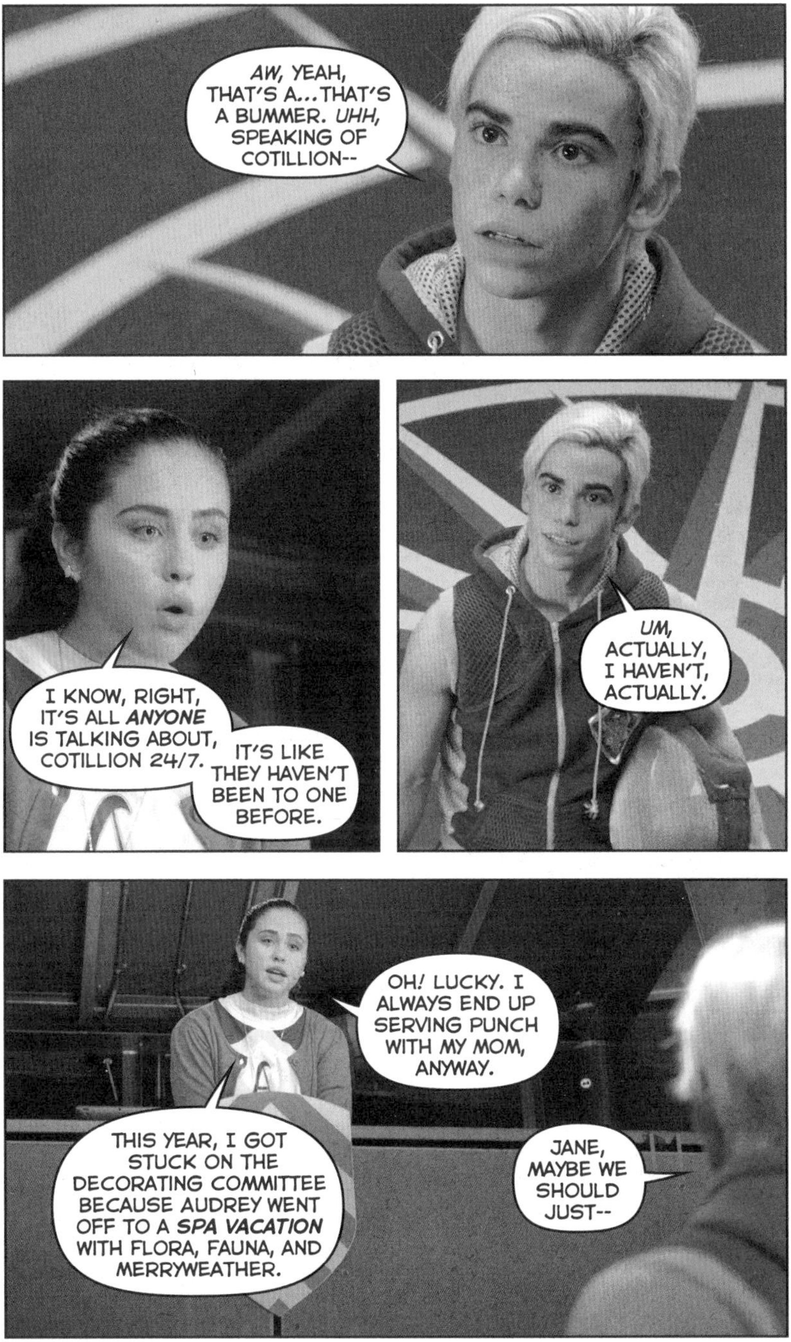
AW, YEAH, THAT'S A...THAT'S A BUMMER. UHH, SPEAKING OF COTILLION--
I KNOW, RIGHT, IT'S ALL ANYONE IS TALKING ABOUT, COTILLION 24/7.
IT'S LIKE THEY HAVEN'T BEEN TO ONE BEFORE.
UM, ACTUALLY, I HAVEN'T, ACTUALLY.
OH! LUCKY. I ALWAYS END UP SERVING PUNCH WITH MY MOM, ANYWAY.
THIS YEAR, I GOT STUCK ON THE DECORATING COMMITTEE BECAUSE AUDREY WENT OFF TO A SPA VACATION WITH FLORA, FAUNA, AND MERRYWEATHER.
JANE, MAYBE WE SHOULD JUST--

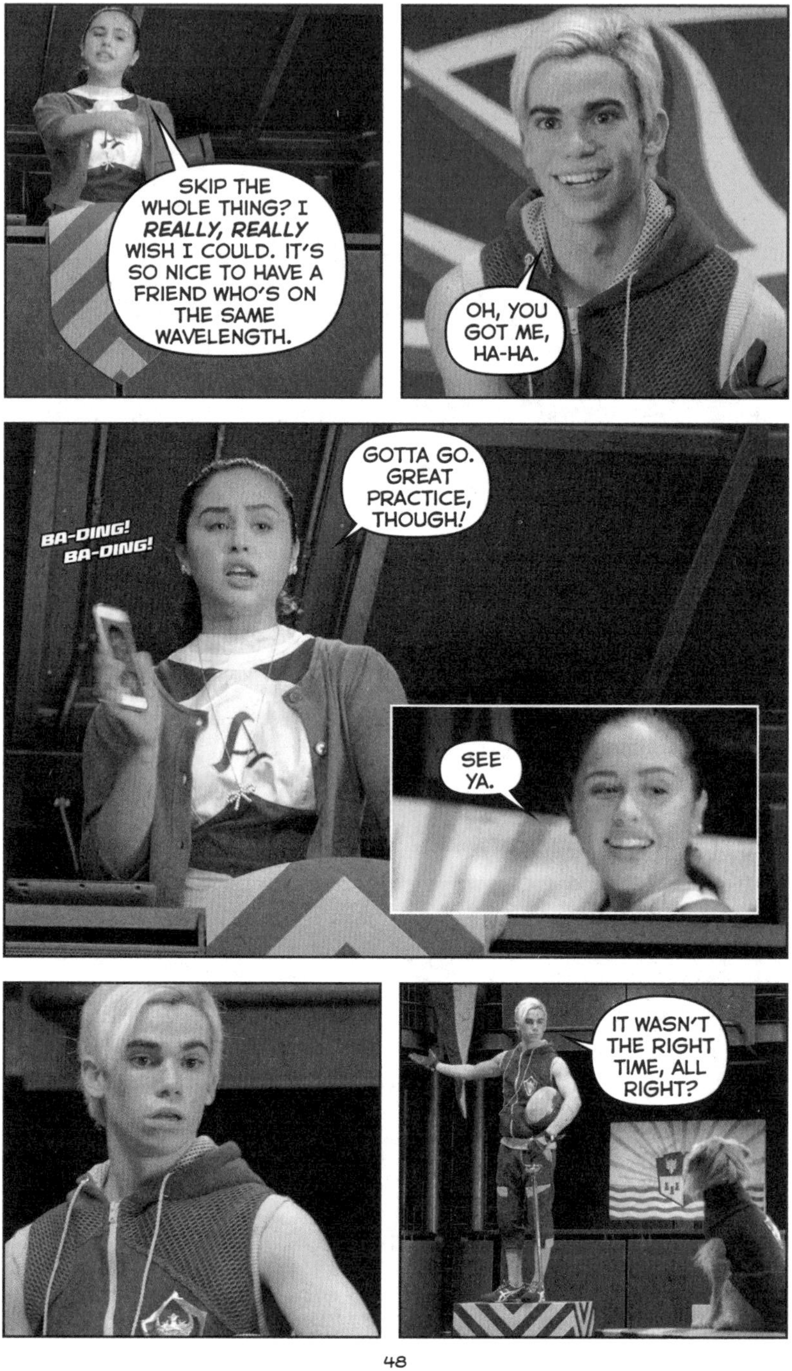
SKIP THE WHOLE THING? I *REALLY, REALLY* WISH I COULD. IT'S SO NICE TO HAVE A FRIEND WHO'S ON THE SAME WAVELENGTH.
OH, YOU GOT ME, HA-HA.
BA-DING! BA-DING!
GOTTA GO. GREAT PRACTICE, THOUGH!
SEE YA.
IT WASN'T THE RIGHT TIME, ALL RIGHT?

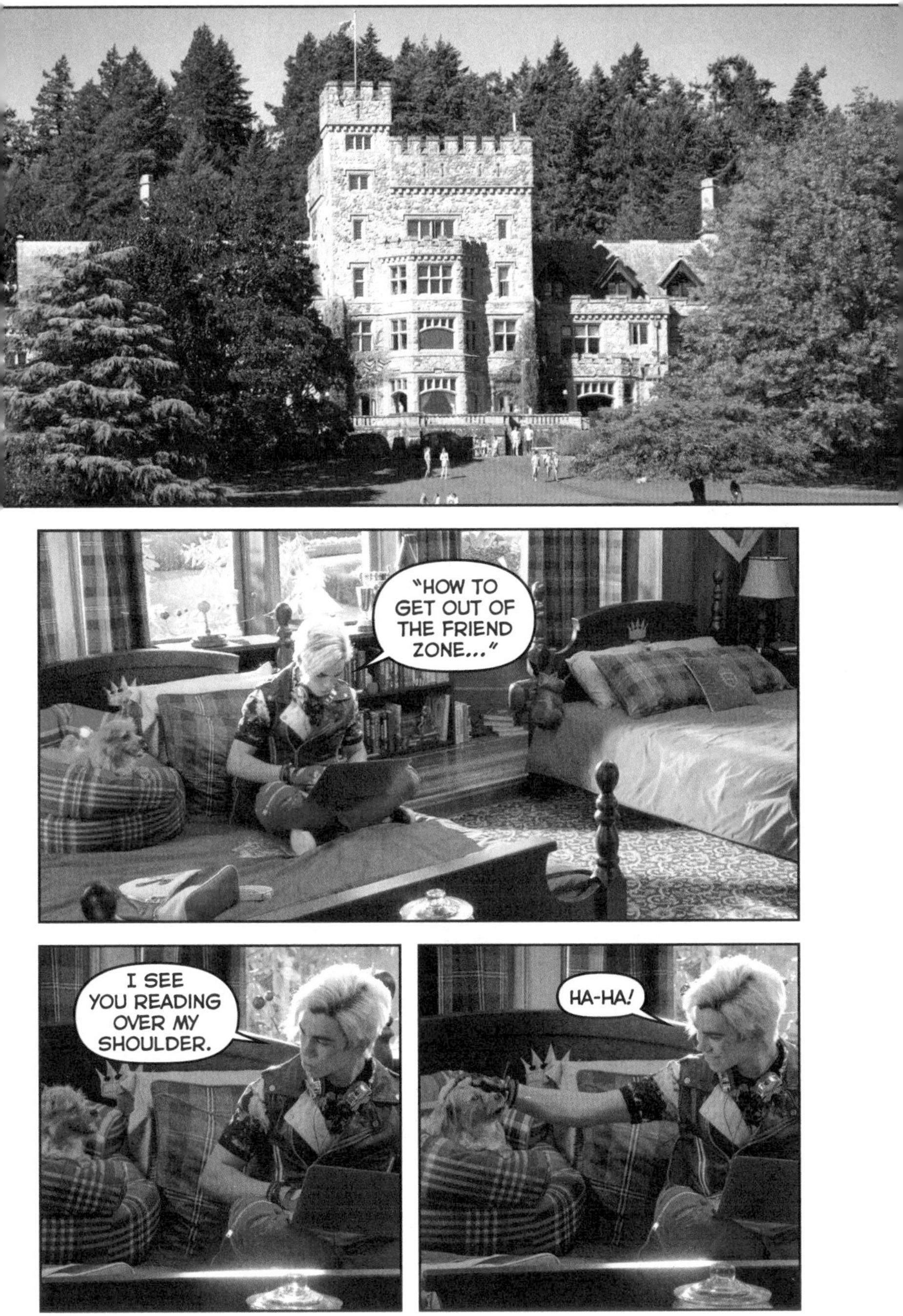
"HOW TO GET OUT OF THE FRIEND ZONE..."
I SEE YOU READING OVER MY SHOULDER.
HA-HA!

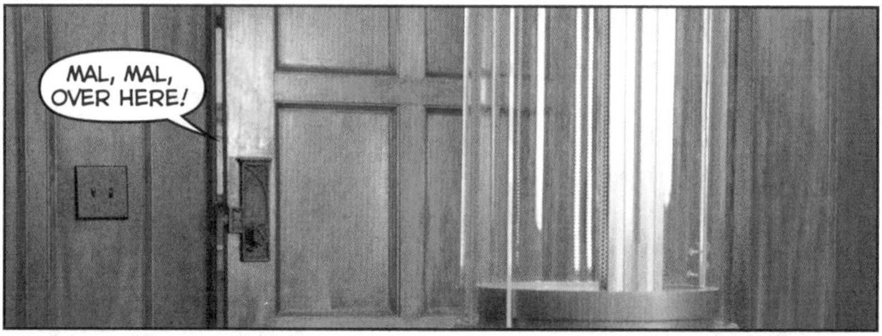
MAL, MAL,
OVER HERE!

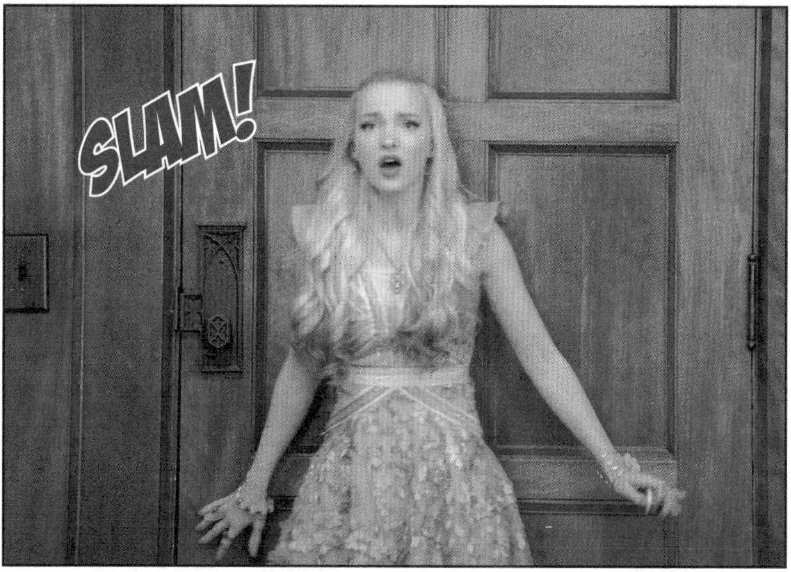
SLAM!

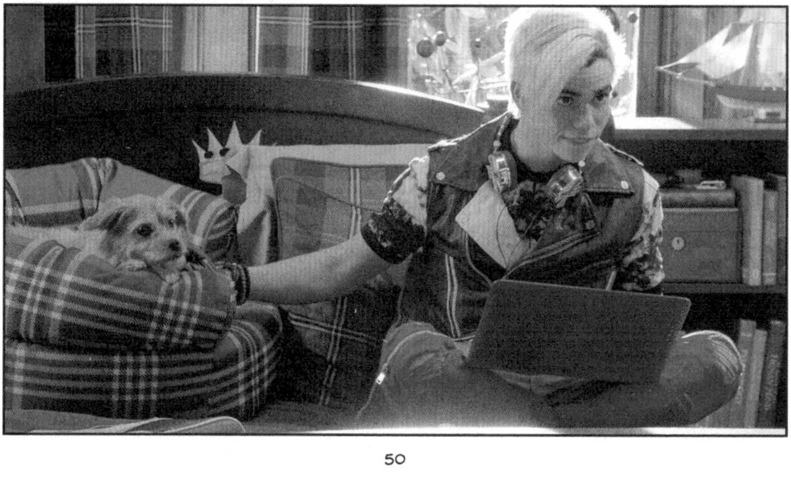

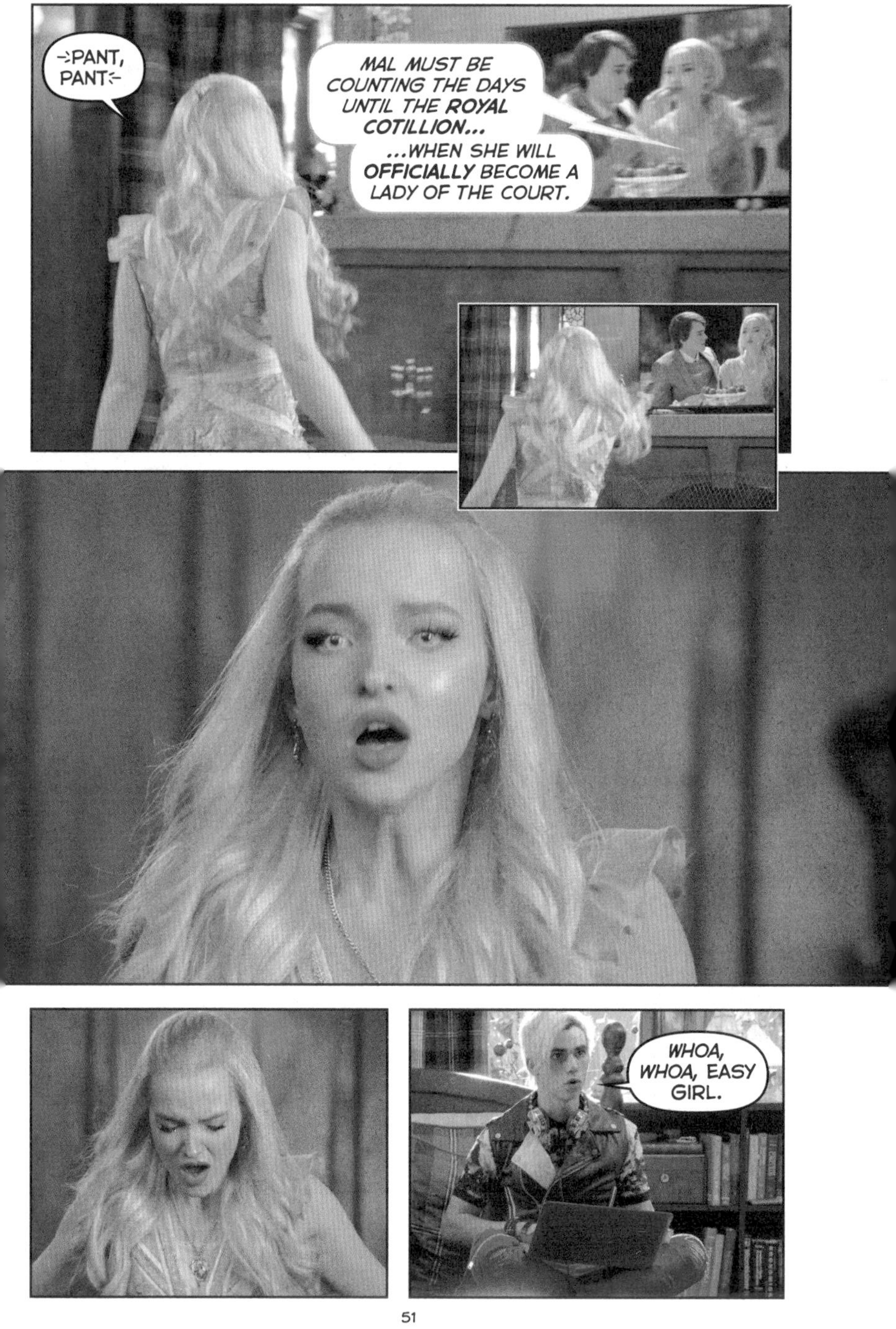
-:PANT, PANT:-
MAL MUST BE COUNTING THE DAYS UNTIL THE **ROYAL** COTILLION...
...WHEN SHE WILL **OFFICIALLY** BECOME A LADY OF THE COURT.
WHOA, WHOA, EASY GIRL.

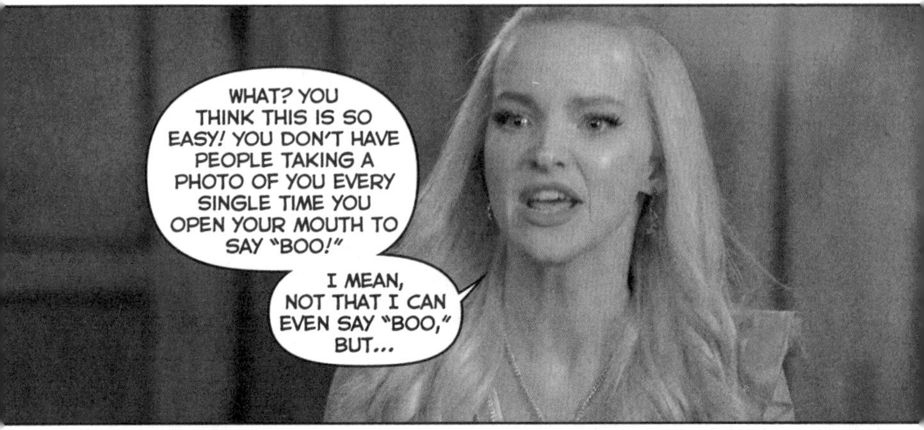
WHAT? YOU THINK THIS IS SO EASY! YOU DON'T HAVE PEOPLE TAKING A PHOTO OF YOU EVERY SINGLE TIME YOU OPEN YOUR MOUTH TO SAY "BOO!"
I MEAN, NOT THAT I CAN EVEN SAY "BOO," BUT...

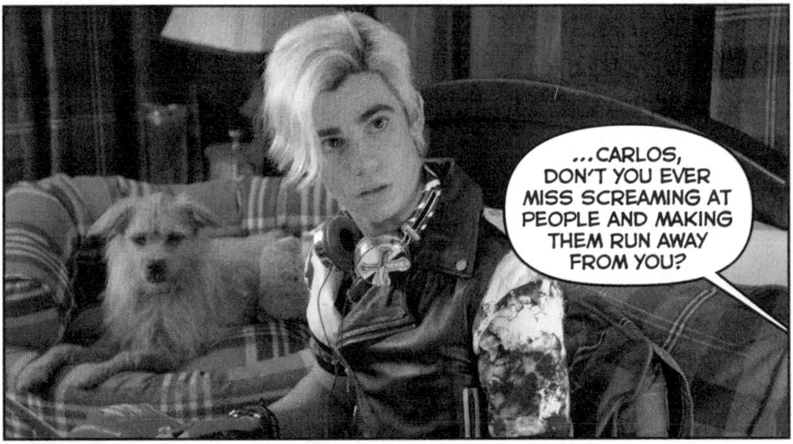
...CARLOS, DON'T YOU EVER MISS SCREAMING AT PEOPLE AND MAKING THEM RUN AWAY FROM YOU?

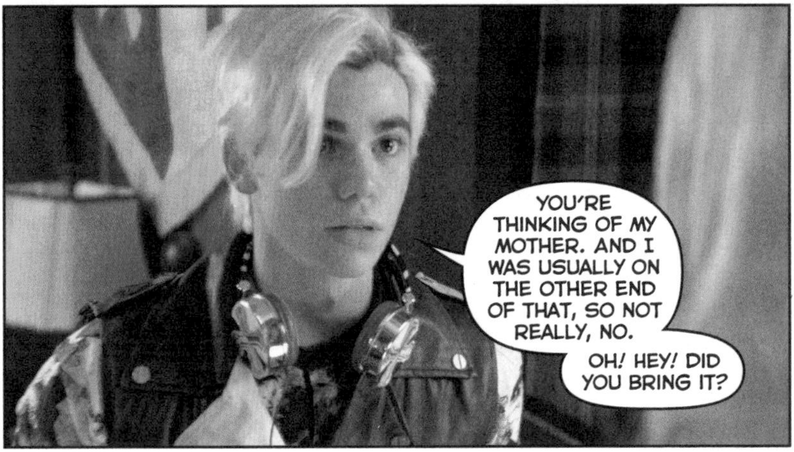
YOU'RE THINKING OF MY MOTHER. AND I WAS USUALLY ON THE OTHER END OF THAT, SO NOT REALLY, NO.
OH! HEY! DID YOU BRING IT?

CREEEEAK

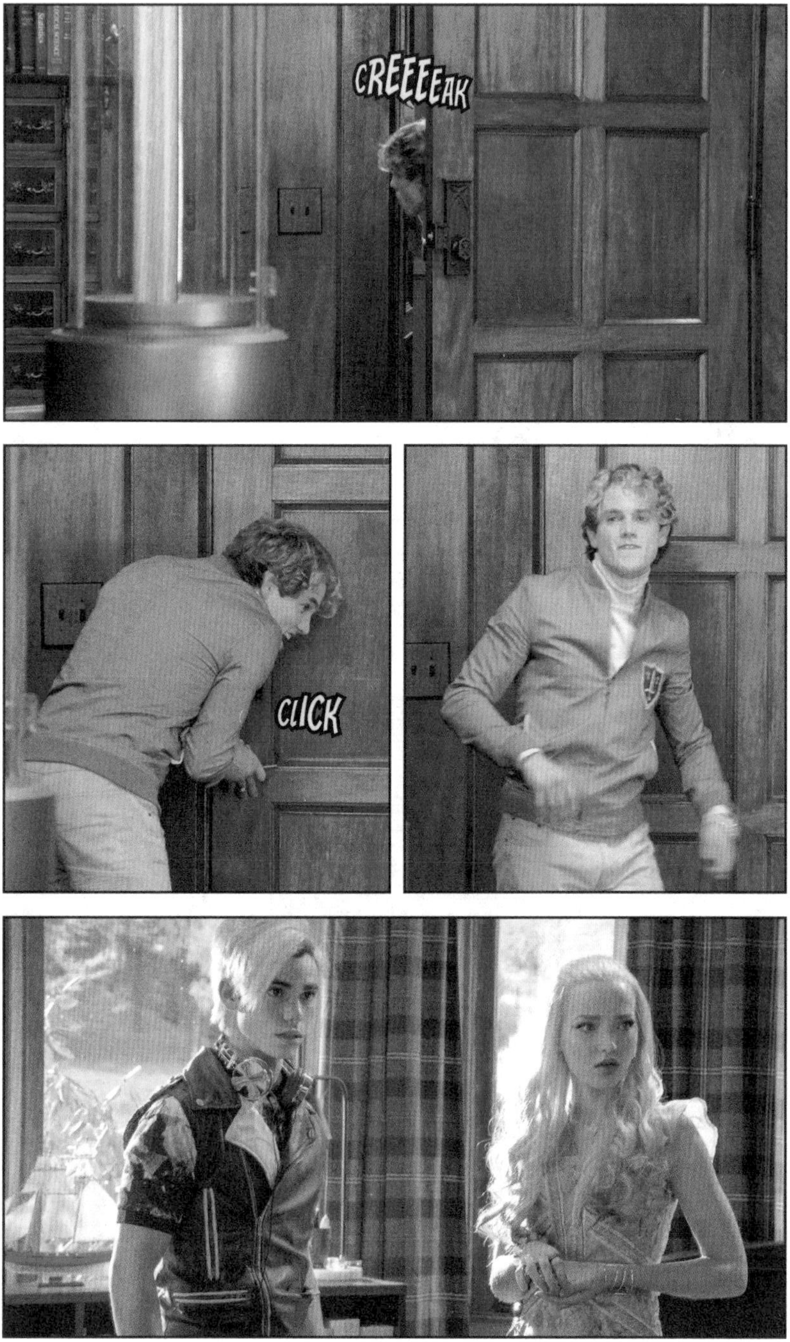
CREEEEAK
CLICK

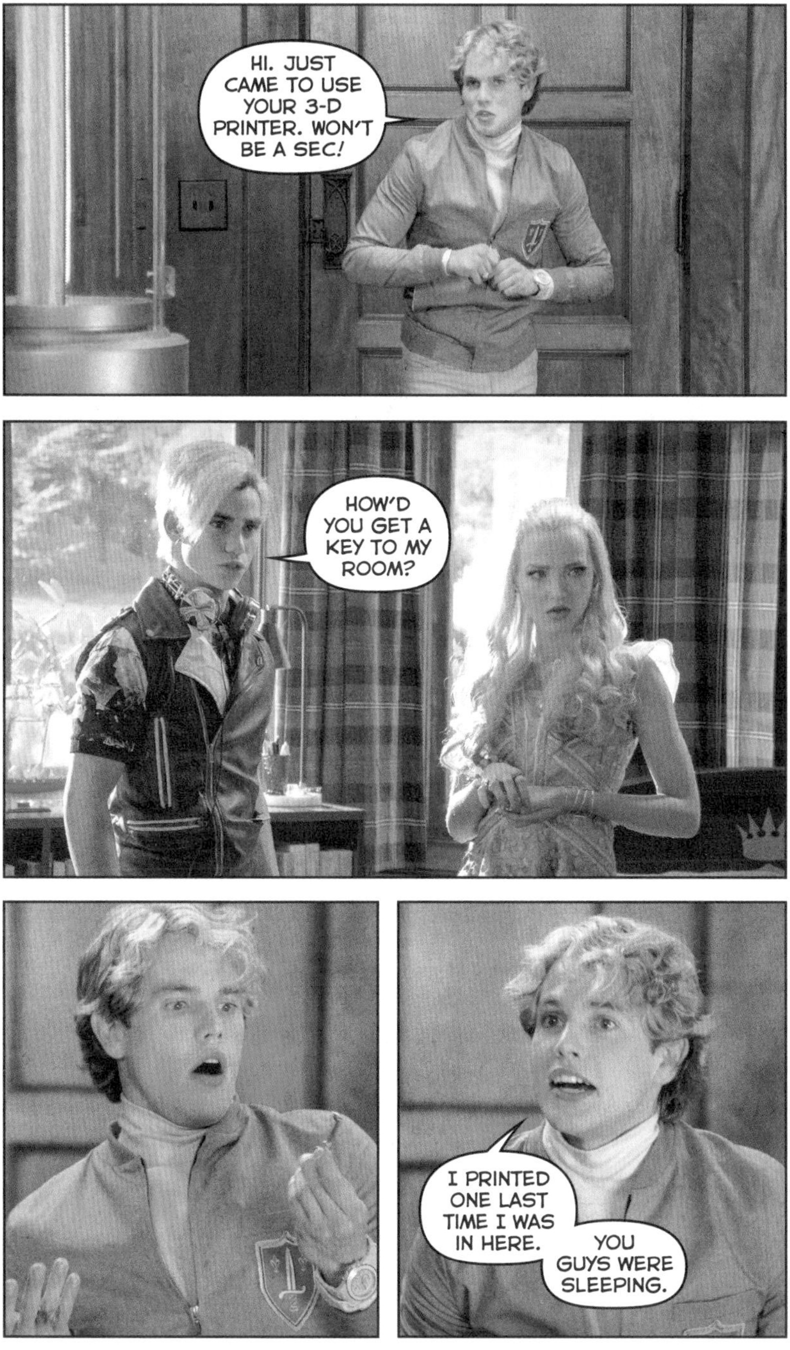
HI. JUST CAME TO USE YOUR 3-D PRINTER. WON'T BE A SEC!
HOW'D YOU GET A KEY TO MY ROOM?
I PRINTED ONE LAST TIME I WAS IN HERE.
YOU GUYS WERE SLEEPING.

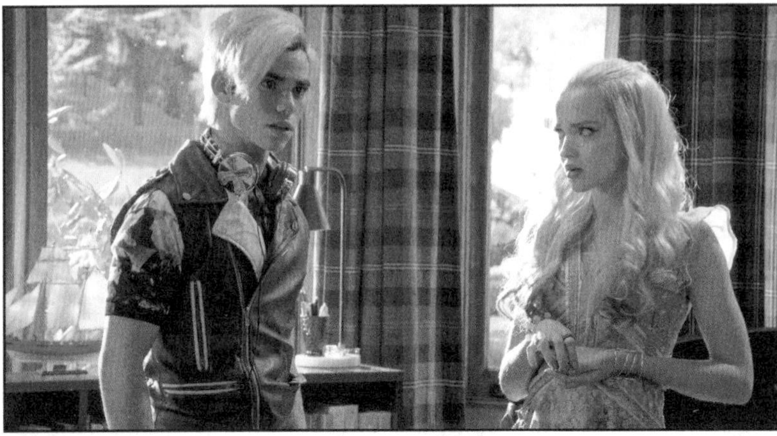

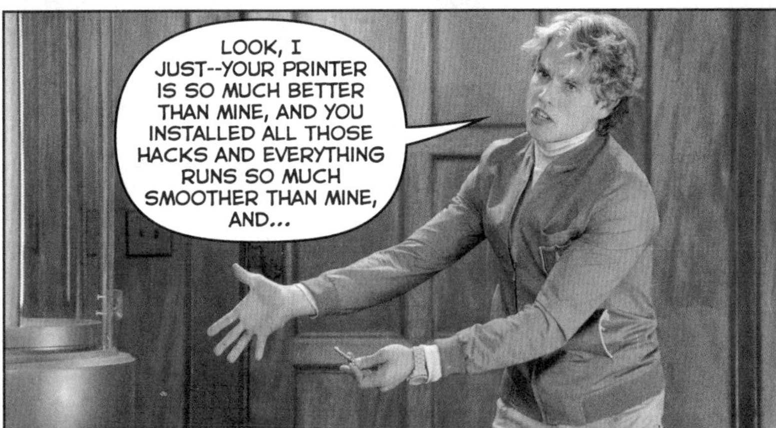
LOOK, I JUST--YOUR PRINTER IS SO MUCH BETTER THAN MINE, AND YOU INSTALLED ALL THOSE HACKS AND EVERYTHING RUNS SO MUCH SMOOTHER THAN MINE, AND...

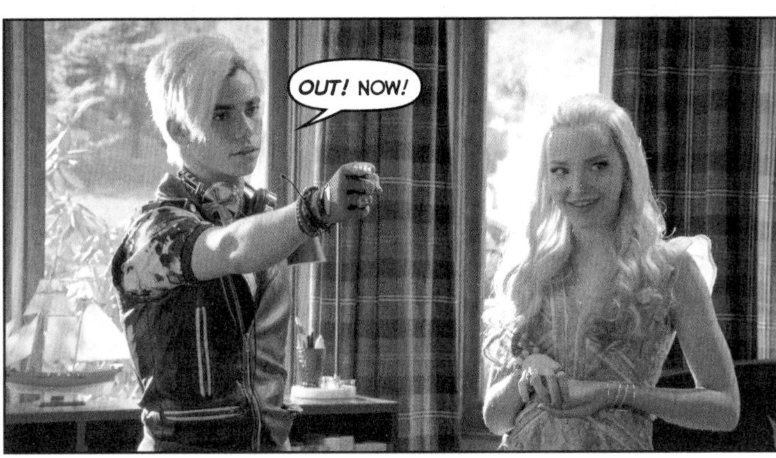
OUT! NOW!

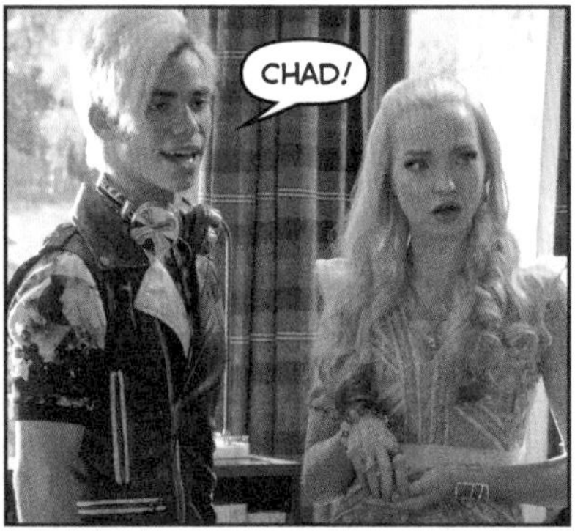
CHAD!

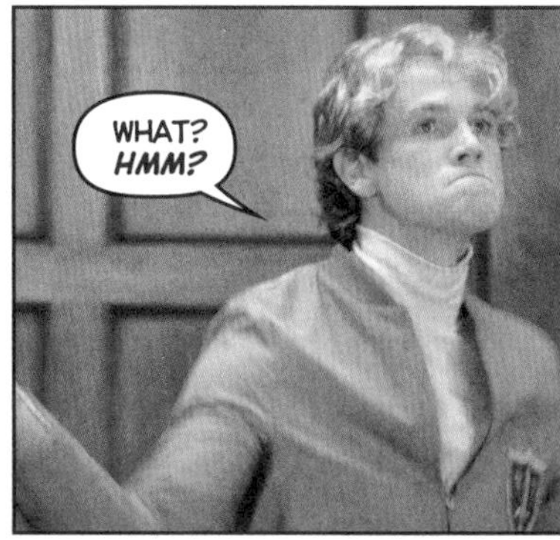
WHAT?
HMM?

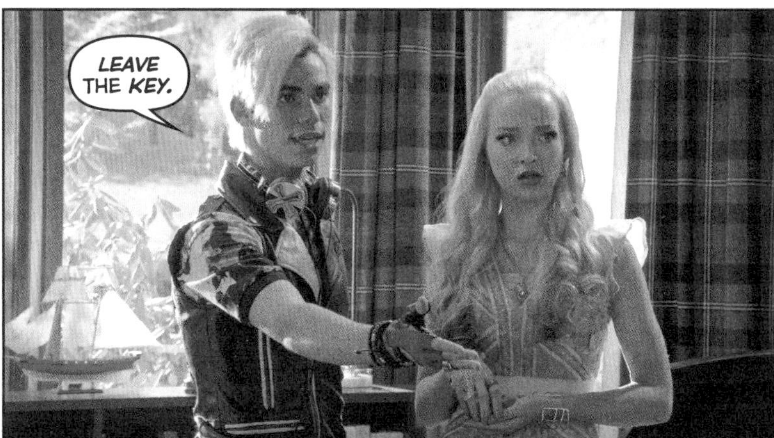
LEAVE THE KEY.

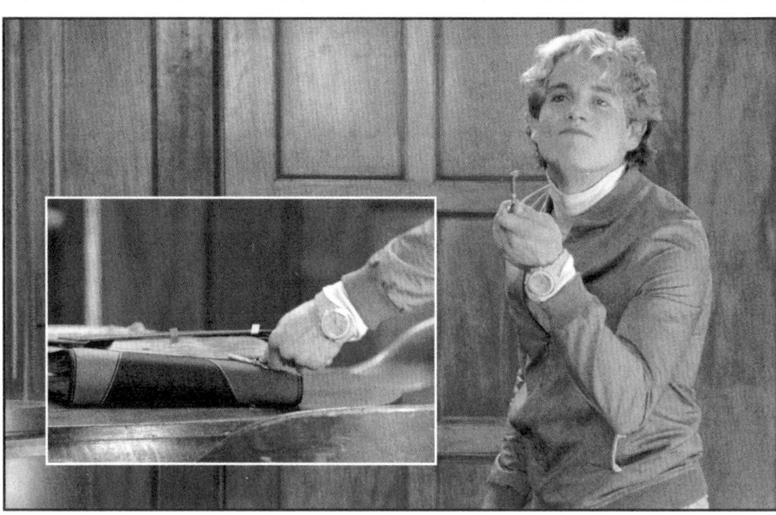

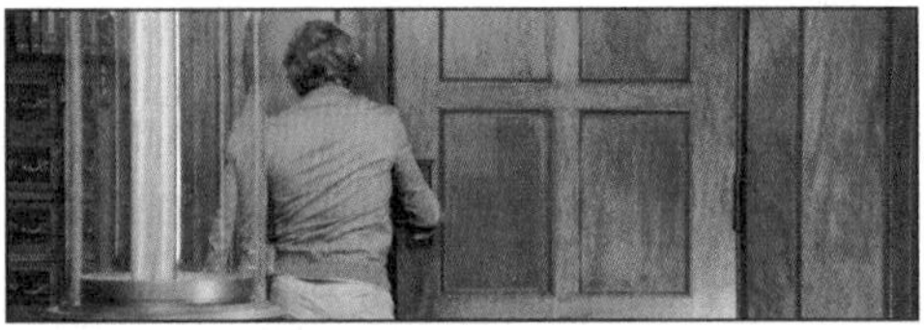

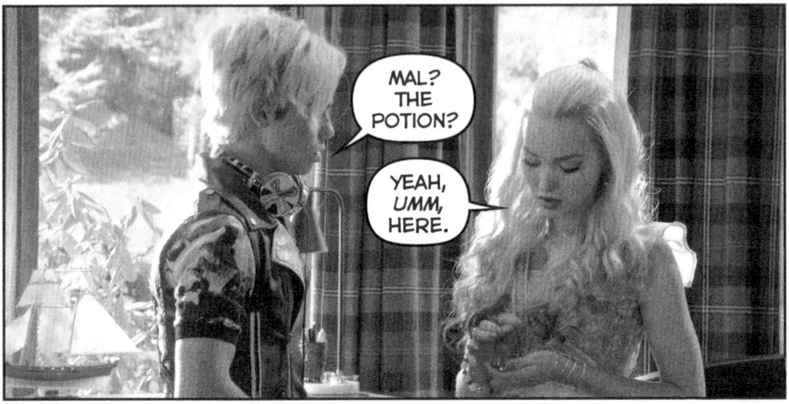
MAL? THE POTION?
YEAH, *UMM,* HERE.

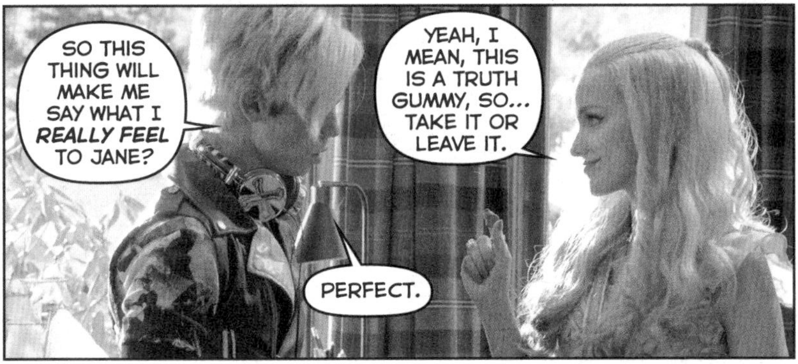
SO THIS THING WILL MAKE ME SAY WHAT I ***REALLY FEEL*** TO JANE?
YEAH, I MEAN, THIS IS A TRUTH GUMMY, SO... TAKE IT OR LEAVE IT.
PERFECT.

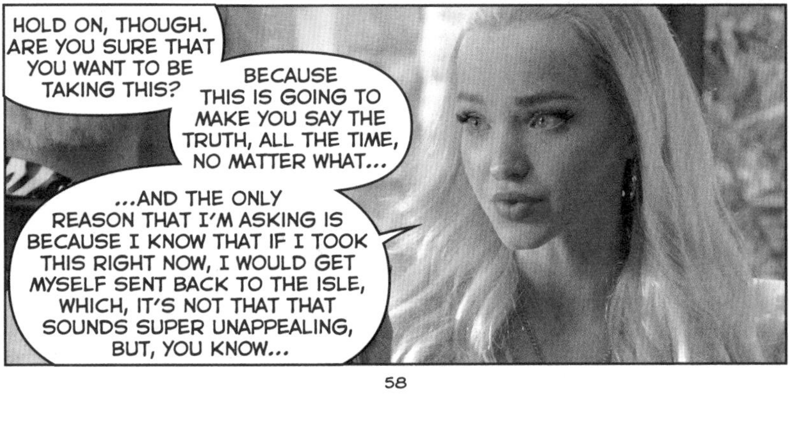
HOLD ON, THOUGH. ARE YOU SURE THAT YOU WANT TO BE TAKING THIS?
BECAUSE THIS IS GOING TO MAKE YOU SAY THE TRUTH, ALL THE TIME, NO MATTER WHAT...
...AND THE ONLY REASON THAT I'M ASKING IS BECAUSE I KNOW THAT IF I TOOK THIS RIGHT NOW, I WOULD GET MYSELF SENT BACK TO THE ISLE, WHICH, IT'S NOT THAT THAT SOUNDS SUPER UNAPPEALING, BUT, YOU KNOW...

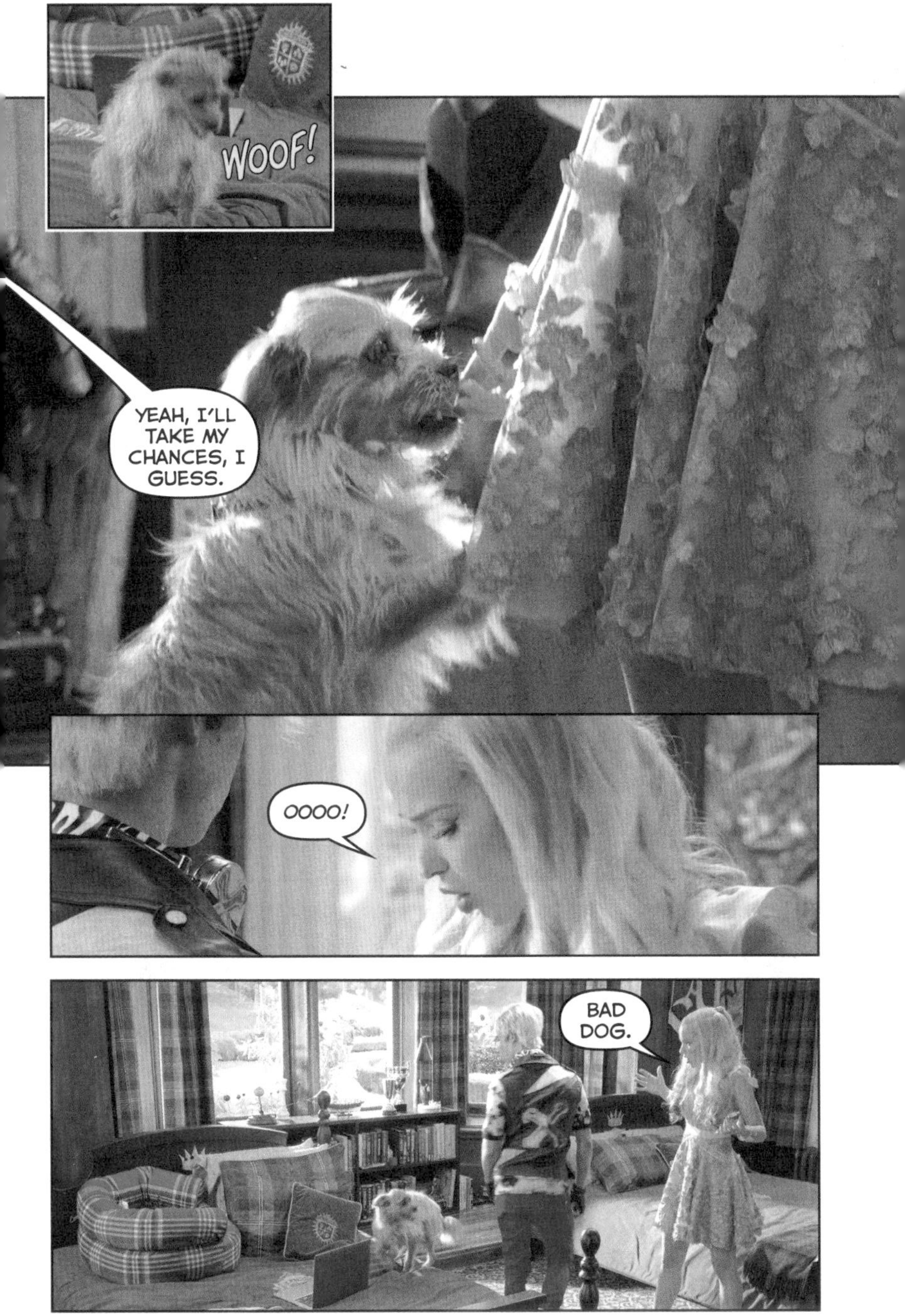
WOOF!
YEAH, I'LL TAKE MY CHANCES, I GUESS.
OOOO!
BAD DOG.

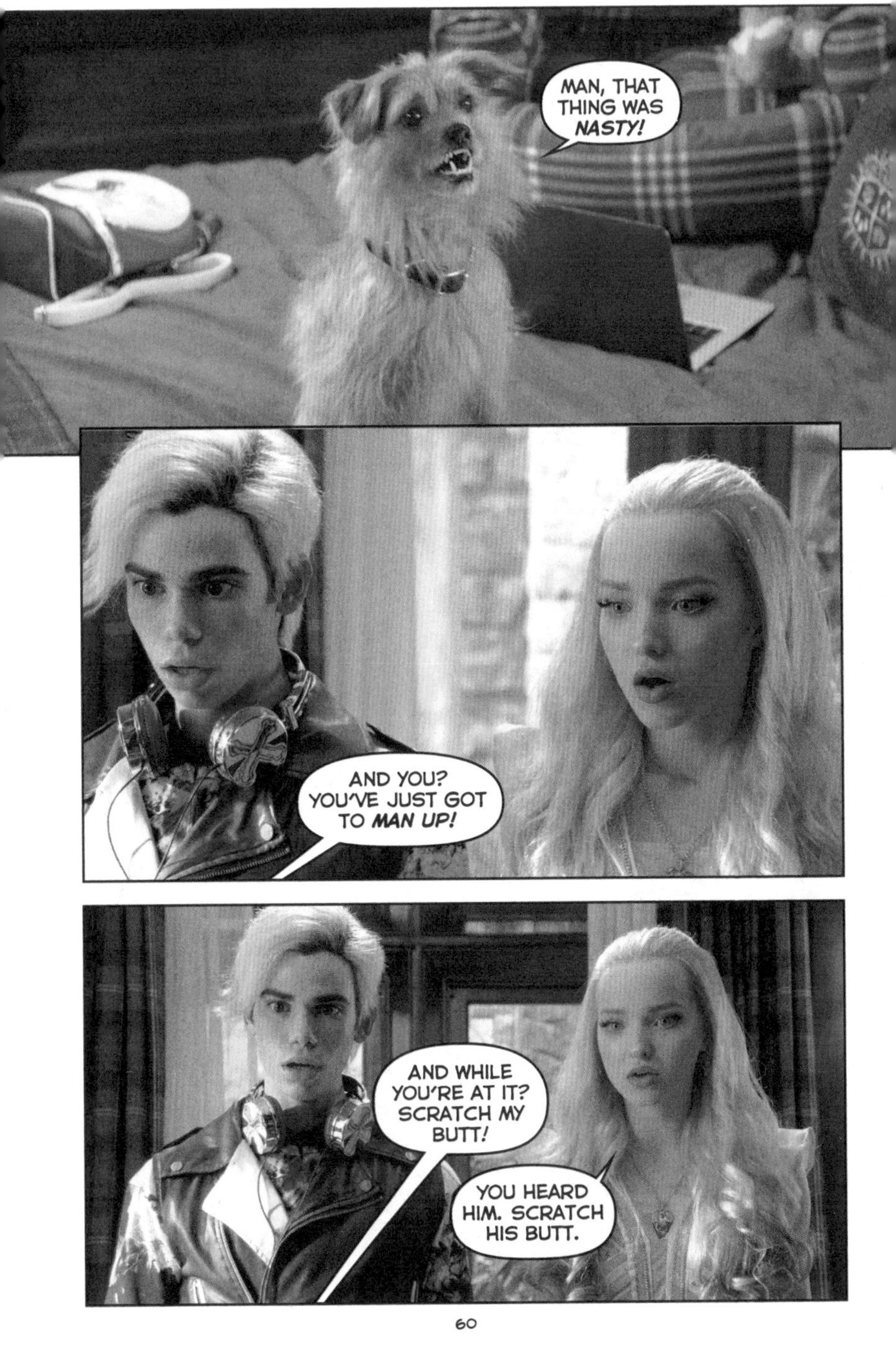
MAN, THAT THING WAS NASTY!
AND YOU? YOU'VE JUST GOT TO MAN UP!
AND WHILE YOU'RE AT IT? SCRATCH MY BUTT!
YOU HEARD HIM. SCRATCH HIS BUTT.

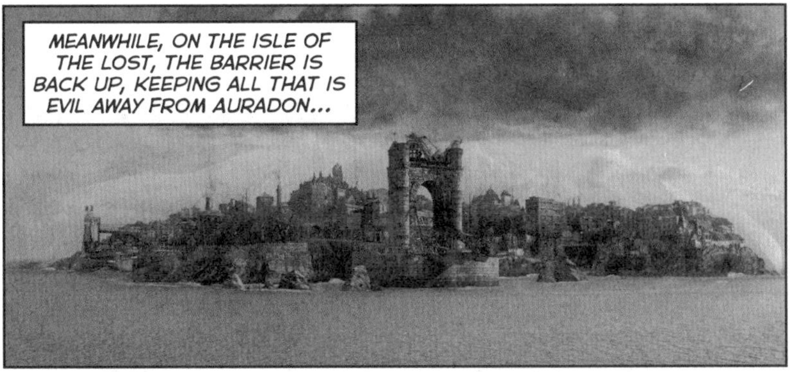
MEANWHILE, ON THE ISLE OF THE LOST, THE BARRIER IS BACK UP, KEEPING ALL THAT IS EVIL AWAY FROM AURADON...

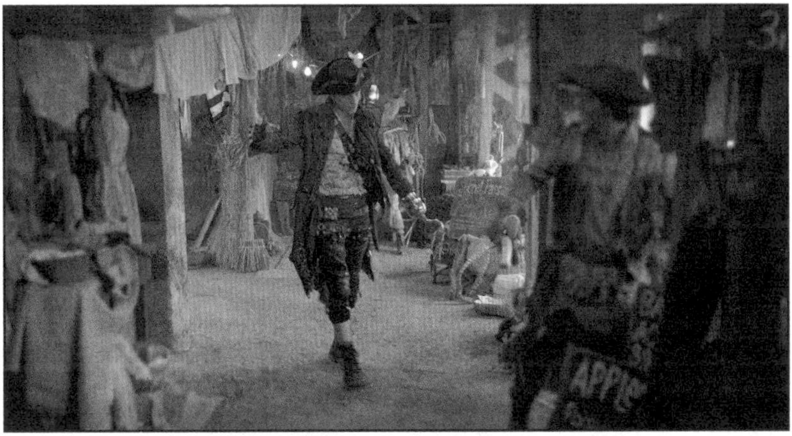

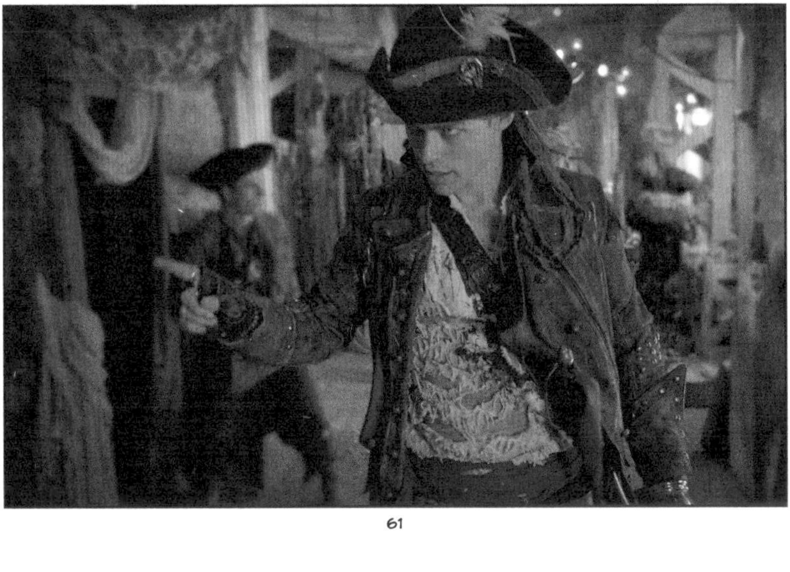

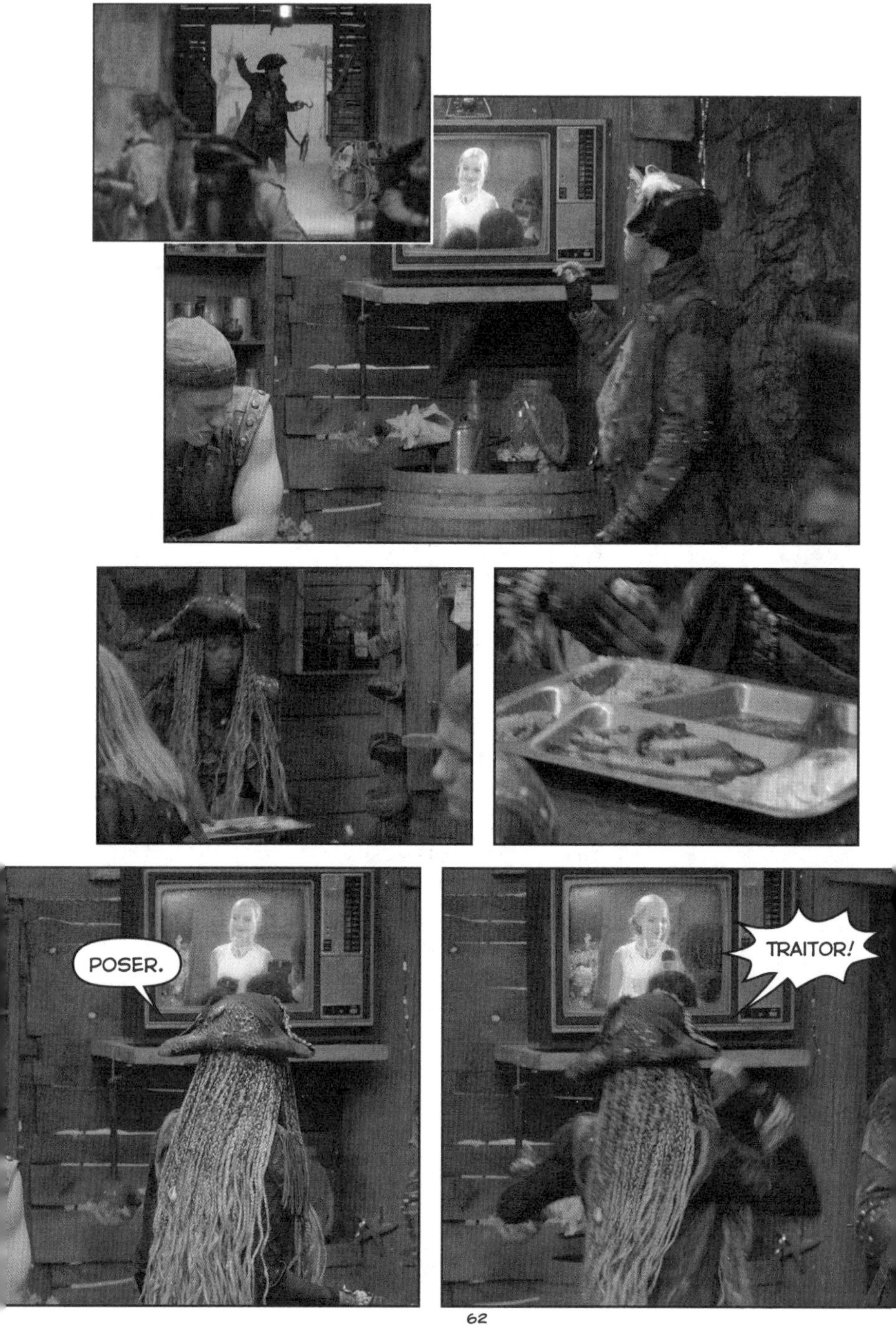
POSER.
TRAITOR!

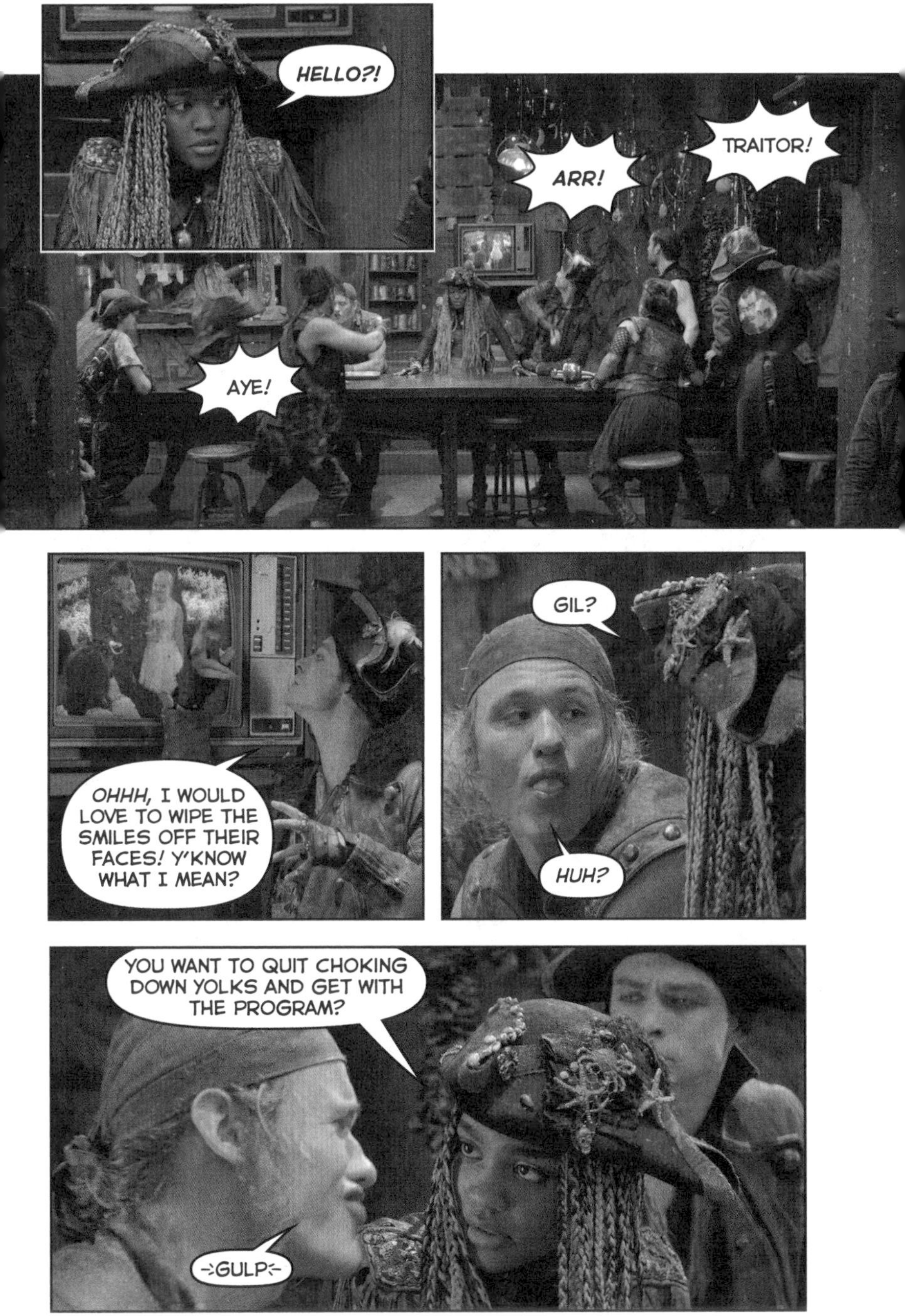
HELLO?!
ARR!
TRAITOR!
AYE!
OHHH, I WOULD LOVE TO WIPE THE SMILES OFF THEIR FACES! Y'KNOW WHAT I MEAN?
GIL?
HUH?
YOU WANT TO QUIT CHOKING DOWN YOLKS AND GET WITH THE PROGRAM?
GULP

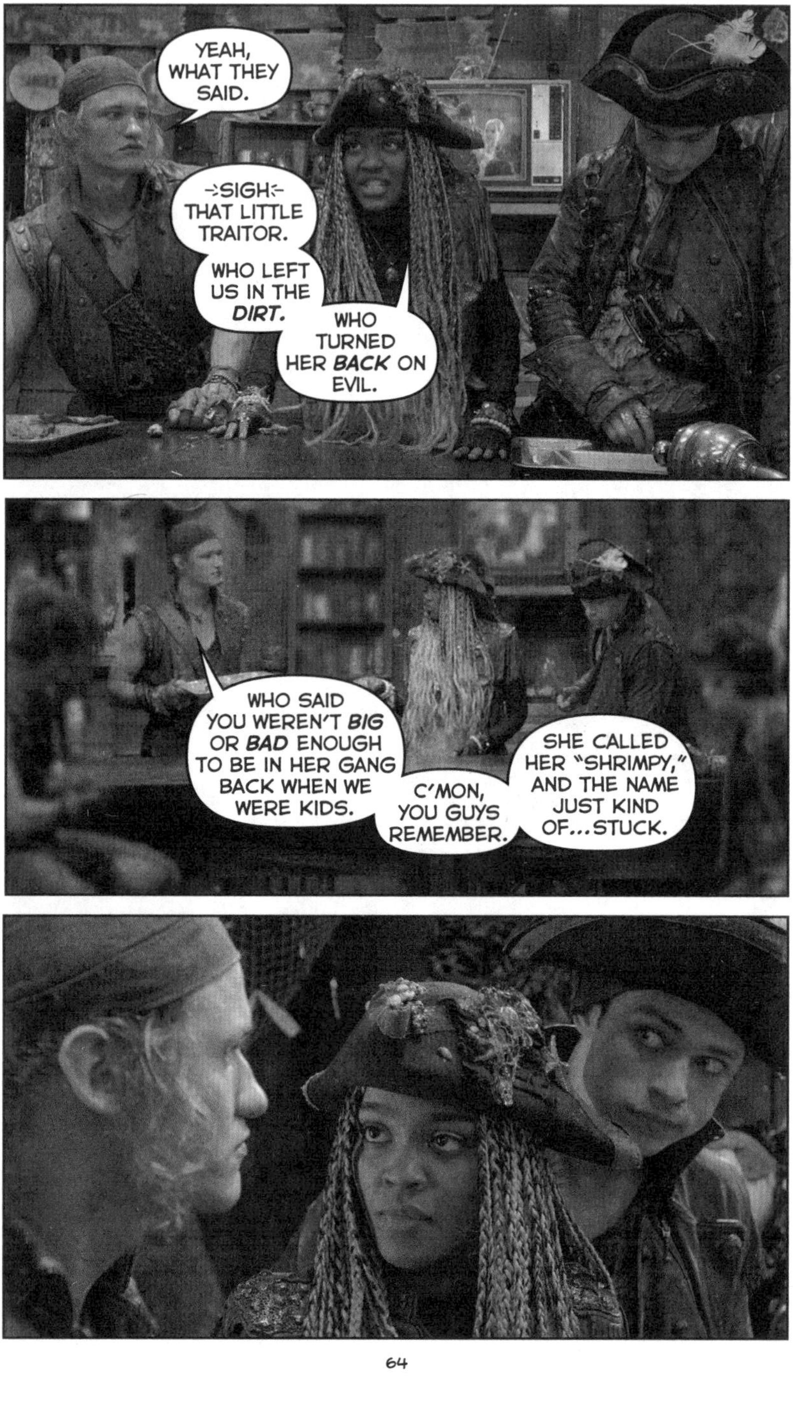
YEAH, WHAT THEY SAID.
SIGH THAT LITTLE TRAITOR.
WHO LEFT US IN THE *DIRT.*
WHO TURNED HER *BACK* ON EVIL.
WHO SAID YOU WEREN'T *BIG* OR *BAD* ENOUGH TO BE IN HER GANG BACK WHEN WE WERE KIDS.
C'MON, YOU GUYS REMEMBER.
SHE CALLED HER "SHRIMPY," AND THE NAME JUST KIND OF...STUCK.

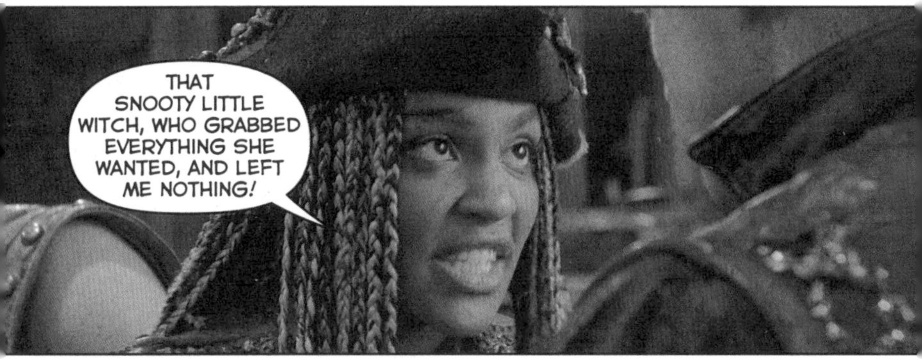
THAT SNOOTY LITTLE WITCH, WHO GRABBED EVERYTHING SHE WANTED, AND LEFT ME NOTHING!

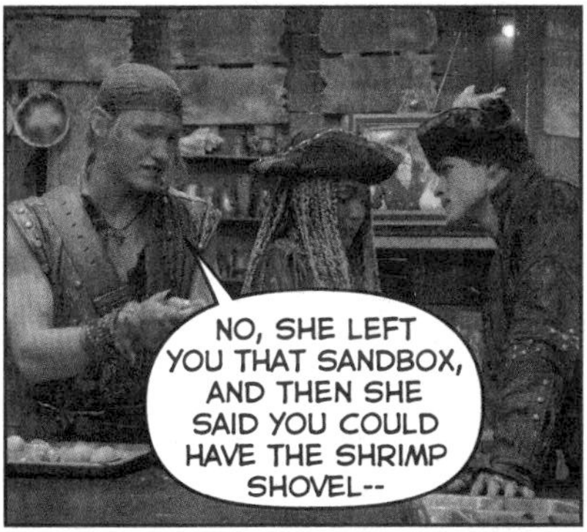
NO, SHE LEFT YOU THAT SANDBOX, AND THEN SHE SAID YOU COULD HAVE THE SHRIMP SHOVEL--

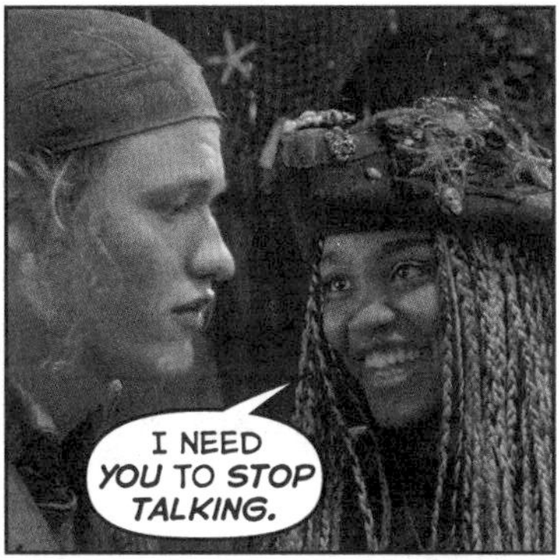
I NEED *YOU* TO *STOP TALKING.*

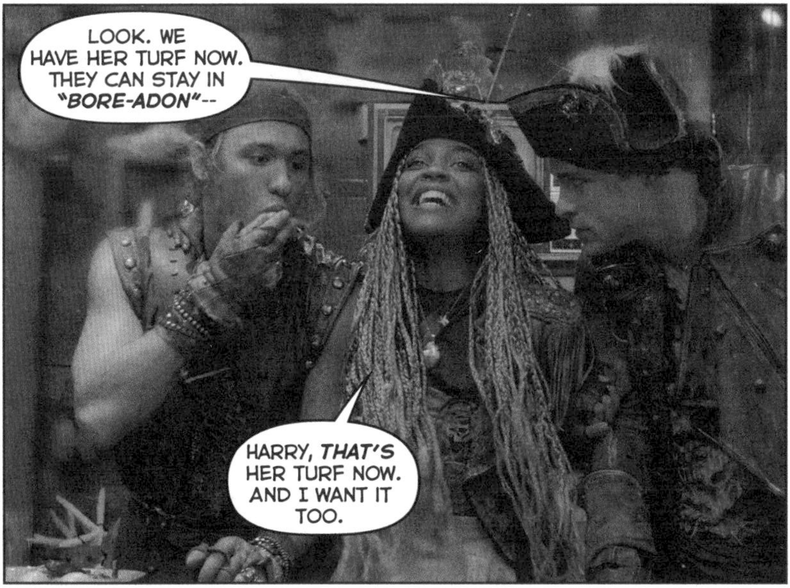
LOOK. WE HAVE HER TURF NOW. THEY CAN STAY IN *"BORE-ADON"*--
HARRY, *THAT'S* HER TURF NOW. AND I WANT IT TOO.

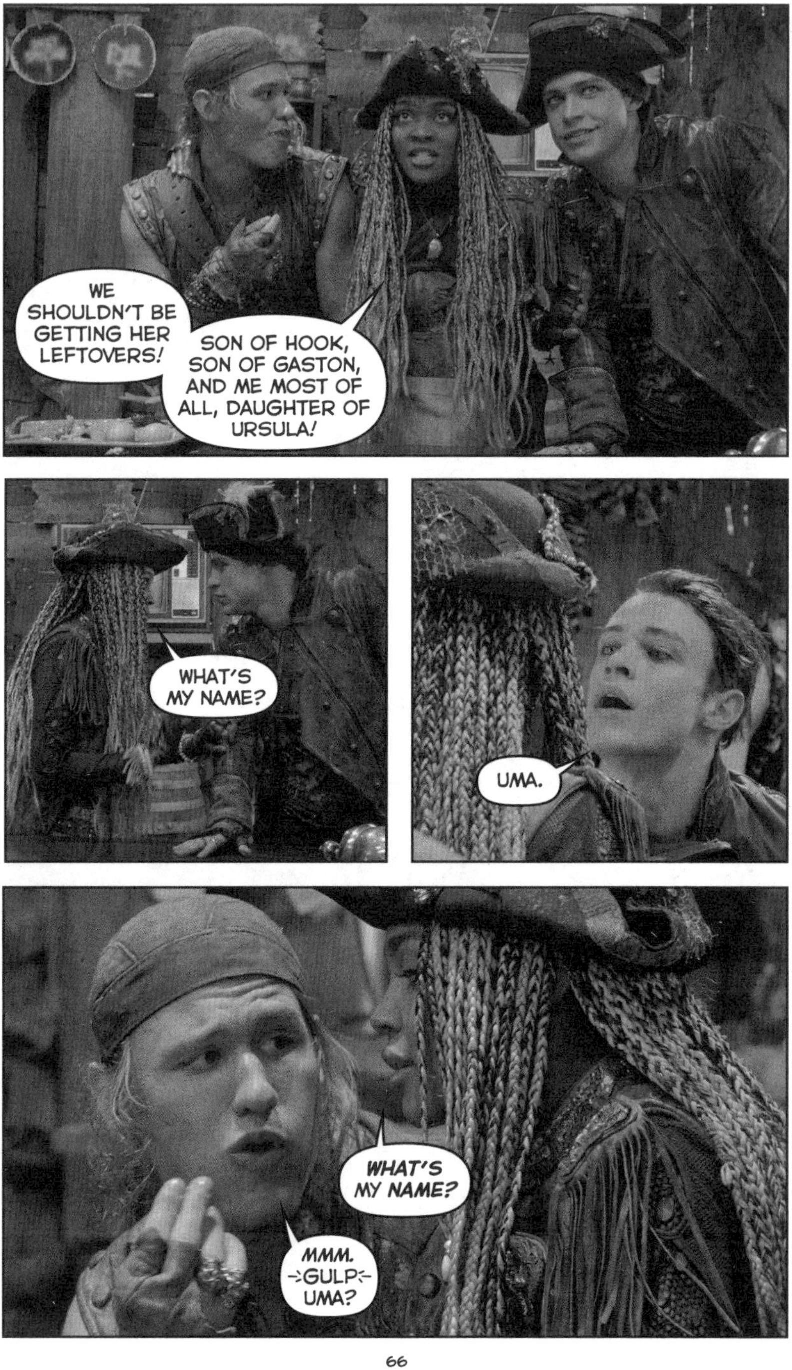
WE SHOULDN'T BE GETTING HER LEFTOVERS!
SON OF HOOK, SON OF GASTON, AND ME MOST OF ALL, DAUGHTER OF URSULA!
WHAT'S MY NAME?
UMA.
WHAT'S MY NAME?
MMM. -GULP- UMA?

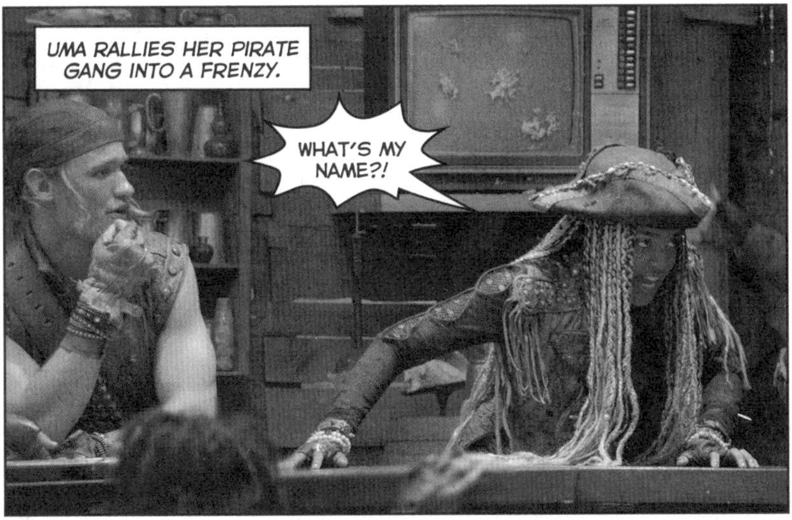
UMA RALLIES HER PIRATE GANG INTO A FRENZY.
WHAT'S MY NAME?!

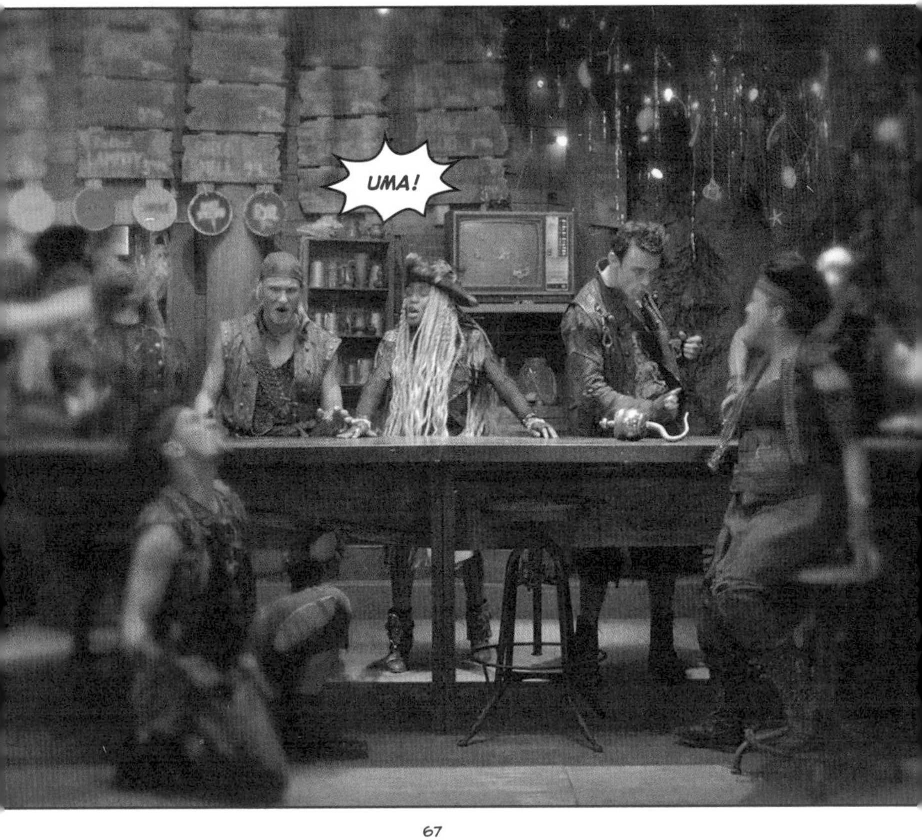
UMA!

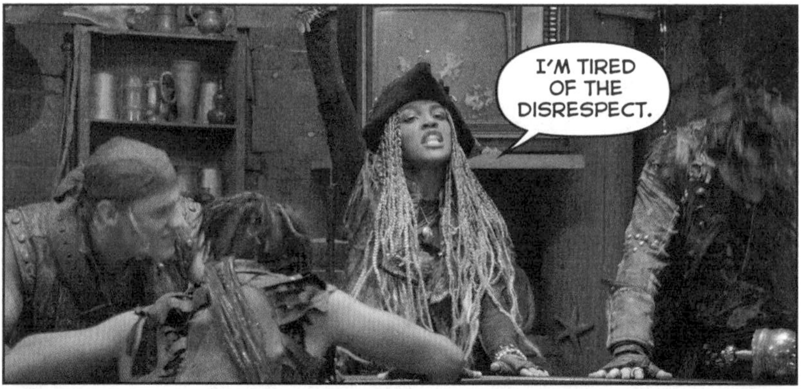
I'M TIRED OF THE DISRESPECT.

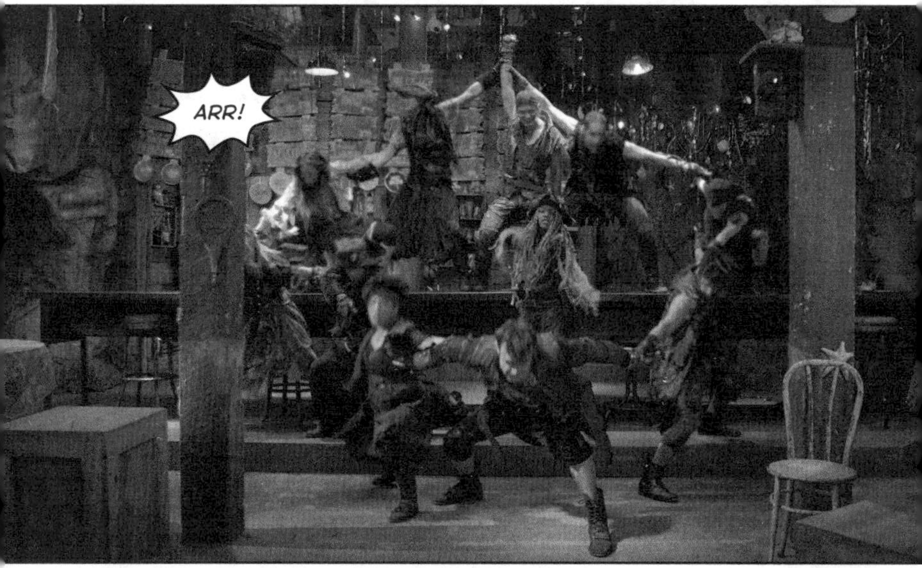
ARR!

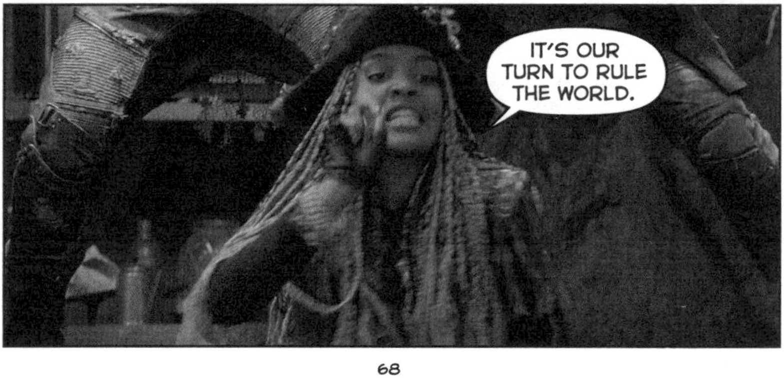
IT'S OUR TURN TO RULE THE WORLD.

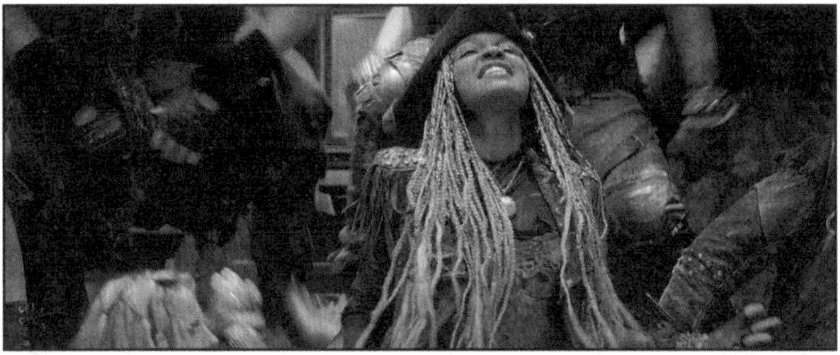

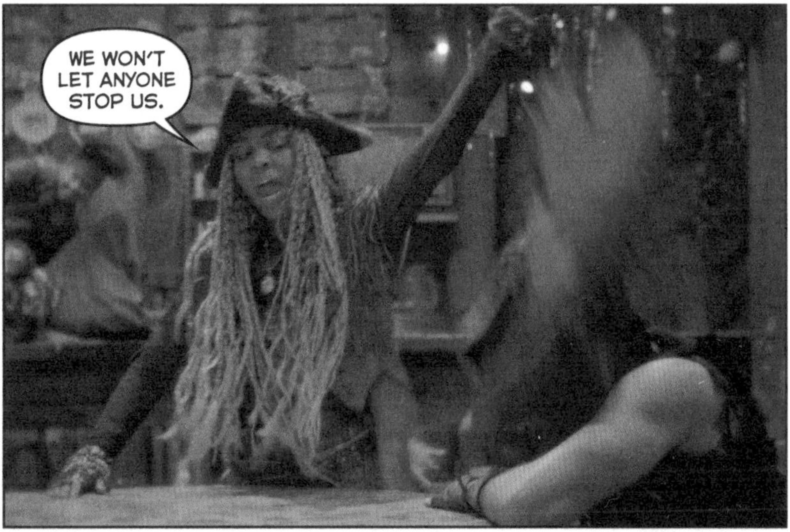
WE WON'T LET ANYONE STOP US.

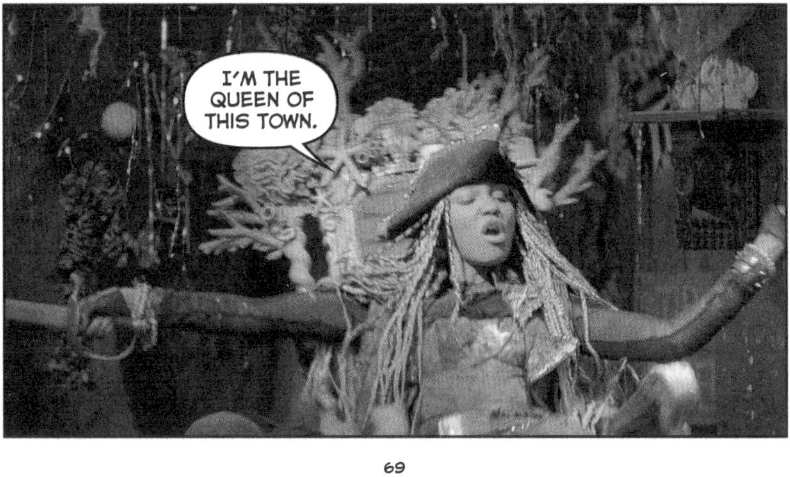
I'M THE QUEEN OF THIS TOWN.

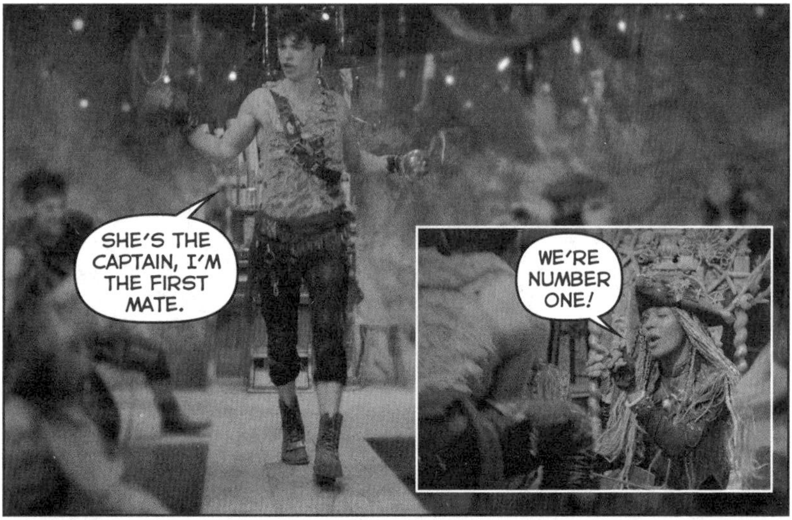
SHE'S THE CAPTAIN, I'M THE FIRST MATE.
WE'RE NUMBER ONE!

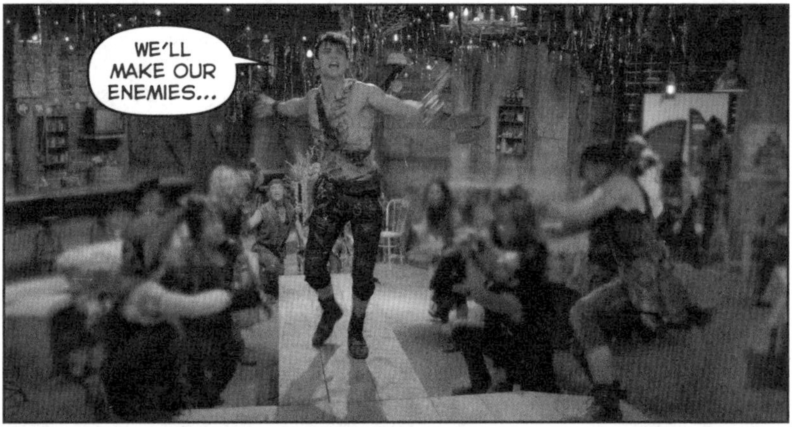
WE'LL MAKE OUR ENEMIES...

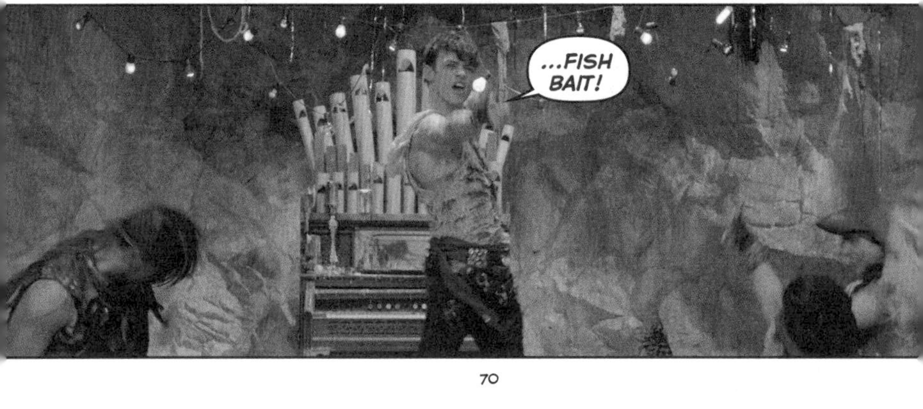
...FISH BAIT!

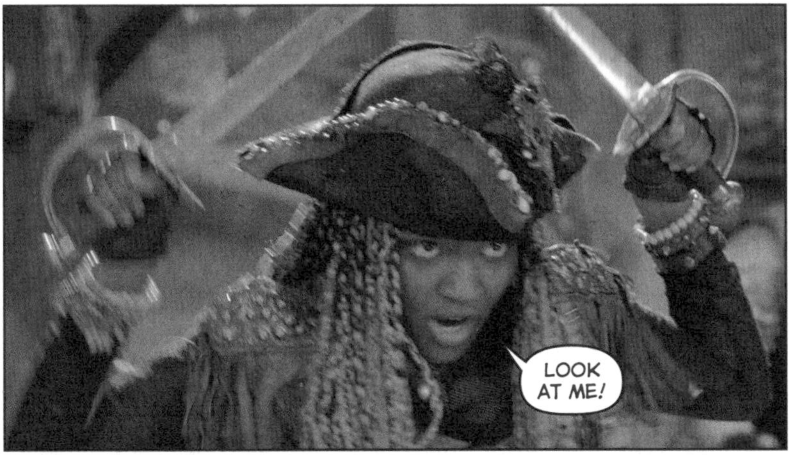
LOOK AT ME!

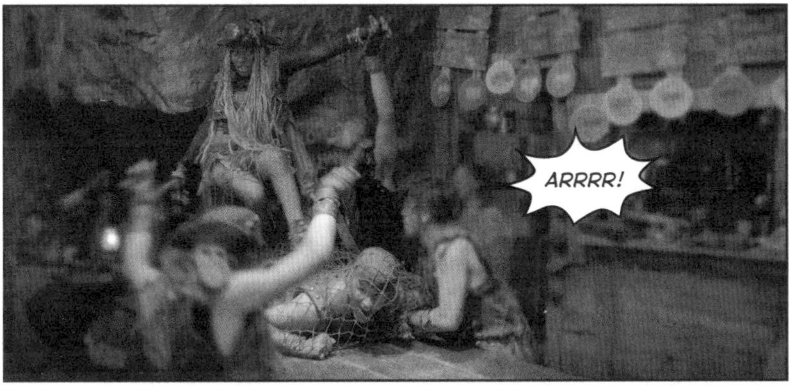
ARRRR!

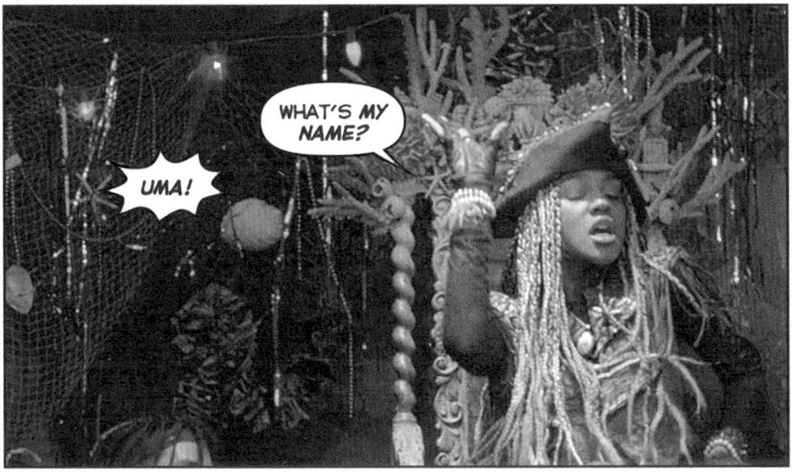
WHAT'S MY NAME?
UMA!

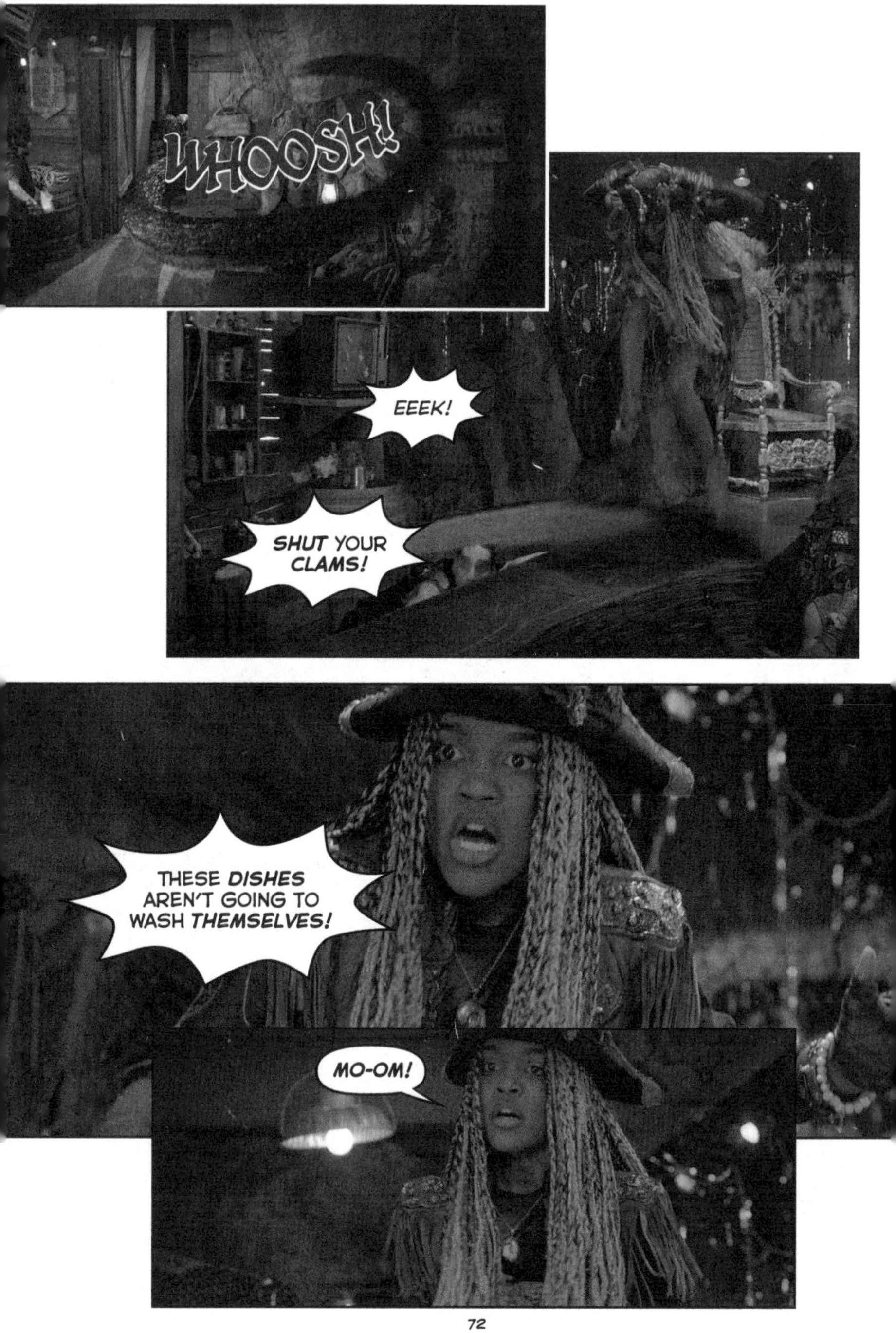
WHOOSH!
EEEK!
SHUT YOUR CLAMS!
THESE DISHES AREN'T GOING TO WASH THEMSELVES!
MO-OM!

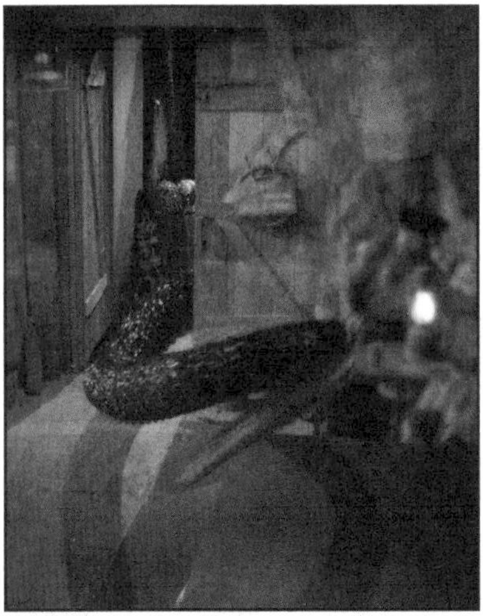

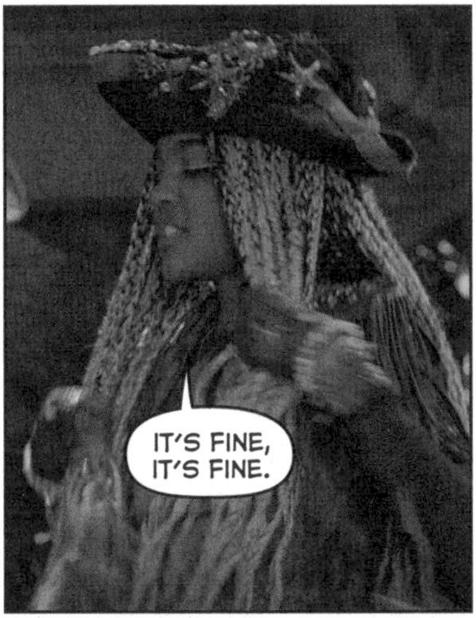
IT'S FINE, IT'S FINE.

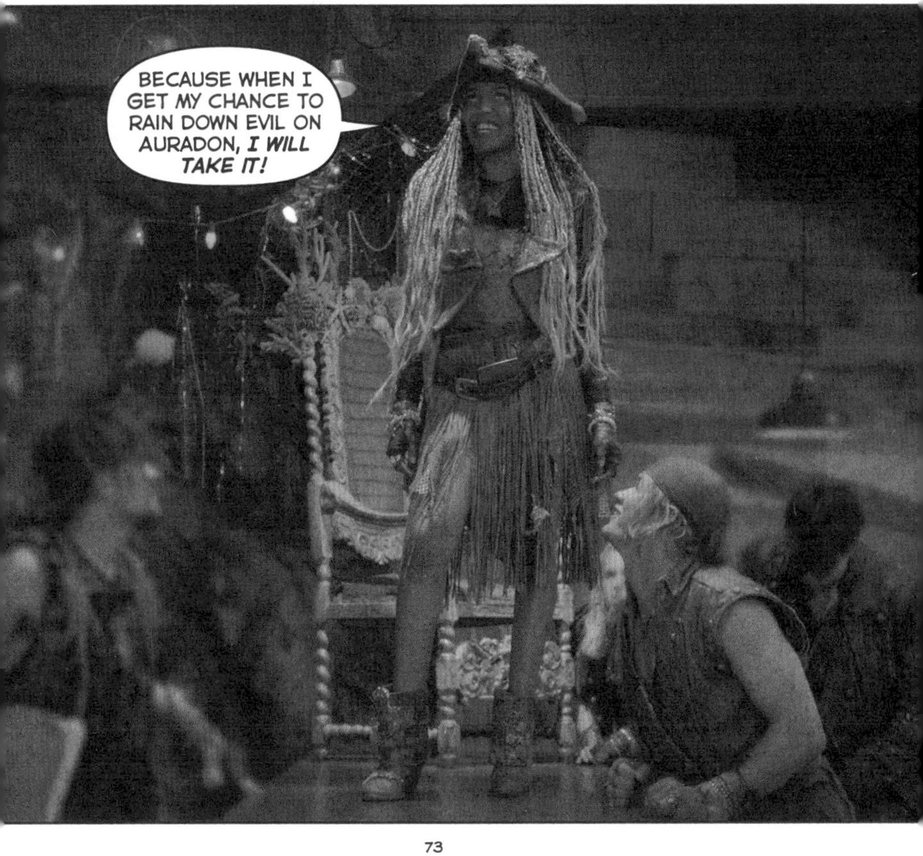
BECAUSE WHEN I GET MY CHANCE TO RAIN DOWN EVIL ON AURADON, *I WILL TAKE IT!*

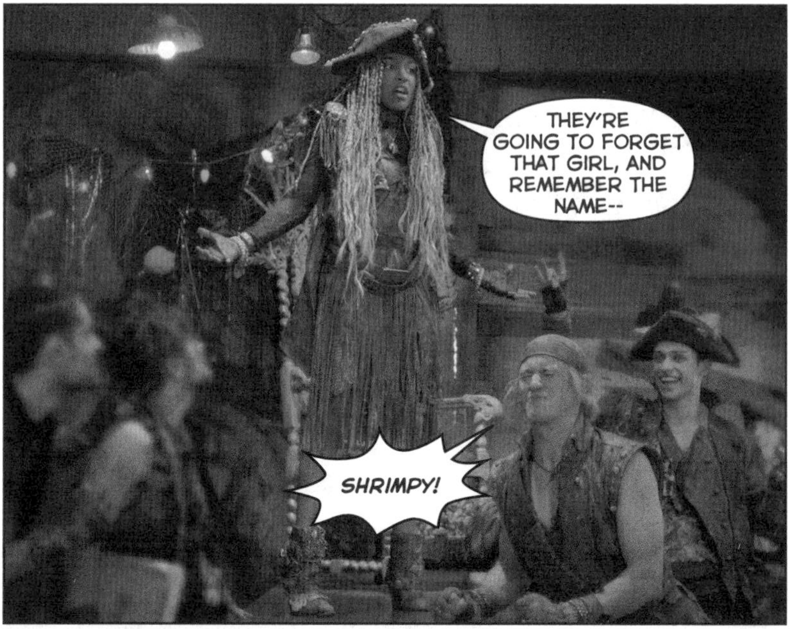
THEY'RE GOING TO FORGET THAT GIRL, AND REMEMBER THE NAME--
SHRIMPY!

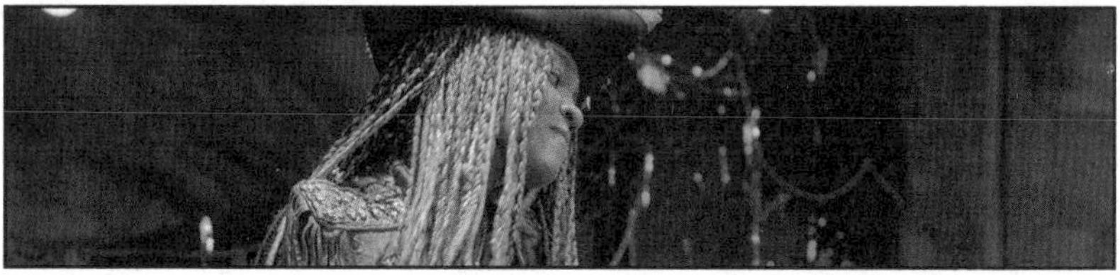

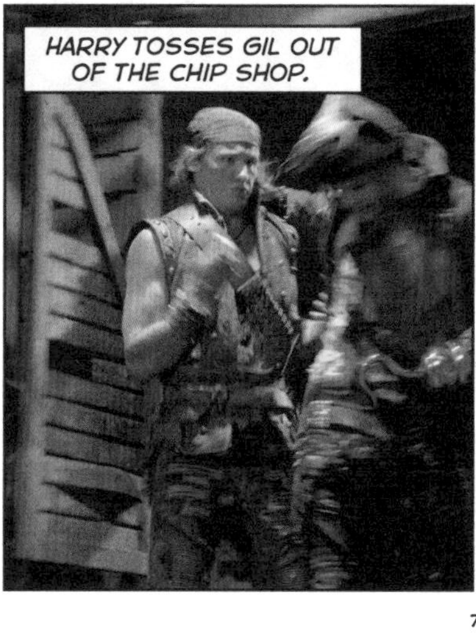
HARRY TOSSES GIL OUT OF THE CHIP SHOP.

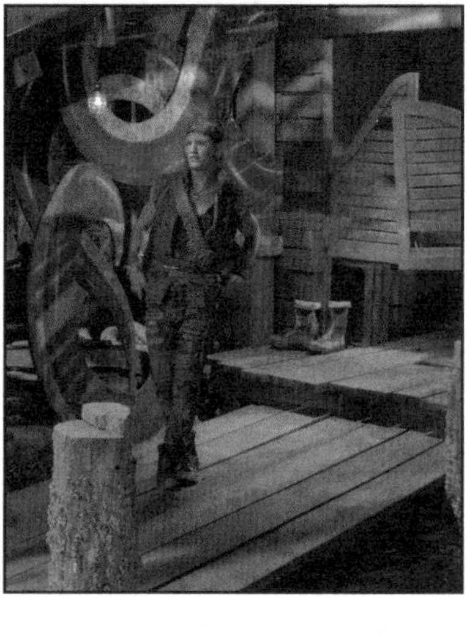

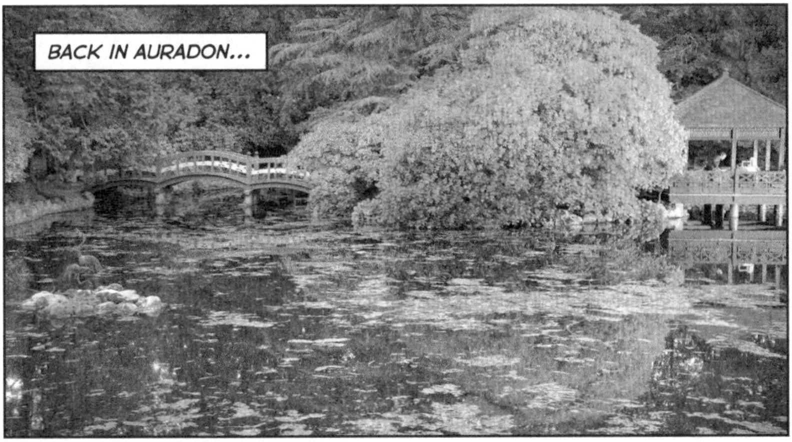
BACK IN AURADON...

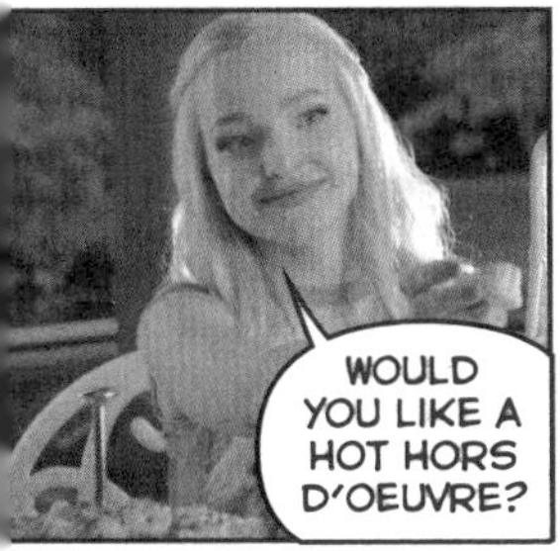
WOULD YOU LIKE A HOT HORS D'OEUVRE?

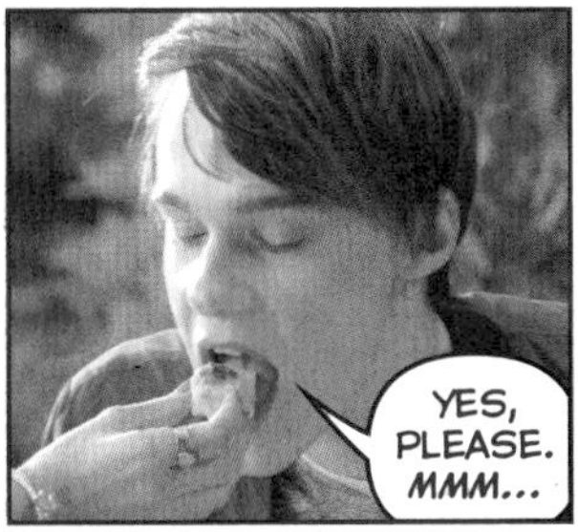
YES, PLEASE. MMM...

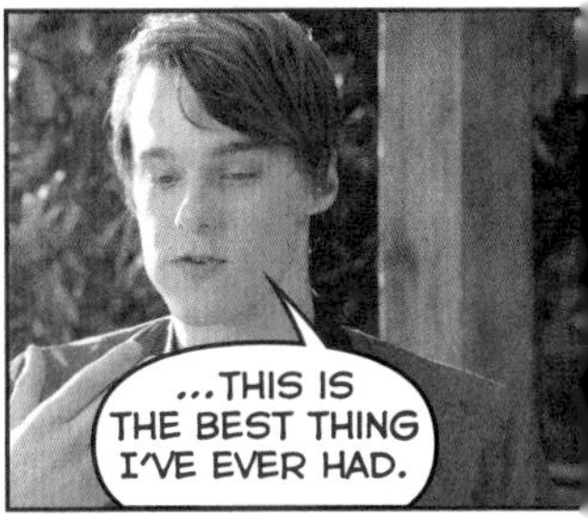
...THIS IS THE BEST THING I'VE EVER HAD.

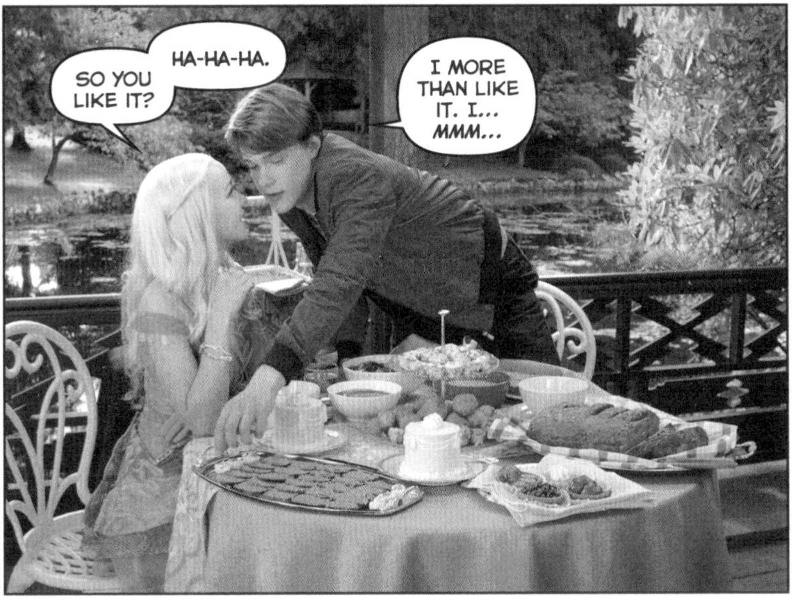
HA-HA-HA.
SO YOU LIKE IT?
I MORE THAN LIKE IT. I... MMM...

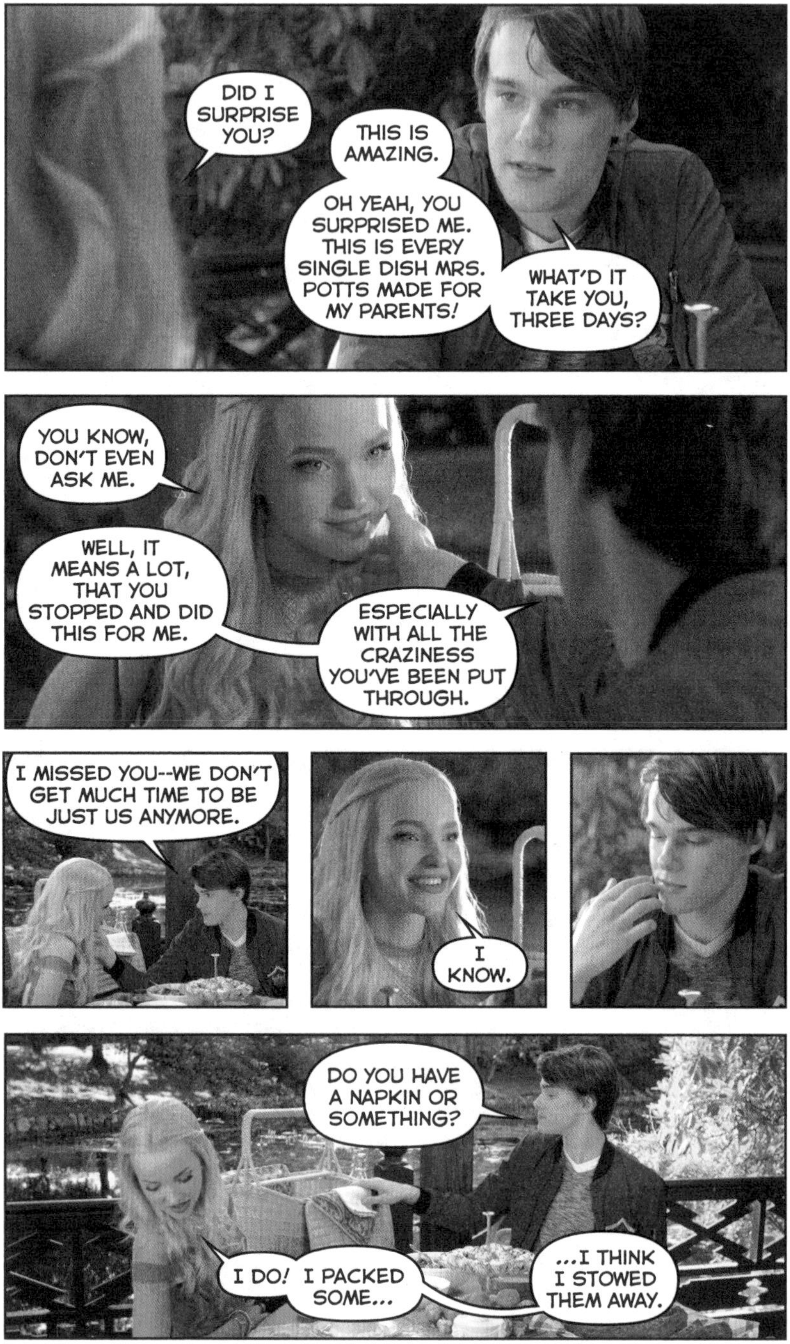

DID I SURPRISE YOU?
THIS IS AMAZING.
OH YEAH, YOU SURPRISED ME. THIS IS EVERY SINGLE DISH MRS. POTTS MADE FOR MY PARENTS!
WHAT'D IT TAKE YOU, THREE DAYS?
YOU KNOW, DON'T EVEN ASK ME.
WELL, IT MEANS A LOT, THAT YOU STOPPED AND DID THIS FOR ME.
ESPECIALLY WITH ALL THE CRAZINESS YOU'VE BEEN PUT THROUGH.
I MISSED YOU--WE DON'T GET MUCH TIME TO BE JUST US ANYMORE.
I KNOW.
DO YOU HAVE A NAPKIN OR SOMETHING?
I DO! I PACKED SOME...
...I THINK I STOWED THEM AWAY.

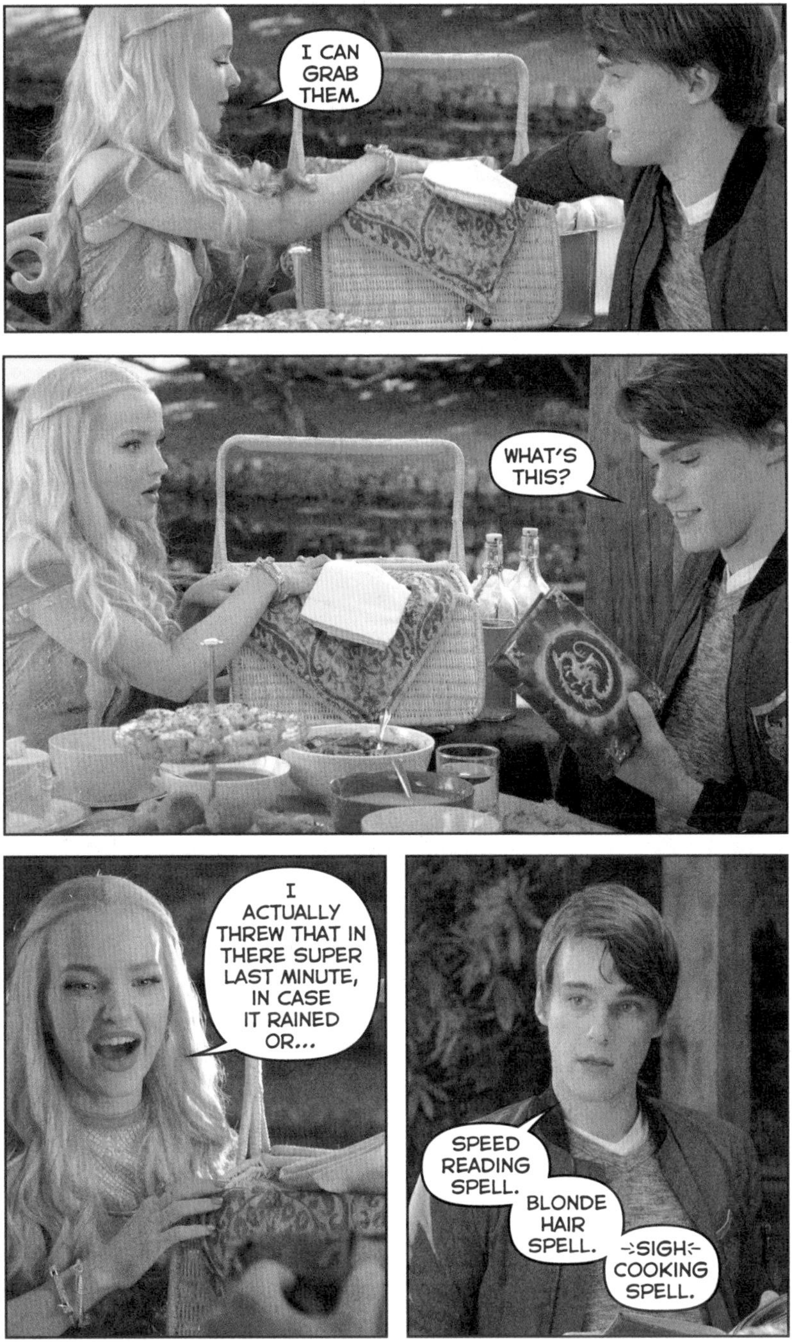
I CAN GRAB THEM.
WHAT'S THIS?
I ACTUALLY THREW THAT IN THERE SUPER LAST MINUTE, IN CASE IT RAINED OR...
SPEED READING SPELL.
BLONDE HAIR SPELL.
SIGH COOKING SPELL.

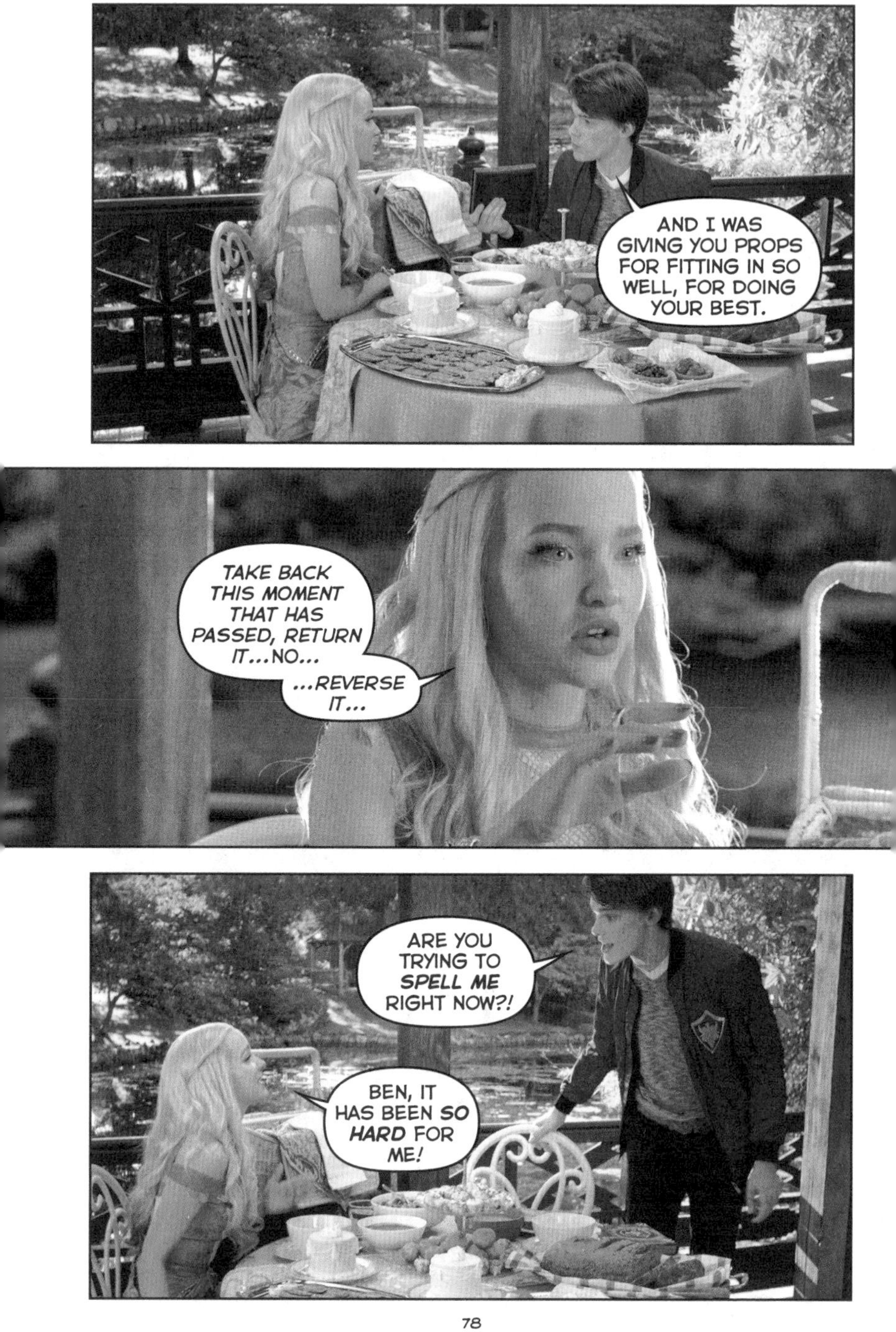
AND I WAS GIVING YOU PROPS FOR FITTING IN SO WELL, FOR DOING YOUR BEST.
TAKE BACK THIS MOMENT THAT HAS PASSED, RETURN IT...NO...
...REVERSE IT...
ARE YOU TRYING TO SPELL ME RIGHT NOW?!
BEN, IT HAS BEEN SO HARD FOR ME!

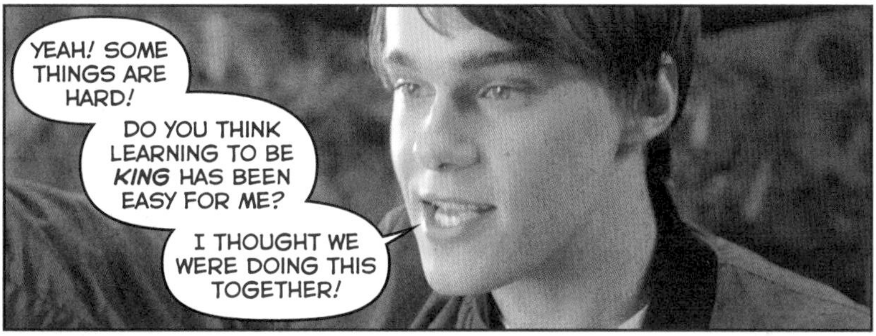
YEAH! SOME THINGS ARE HARD!
DO YOU THINK LEARNING TO BE *KING* HAS BEEN EASY FOR ME?
I THOUGHT WE WERE DOING THIS TOGETHER!

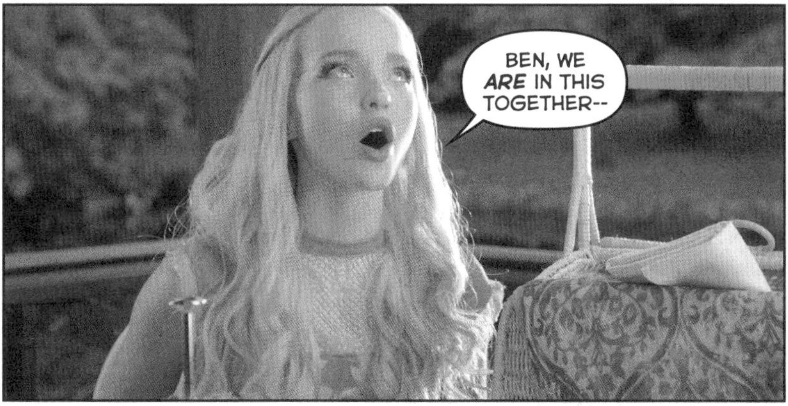
BEN, WE *ARE* IN THIS TOGETHER--

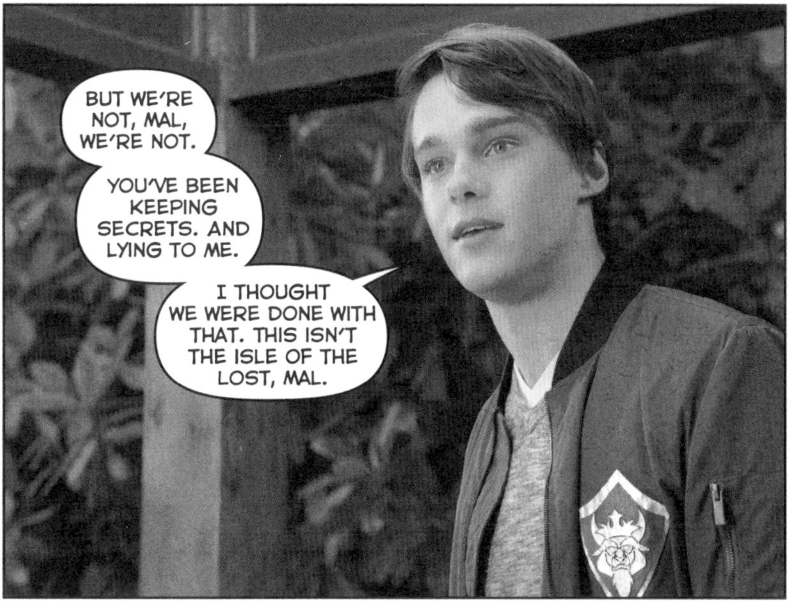
BUT WE'RE NOT, MAL, WE'RE NOT.
YOU'VE BEEN KEEPING SECRETS. AND LYING TO ME.
I THOUGHT WE WERE DONE WITH THAT. THIS ISN'T THE ISLE OF THE LOST, MAL.

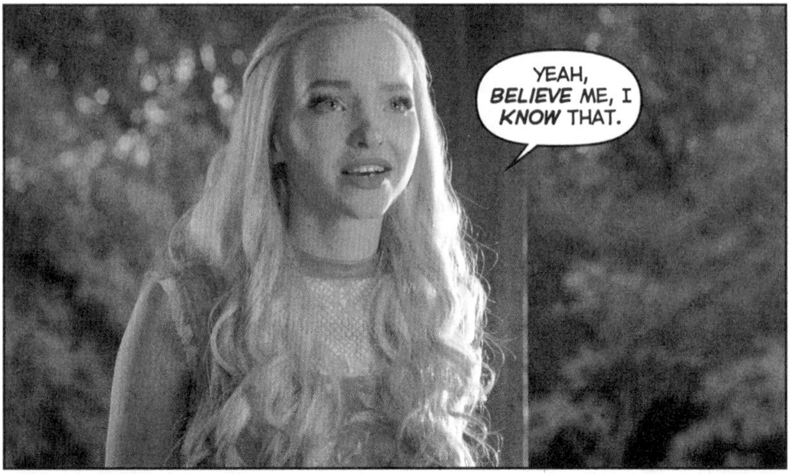
YEAH, BELIEVE ME, I KNOW THAT.

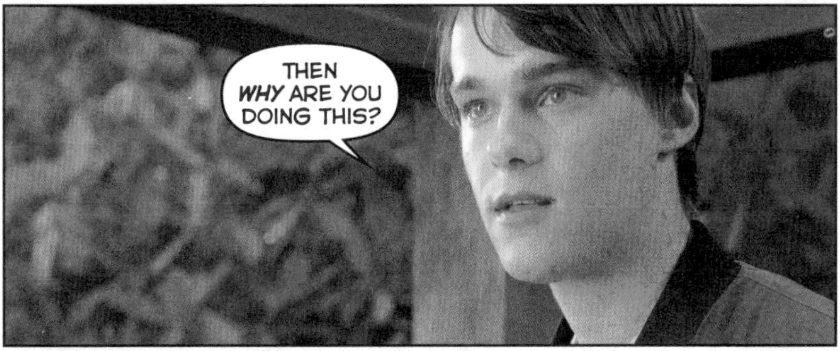
THEN WHY ARE YOU DOING THIS?

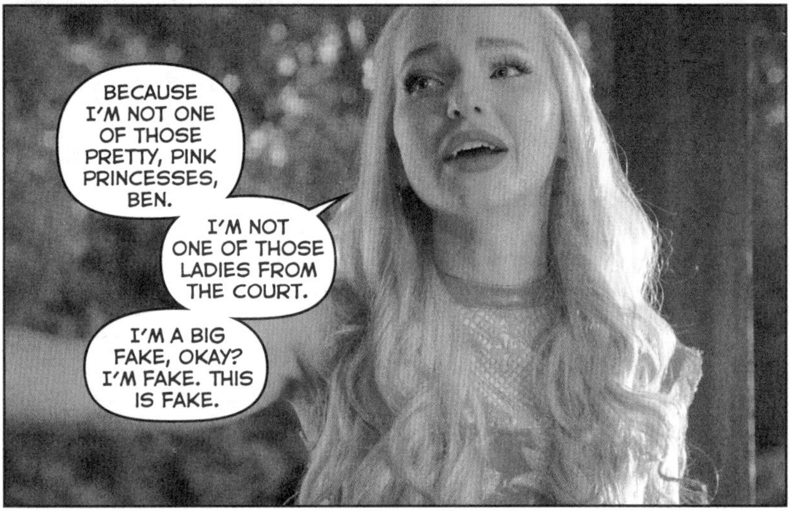
BECAUSE I'M NOT ONE OF THOSE PRETTY, PINK PRINCESSES, BEN.
I'M NOT ONE OF THOSE LADIES FROM THE COURT.
I'M A BIG FAKE, OKAY? I'M FAKE. THIS IS FAKE.

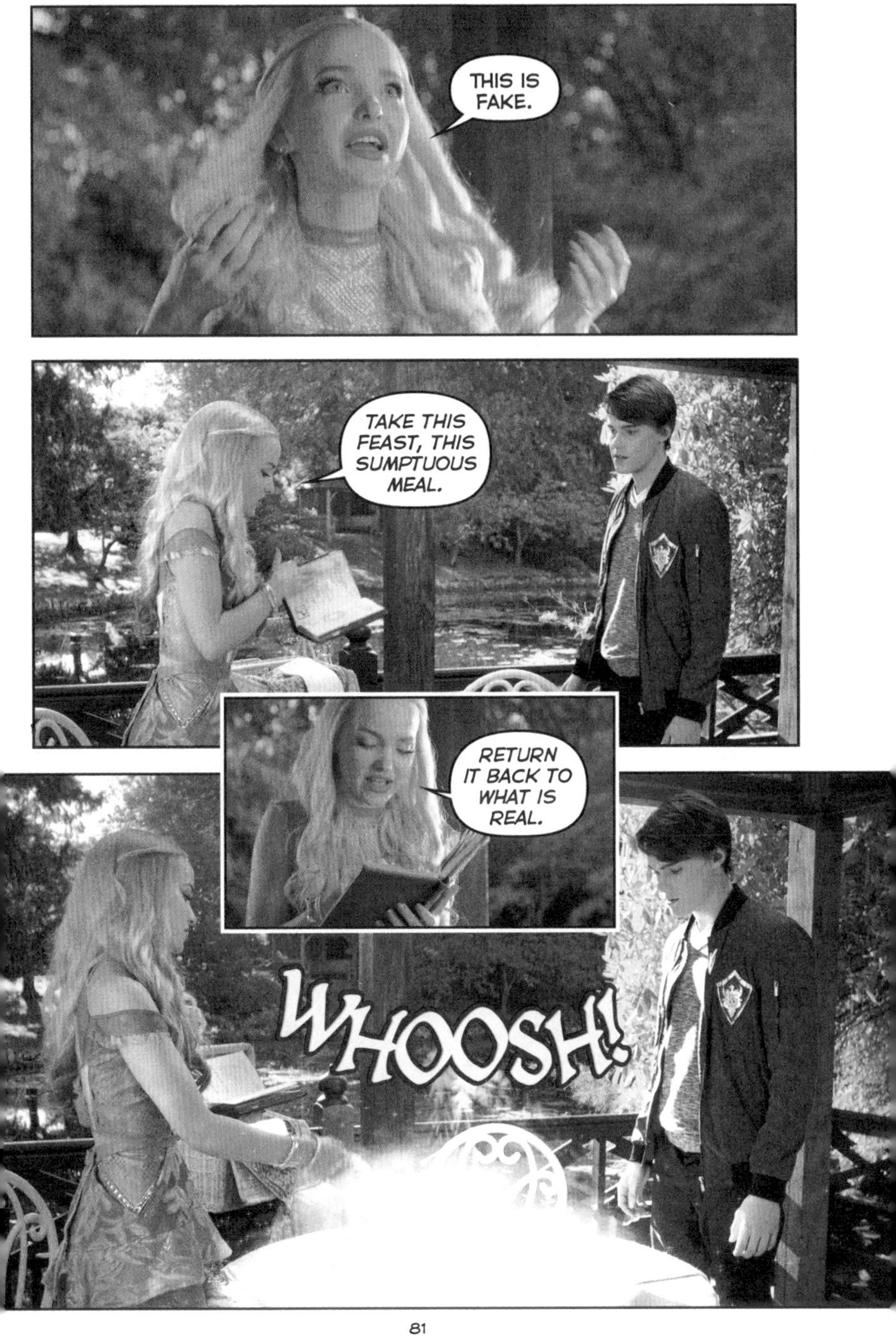
THIS IS FAKE.
TAKE THIS FEAST, THIS SUMPTUOUS MEAL.
RETURN IT BACK TO WHAT IS REAL.
WHOOSH!

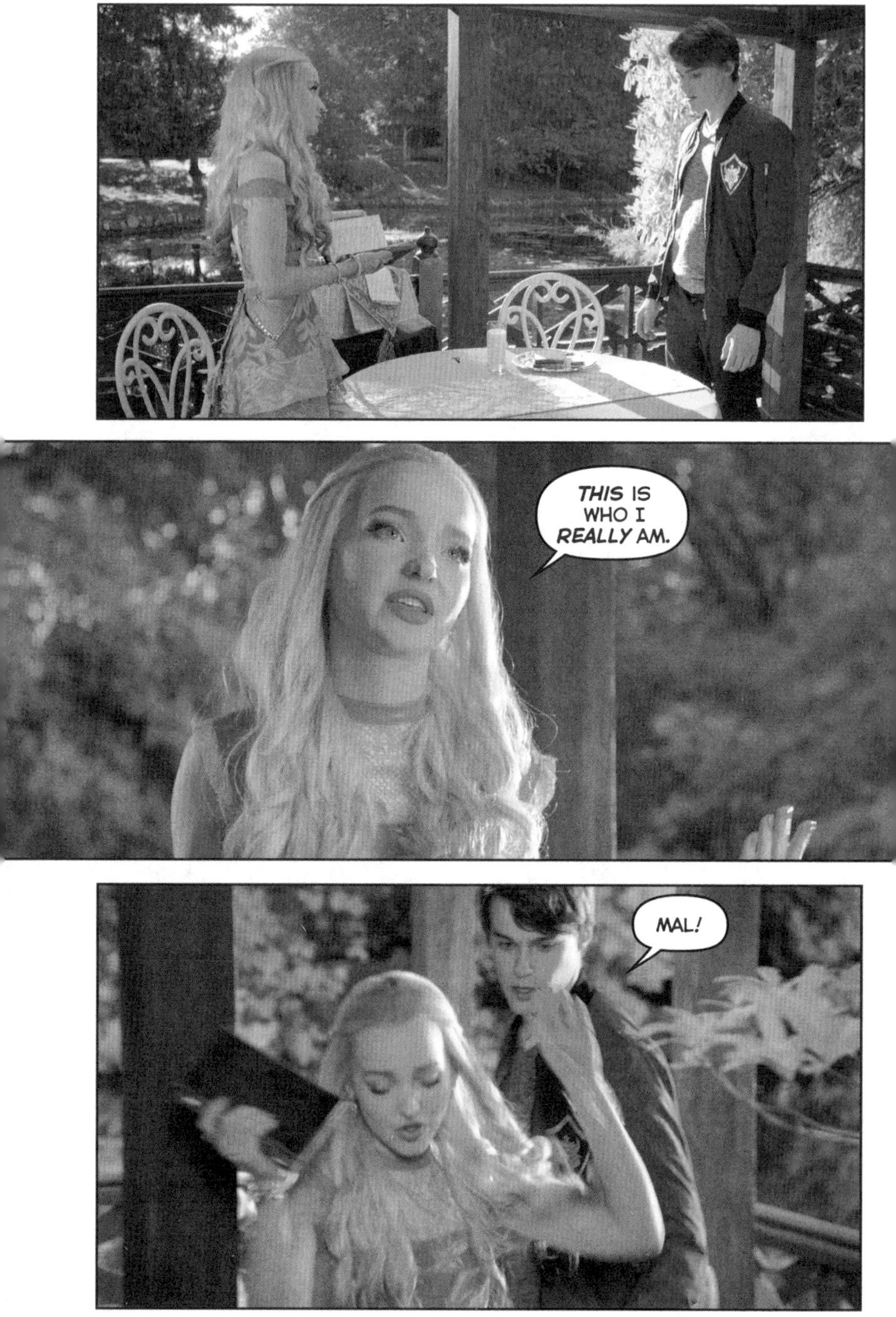
THIS IS WHO I REALLY AM.
MAL!

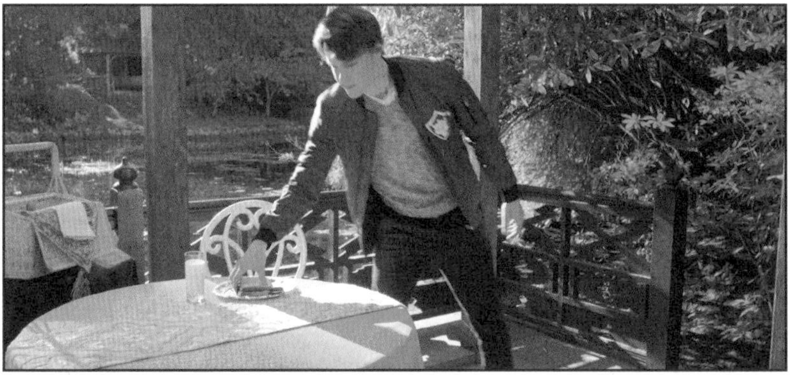

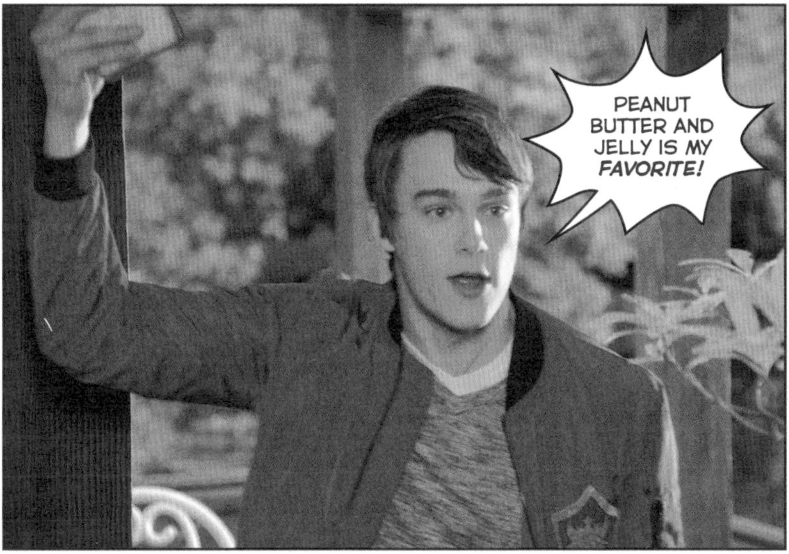
PEANUT BUTTER AND JELLY IS MY *FAVORITE!*

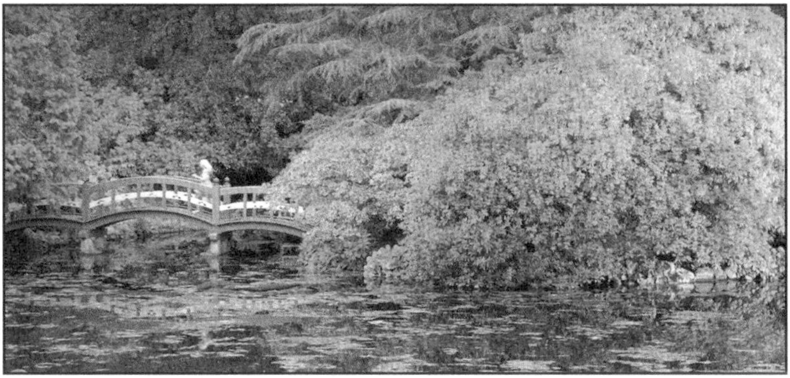

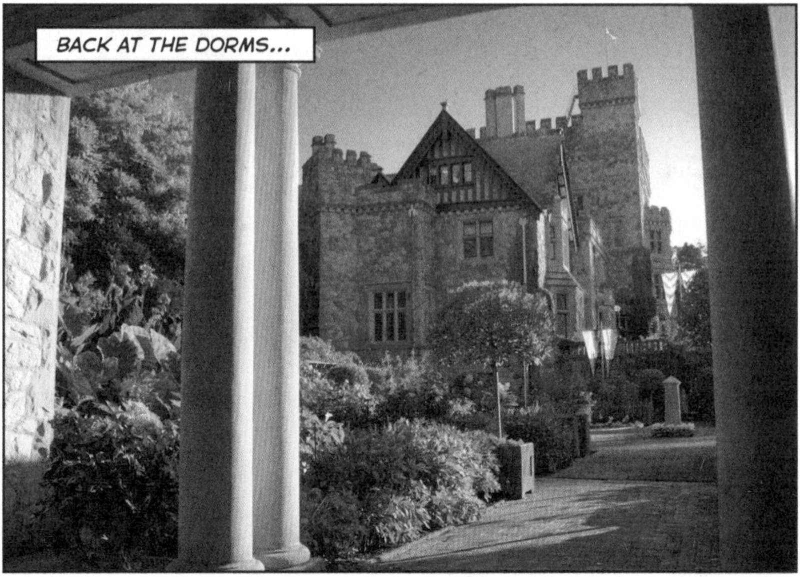
BACK AT THE DORMS...

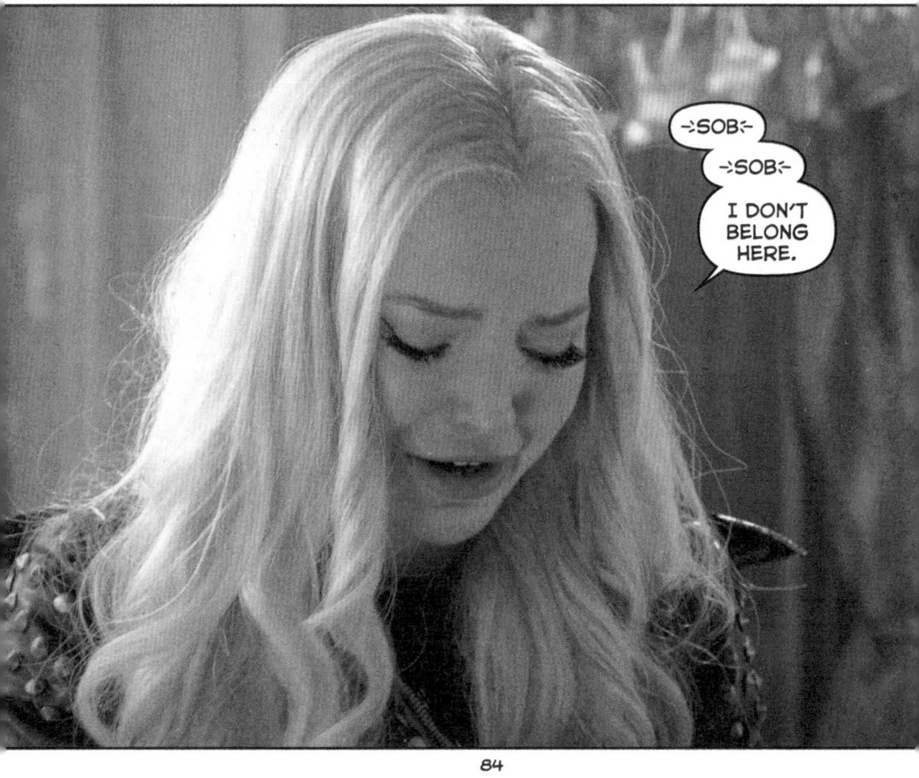
-SOB-
-SOB-
I DON'T BELONG HERE.

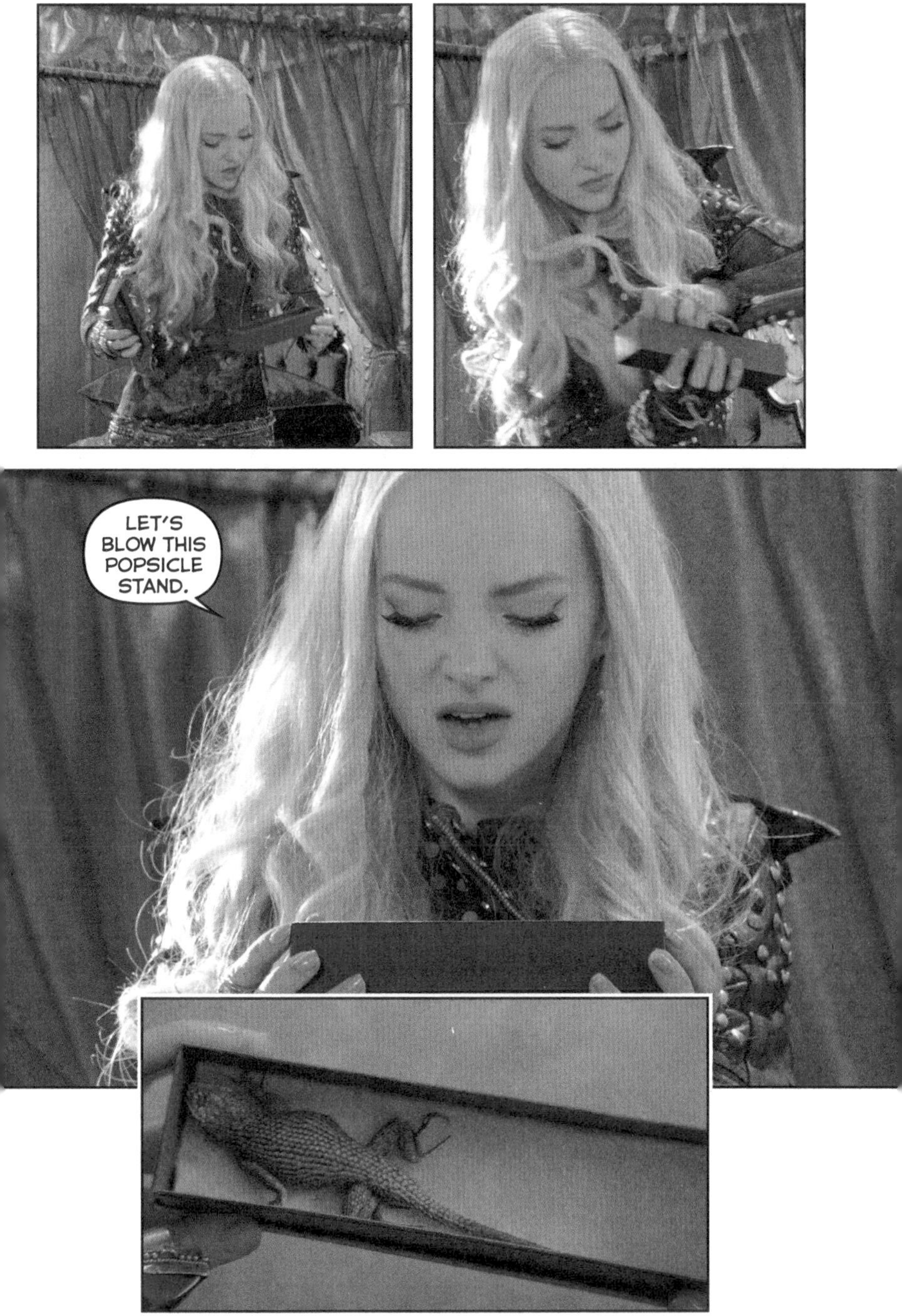
LET'S BLOW THIS POPSICLE STAND.

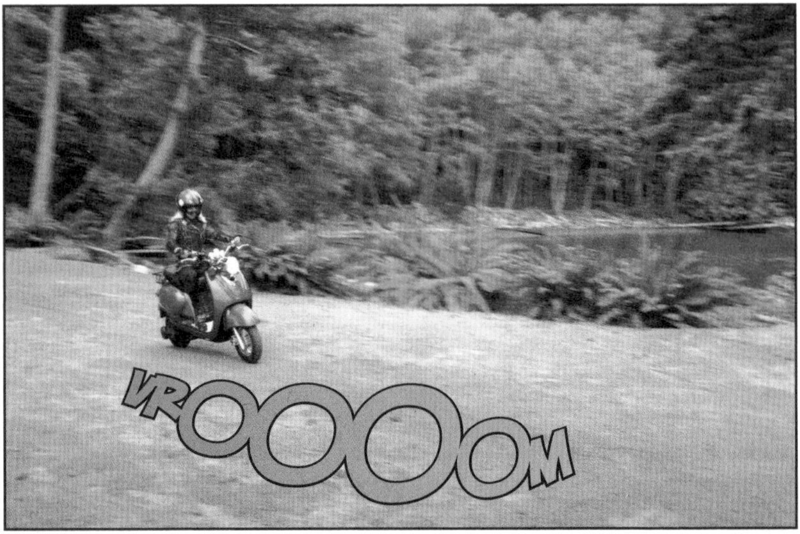
VROOOOOM

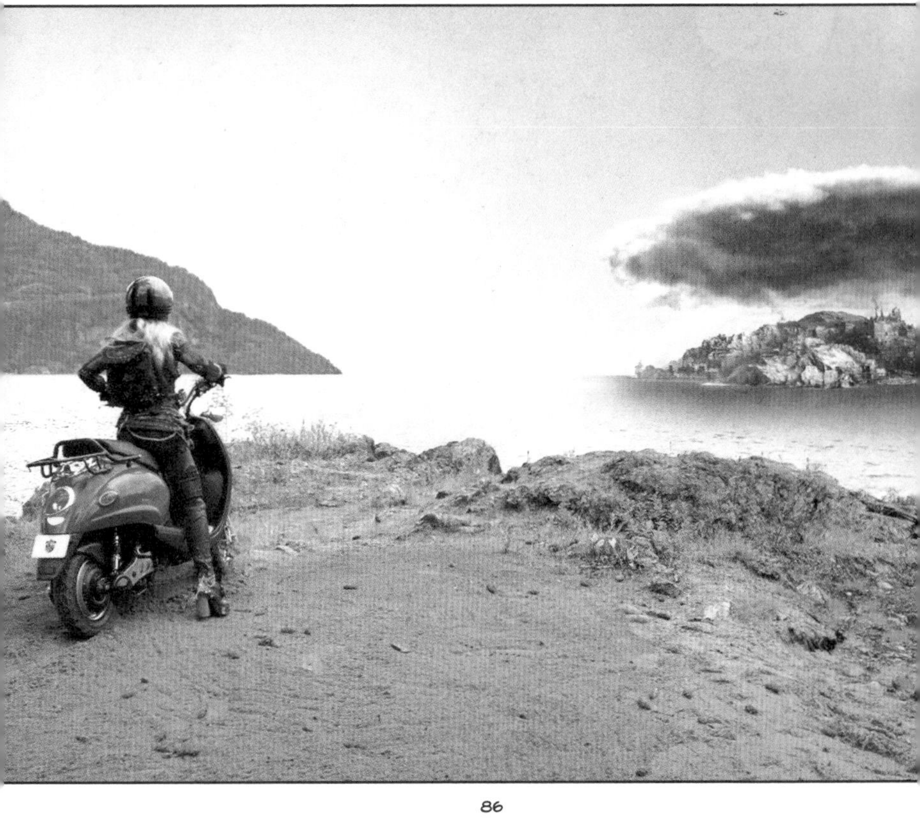

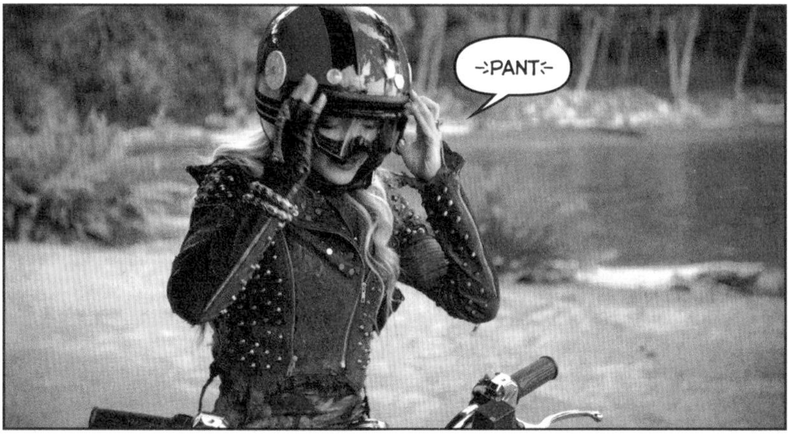
PANT

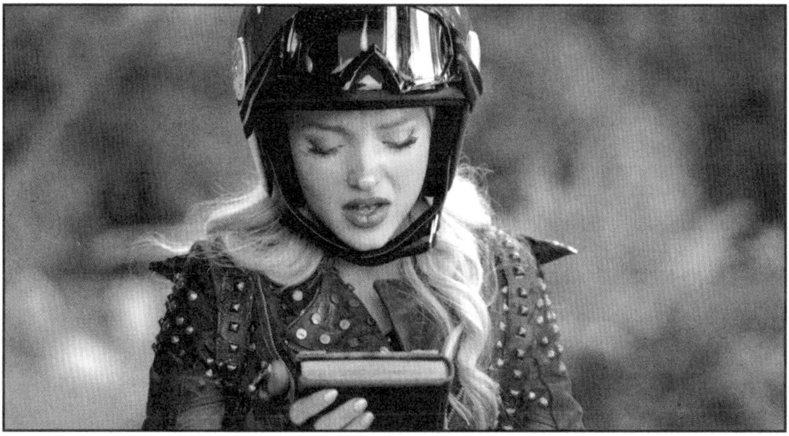

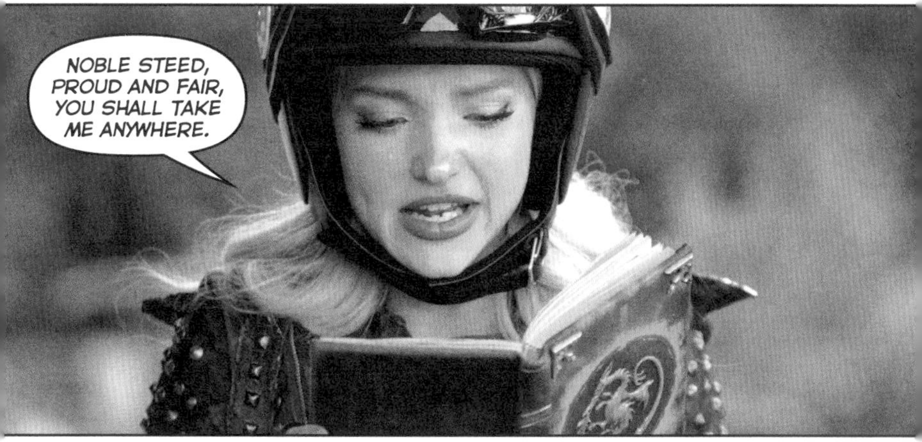
NOBLE STEED, PROUD AND FAIR, YOU SHALL TAKE ME ANYWHERE.

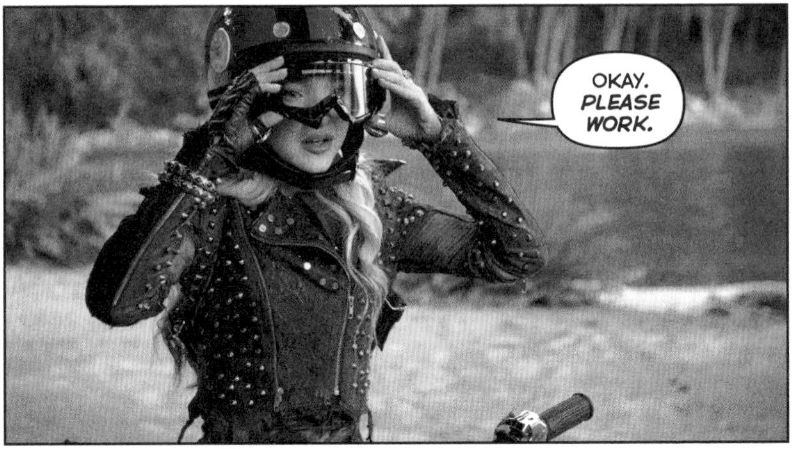
OKAY. PLEASE WORK.

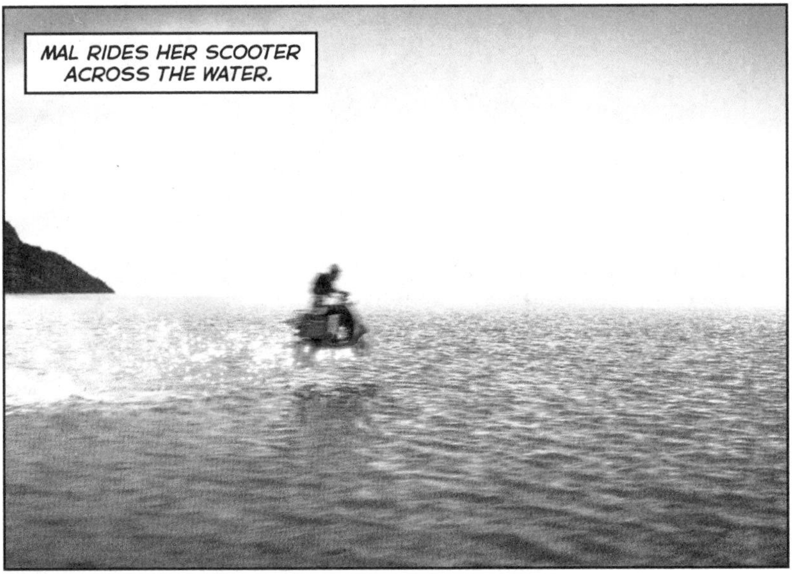
MAL RIDES HER SCOOTER ACROSS THE WATER.

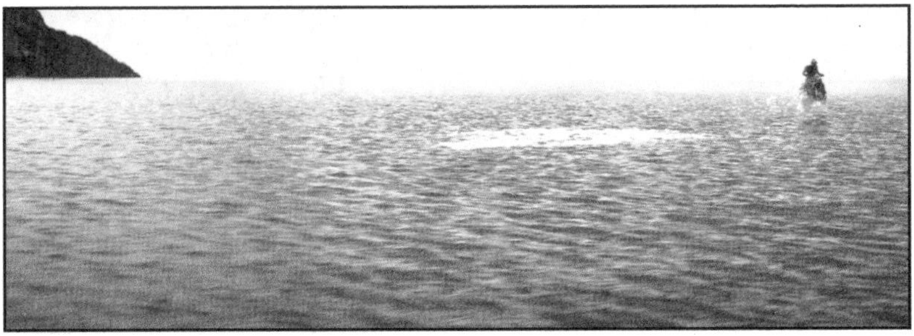

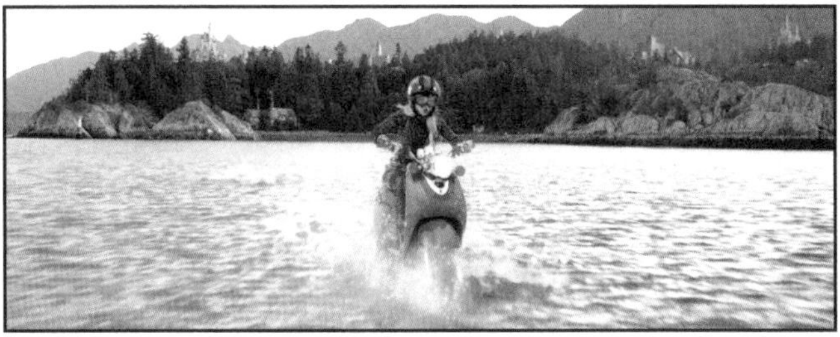

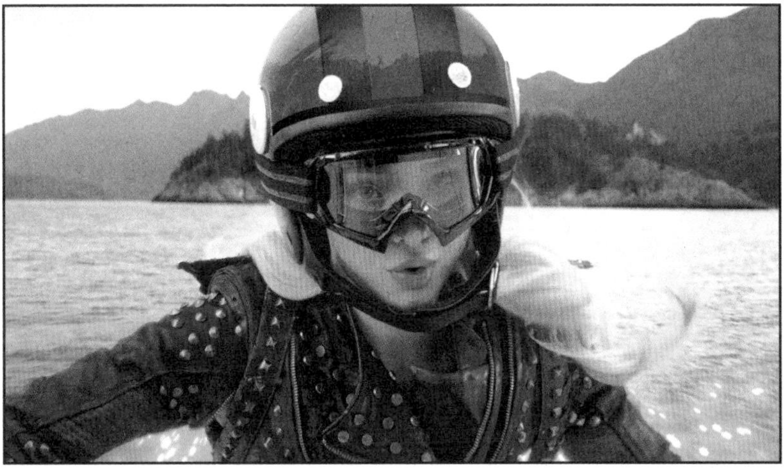

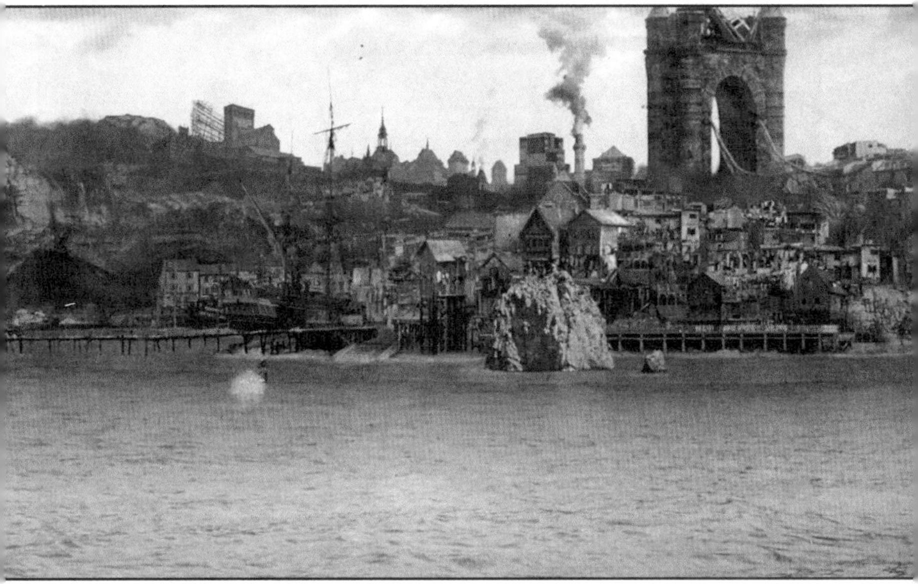

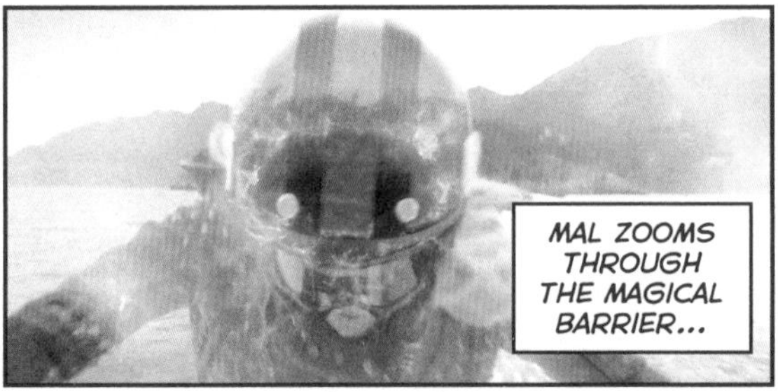
MAL ZOOMS THROUGH THE MAGICAL BARRIER...

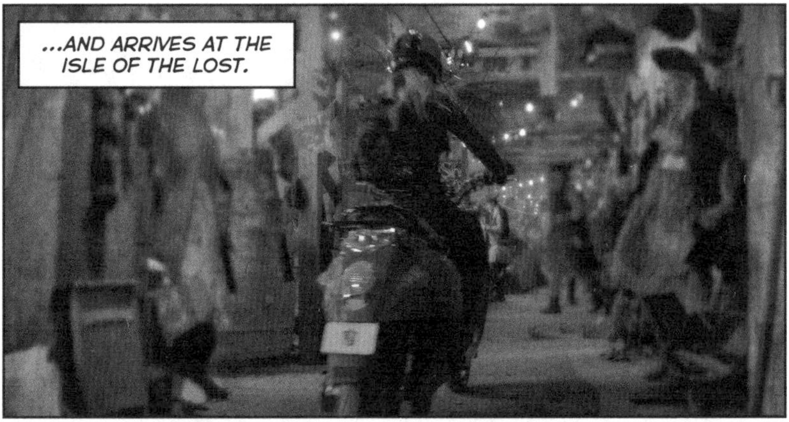
...AND ARRIVES AT THE ISLE OF THE LOST.

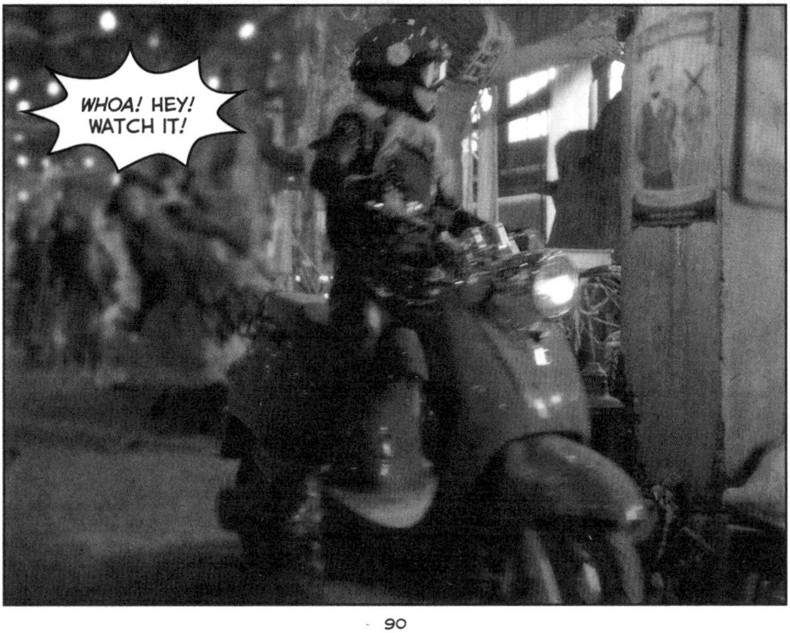
WHOA! HEY! WATCH IT!

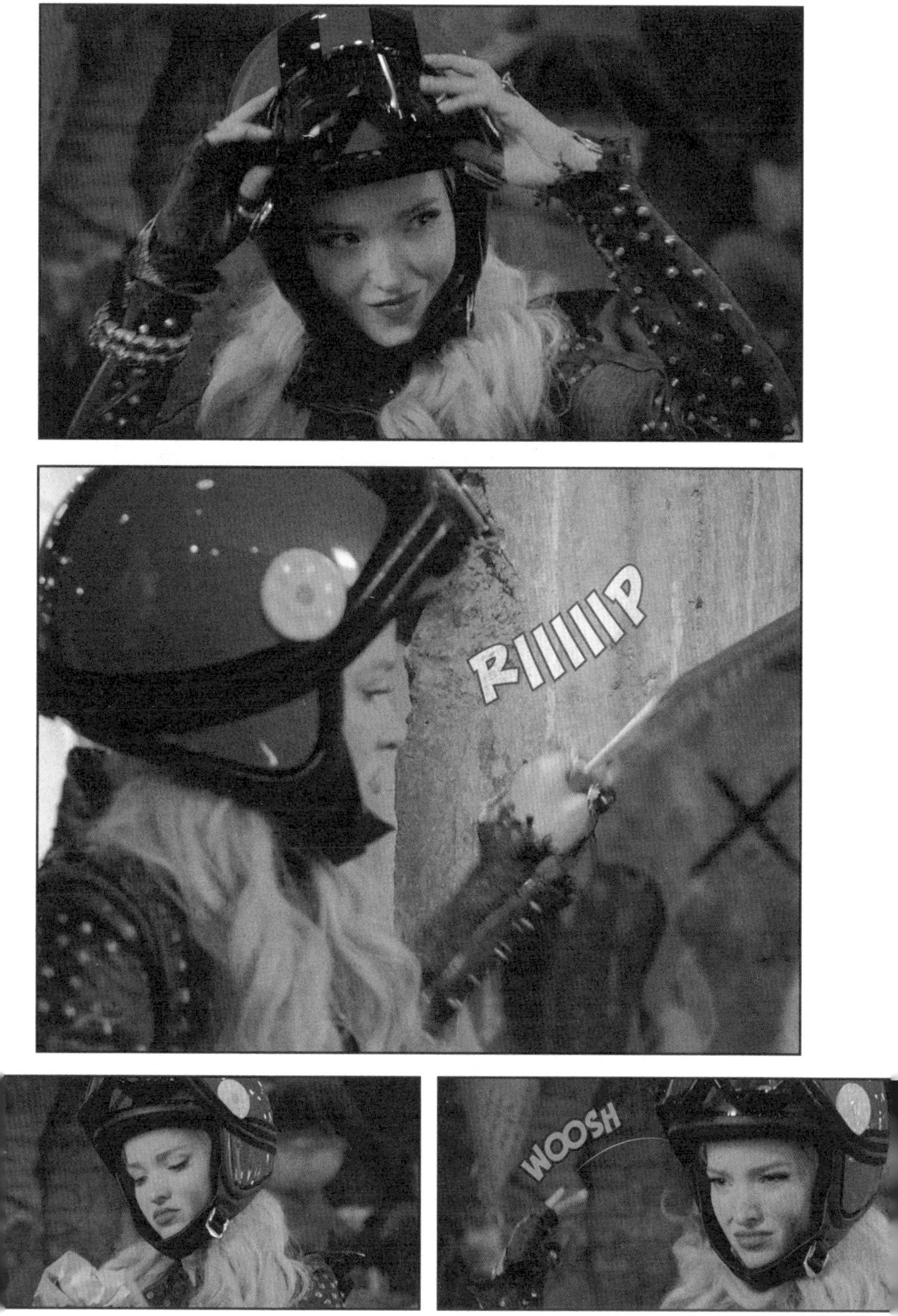
RIIIIIP
WOOSH

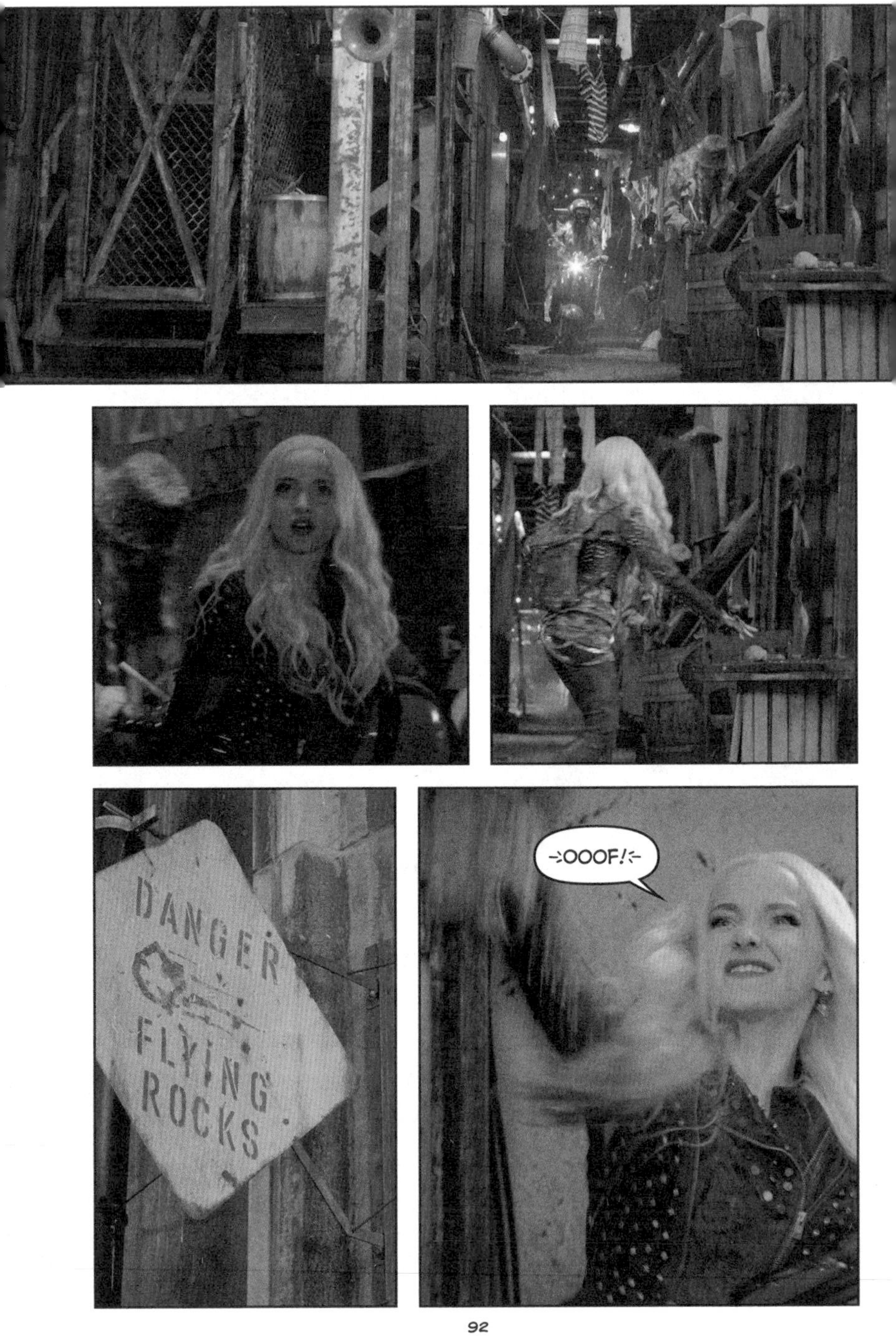
DANGER
FLYING
ROCKS
-OOOF!-

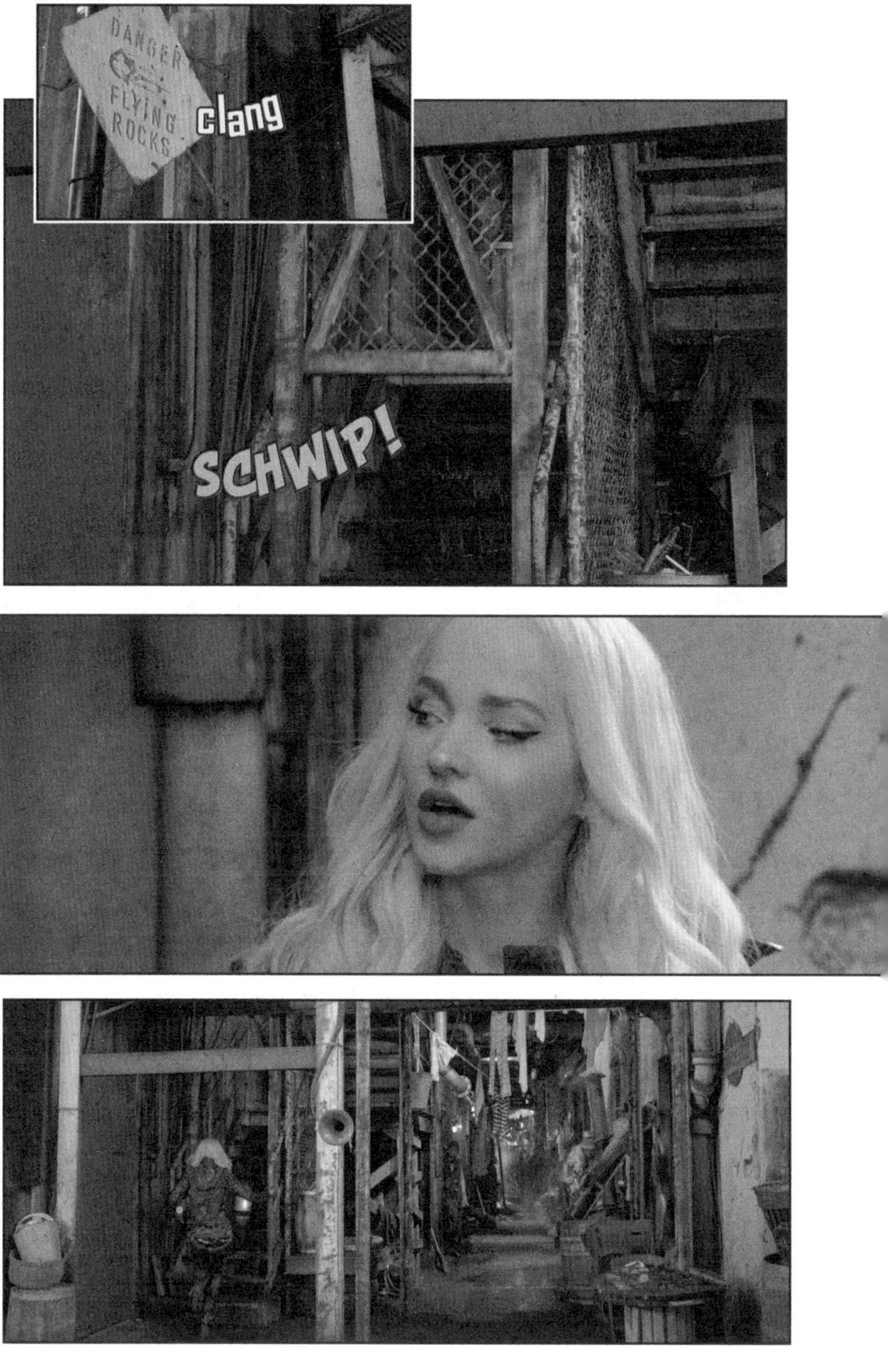
DANGER
FLYING ROCKS
clang
SCHWIP!

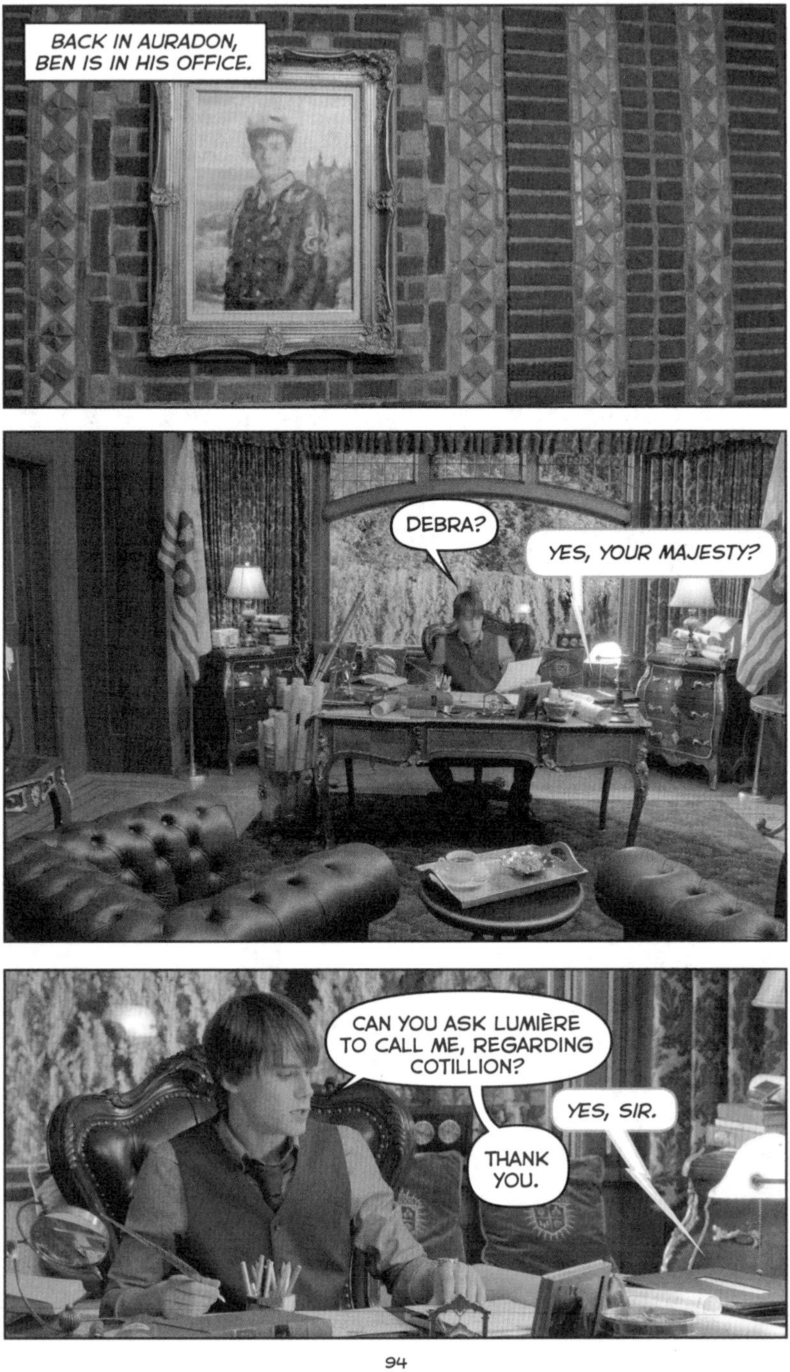
BACK IN AURADON, BEN IS IN HIS OFFICE.
DEBRA?
YES, YOUR MAJESTY?
CAN YOU ASK LUMIÈRE TO CALL ME, REGARDING COTILLION?
YES, SIR.
THANK YOU.

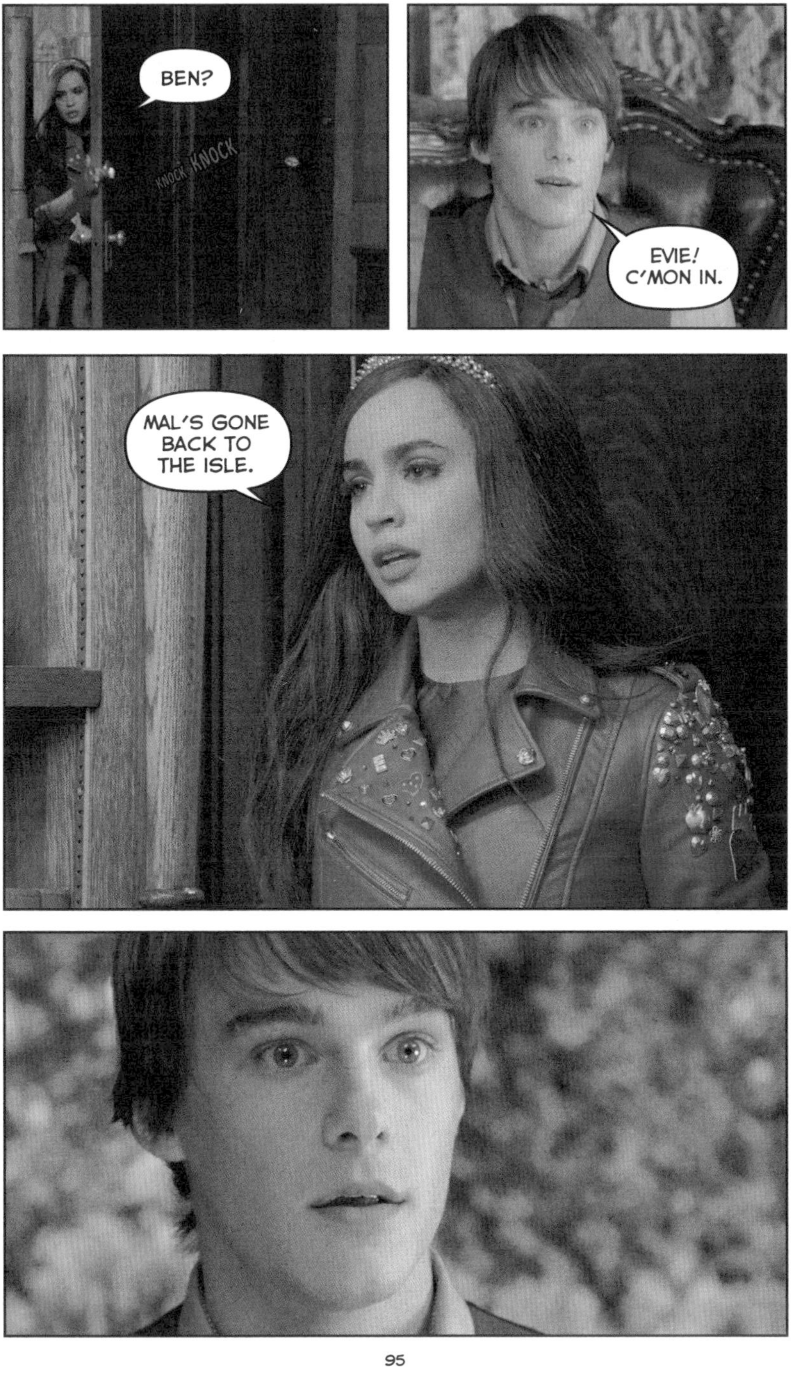
BEN?
KNOCK KNOCK
EVIE! C'MON IN.
MAL'S GONE BACK TO THE ISLE.

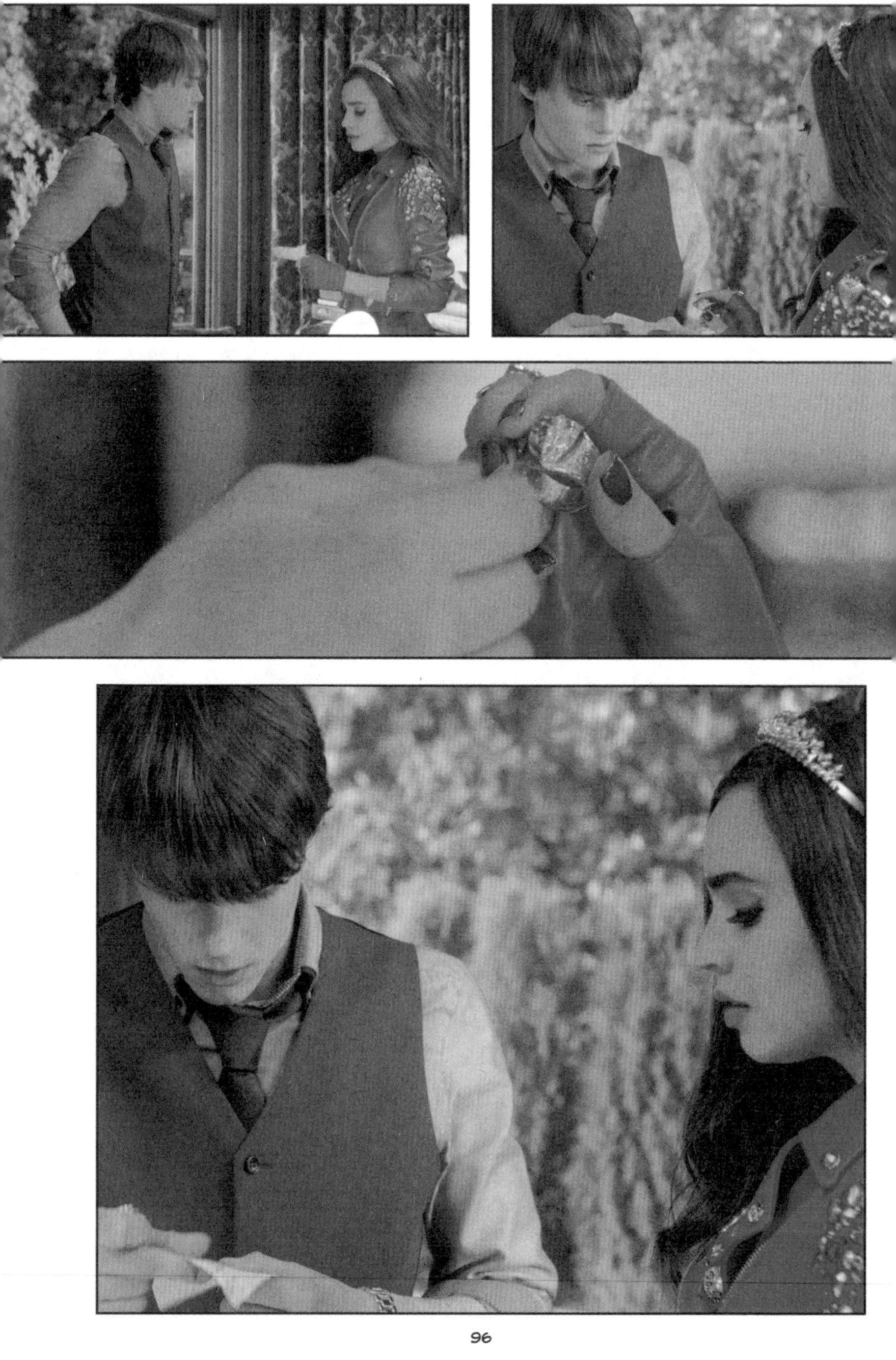

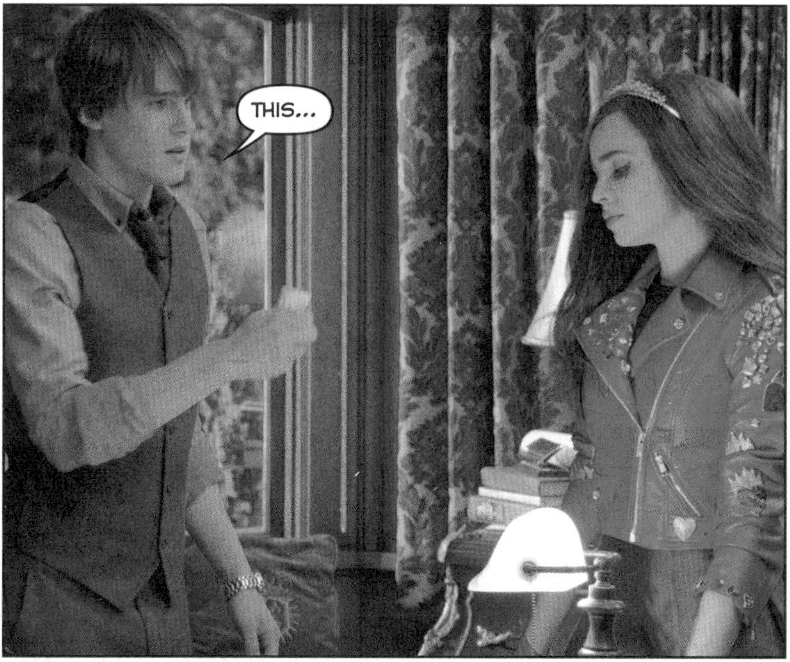
THIS...

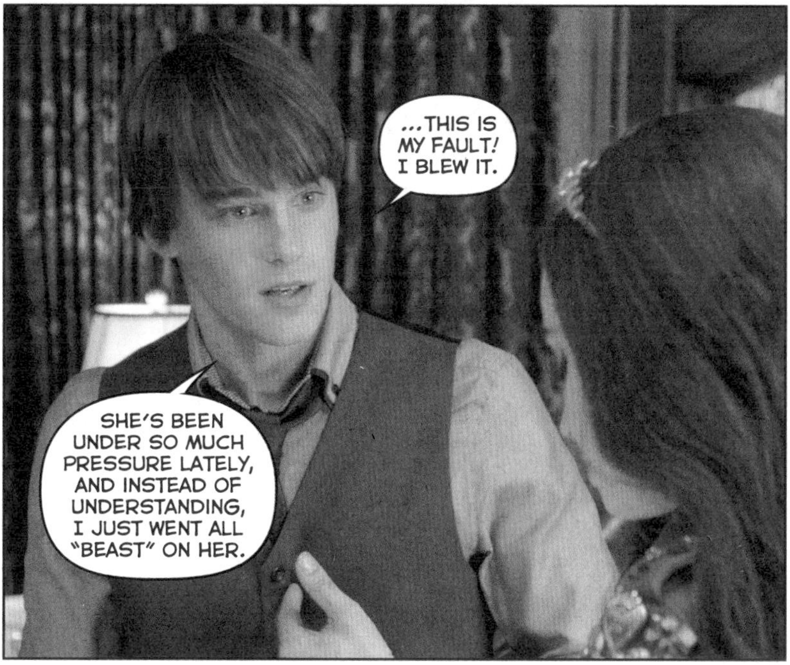
...THIS IS MY FAULT! I BLEW IT.
SHE'S BEEN UNDER SO MUCH PRESSURE LATELY, AND INSTEAD OF UNDERSTANDING, I JUST WENT ALL "BEAST" ON HER.

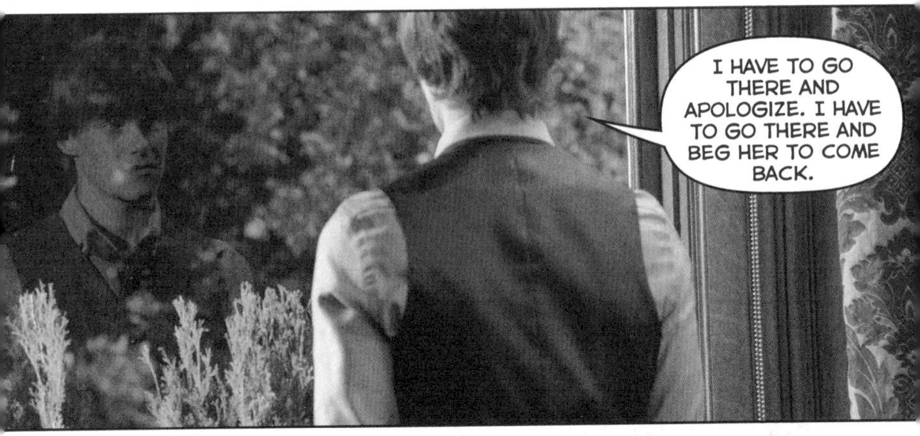
I HAVE TO GO THERE AND APOLOGIZE. I HAVE TO GO THERE AND BEG HER TO COME BACK.

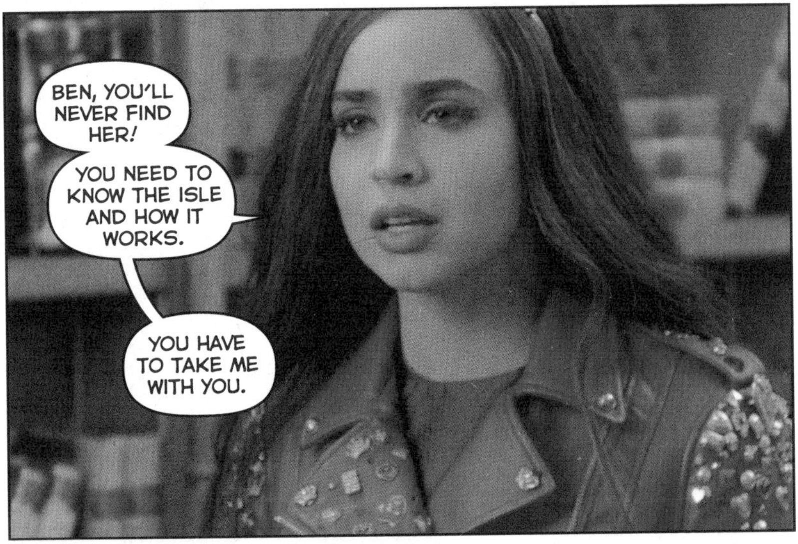
BEN, YOU'LL NEVER FIND HER!
YOU NEED TO KNOW THE ISLE AND HOW IT WORKS.
YOU HAVE TO TAKE ME WITH YOU.

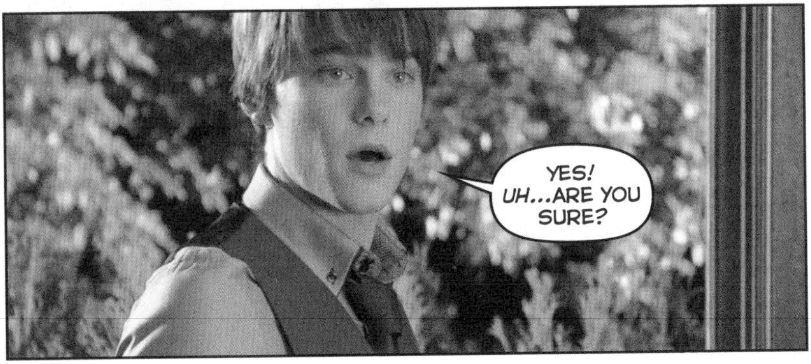
YES! UH...ARE YOU SURE?

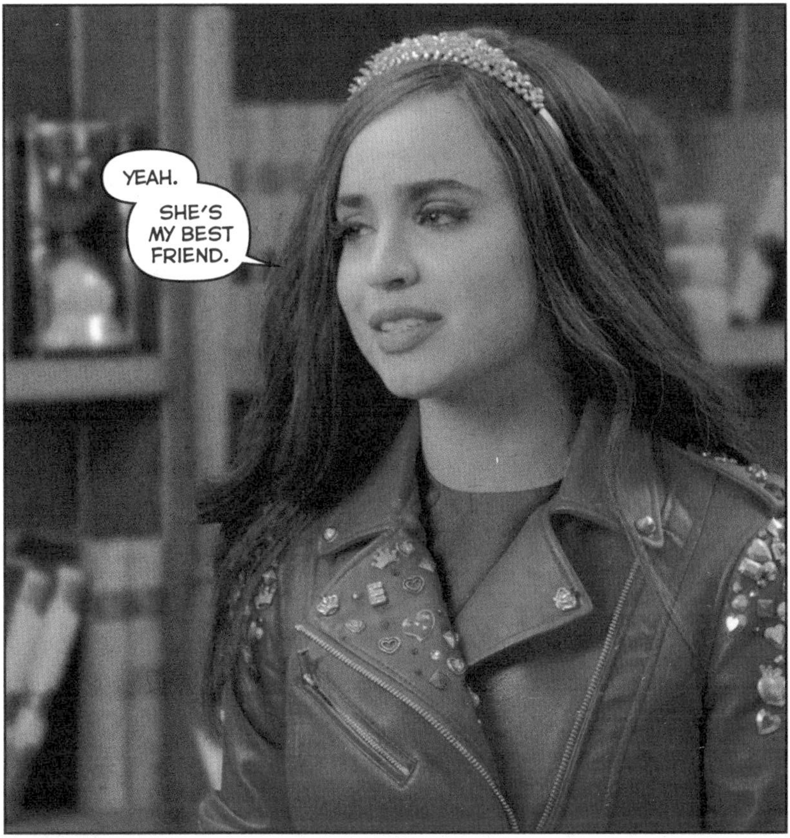
YEAH.
SHE'S MY BEST FRIEND.

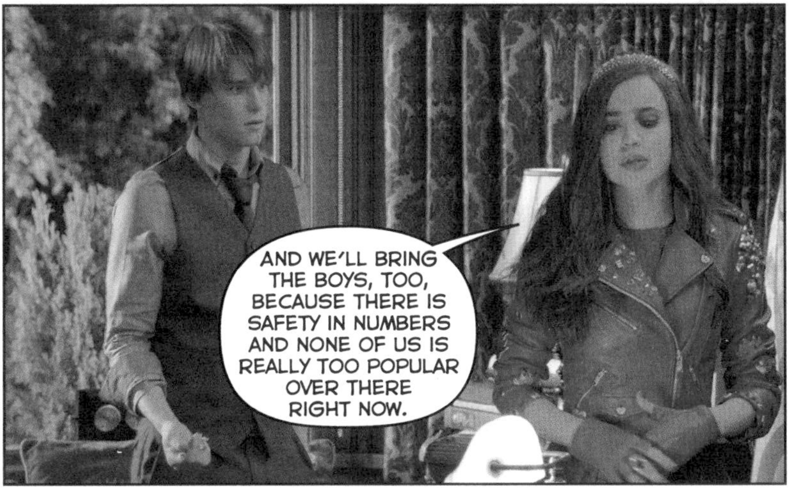
AND WE'LL BRING THE BOYS, TOO, BECAUSE THERE IS SAFETY IN NUMBERS AND NONE OF US IS REALLY TOO POPULAR OVER THERE RIGHT NOW.

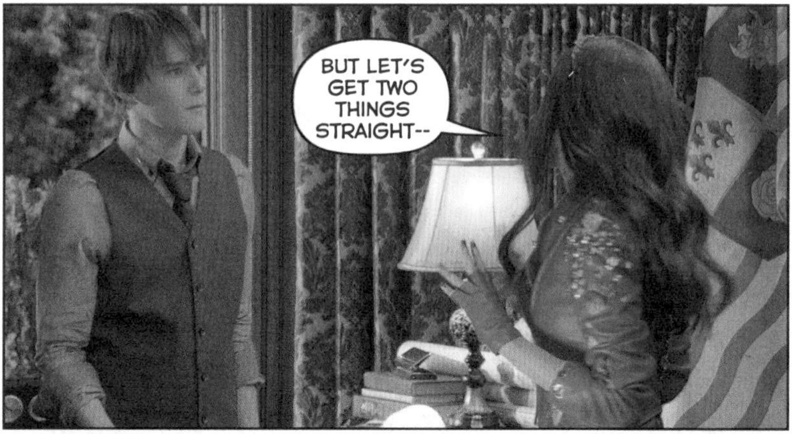
BUT LET'S GET TWO THINGS STRAIGHT--

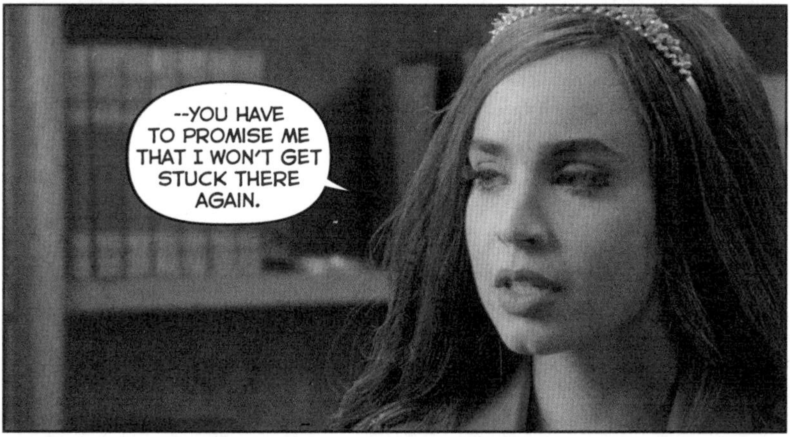
--YOU HAVE TO PROMISE ME THAT I WON'T GET STUCK THERE AGAIN.

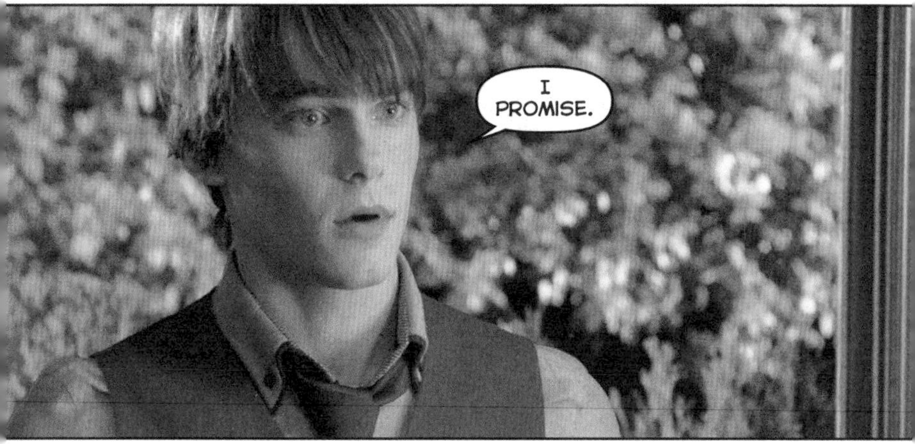
I PROMISE.

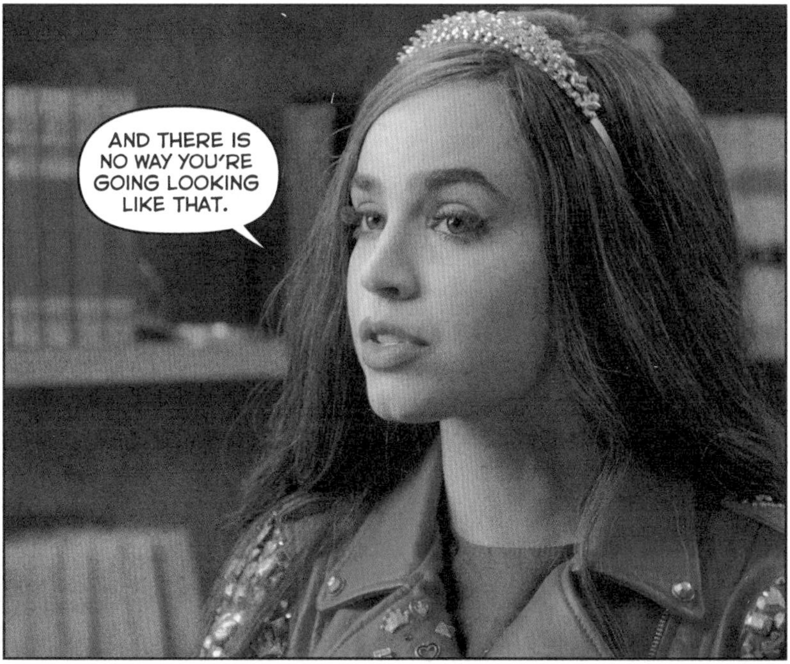
AND THERE IS NO WAY YOU'RE GOING LOOKING LIKE THAT.

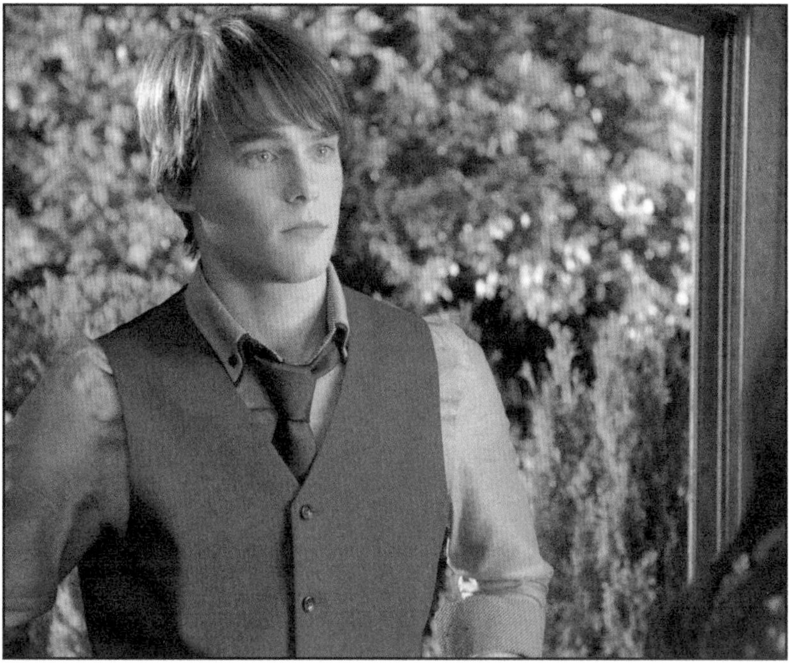

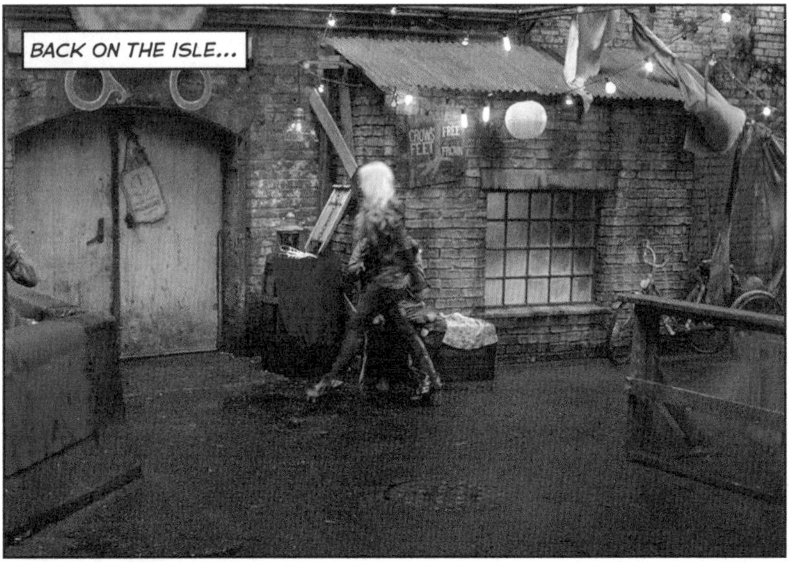
BACK ON THE ISLE...

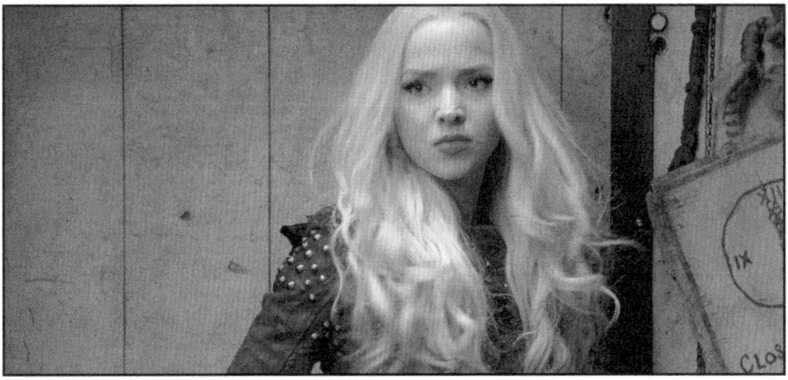

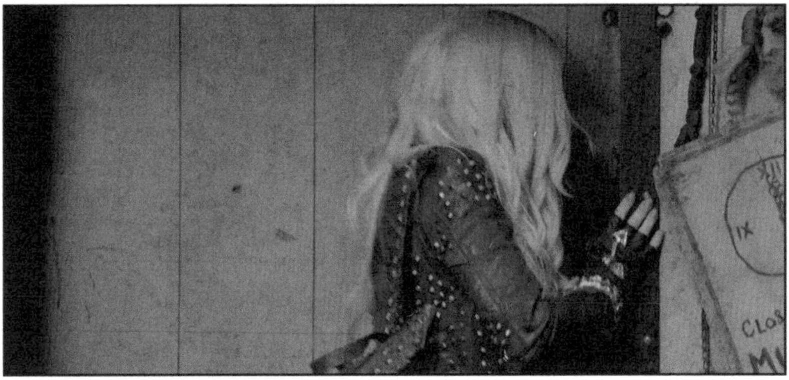

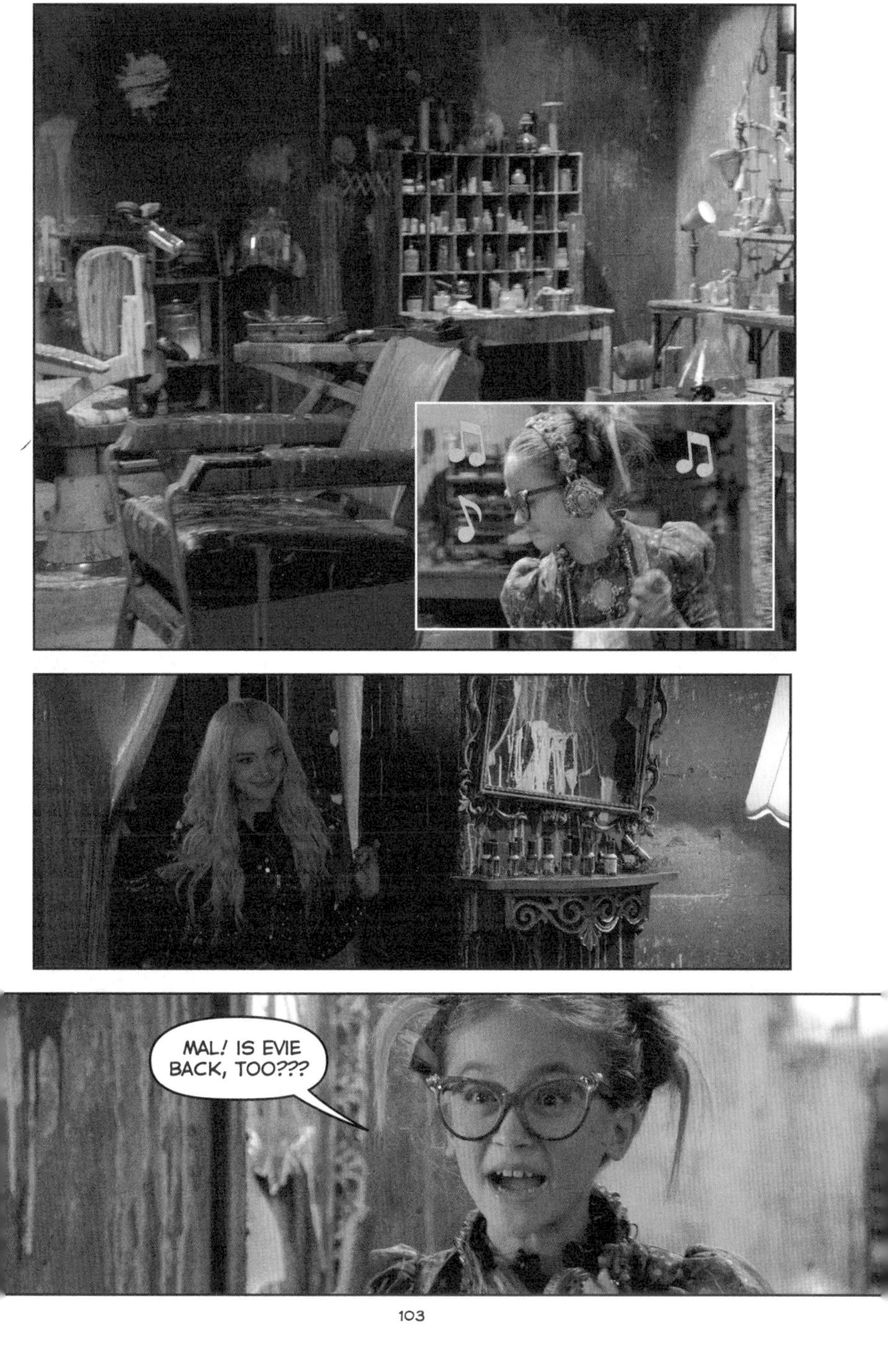
MAL! IS EVIE BACK, TOO???

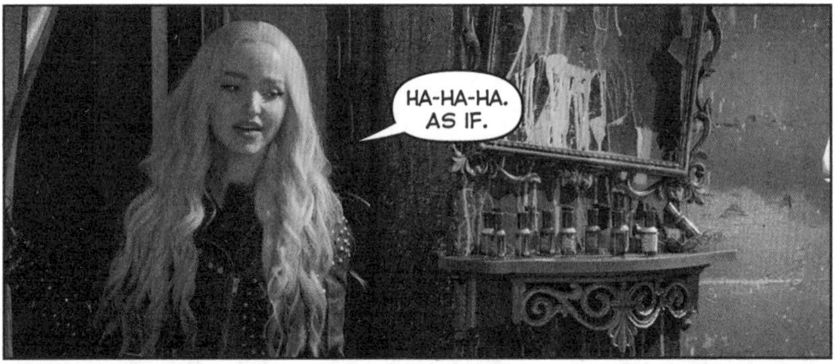
HA-HA-HA. AS IF.

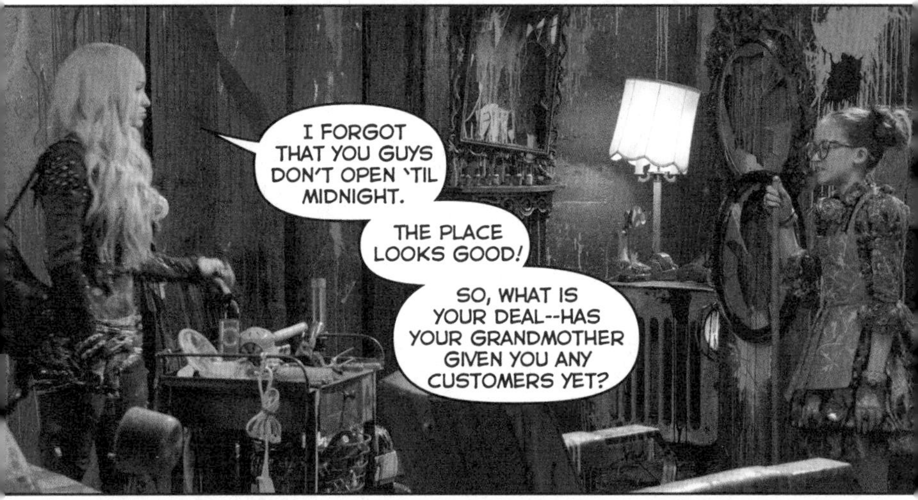
I FORGOT THAT YOU GUYS DON'T OPEN 'TIL MIDNIGHT.
THE PLACE LOOKS GOOD!
SO, WHAT IS YOUR DEAL--HAS YOUR GRANDMOTHER GIVEN YOU ANY CUSTOMERS YET?

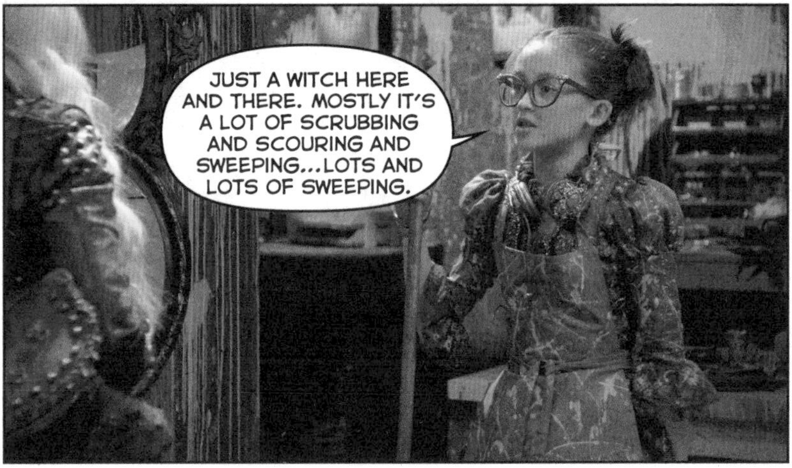
JUST A WITCH HERE AND THERE. MOSTLY IT'S A LOT OF SCRUBBING AND SCOURING AND SWEEPING...LOTS AND LOTS OF SWEEPING.

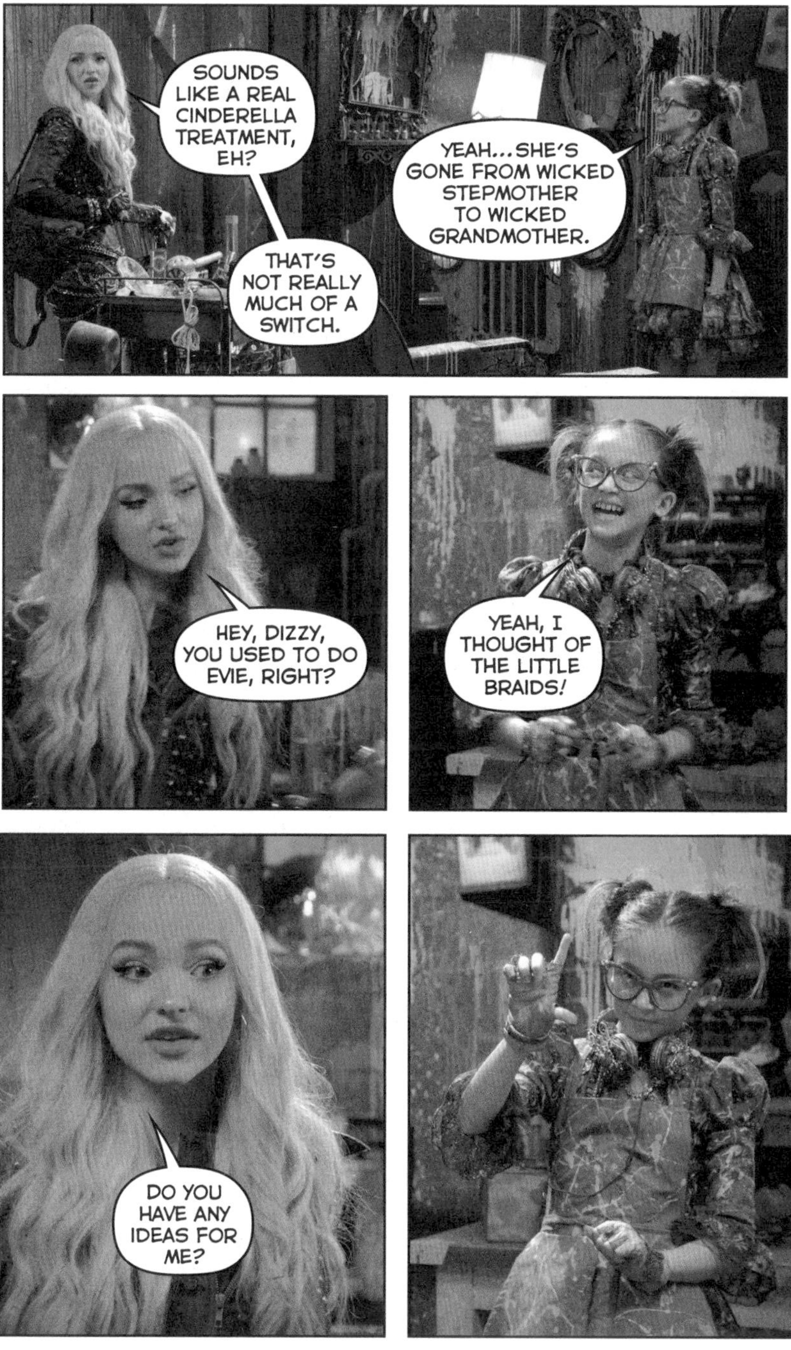
SOUNDS LIKE A REAL CINDERELLA TREATMENT, EH?
YEAH...SHE'S GONE FROM WICKED STEPMOTHER TO WICKED GRANDMOTHER.
THAT'S NOT REALLY MUCH OF A SWITCH.
HEY, DIZZY, YOU USED TO DO EVIE, RIGHT?
YEAH, I THOUGHT OF THE LITTLE BRAIDS!
DO YOU HAVE ANY IDEAS FOR ME?

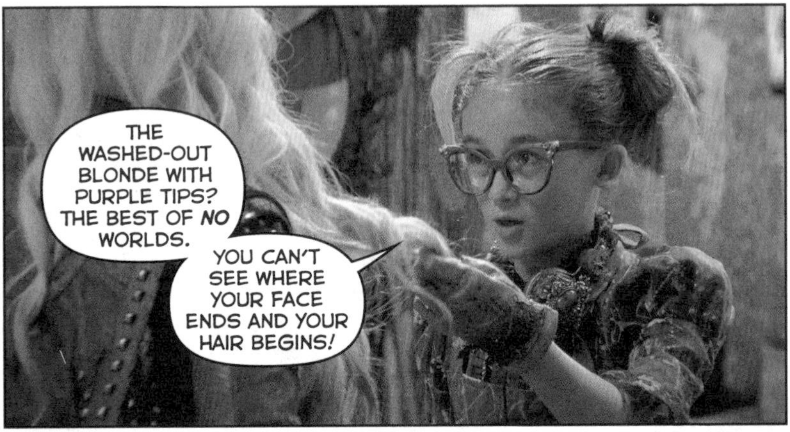
THE WASHED-OUT BLONDE WITH PURPLE TIPS? THE BEST OF NO WORLDS.
YOU CAN'T SEE WHERE YOUR FACE ENDS AND YOUR HAIR BEGINS!

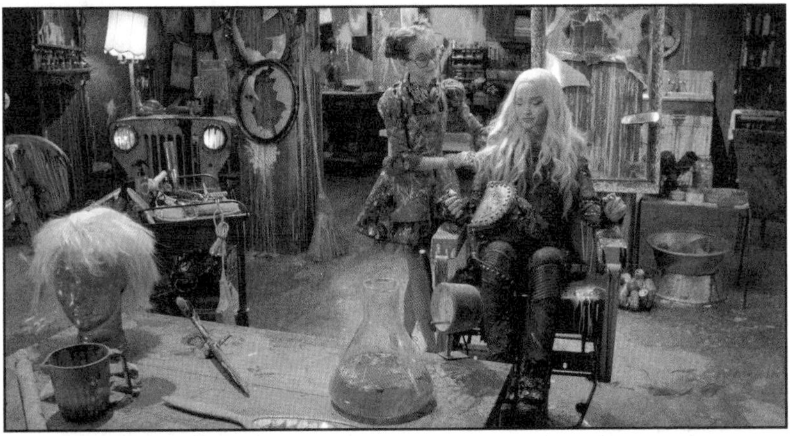

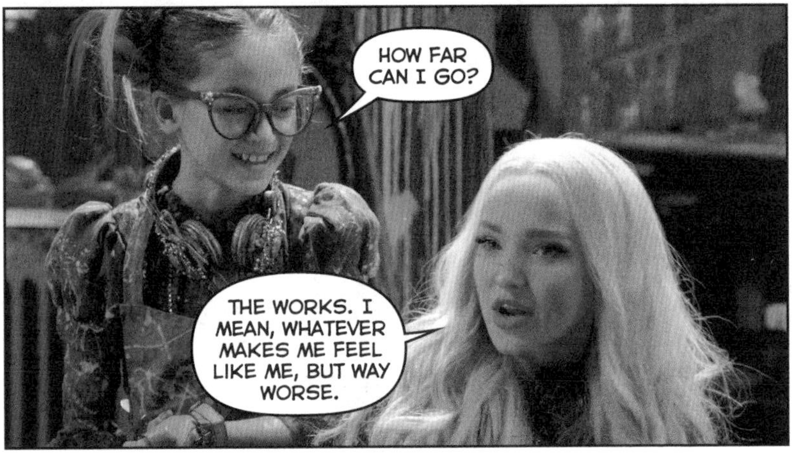
HOW FAR CAN I GO?
THE WORKS. I MEAN, WHATEVER MAKES ME FEEL LIKE ME, BUT WAY WORSE.

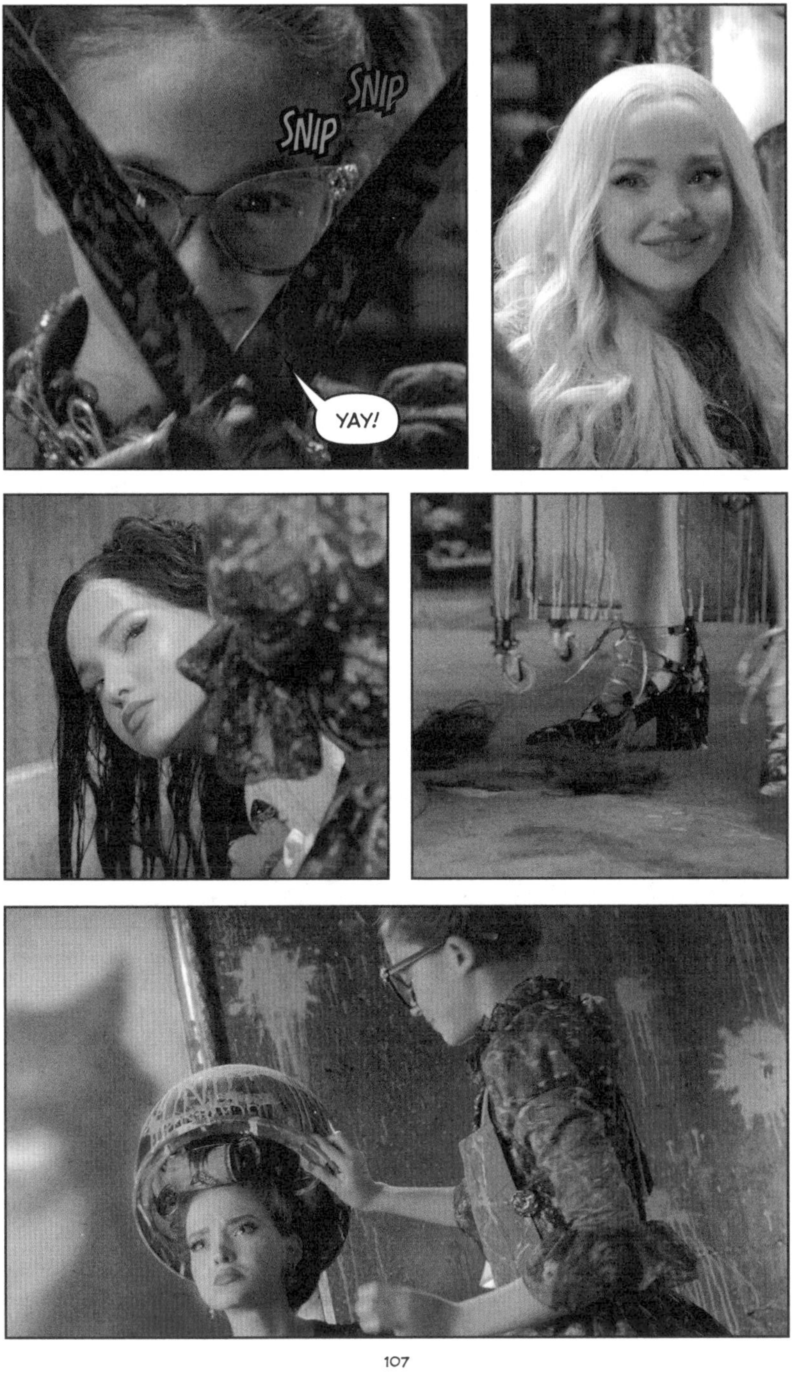
SNIP
SNIP
YAY!

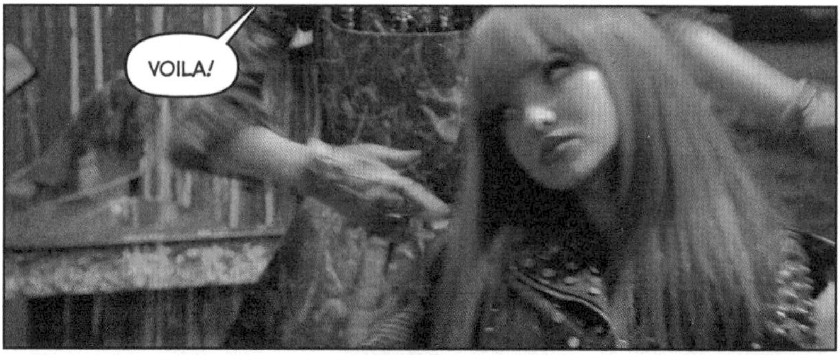
VOILA!

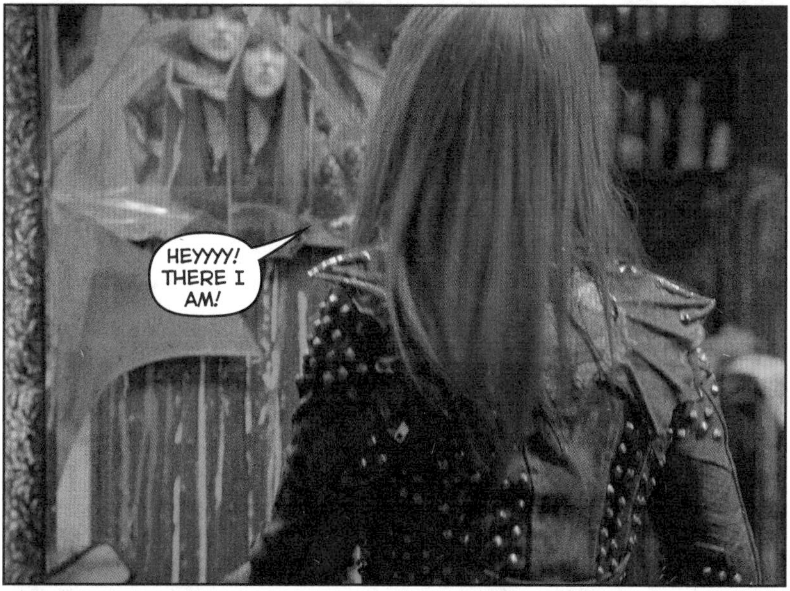
HEYYYY! THERE I AM!

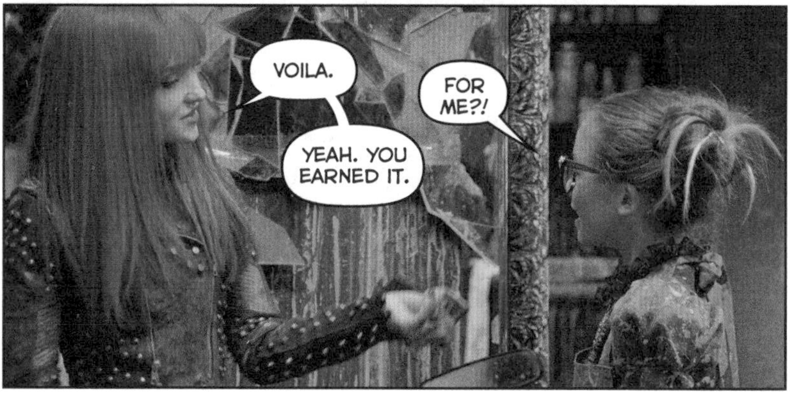
VOILA.
FOR ME?!
YEAH. YOU EARNED IT.

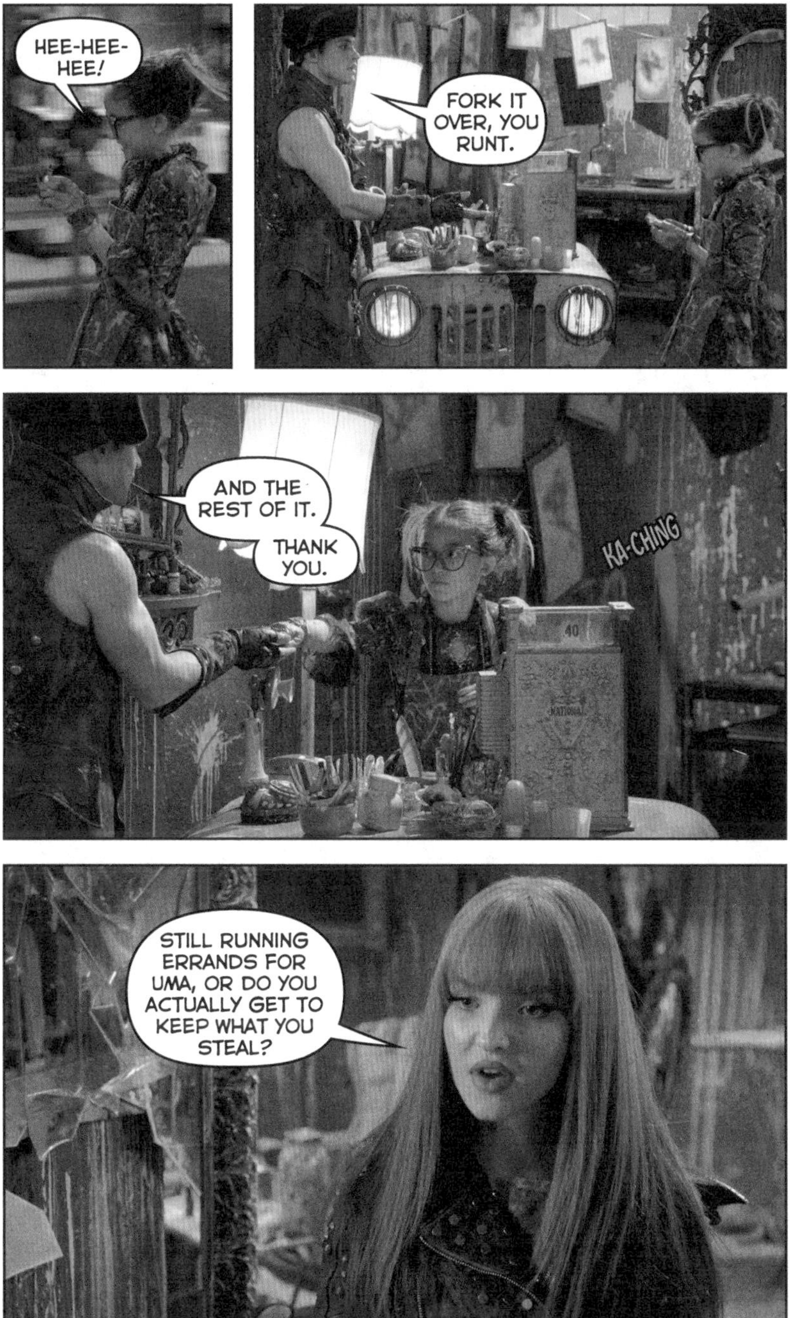
HEE-HEE-HEE!
FORK IT OVER, YOU RUNT.
AND THE REST OF IT.
THANK YOU.
KA-CHING
STILL RUNNING ERRANDS FOR UMA, OR DO YOU ACTUALLY GET TO KEEP WHAT YOU STEAL?

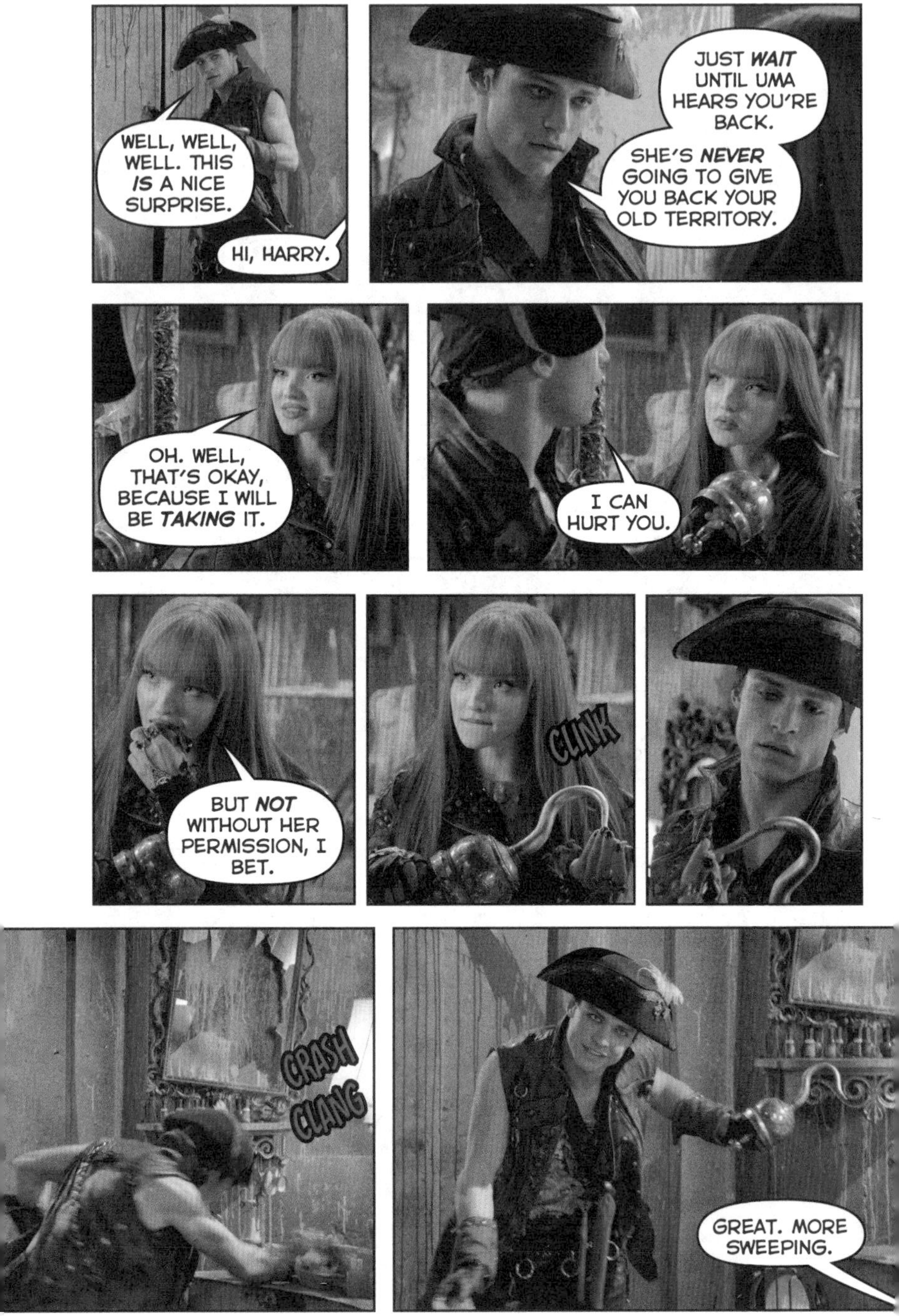
WELL, WELL, WELL. THIS *IS* A NICE SURPRISE.
HI, HARRY.
JUST *WAIT* UNTIL UMA HEARS YOU'RE BACK.
SHE'S *NEVER* GOING TO GIVE YOU BACK YOUR OLD TERRITORY.
OH. WELL, THAT'S OKAY, BECAUSE I WILL BE *TAKING* IT.
I CAN HURT YOU.
BUT *NOT* WITHOUT HER PERMISSION, I BET.
CLINK
CRASH
CLANG
GREAT. MORE SWEEPING.

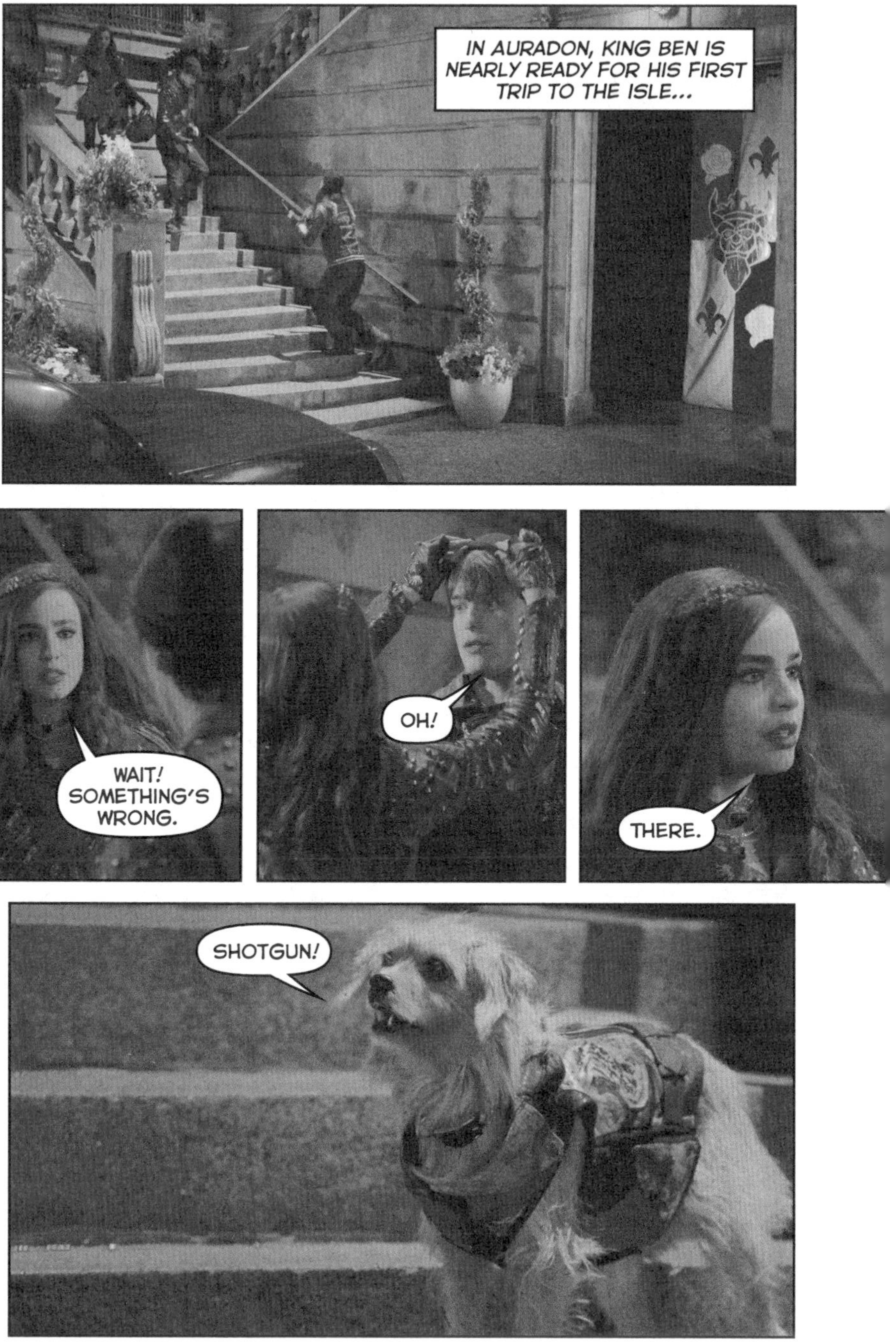
IN AURADON, KING BEN IS NEARLY READY FOR HIS FIRST TRIP TO THE ISLE...
WAIT! SOMETHING'S WRONG.
OH!
THERE.
SHOTGUN!

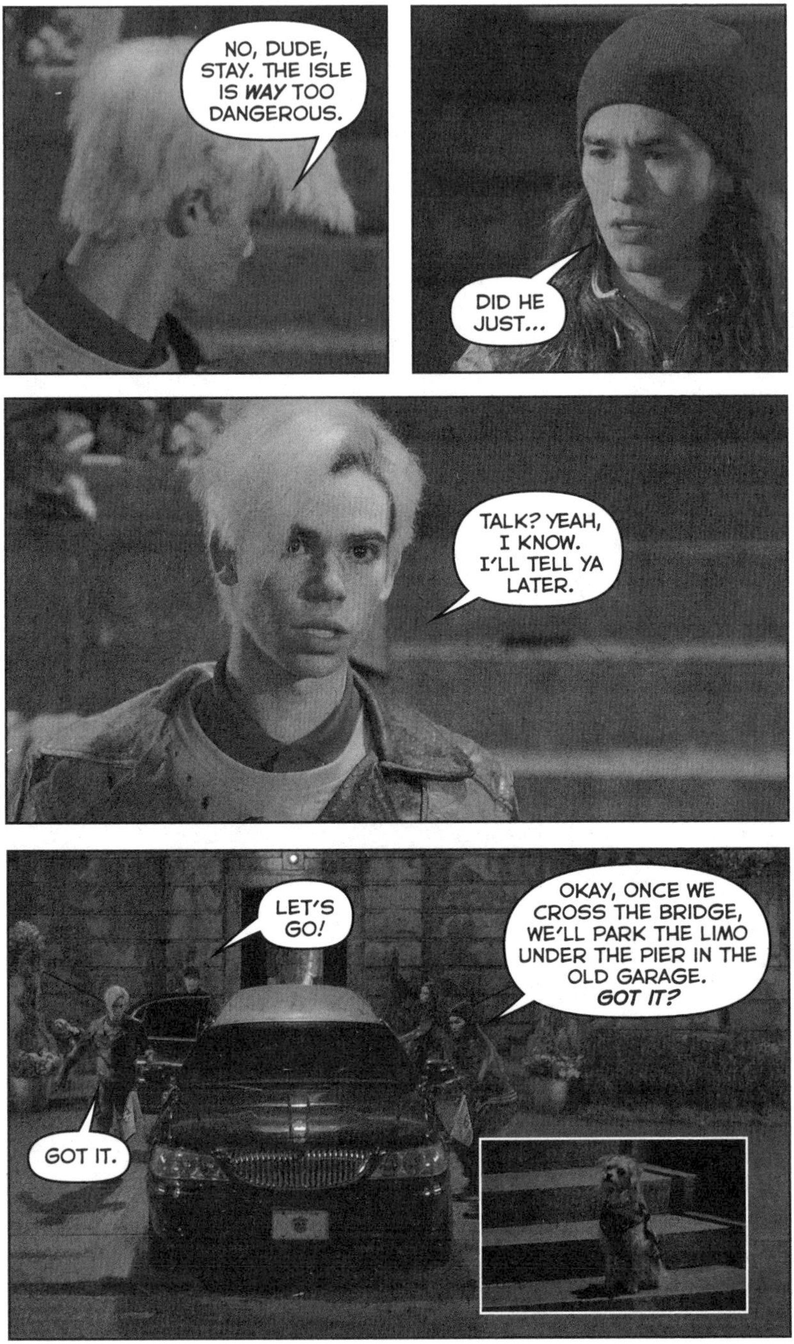
NO, DUDE, STAY. THE ISLE IS *WAY* TOO DANGEROUS.
DID HE JUST...
TALK? YEAH, I KNOW. I'LL TELL YA LATER.
LET'S GO!
OKAY, ONCE WE CROSS THE BRIDGE, WE'LL PARK THE LIMO UNDER THE PIER IN THE OLD GARAGE. *GOT IT?*
GOT IT.

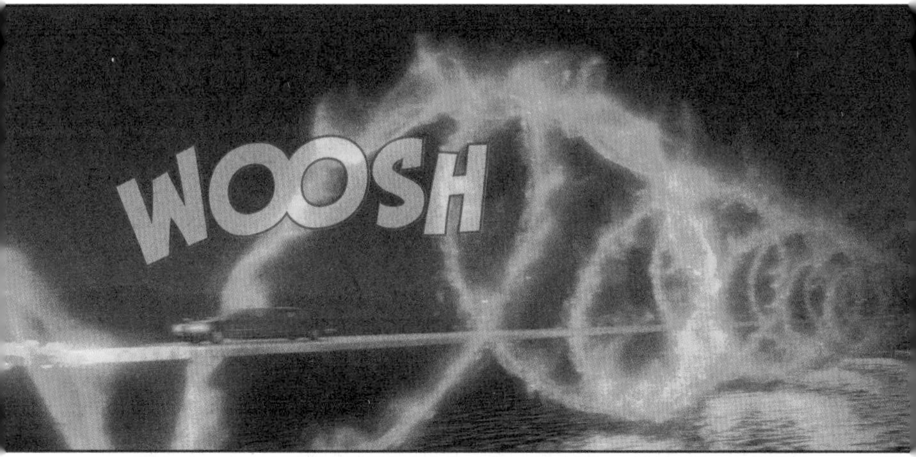
WOOSH

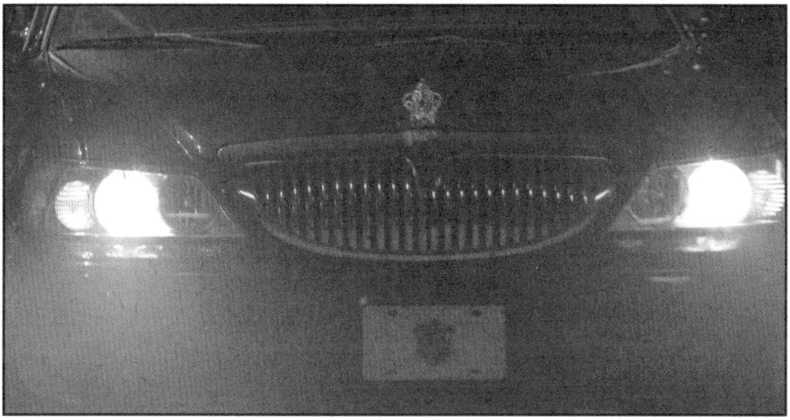

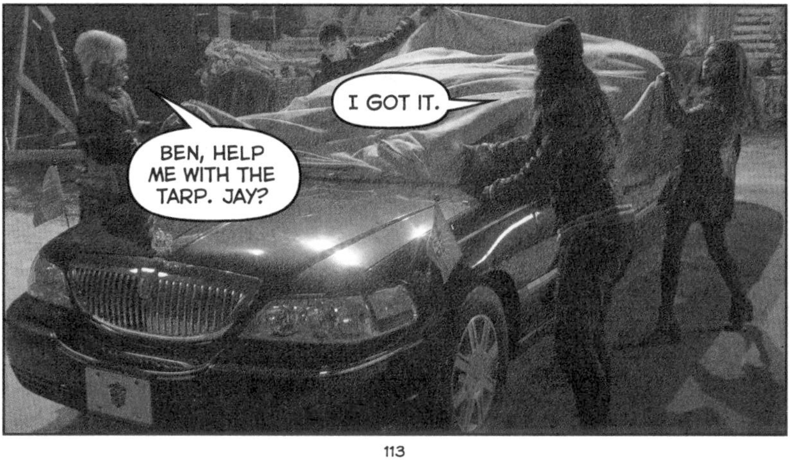
BEN, HELP ME WITH THE TARP. JAY?
I GOT IT.

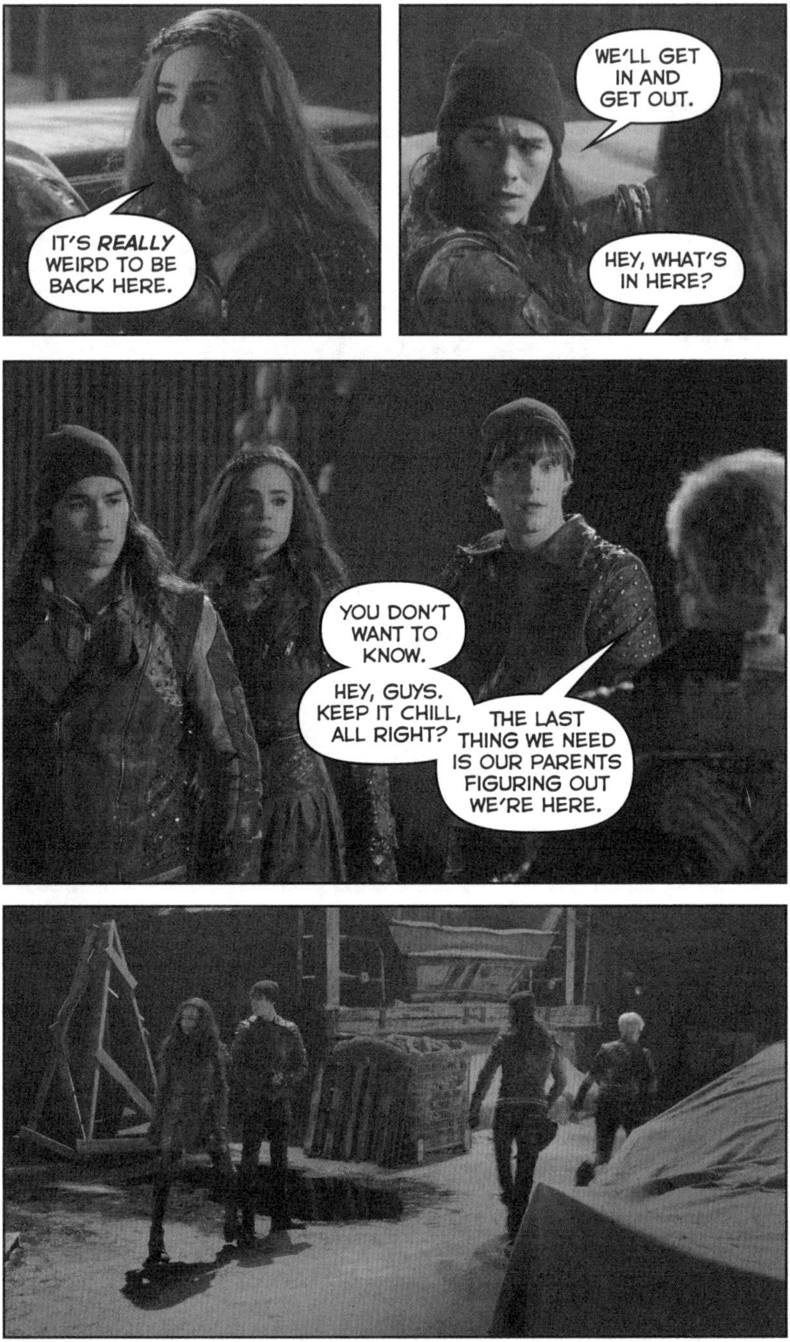

IT'S *REALLY* WEIRD TO BE BACK HERE.
WE'LL GET IN AND GET OUT.
HEY, WHAT'S IN HERE?
YOU DON'T WANT TO KNOW.
HEY, GUYS. KEEP IT CHILL, ALL RIGHT?
THE LAST THING WE NEED IS OUR PARENTS FIGURING OUT WE'RE HERE.

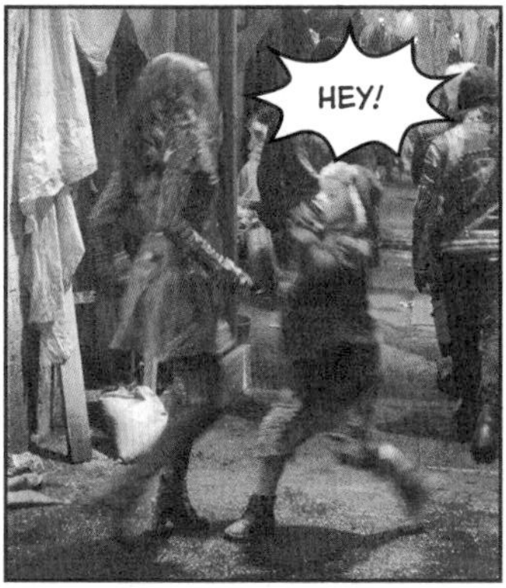
HEY!

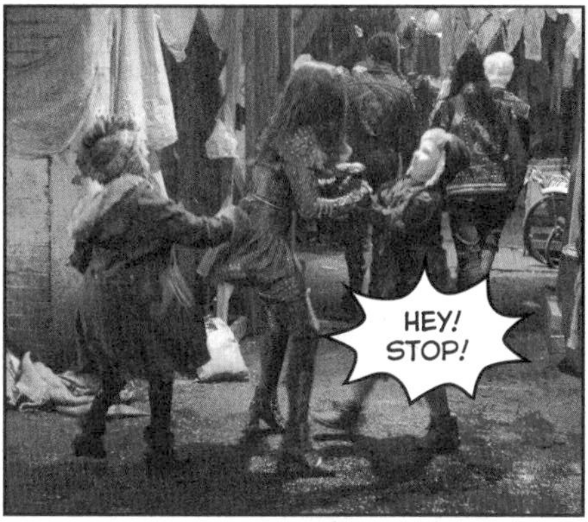
HEY!
STOP!

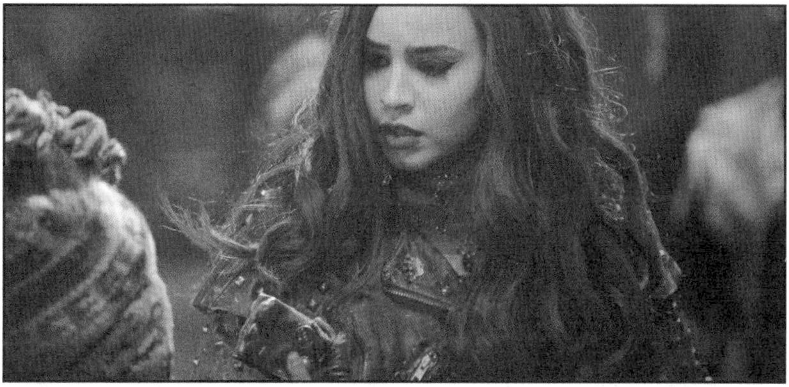

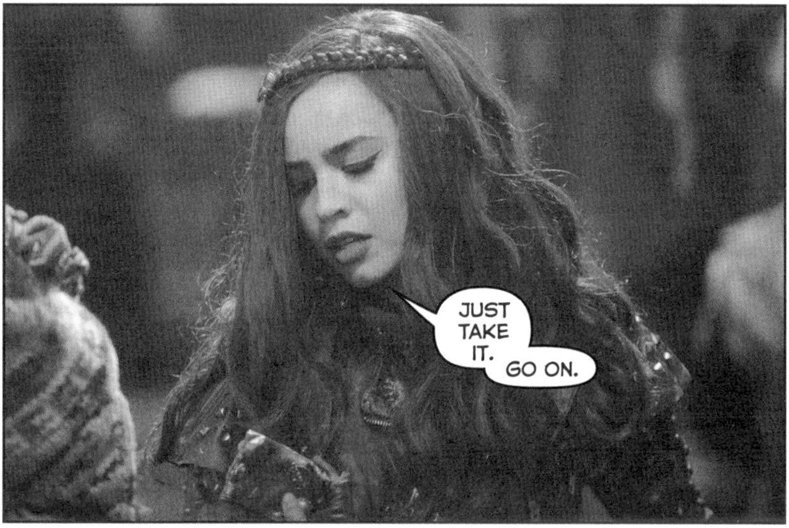
JUST TAKE IT.
GO ON.

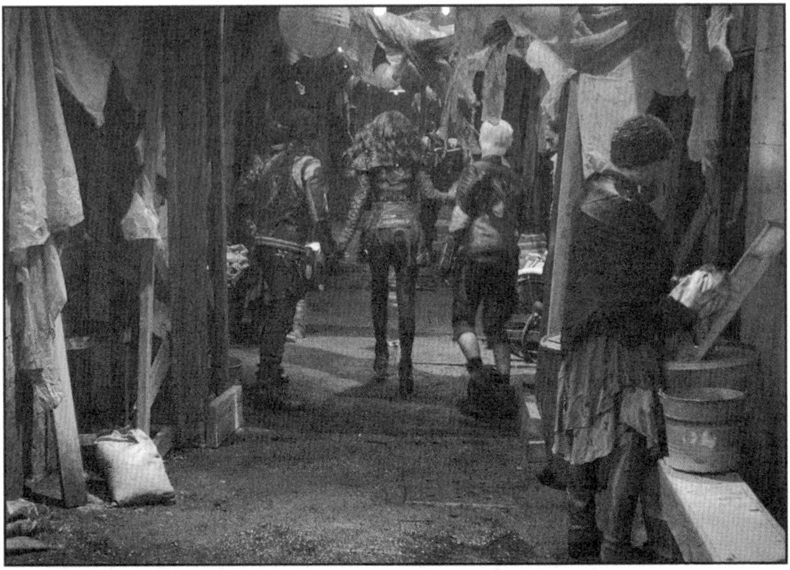

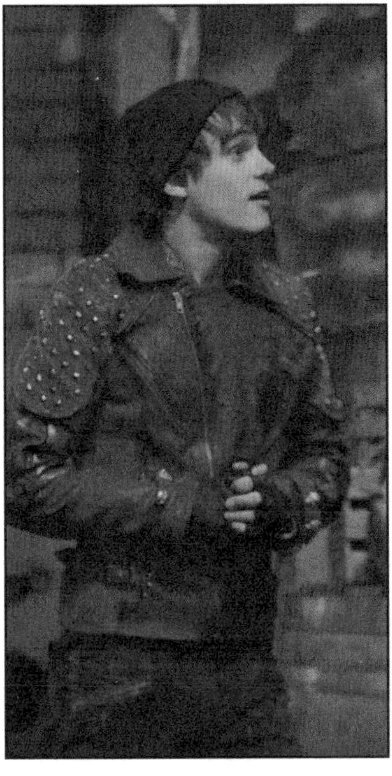

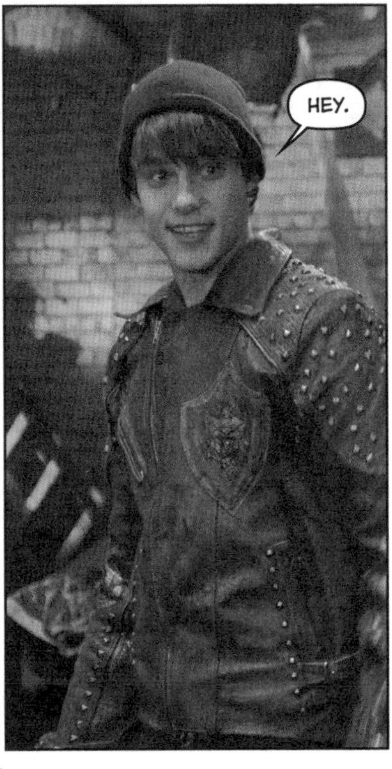
HEY.

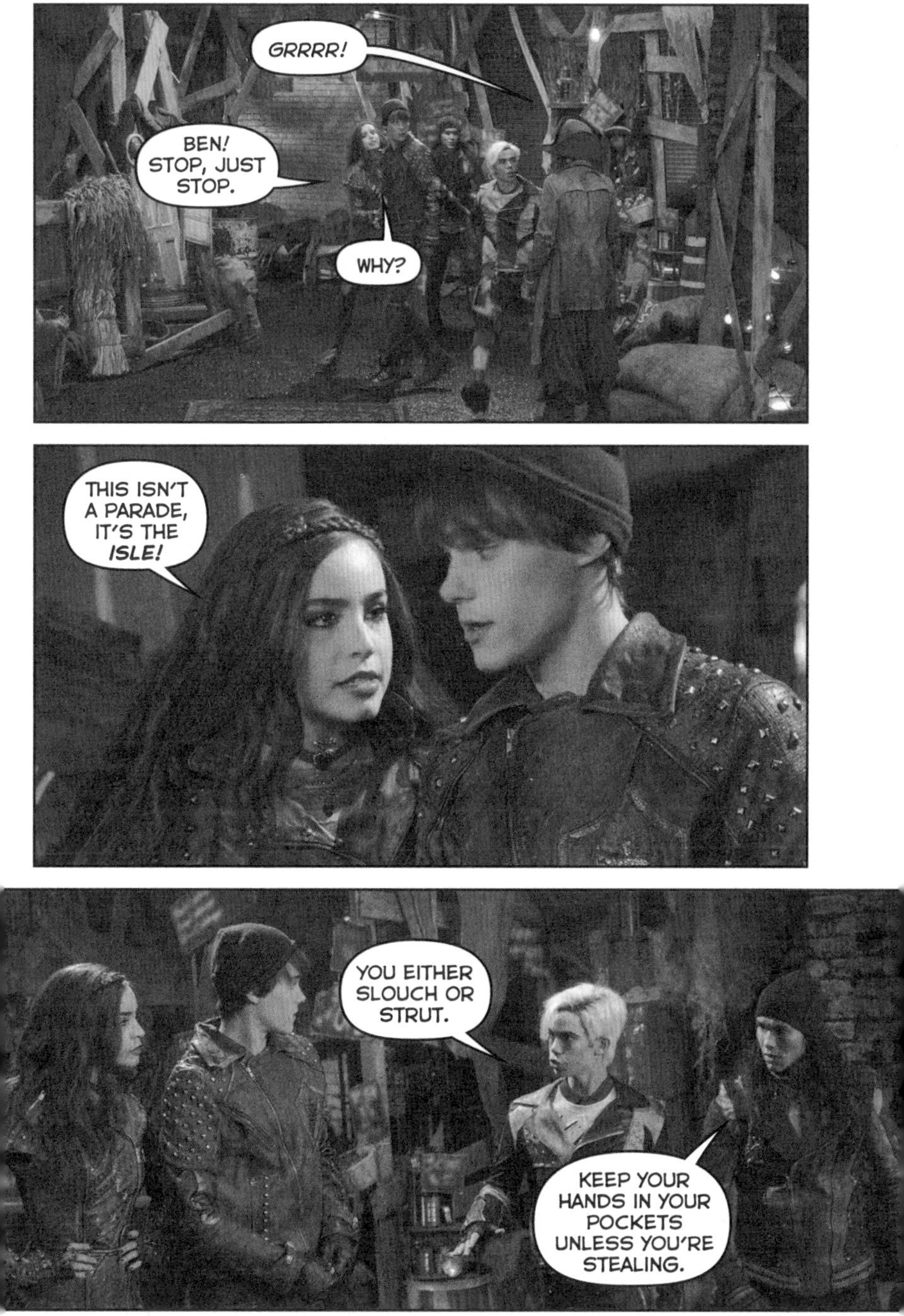
GRRRR!
BEN! STOP, JUST STOP.
WHY?
THIS ISN'T A PARADE, IT'S THE *ISLE!*
YOU EITHER SLOUCH OR STRUT.
KEEP YOUR HANDS IN YOUR POCKETS UNLESS YOU'RE STEALING.

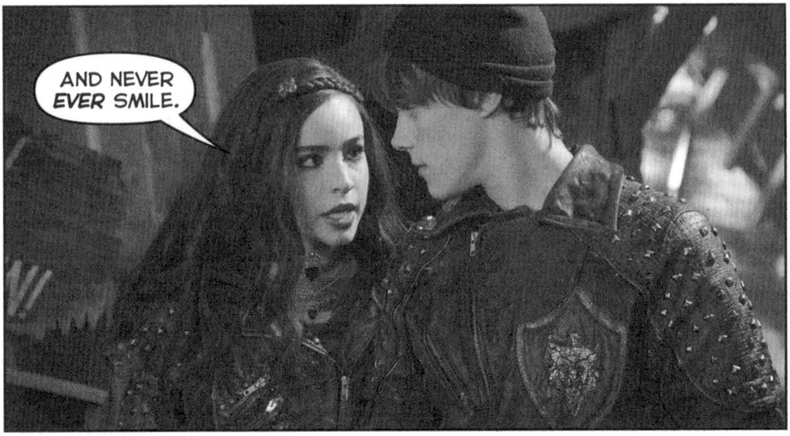
AND NEVER *EVER* SMILE.

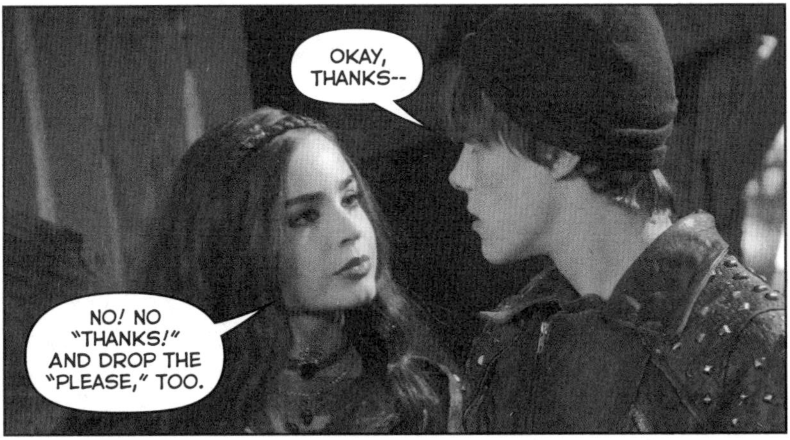
OKAY, THANKS--
NO! NO "THANKS!" AND DROP THE "PLEASE," TOO.

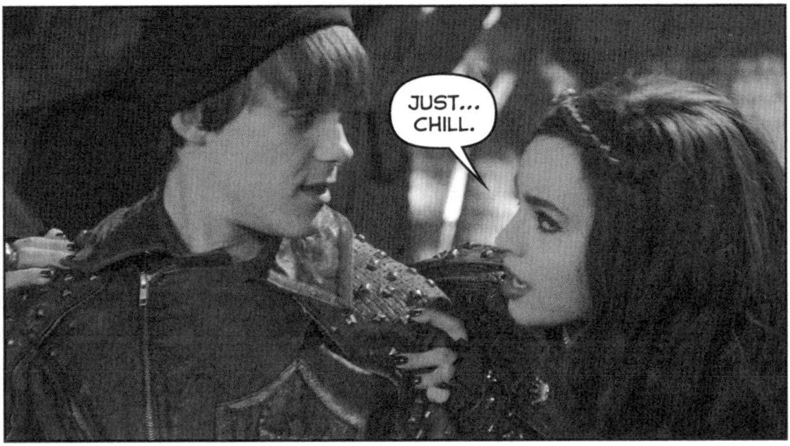
JUST... CHILL.

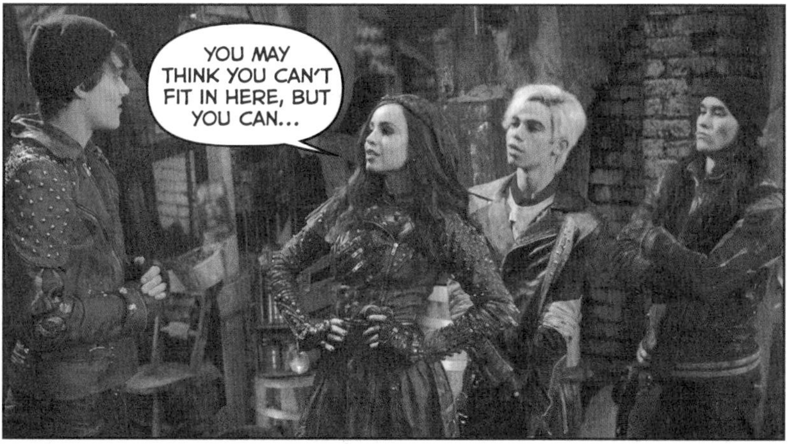
YOU MAY THINK YOU CAN'T FIT IN HERE, BUT YOU CAN...

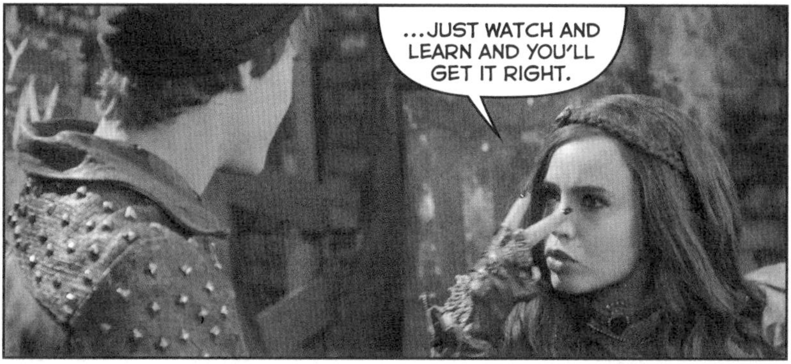
...JUST WATCH AND LEARN AND YOU'LL GET IT RIGHT.

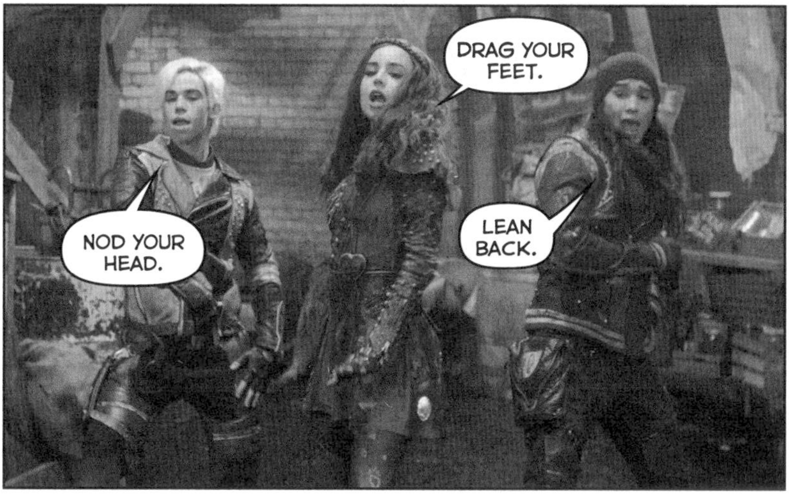
DRAG YOUR FEET.
NOD YOUR HEAD.
LEAN BACK.

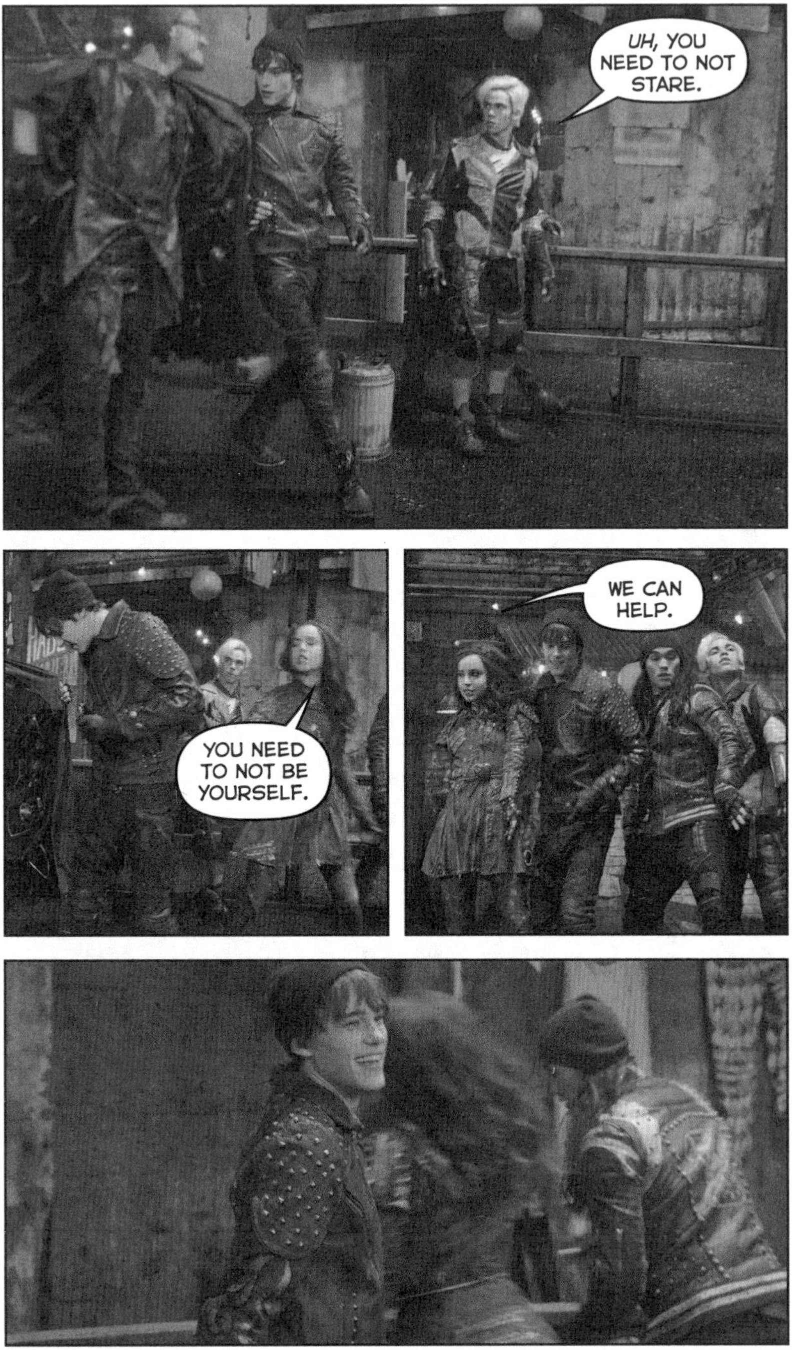
UH, YOU NEED TO NOT STARE.
YOU NEED TO NOT BE YOURSELF.
WE CAN HELP.

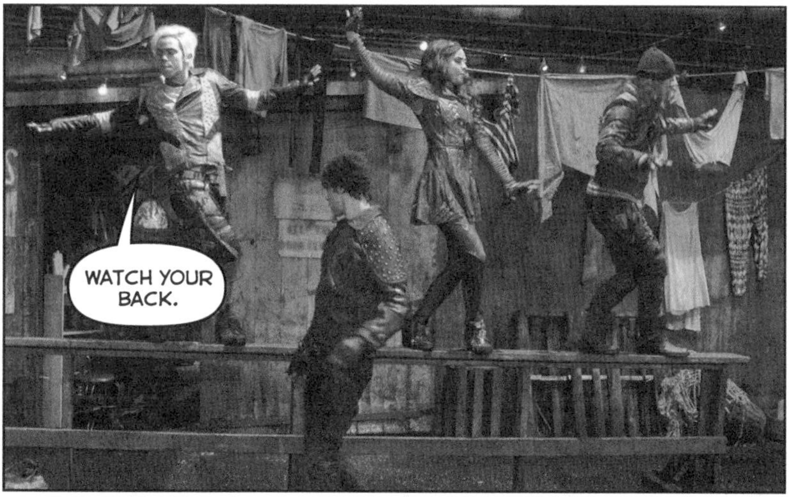
WATCH YOUR BACK.

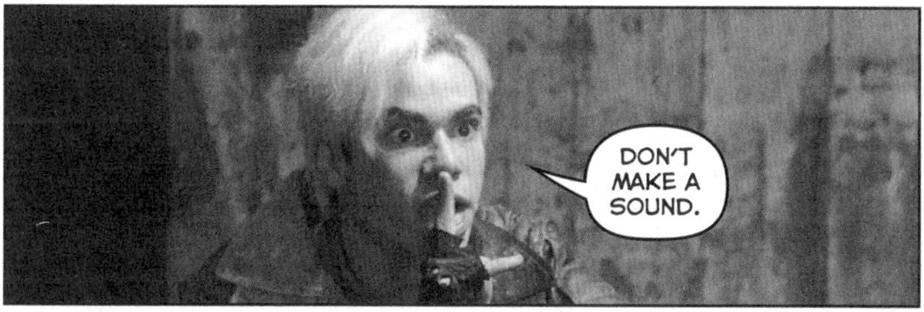
DON'T MAKE A SOUND.

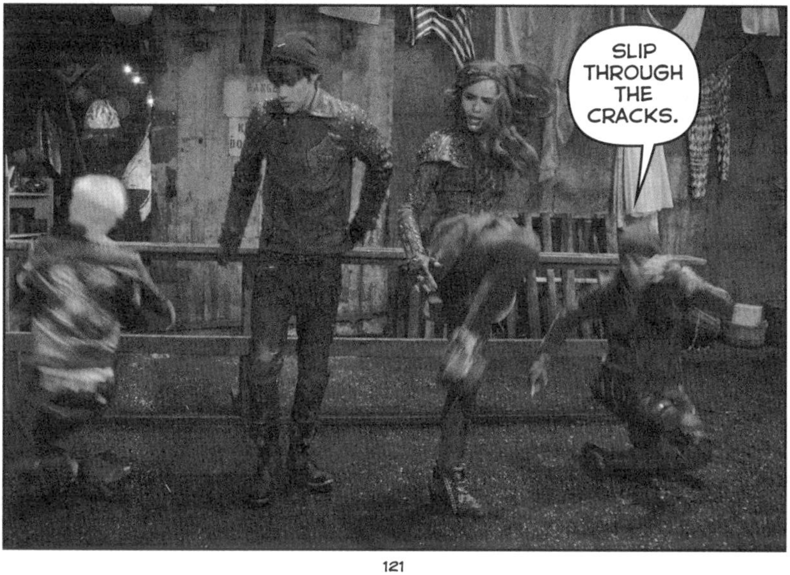
SLIP THROUGH THE CRACKS.

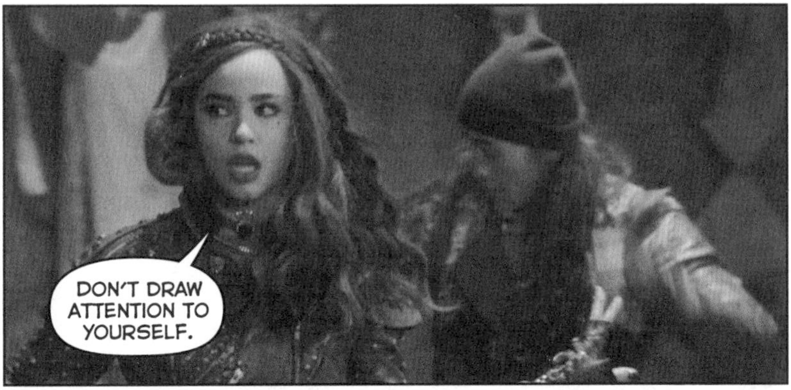
DON'T DRAW ATTENTION TO YOURSELF.

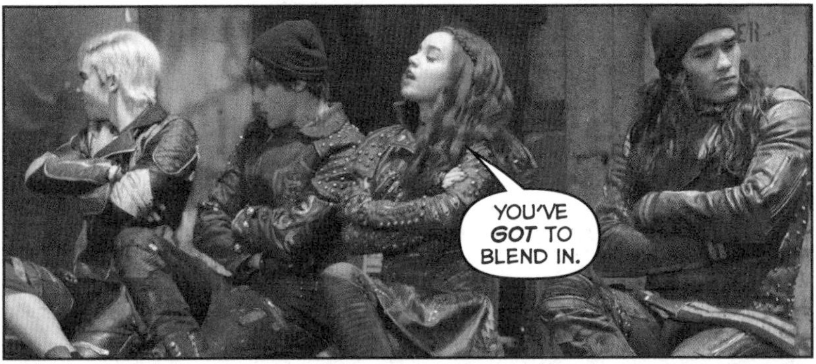
YOU'VE ***GOT*** TO BLEND IN.

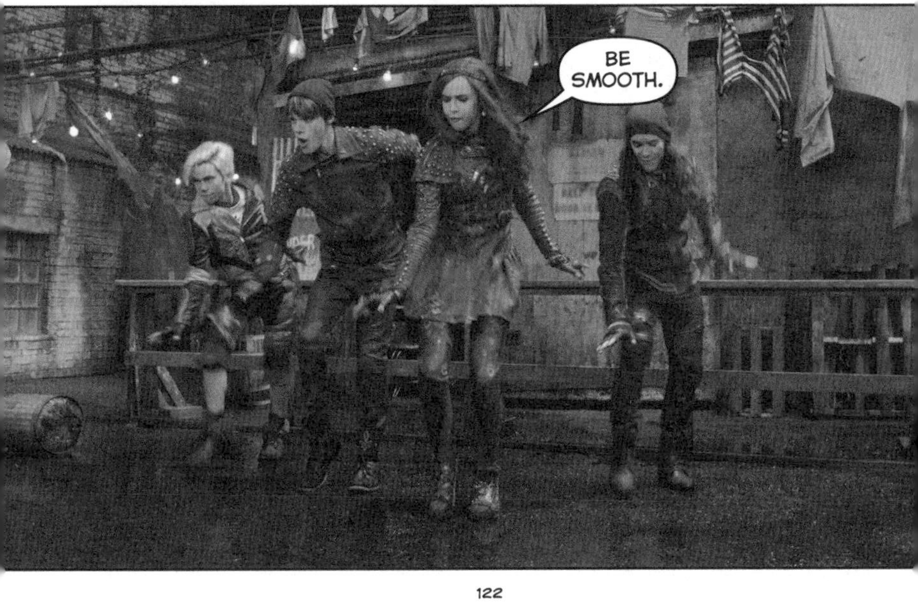
BE SMOOTH.

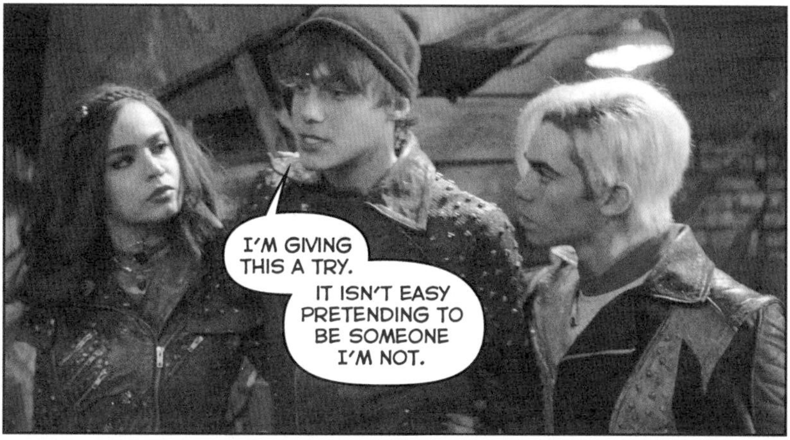
I'M GIVING THIS A TRY.
IT ISN'T EASY PRETENDING TO BE SOMEONE I'M NOT.

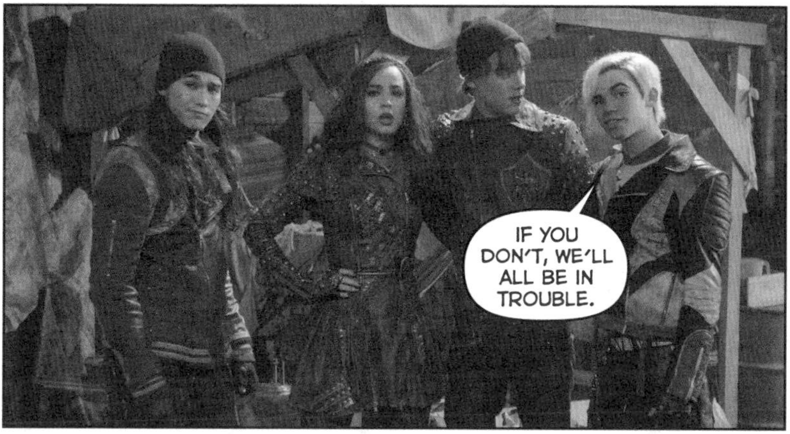
IF YOU DON'T, WE'LL ALL BE IN TROUBLE.

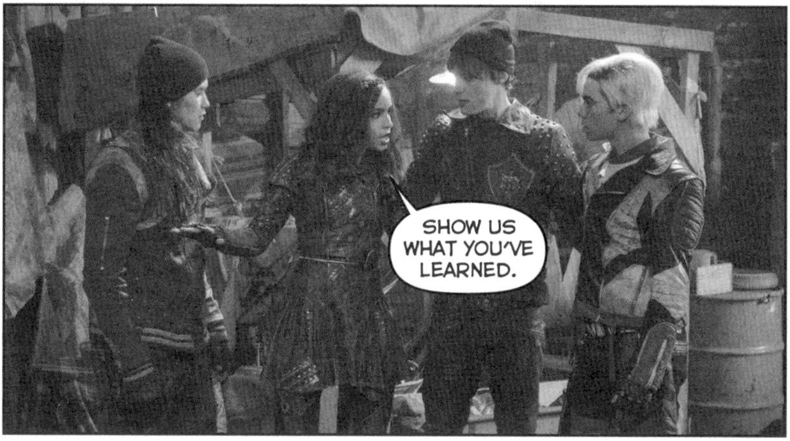
SHOW US WHAT YOU'VE LEARNED.

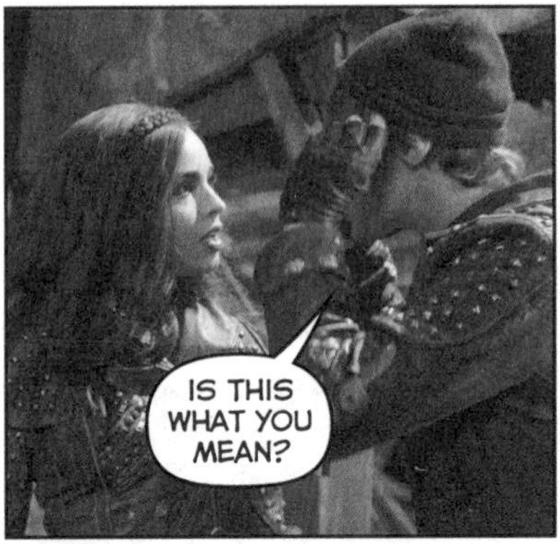
IS THIS WHAT YOU MEAN?

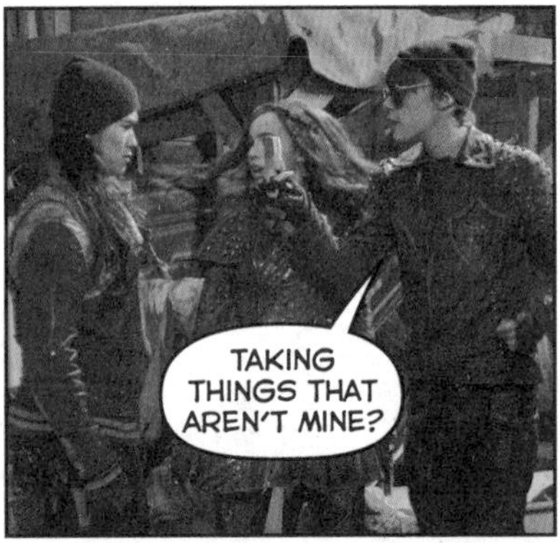
TAKING THINGS THAT AREN'T MINE?

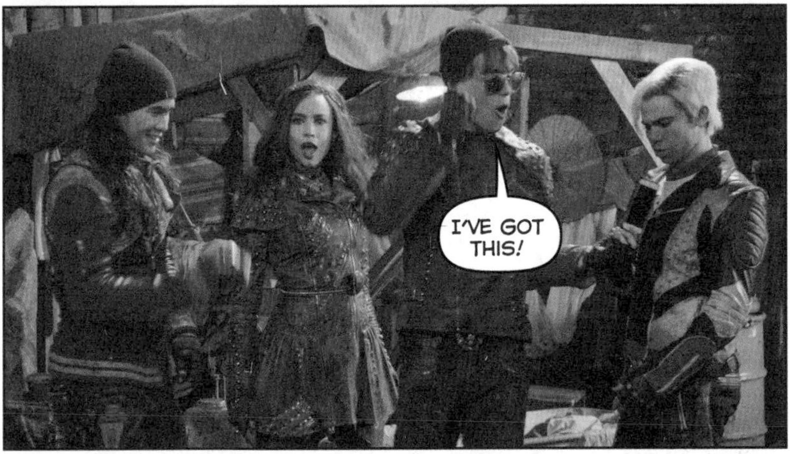
I'VE GOT THIS!

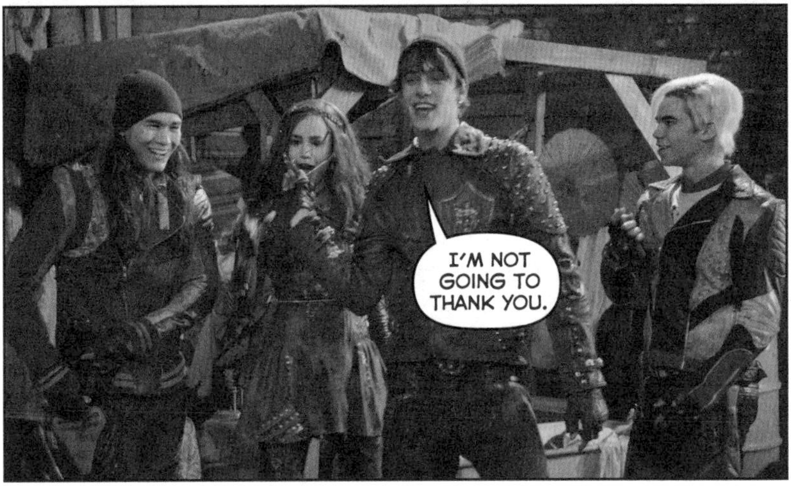
I'M NOT GOING TO THANK YOU.

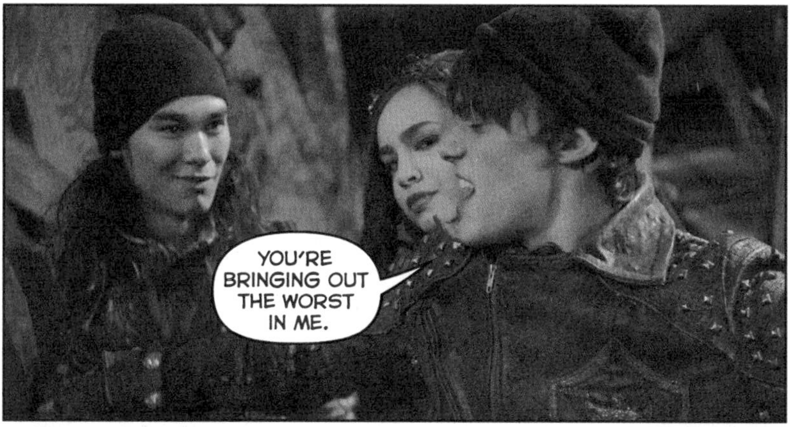
YOU'RE BRINGING OUT THE WORST IN ME.

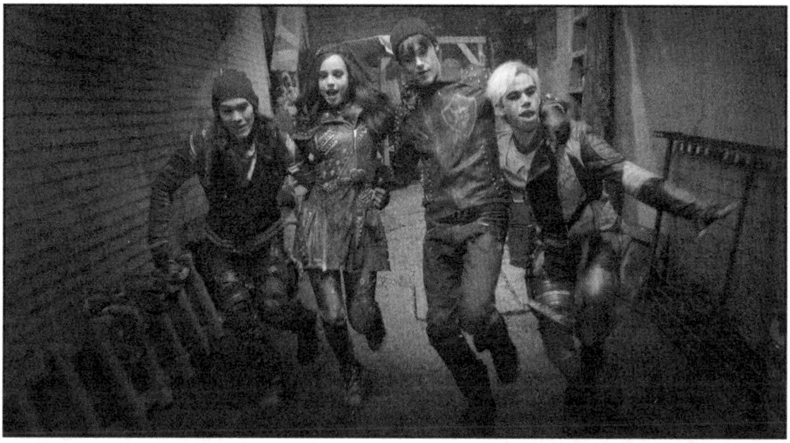

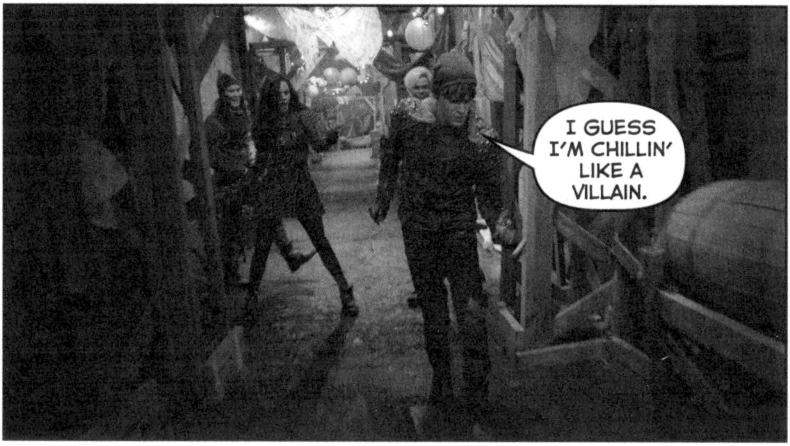
I GUESS I'M CHILLIN' LIKE A VILLAIN.

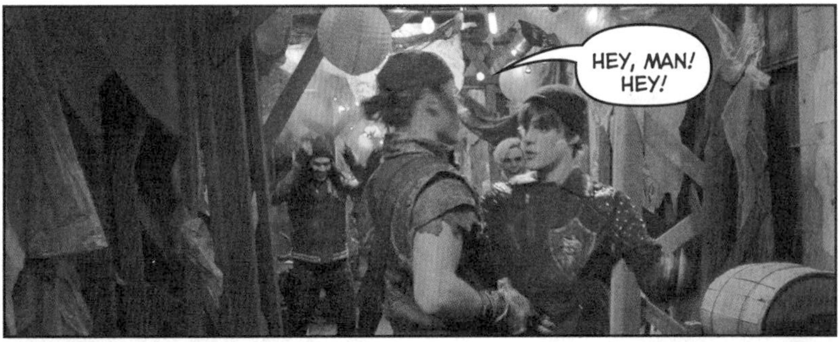
HEY, MAN! HEY!

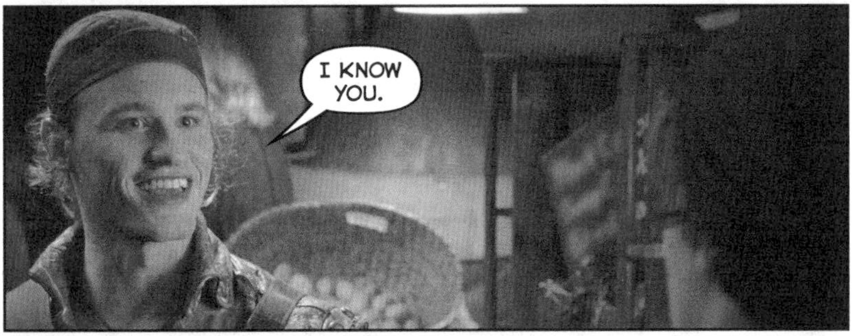
I KNOW YOU.

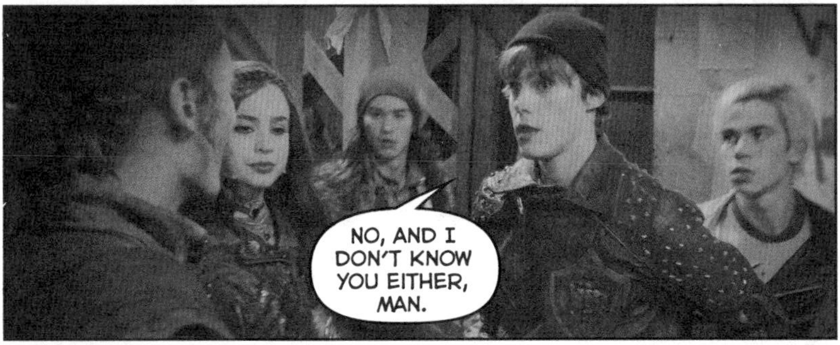
NO, AND I DON'T KNOW YOU EITHER, MAN.

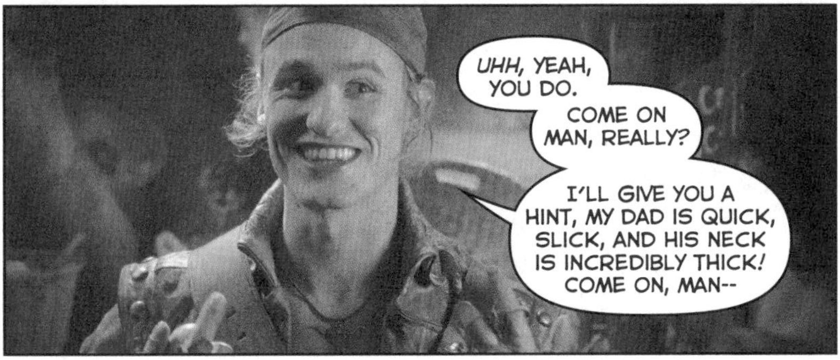
UHH, YEAH, YOU DO.
COME ON MAN, REALLY?
I'LL GIVE YOU A HINT, MY DAD IS QUICK, SLICK, AND HIS NECK IS INCREDIBLY THICK! COME ON, MAN--

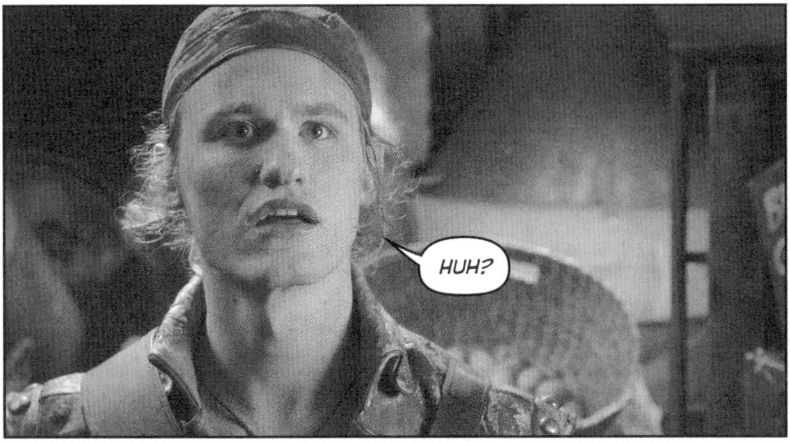
HUH?

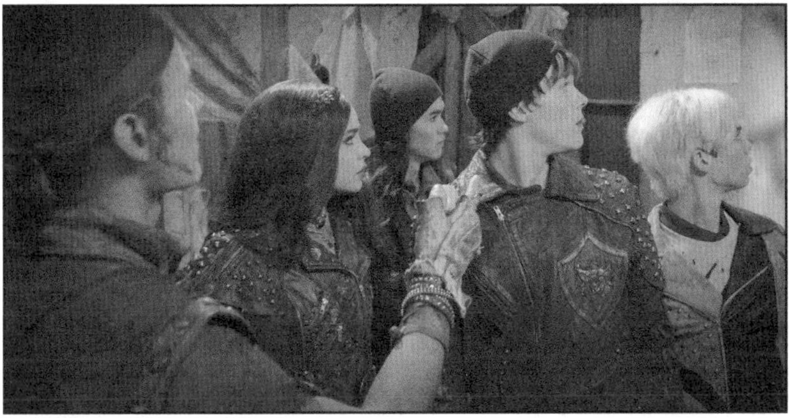

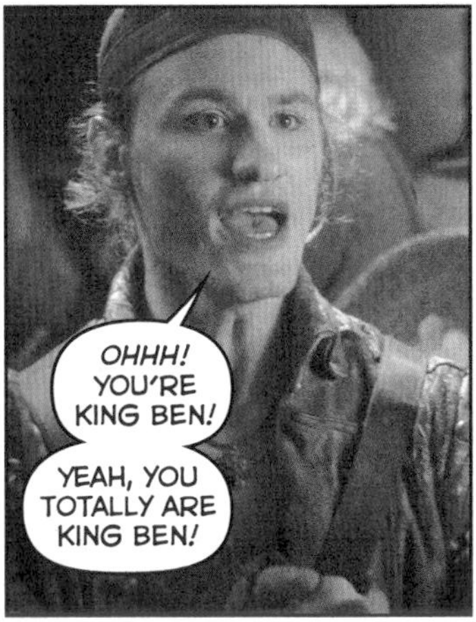
OHHH! YOU'RE KING BEN!
YEAH, YOU TOTALLY ARE KING BEN!

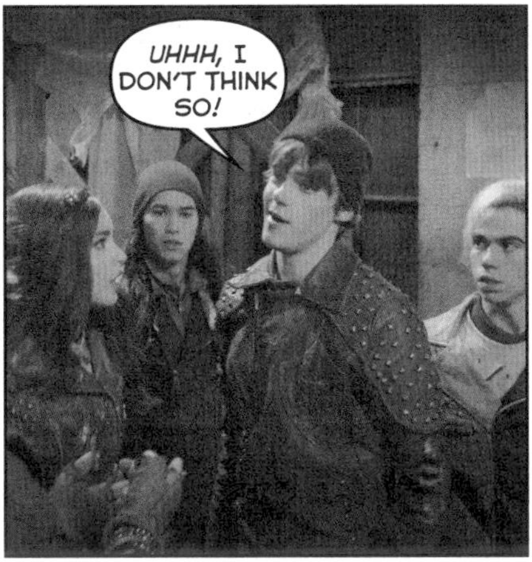
UHHH, I DON'T THINK SO!

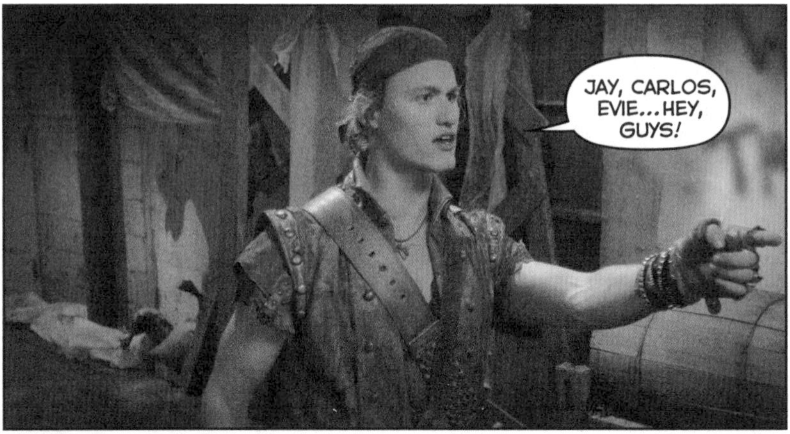
JAY, CARLOS, EVIE...HEY, GUYS!

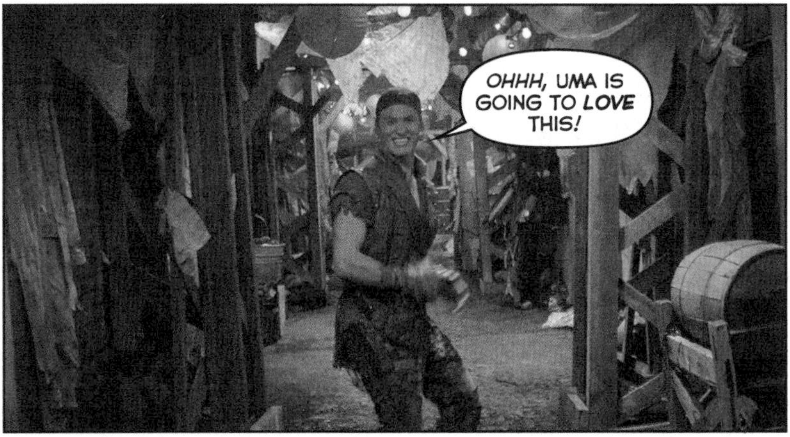
OHHH, UMA IS GOING TO ***LOVE*** THIS!

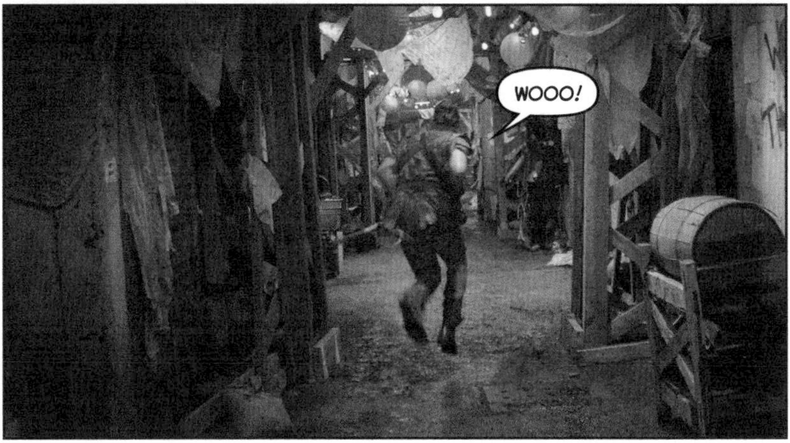
WOOO!

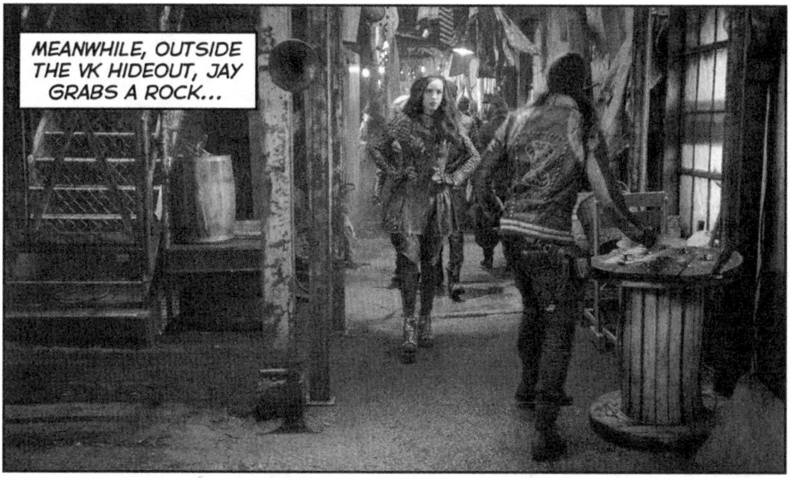
MEANWHILE, OUTSIDE THE VK HIDEOUT, JAY GRABS A ROCK...

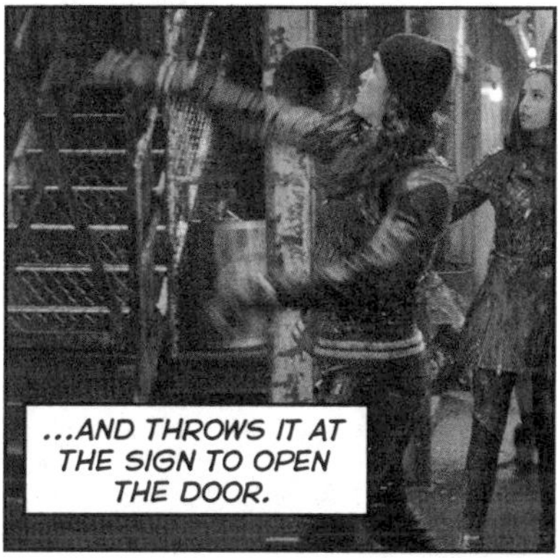
...AND THROWS IT AT THE SIGN TO OPEN THE DOOR.

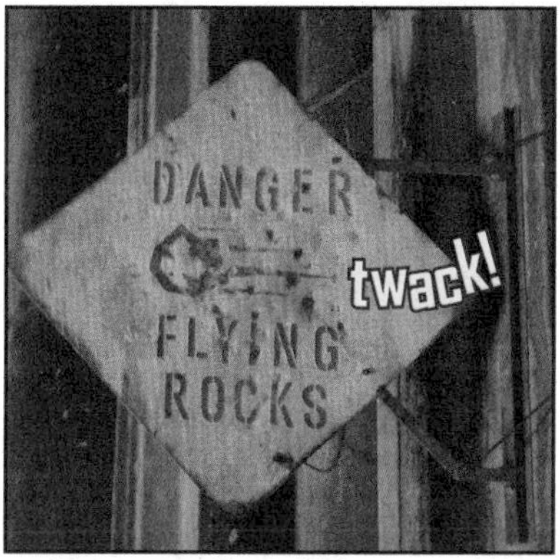
DANGER
FLYING ROCKS
twack!

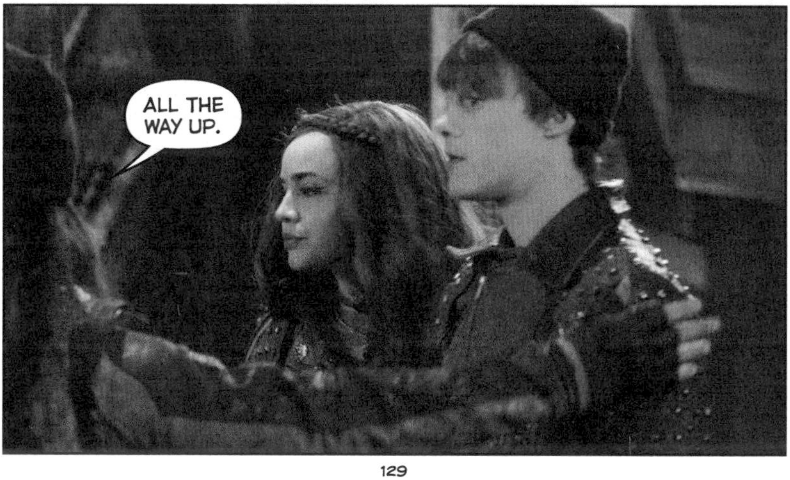
ALL THE WAY UP.

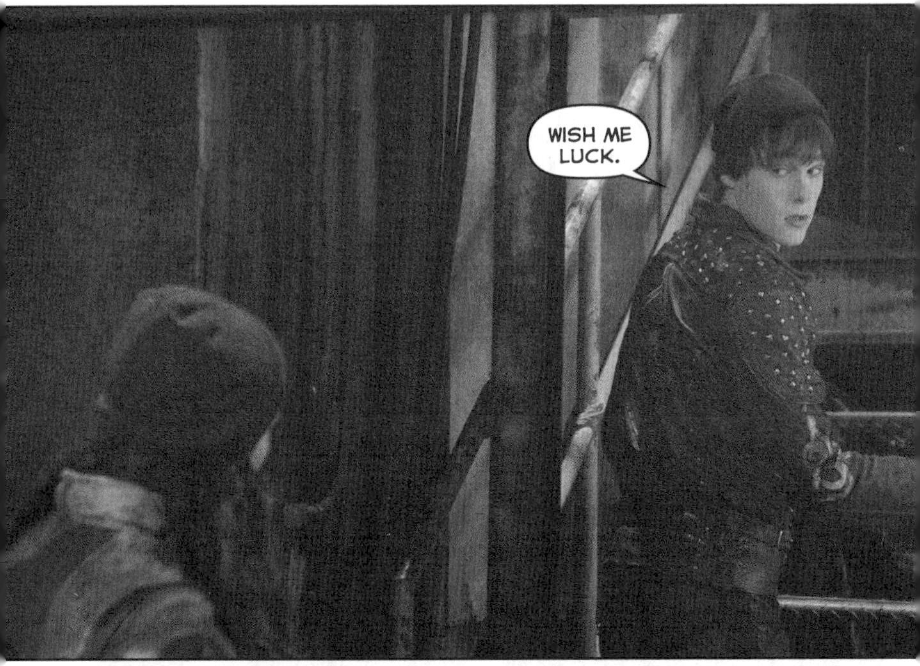
WISH ME LUCK.

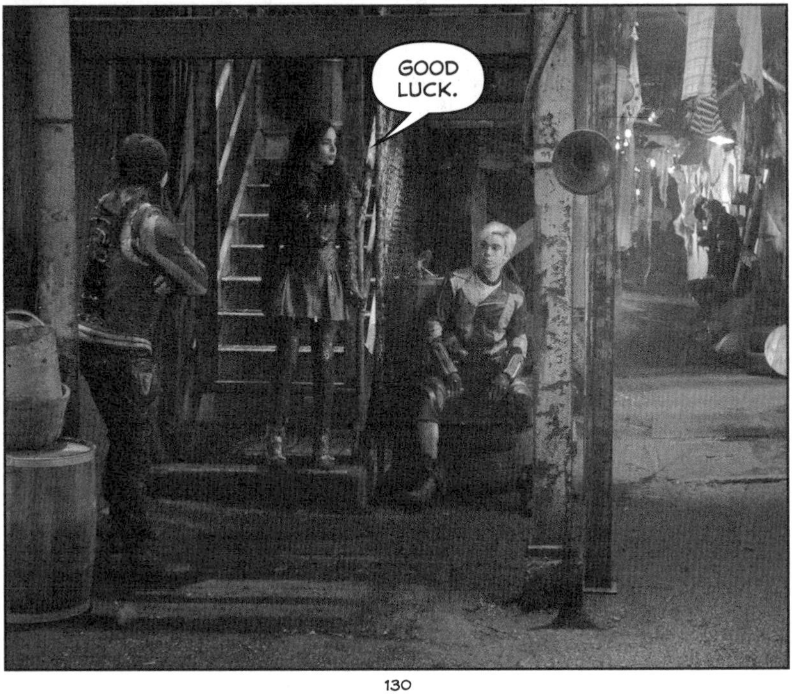
GOOD LUCK.

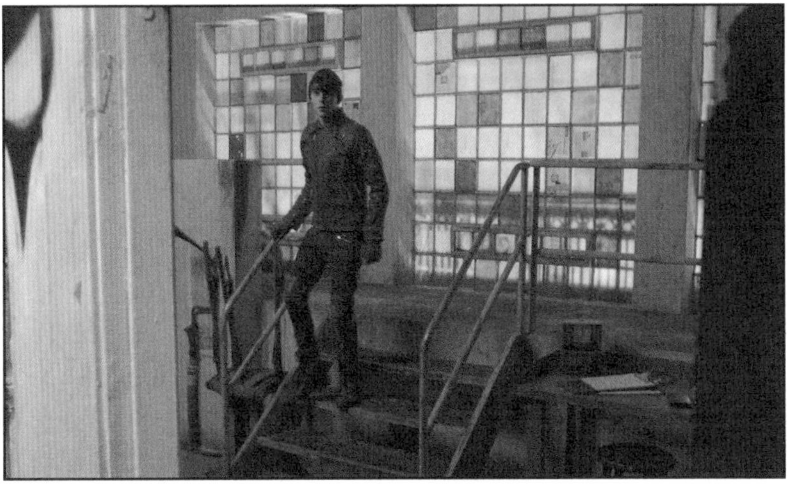

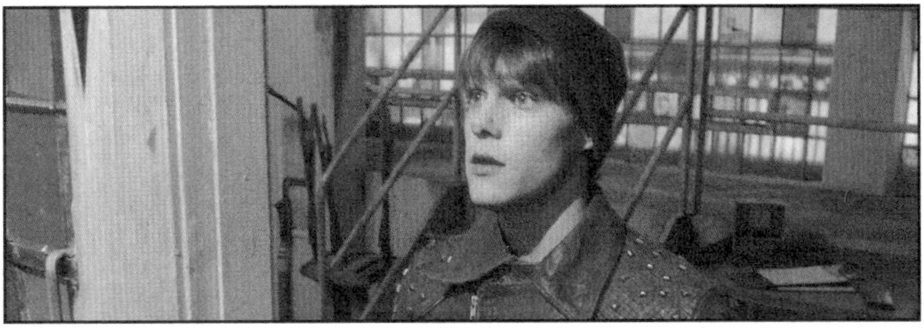

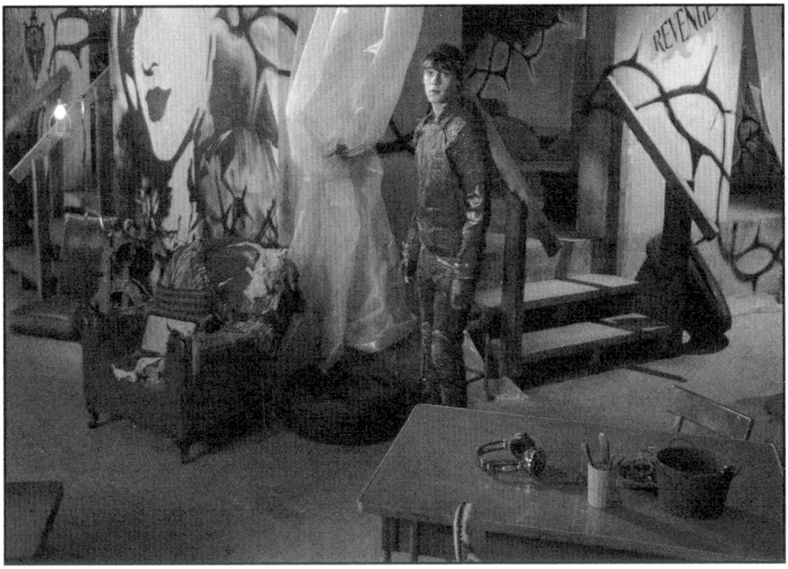
REVENG

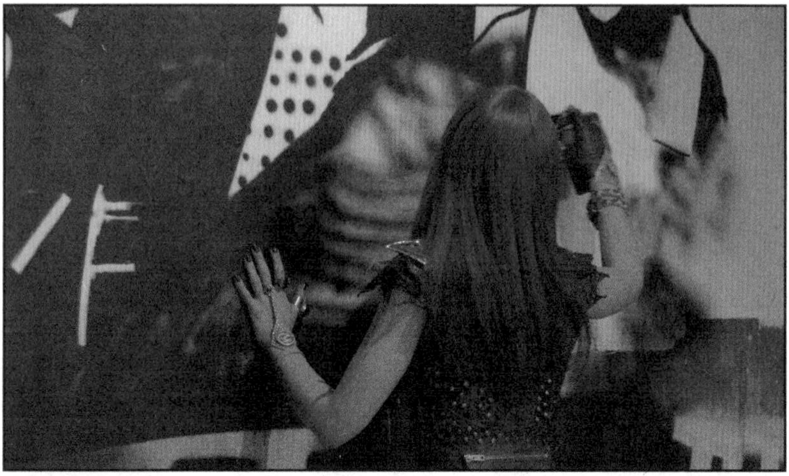

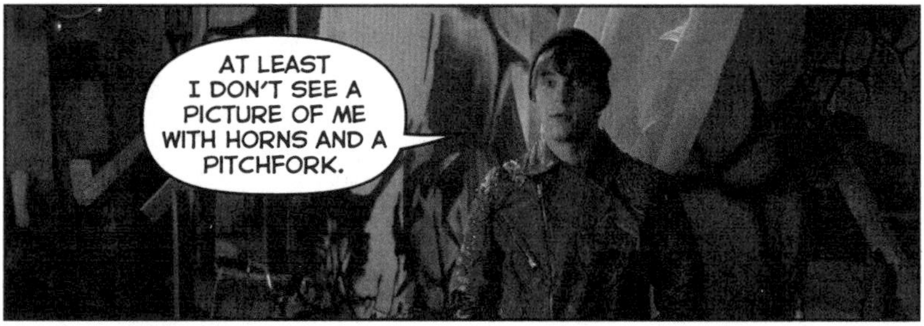
AT LEAST I DON'T SEE A PICTURE OF ME WITH HORNS AND A PITCHFORK.

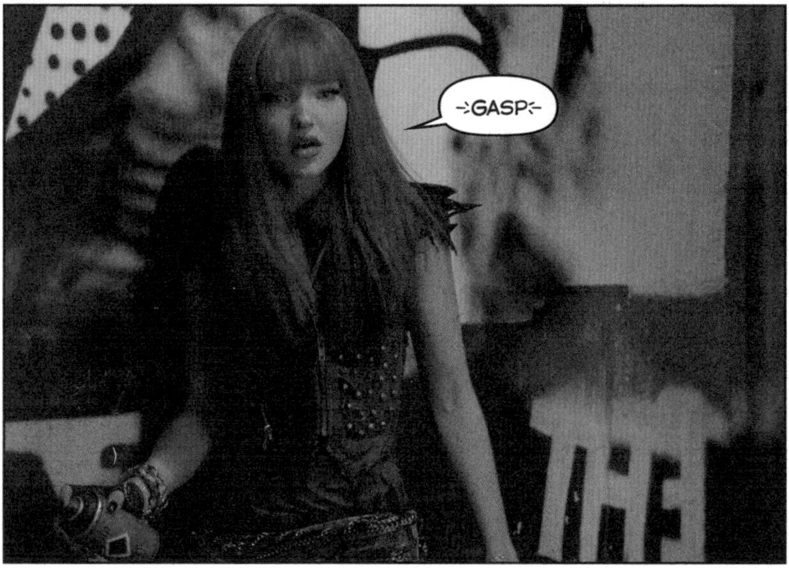
-GASP-

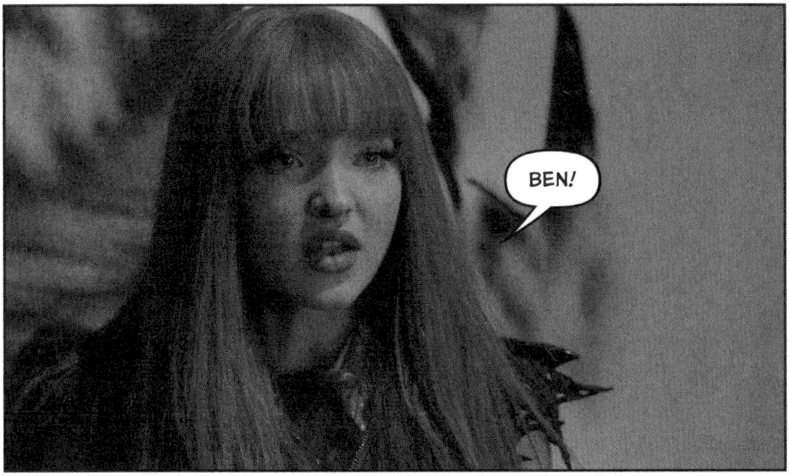
BEN!

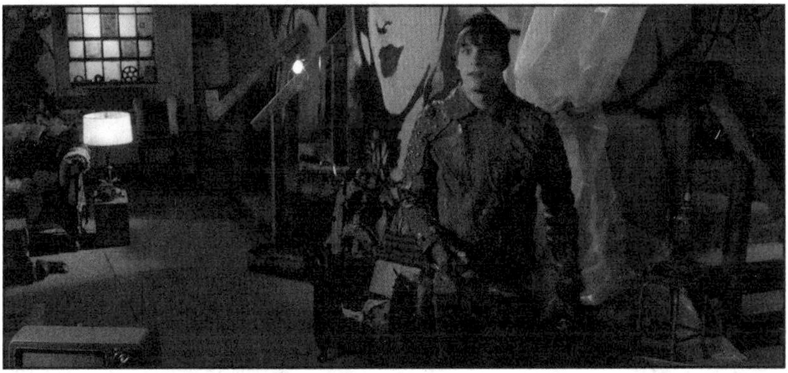

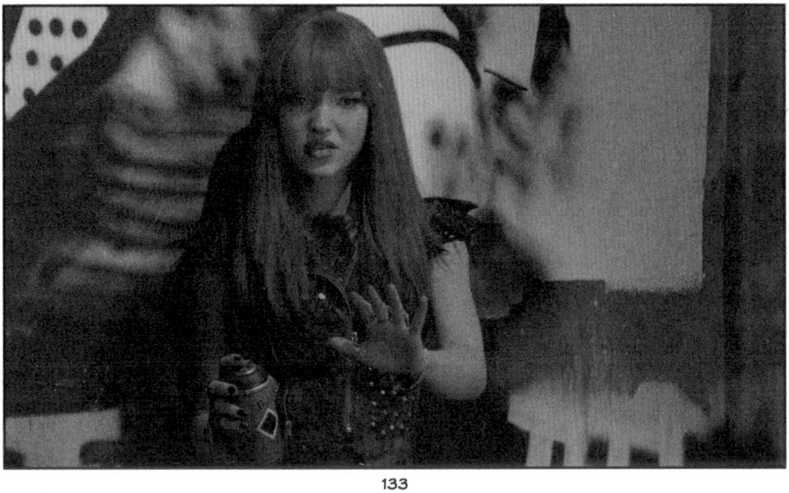

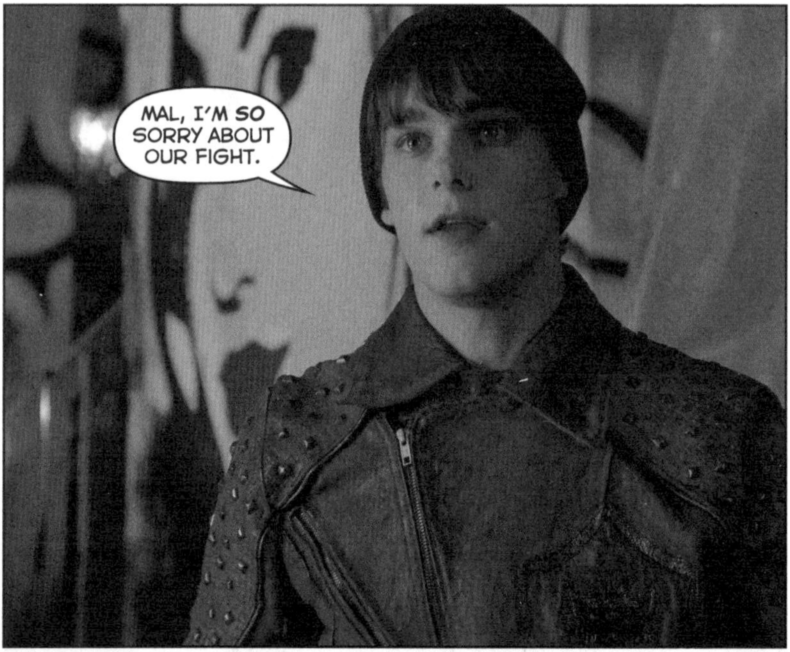
MAL, I'M SO SORRY ABOUT OUR FIGHT.

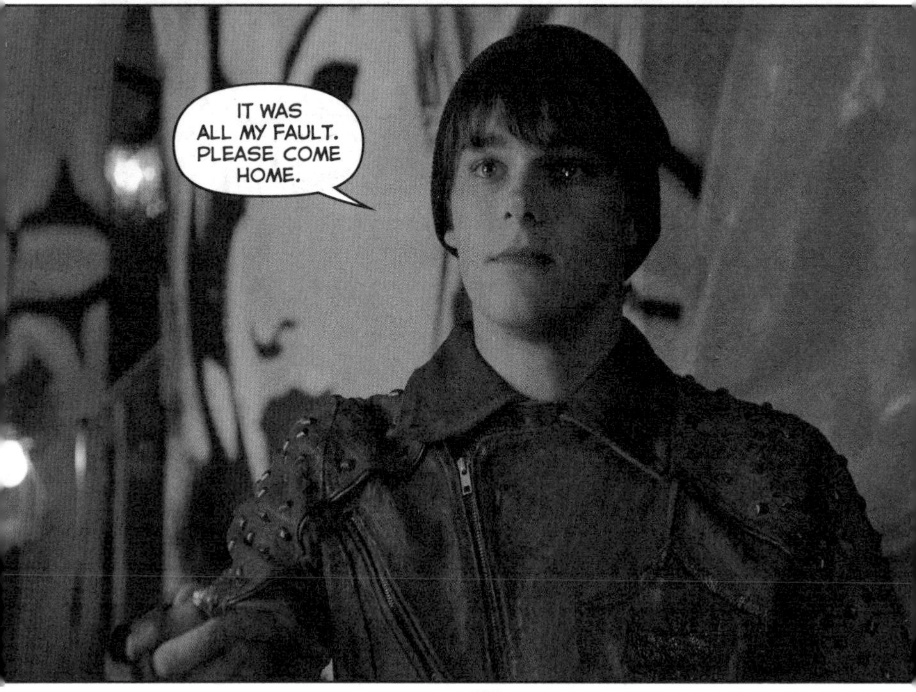
IT WAS ALL MY FAULT. PLEASE COME HOME.

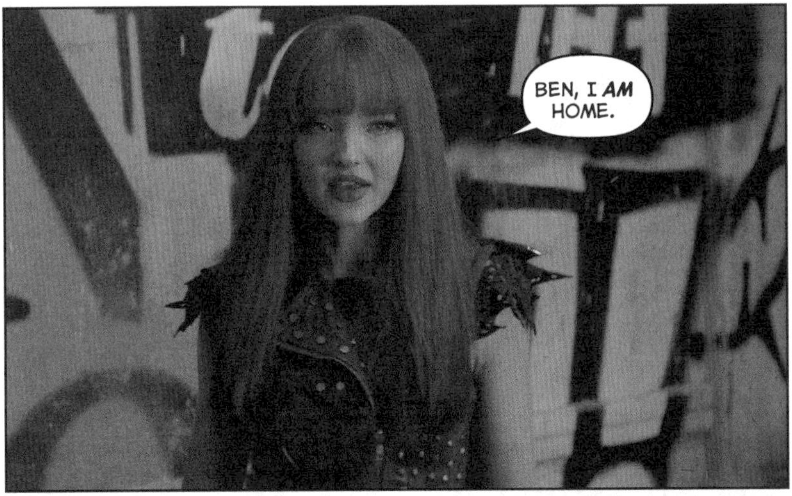
BEN, I *AM* HOME.

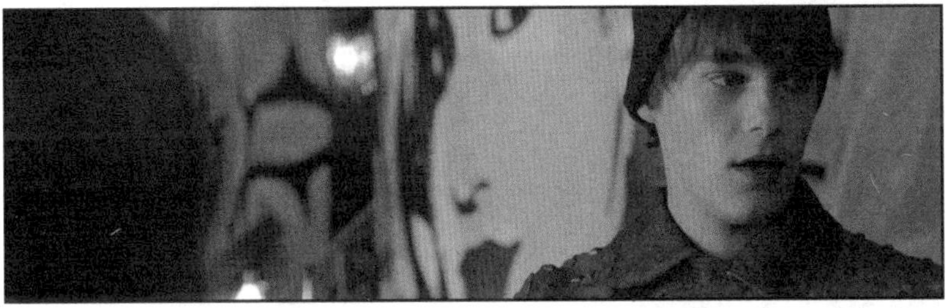

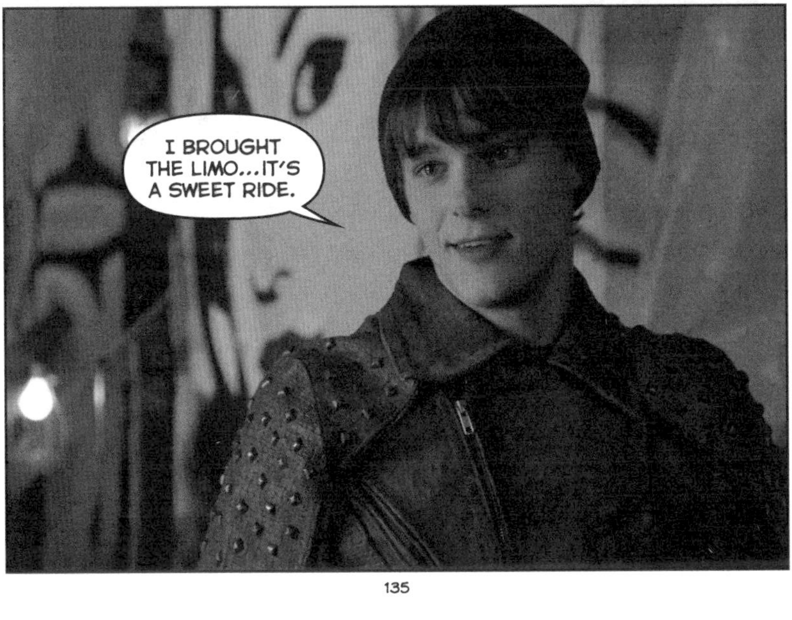
I BROUGHT THE LIMO...IT'S A SWEET RIDE.

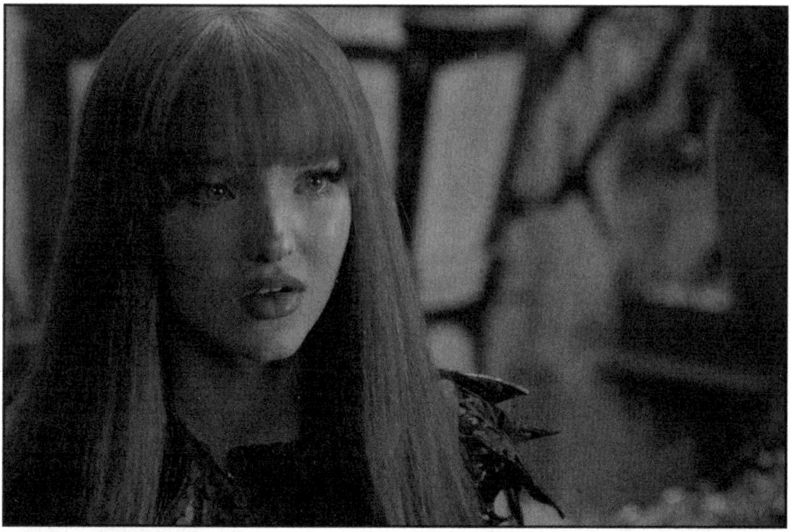

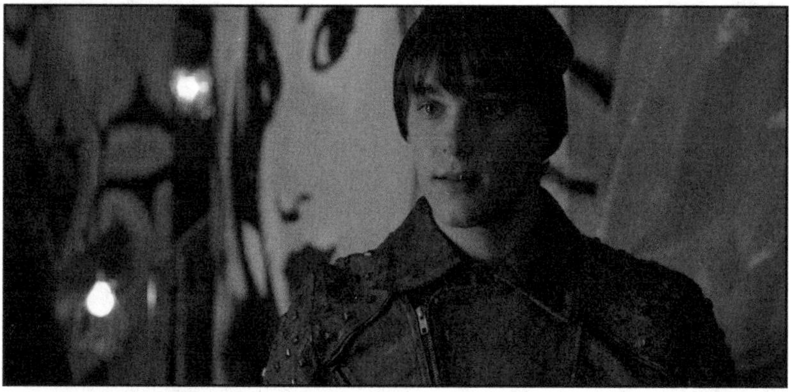

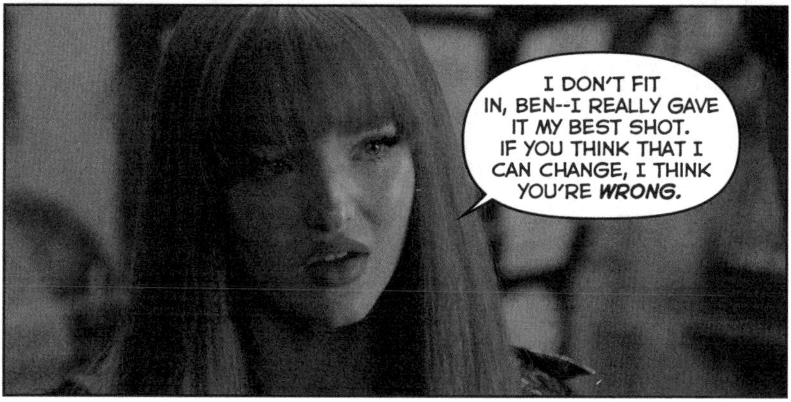
I DON'T FIT IN, BEN--I REALLY GAVE IT MY BEST SHOT. IF YOU THINK THAT I CAN CHANGE, I THINK YOU'RE ***WRONG.***

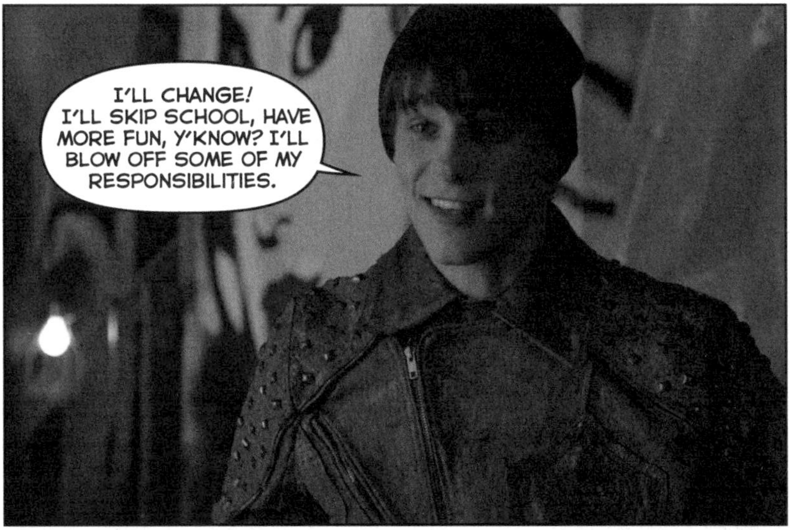
I'LL CHANGE! I'LL SKIP SCHOOL, HAVE MORE FUN, Y'KNOW? I'LL BLOW OFF SOME OF MY RESPONSIBILITIES.

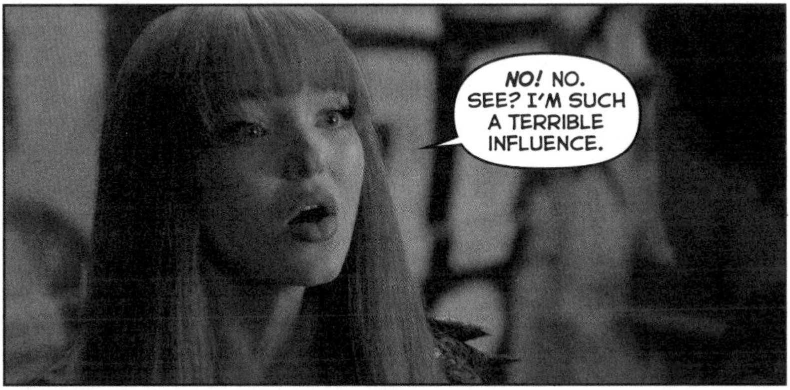
NO! NO. SEE? I'M SUCH A TERRIBLE INFLUENCE.

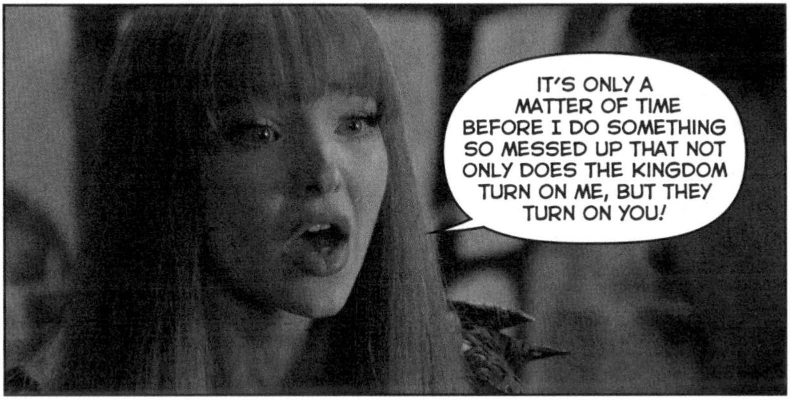
IT'S ONLY A MATTER OF TIME BEFORE I DO SOMETHING SO MESSED UP THAT NOT ONLY DOES THE KINGDOM TURN ON ME, BUT THEY TURN ON YOU!

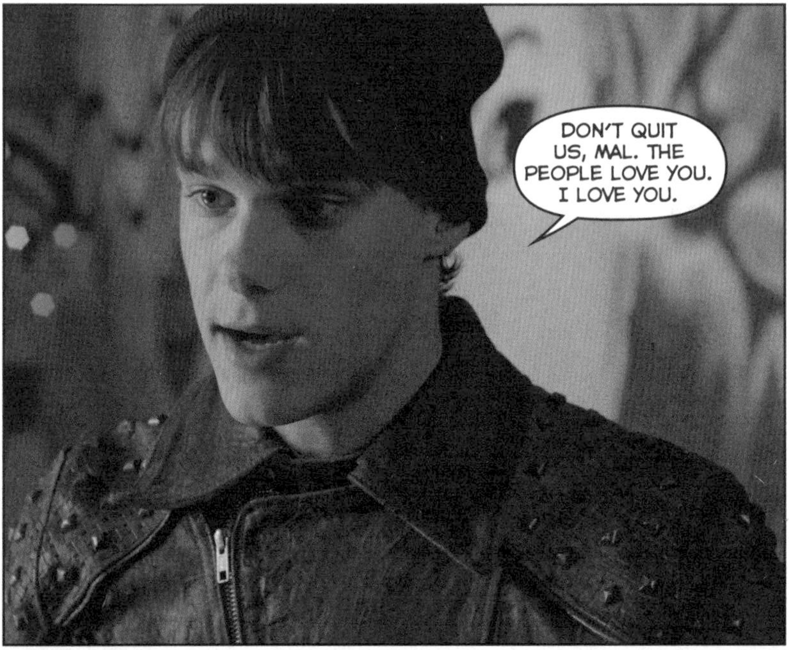
DON'T QUIT
US, MAL. THE
PEOPLE LOVE YOU.
I LOVE YOU.

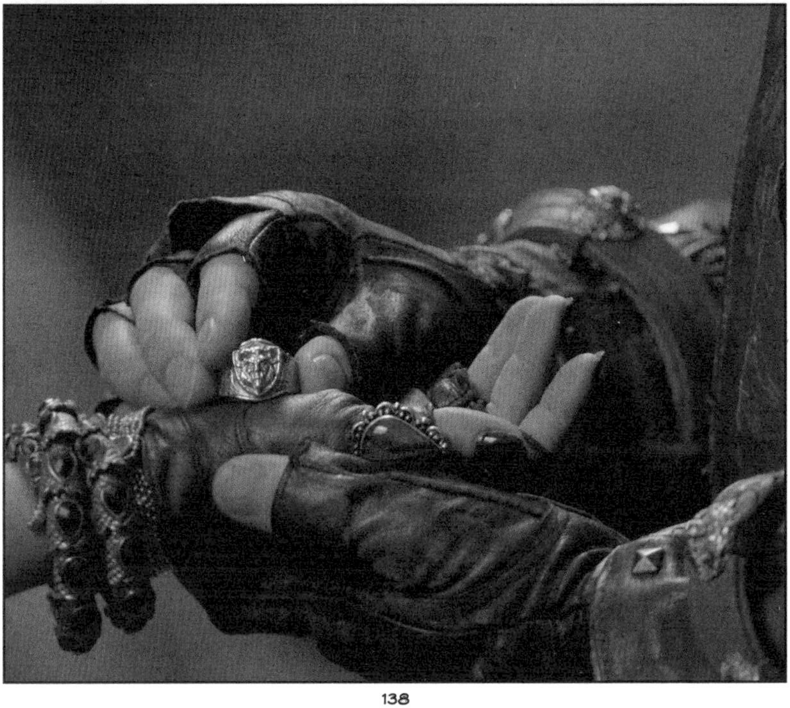

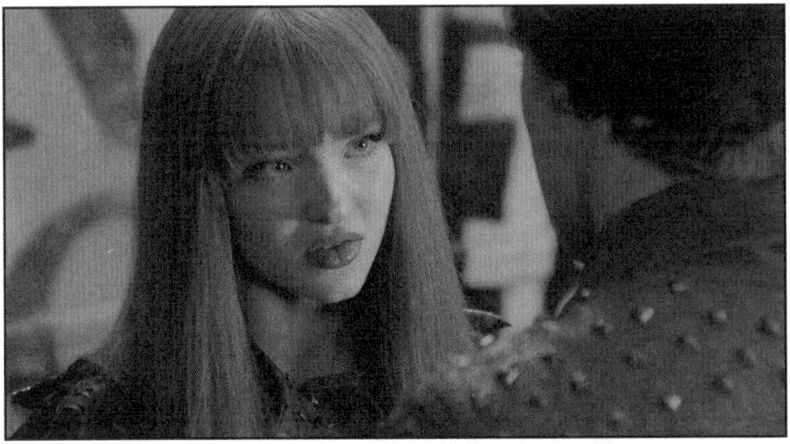

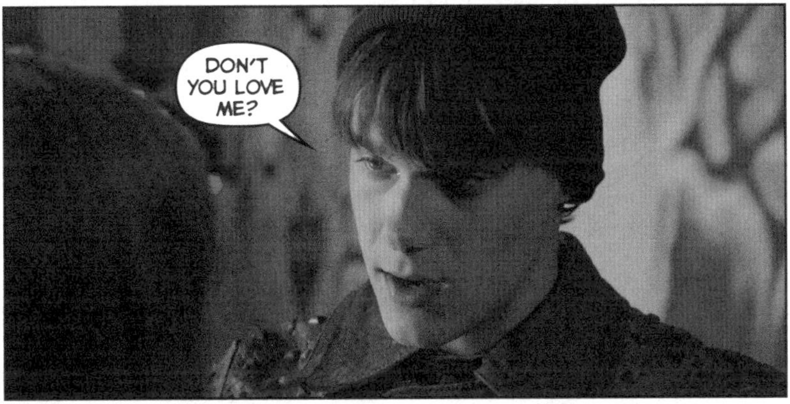
DON'T YOU LOVE ME?

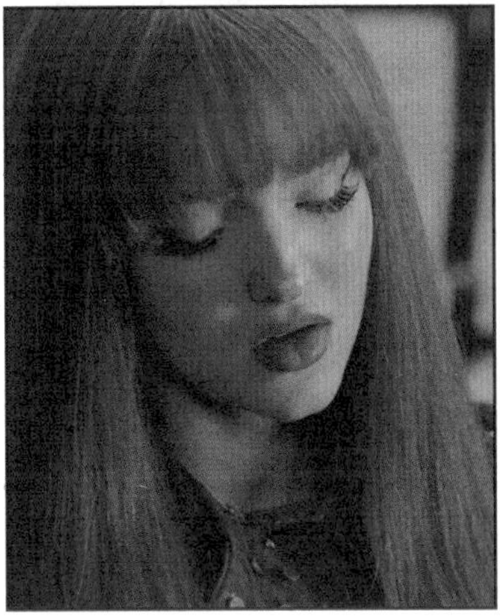

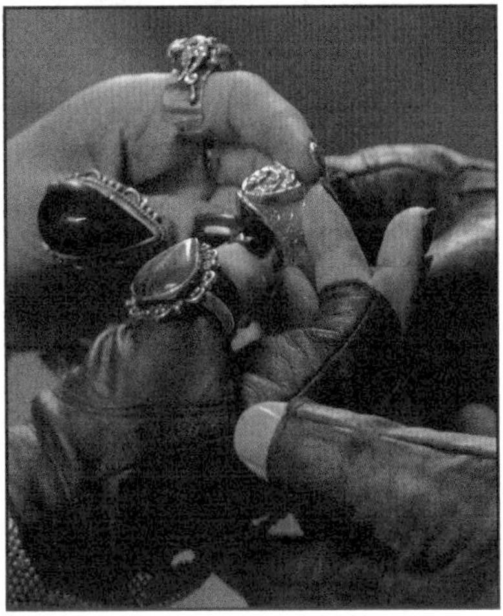

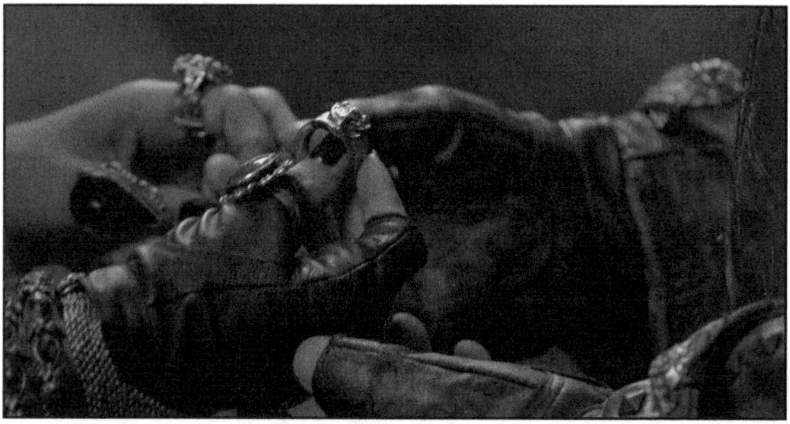
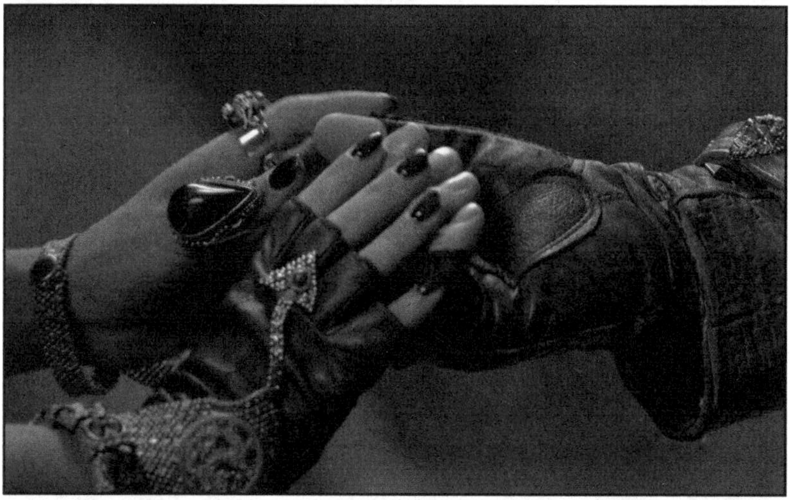
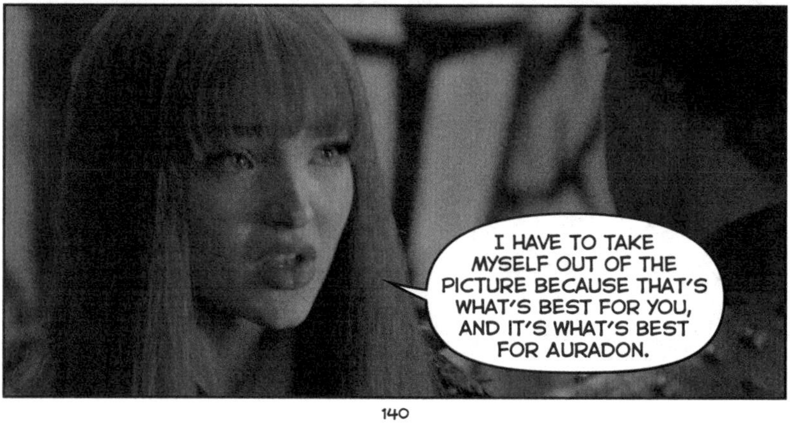
I HAVE TO TAKE MYSELF OUT OF THE PICTURE BECAUSE THAT'S WHAT'S BEST FOR YOU, AND IT'S WHAT'S BEST FOR AURADON.

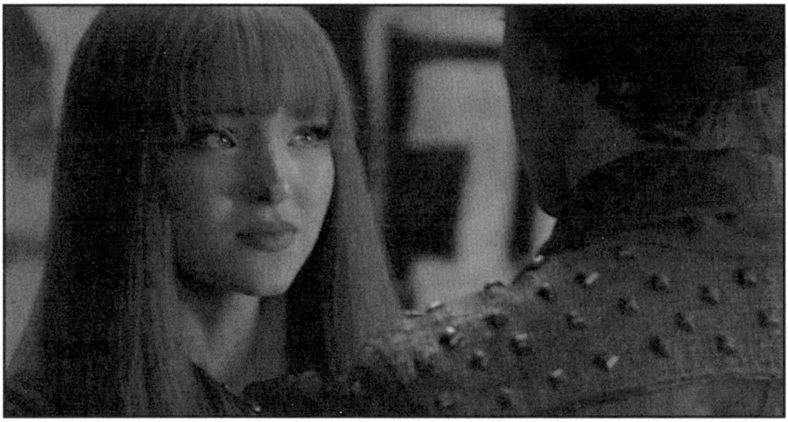

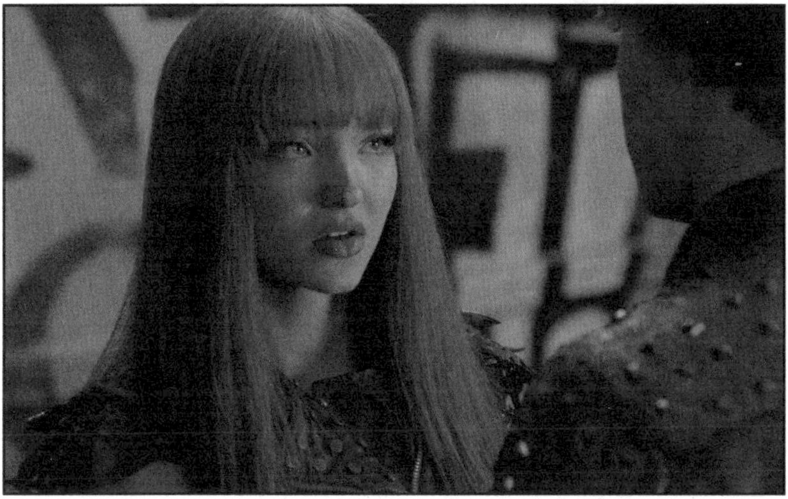

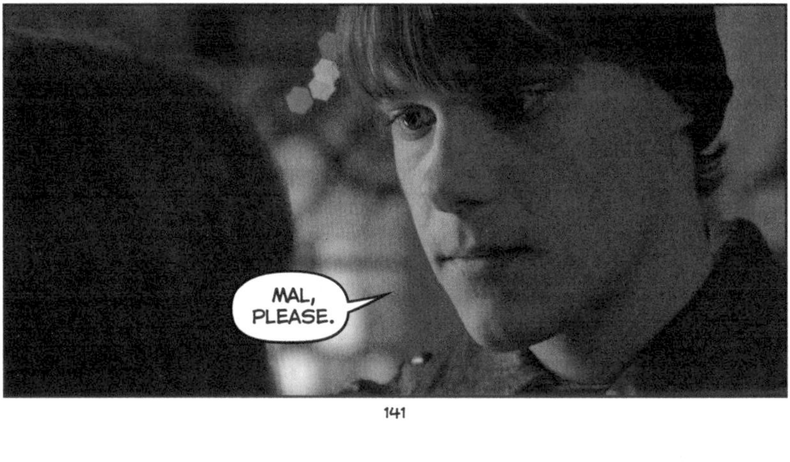

MAL, PLEASE.

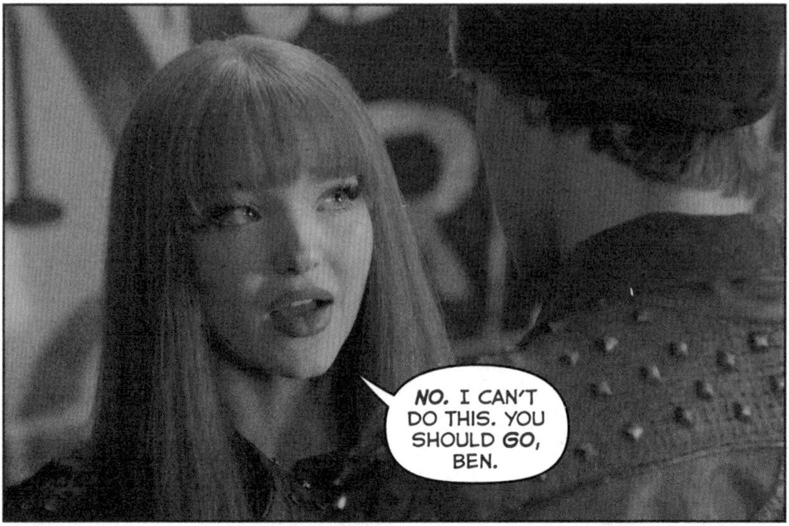
NO. I CAN'T DO THIS. YOU SHOULD GO, BEN.
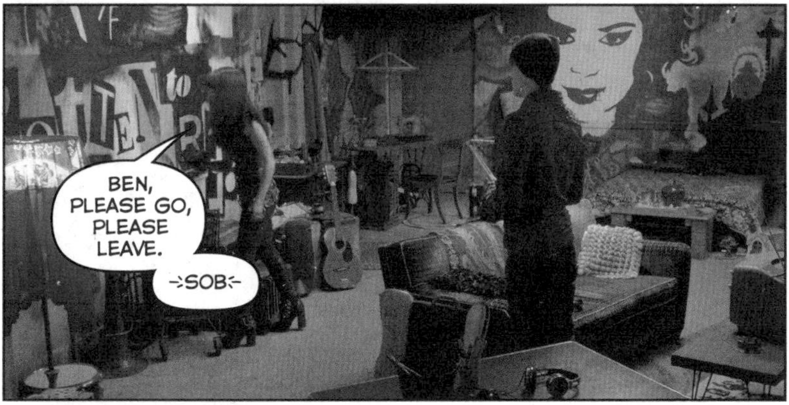
BEN, PLEASE GO, PLEASE LEAVE.
SOB
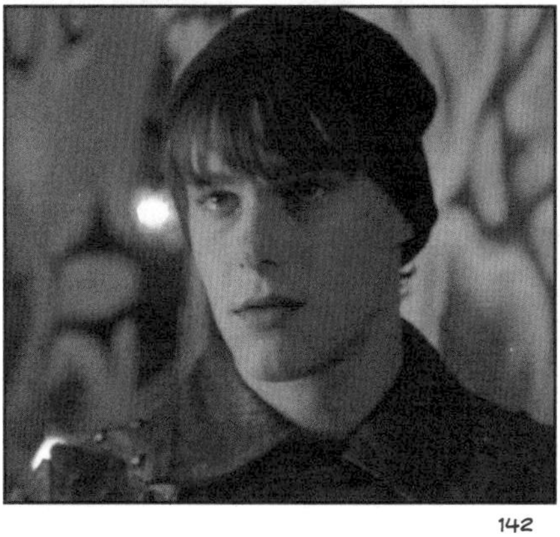
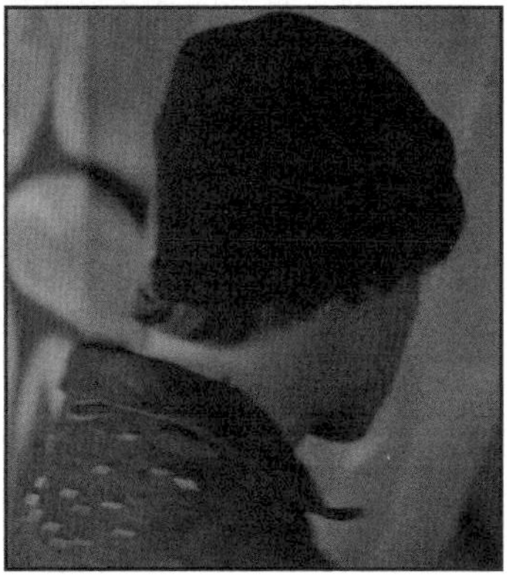

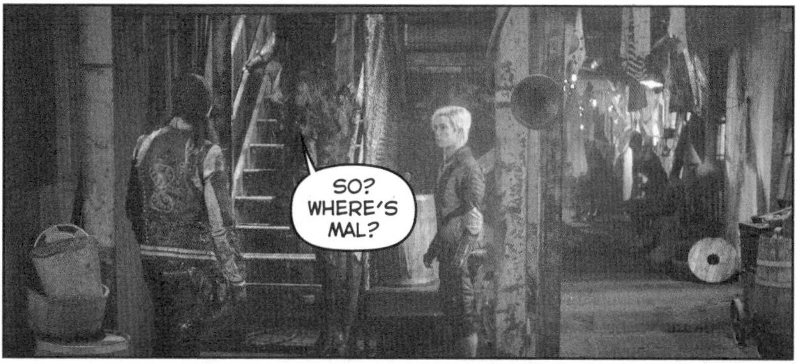
SO? WHERE'S MAL?

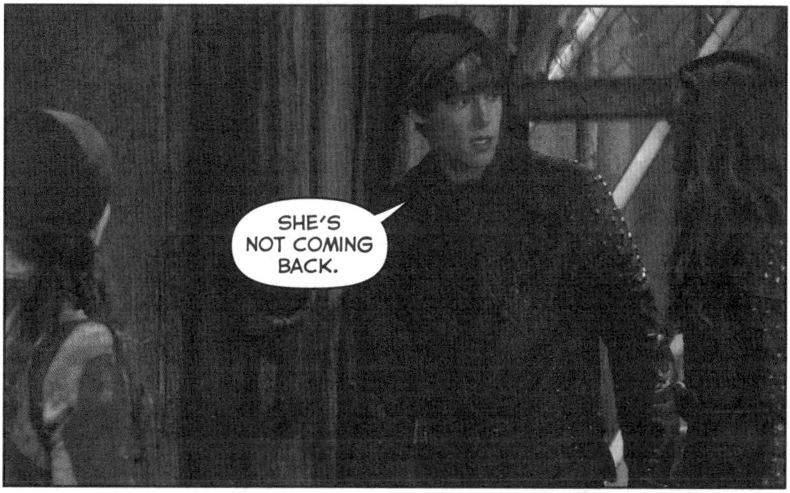
SHE'S NOT COMING BACK.

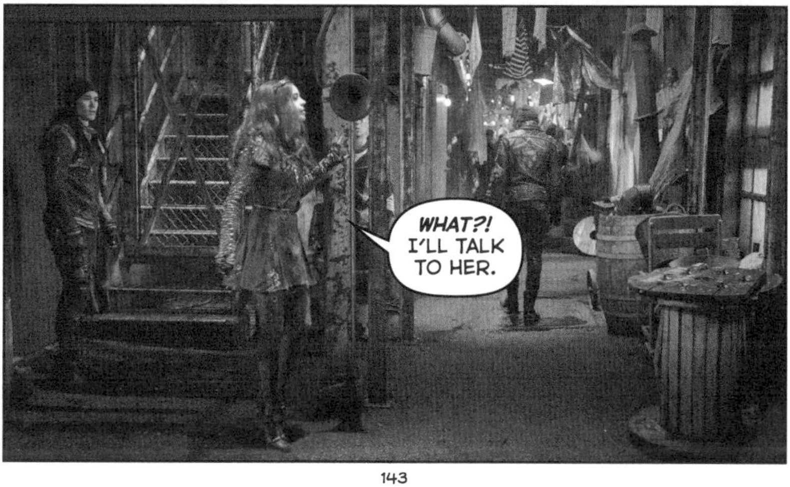
WHAT?! I'LL TALK TO HER.

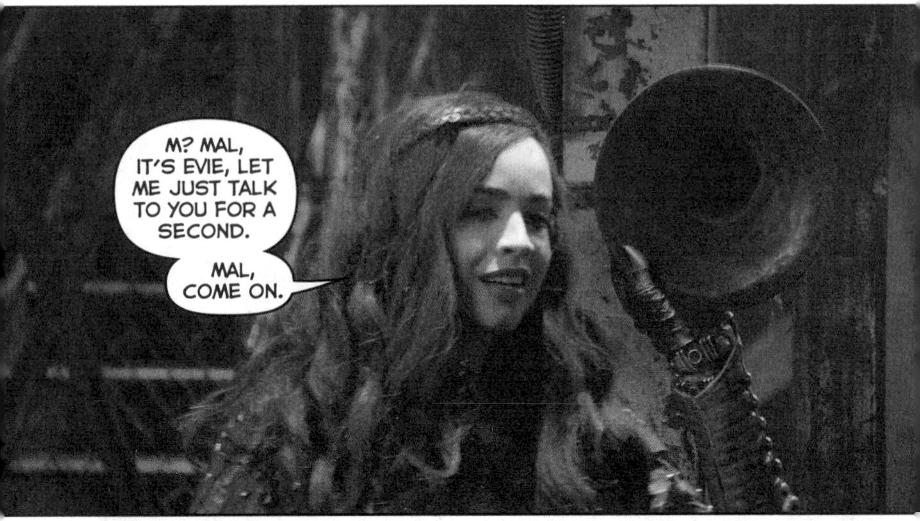
M? MAL, IT'S EVIE, LET ME JUST TALK TO YOU FOR A SECOND.
MAL, COME ON.

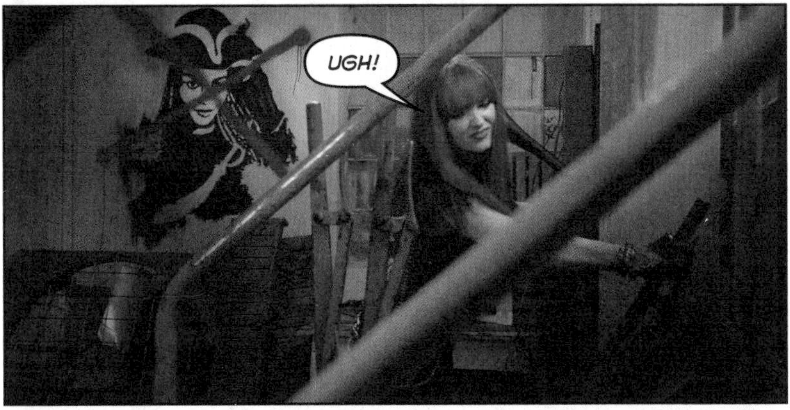
UGH!

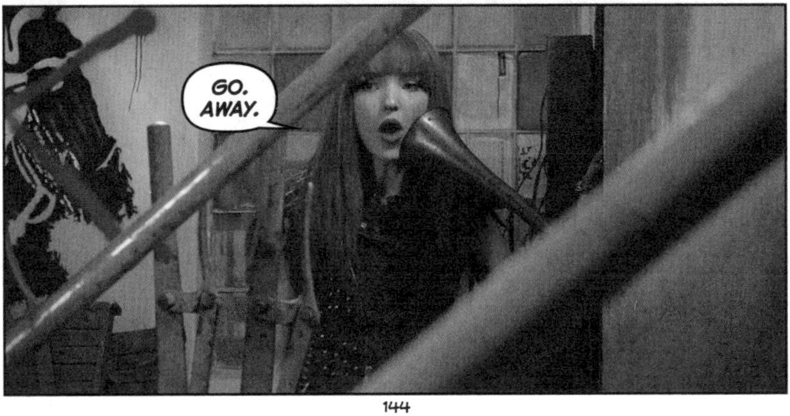
GO. AWAY.

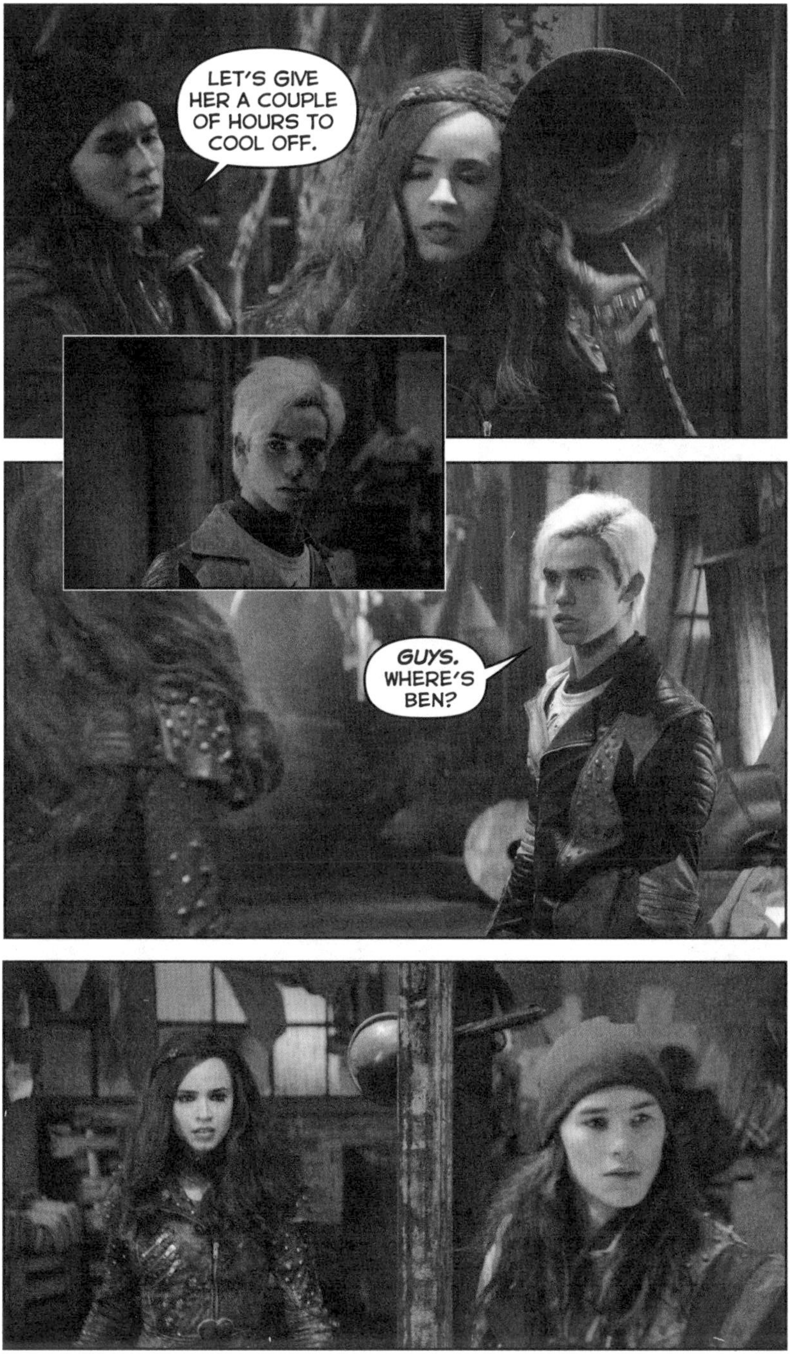
LET'S GIVE HER A COUPLE OF HOURS TO COOL OFF.
GUYS. WHERE'S BEN?

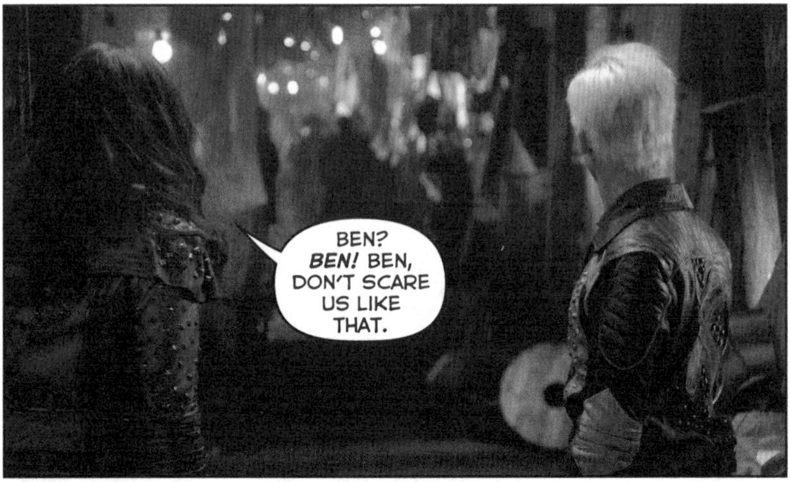
BEN? *BEN!* BEN, DON'T SCARE US LIKE THAT.

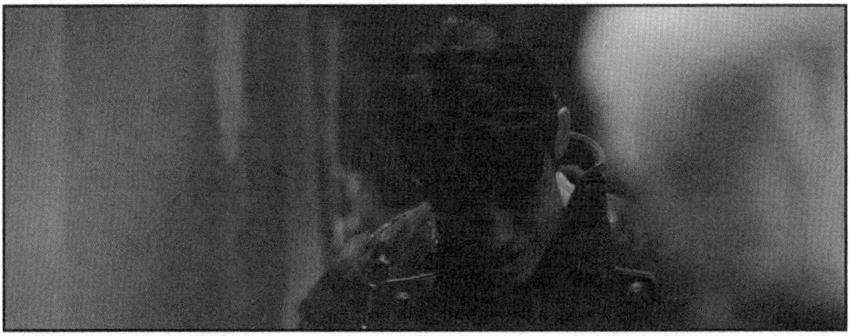

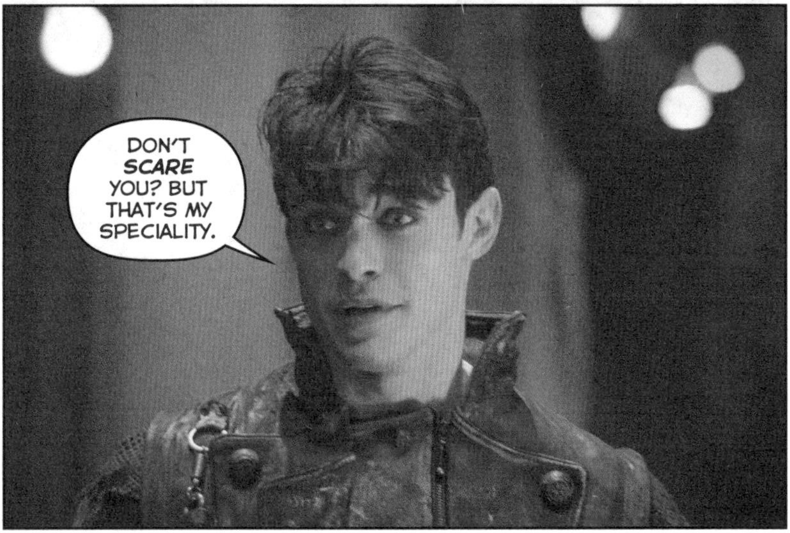
DON'T *SCARE* YOU? BUT THAT'S MY SPECIALITY.

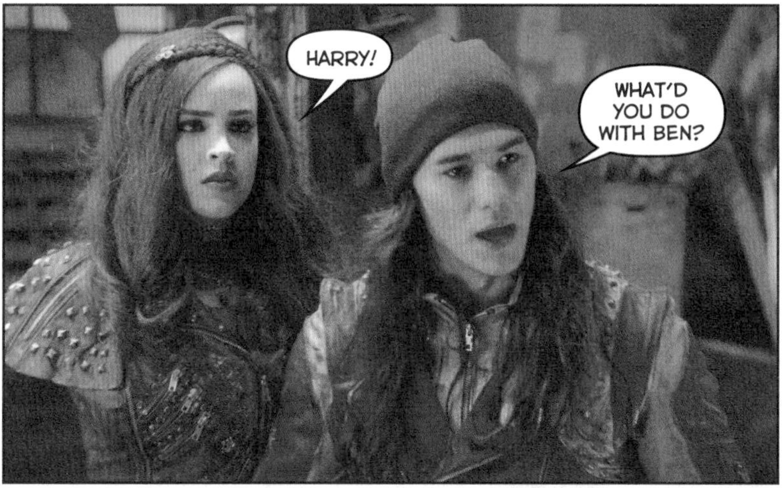
HARRY!
WHAT'D YOU DO WITH BEN?

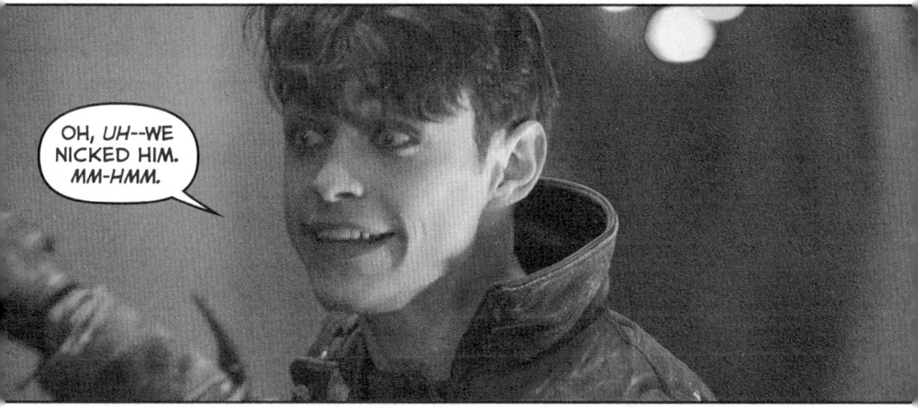
OH, *UH*--WE NICKED HIM. *MM-HMM.*

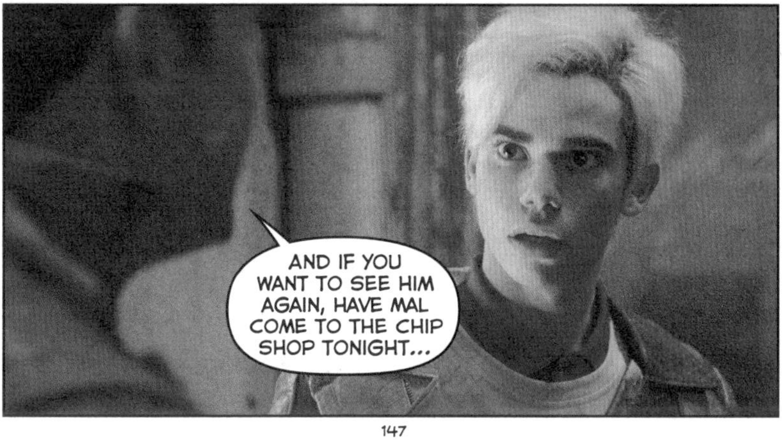
AND IF YOU WANT TO SEE HIM AGAIN, HAVE MAL COME TO THE CHIP SHOP TONIGHT...

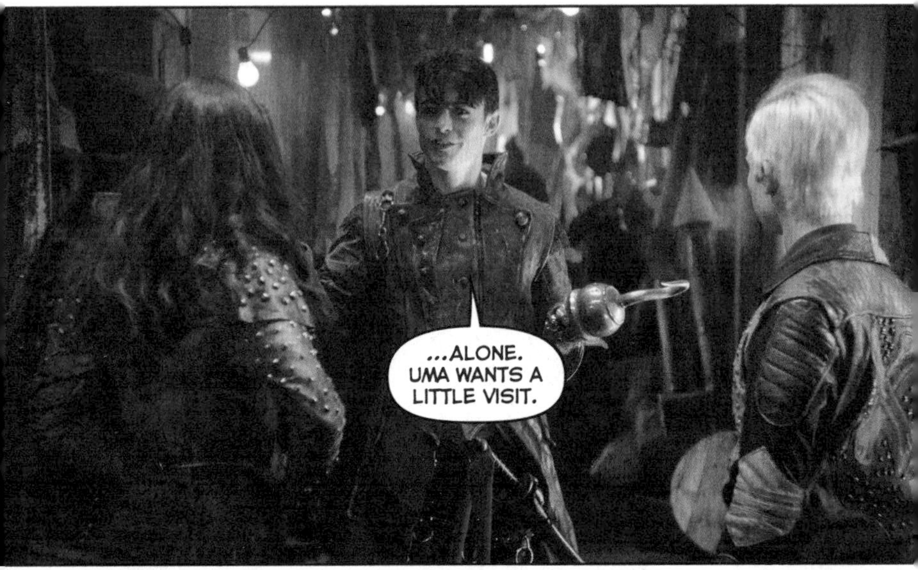
...ALONE. UMA WANTS A LITTLE VISIT.

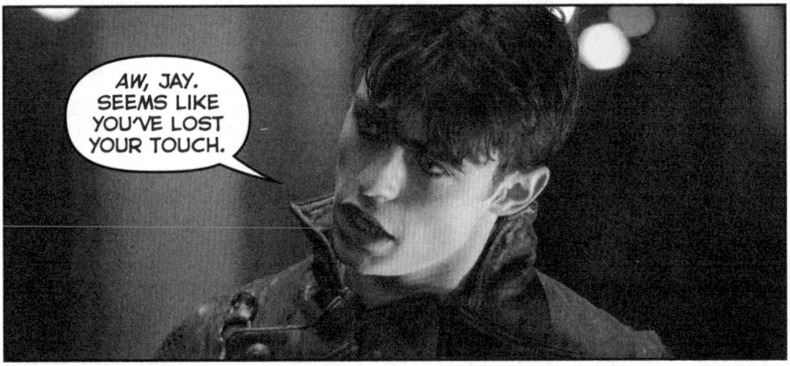
AW, JAY. SEEMS LIKE YOU'VE LOST YOUR TOUCH.

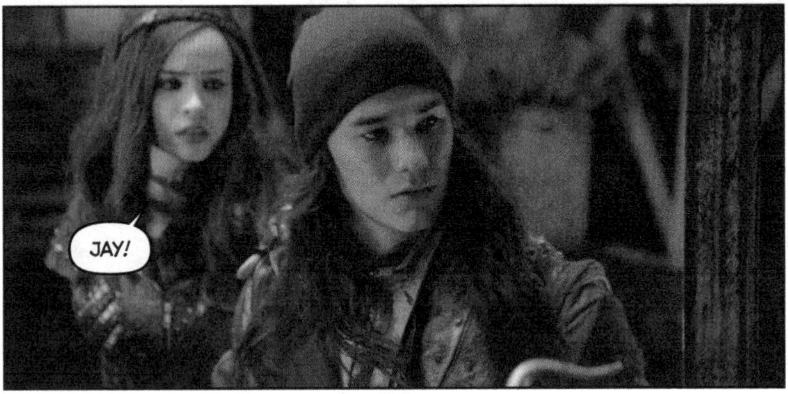
JAY!

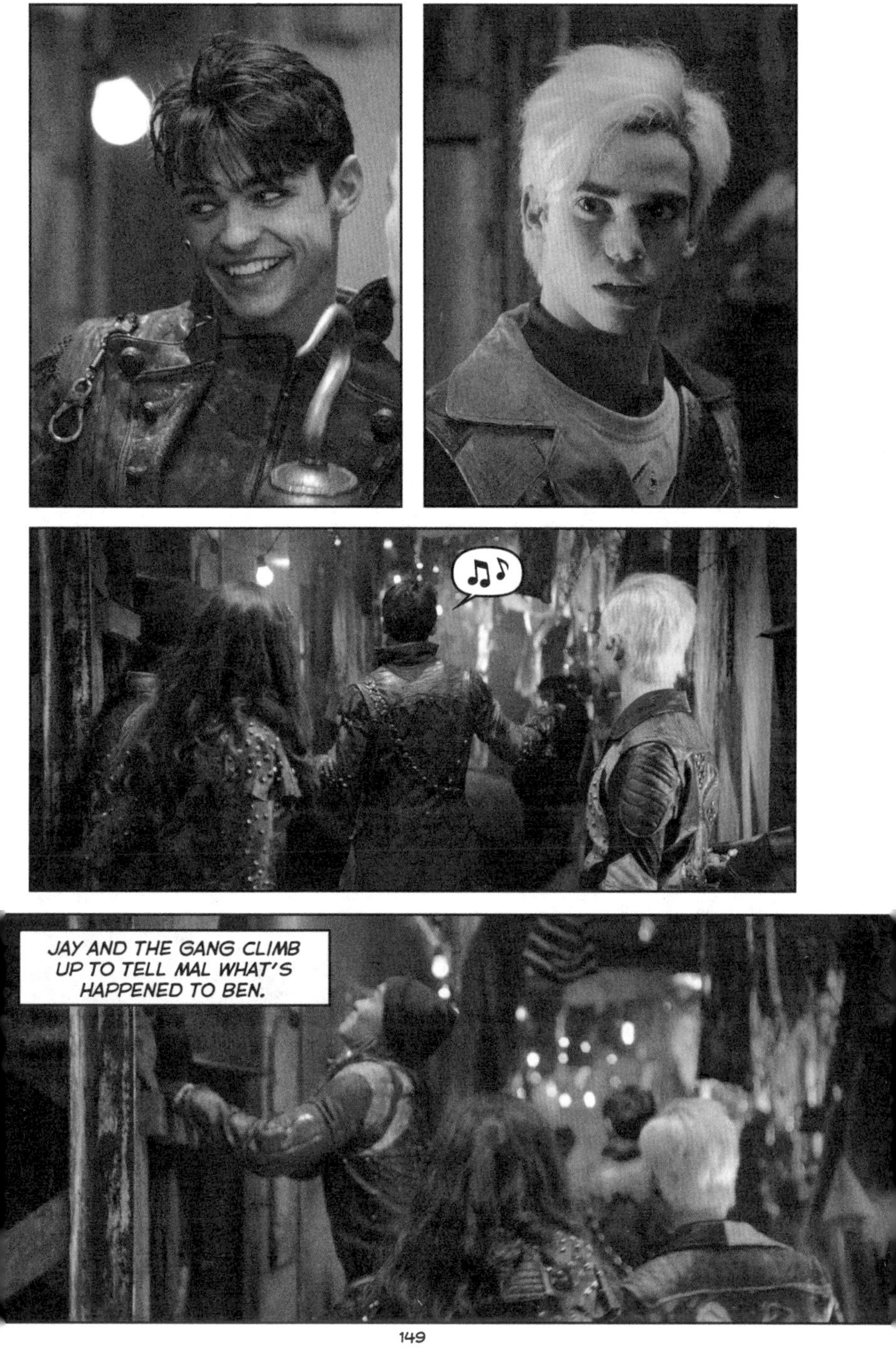
♫♪
JAY AND THE GANG CLIMB UP TO TELL MAL WHAT'S HAPPENED TO BEN.

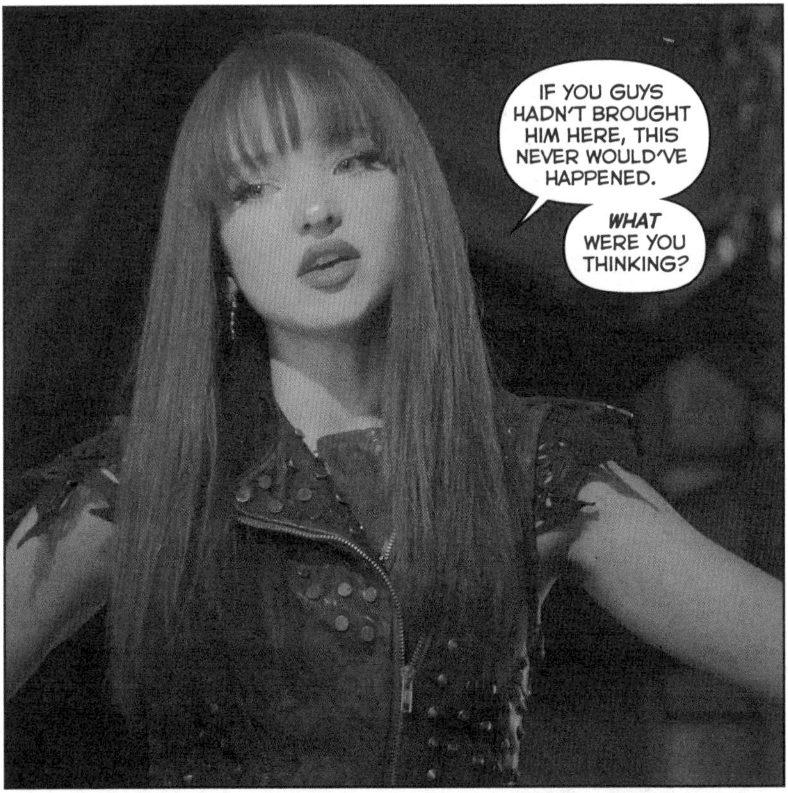
IF YOU GUYS HADN'T BROUGHT HIM HERE, THIS NEVER WOULD'VE HAPPENED.
WHAT WERE YOU THINKING?

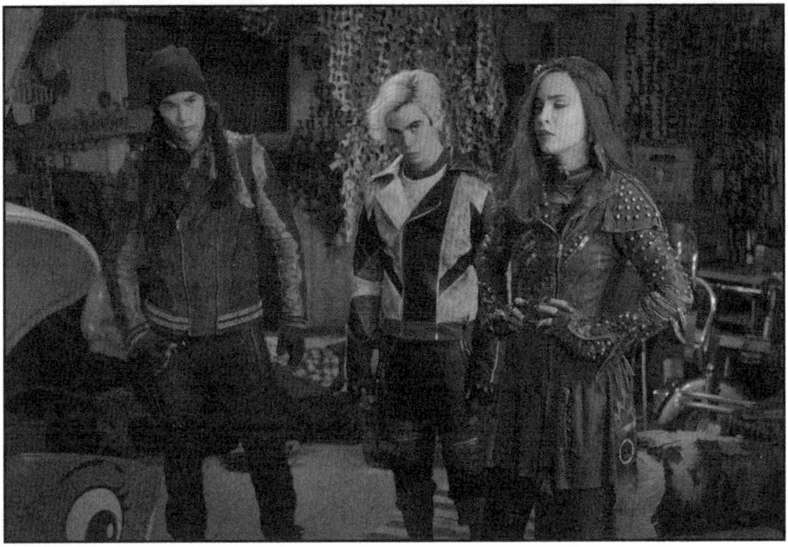

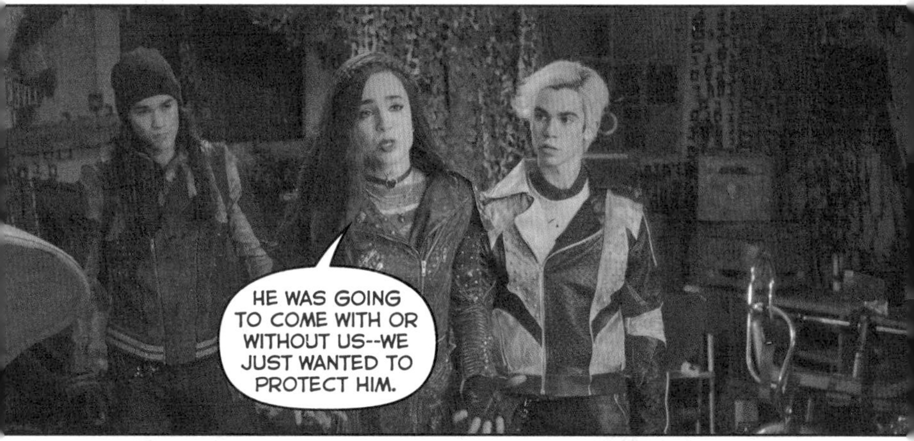
HE WAS GOING TO COME WITH OR WITHOUT US--WE JUST WANTED TO PROTECT HIM.

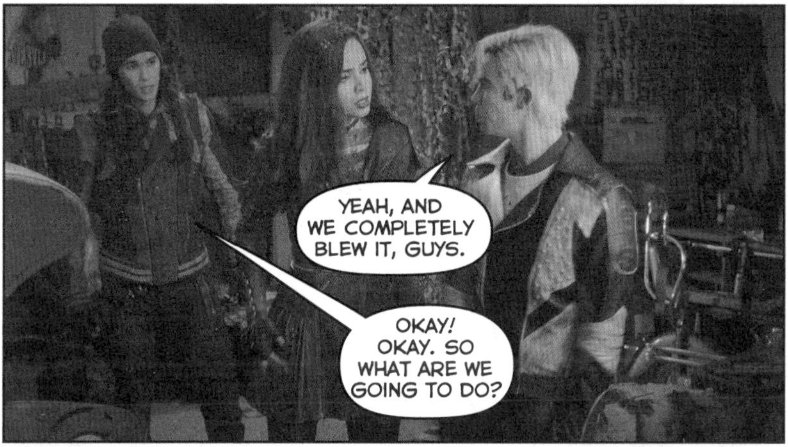
YEAH, AND WE COMPLETELY BLEW IT, GUYS.
OKAY! OKAY. SO WHAT ARE WE GOING TO DO?

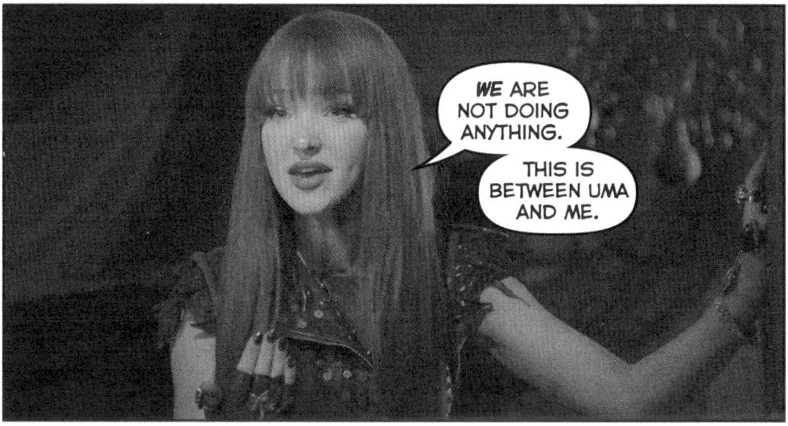
WE ARE NOT DOING ANYTHING.
THIS IS BETWEEN UMA AND ME.

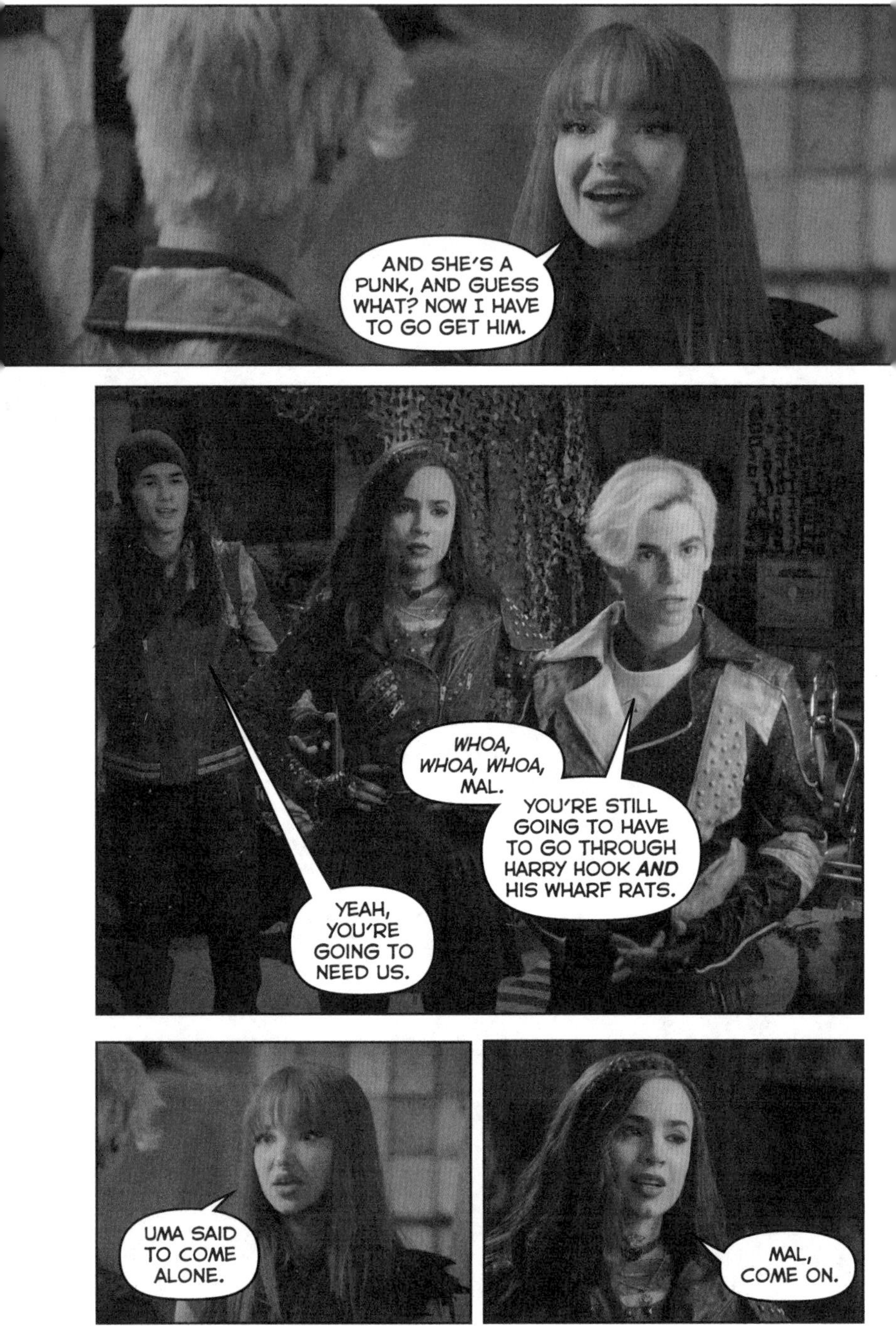
AND SHE'S A PUNK, AND GUESS WHAT? NOW I HAVE TO GO GET HIM.
WHOA, WHOA, WHOA, MAL.
YOU'RE STILL GOING TO HAVE TO GO THROUGH HARRY HOOK ***AND*** HIS WHARF RATS.
YEAH, YOU'RE GOING TO NEED US.
UMA SAID TO COME ALONE.
MAL, COME ON.

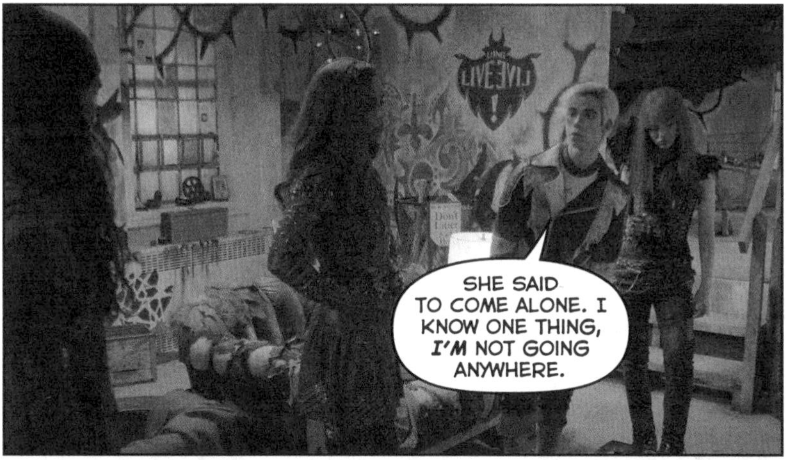
LIVE EVIL !
SHE SAID TO COME ALONE. I KNOW ONE THING, *I'M* NOT GOING ANYWHERE.

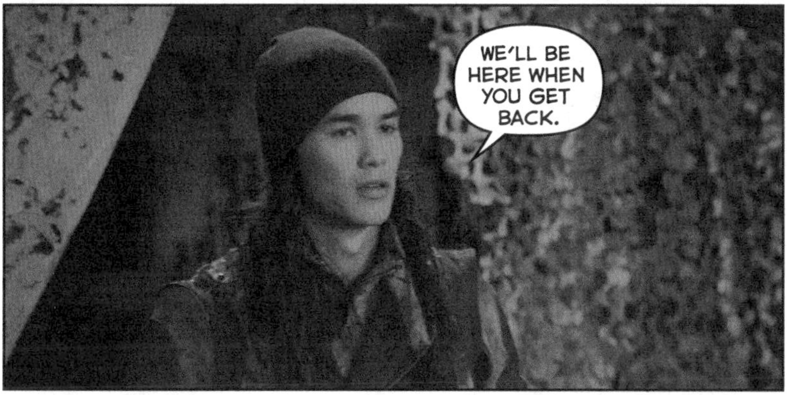
WE'LL BE HERE WHEN YOU GET BACK.

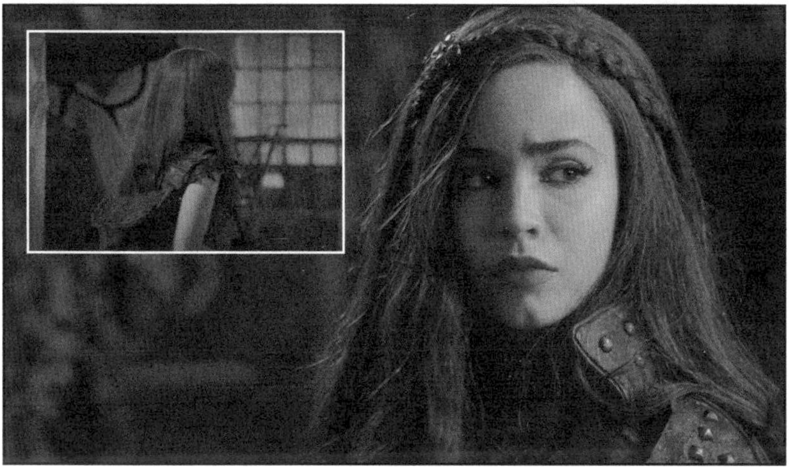

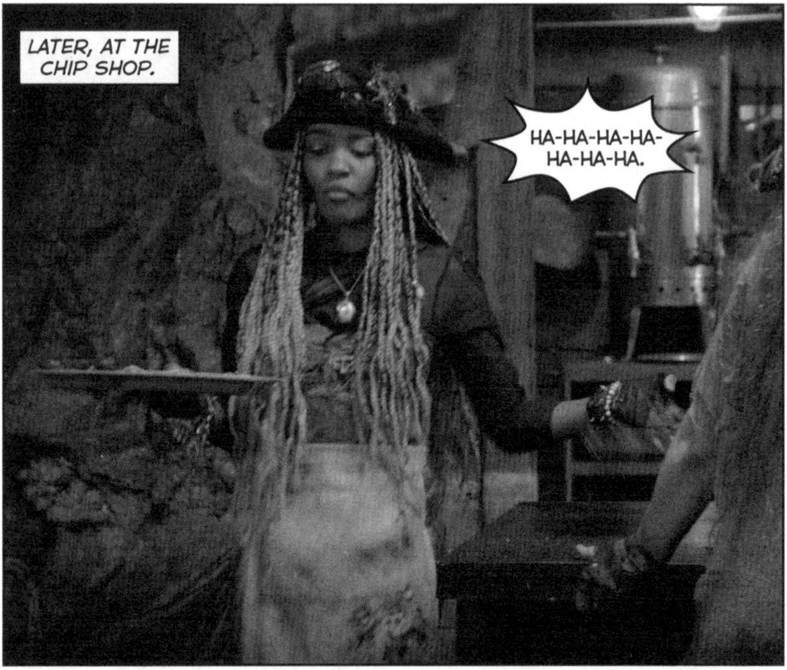
LATER, AT THE CHIP SHOP.
HA-HA-HA-HA-HA-HA-HA.

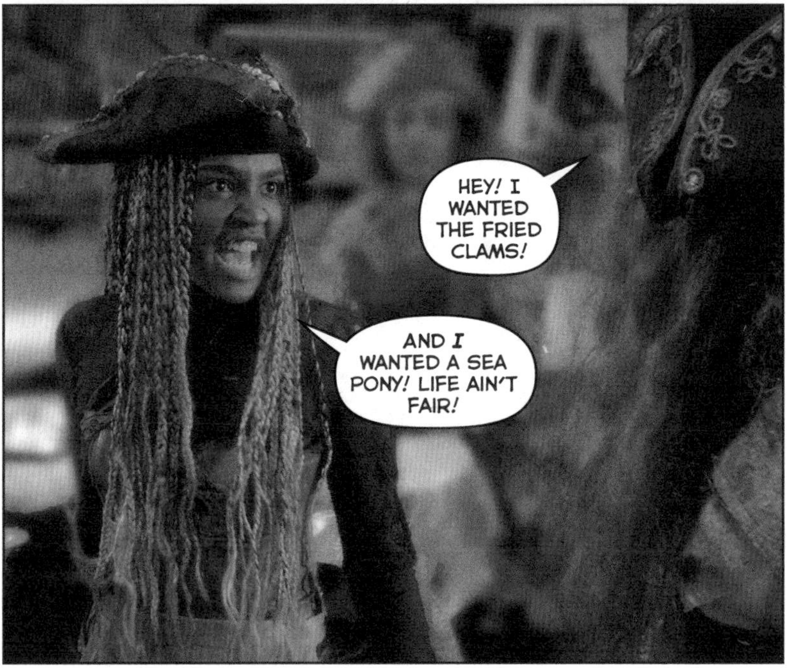
HEY! I WANTED THE FRIED CLAMS!
AND I WANTED A SEA PONY! LIFE AIN'T FAIR!

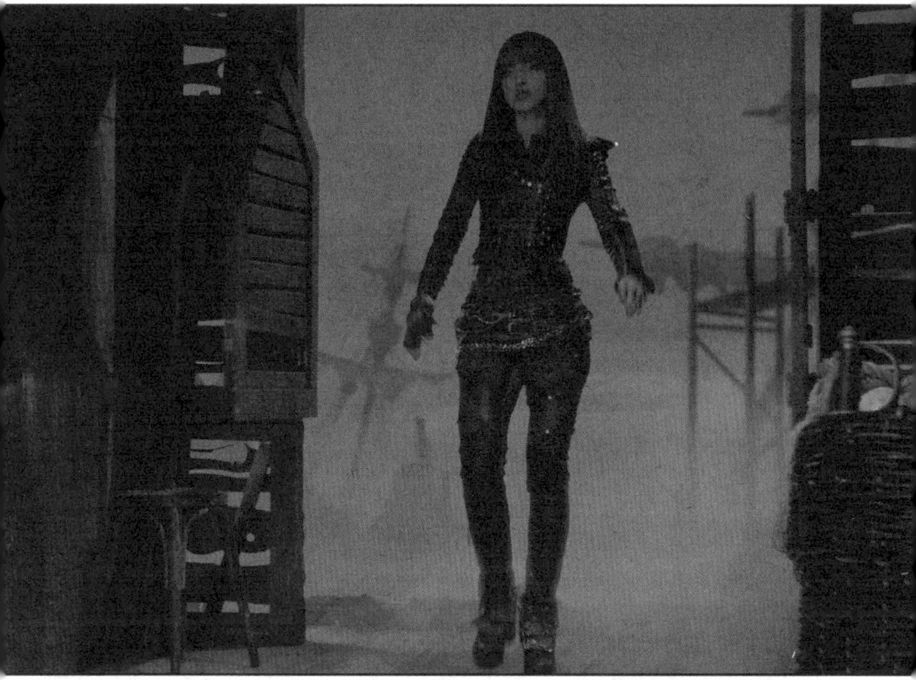

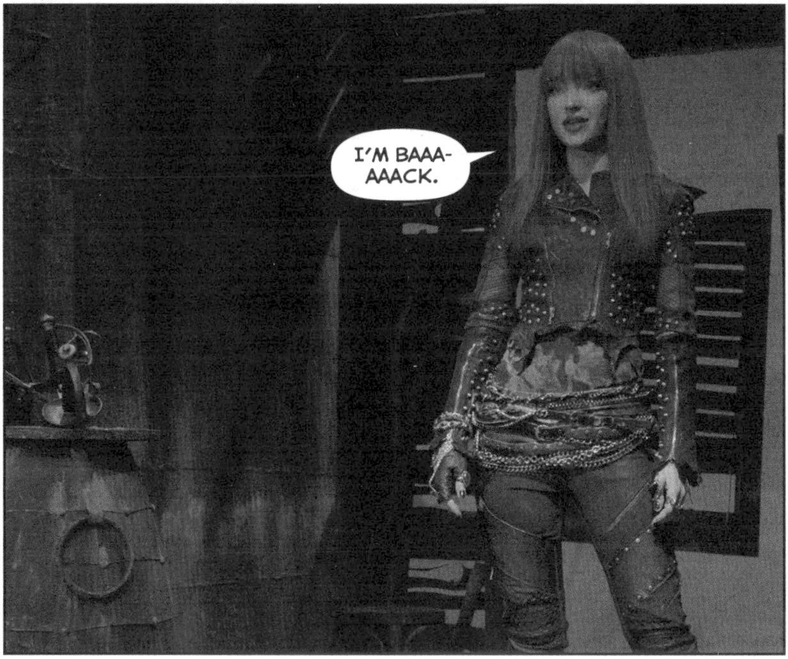
I'M BAAA-
AAACK.

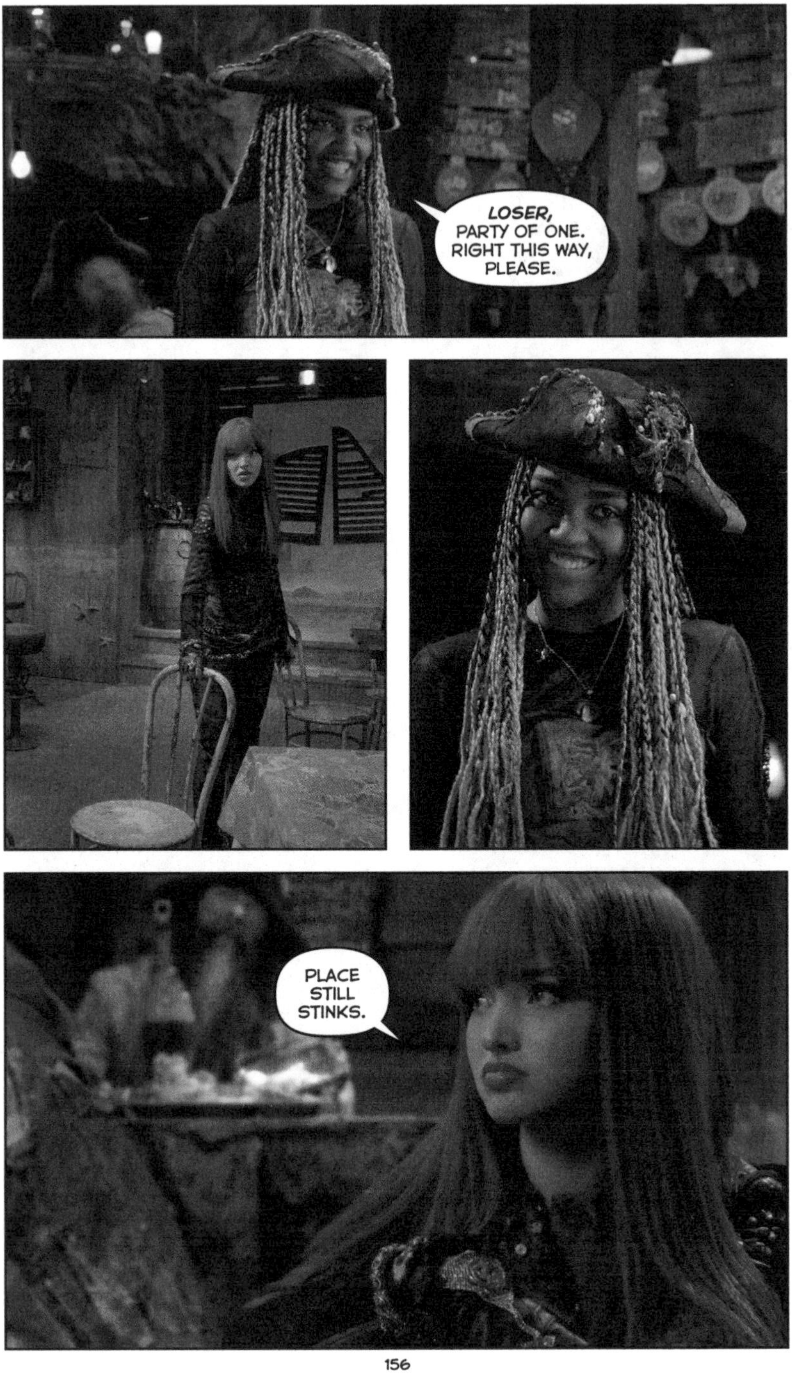
LOSER, PARTY OF ONE. RIGHT THIS WAY, PLEASE.
PLACE STILL STINKS.

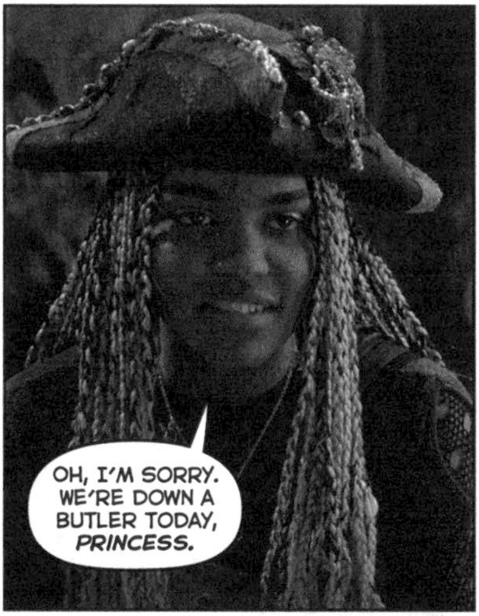
OH, I'M SORRY. WE'RE DOWN A BUTLER TODAY, *PRINCESS.*

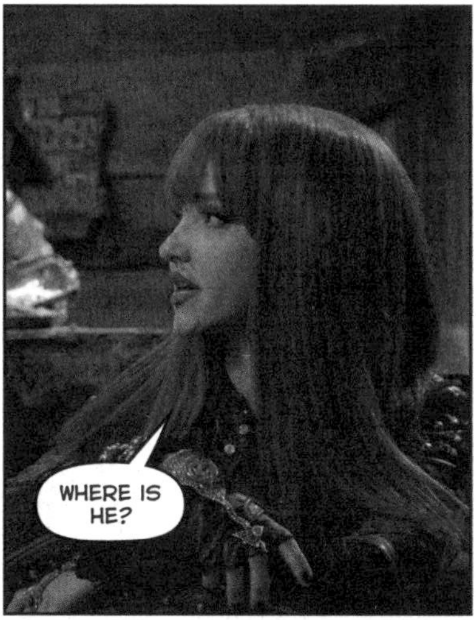
WHERE IS HE?

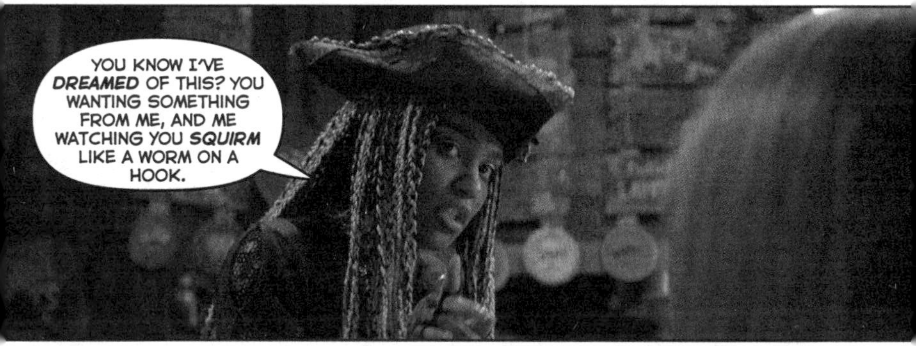
YOU KNOW I'VE *DREAMED* OF THIS? YOU WANTING SOMETHING FROM ME, AND ME WATCHING YOU *SQUIRM* LIKE A WORM ON A HOOK.

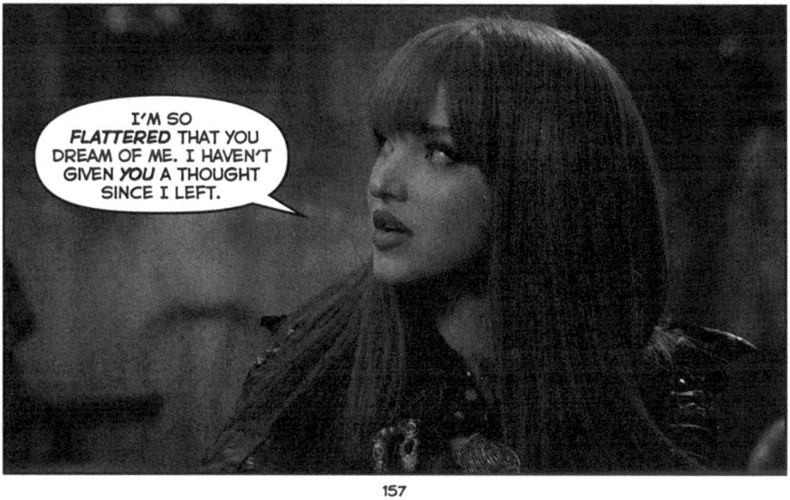
I'M SO *FLATTERED* THAT YOU DREAM OF ME. I HAVEN'T GIVEN *YOU* A THOUGHT SINCE I LEFT.

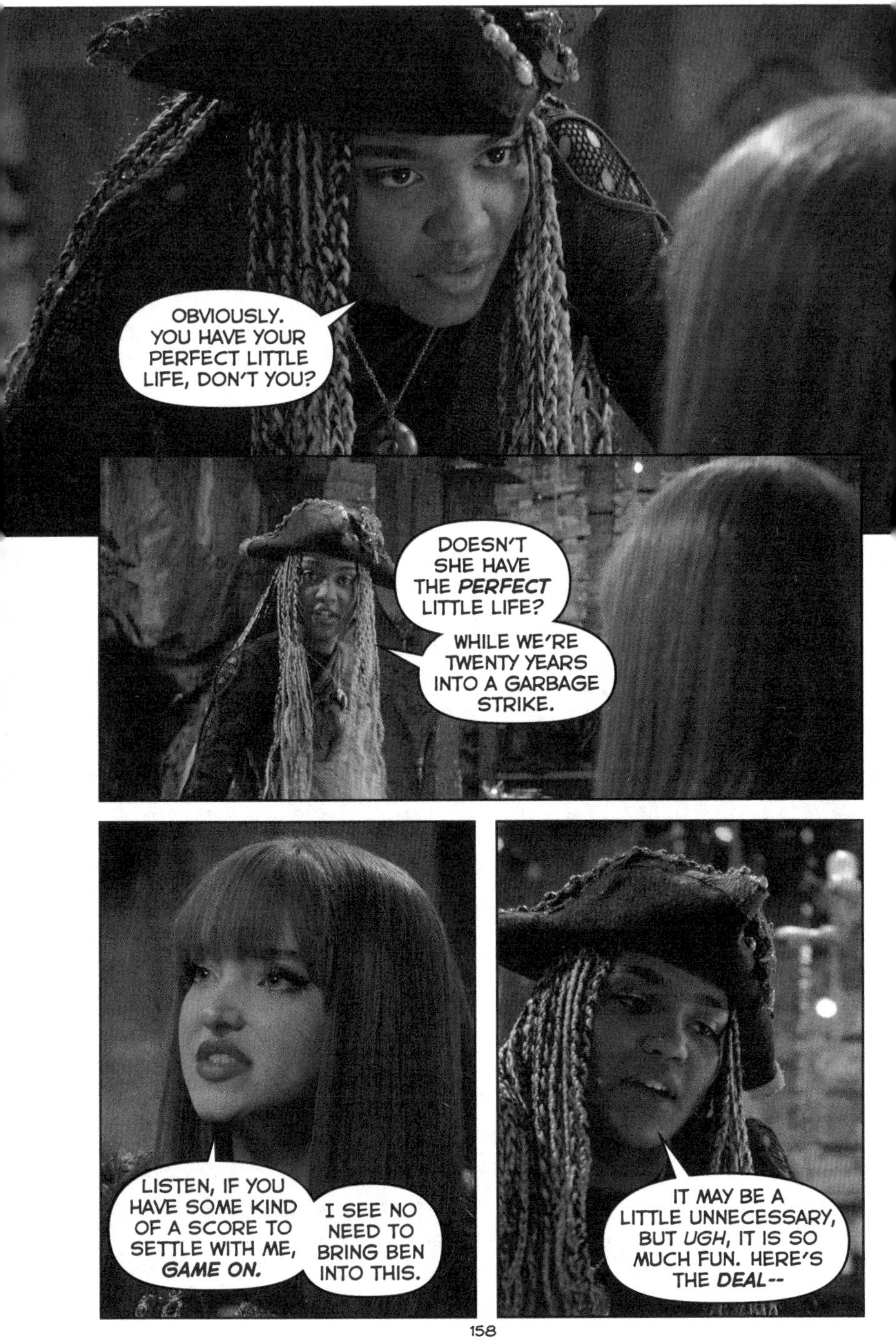
OBVIOUSLY. YOU HAVE YOUR PERFECT LITTLE LIFE, DON'T YOU?
DOESN'T SHE HAVE THE *PERFECT* LITTLE LIFE?
WHILE WE'RE TWENTY YEARS INTO A GARBAGE STRIKE.
LISTEN, IF YOU HAVE SOME KIND OF A SCORE TO SETTLE WITH ME, ***GAME ON.***
I SEE NO NEED TO BRING BEN INTO THIS.
IT MAY BE A LITTLE UNNECESSARY, BUT *UGH*, IT IS SO MUCH FUN. HERE'S THE ***DEAL***--

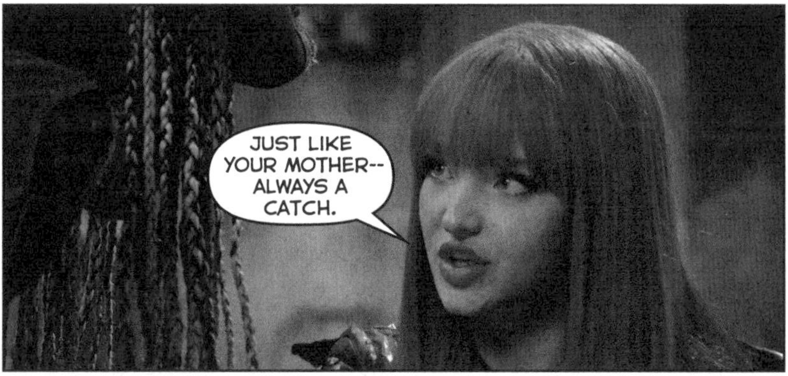
JUST LIKE YOUR MOTHER-- ALWAYS A CATCH.

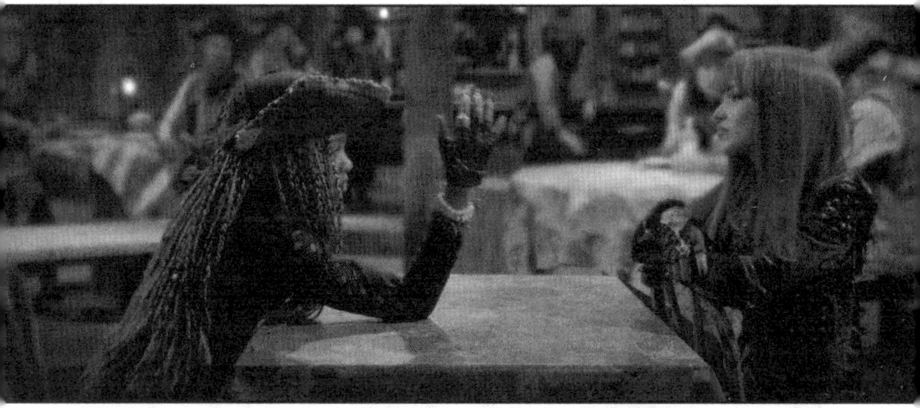

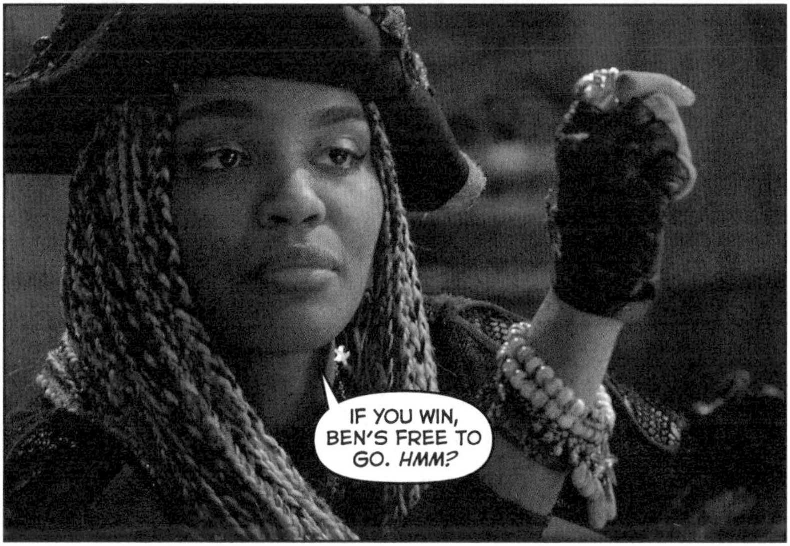
IF YOU WIN, BEN'S FREE TO GO. *HMM?*

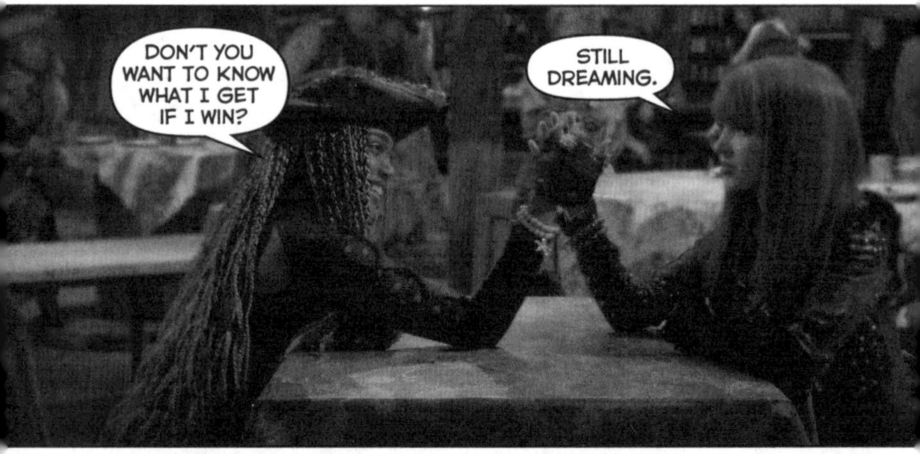
DON'T YOU WANT TO KNOW WHAT I GET IF I WIN?
STILL DREAMING.

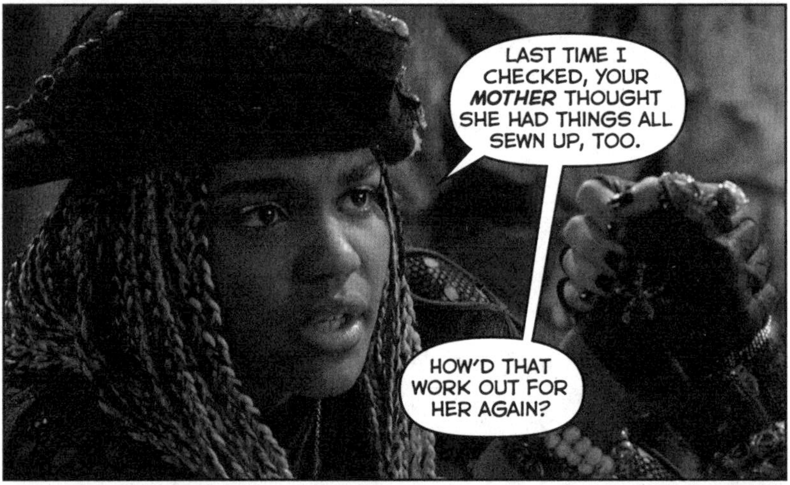
LAST TIME I CHECKED, YOUR *MOTHER* THOUGHT SHE HAD THINGS ALL SEWN UP, TOO.
HOW'D THAT WORK OUT FOR HER AGAIN?

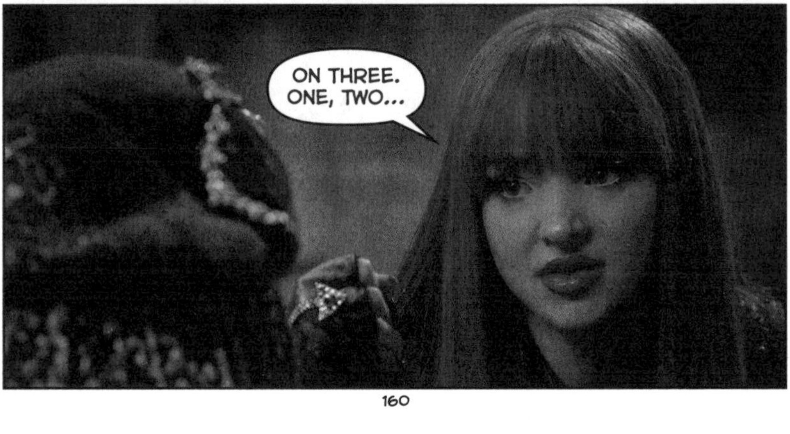
ON THREE. ONE, TWO...

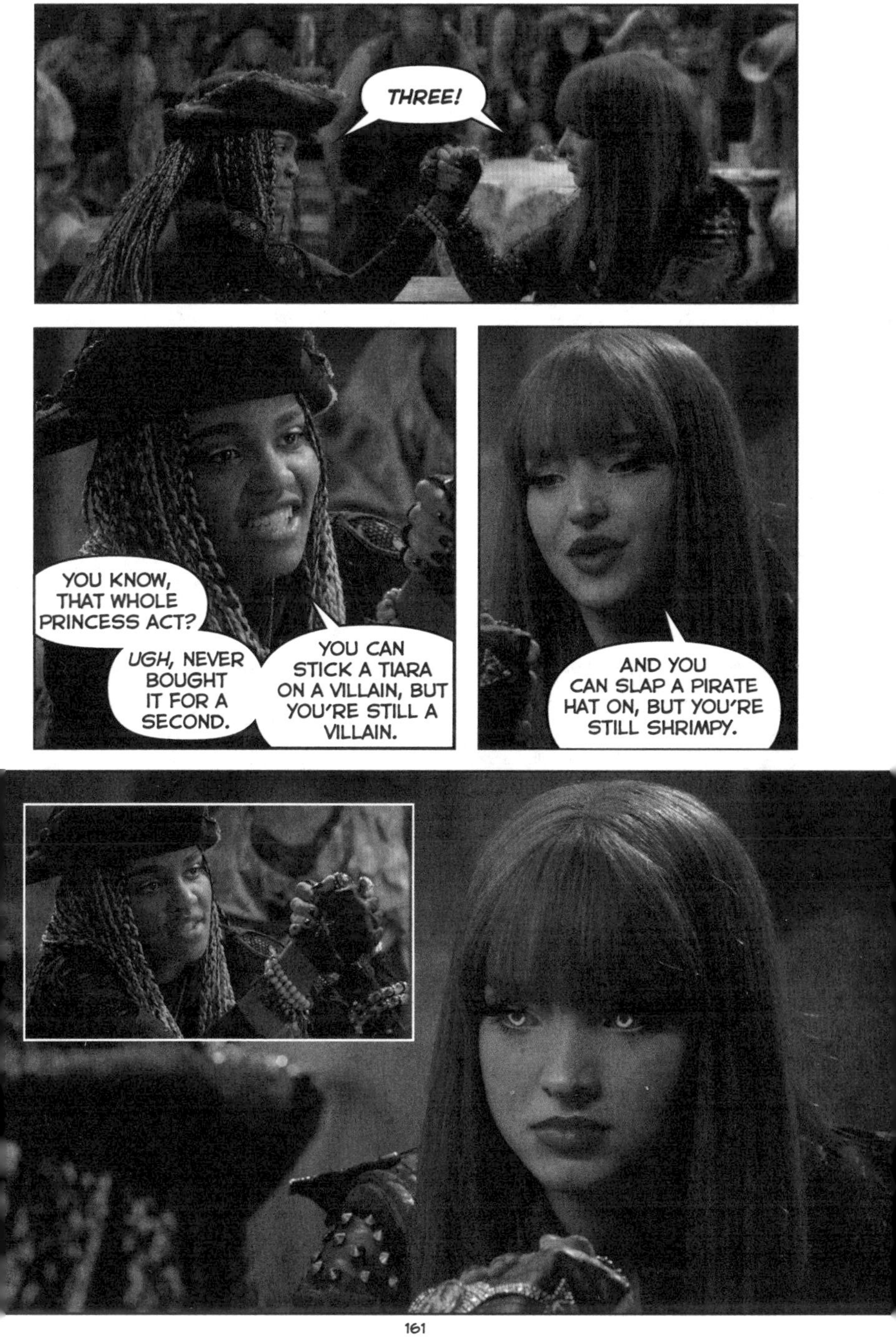
THREE!
YOU KNOW, THAT WHOLE PRINCESS ACT?
UGH, NEVER BOUGHT IT FOR A SECOND.
YOU CAN STICK A TIARA ON A VILLAIN, BUT YOU'RE STILL A VILLAIN.
AND YOU CAN SLAP A PIRATE HAT ON, BUT YOU'RE STILL SHRIMPY.

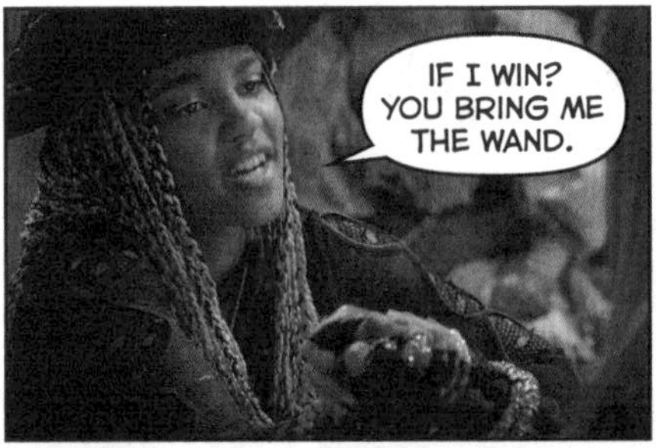
IF I WIN? YOU BRING ME THE WAND.
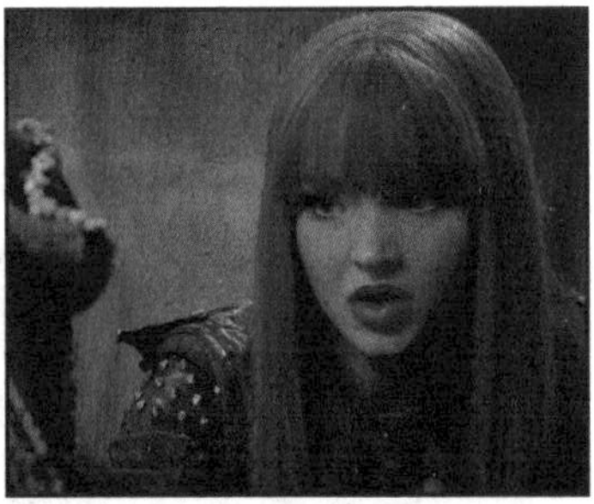
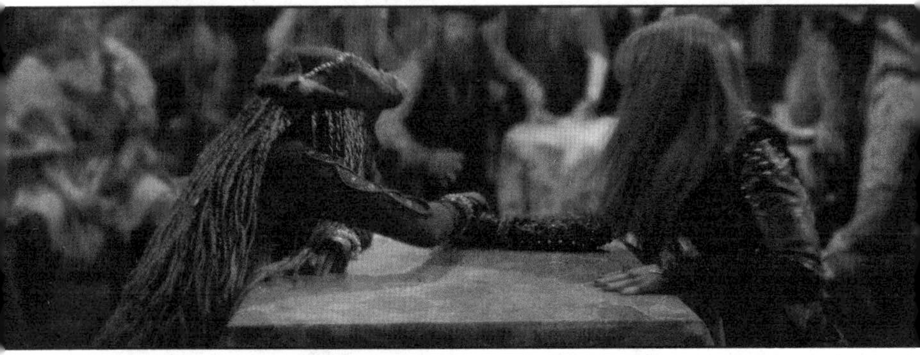
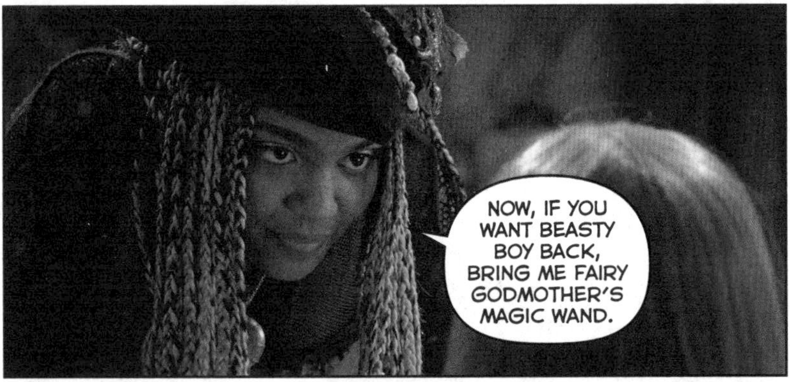
NOW, IF YOU WANT BEASTY BOY BACK, BRING ME FAIRY GODMOTHER'S MAGIC WAND.
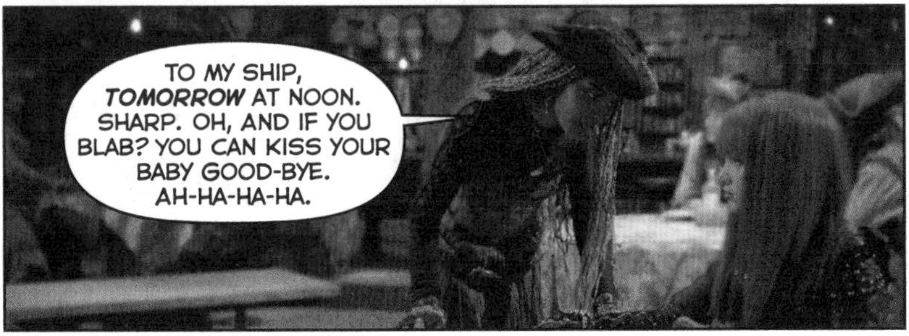
TO MY SHIP, TOMORROW AT NOON. SHARP. OH, AND IF YOU BLAB? YOU CAN KISS YOUR BABY GOOD-BYE. AH-HA-HA-HA.

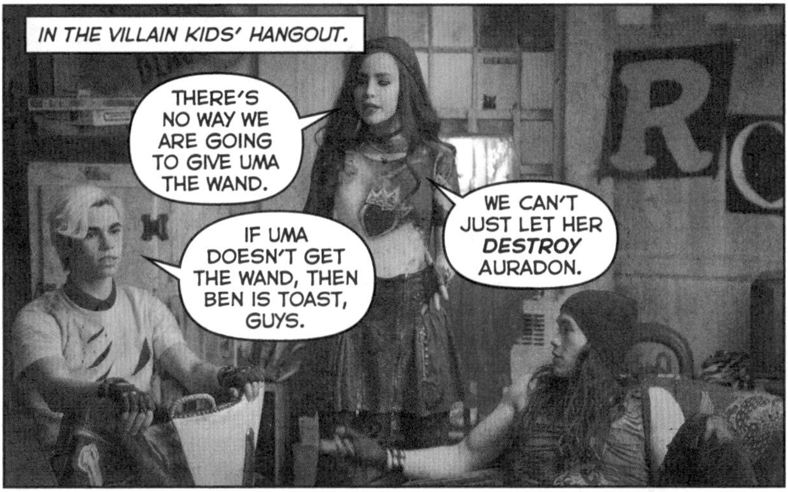
IN THE VILLAIN KIDS' HANGOUT.
THERE'S NO WAY WE ARE GOING TO GIVE UMA THE WAND.
WE CAN'T JUST LET HER *DESTROY* AURADON.
IF UMA DOESN'T GET THE WAND, THEN BEN IS TOAST, GUYS.

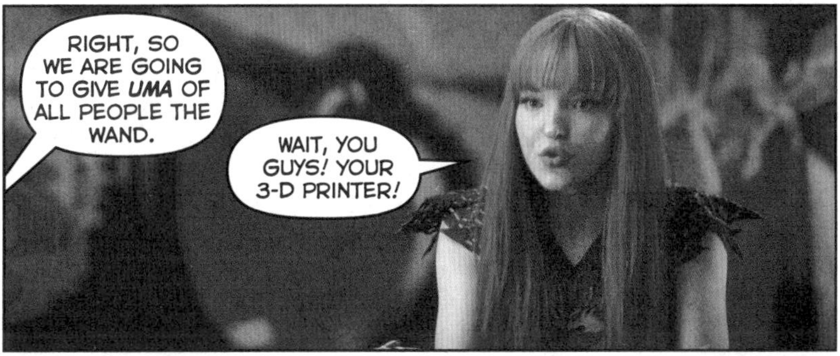
RIGHT, SO WE ARE GOING TO GIVE *UMA* OF ALL PEOPLE THE WAND.
WAIT, YOU GUYS! YOUR 3-D PRINTER!

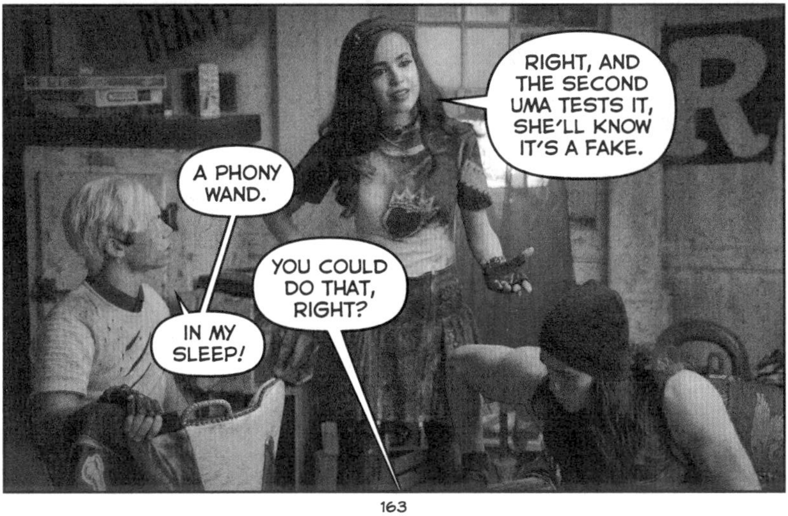
RIGHT, AND THE SECOND UMA TESTS IT, SHE'LL KNOW IT'S A FAKE.
A PHONY WAND.
YOU COULD DO THAT, RIGHT?
IN MY SLEEP!

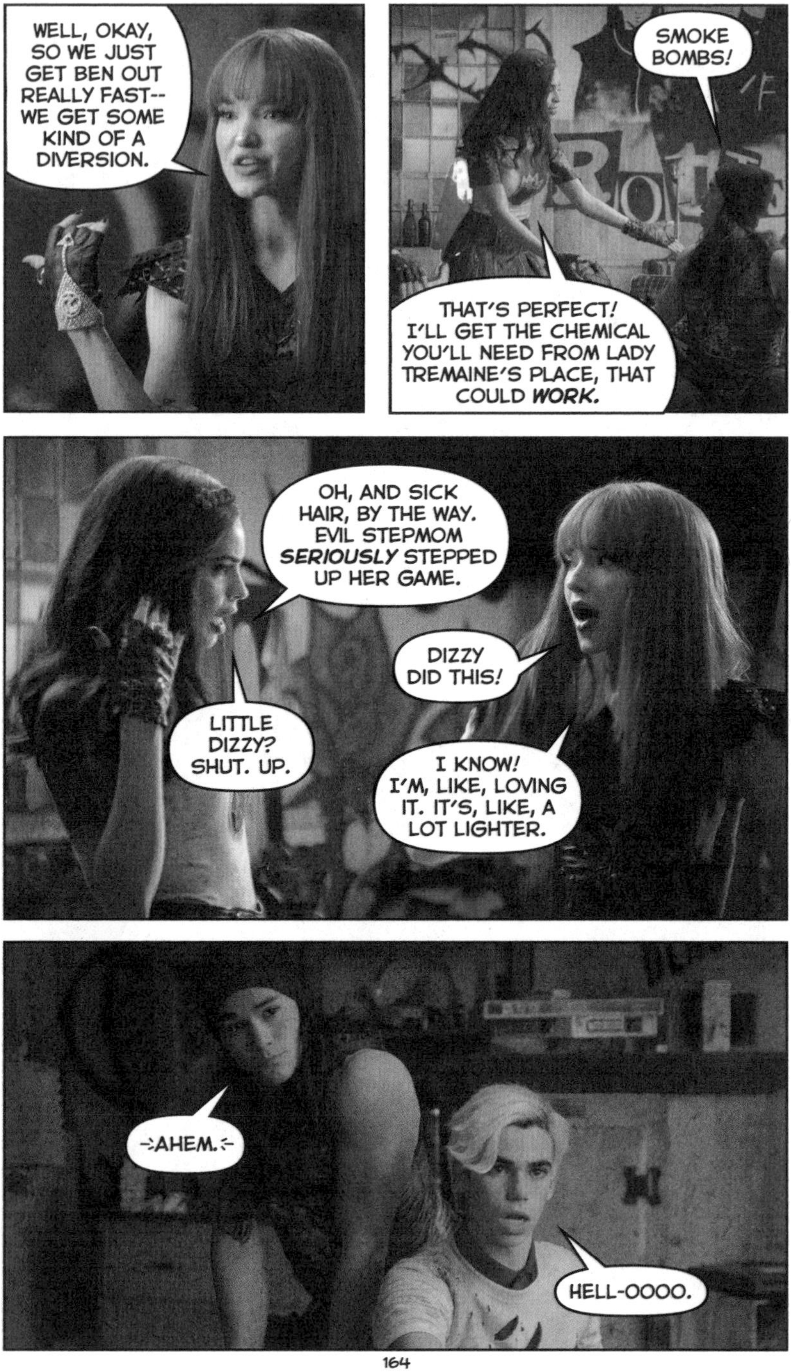
WELL, OKAY, SO WE JUST GET BEN OUT REALLY FAST-- WE GET SOME KIND OF A DIVERSION.
SMOKE BOMBS!
THAT'S PERFECT! I'LL GET THE CHEMICAL YOU'LL NEED FROM LADY TREMAINE'S PLACE, THAT COULD *WORK.*
OH, AND SICK HAIR, BY THE WAY. EVIL STEPMOM *SERIOUSLY* STEPPED UP HER GAME.
DIZZY DID THIS!
LITTLE DIZZY? SHUT. UP.
I KNOW! I'M, LIKE, LOVING IT. IT'S, LIKE, A LOT LIGHTER.
AHEM.
HELL-OOOO.

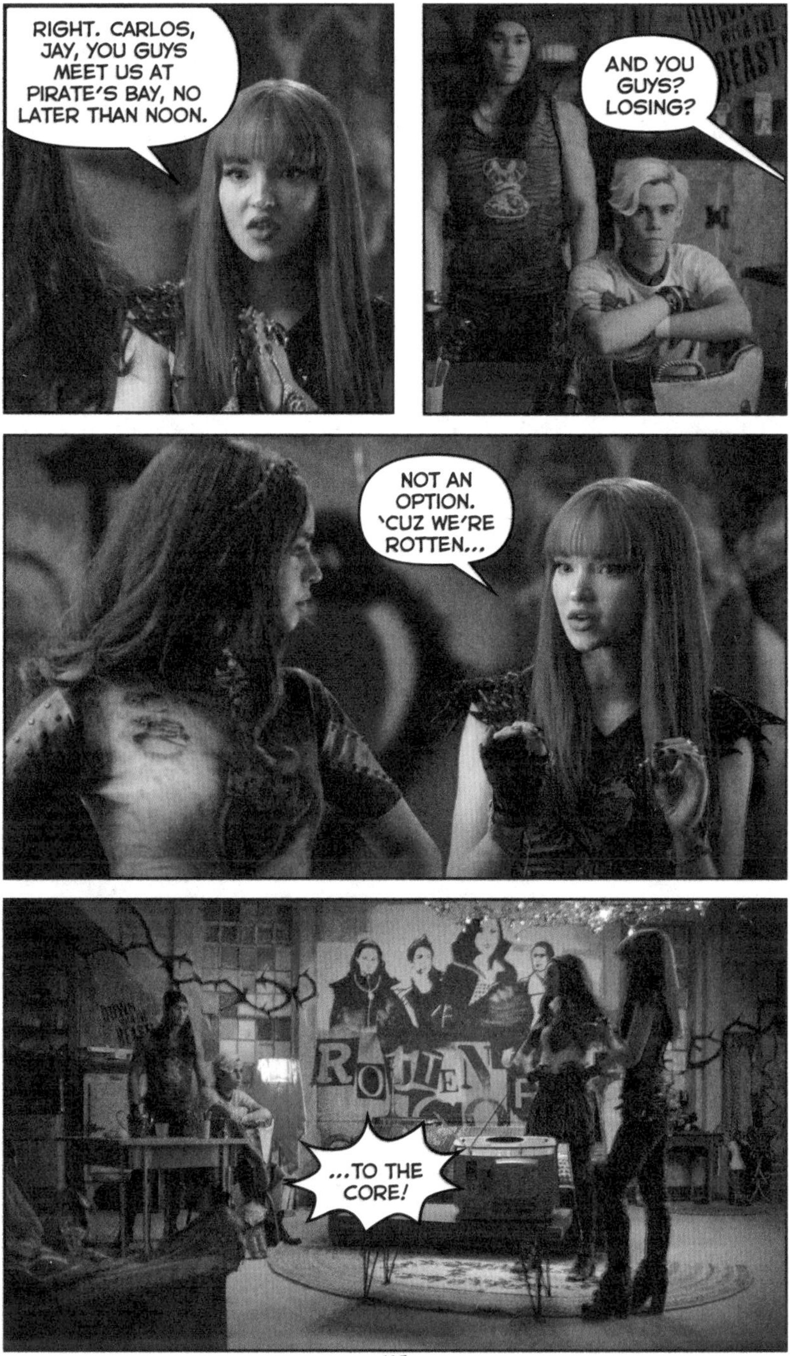
RIGHT. CARLOS, JAY, YOU GUYS MEET US AT PIRATE'S BAY, NO LATER THAN NOON.
AND YOU GUYS? LOSING?
NOT AN OPTION. 'CUZ WE'RE ROTTEN...
...TO THE CORE!

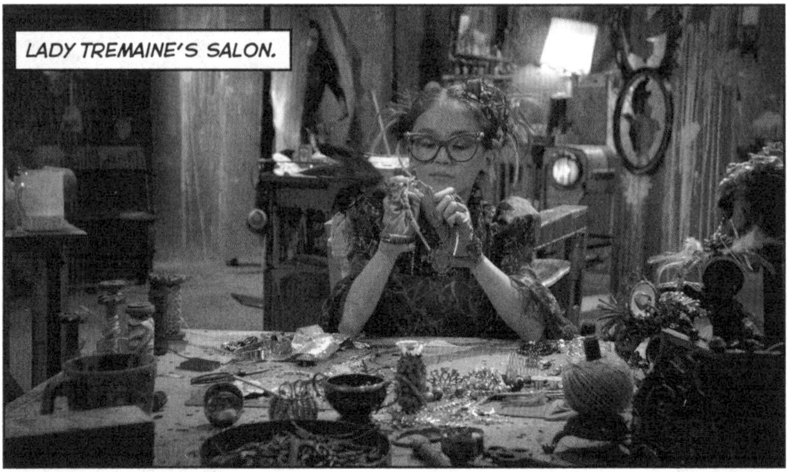
LADY TREMAINE'S SALON.

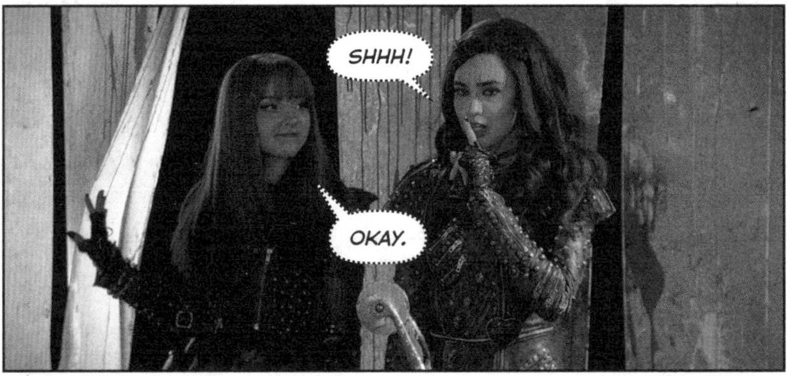
SHHH!
OKAY.

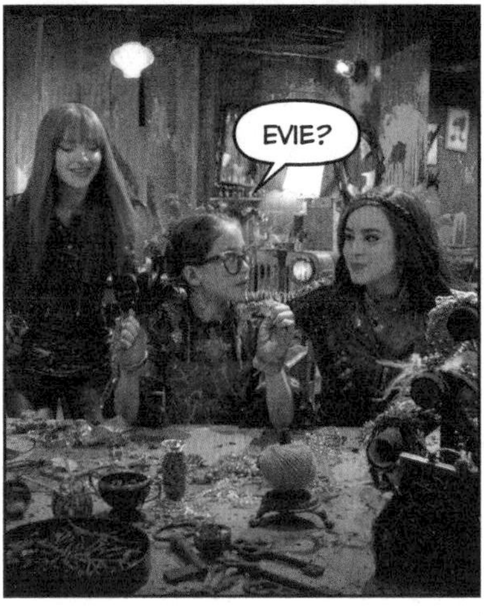
EVIE?

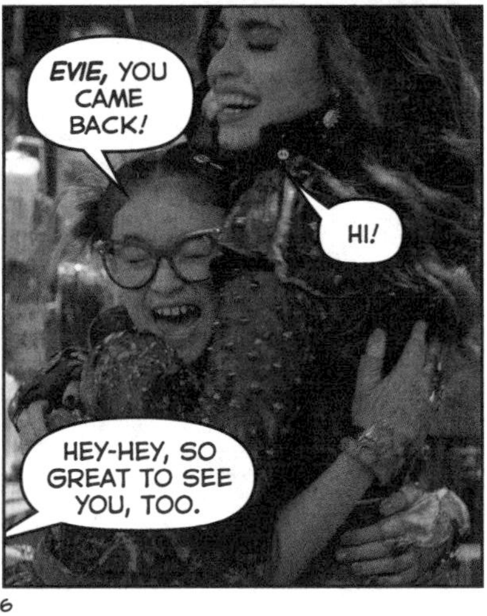
EVIE, YOU CAME BACK!
HI!
HEY-HEY, SO GREAT TO SEE YOU, TOO.

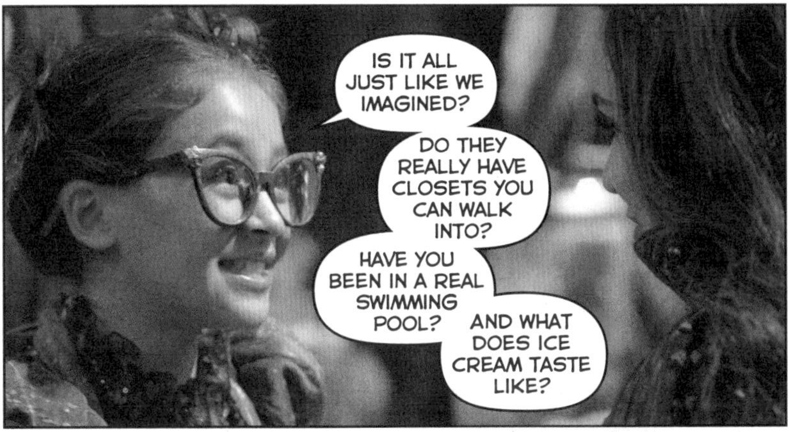
IS IT ALL JUST LIKE WE IMAGINED?
DO THEY REALLY HAVE CLOSETS YOU CAN WALK INTO?
HAVE YOU BEEN IN A REAL SWIMMING POOL?
AND WHAT DOES ICE CREAM TASTE LIKE?

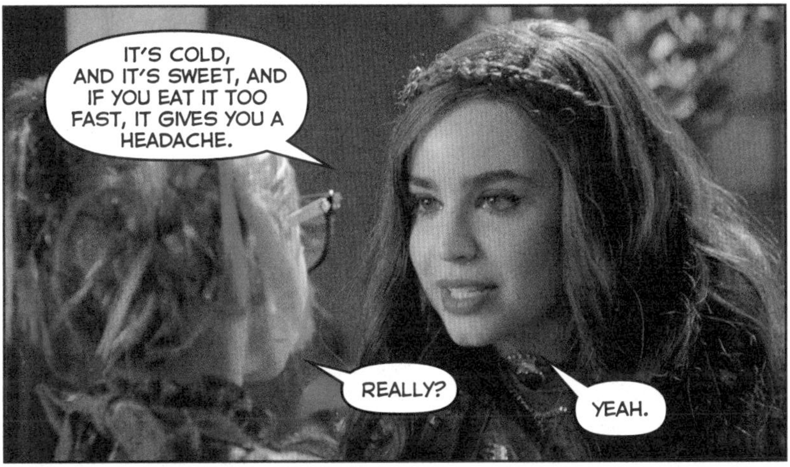
IT'S COLD, AND IT'S SWEET, AND IF YOU EAT IT TOO FAST, IT GIVES YOU A HEADACHE.
REALLY?
YEAH.

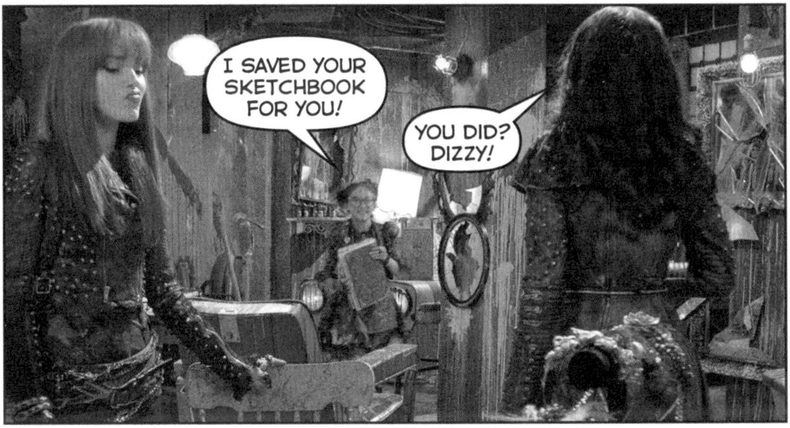
I SAVED YOUR SKETCHBOOK FOR YOU!
YOU DID? DIZZY!

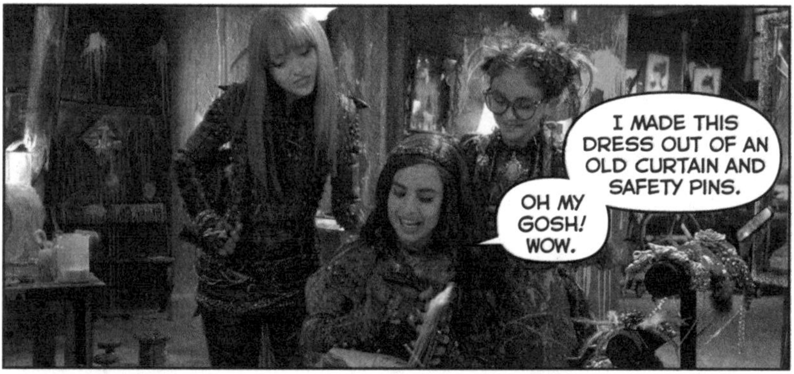
I MADE THIS DRESS OUT OF AN OLD CURTAIN AND SAFETY PINS.
OH MY GOSH! WOW.

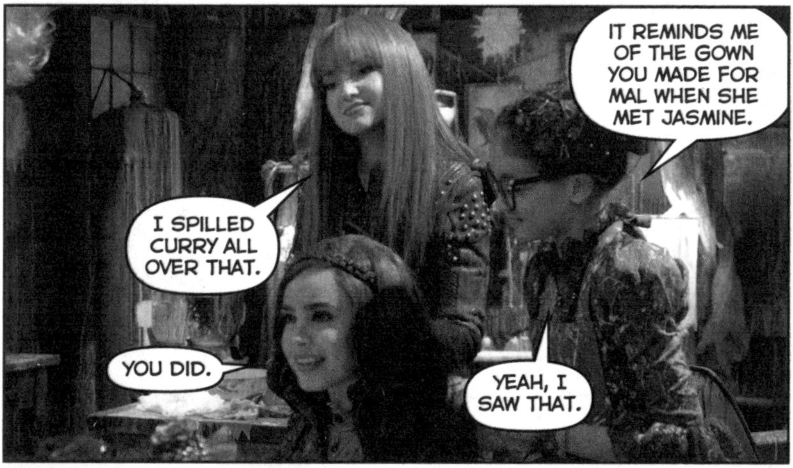
IT REMINDS ME OF THE GOWN YOU MADE FOR MAL WHEN SHE MET JASMINE.
I SPILLED CURRY ALL OVER THAT.
YOU DID.
YEAH, I SAW THAT.

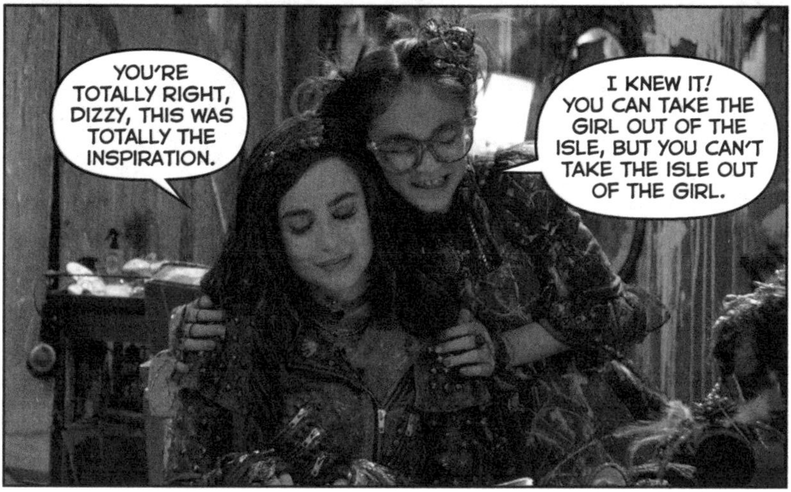
YOU'RE TOTALLY RIGHT, DIZZY, THIS WAS TOTALLY THE INSPIRATION.
I KNEW IT! YOU CAN TAKE THE GIRL OUT OF THE ISLE, BUT YOU CAN'T TAKE THE ISLE OUT OF THE GIRL.

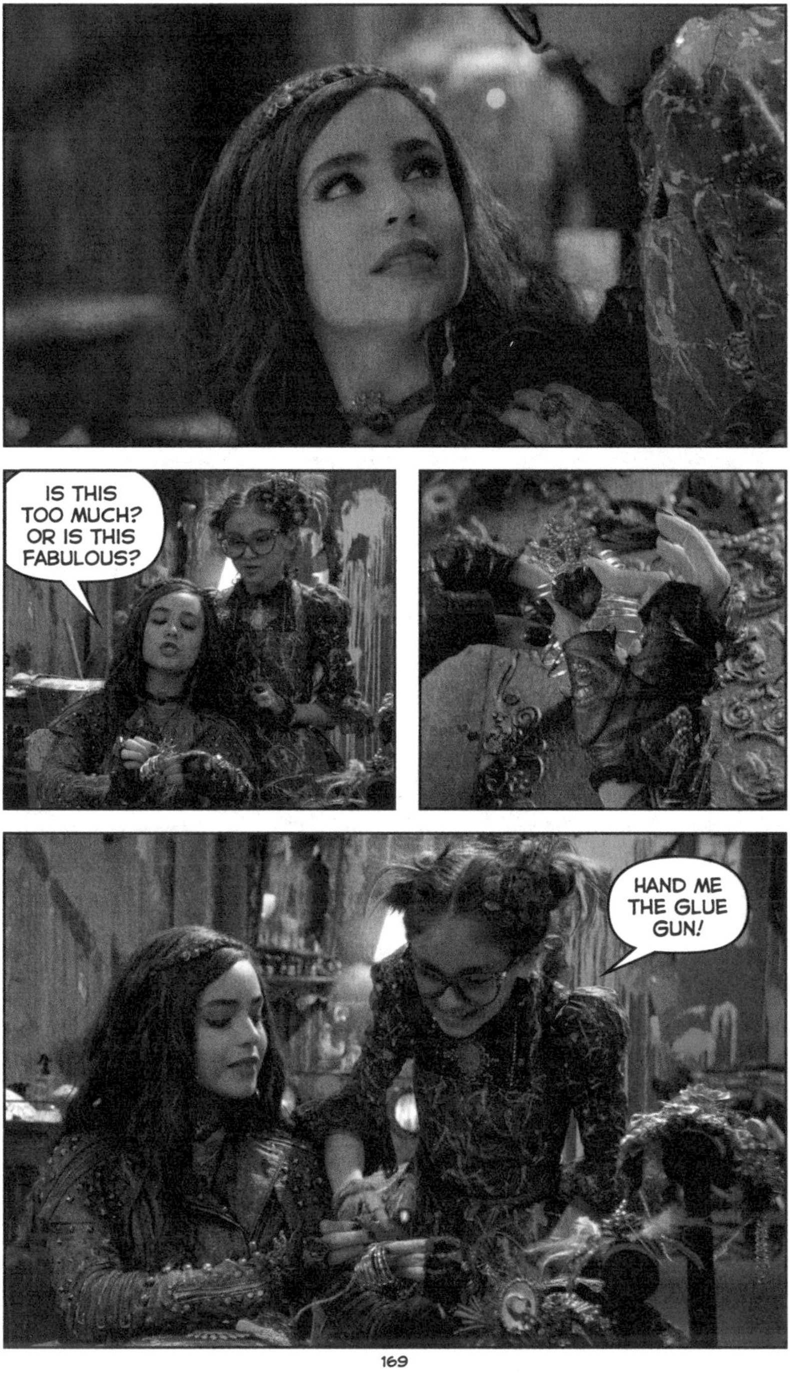
IS THIS TOO MUCH? OR IS THIS FABULOUS?
HAND ME THE GLUE GUN!

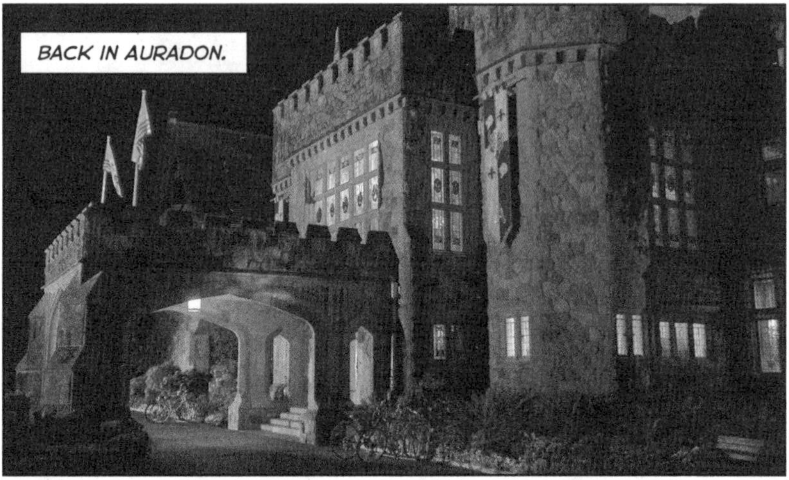
BACK IN AURADON.

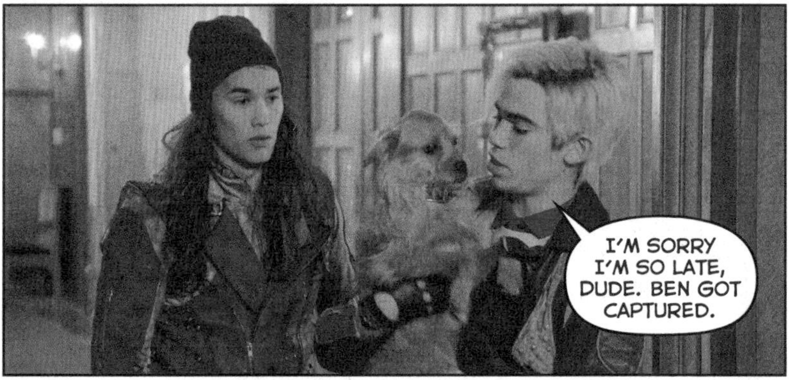
I'M SORRY I'M SO LATE, DUDE. BEN GOT CAPTURED.

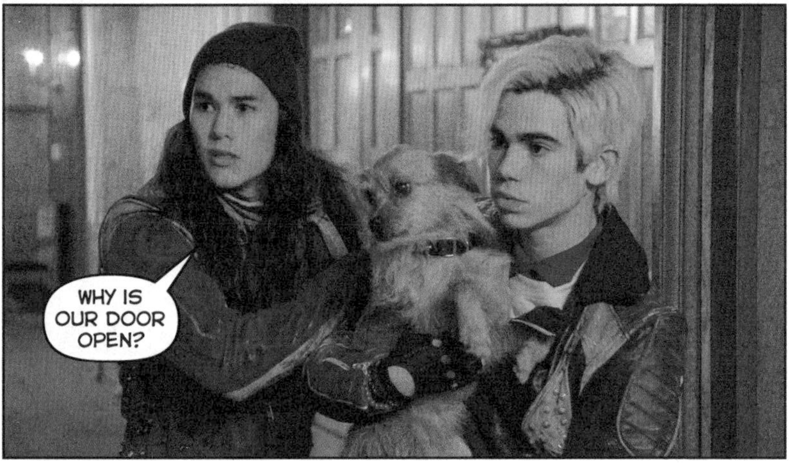
WHY IS OUR DOOR OPEN?

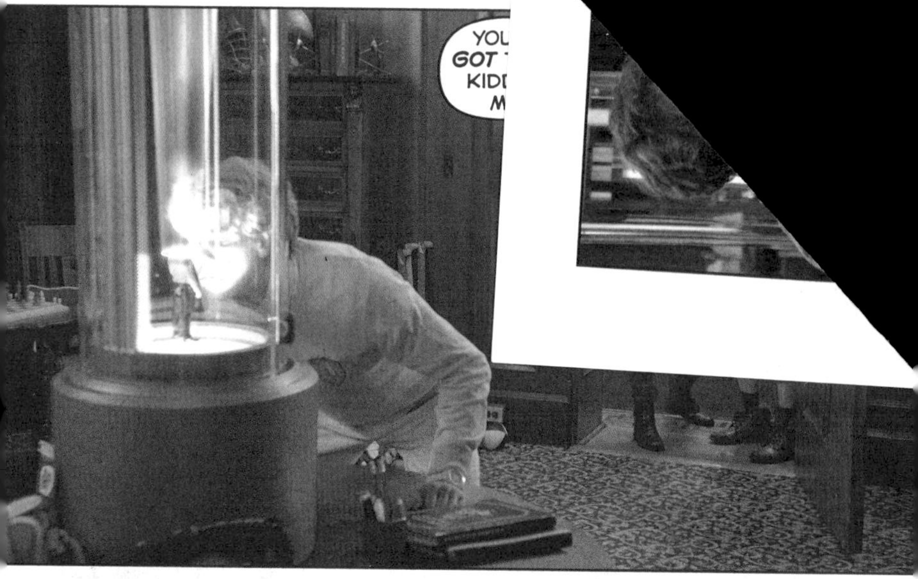
YOU
GOT
KIDD
M

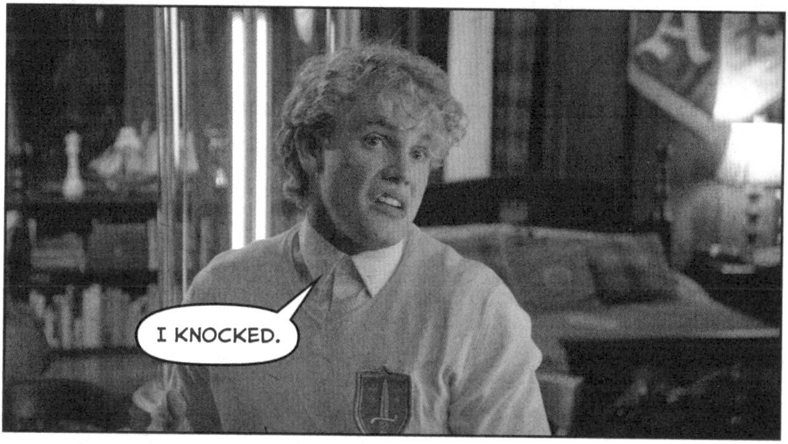
I KNOCKED.

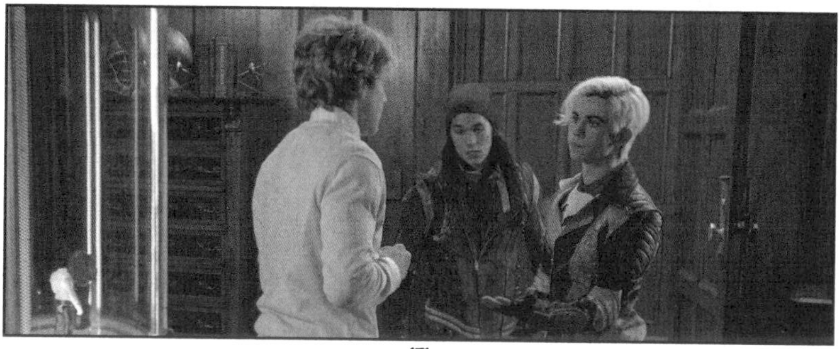

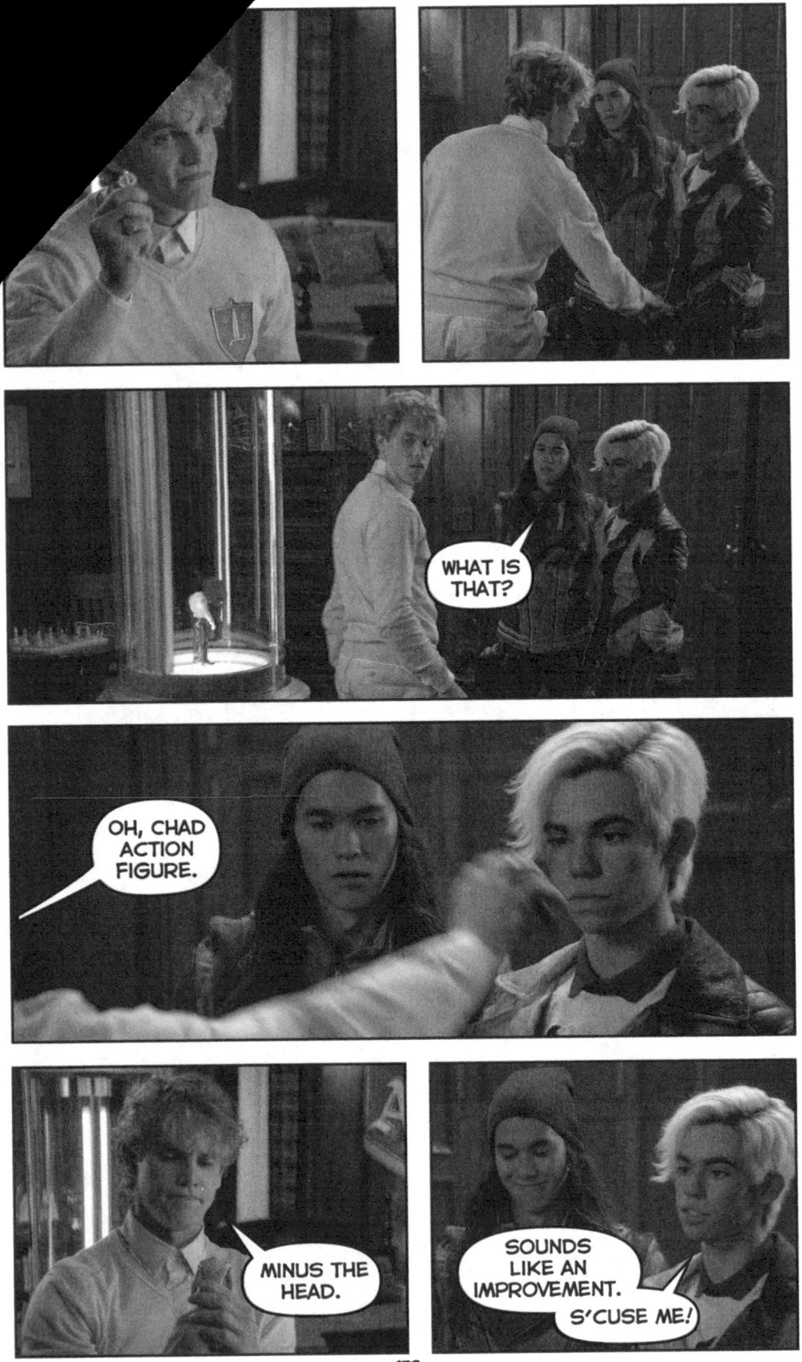
WHAT IS THAT?
OH, CHAD ACTION FIGURE.
MINUS THE HEAD.
SOUNDS LIKE AN IMPROVEMENT.
S'CUSE ME!

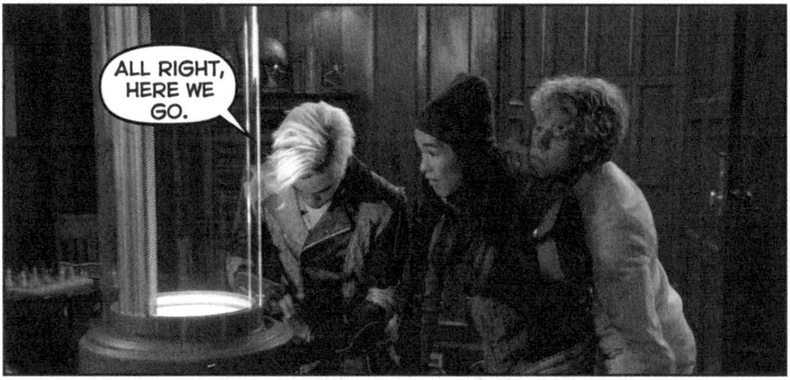
ALL RIGHT, HERE WE GO.

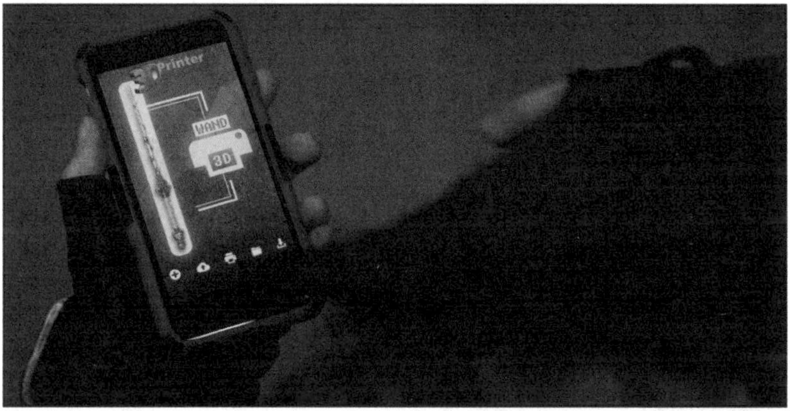
Printer
WAND
3D

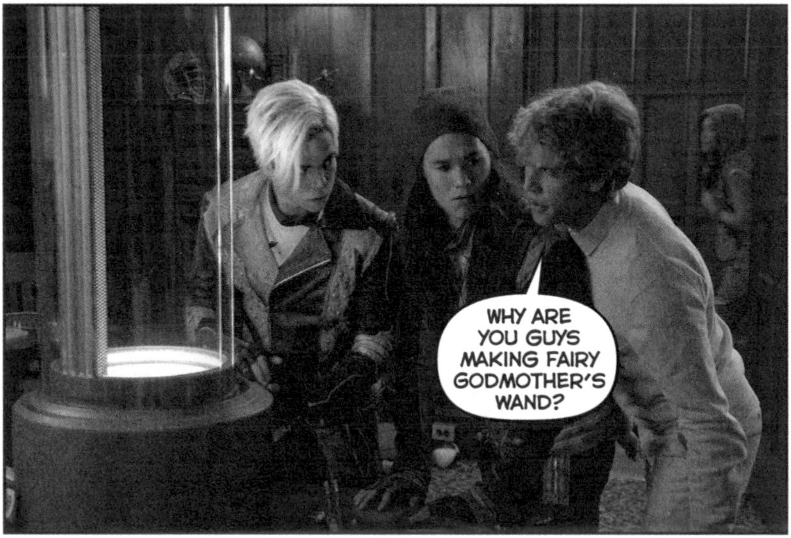
WHY ARE YOU GUYS MAKING FAIRY GODMOTHER'S WAND?

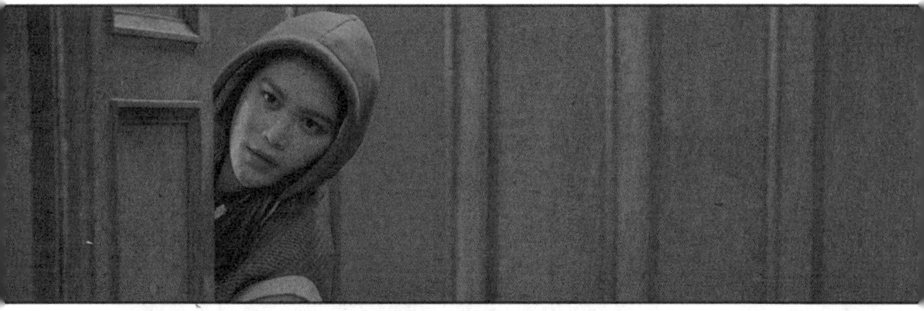

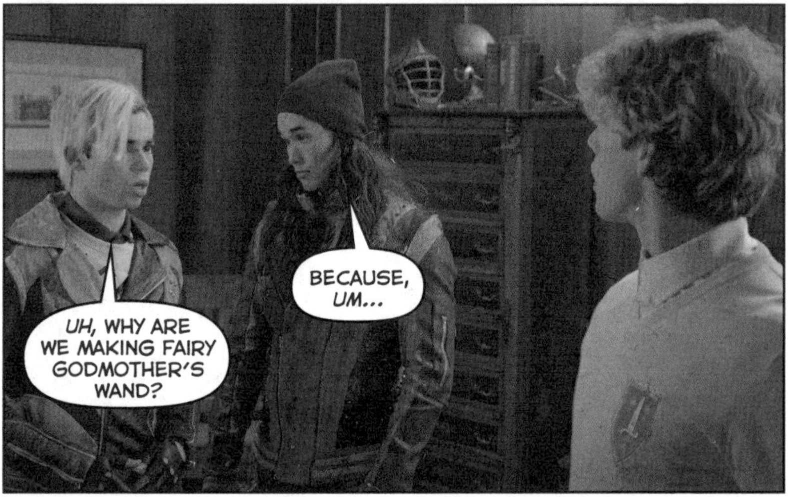
UH, WHY ARE WE MAKING FAIRY GODMOTHER'S WAND?
BECAUSE, UM...

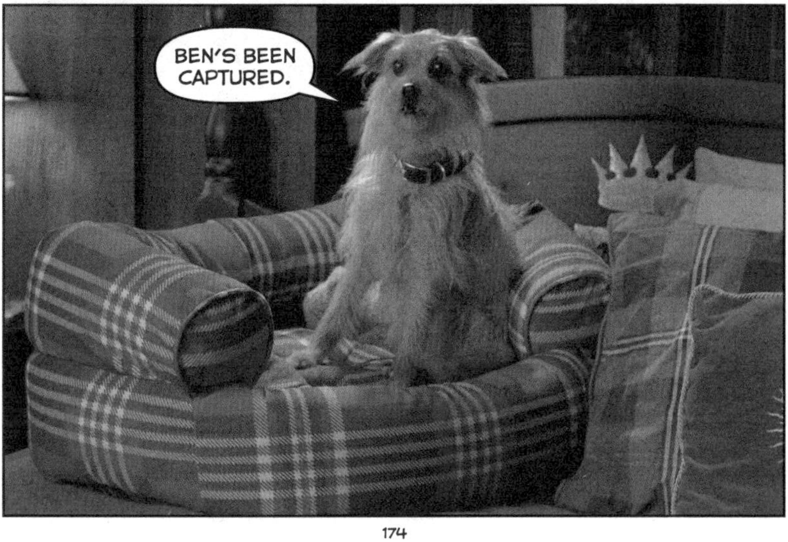
BEN'S BEEN CAPTURED.

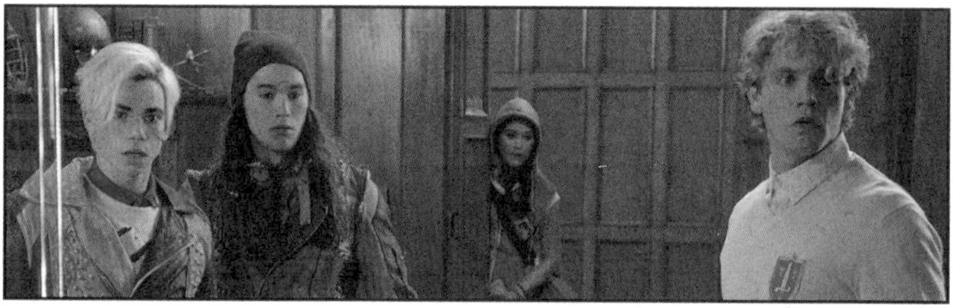

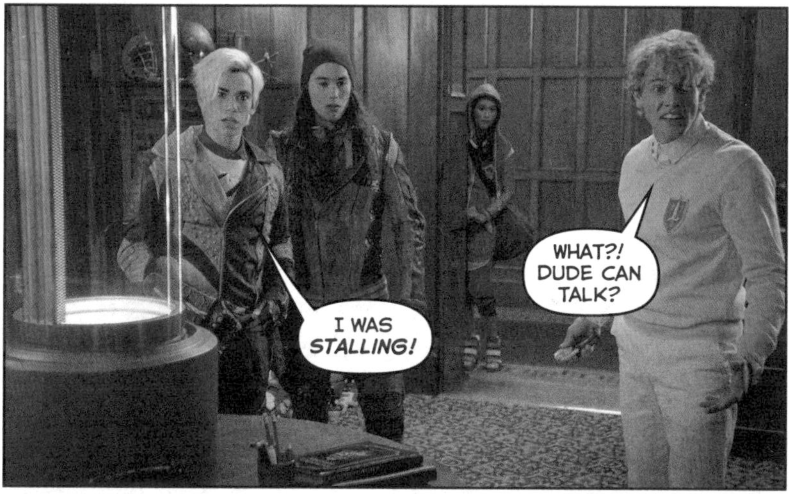
WHAT?! DUDE CAN TALK?
I WAS *STALLING!*

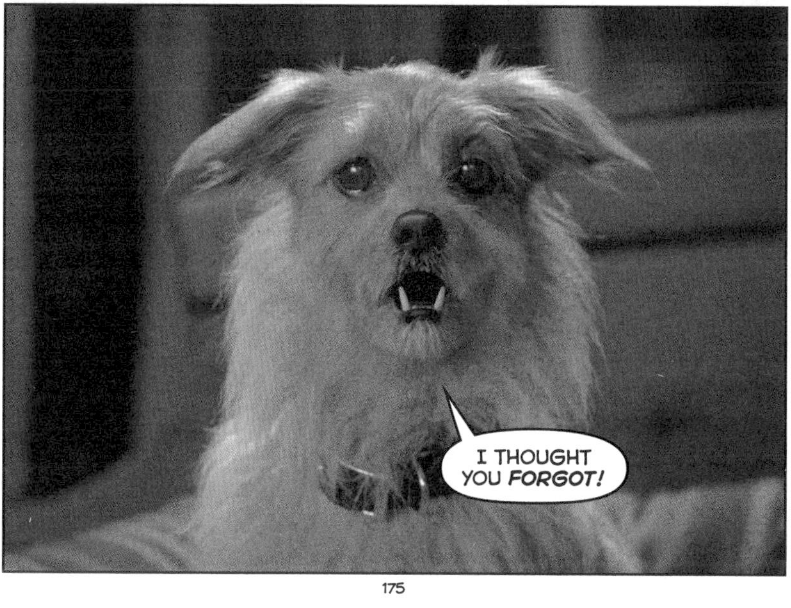
I THOUGHT YOU *FORGOT!*

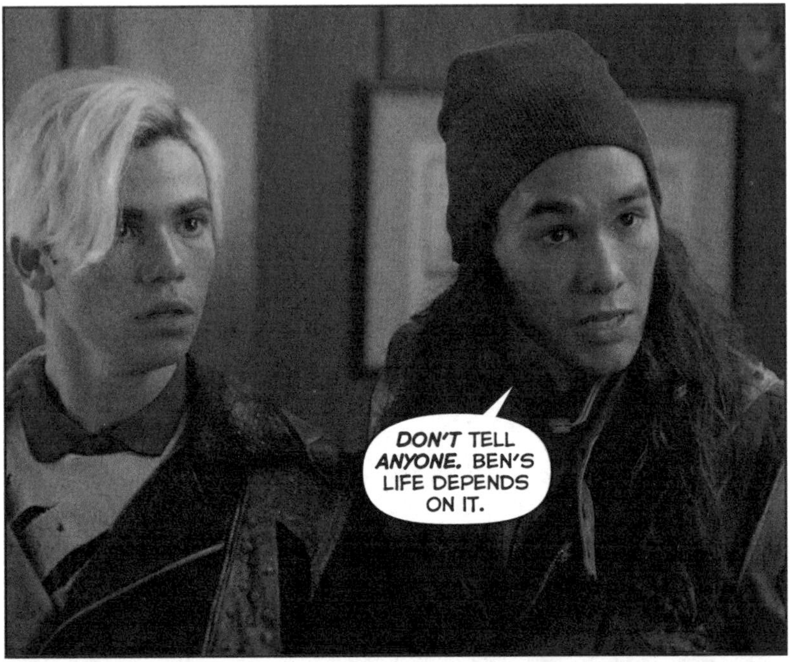
DON'T TELL ANYONE. BEN'S LIFE DEPENDS ON IT.

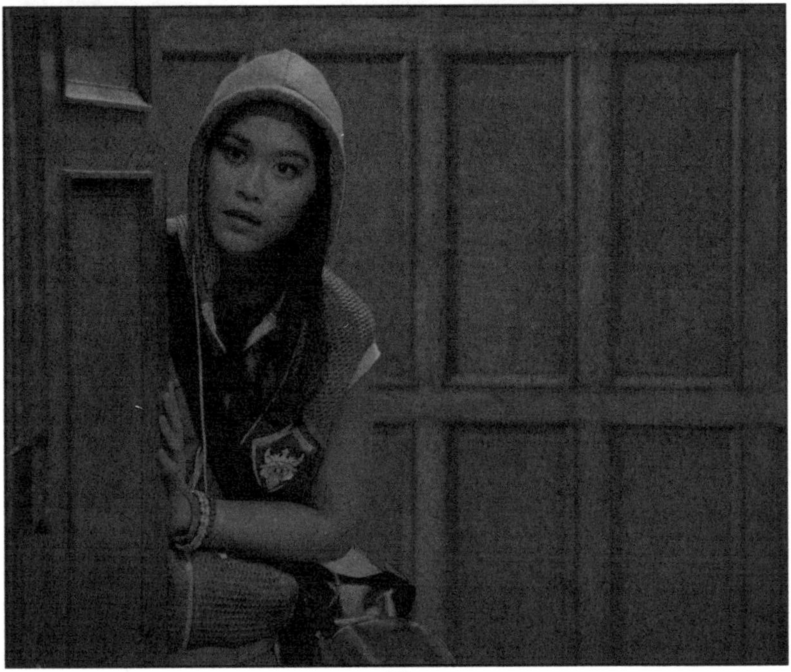

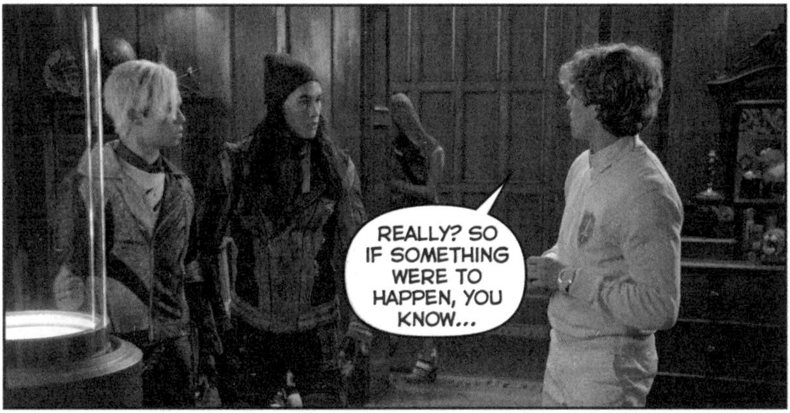
REALLY? SO IF SOMETHING WERE TO HAPPEN, YOU KNOW...

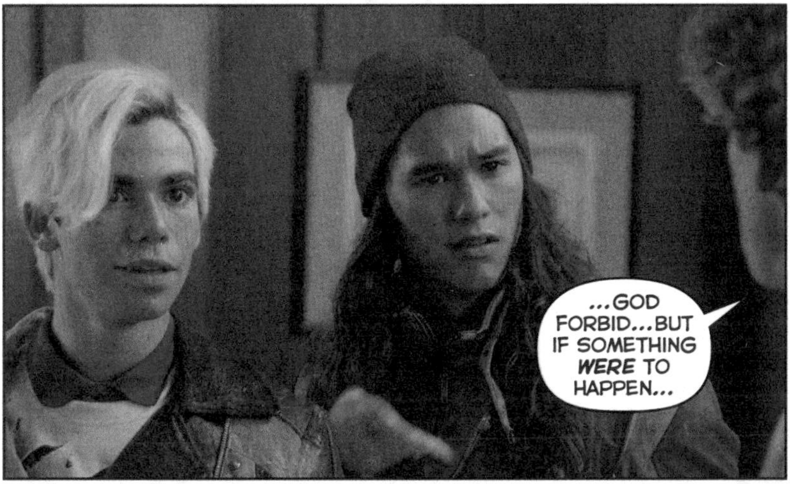
...GOD FORBID...BUT IF SOMETHING *WERE* TO HAPPEN...

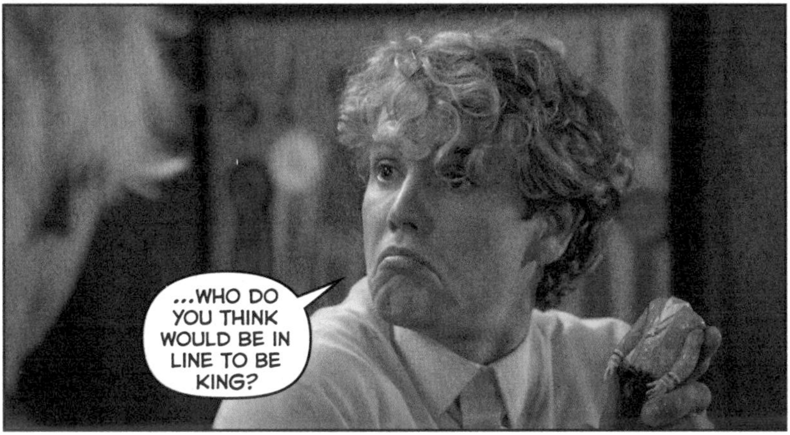
...WHO DO YOU THINK WOULD BE IN LINE TO BE KING?

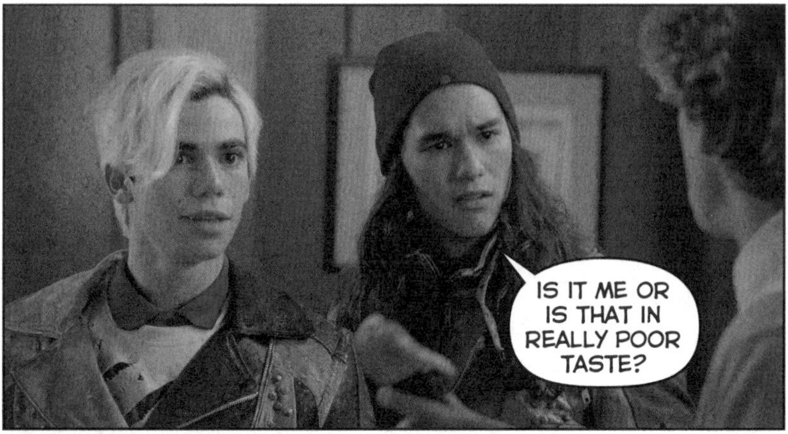
IS IT ME OR IS THAT IN REALLY POOR TASTE?

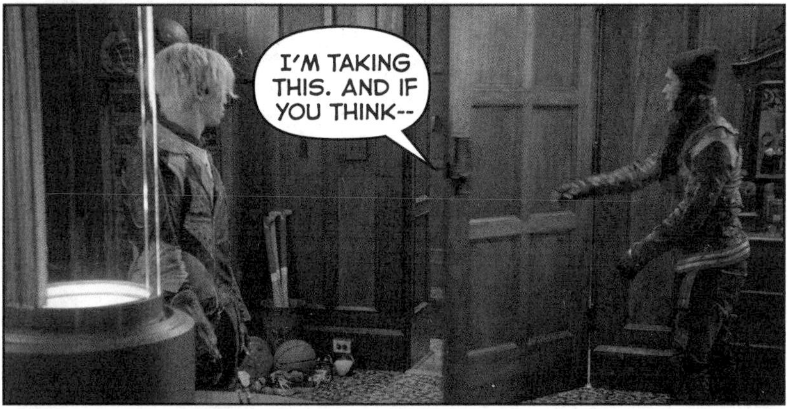
I'M TAKING THIS. AND IF YOU THINK--

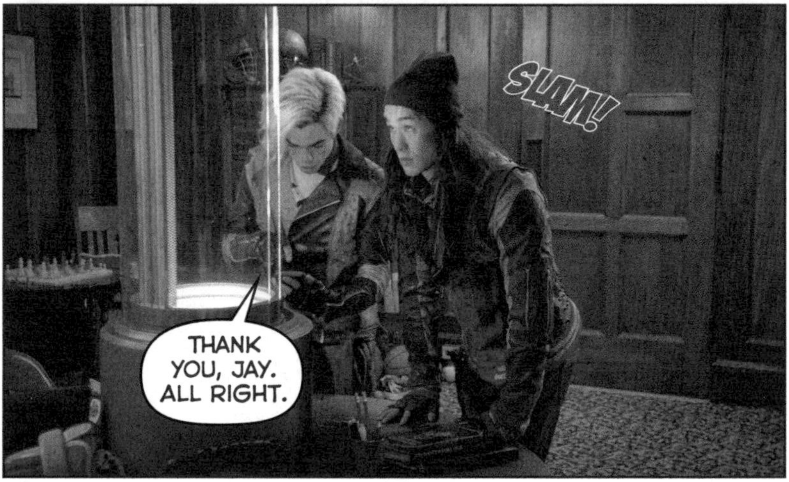
SLAM!
THANK YOU, JAY. ALL RIGHT.

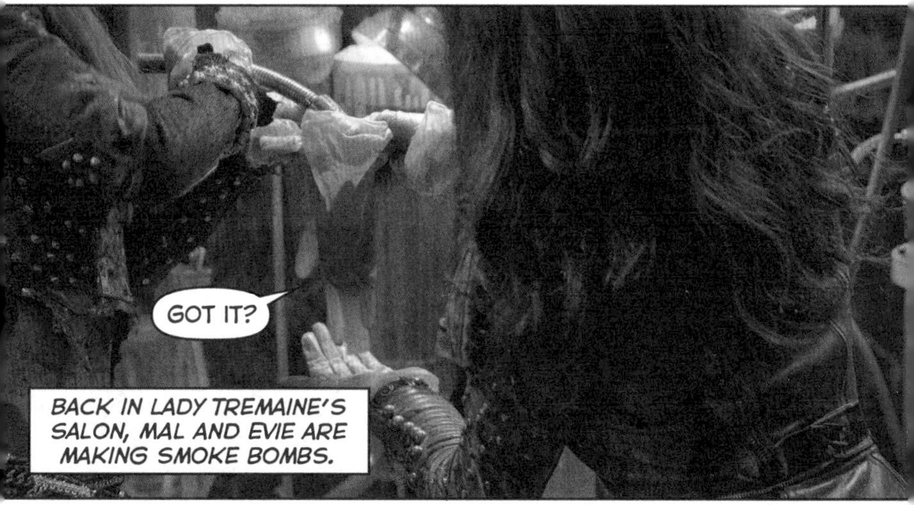
GOT IT?
BACK IN LADY TREMAINE'S SALON, MAL AND EVIE ARE MAKING SMOKE BOMBS.

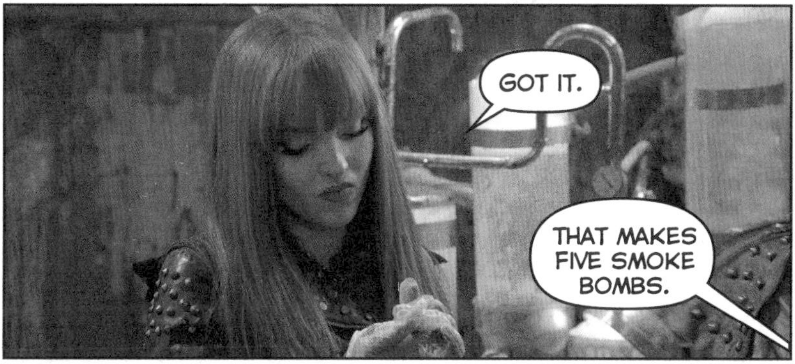
GOT IT.
THAT MAKES FIVE SMOKE BOMBS.

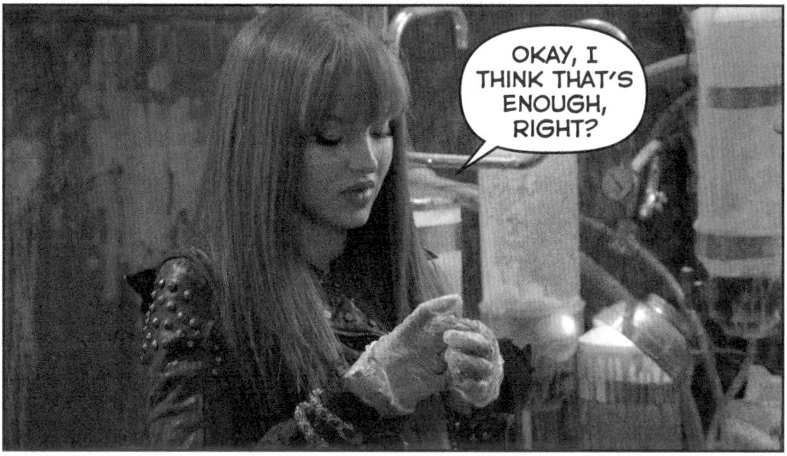
OKAY, I THINK THAT'S ENOUGH, RIGHT?

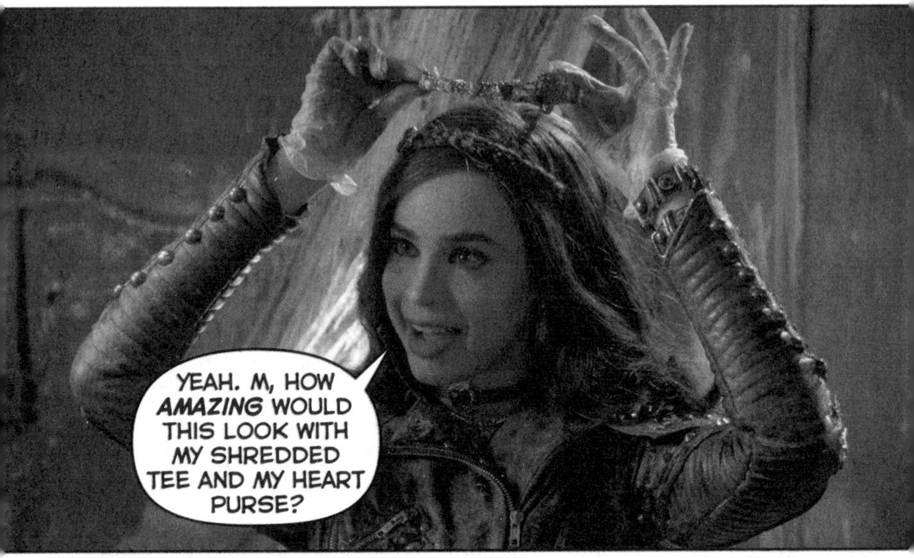
YEAH. M, HOW *AMAZING* WOULD THIS LOOK WITH MY SHREDDED TEE AND MY HEART PURSE?

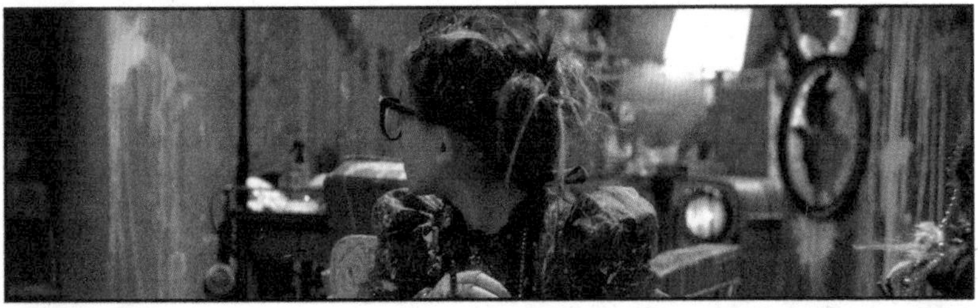

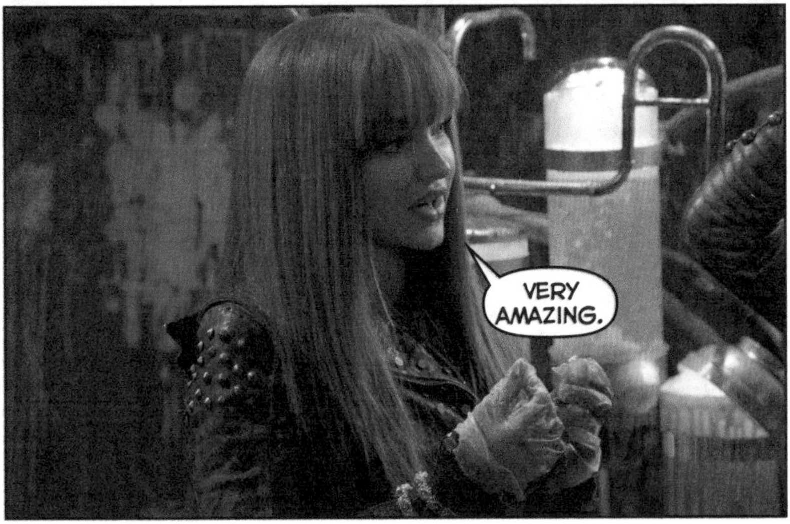
VERY AMAZING.

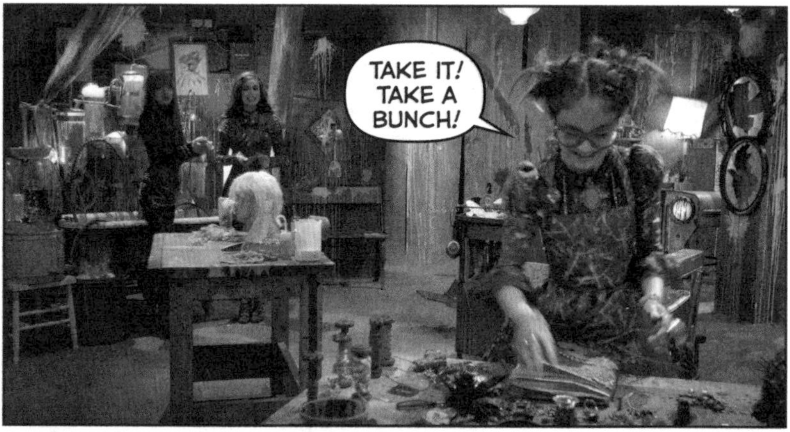
TAKE IT! TAKE A BUNCH!

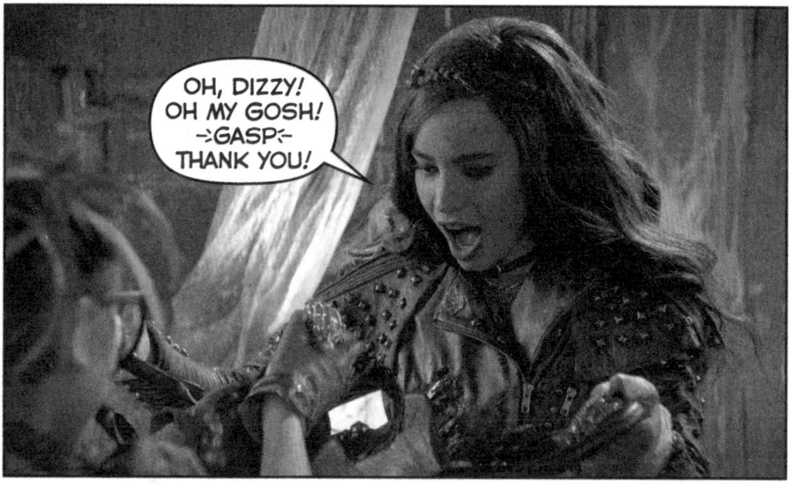
OH, DIZZY! OH MY GOSH! ⇝GASP⇜ THANK YOU!

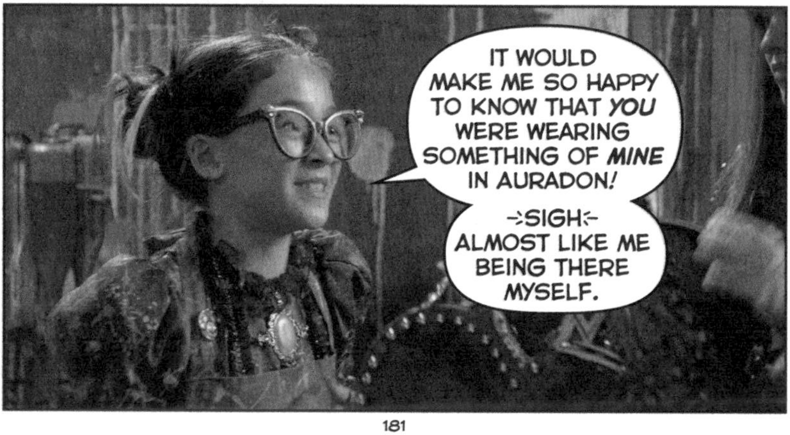
IT WOULD MAKE ME SO HAPPY TO KNOW THAT *YOU* WERE WEARING SOMETHING OF *MINE* IN AURADON!
⇝SIGH⇜ ALMOST LIKE ME BEING THERE MYSELF.

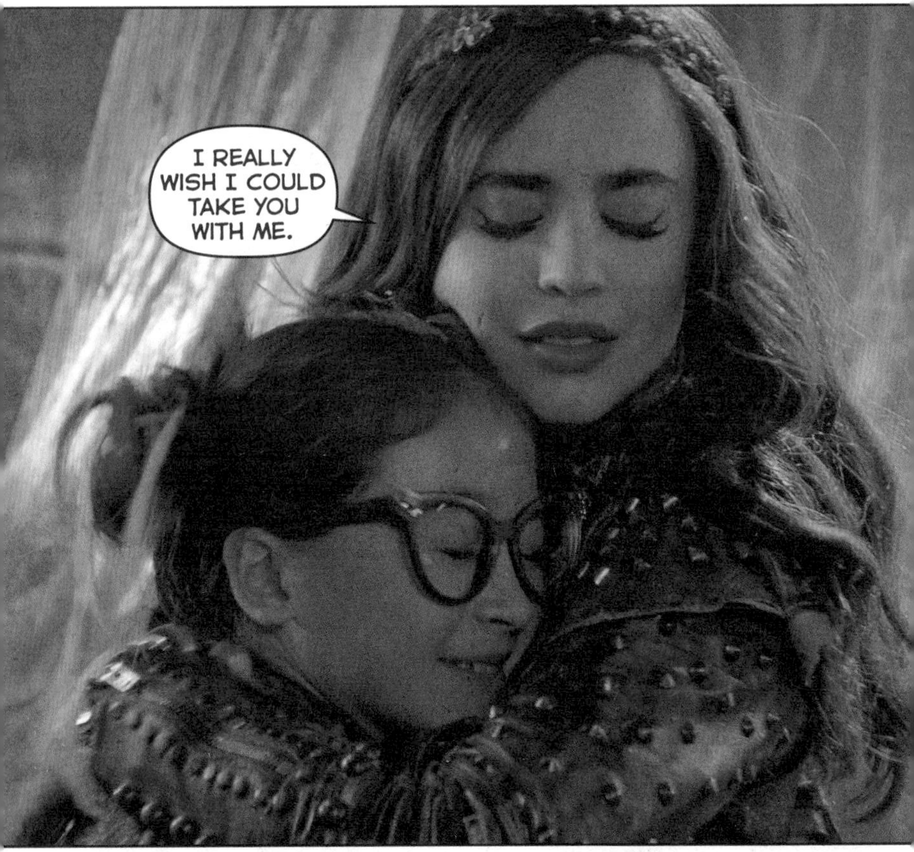
I REALLY WISH I COULD TAKE YOU WITH ME.

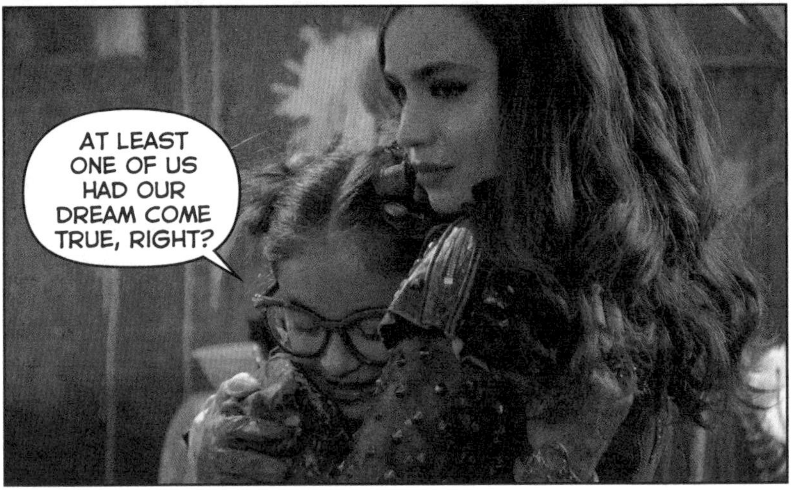
AT LEAST ONE OF US HAD OUR DREAM COME TRUE, RIGHT?

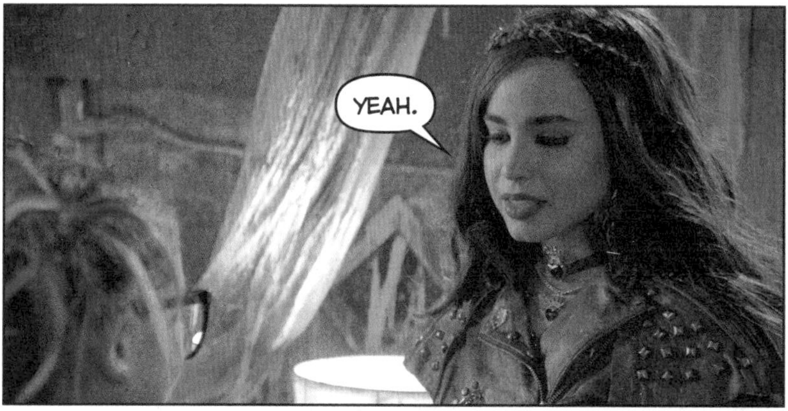
YEAH.

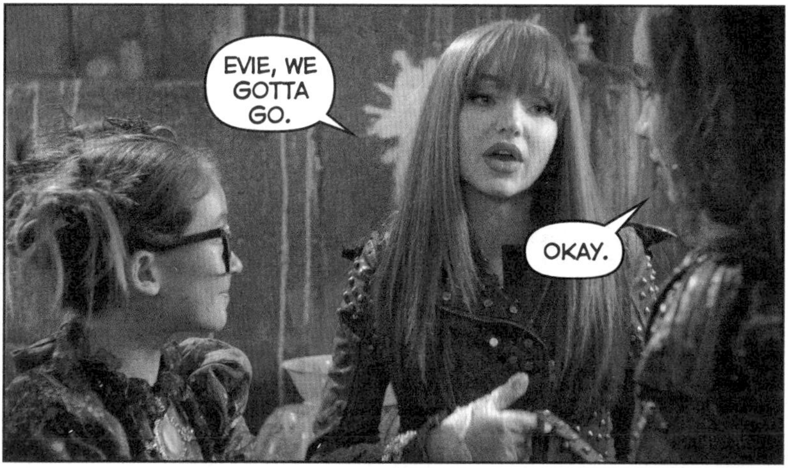
EVIE, WE GOTTA GO.
OKAY.

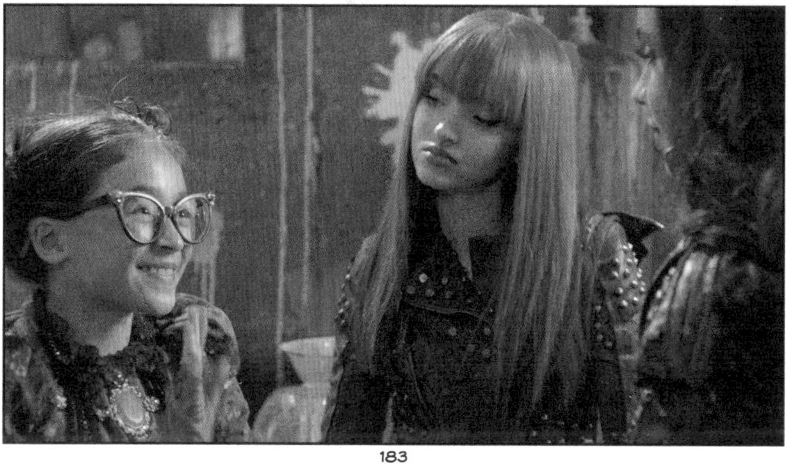

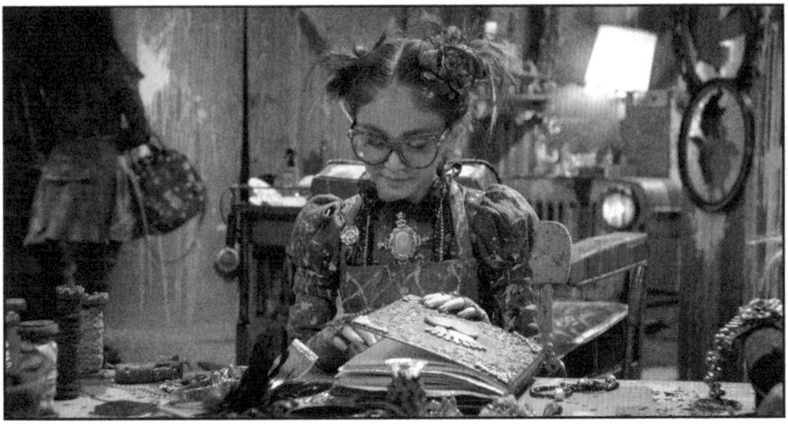

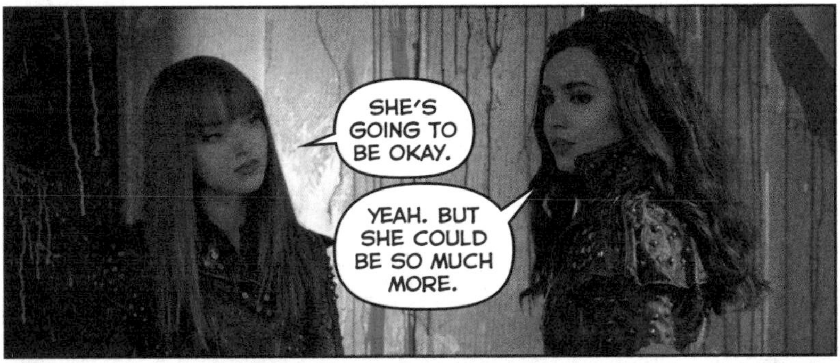
SHE'S GOING TO BE OKAY.
YEAH. BUT SHE COULD BE SO MUCH MORE.

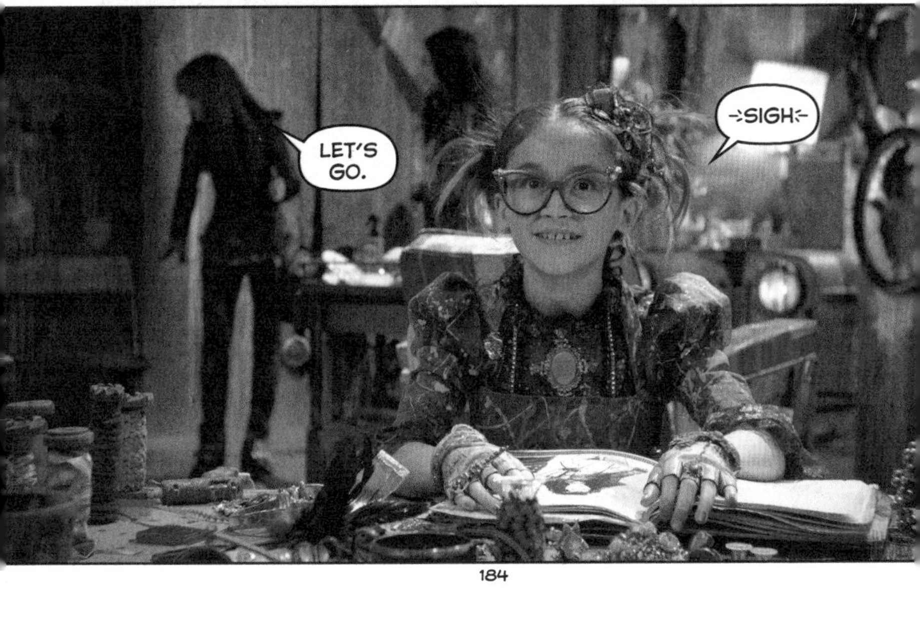
LET'S GO.
SIGH

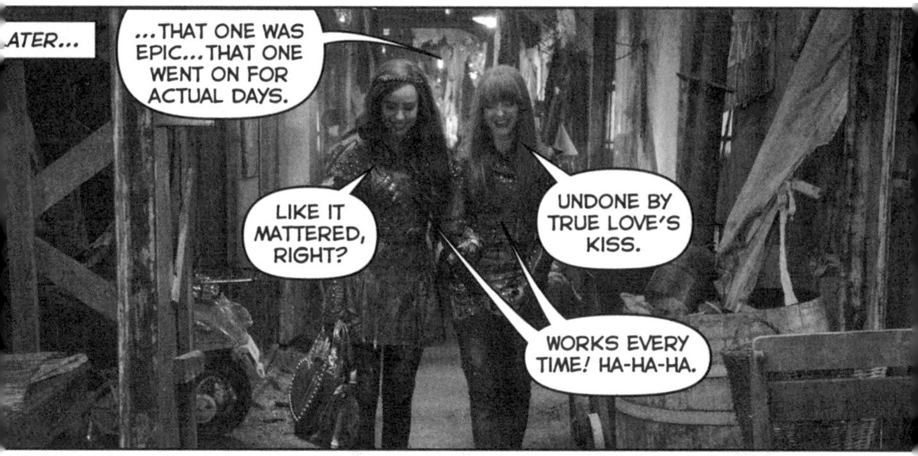
ATER...
...THAT ONE WAS EPIC...THAT ONE WENT ON FOR ACTUAL DAYS.
LIKE IT MATTERED, RIGHT?
UNDONE BY TRUE LOVE'S KISS.
WORKS EVERY TIME! HA-HA-HA.

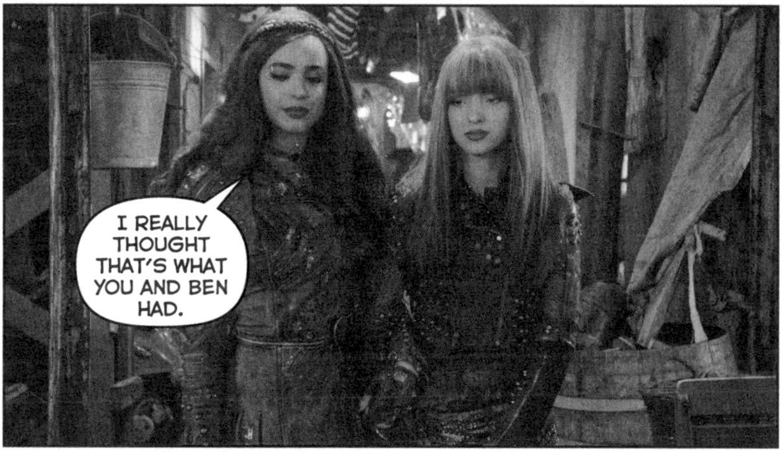
I REALLY THOUGHT THAT'S WHAT YOU AND BEN HAD.

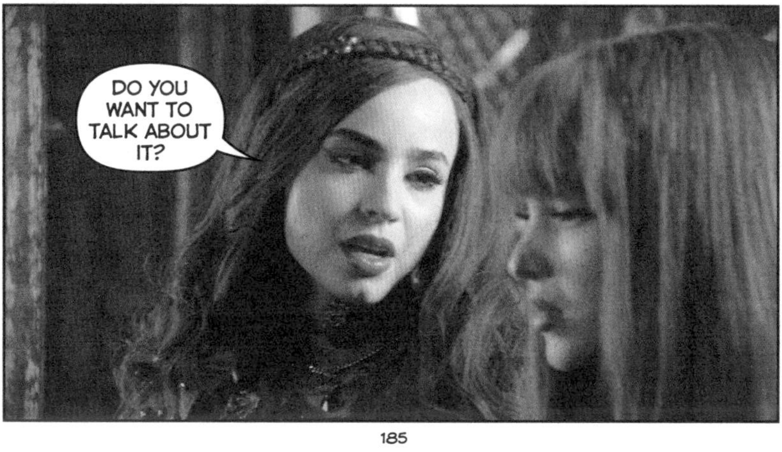
DO YOU WANT TO TALK ABOUT IT?

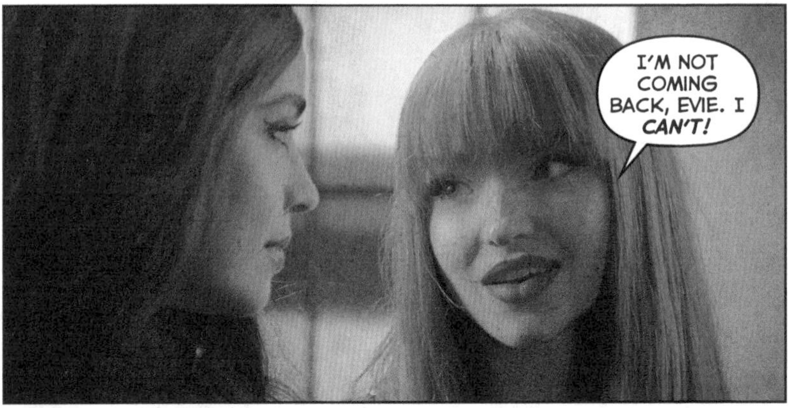
I'M NOT COMING BACK, EVIE. I *CAN'T!*

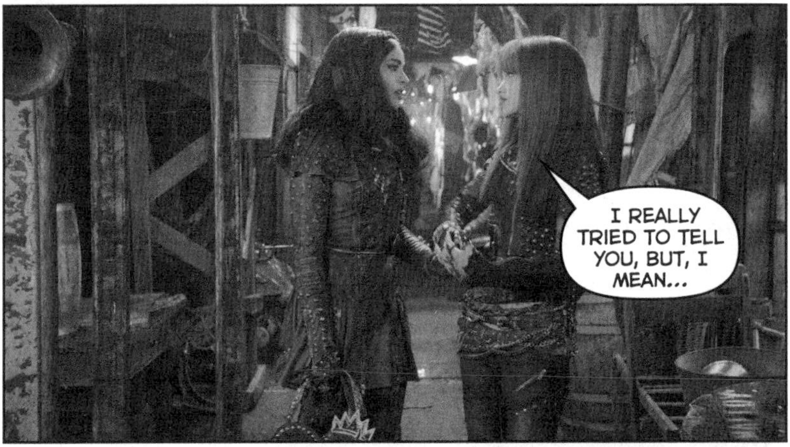
I REALLY TRIED TO TELL YOU, BUT, I MEAN...

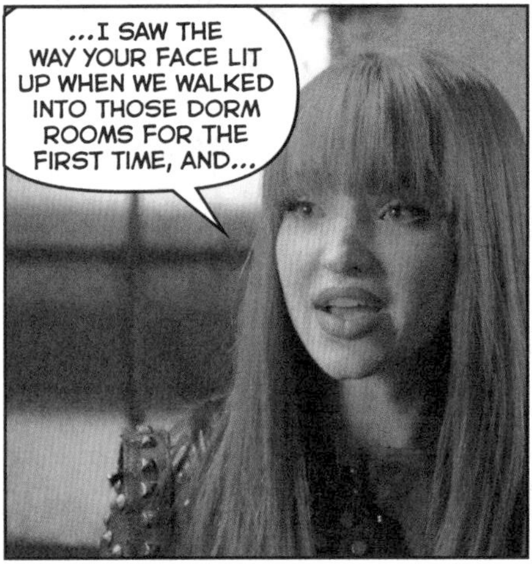
...I SAW THE WAY YOUR FACE LIT UP WHEN WE WALKED INTO THOSE DORM ROOMS FOR THE FIRST TIME, AND...

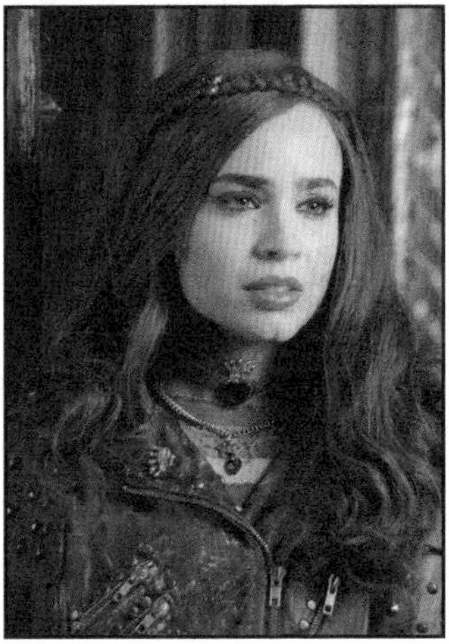

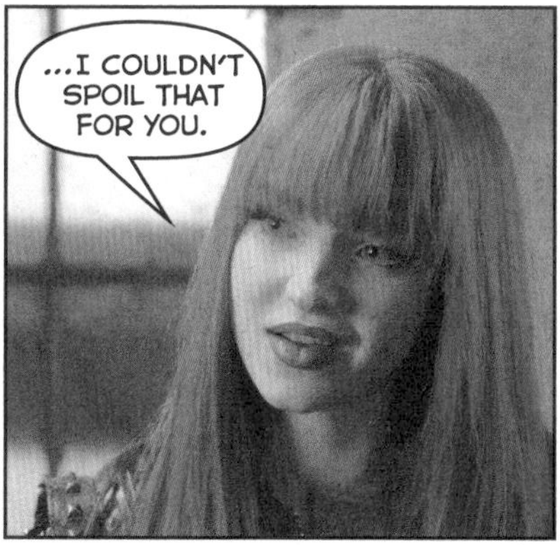
...I COULDN'T SPOIL THAT FOR YOU.

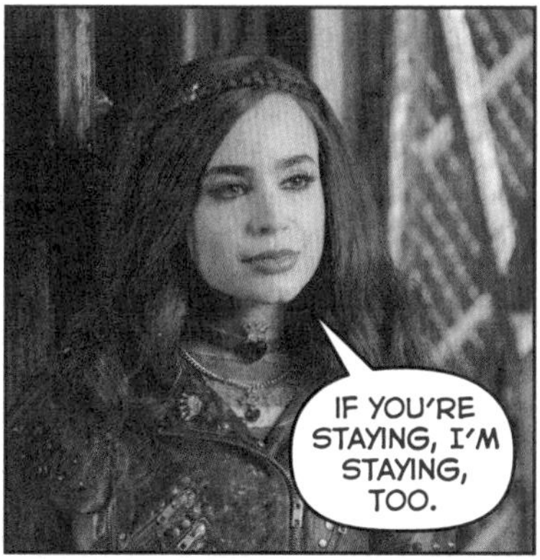
IF YOU'RE STAYING, I'M STAYING, TOO.

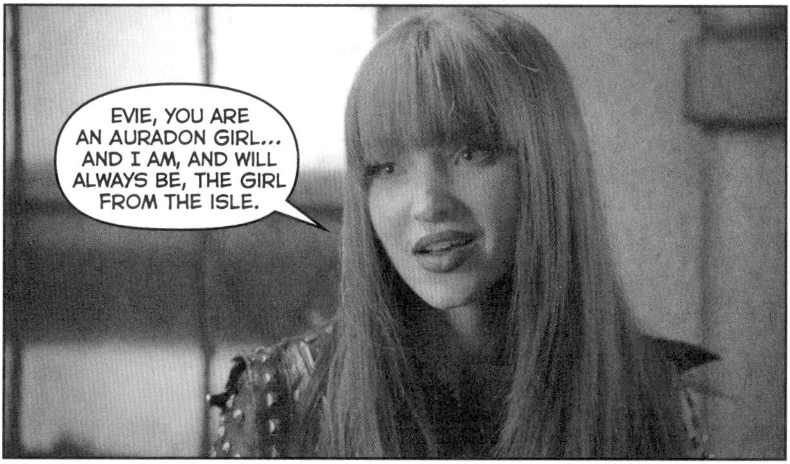
EVIE, YOU ARE AN AURADON GIRL... AND I AM, AND WILL ALWAYS BE, THE GIRL FROM THE ISLE.

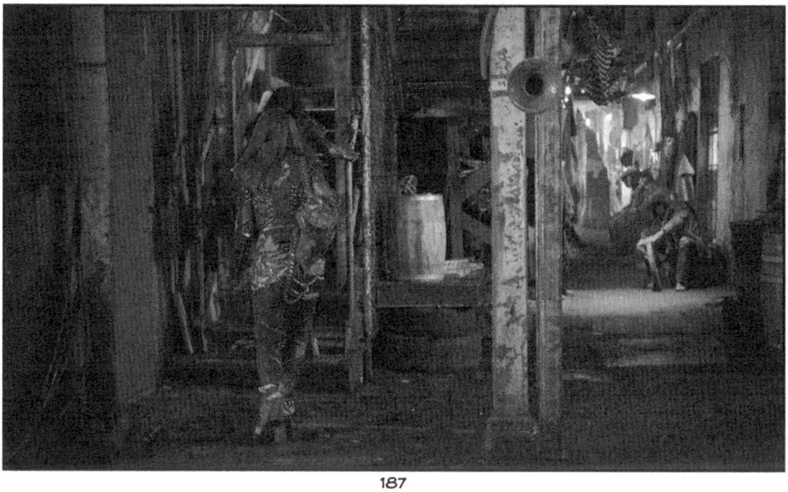

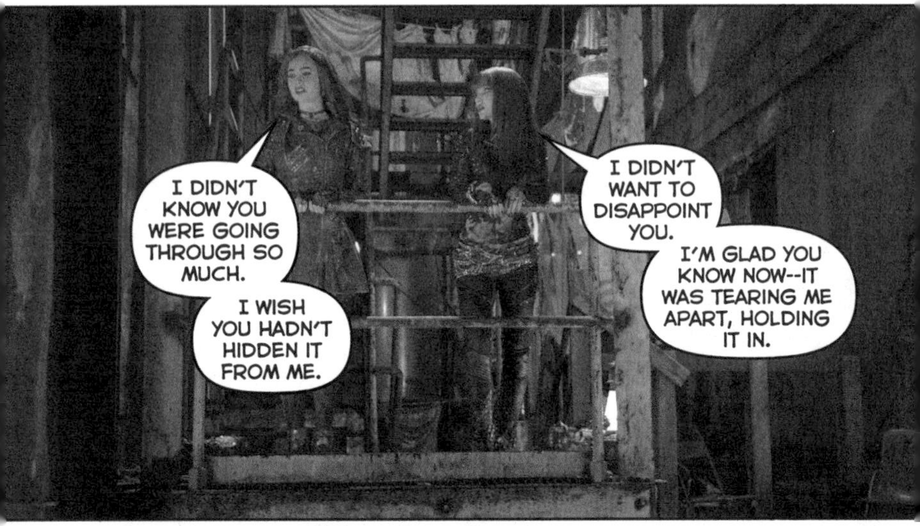
I DIDN'T KNOW YOU WERE GOING THROUGH SO MUCH.
I WISH YOU HADN'T HIDDEN IT FROM ME.
I DIDN'T WANT TO DISAPPOINT YOU.
I'M GLAD YOU KNOW NOW--IT WAS TEARING ME APART, HOLDING IT IN.

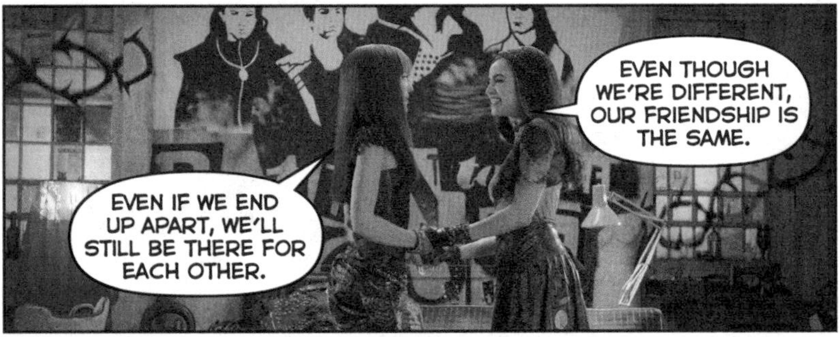
EVEN THOUGH WE'RE DIFFERENT, OUR FRIENDSHIP IS THE SAME.
EVEN IF WE END UP APART, WE'LL STILL BE THERE FOR EACH OTHER.

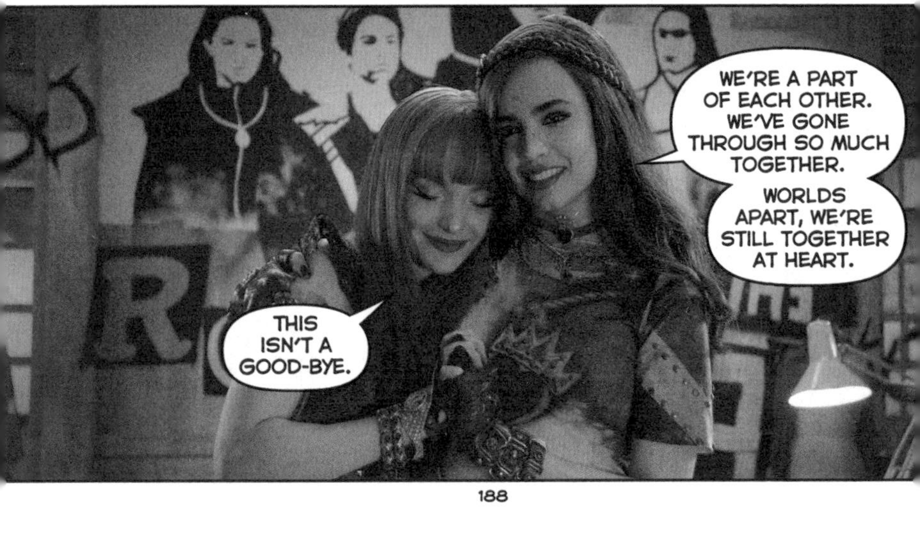
WE'RE A PART OF EACH OTHER. WE'VE GONE THROUGH SO MUCH TOGETHER.
WORLDS APART, WE'RE STILL TOGETHER AT HEART.
THIS ISN'T A GOOD-BYE.

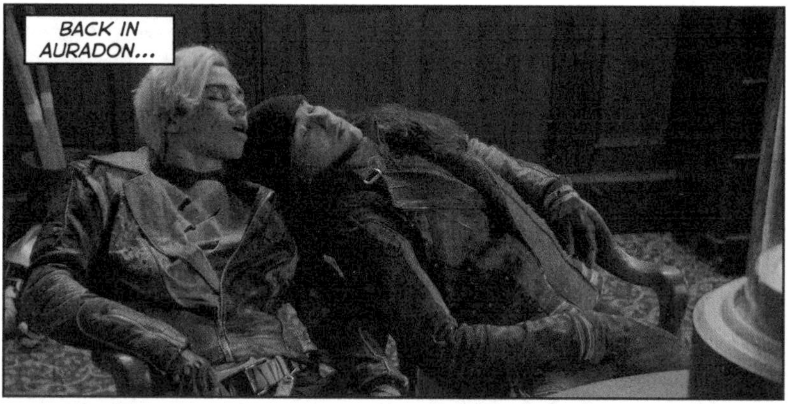
BACK IN AURADON...

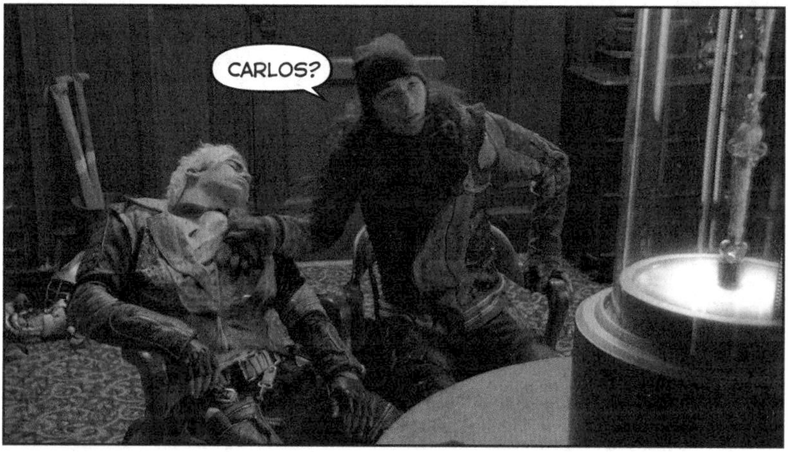
CARLOS?

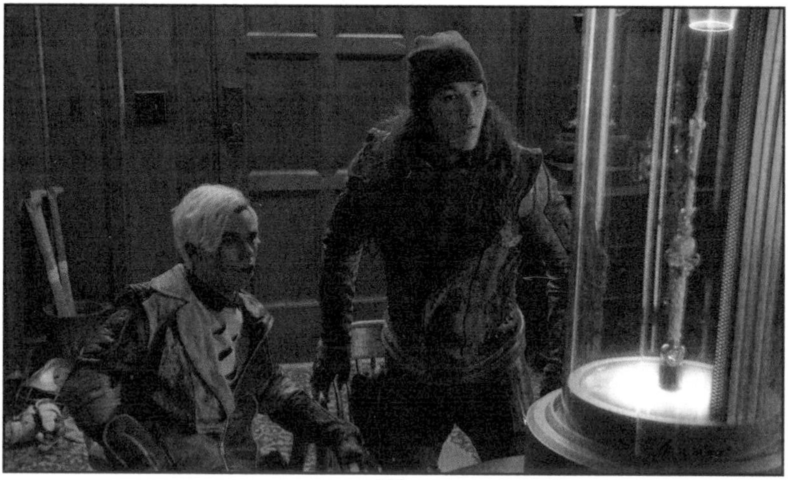

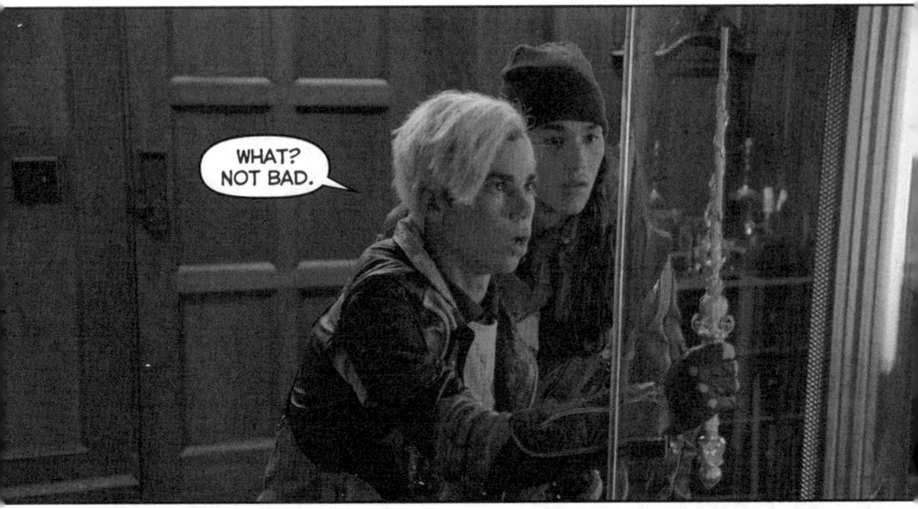
WHAT?
NOT BAD.

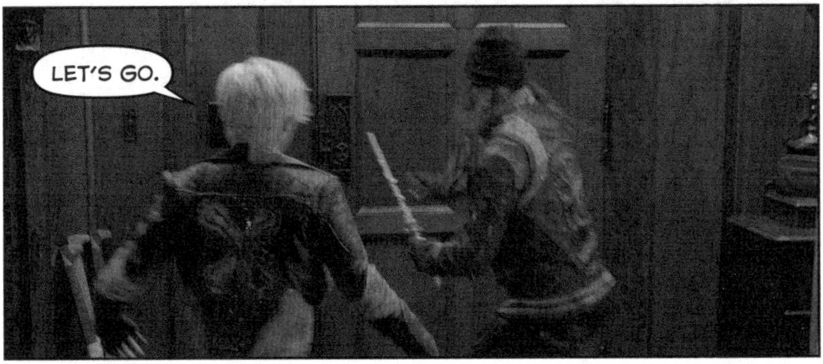
LET'S GO.

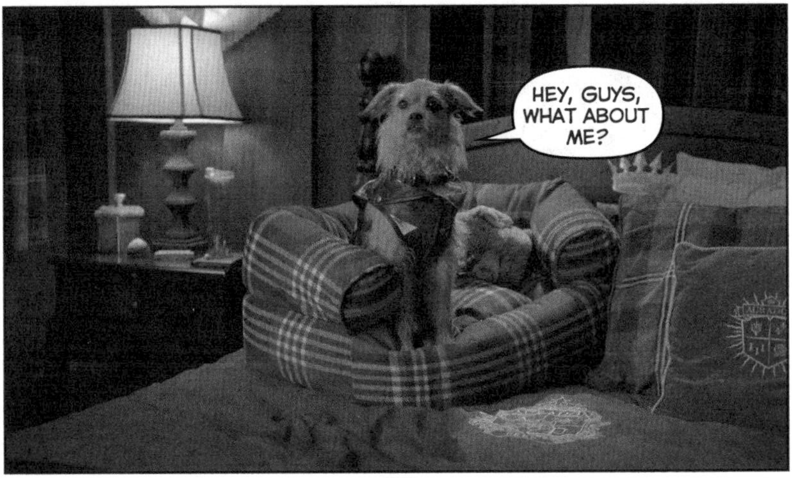
HEY, GUYS,
WHAT ABOUT
ME?

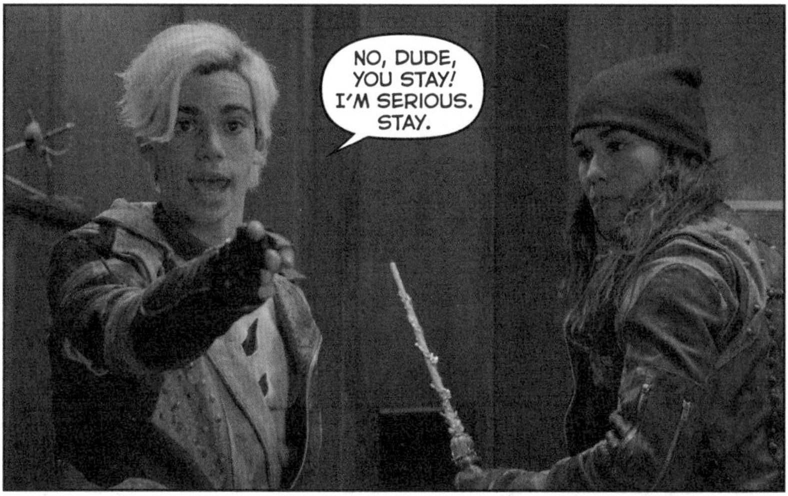
NO, DUDE, YOU STAY! I'M SERIOUS. STAY.

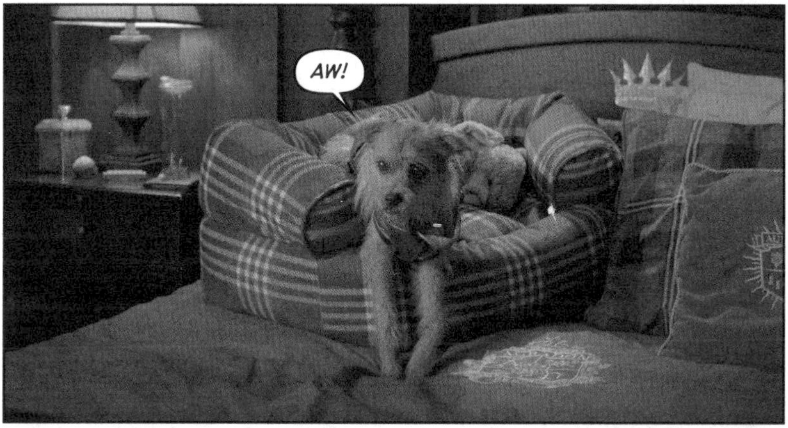
AW!

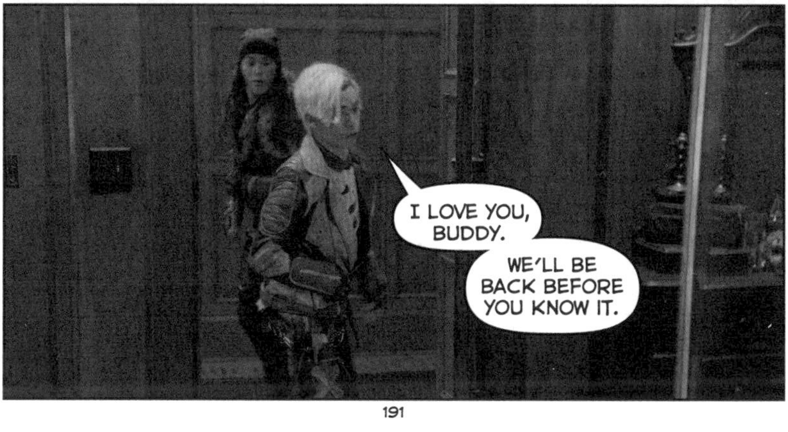
I LOVE YOU, BUDDY.
WE'LL BE BACK BEFORE YOU KNOW IT.

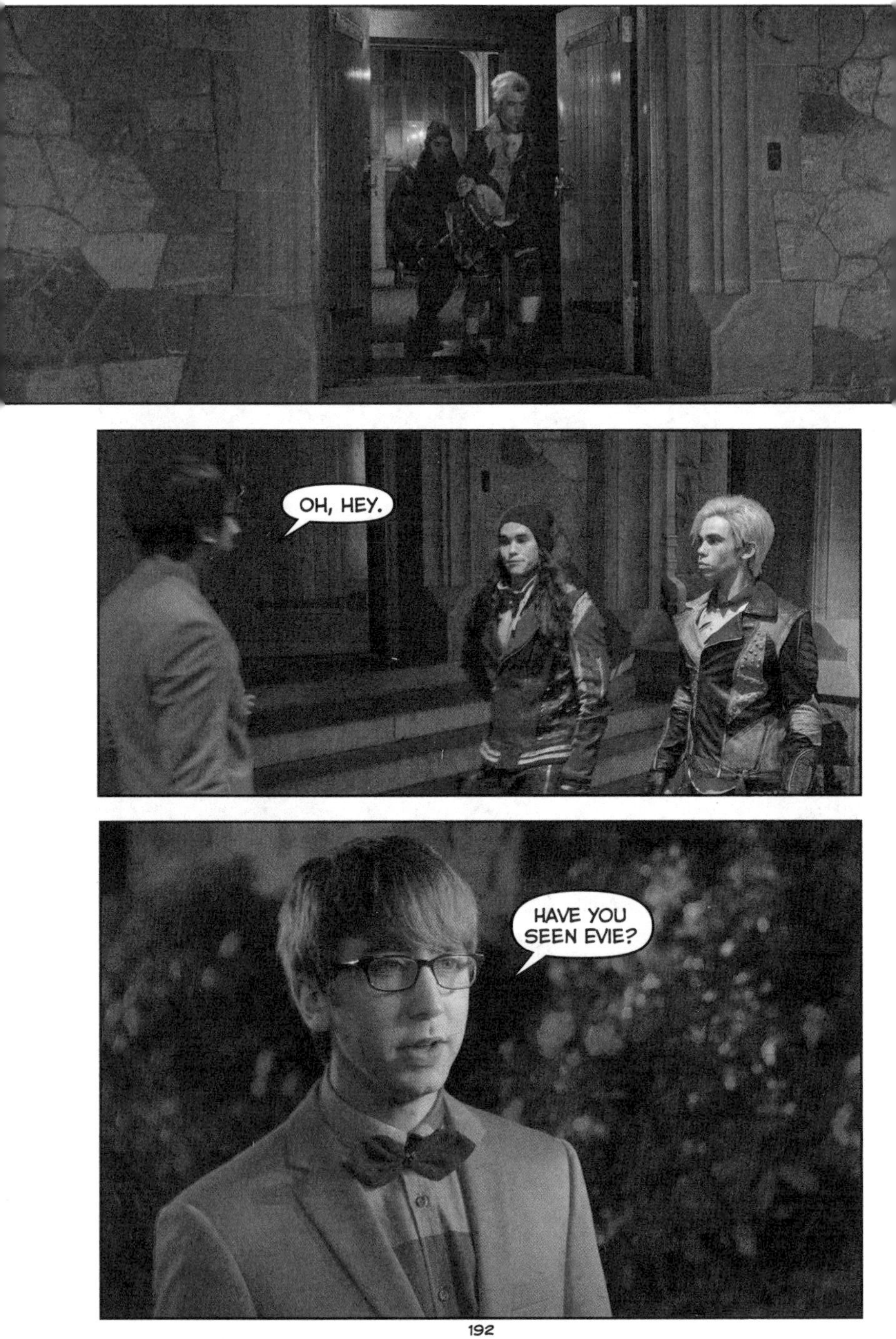
OH, HEY.
HAVE YOU SEEN EVIE?

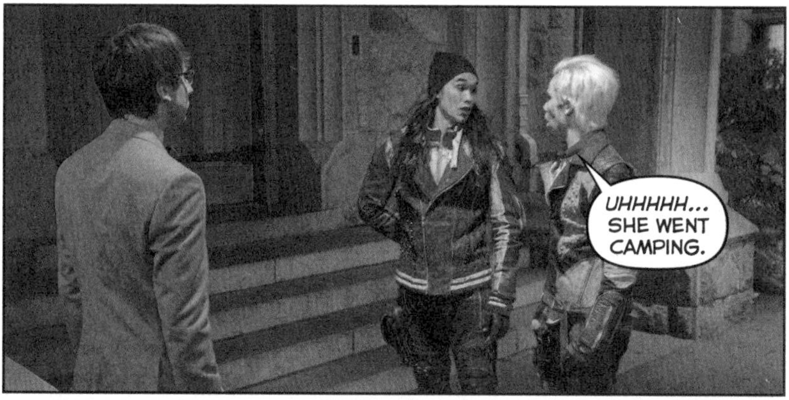
UHHHHH...
SHE WENT
CAMPING.

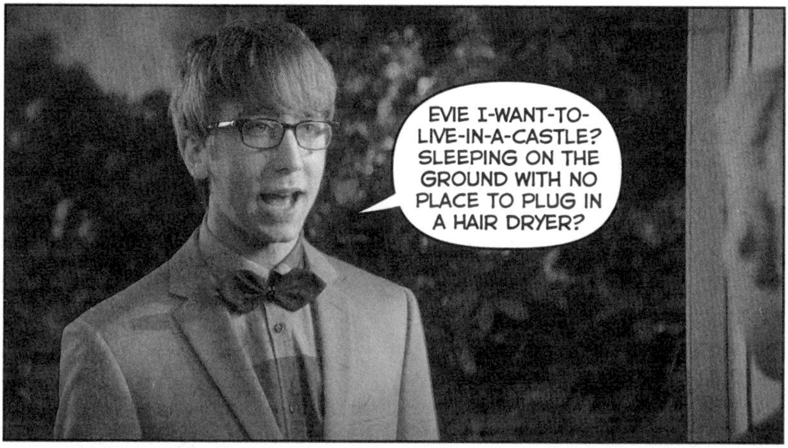
EVIE I-WANT-TO-
LIVE-IN-A-CASTLE?
SLEEPING ON THE
GROUND WITH NO
PLACE TO PLUG IN
A HAIR DRYER?

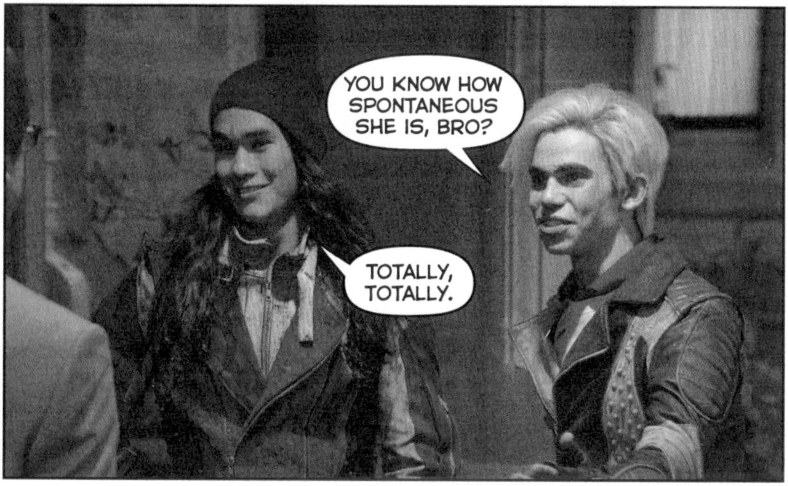
YOU KNOW HOW
SPONTANEOUS
SHE IS, BRO?
TOTALLY,
TOTALLY.

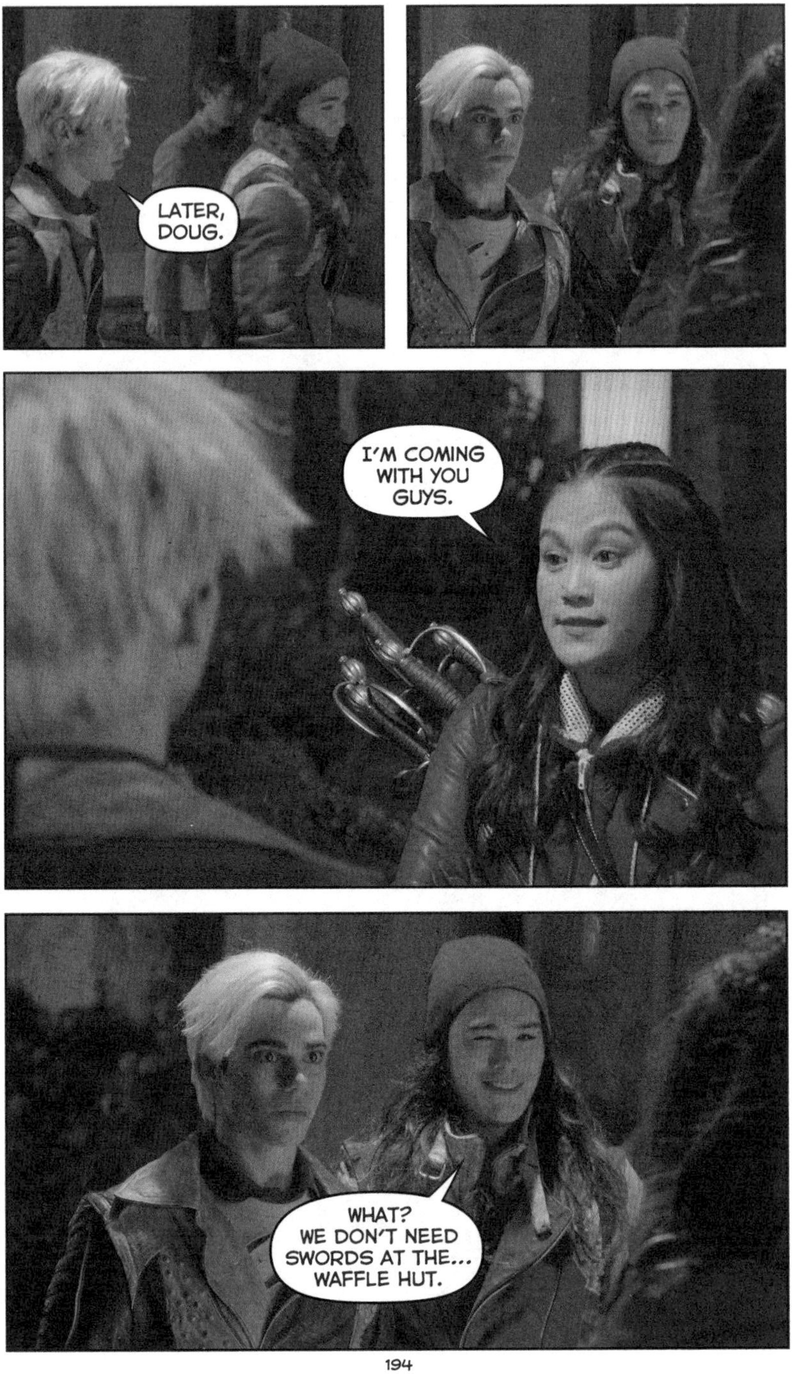
LATER, DOUG.
I'M COMING WITH YOU GUYS.
WHAT? WE DON'T NEED SWORDS AT THE... WAFFLE HUT.

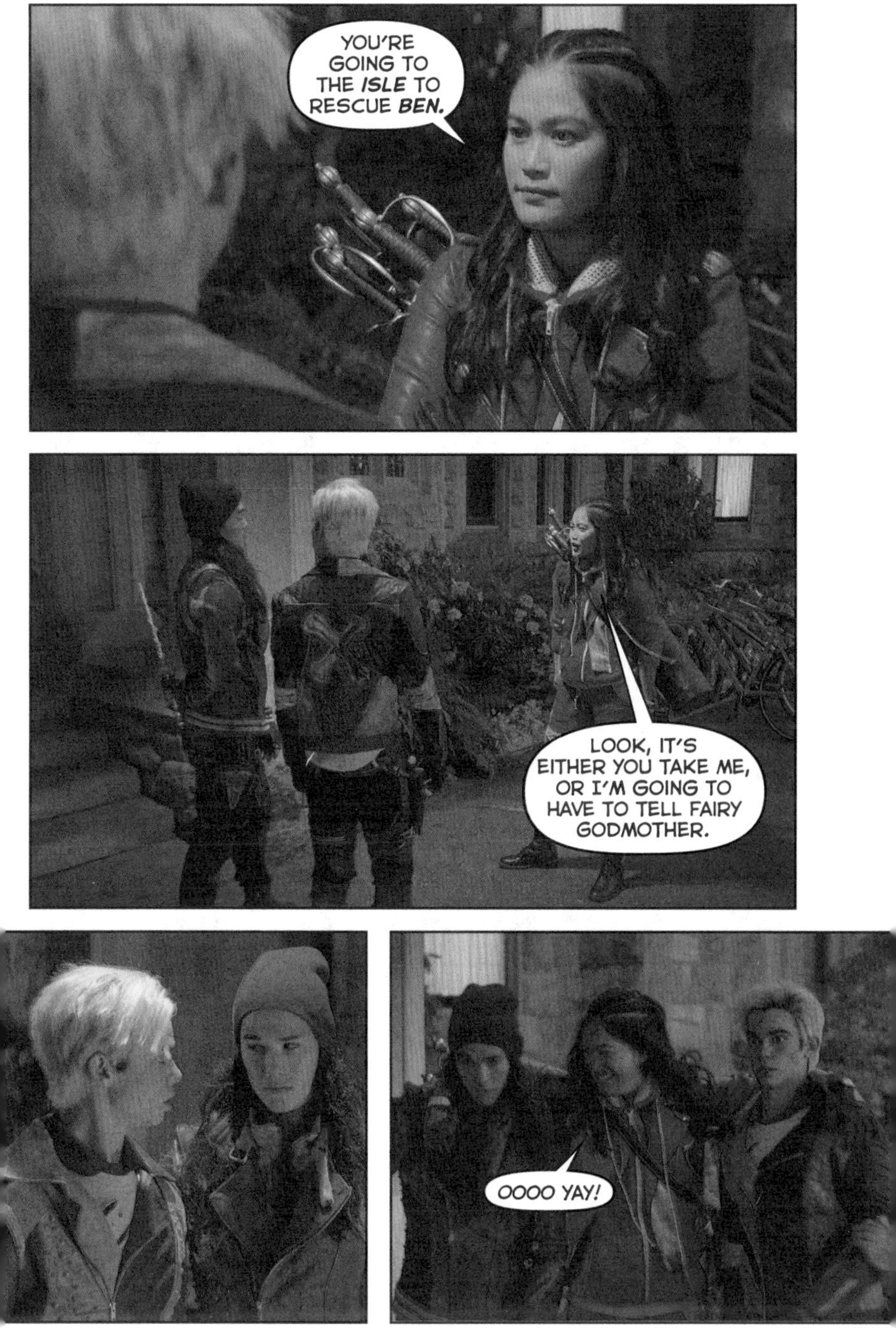
YOU'RE GOING TO THE *ISLE* TO RESCUE *BEN.*
LOOK, IT'S EITHER YOU TAKE ME, OR I'M GOING TO HAVE TO TELL FAIRY GODMOTHER.
OOOO YAY!

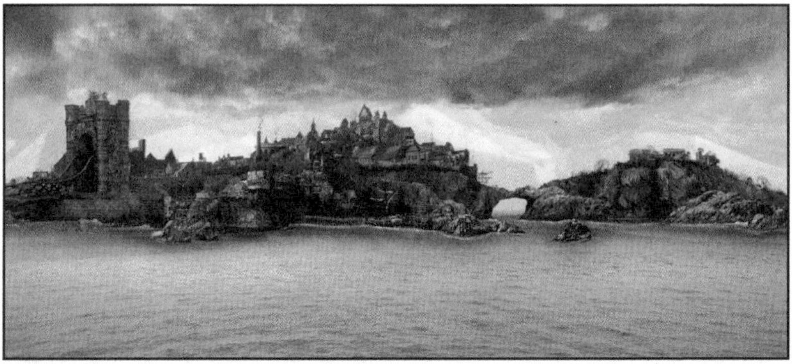

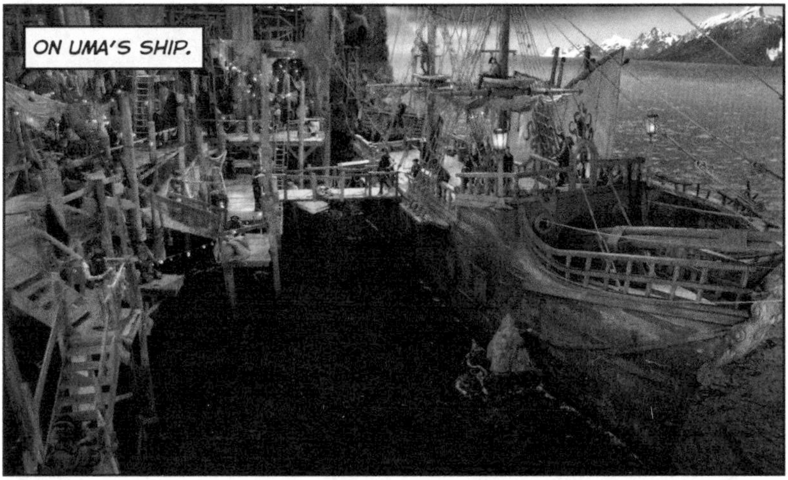
ON UMA'S SHIP.

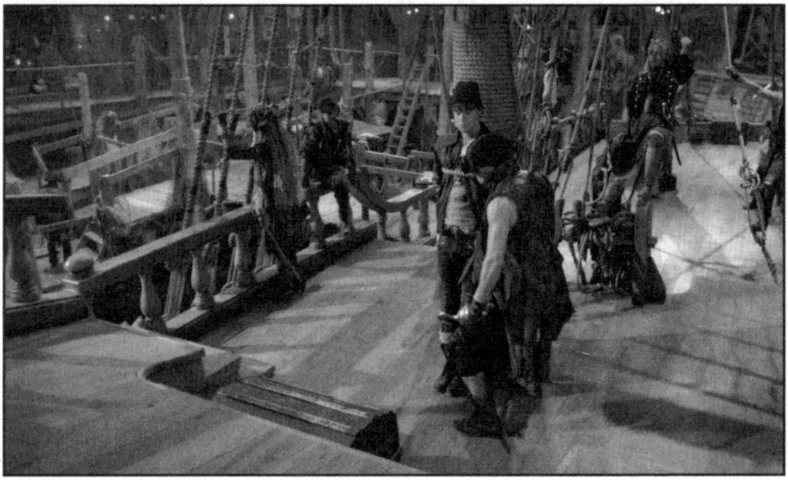

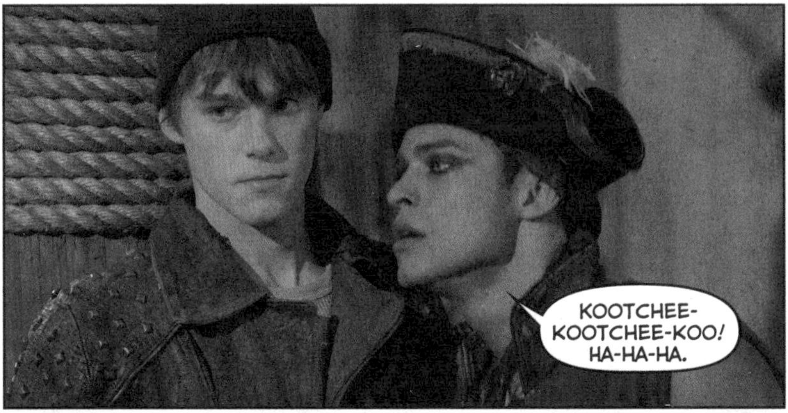
KOOTCHEE-KOOTCHEE-KOO! HA-HA-HA.

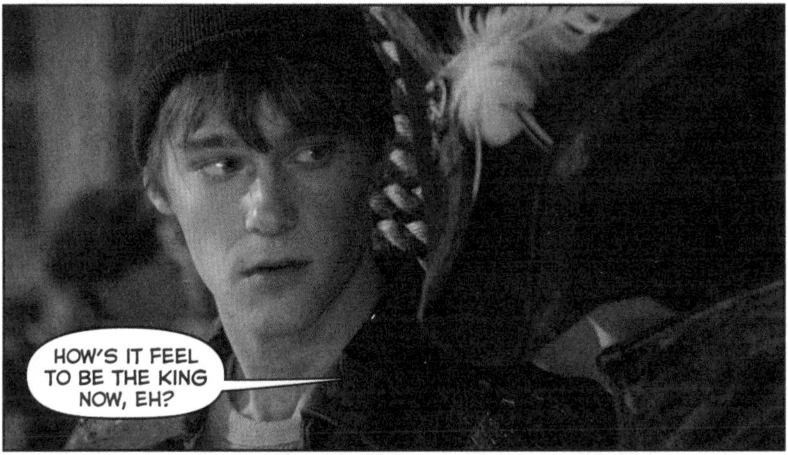
HOW'S IT FEEL TO BE THE KING NOW, EH?

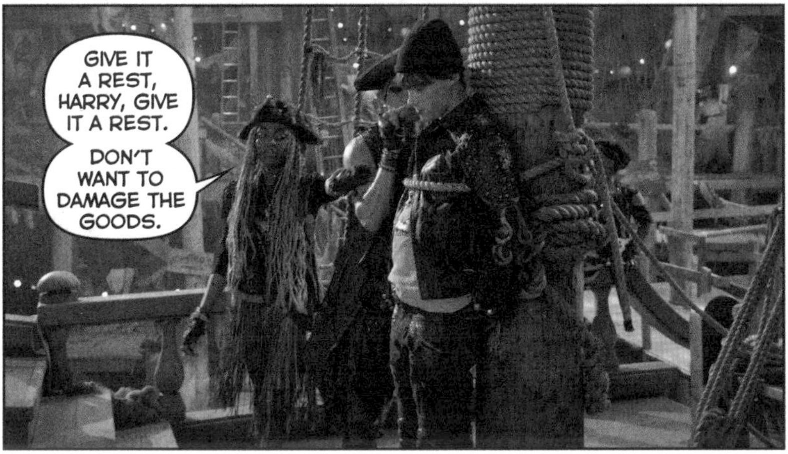
GIVE IT A REST, HARRY, GIVE IT A REST.
DON'T WANT TO DAMAGE THE GOODS.

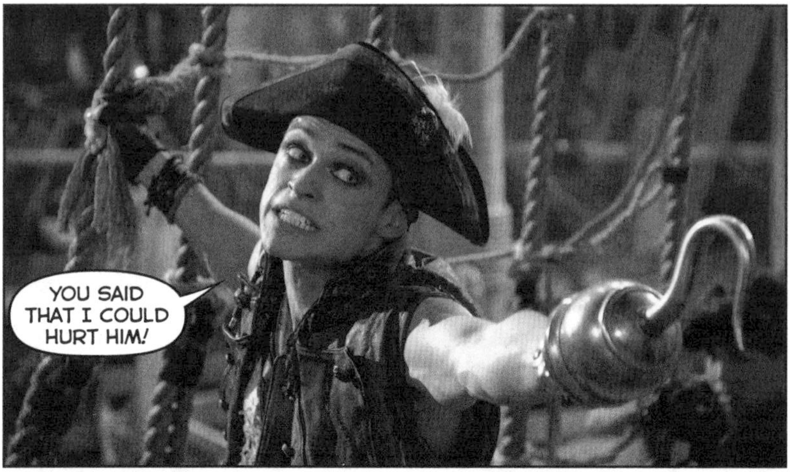
YOU SAID THAT I COULD HURT HIM!

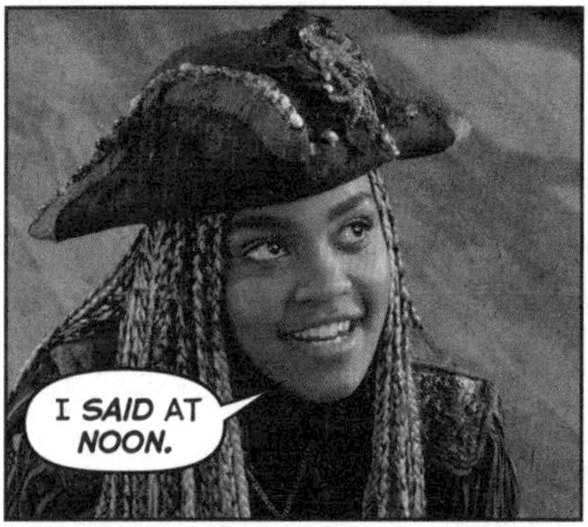
I *SAID* AT *NOON.*

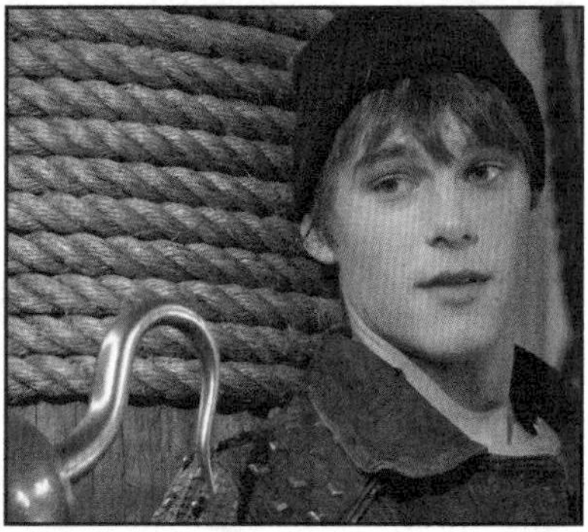

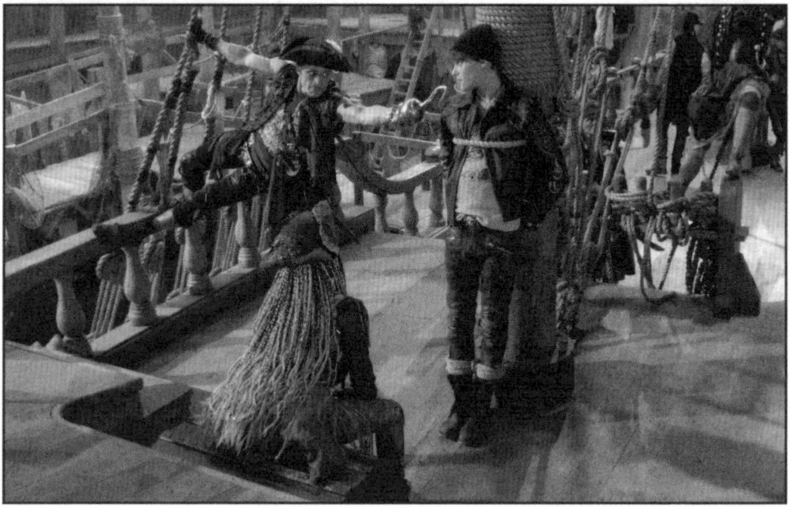

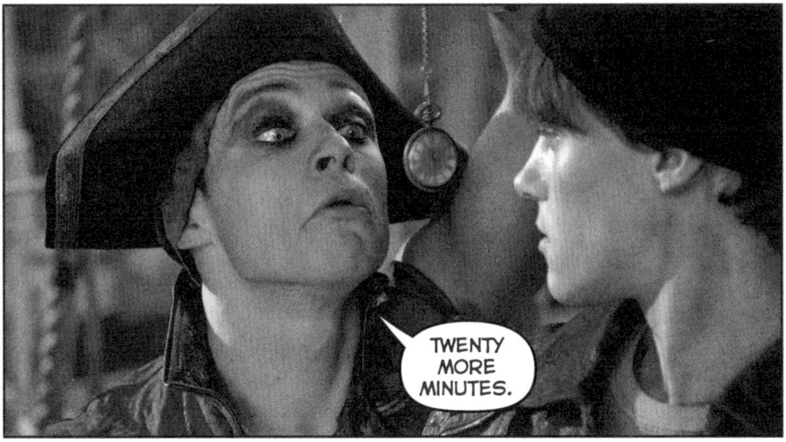
TWENTY MORE MINUTES.

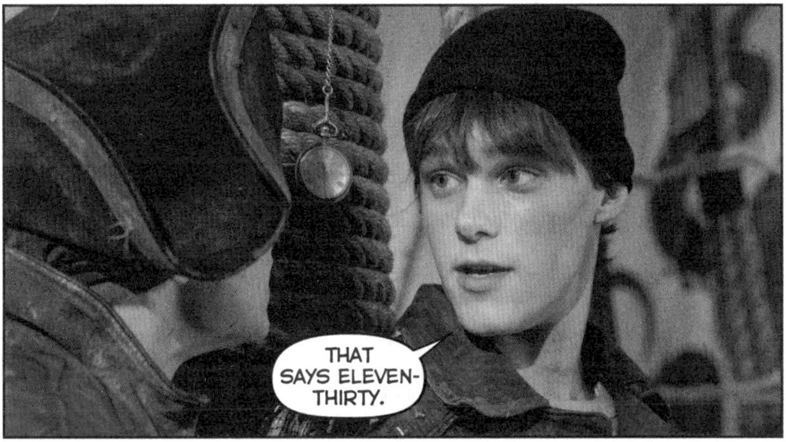
THAT SAYS ELEVEN-THIRTY.

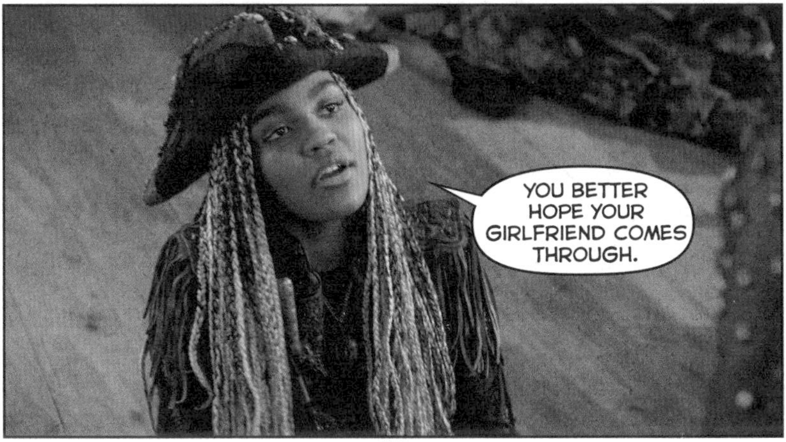
YOU BETTER HOPE YOUR GIRLFRIEND COMES THROUGH.

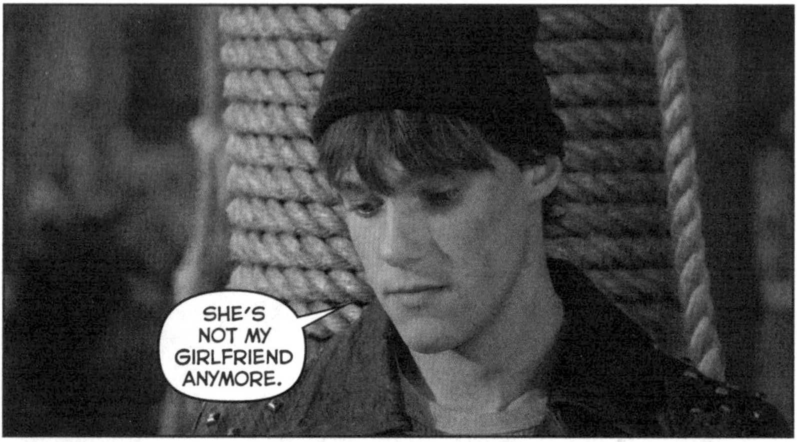
SHE'S NOT MY GIRLFRIEND ANYMORE.

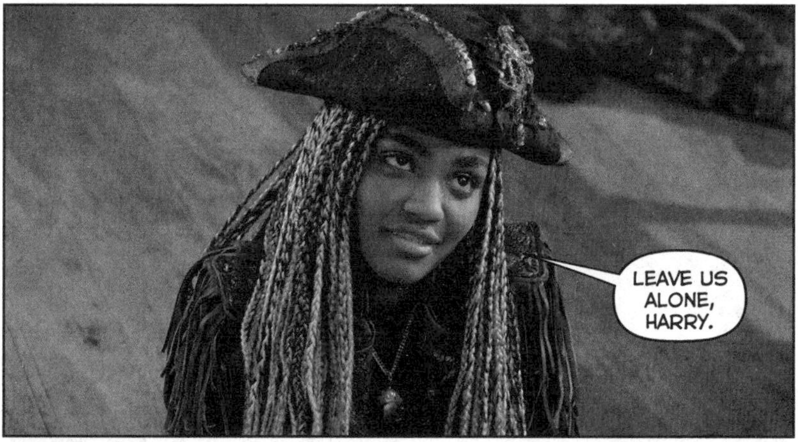
LEAVE US ALONE, HARRY.

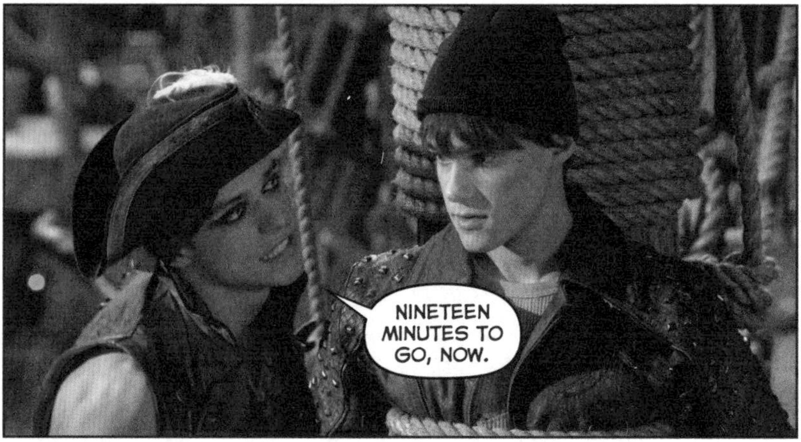
NINETEEN MINUTES TO GO, NOW.

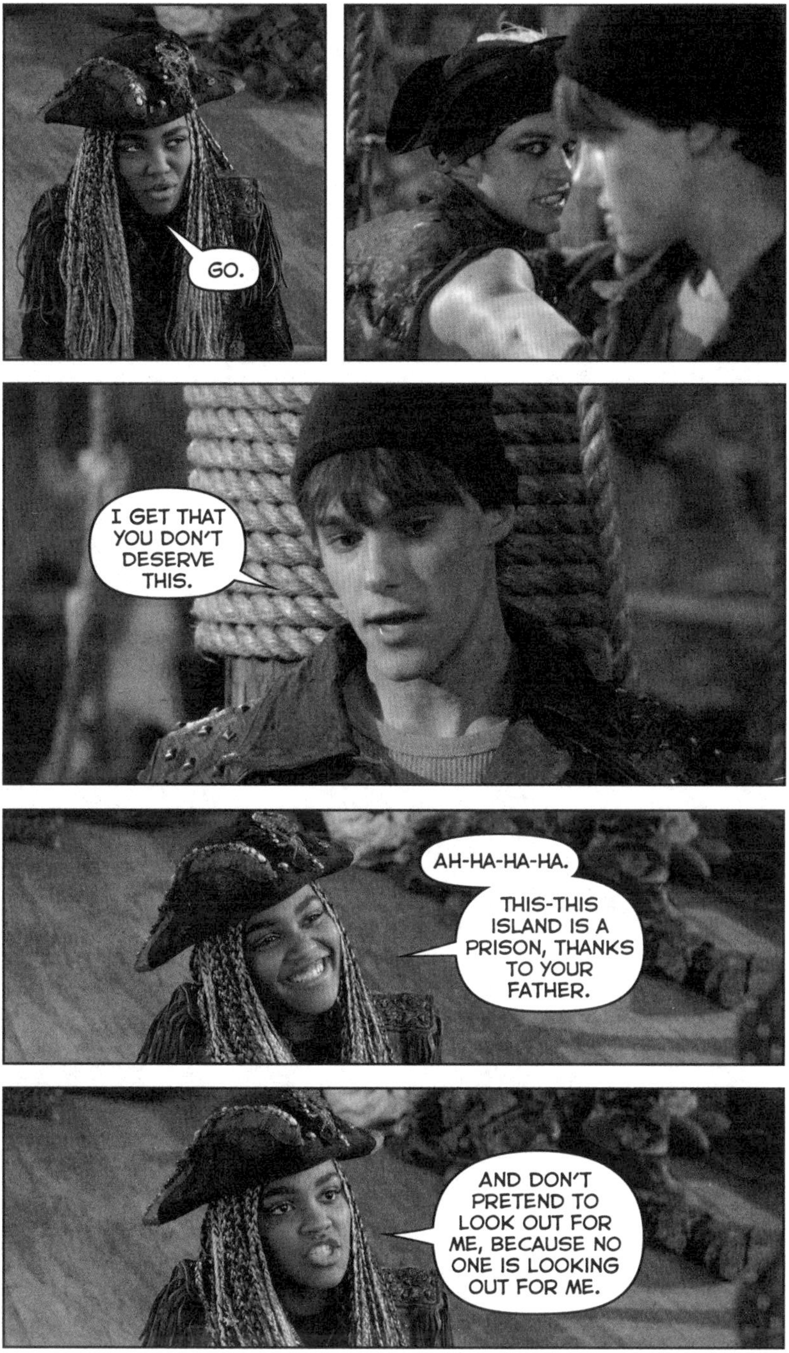
GO.
I GET THAT YOU DON'T DESERVE THIS.
AH-HA-HA-HA.
THIS-THIS ISLAND IS A PRISON, THANKS TO YOUR FATHER.
AND DON'T PRETEND TO LOOK OUT FOR ME, BECAUSE NO ONE IS LOOKING OUT FOR ME.

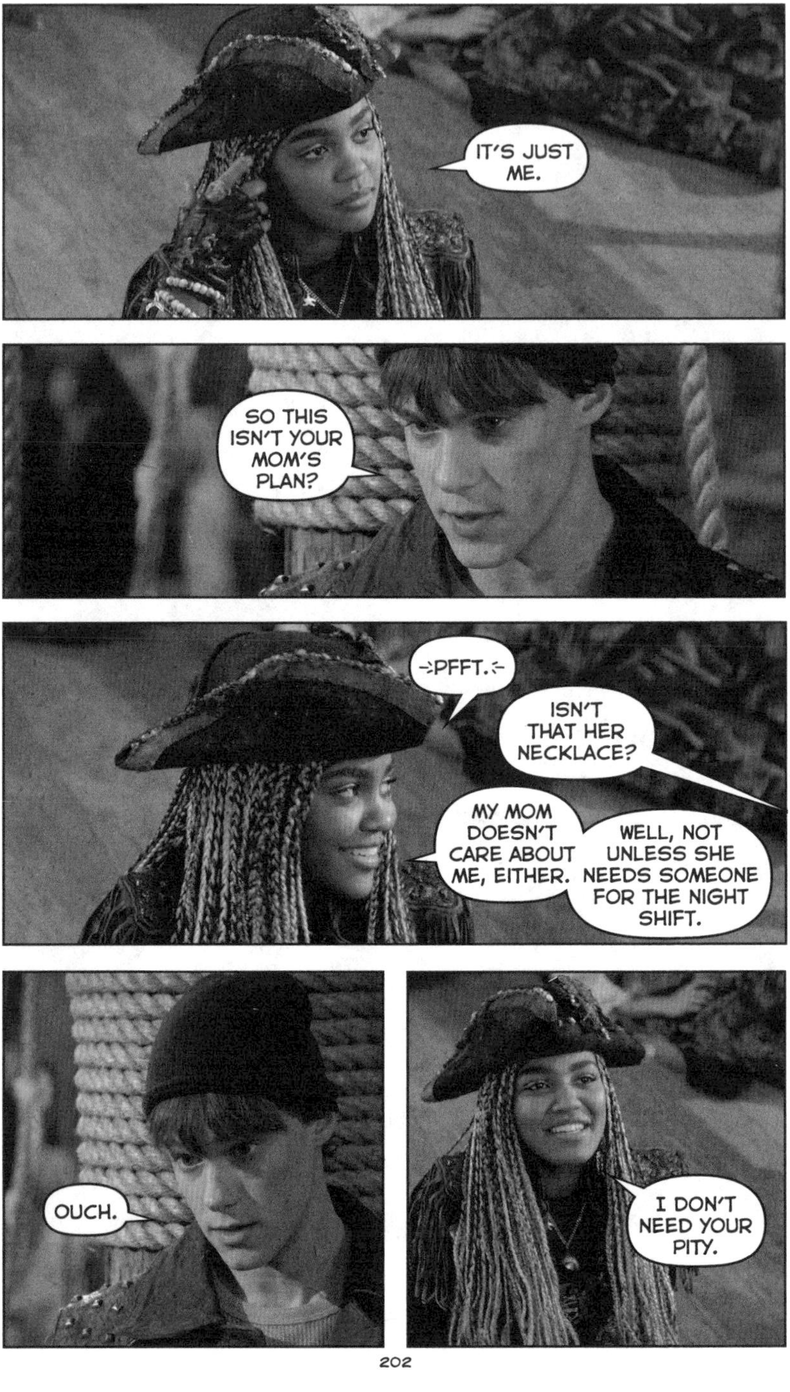
IT'S JUST ME.
SO THIS ISN'T YOUR MOM'S PLAN?
PFFT.
ISN'T THAT HER NECKLACE?
MY MOM DOESN'T CARE ABOUT ME, EITHER.
WELL, NOT UNLESS SHE NEEDS SOMEONE FOR THE NIGHT SHIFT.
OUCH.
I DON'T NEED YOUR PITY.

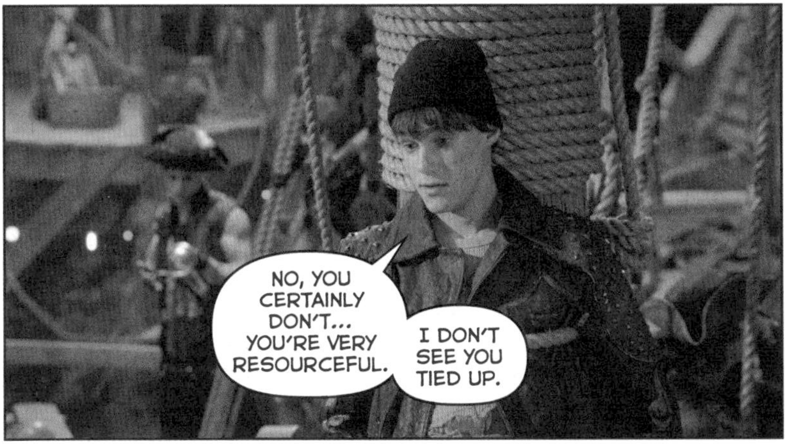
NO, YOU CERTAINLY DON'T... YOU'RE VERY RESOURCEFUL.
I DON'T SEE YOU TIED UP.

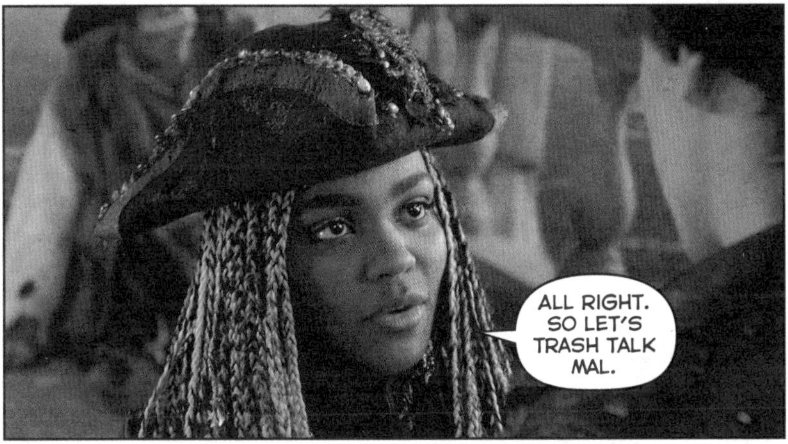
ALL RIGHT. SO LET'S TRASH TALK MAL.

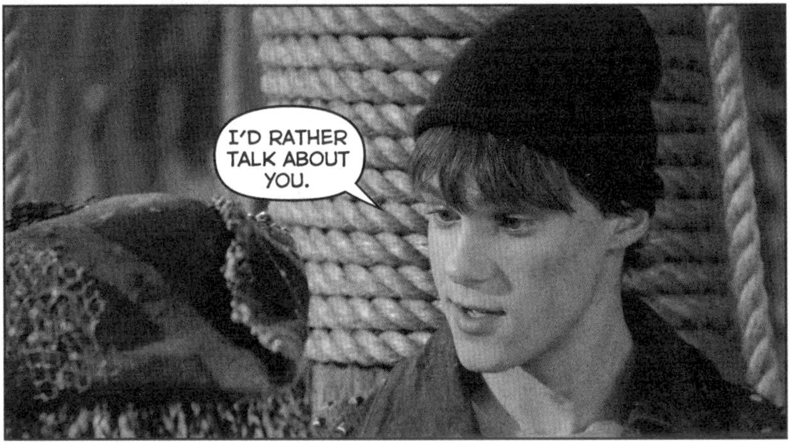
I'D RATHER TALK ABOUT YOU.

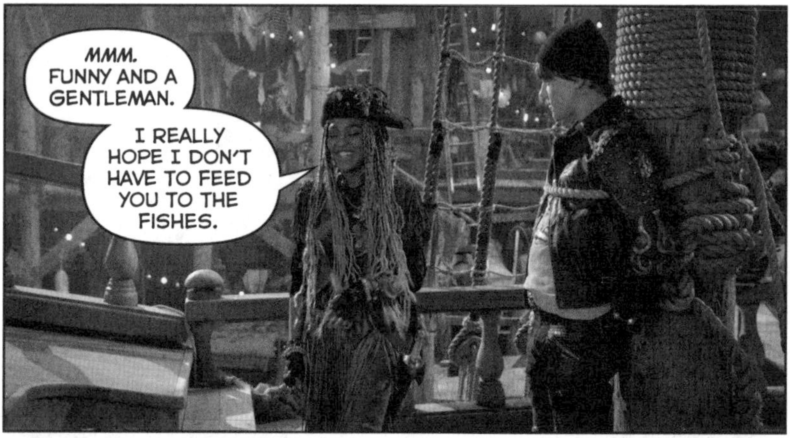
MMM. FUNNY AND A GENTLEMAN.
I REALLY HOPE I DON'T HAVE TO FEED YOU TO THE FISHES.

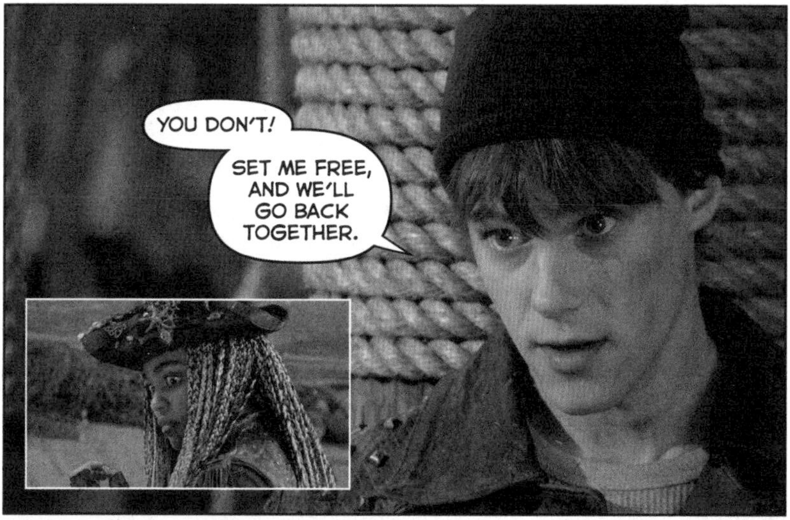
YOU DON'T!
SET ME FREE, AND WE'LL GO BACK TOGETHER.

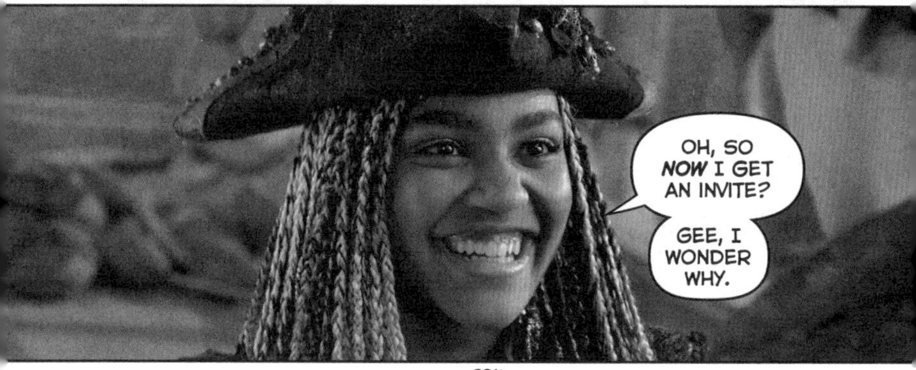
OH, SO *NOW* I GET AN INVITE?
GEE, I WONDER WHY.

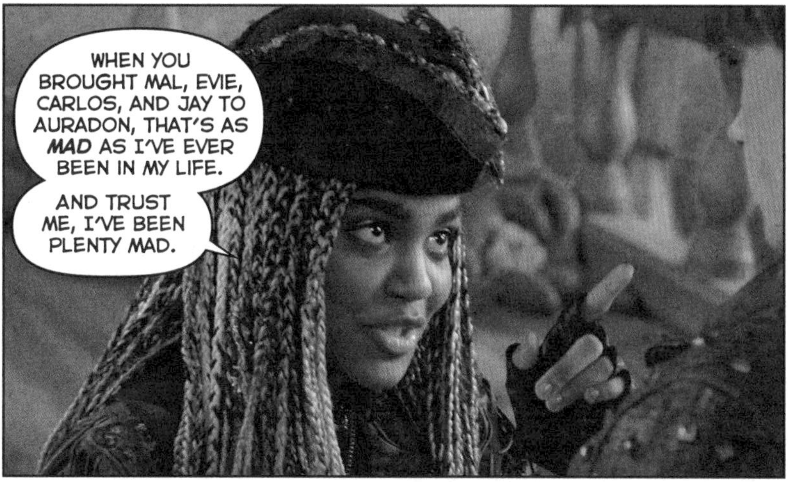
WHEN YOU BROUGHT MAL, EVIE, CARLOS, AND JAY TO AURADON, THAT'S AS ***MAD*** AS I'VE EVER BEEN IN MY LIFE.
AND TRUST ME, I'VE BEEN PLENTY MAD.

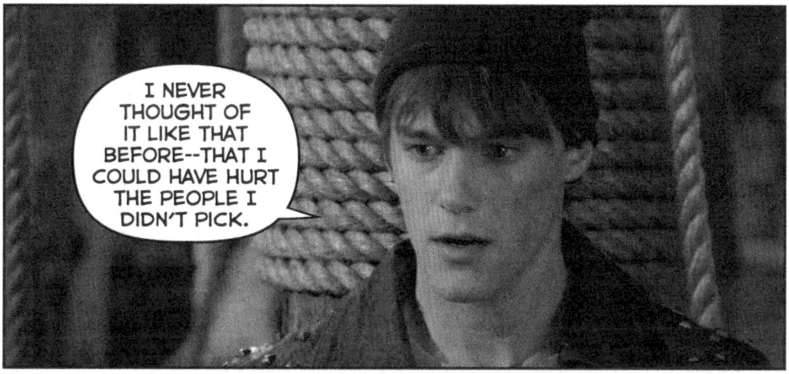
I NEVER THOUGHT OF IT LIKE THAT BEFORE--THAT I COULD HAVE HURT THE PEOPLE I DIDN'T PICK.

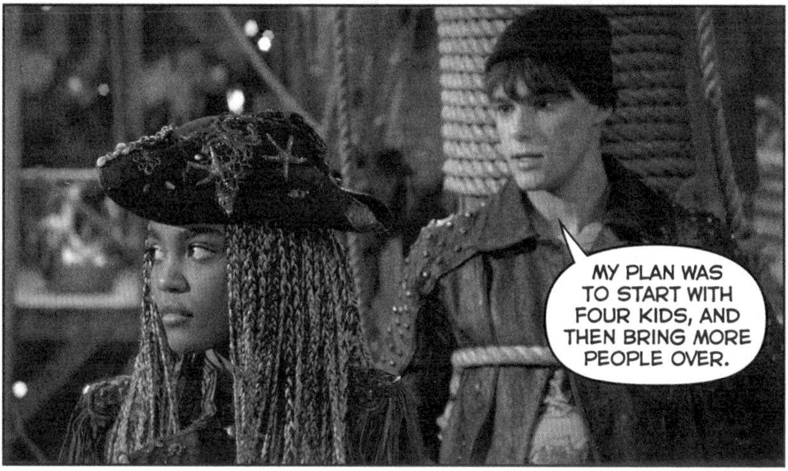
MY PLAN WAS TO START WITH FOUR KIDS, AND THEN BRING MORE PEOPLE OVER.

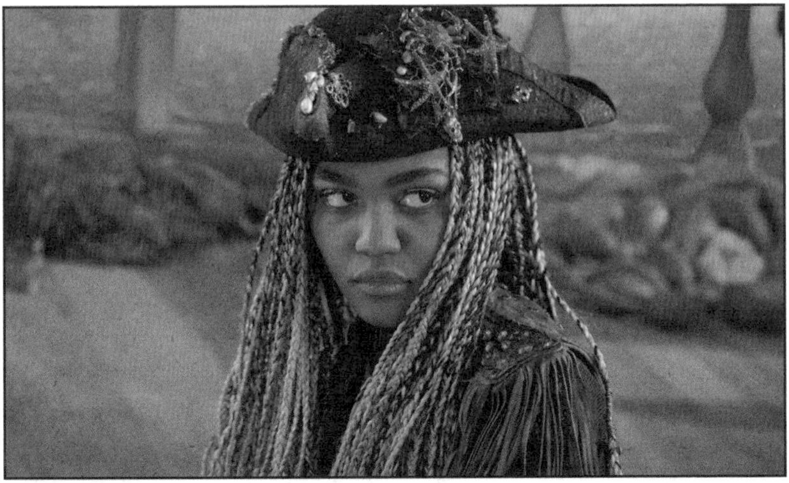

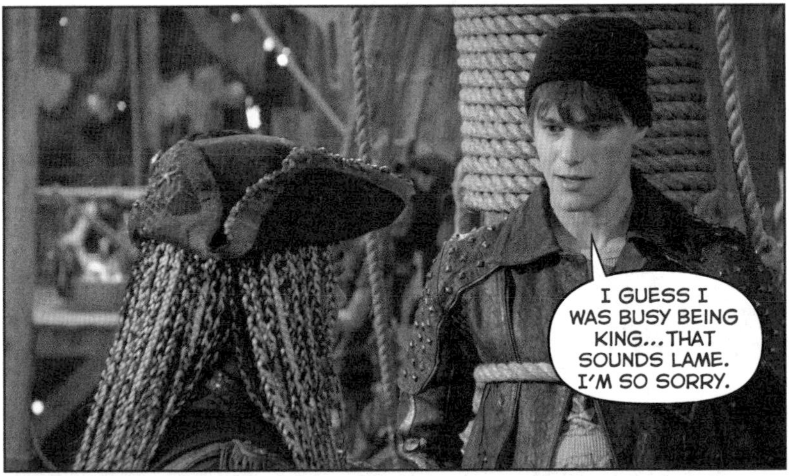
I GUESS I WAS BUSY BEING KING...THAT SOUNDS LAME. I'M SO SORRY.

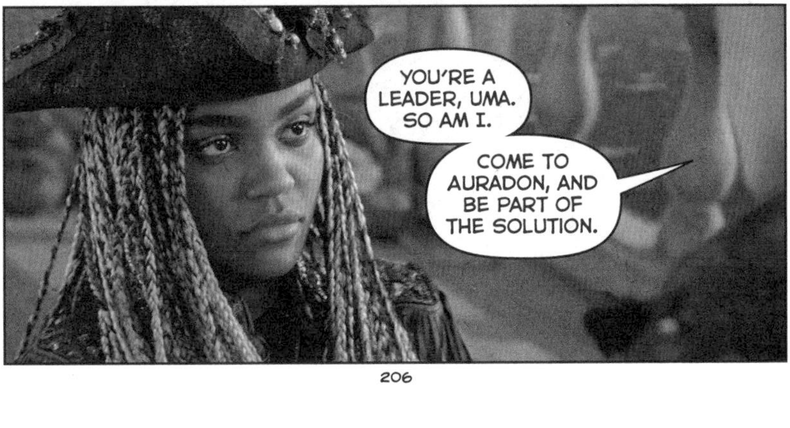
YOU'RE A LEADER, UMA. SO AM I.
COME TO AURADON, AND BE PART OF THE SOLUTION.

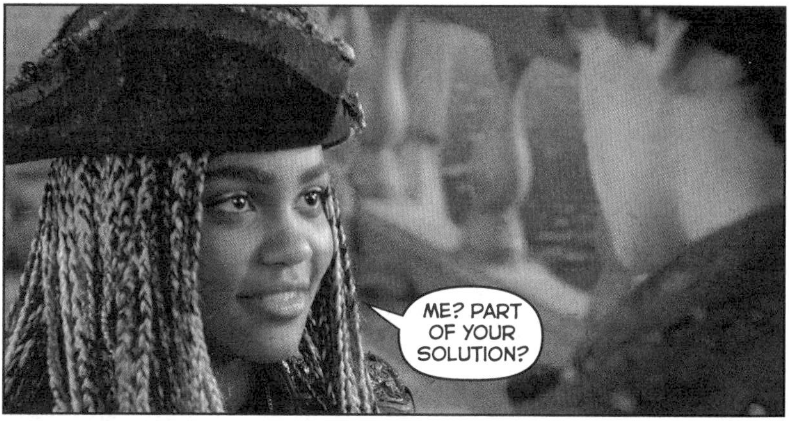
ME? PART OF YOUR SOLUTION?

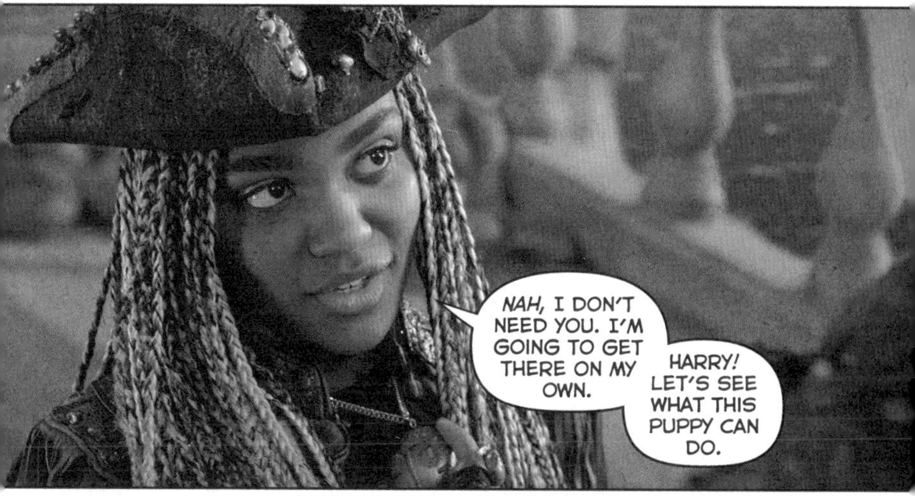
NAH, I DON'T NEED YOU. I'M GOING TO GET THERE ON MY OWN.
HARRY! LET'S SEE WHAT THIS PUPPY CAN DO.

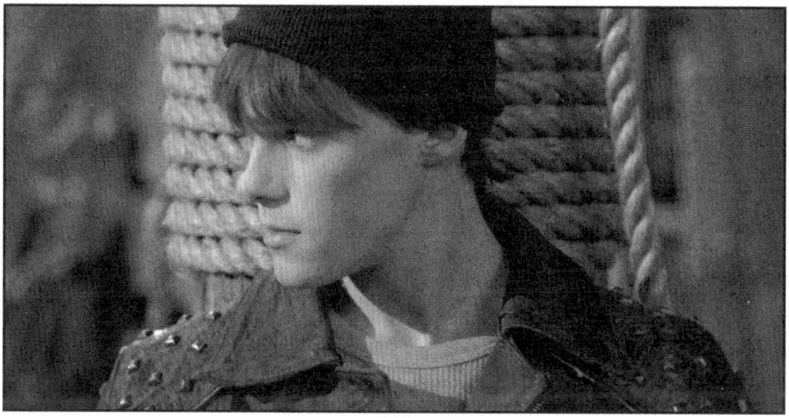

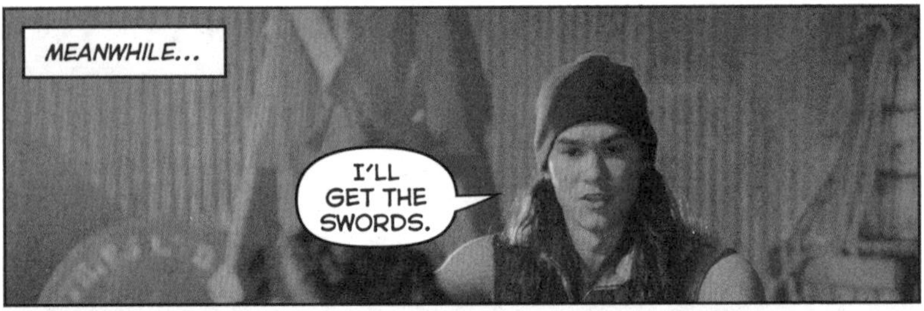
MEANWHILE...
I'LL GET THE SWORDS.

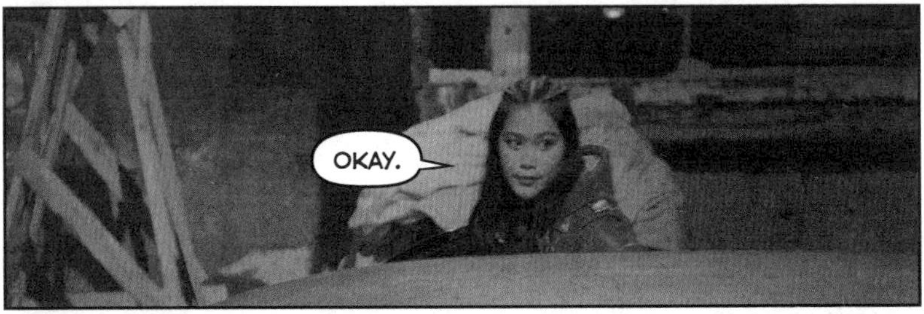
OKAY.

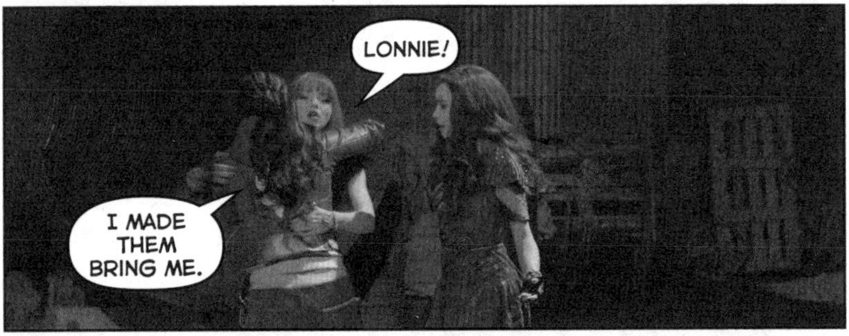
LONNIE!
I MADE THEM BRING ME.

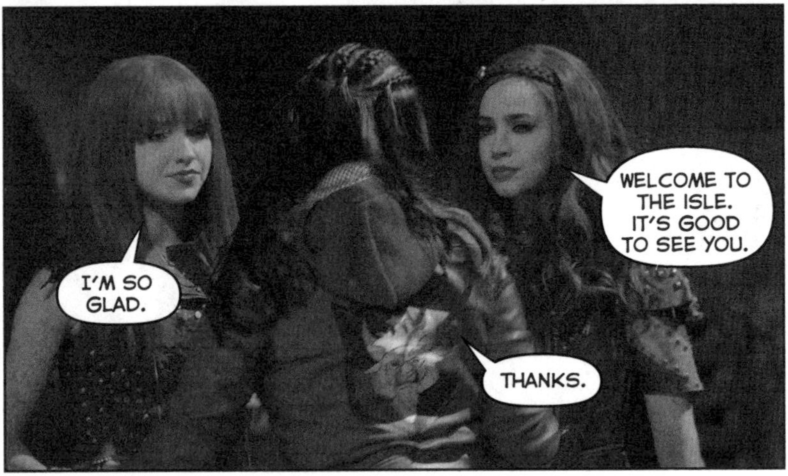
WELCOME TO THE ISLE. IT'S GOOD TO SEE YOU.
I'M SO GLAD.
THANKS.

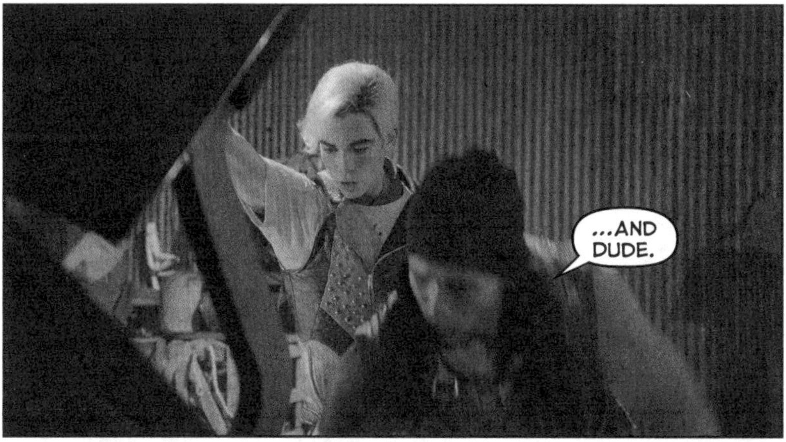
...AND
DUDE.

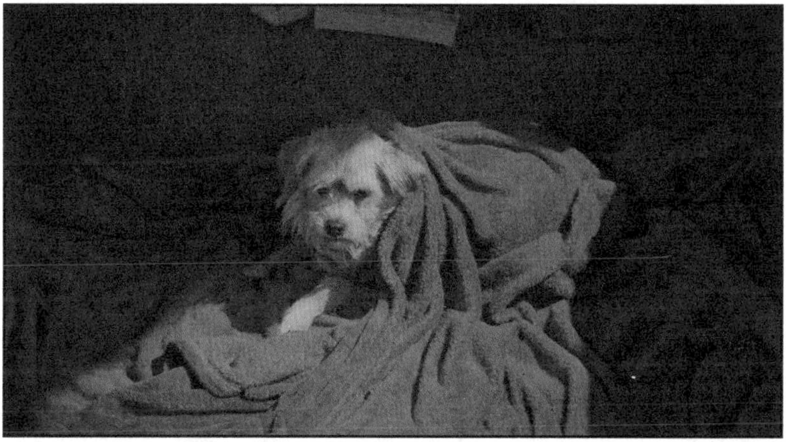

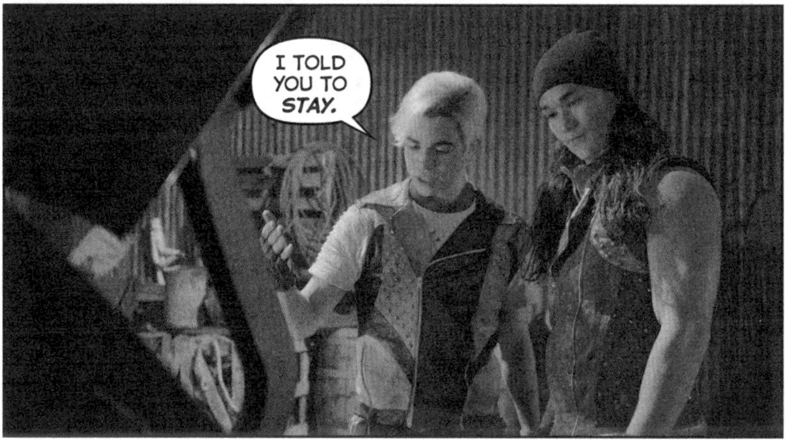
I TOLD
YOU TO
STAY.

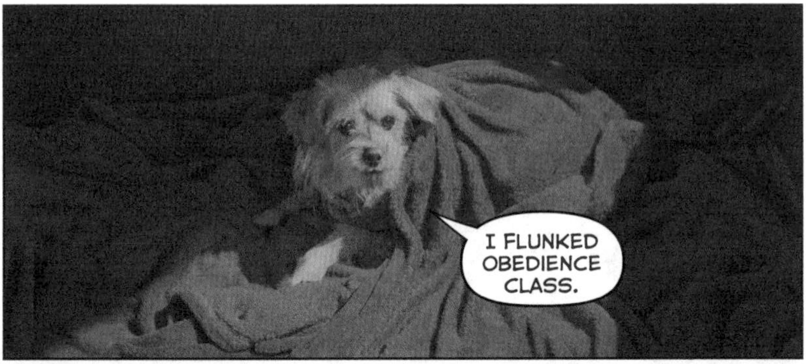
I FLUNKED OBEDIENCE CLASS.

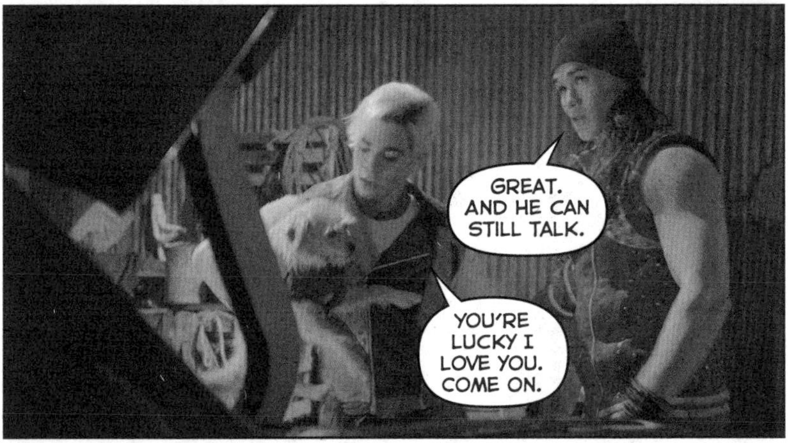
GREAT. AND HE CAN STILL TALK.
YOU'RE LUCKY I LOVE YOU. COME ON.

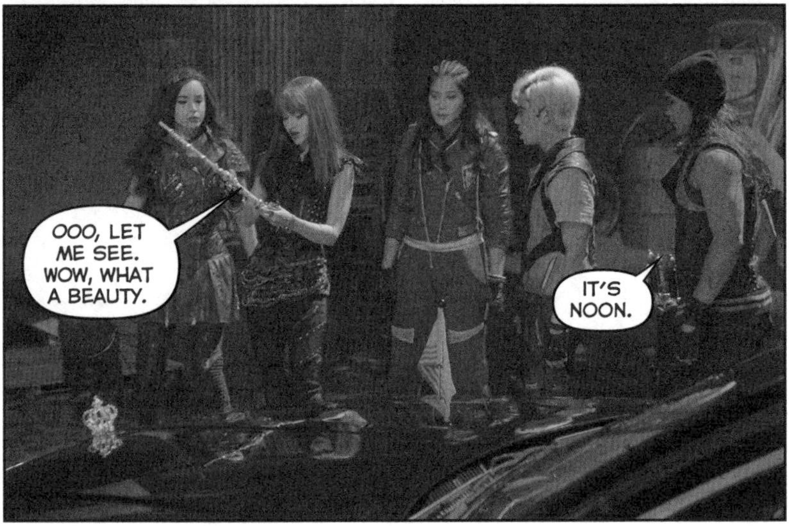
OOO, LET ME SEE. WOW, WHAT A BEAUTY.
IT'S NOON.

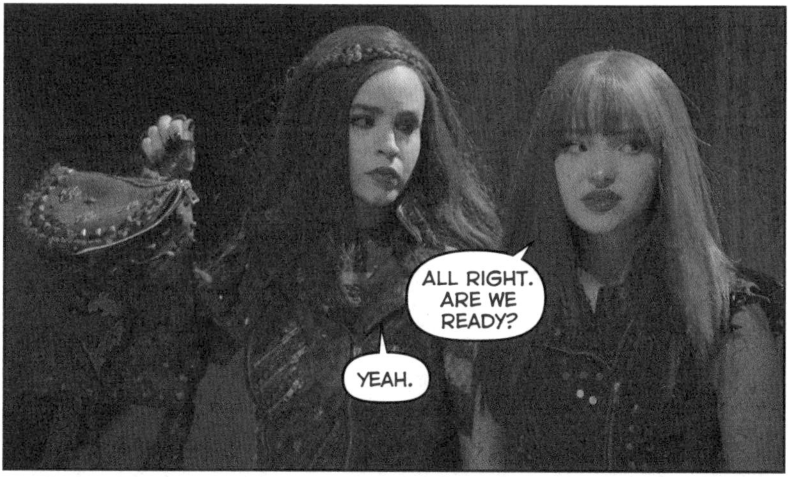
ALL RIGHT. ARE WE READY?
YEAH.

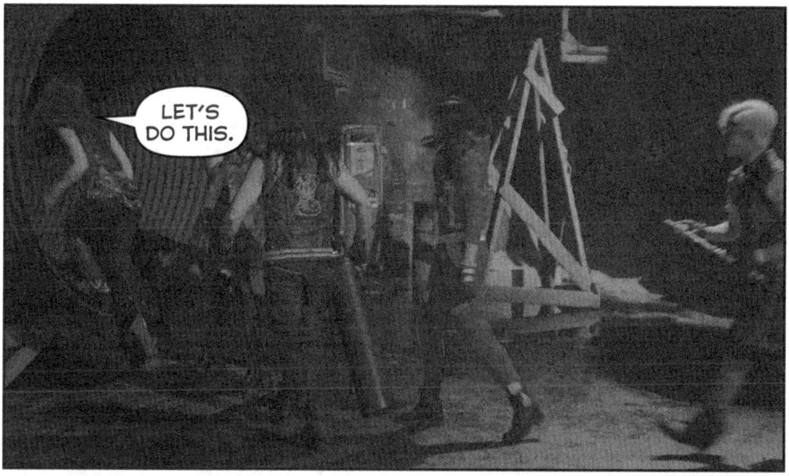
LET'S DO THIS.

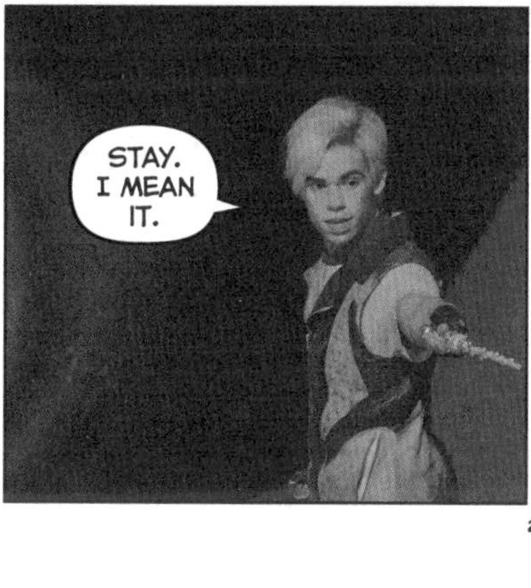
STAY. I MEAN IT.

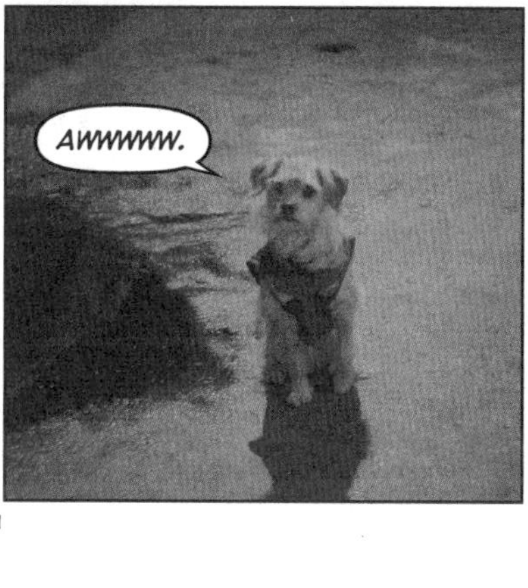
AWWWWW.

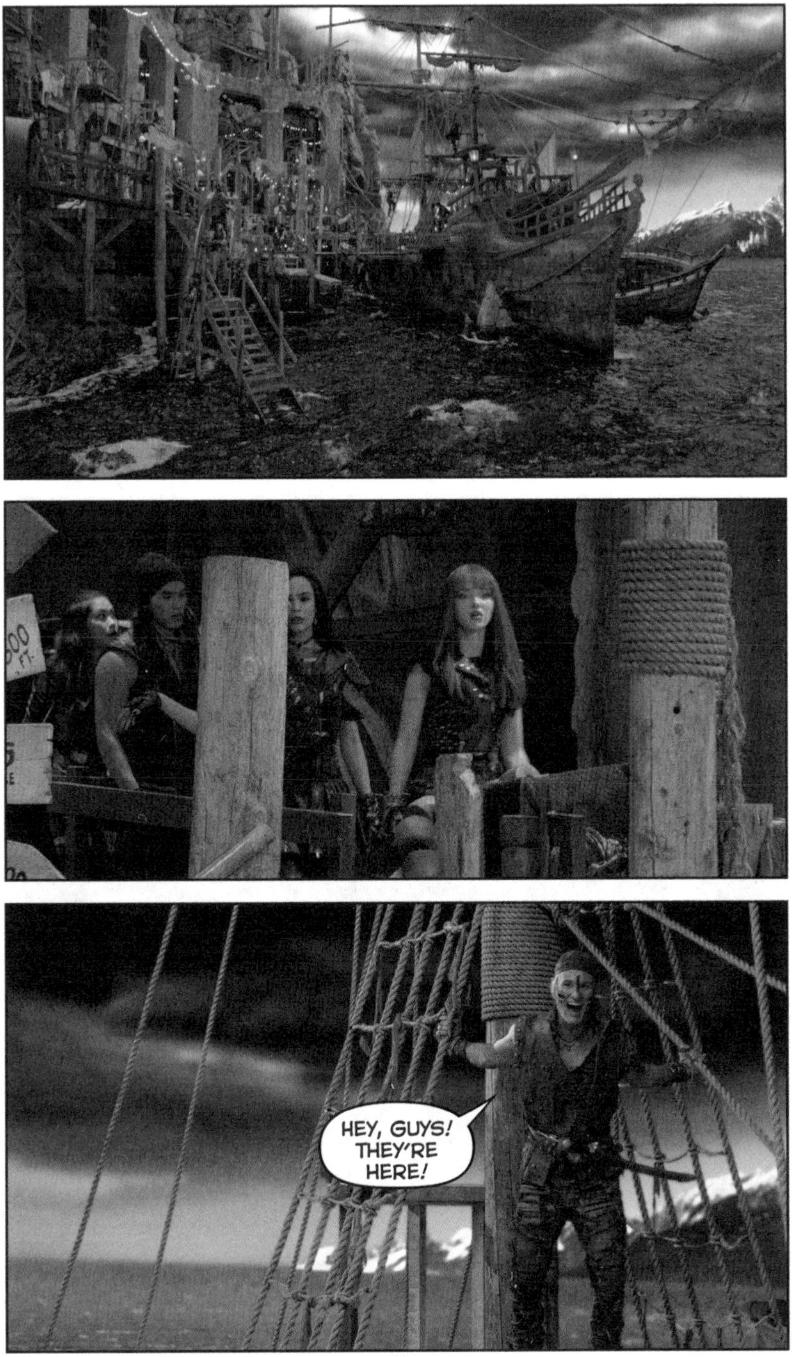
HEY, GUYS!
THEY'RE
HERE!

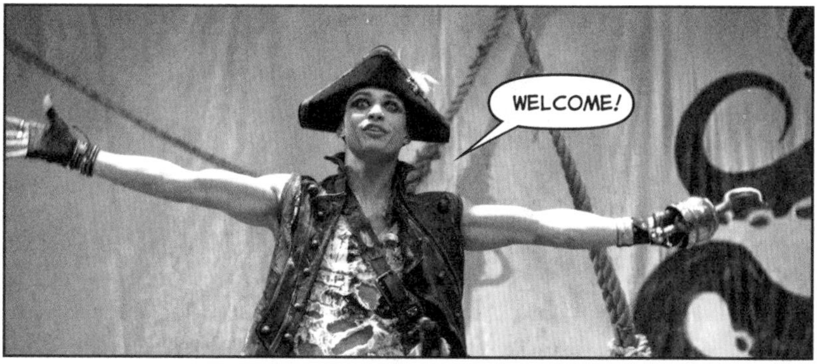
WELCOME!

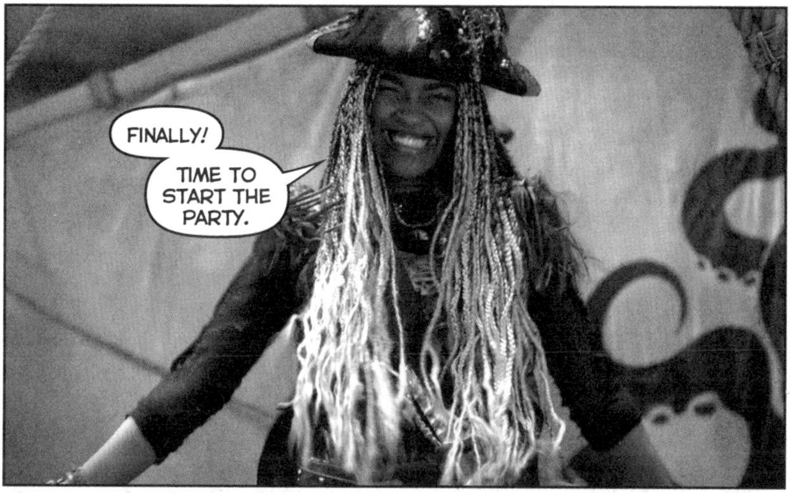
FINALLY!
TIME TO START THE PARTY.

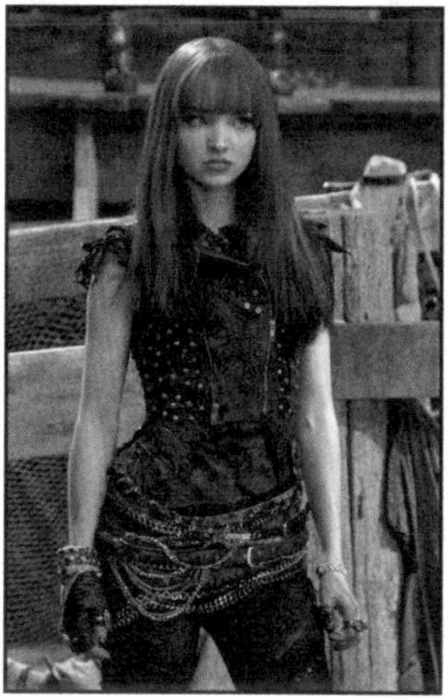

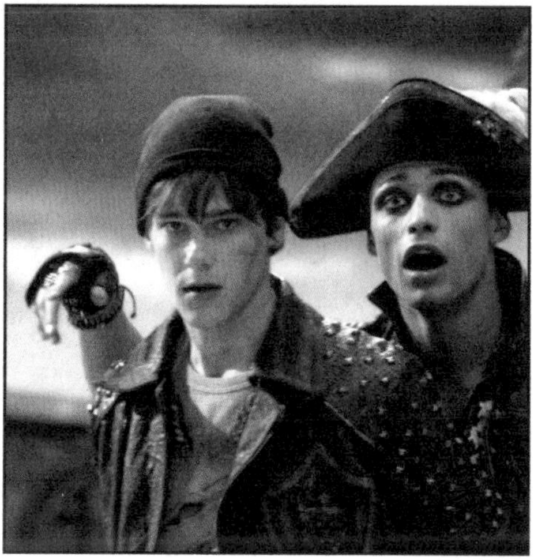

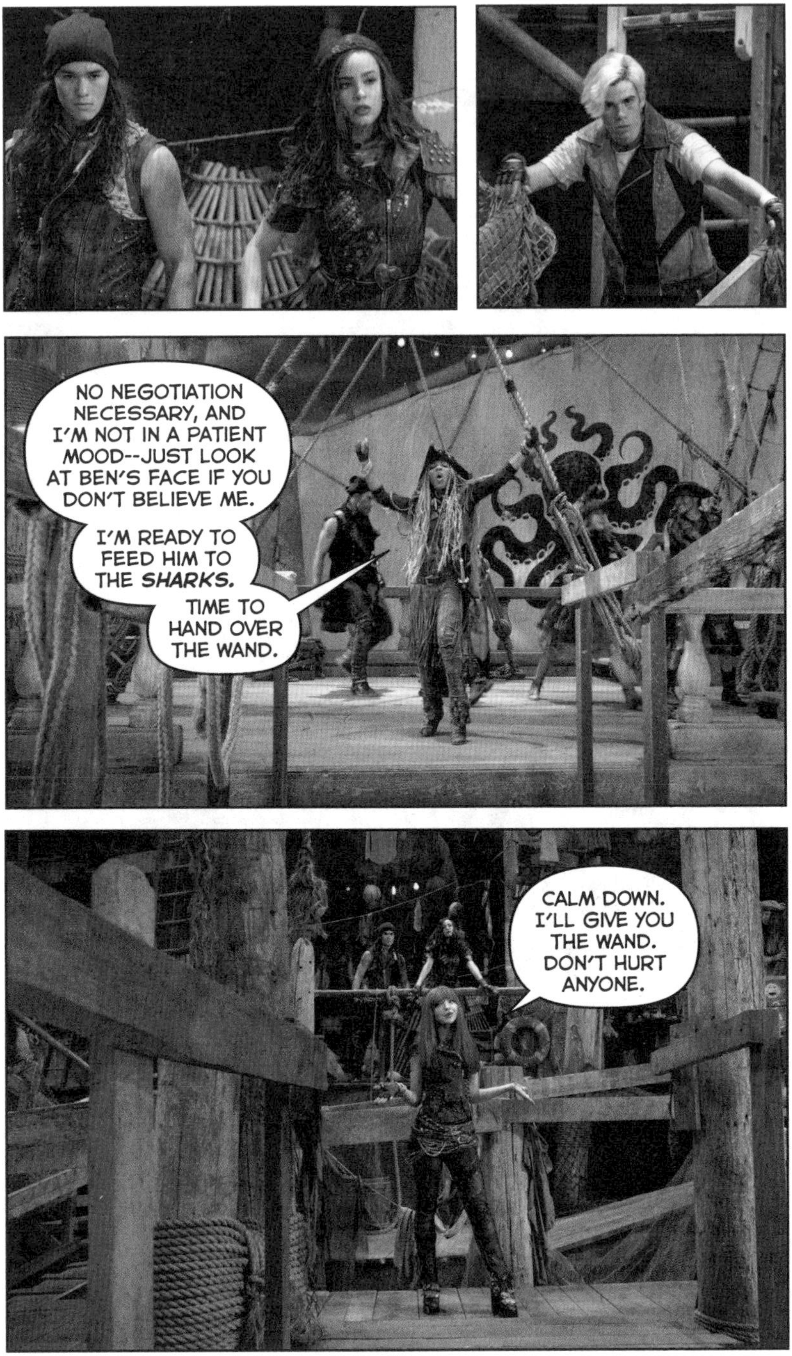
NO NEGOTIATION NECESSARY, AND I'M NOT IN A PATIENT MOOD--JUST LOOK AT BEN'S FACE IF YOU DON'T BELIEVE ME.
I'M READY TO FEED HIM TO THE *SHARKS.*
TIME TO HAND OVER THE WAND.
CALM DOWN. I'LL GIVE YOU THE WAND. DON'T HURT ANYONE.

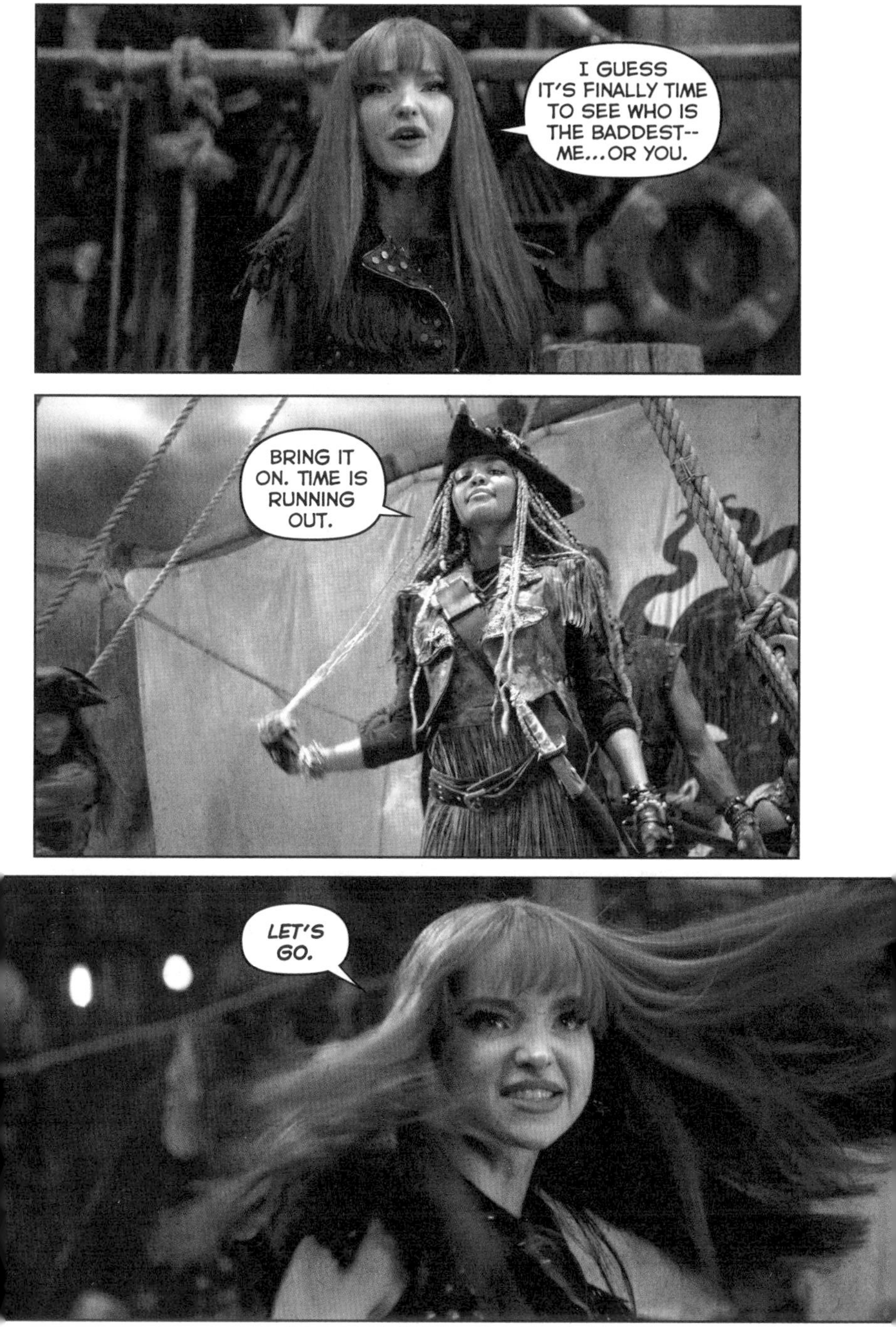
I GUESS IT'S FINALLY TIME TO SEE WHO IS THE BADDEST-- ME...OR YOU.
BRING IT ON. TIME IS RUNNING OUT.
LET'S GO.

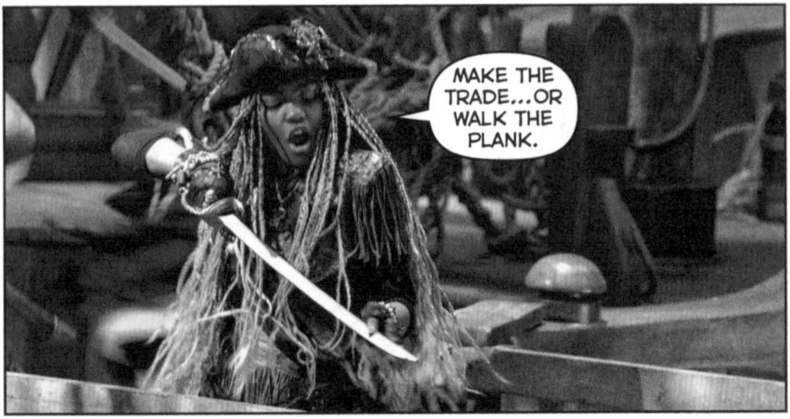
MAKE THE TRADE...OR WALK THE PLANK.

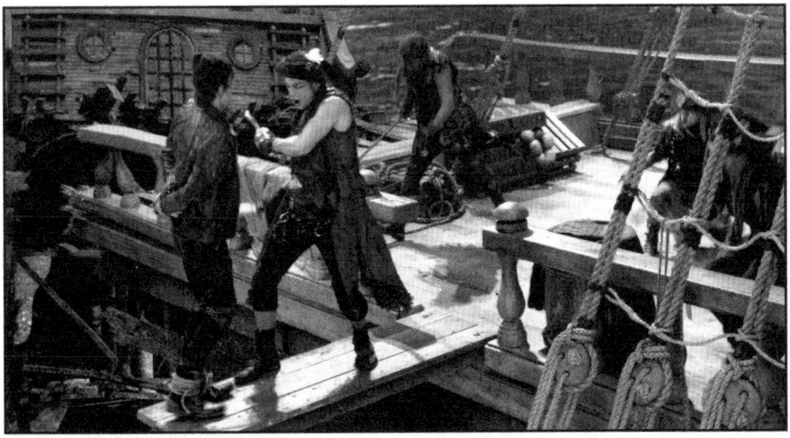

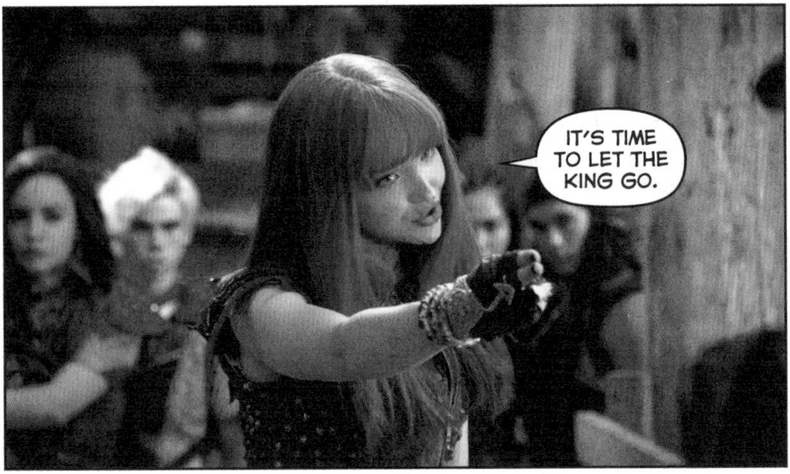
IT'S TIME TO LET THE KING GO.

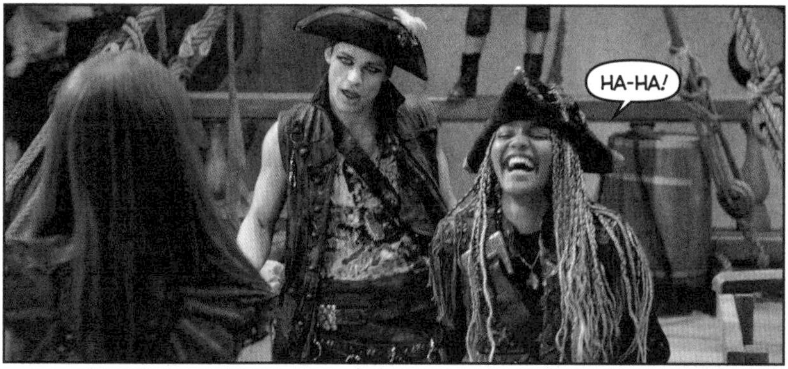
HA-HA!

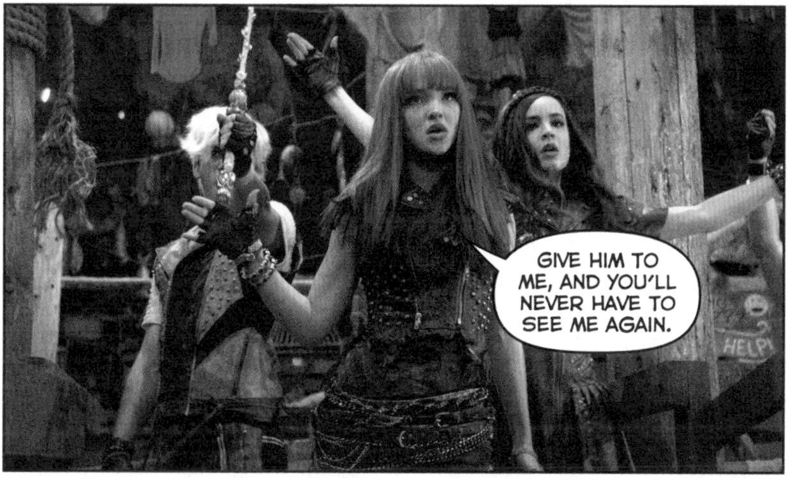
GIVE HIM TO ME, AND YOU'LL NEVER HAVE TO SEE ME AGAIN.
HELP

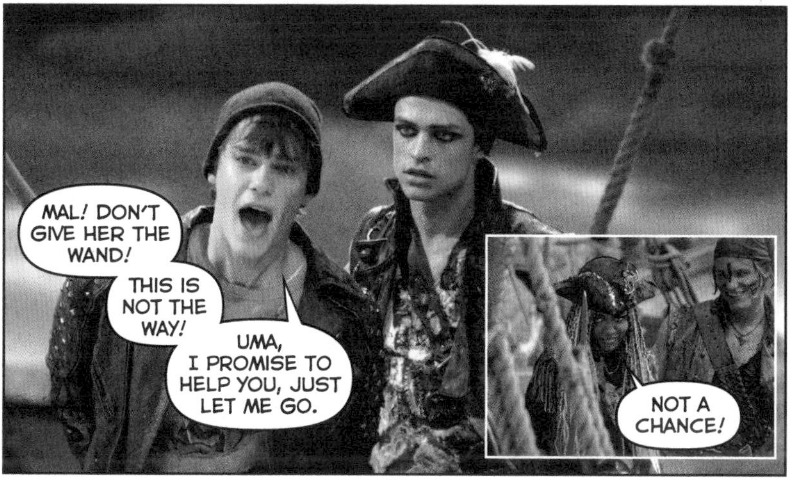
MAL! DON'T GIVE HER THE WAND!
THIS IS NOT THE WAY!
UMA, I PROMISE TO HELP YOU, JUST LET ME GO.
NOT A CHANCE!

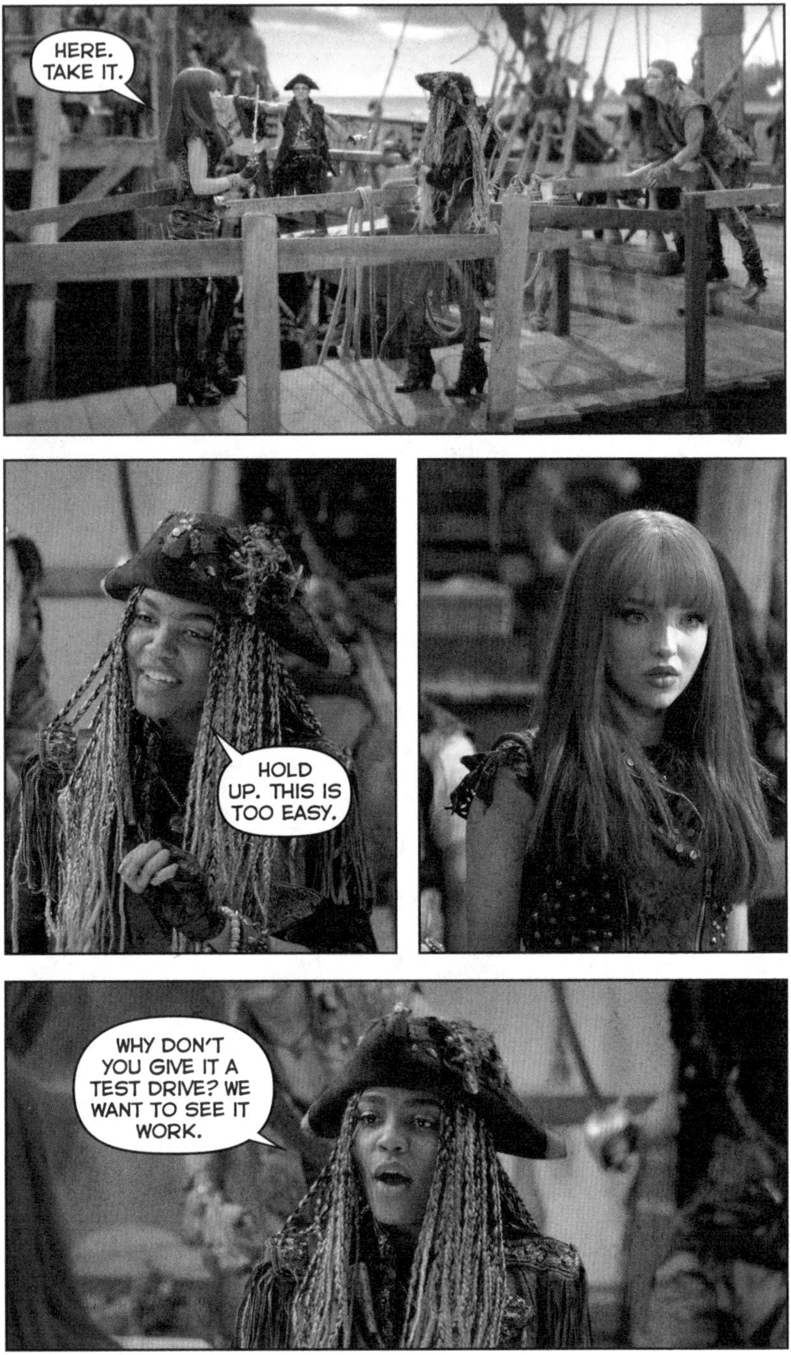
HERE. TAKE IT.
HOLD UP. THIS IS TOO EASY.
WHY DON'T YOU GIVE IT A TEST DRIVE? WE WANT TO SEE IT WORK.

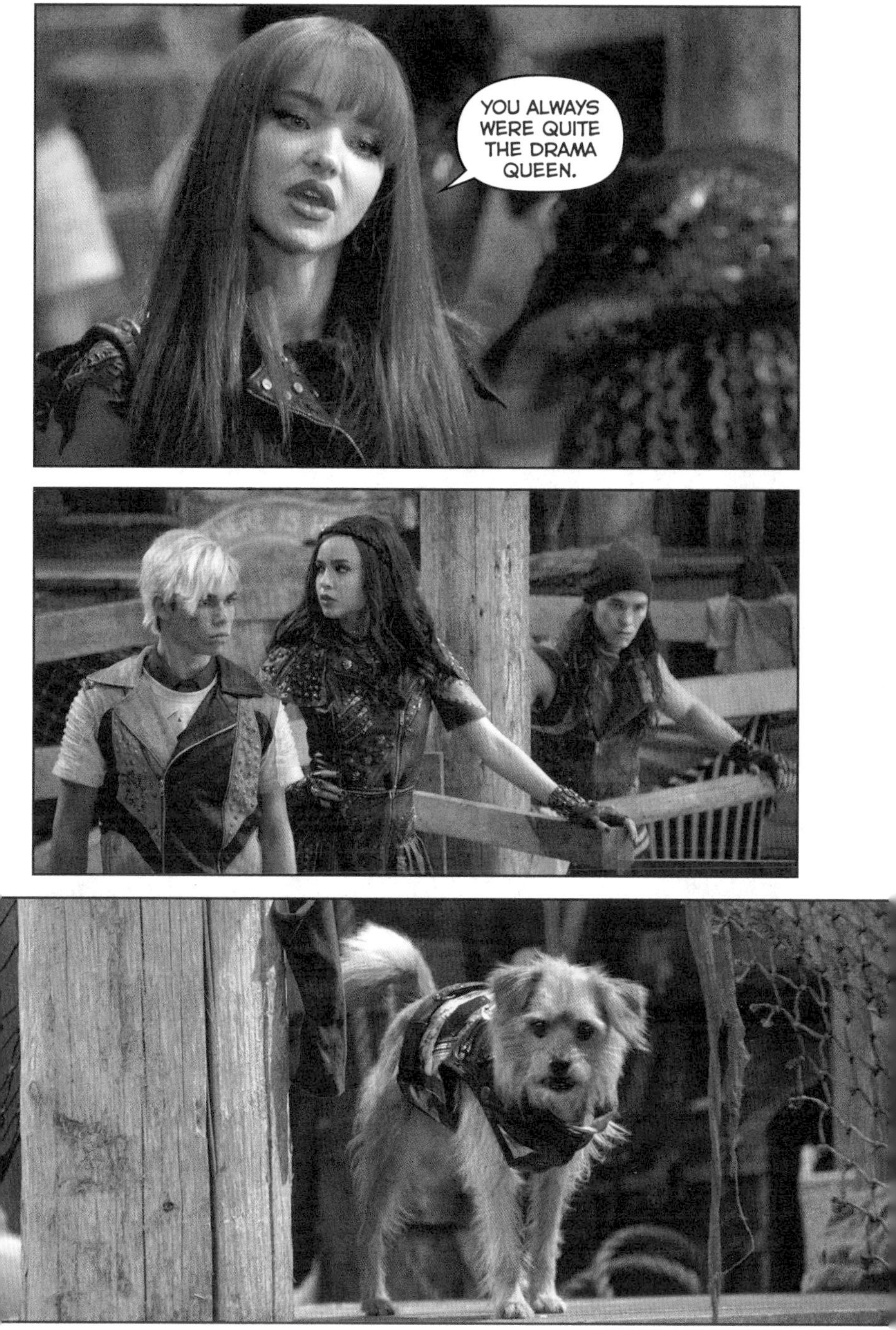
YOU ALWAYS WERE QUITE THE DRAMA QUEEN.

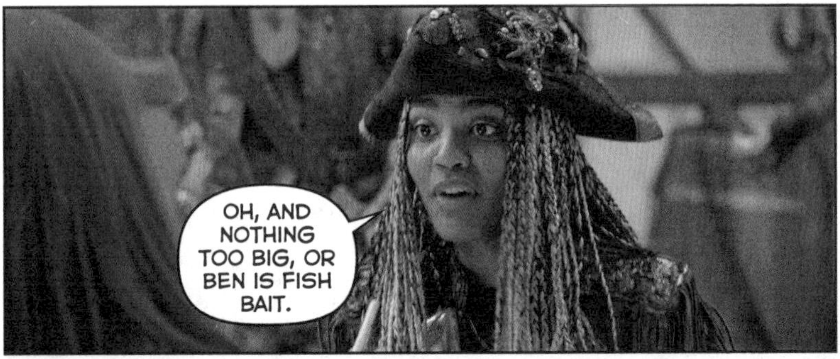
OH, AND NOTHING TOO BIG, OR BEN IS FISH BAIT.

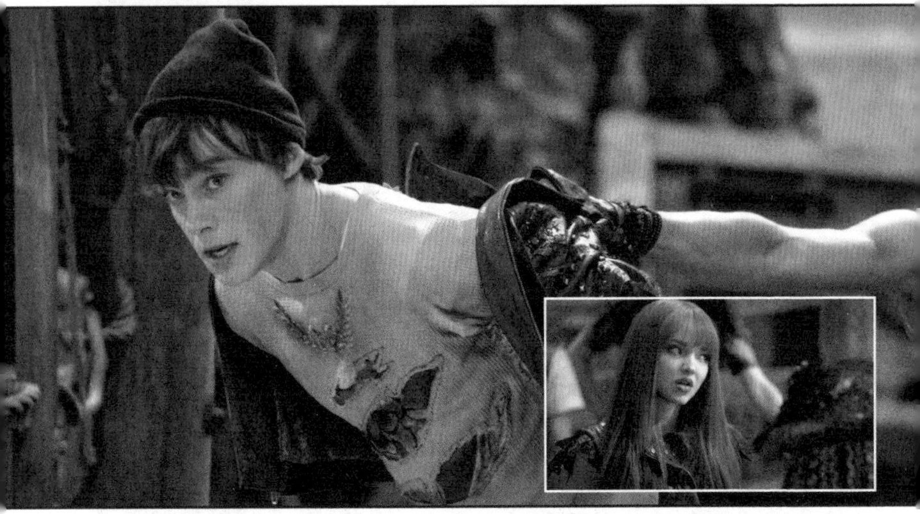

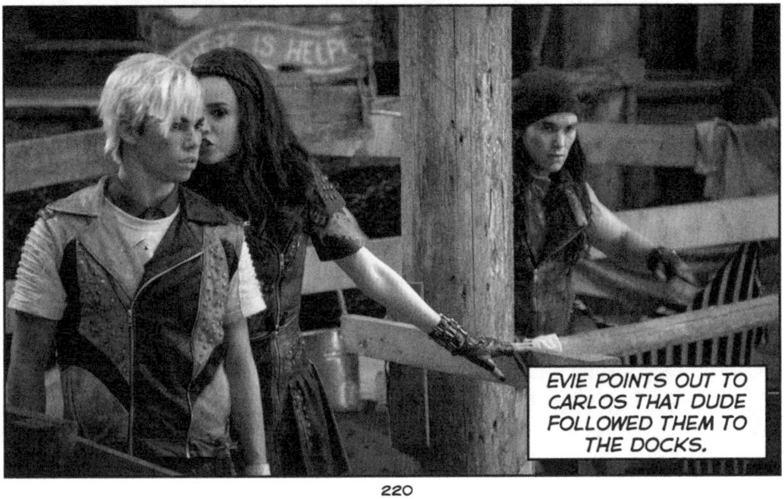
EVIE POINTS OUT TO CARLOS THAT DUDE FOLLOWED THEM TO THE DOCKS.

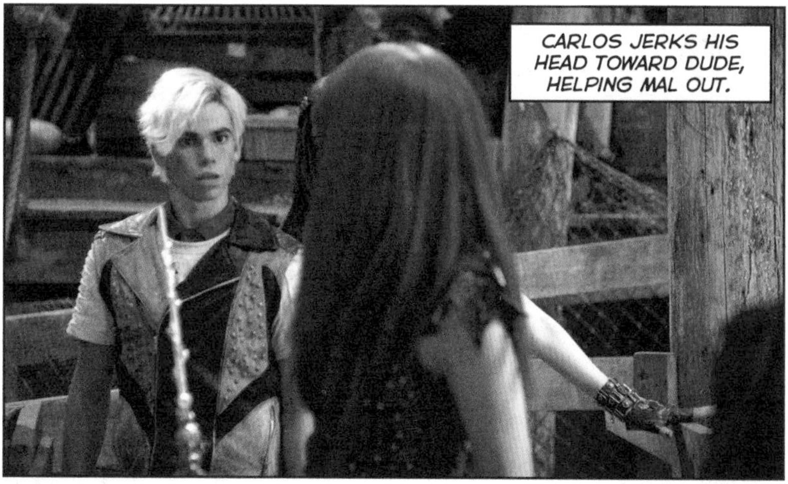
CARLOS JERKS HIS HEAD TOWARD DUDE, HELPING MAL OUT.

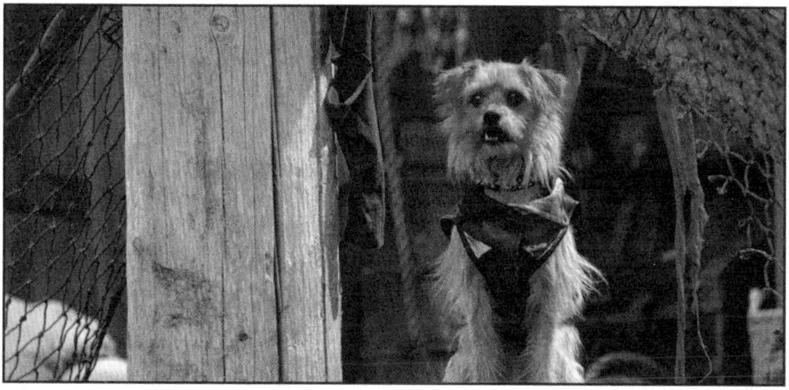

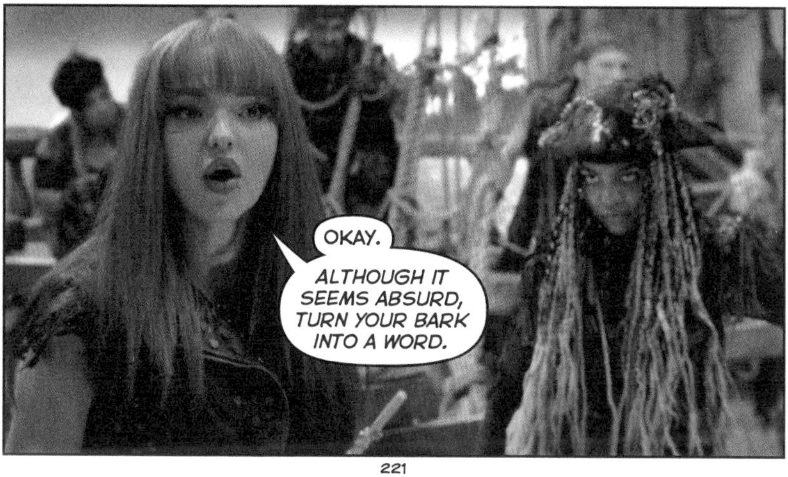
OKAY.
ALTHOUGH IT SEEMS ABSURD, TURN YOUR BARK INTO A WORD.

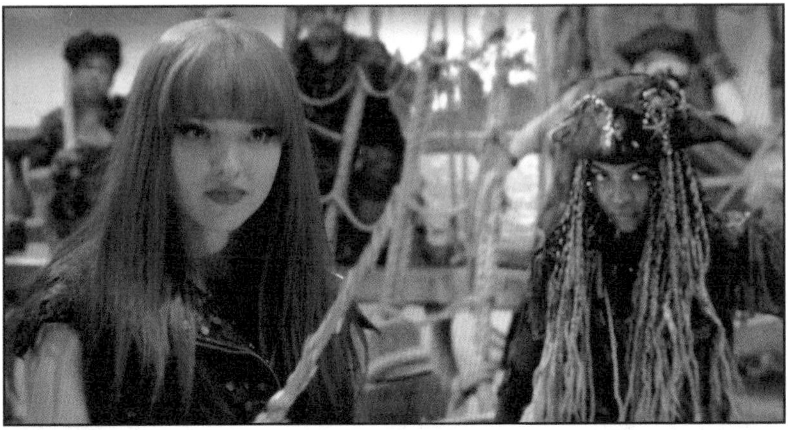

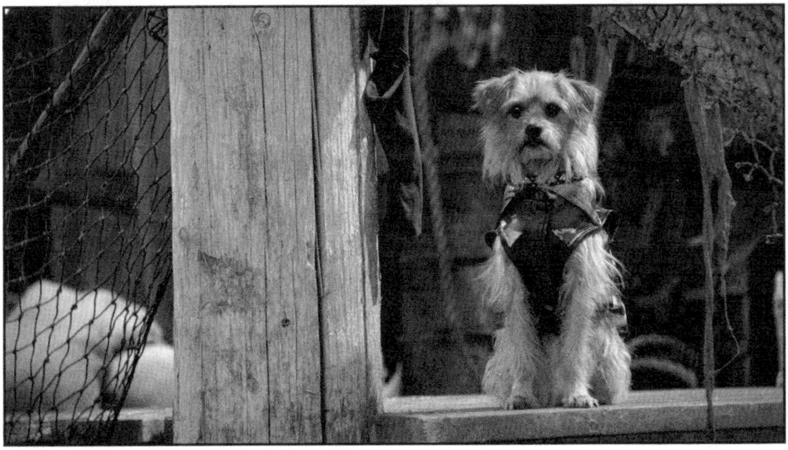

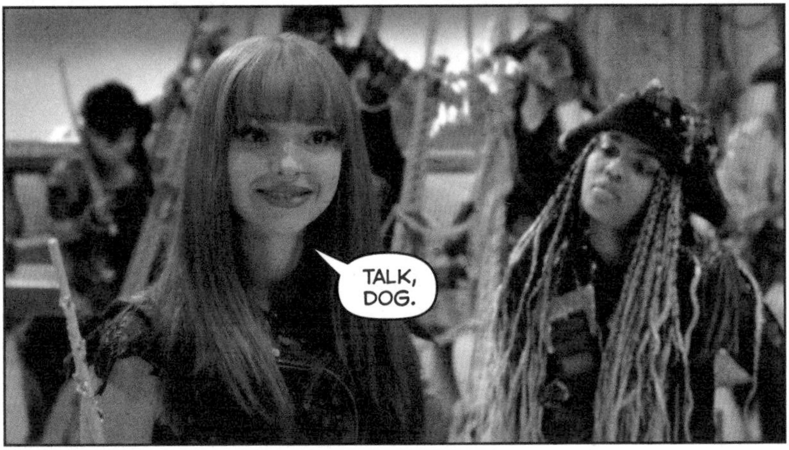
TALK, DOG.

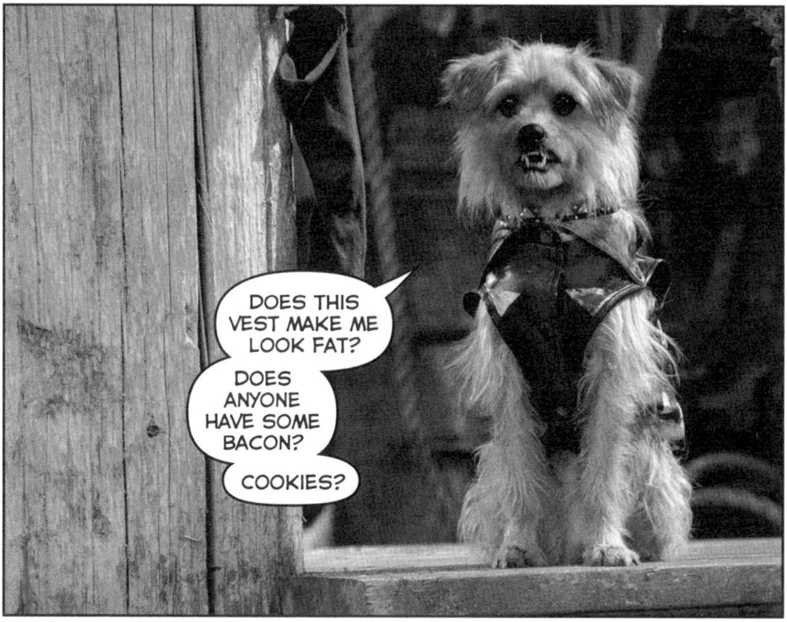
DOES THIS VEST MAKE ME LOOK FAT?
DOES ANYONE HAVE SOME BACON?
COOKIES?

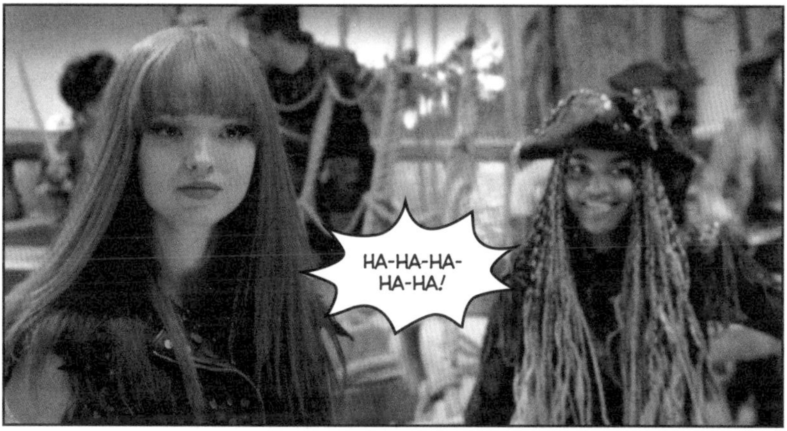
HA-HA-HA-HA-HA!

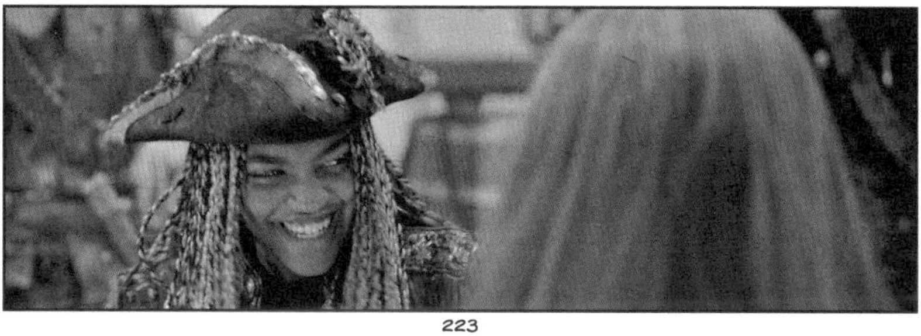

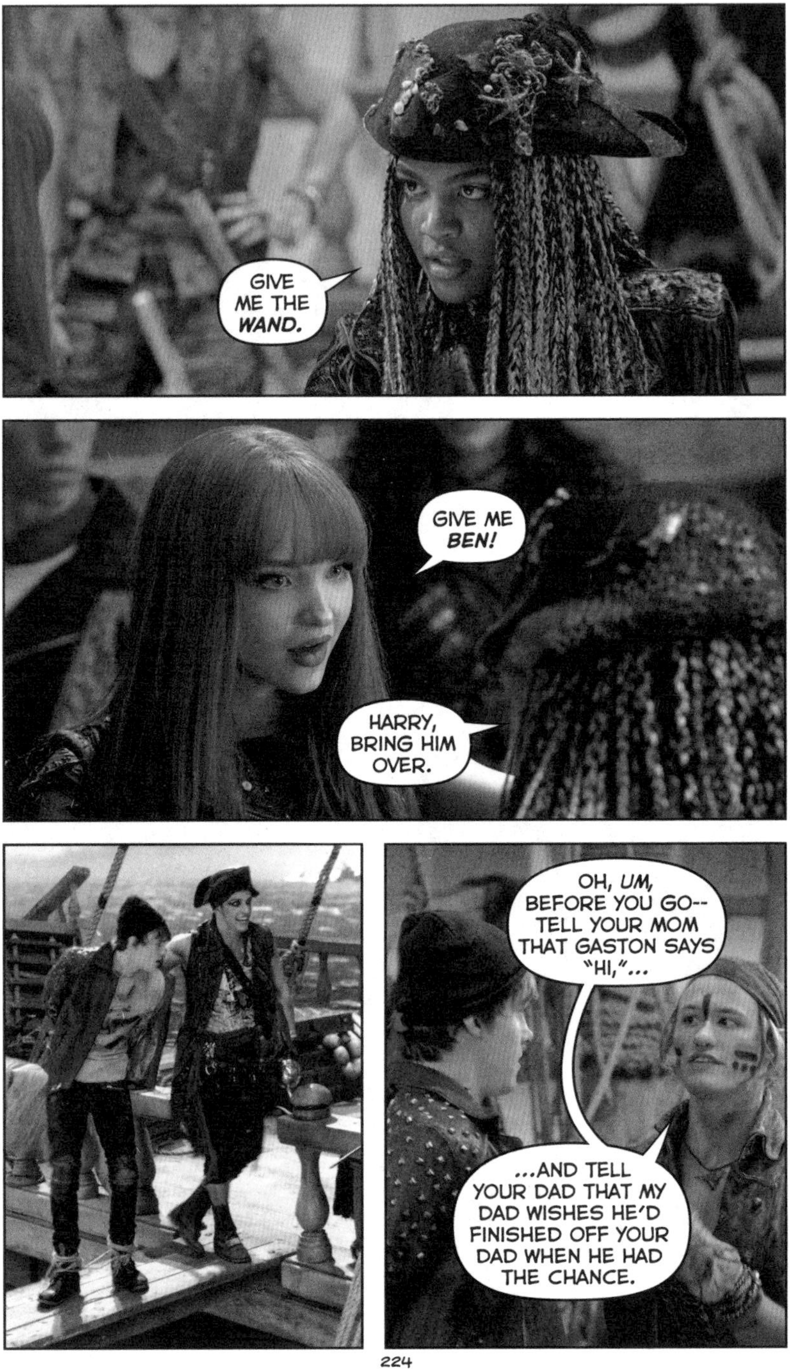
GIVE ME THE *WAND.*
GIVE ME *BEN!*
HARRY, BRING HIM OVER.
OH, *UM,* BEFORE YOU GO-- TELL YOUR MOM THAT GASTON SAYS "HI,"...
...AND TELL YOUR DAD THAT MY DAD WISHES HE'D FINISHED OFF YOUR DAD WHEN HE HAD THE CHANCE.

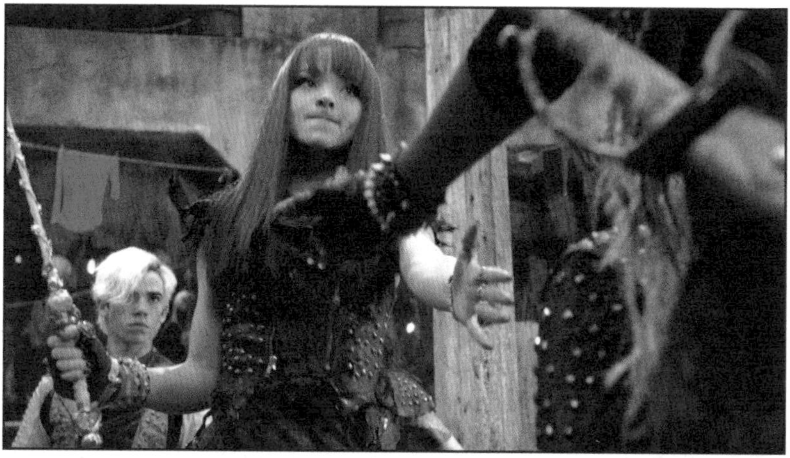

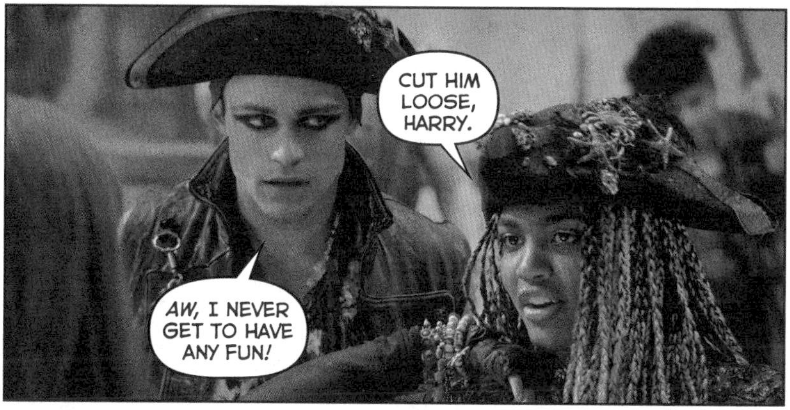
CUT HIM LOOSE, HARRY.
AW, I NEVER GET TO HAVE ANY FUN!

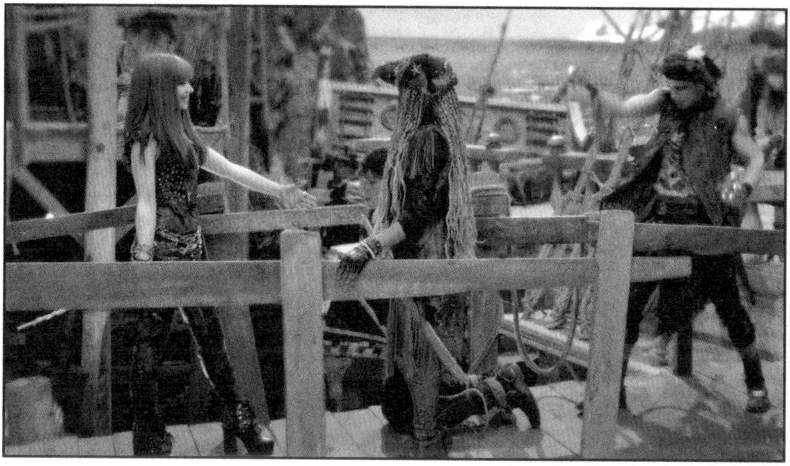

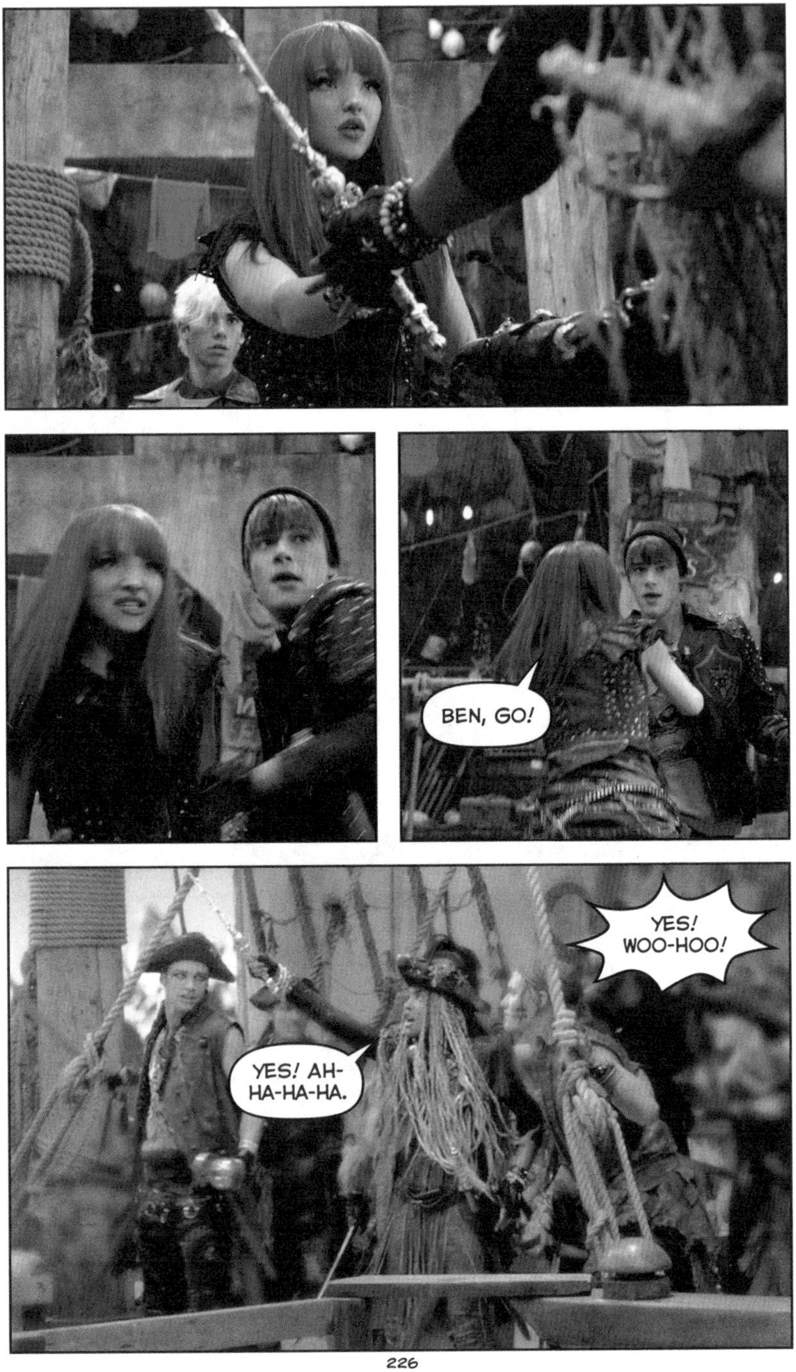
BEN, GO!
YES! WOO-HOO!
YES! AH-HA-HA-HA.

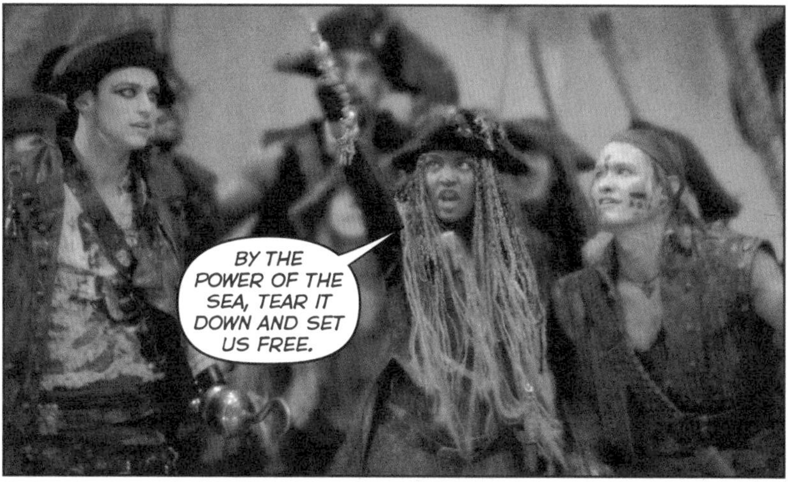
BY THE POWER OF THE SEA, TEAR IT DOWN AND SET US FREE.

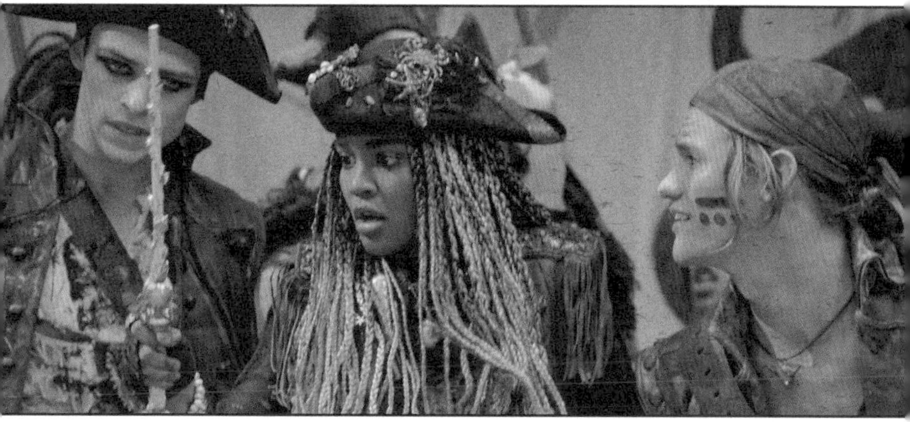

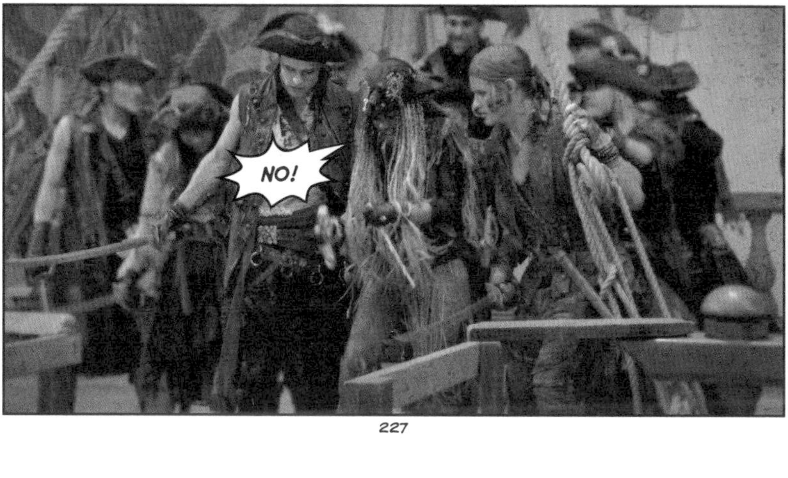
NO!

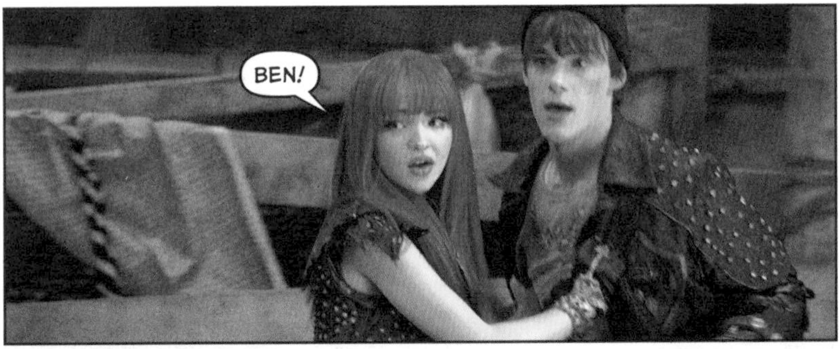
BEN!

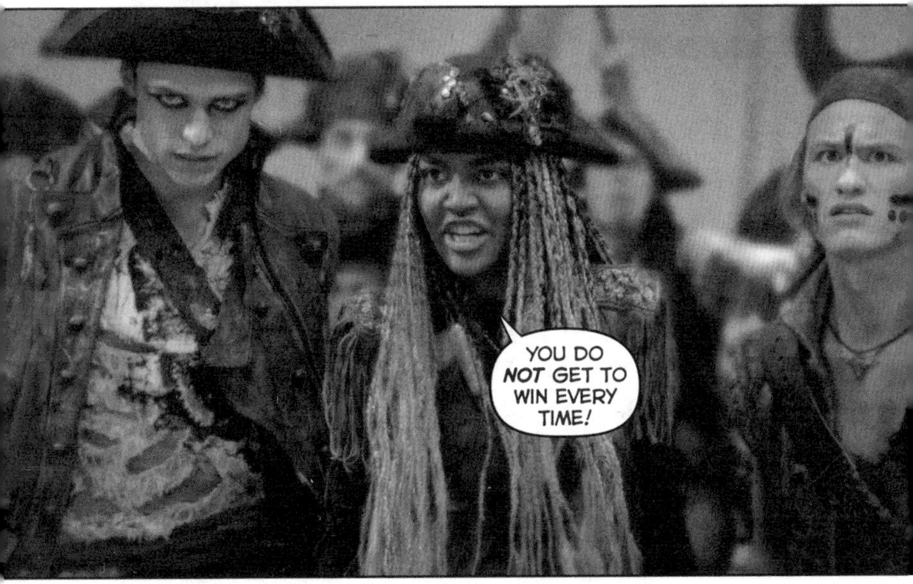
YOU DO ***NOT*** GET TO WIN EVERY TIME!

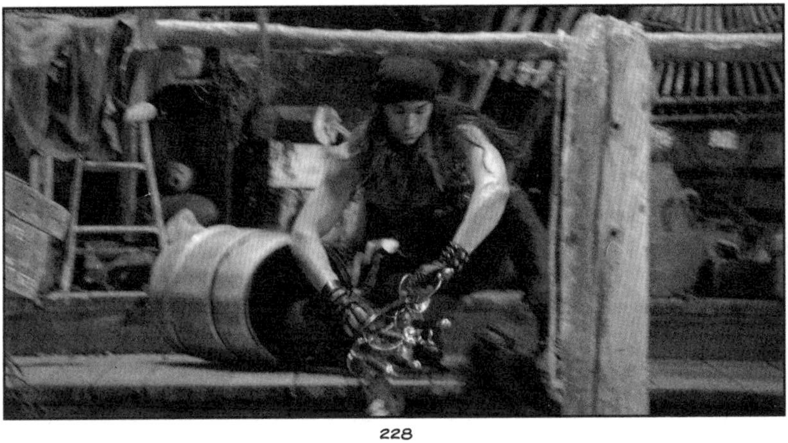

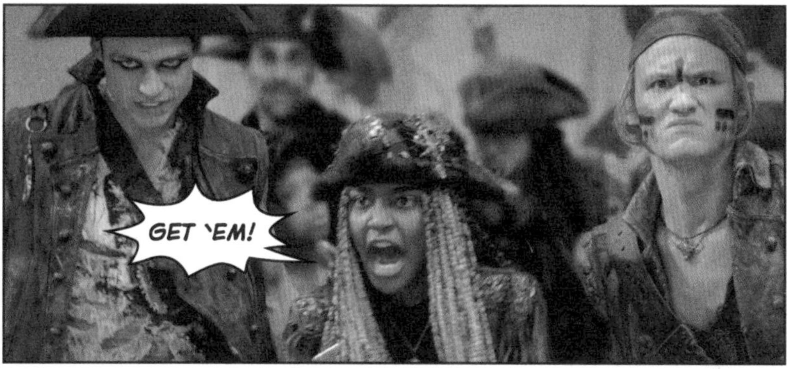
GET 'EM!

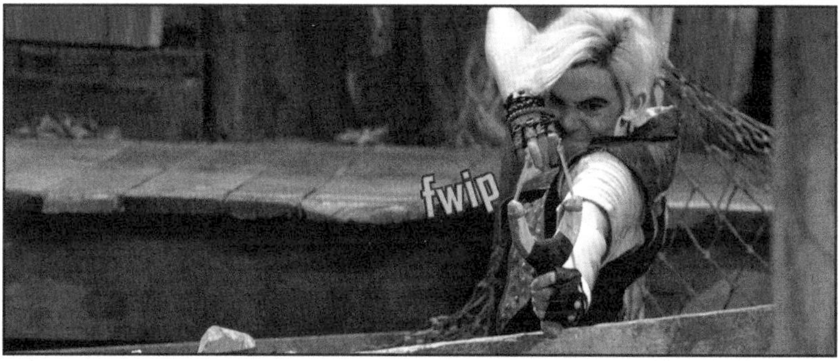
fwip

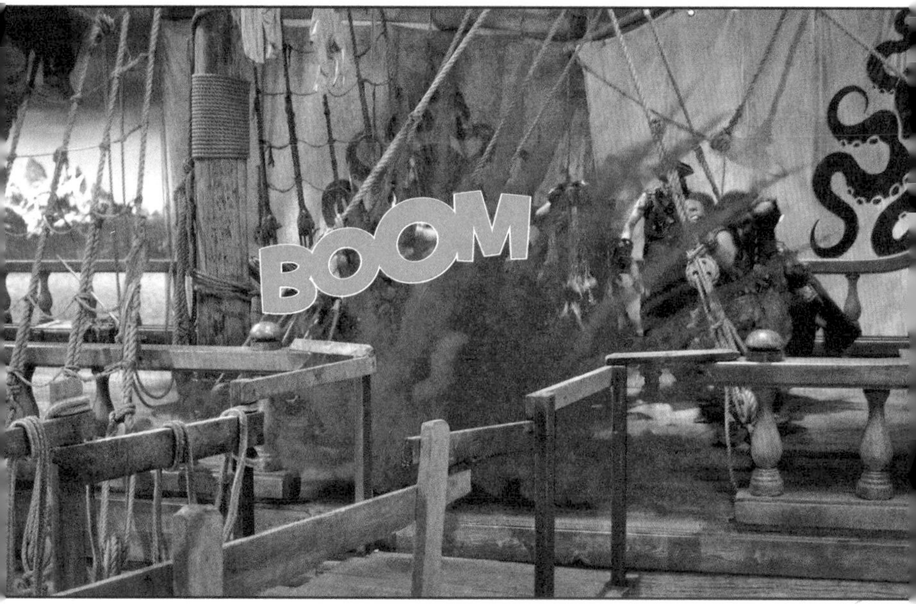
BOOM

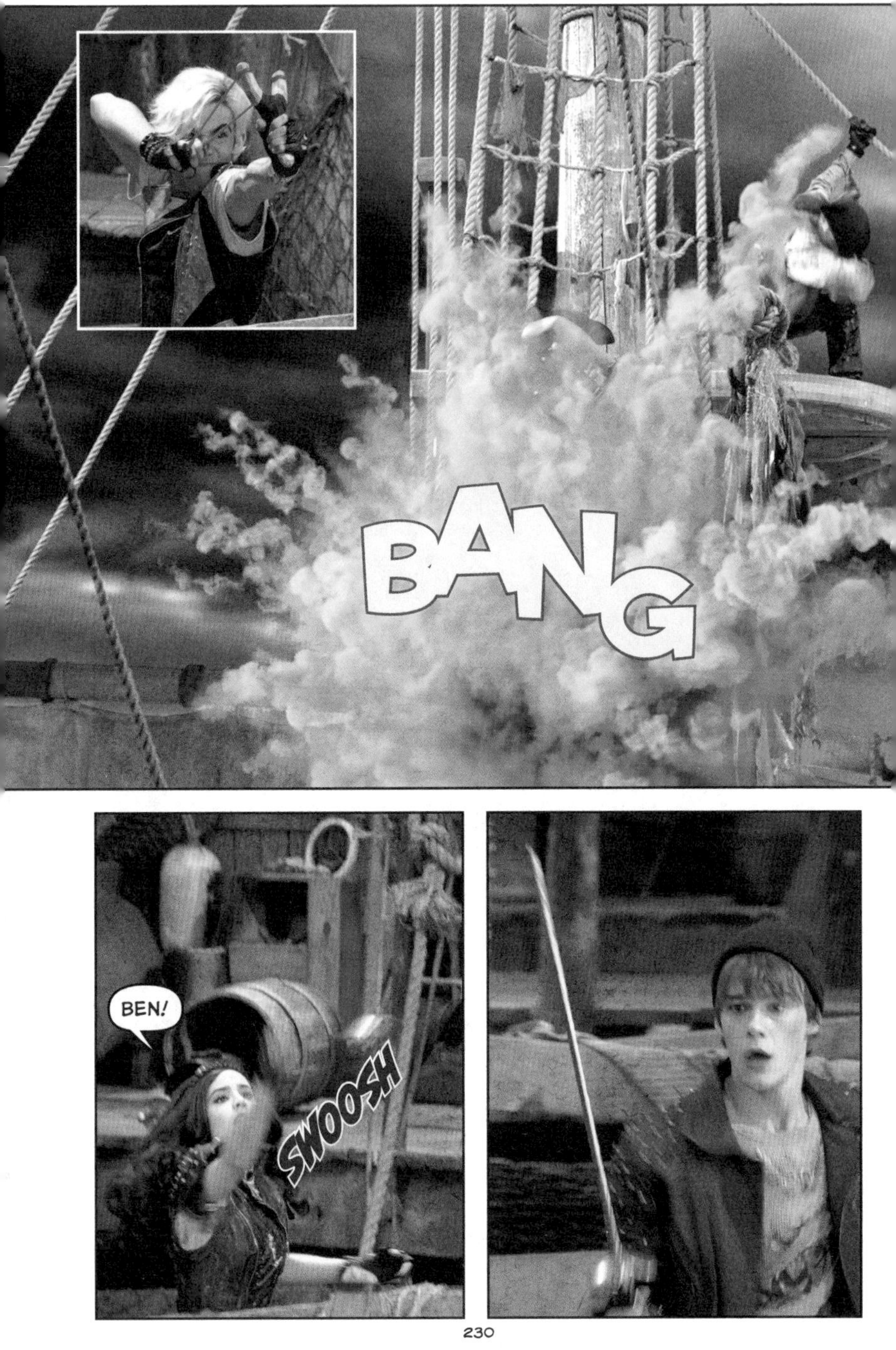
BANG
BEN!
SWOOSH

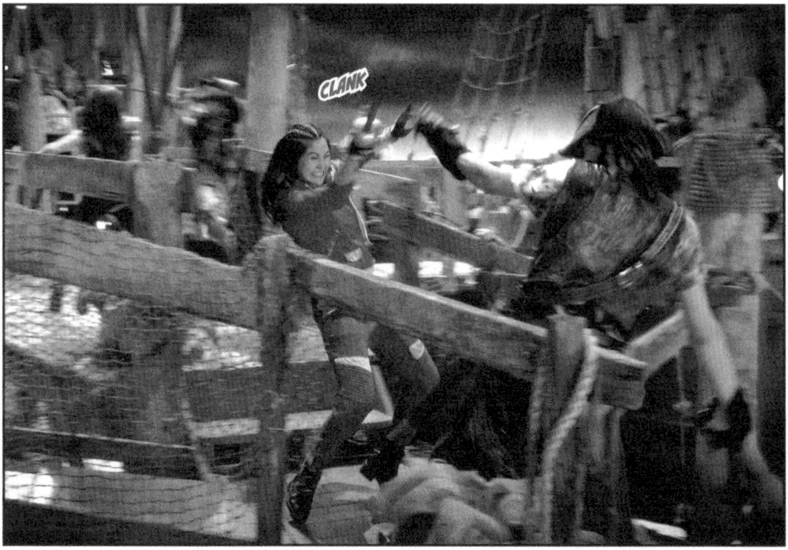
CLANK

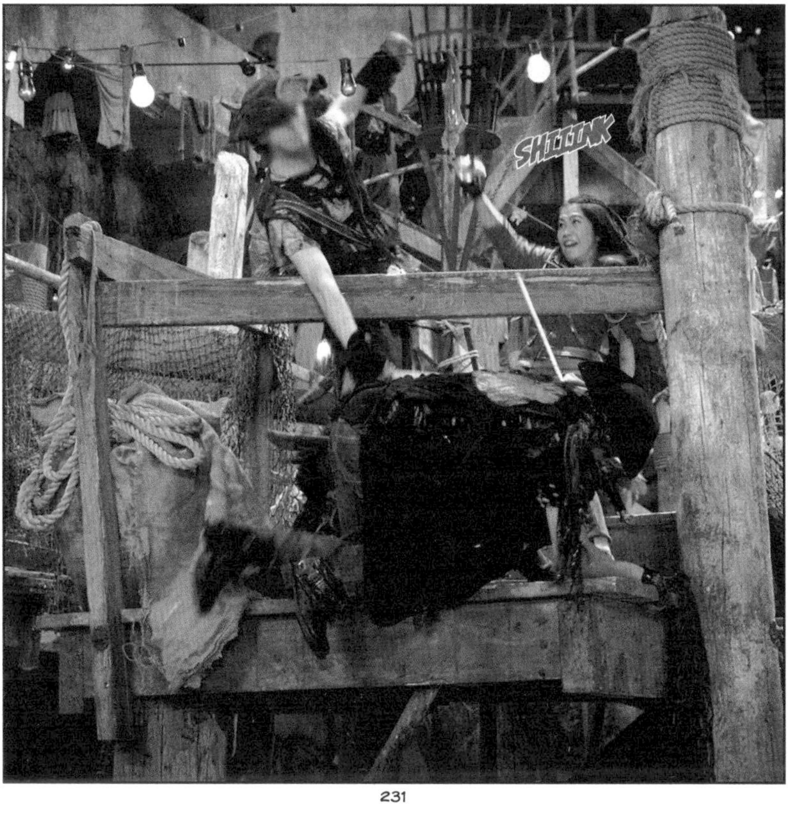
SHIIINK

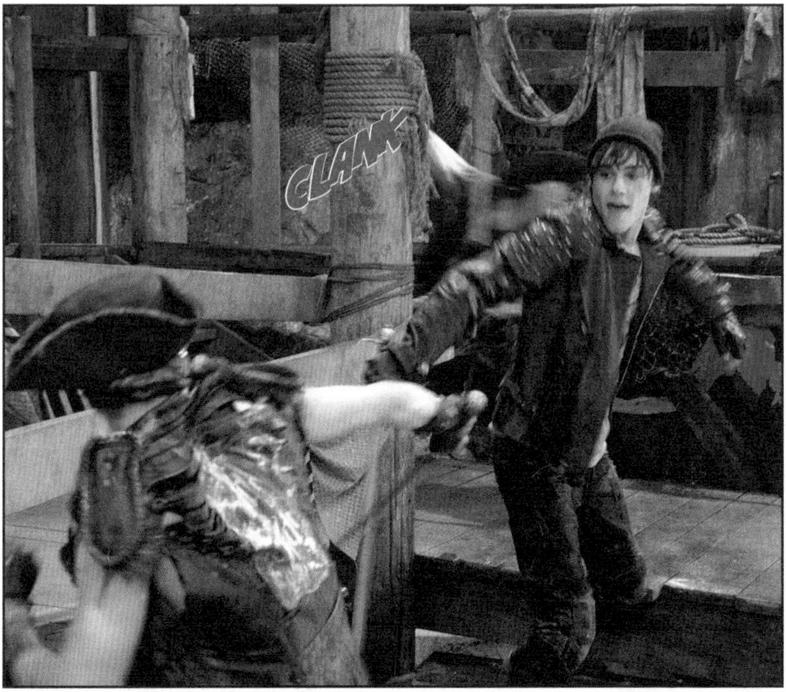
CLANK

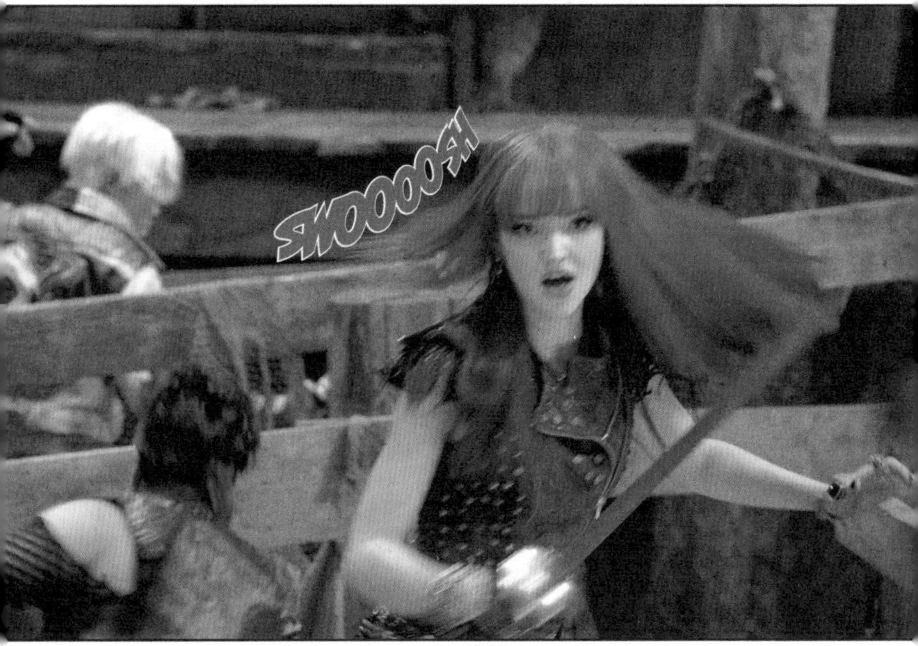
SWOOOOSH

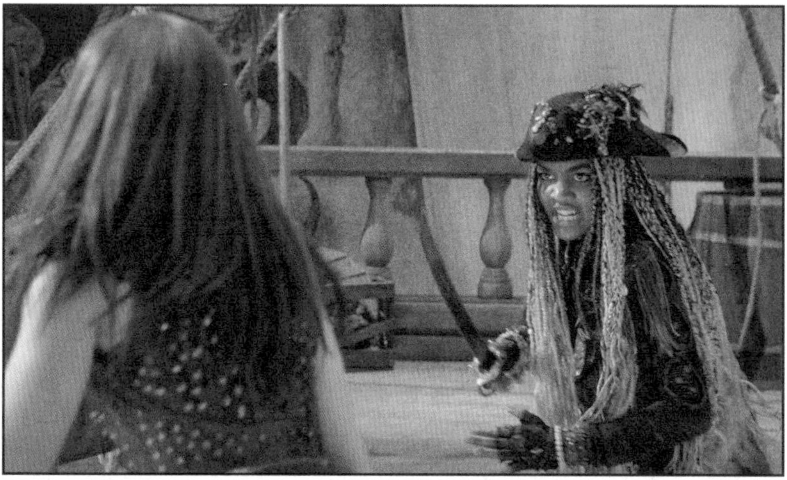

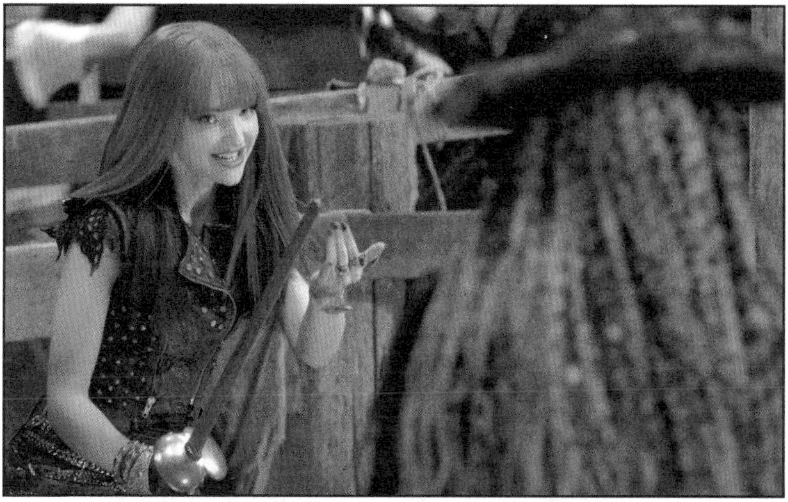

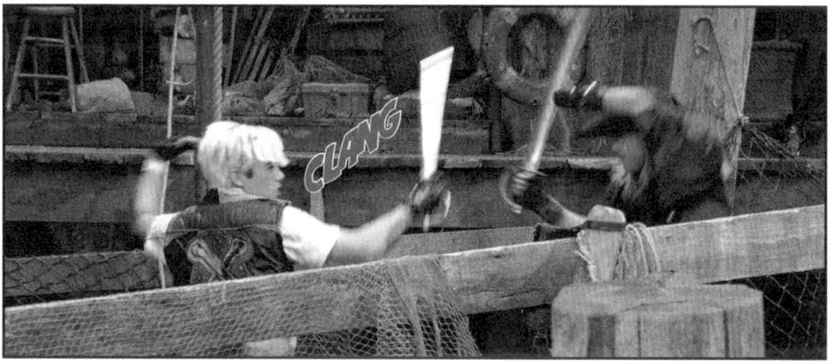
CLANG

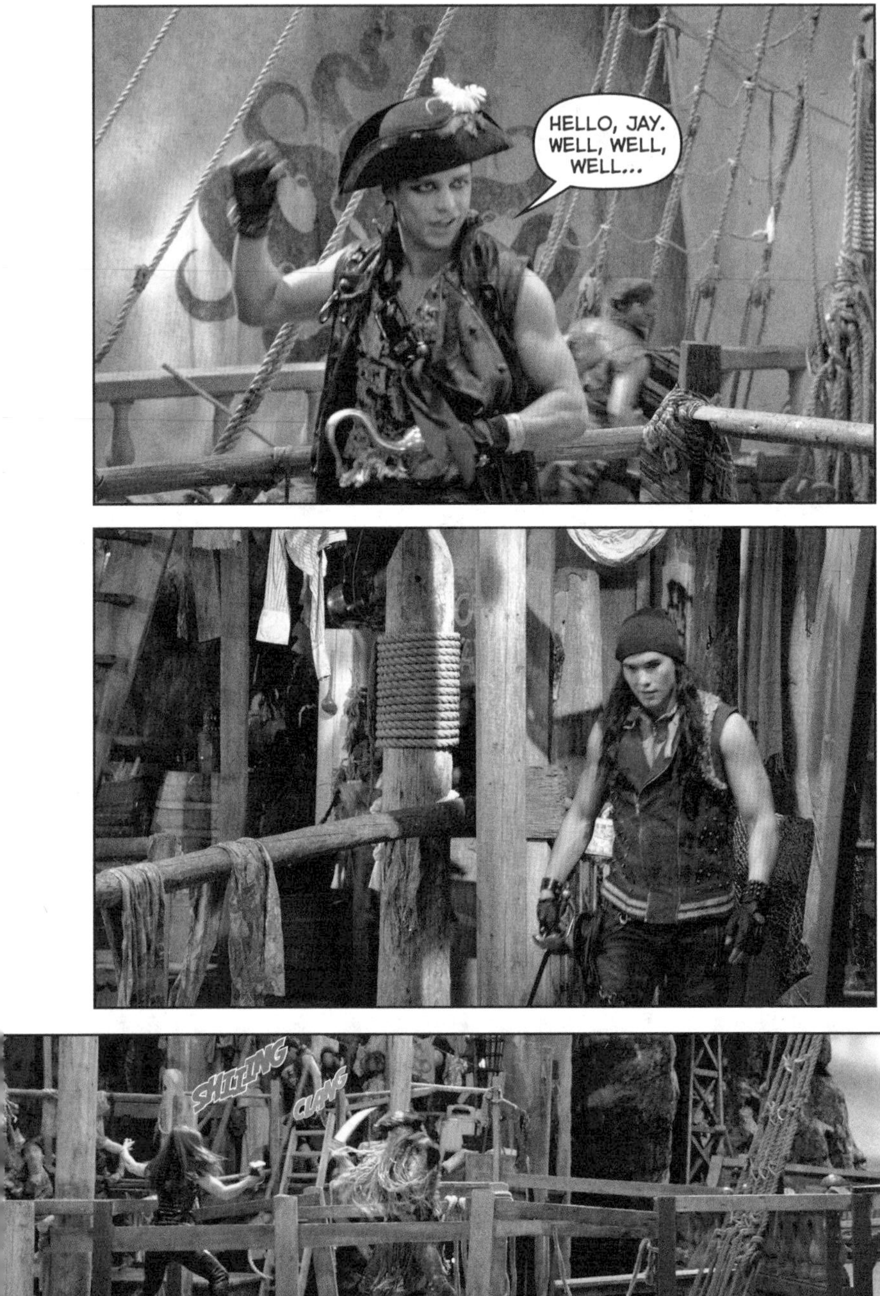
HELLO, JAY.
WELL, WELL,
WELL...
SHIIING
CLANG

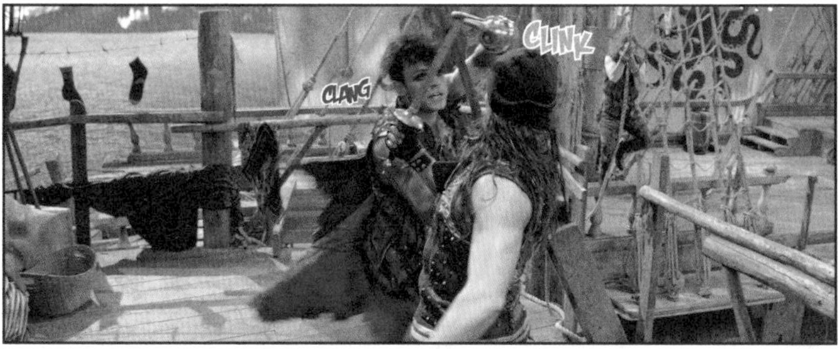
CLANG
CLINK

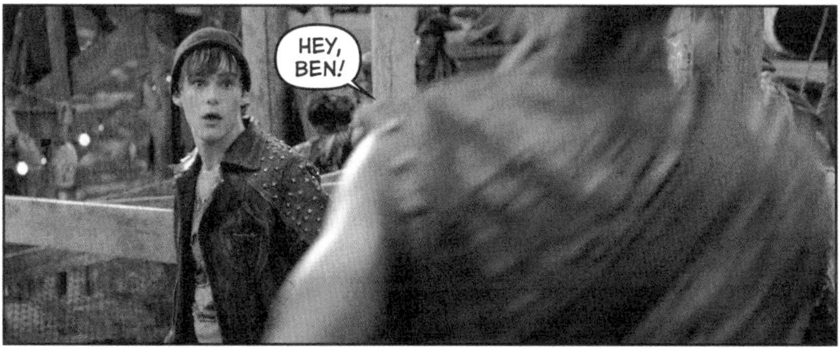
HEY, BEN!

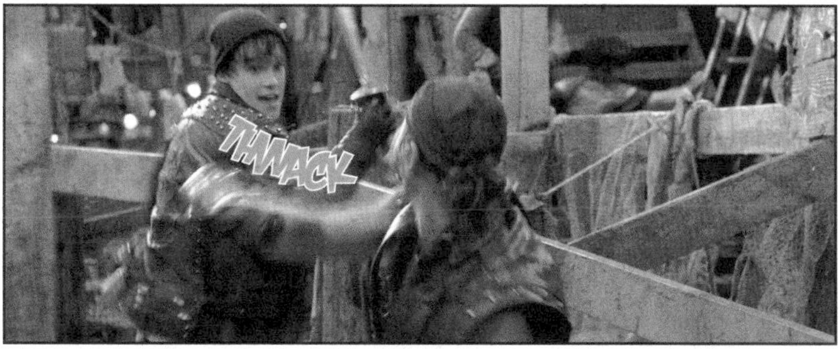
THWACK

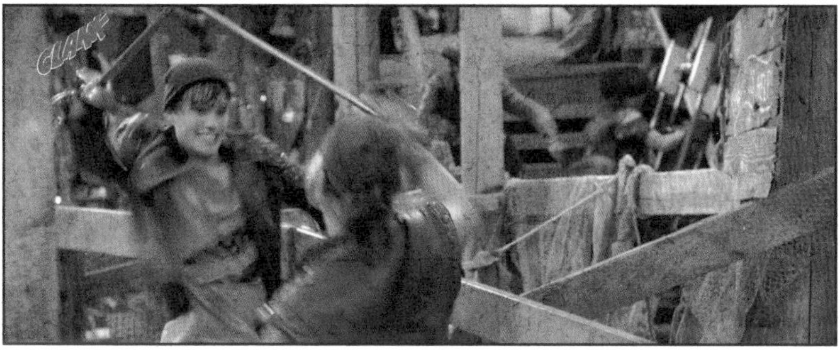
CLANK

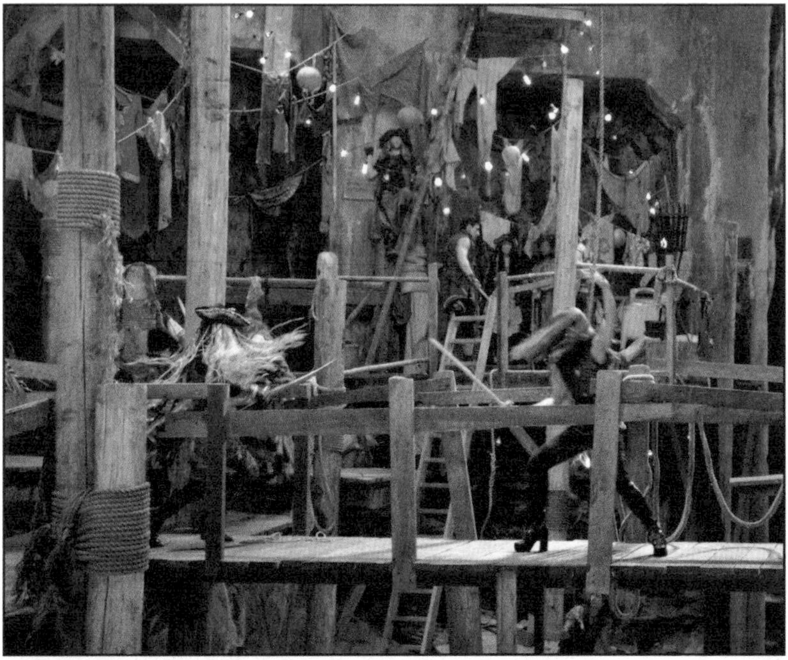

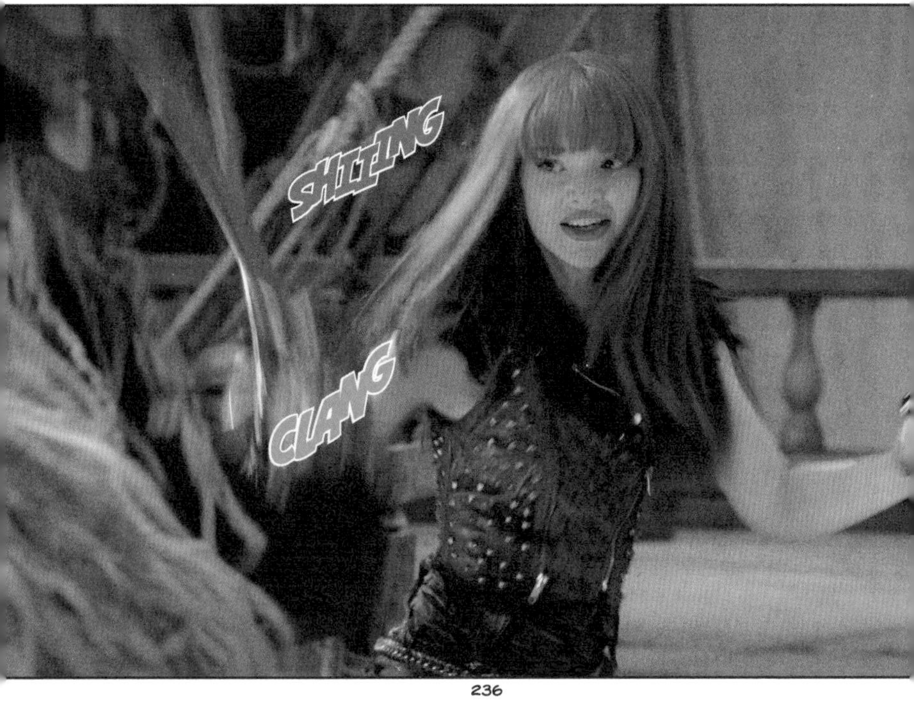
SHIIING
CLANG

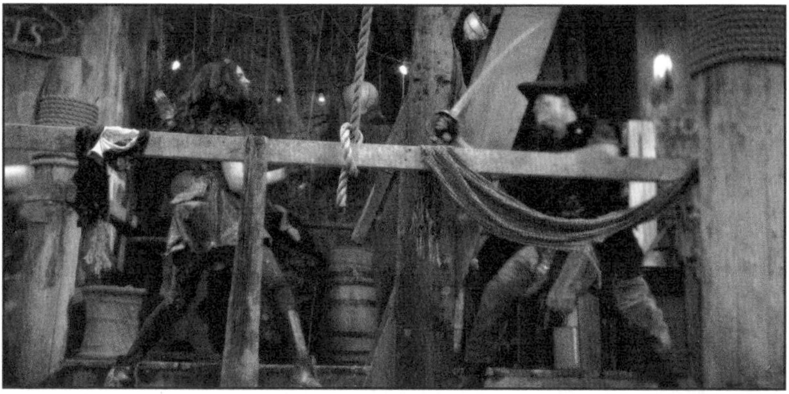

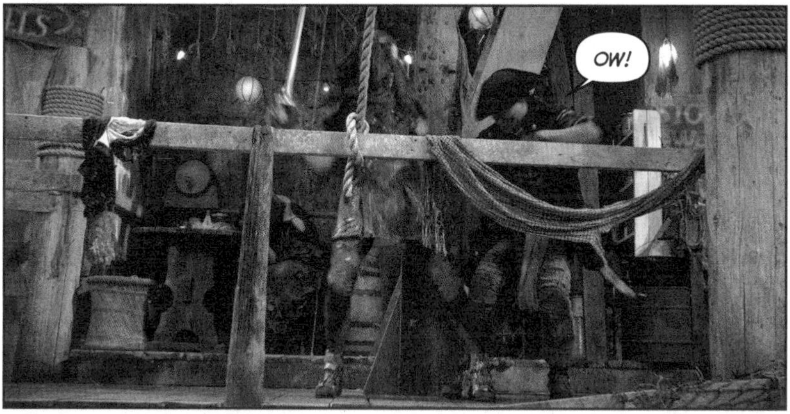
OW!

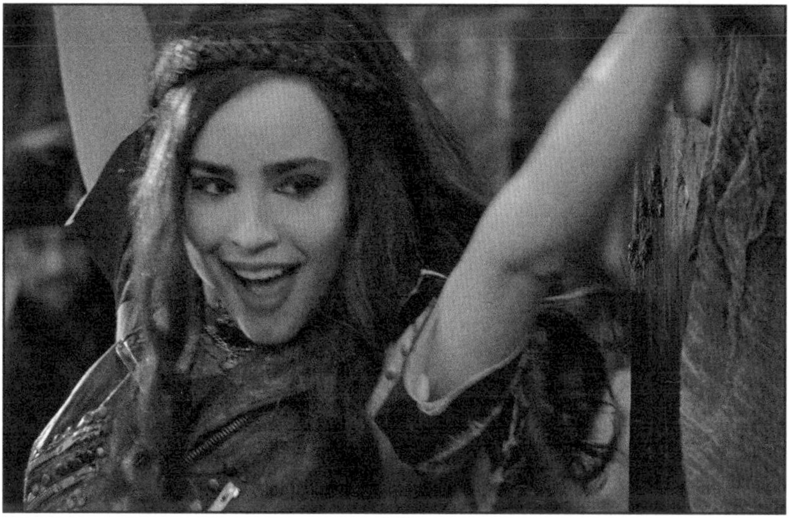

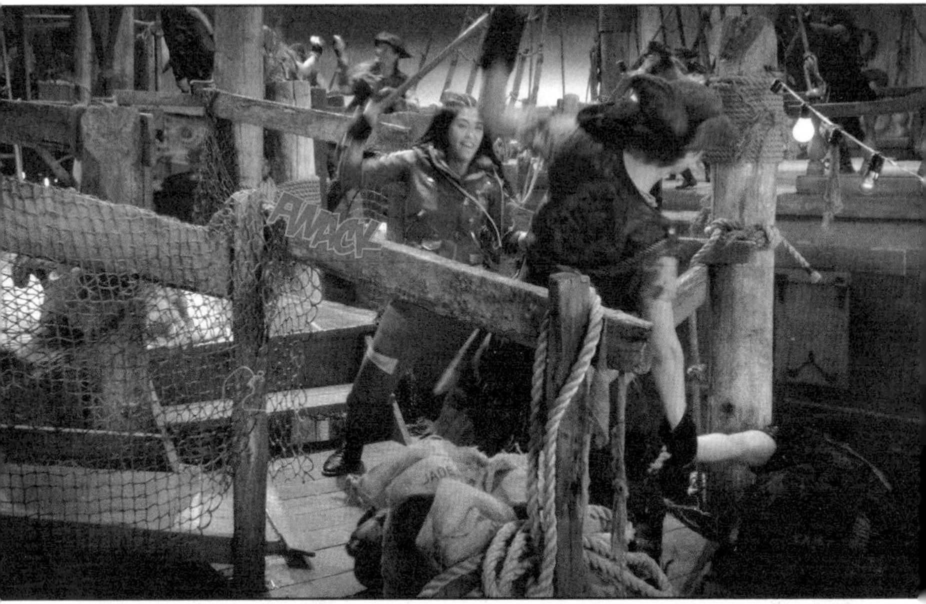

FWACK

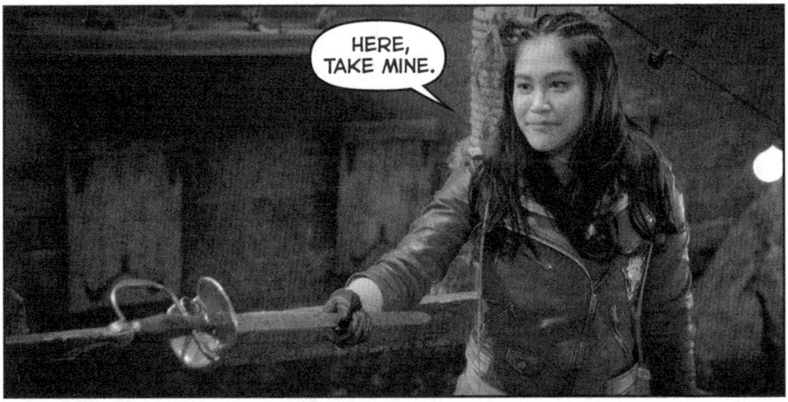

HERE, TAKE MINE.

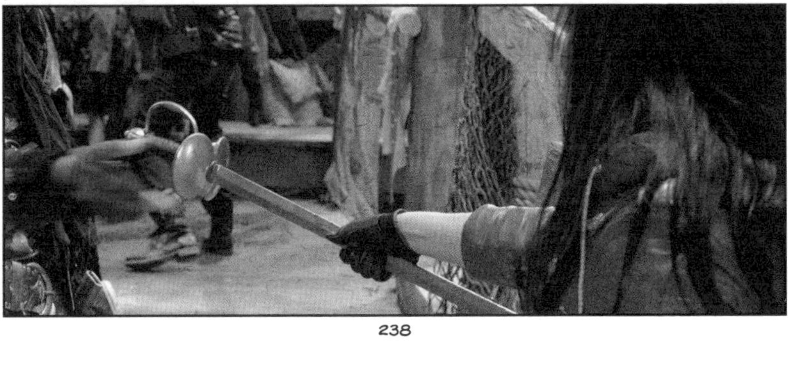

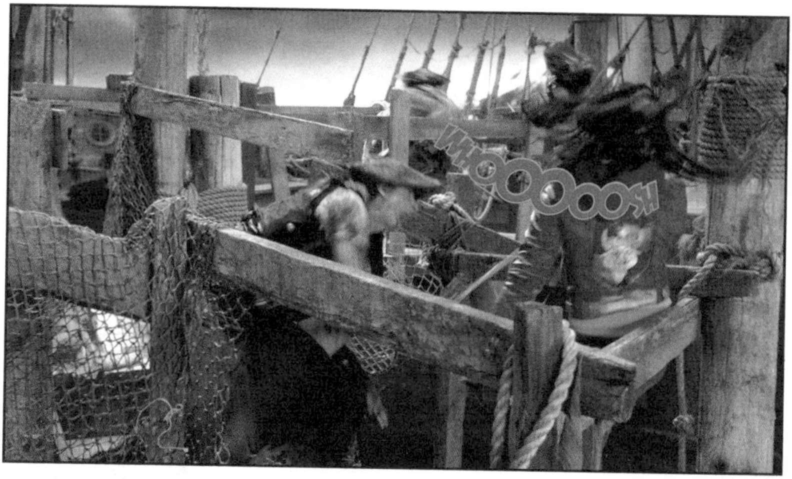
WHOOOOOSH

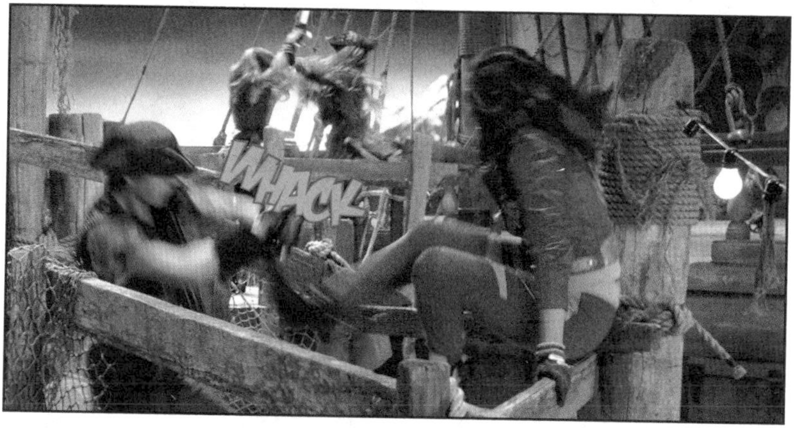
WHACK

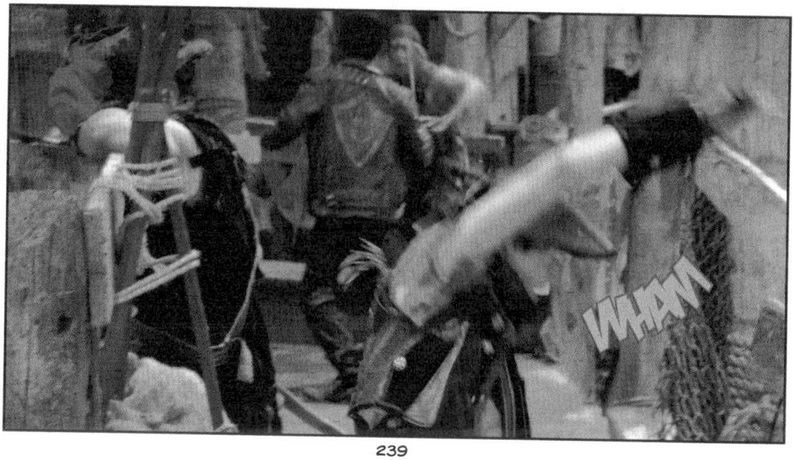
WHAM

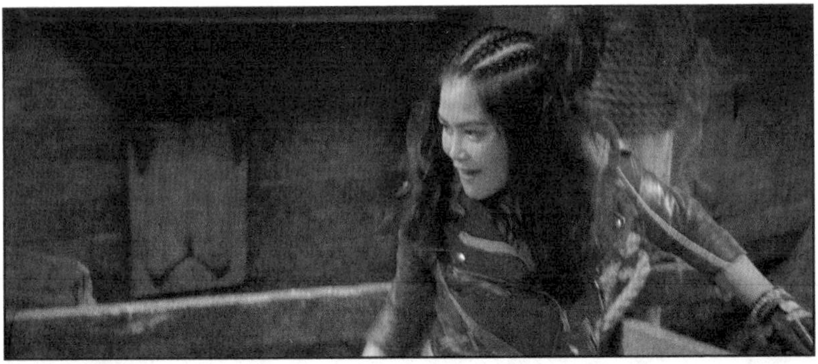

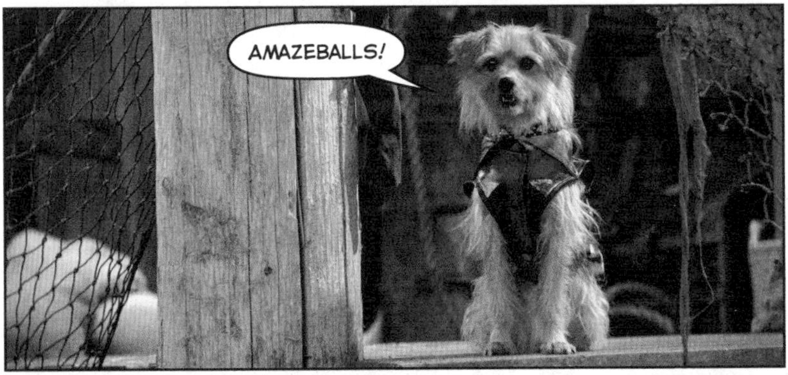
AMAZEBALLS!

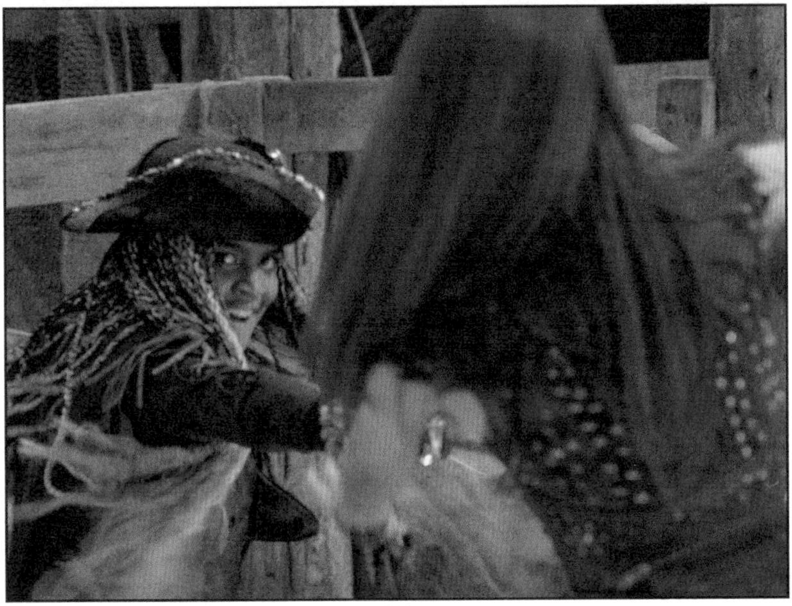

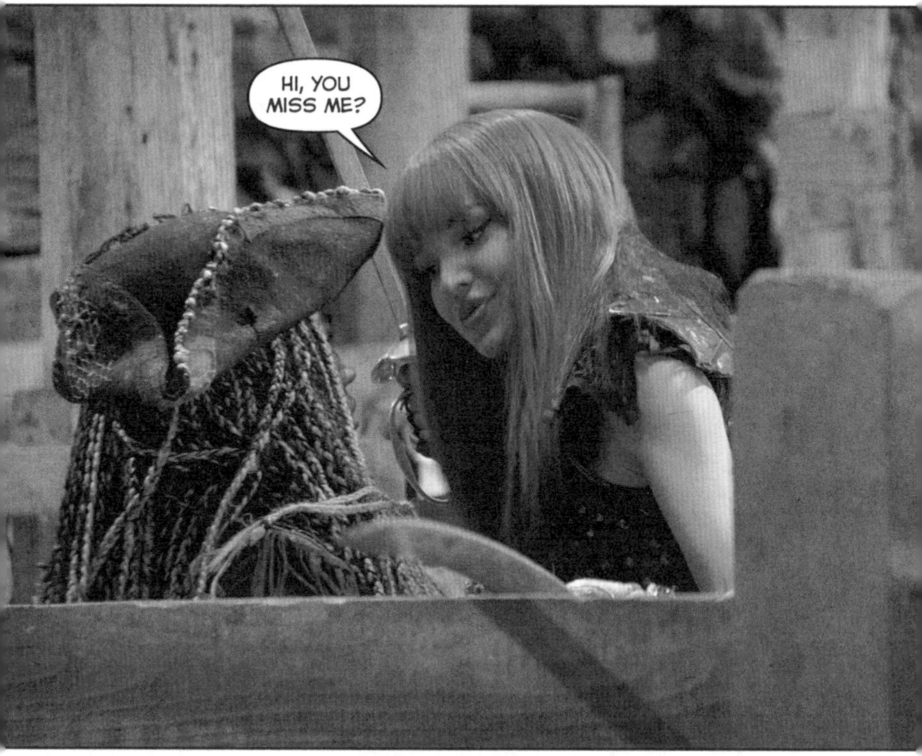
HI, YOU
MISS ME?

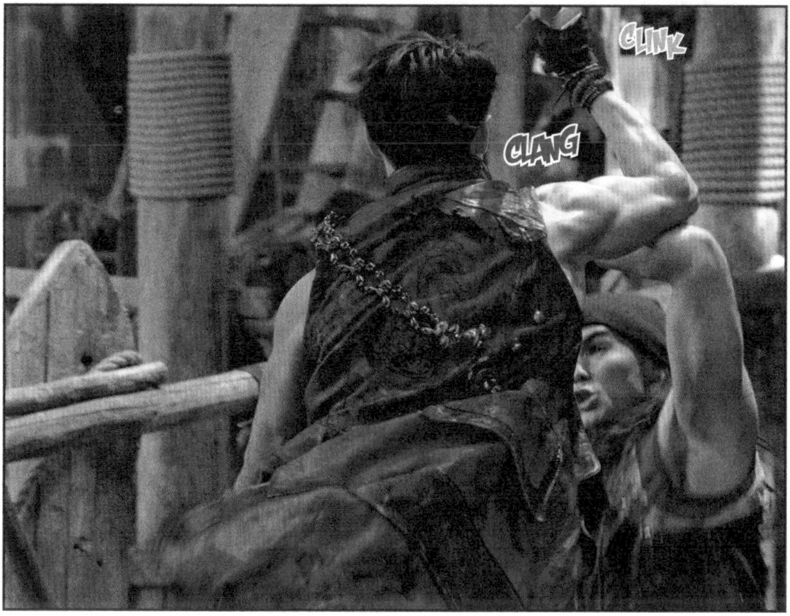
CLINK
CLANG

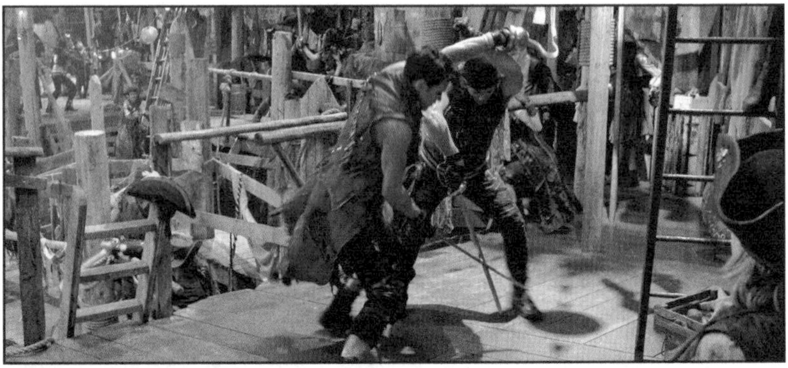
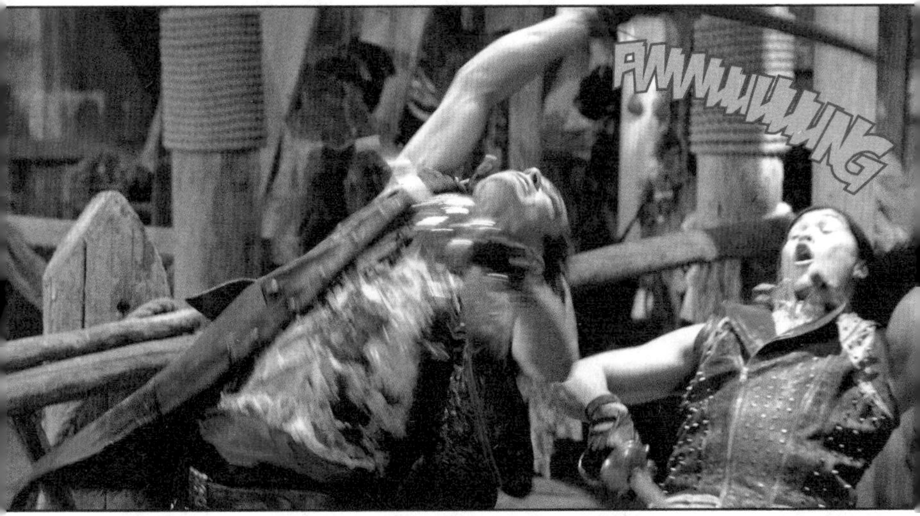
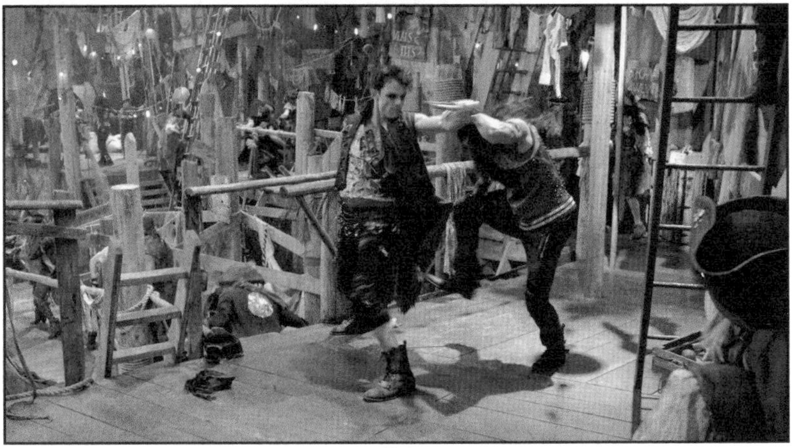

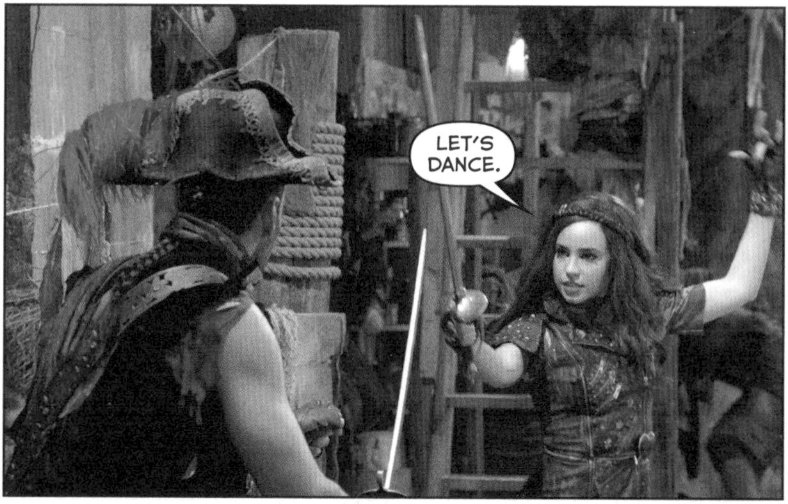
LET'S DANCE.

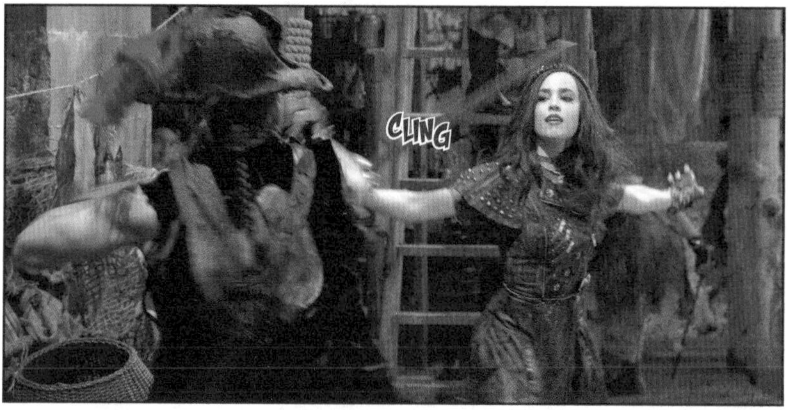
CLING

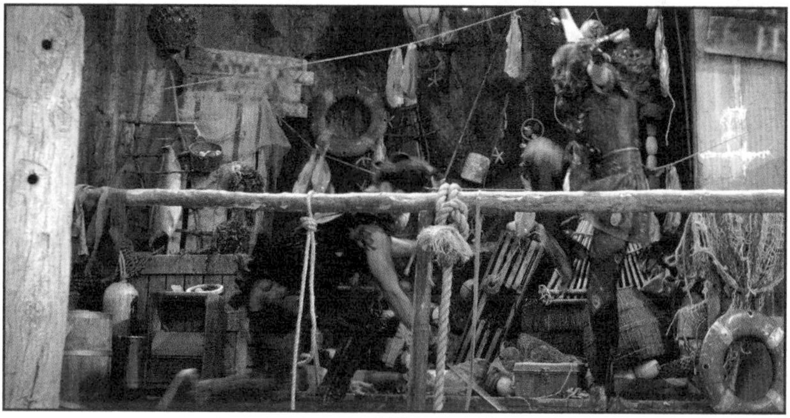

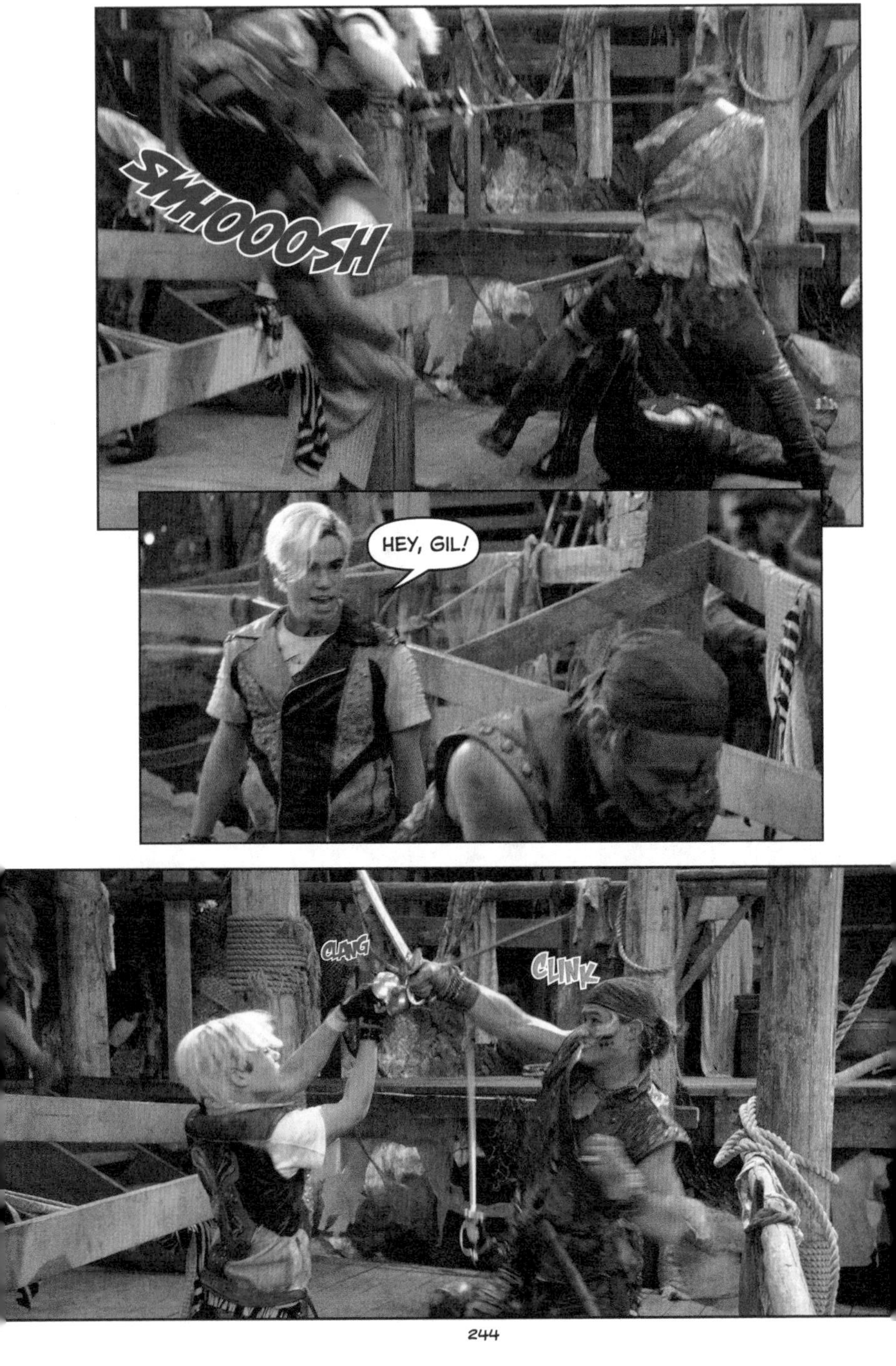
SWHOOOSH
HEY, GIL!
CLANG
CLINK

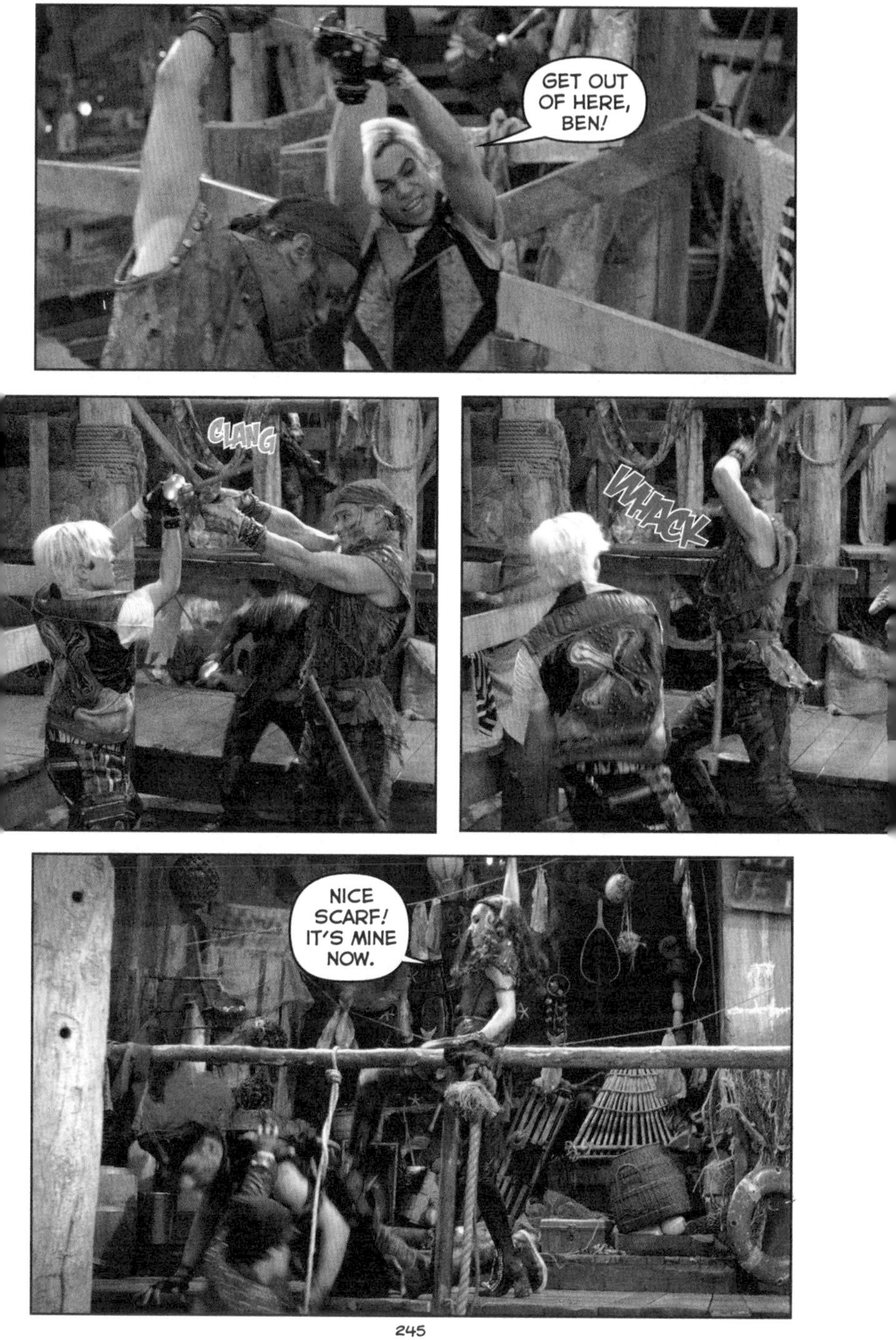

GET OUT OF HERE, BEN!
CLANG
WHACK
NICE SCARF! IT'S MINE NOW.

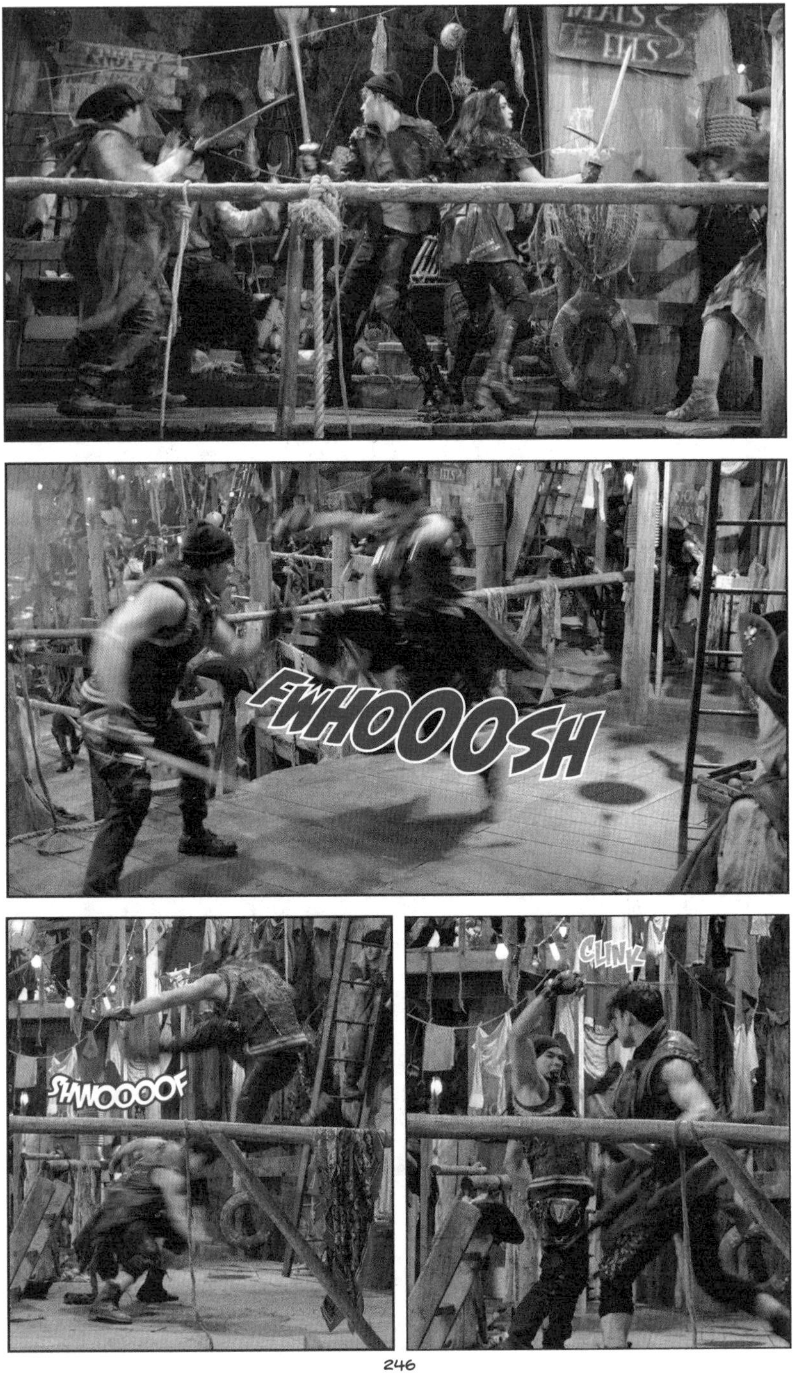
FWHOOOSH
SHWOOOOF
CLINK

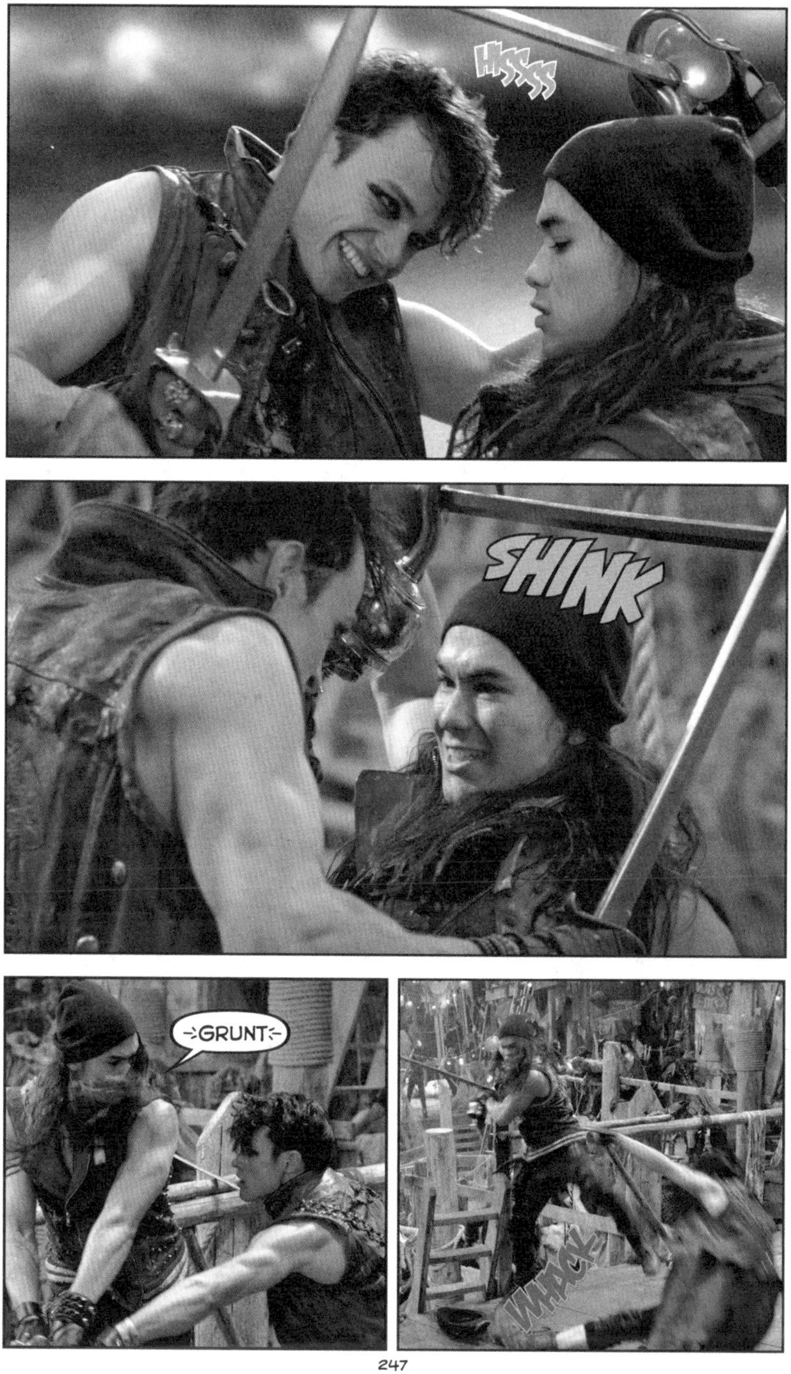
HISSSS
SHINK
GRUNT
WHACK

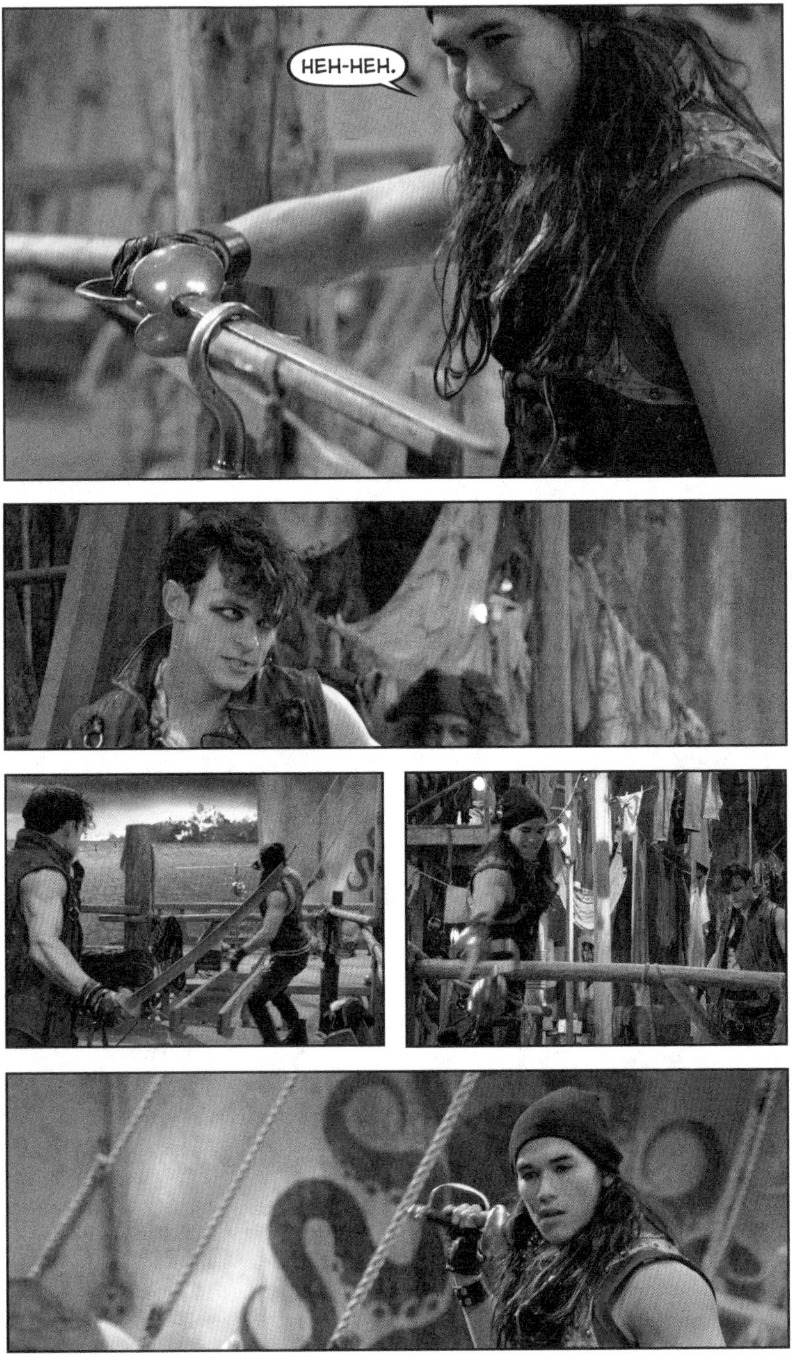
HEH-HEH.

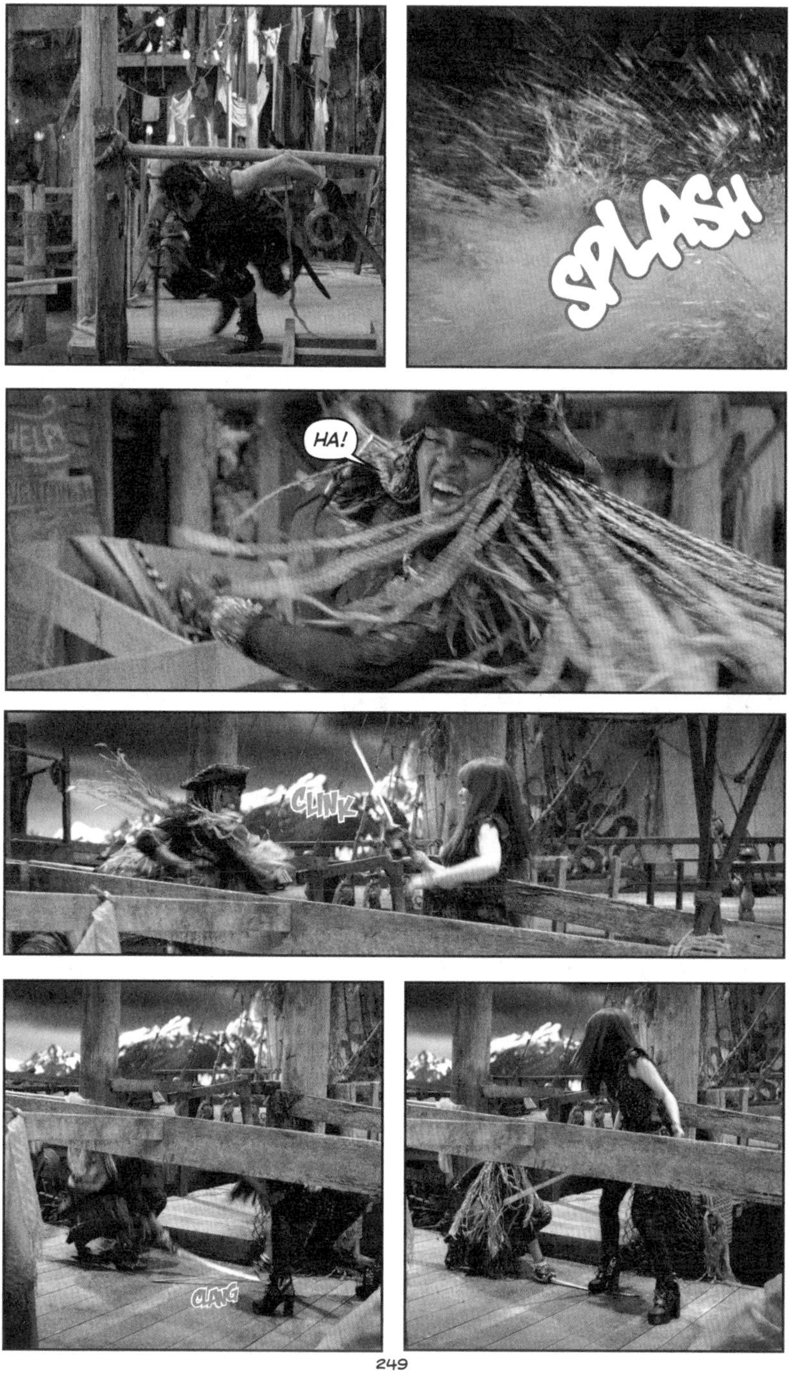
SPLASH
HA!
CLINK
CLANG

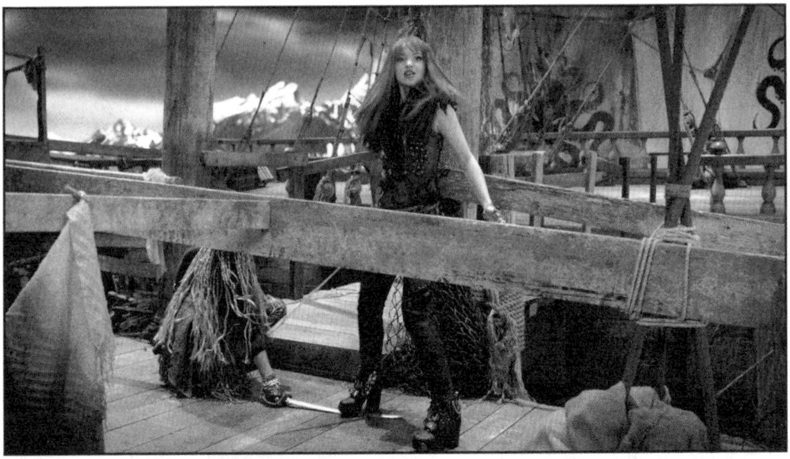

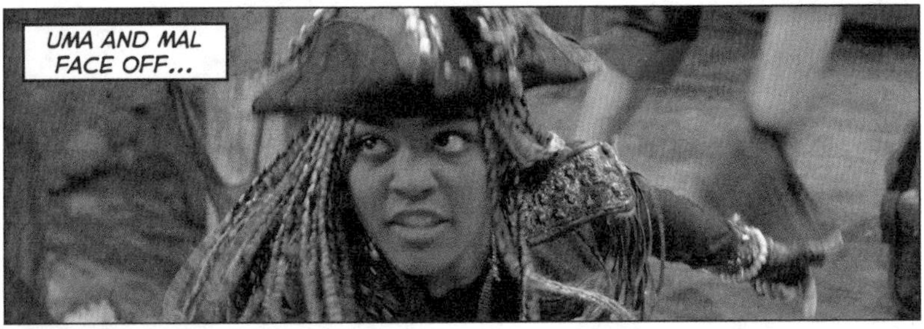
UMA AND MAL FACE OFF...

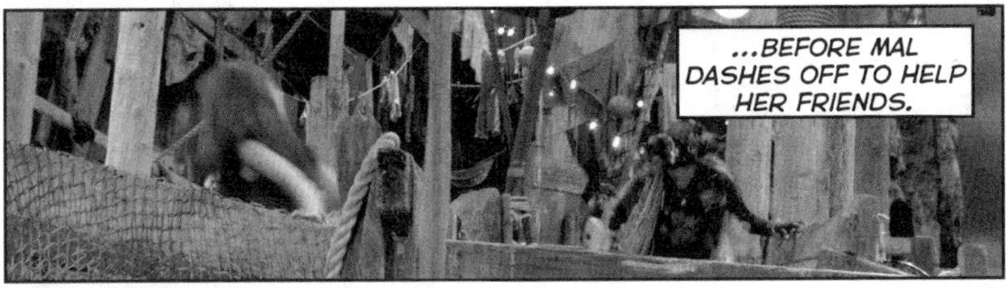
...BEFORE MAL DASHES OFF TO HELP HER FRIENDS.

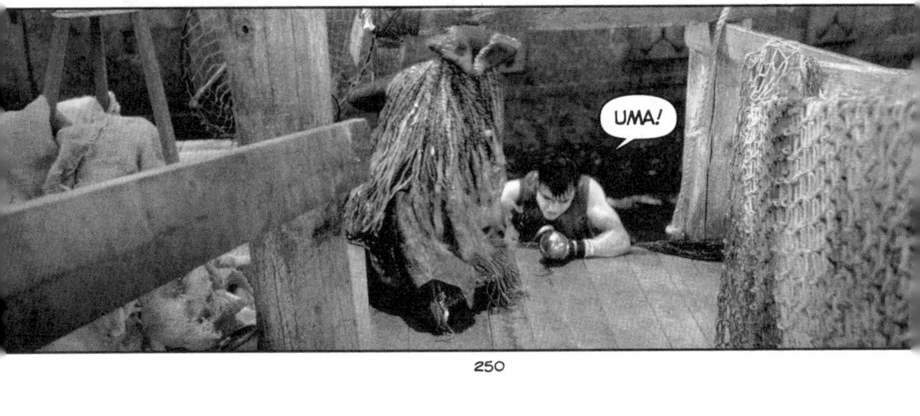
UMA!

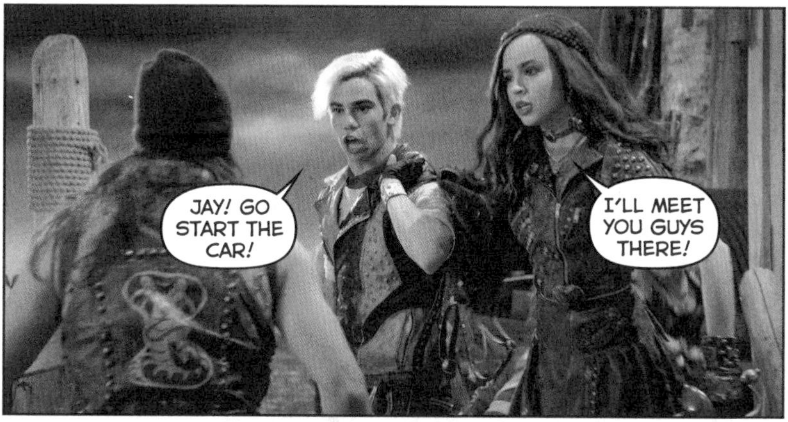
JAY! GO START THE CAR!
I'LL MEET YOU GUYS THERE!

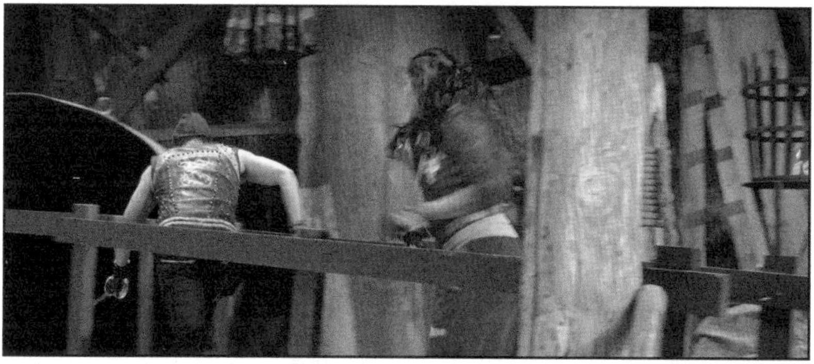

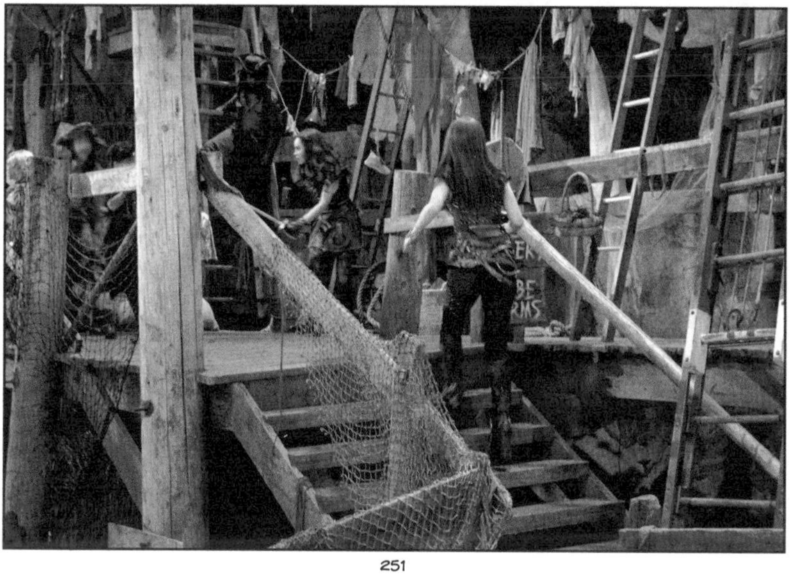

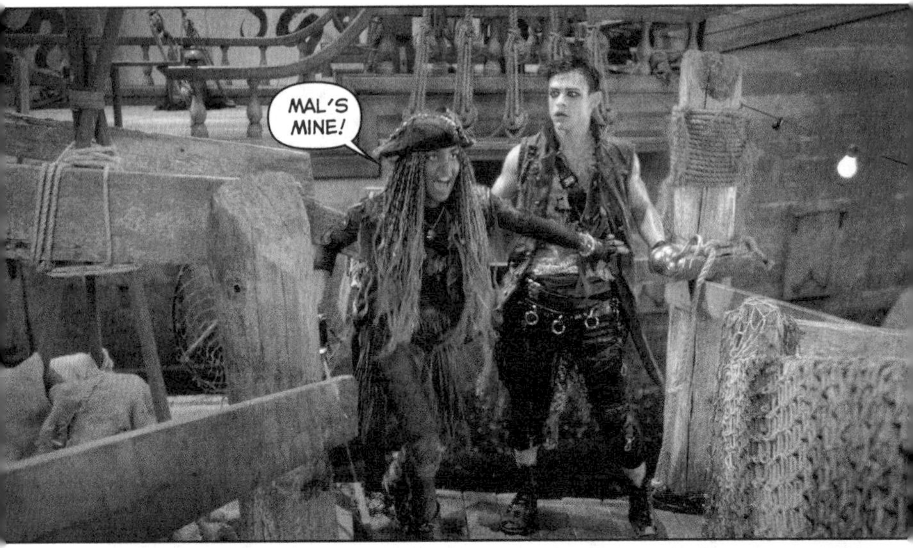
MAL'S MINE!

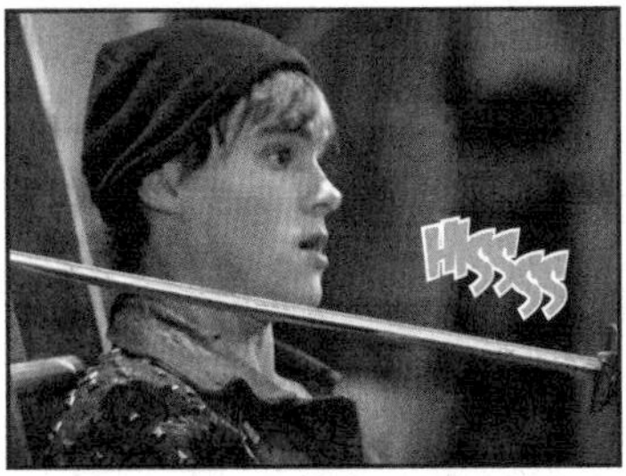
HISSSS

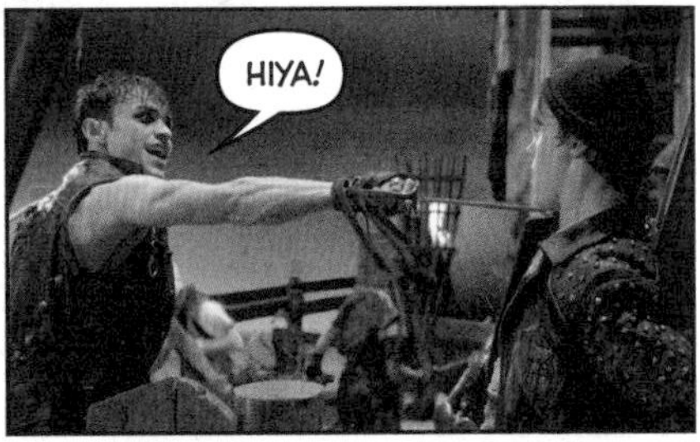
HIYA!

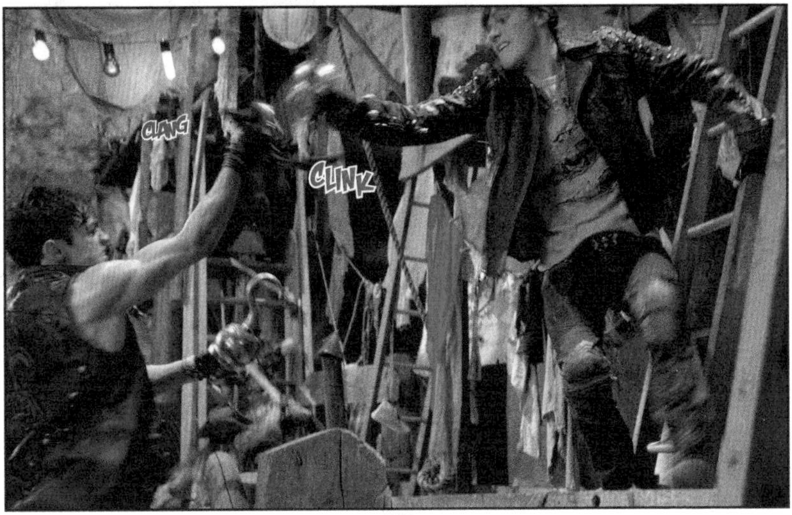
CLANG
CLINK

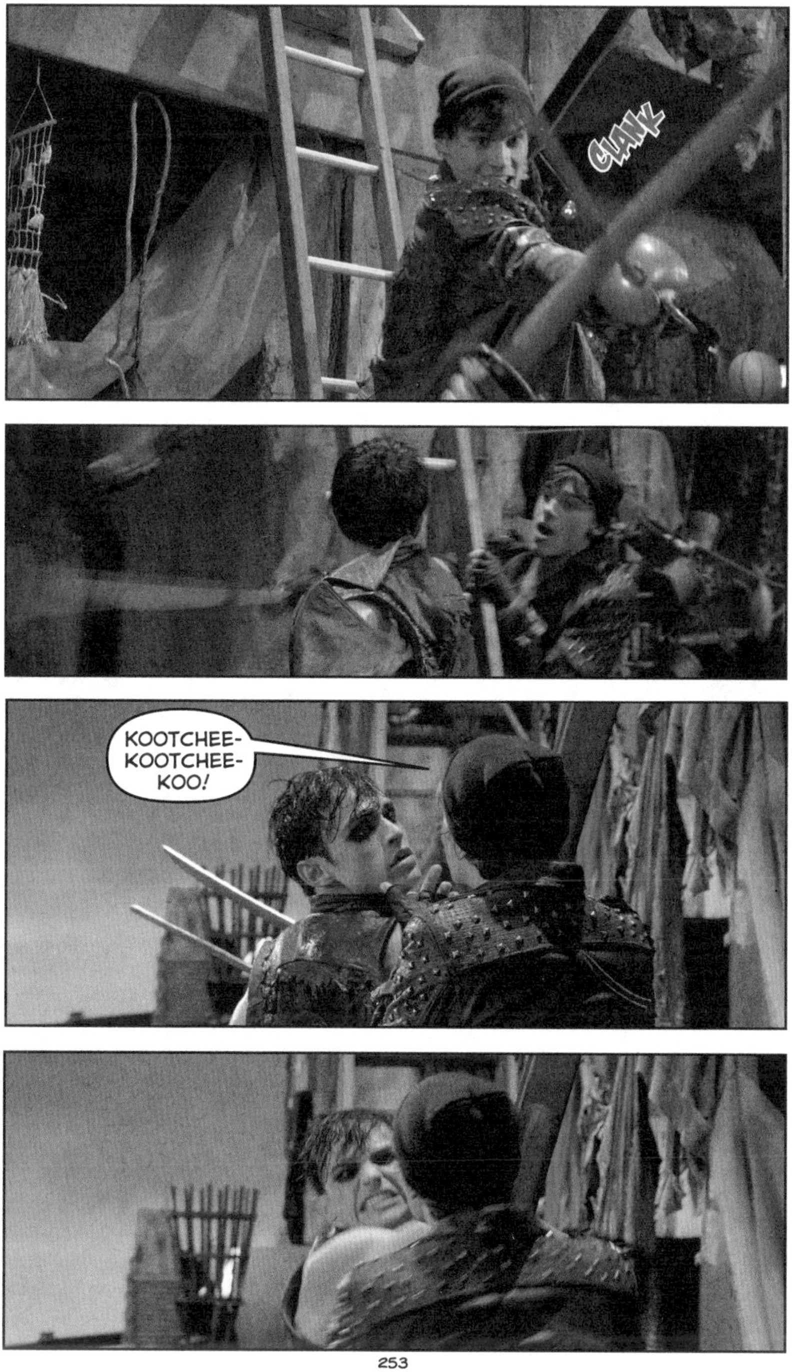
CLANK
KOOTCHEE-KOOTCHEE-KOO!

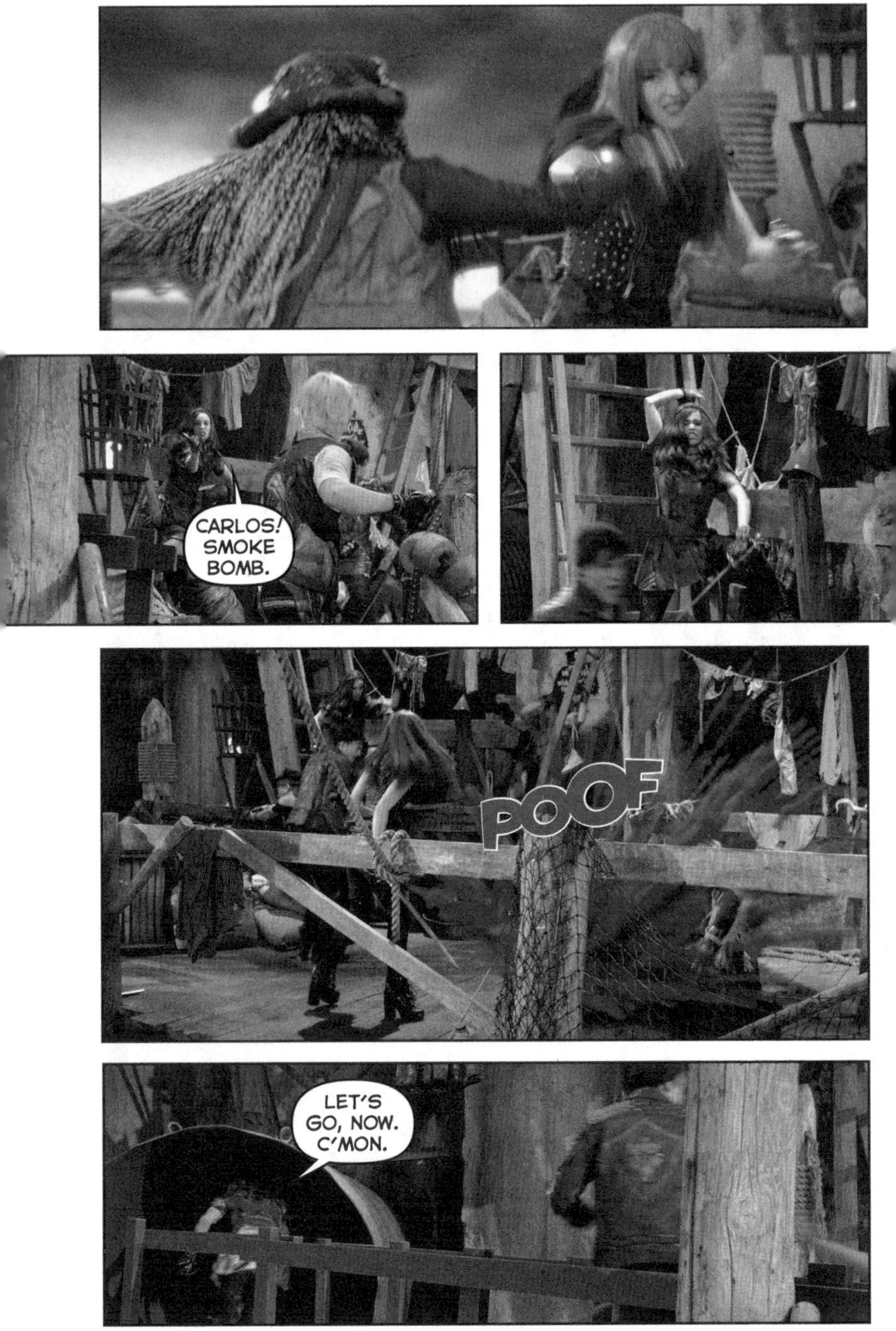
CARLOS! SMOKE BOMB.
POOF
LET'S GO, NOW. C'MON.

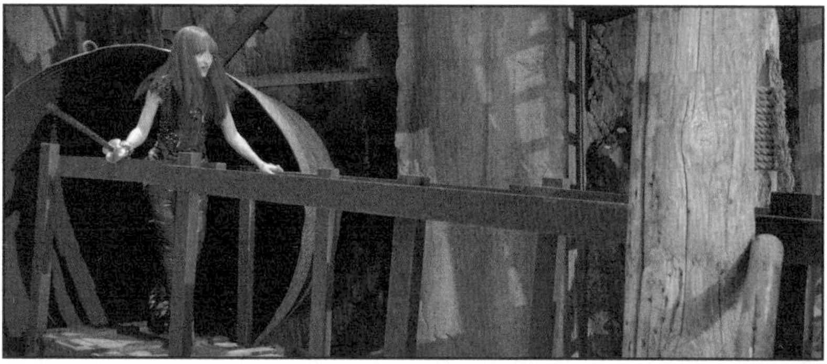

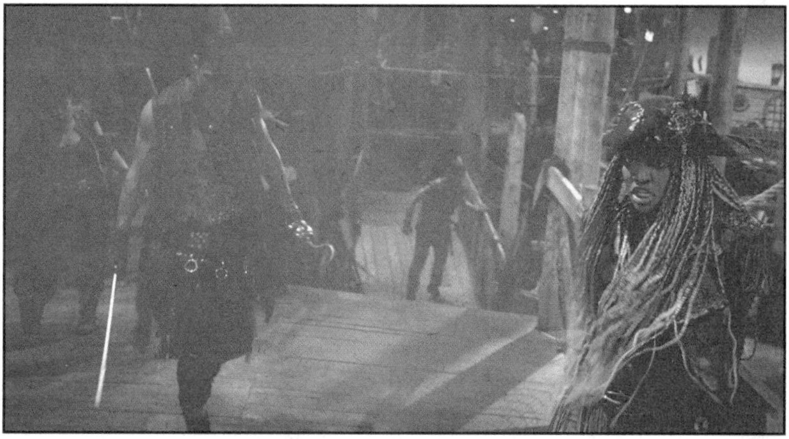

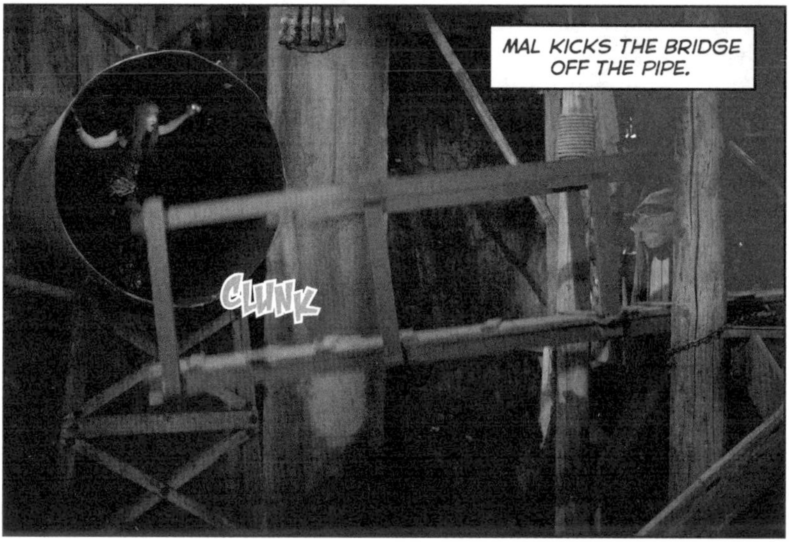
MAL KICKS THE BRIDGE OFF THE PIPE.
CLUNK

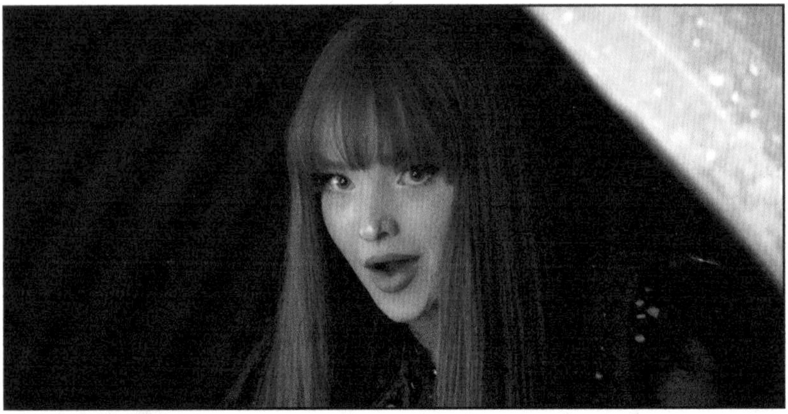

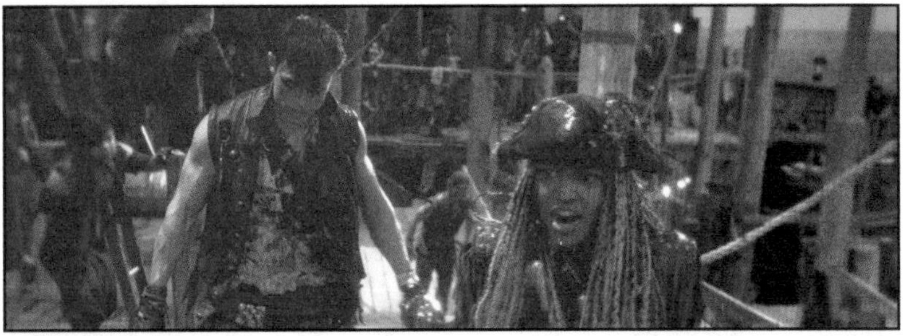

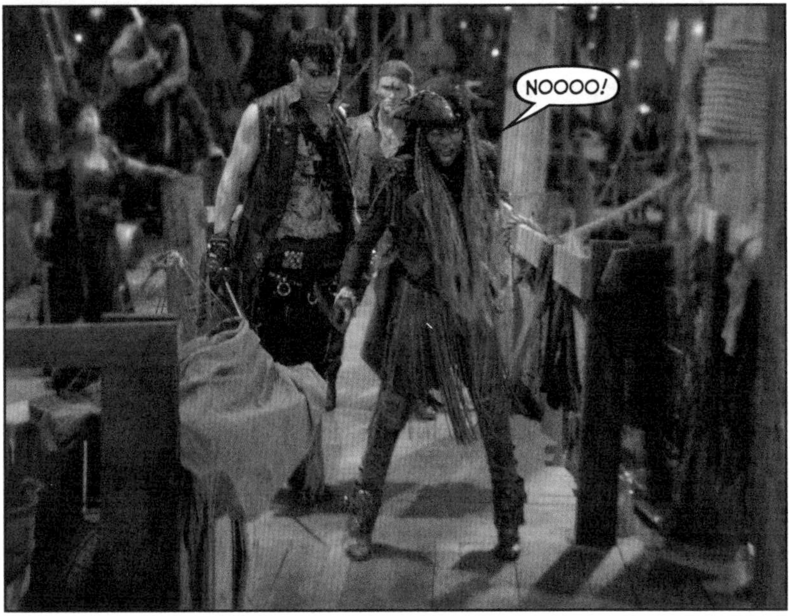

NOOOO!

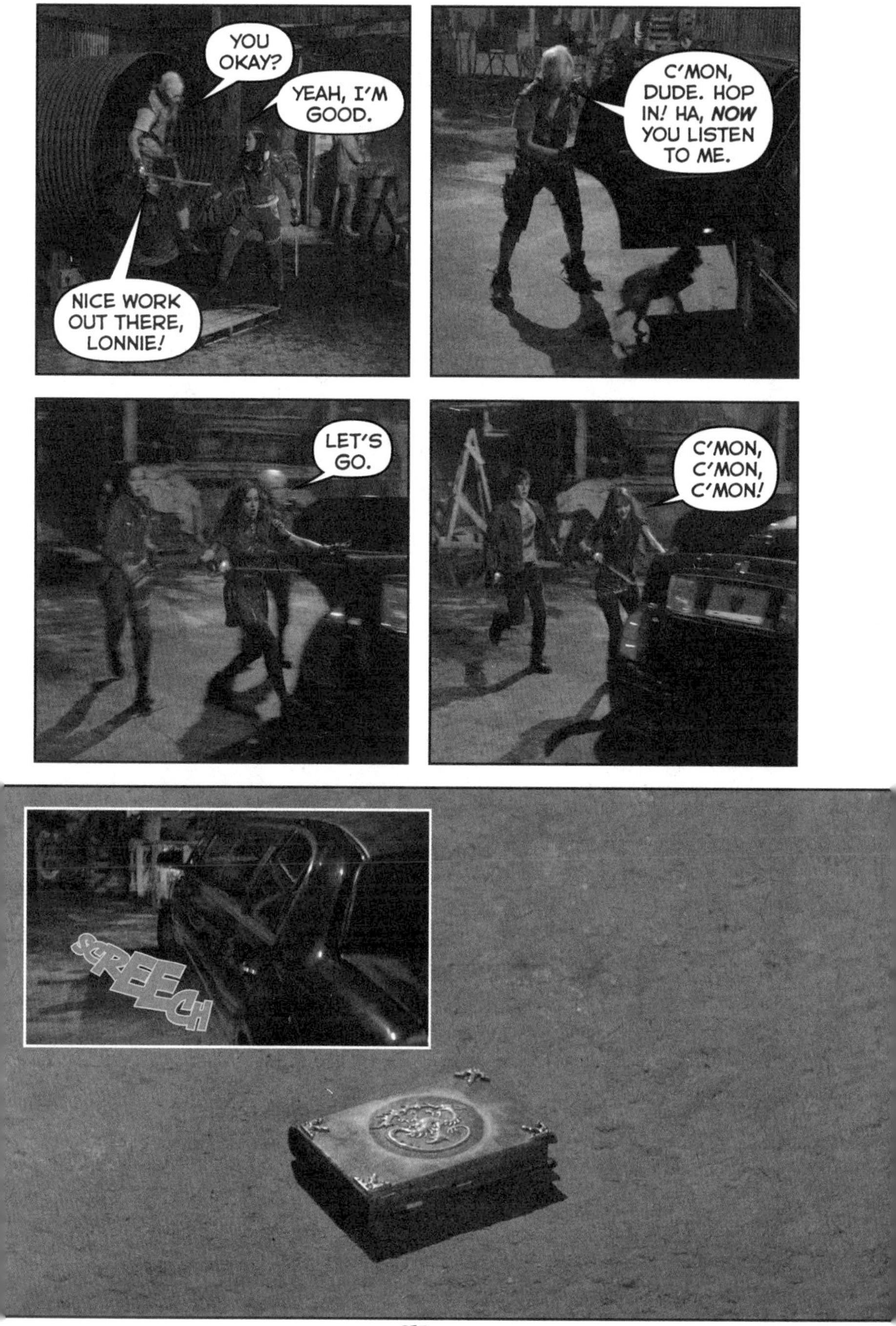
YOU OKAY?
YEAH, I'M GOOD.
NICE WORK OUT THERE, LONNIE!
C'MON, DUDE. HOP IN! HA, *NOW* YOU LISTEN TO ME.
LET'S GO.
C'MON, C'MON, C'MON!
SCREECH

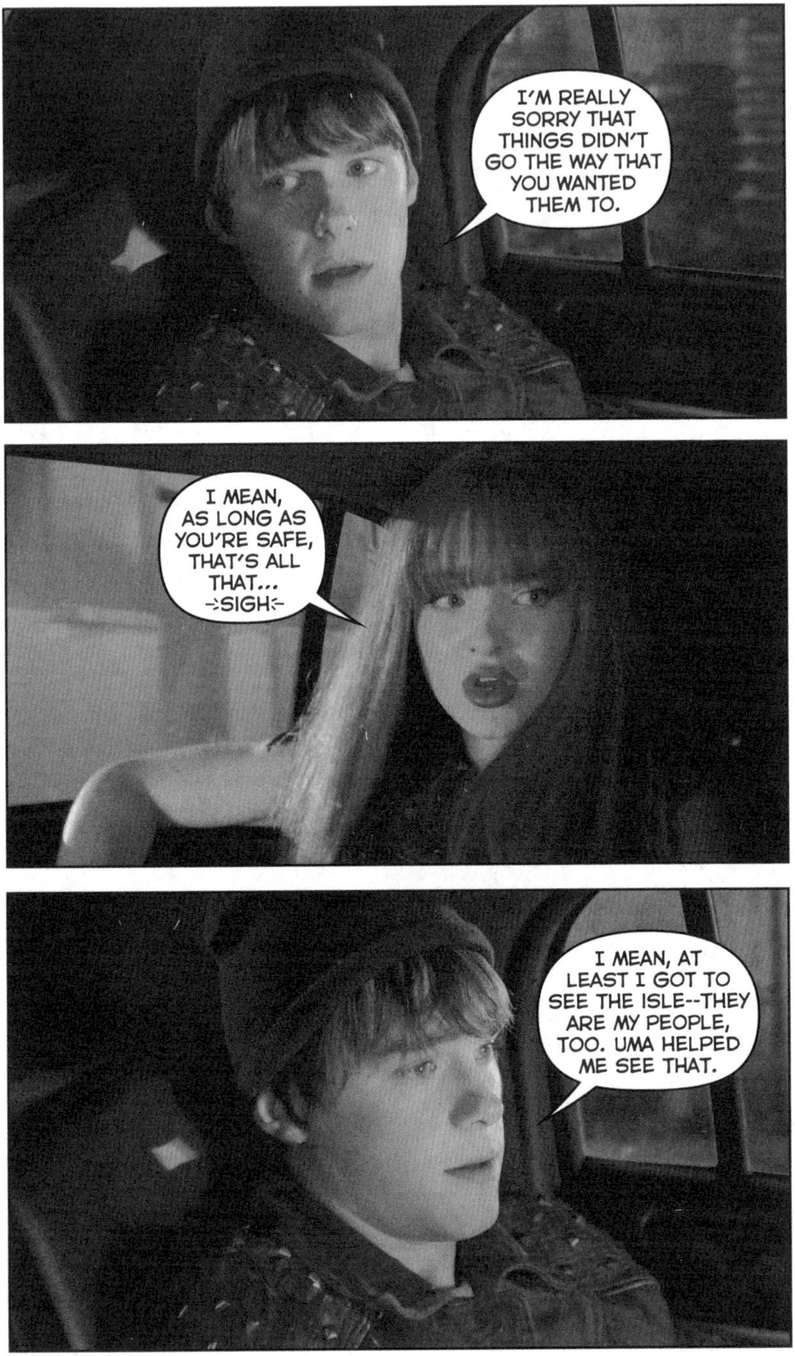
I'M REALLY SORRY THAT THINGS DIDN'T GO THE WAY THAT YOU WANTED THEM TO.
I MEAN, AS LONG AS YOU'RE SAFE, THAT'S ALL THAT... -SIGH-
I MEAN, AT LEAST I GOT TO SEE THE ISLE--THEY ARE MY PEOPLE, TOO. UMA HELPED ME SEE THAT.

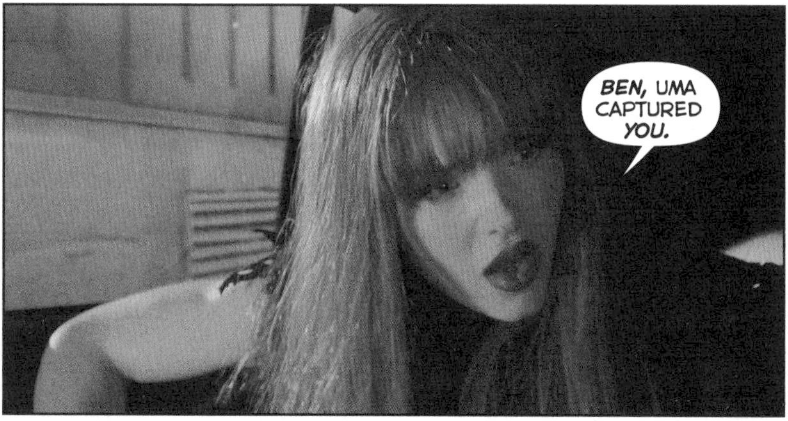
BEN, UMA CAPTURED YOU.

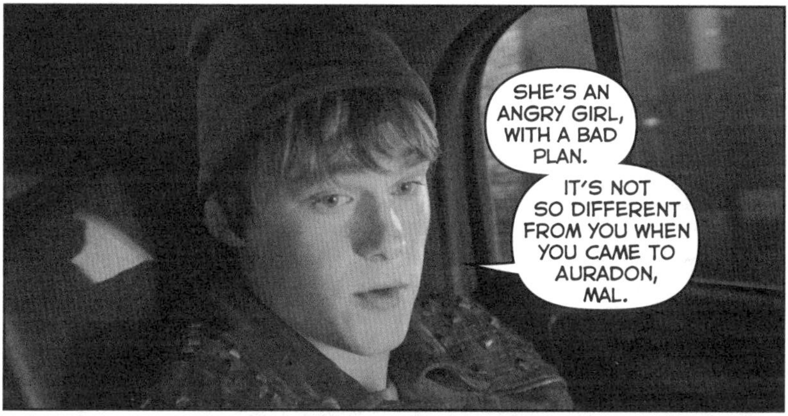
SHE'S AN ANGRY GIRL, WITH A BAD PLAN.
IT'S NOT SO DIFFERENT FROM YOU WHEN YOU CAME TO AURADON, MAL.

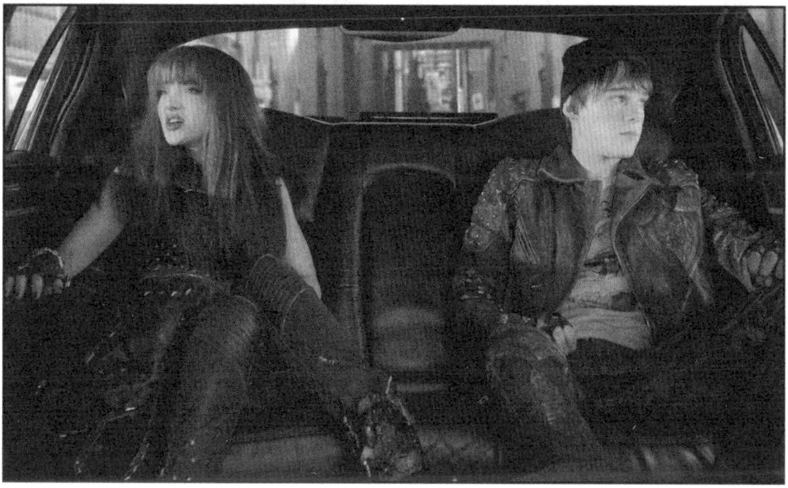

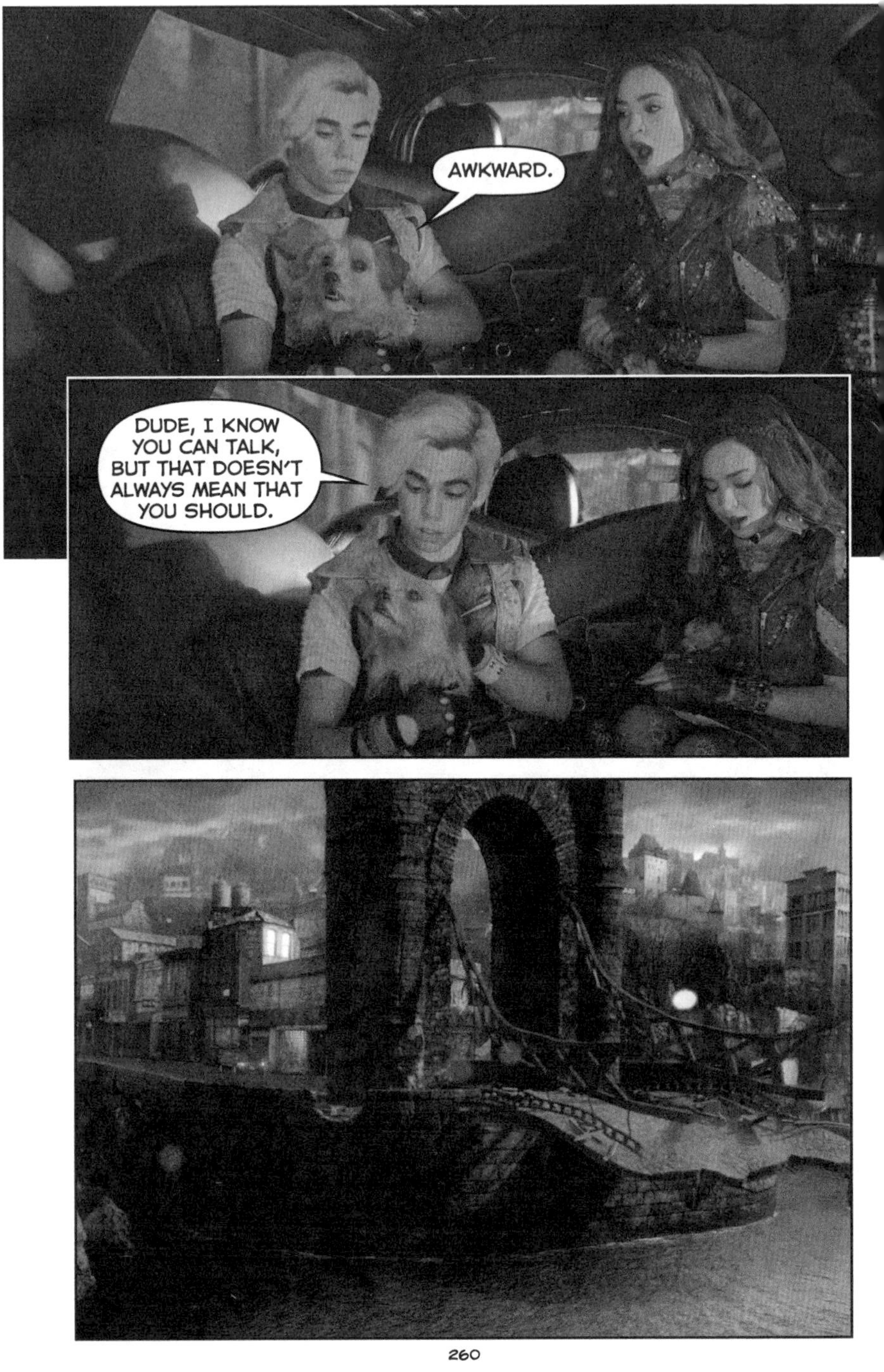
AWKWARD.
DUDE, I KNOW YOU CAN TALK, BUT THAT DOESN'T ALWAYS MEAN THAT YOU SHOULD.

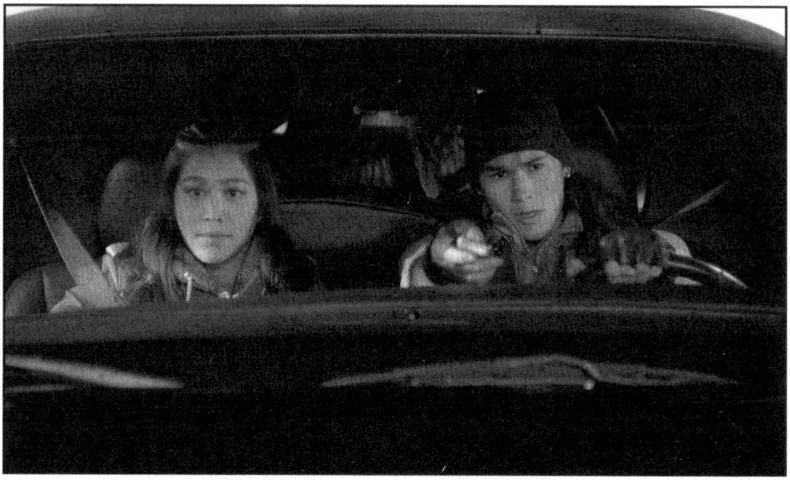

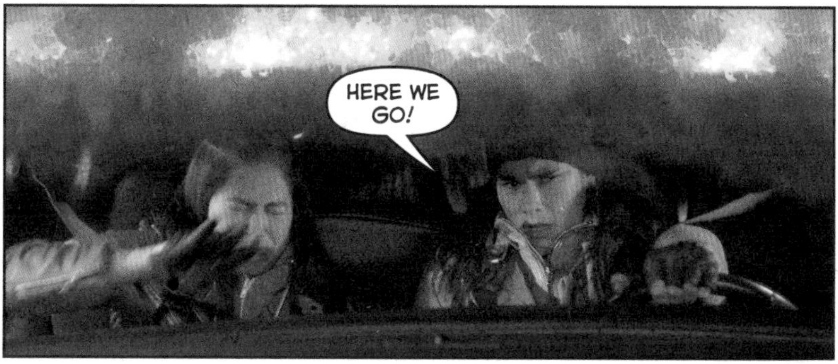
HERE WE GO!

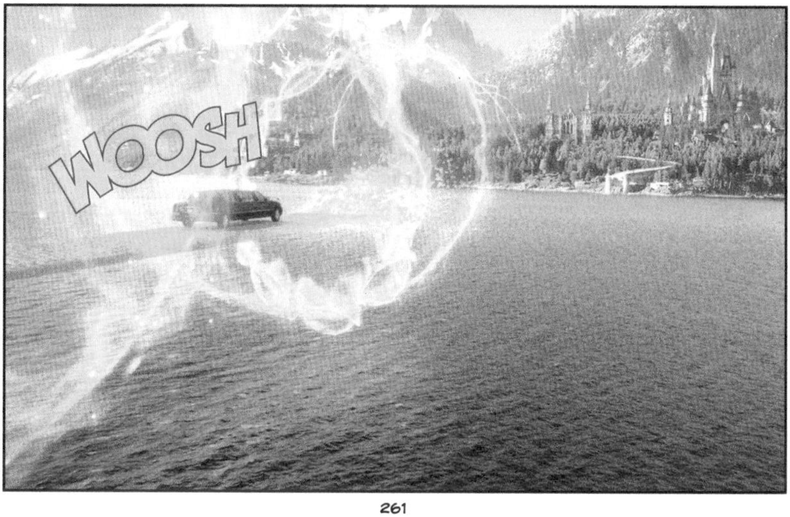
WOOSH

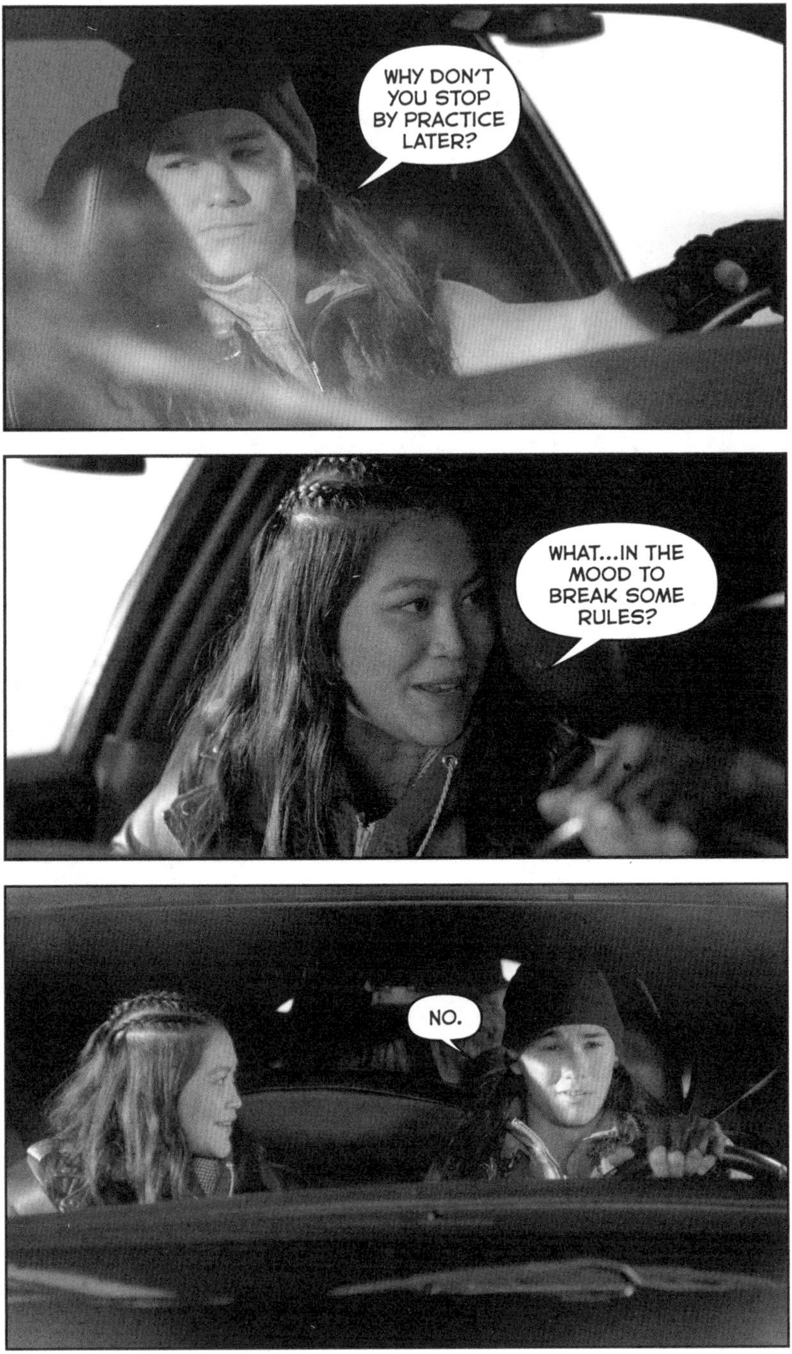
WHY DON'T YOU STOP BY PRACTICE LATER?
WHAT...IN THE MOOD TO BREAK SOME RULES?
NO.

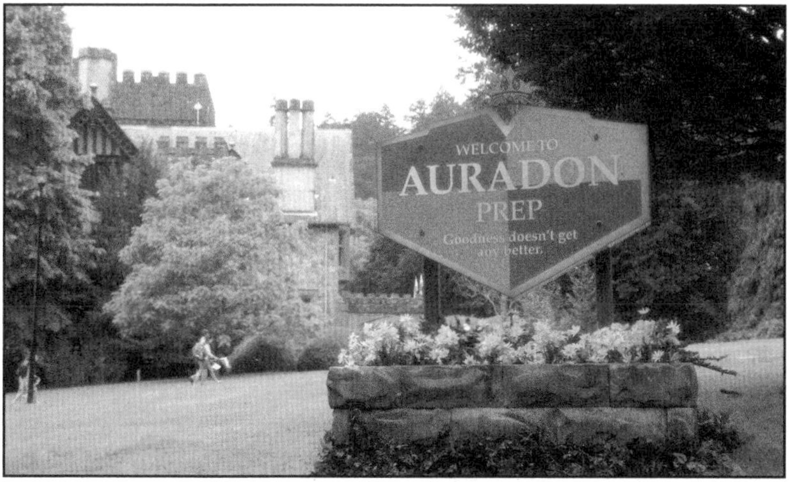
WELCOME TO
AURADON
PREP
Goodness doesn't get any better.

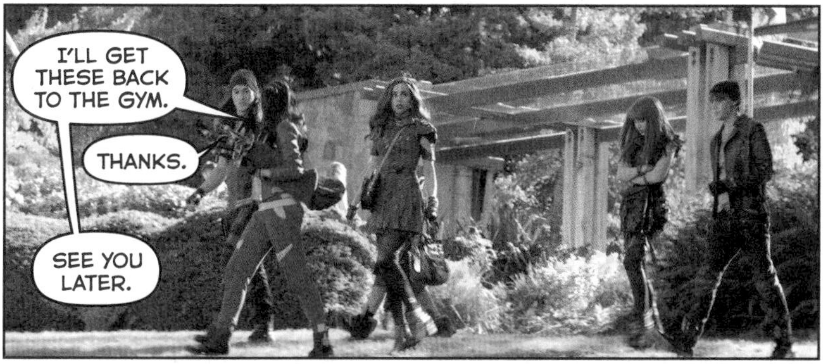
I'LL GET THESE BACK TO THE GYM.
THANKS.
SEE YOU LATER.

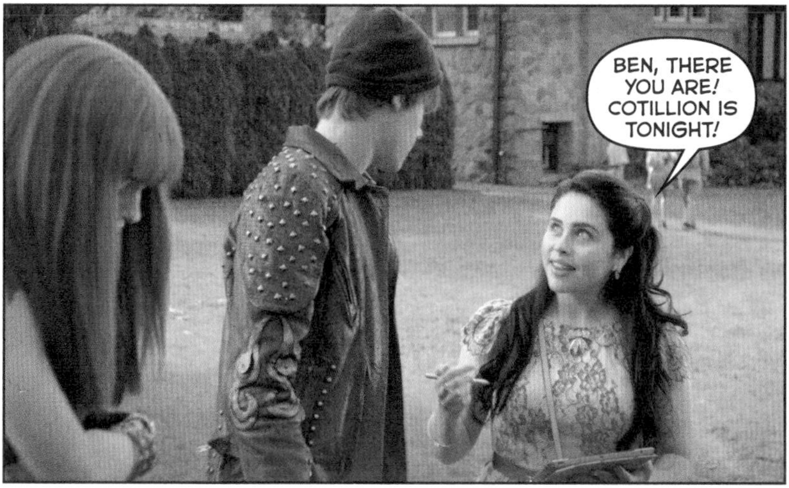
BEN, THERE YOU ARE! COTILLION IS TONIGHT!

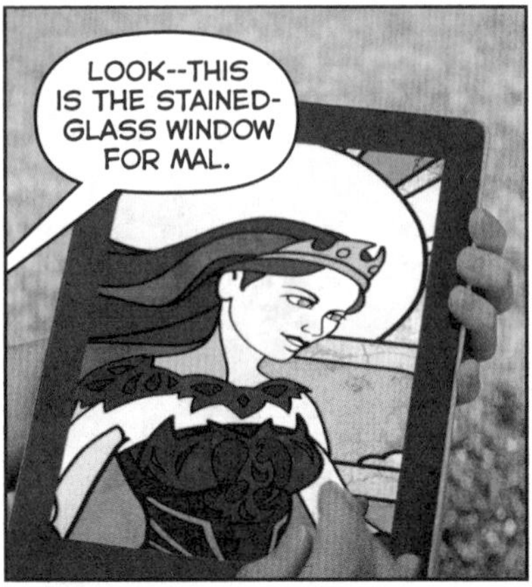
LOOK--THIS IS THE STAINED-GLASS WINDOW FOR MAL.

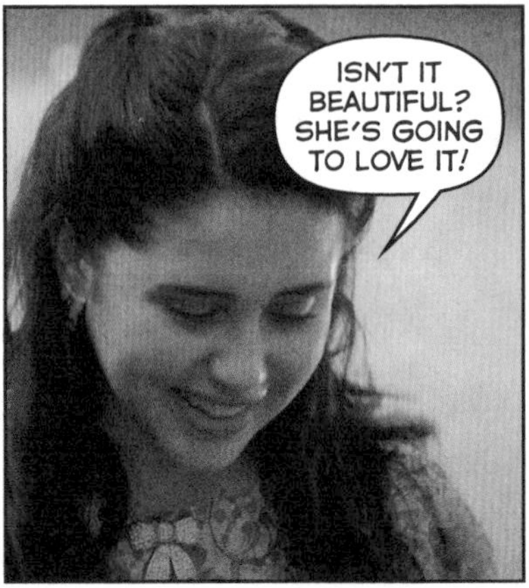
ISN'T IT BEAUTIFUL? SHE'S GOING TO LOVE IT!

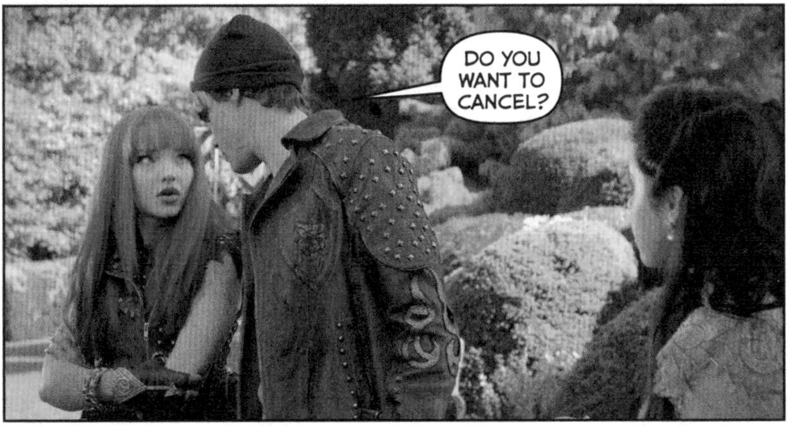
DO YOU WANT TO CANCEL?

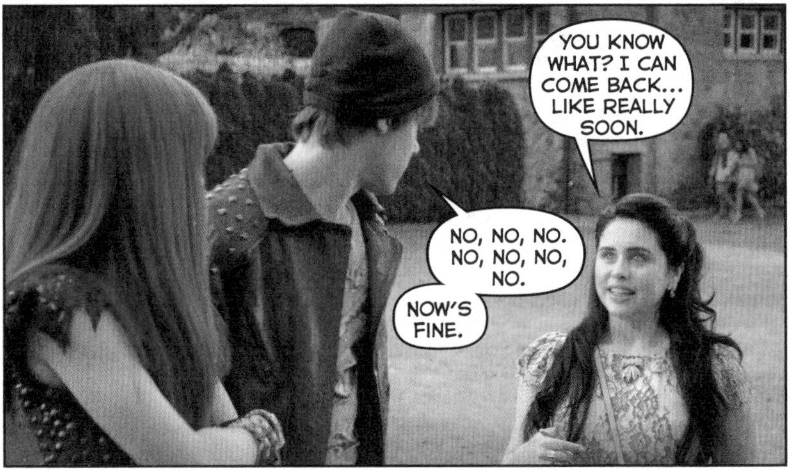
YOU KNOW WHAT? I CAN COME BACK... LIKE REALLY SOON.
NO, NO, NO. NO, NO, NO, NO.
NOW'S FINE.

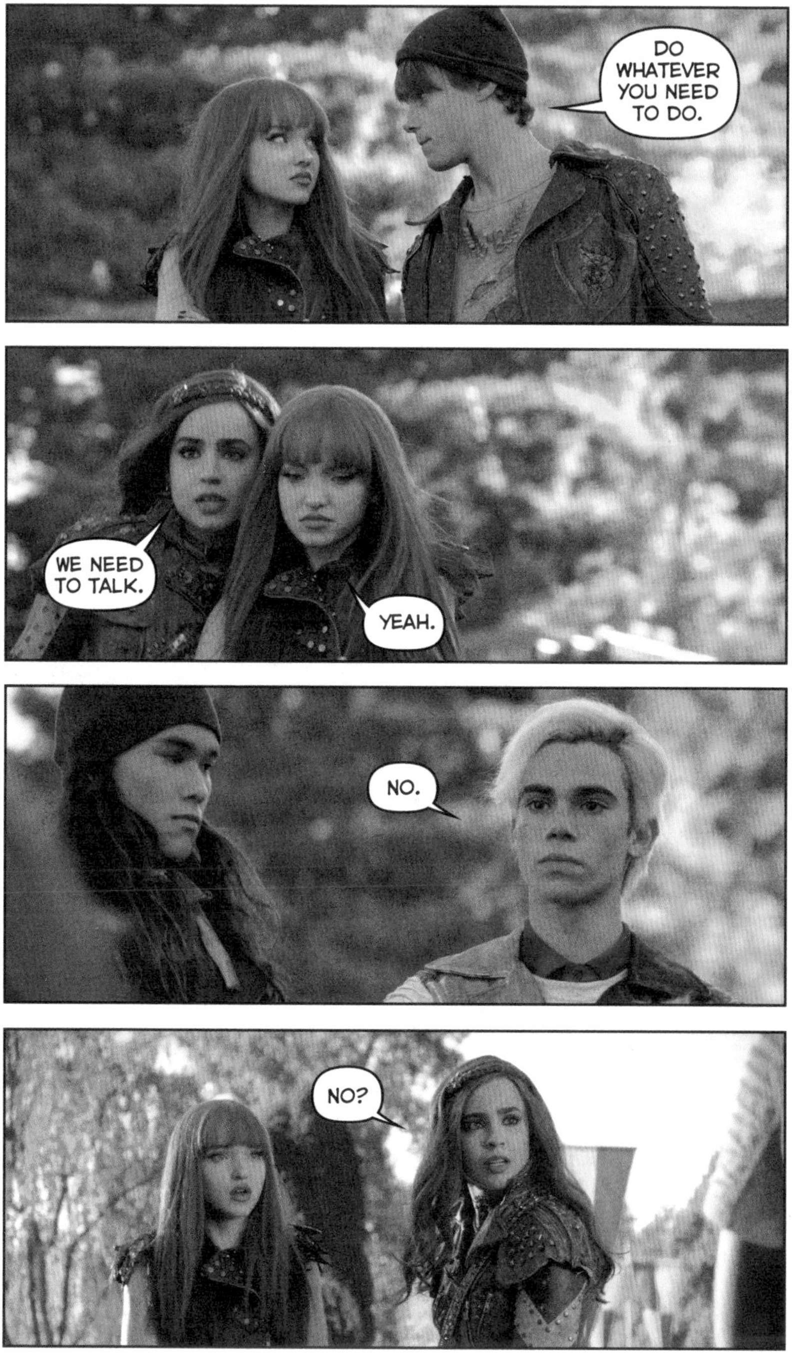
DO WHATEVER YOU NEED TO DO.
WE NEED TO TALK.
YEAH.
NO.
NO?

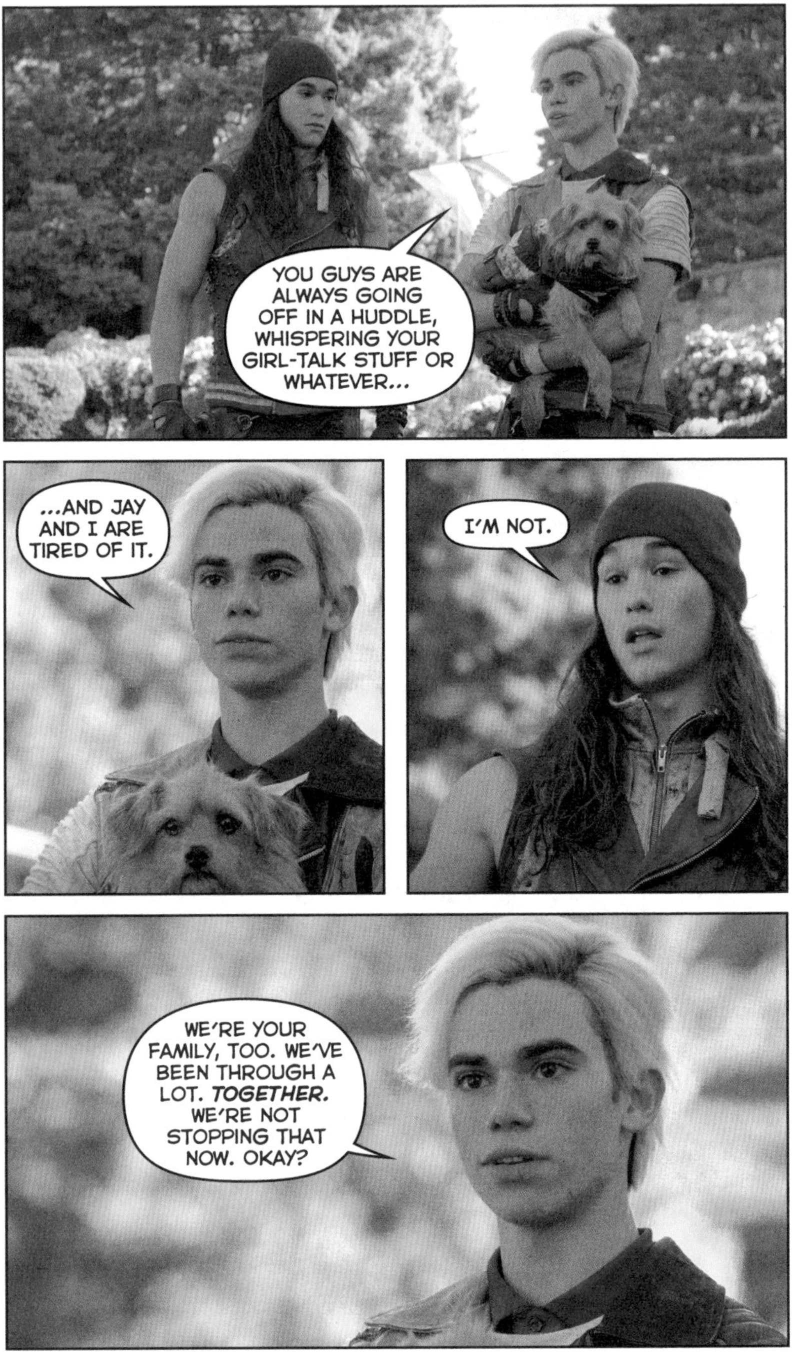
YOU GUYS ARE ALWAYS GOING OFF IN A HUDDLE, WHISPERING YOUR GIRL-TALK STUFF OR WHATEVER...
...AND JAY AND I ARE TIRED OF IT.
I'M NOT.
WE'RE YOUR FAMILY, TOO. WE'VE BEEN THROUGH A LOT. *TOGETHER.* WE'RE NOT STOPPING THAT NOW. OKAY?

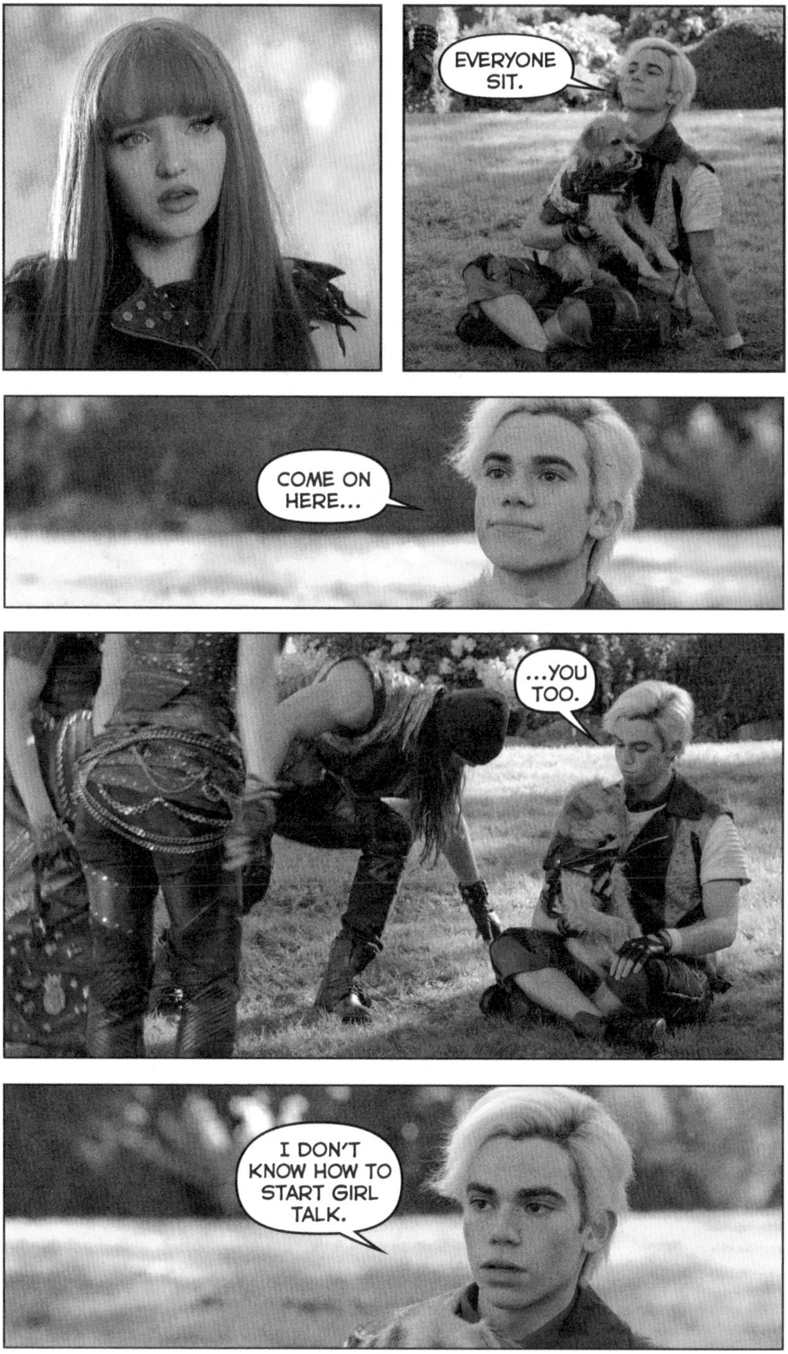
EVERYONE SIT.
COME ON HERE...
...YOU TOO.
I DON'T KNOW HOW TO START GIRL TALK.

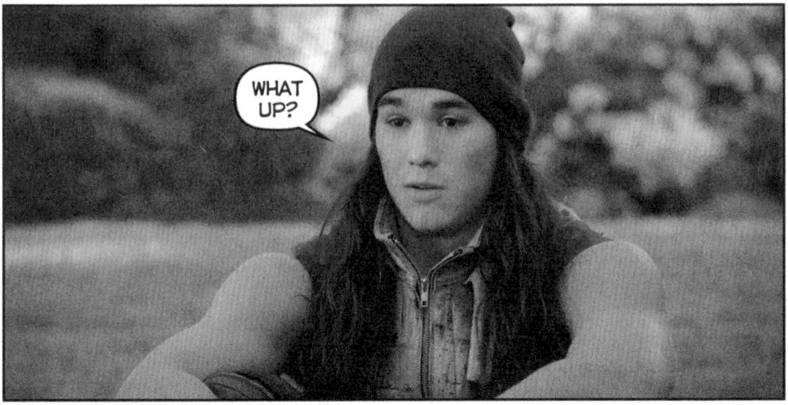
WHAT UP?

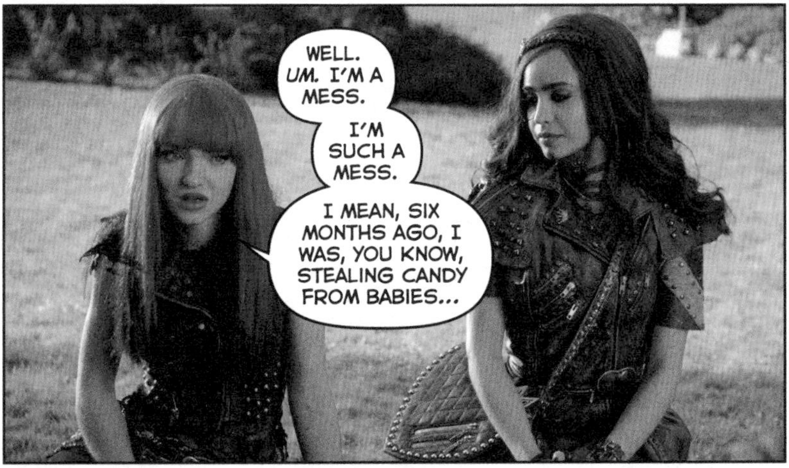
WELL. *UM.* I'M A MESS.
I'M SUCH A MESS.
I MEAN, SIX MONTHS AGO, I WAS, YOU KNOW, STEALING CANDY FROM BABIES...

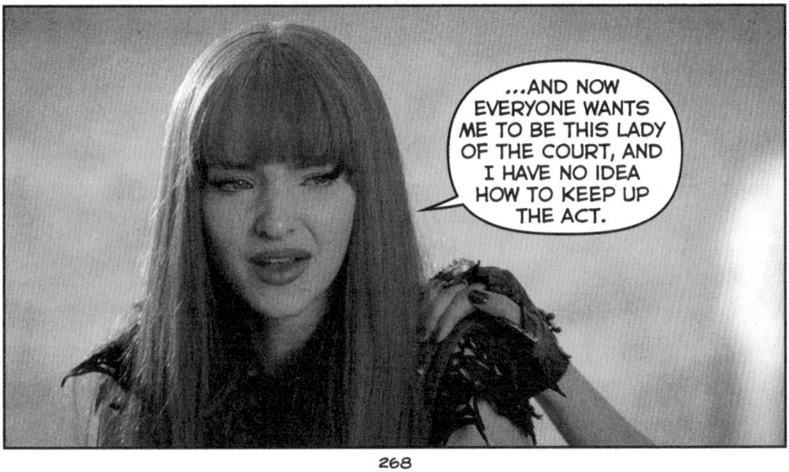
...AND NOW EVERYONE WANTS ME TO BE THIS LADY OF THE COURT, AND I HAVE NO IDEA HOW TO KEEP UP THE ACT.

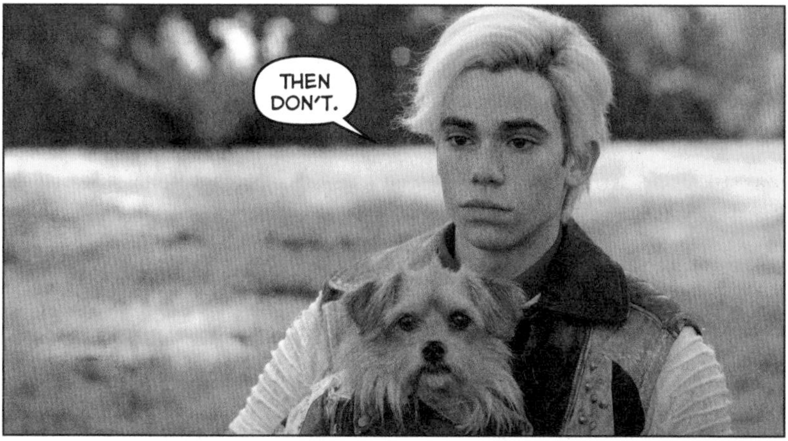
THEN DON'T.

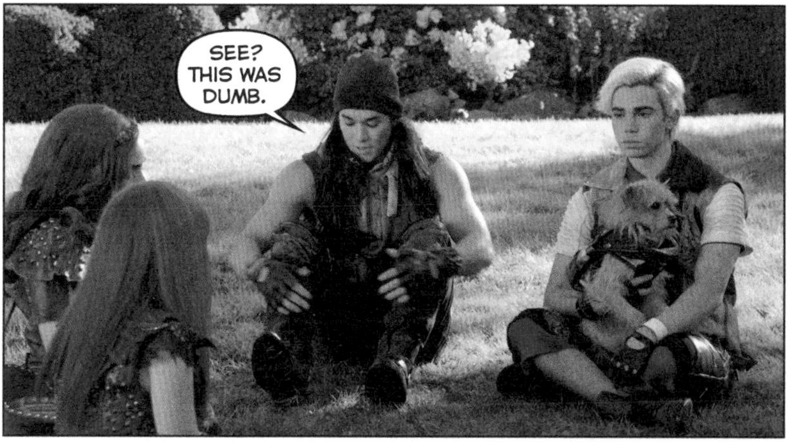
SEE? THIS WAS DUMB.

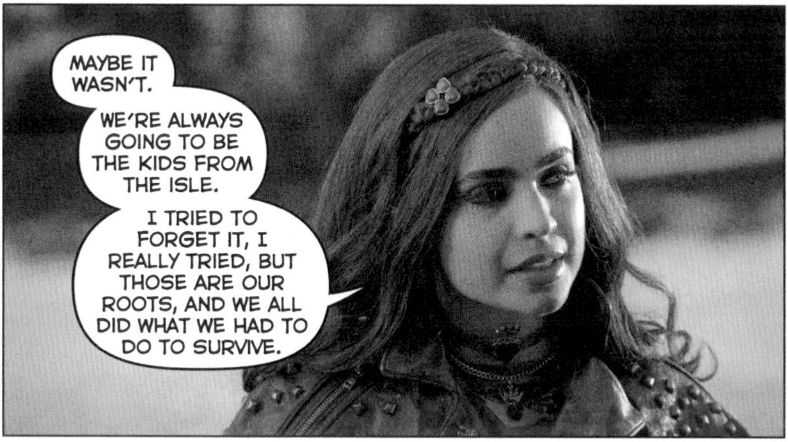
MAYBE IT WASN'T.
WE'RE ALWAYS GOING TO BE THE KIDS FROM THE ISLE.
I TRIED TO FORGET IT, I REALLY TRIED, BUT THOSE ARE OUR ROOTS, AND WE ALL DID WHAT WE HAD TO DO TO SURVIVE.

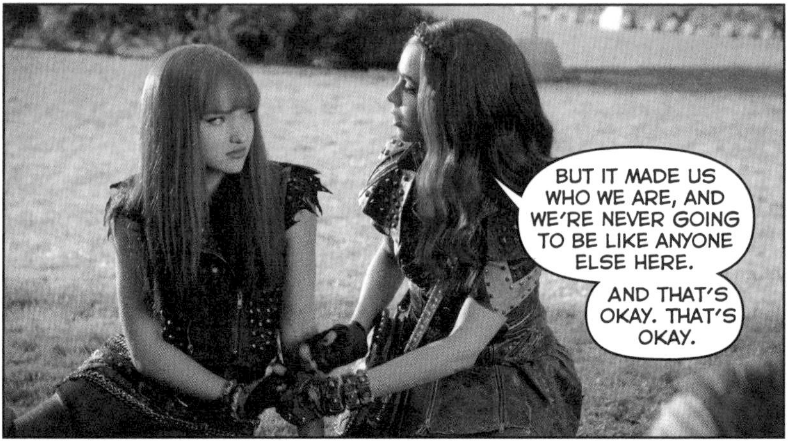
BUT IT MADE US WHO WE ARE, AND WE'RE NEVER GOING TO BE LIKE ANYONE ELSE HERE.
AND THAT'S OKAY. THAT'S OKAY.

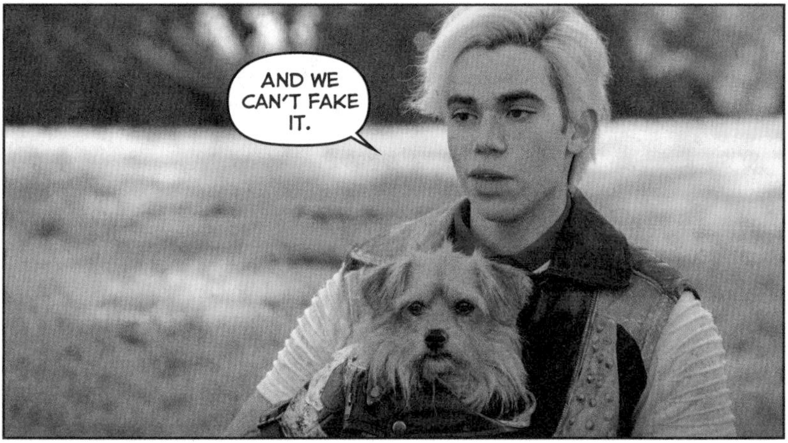
AND WE CAN'T FAKE IT.

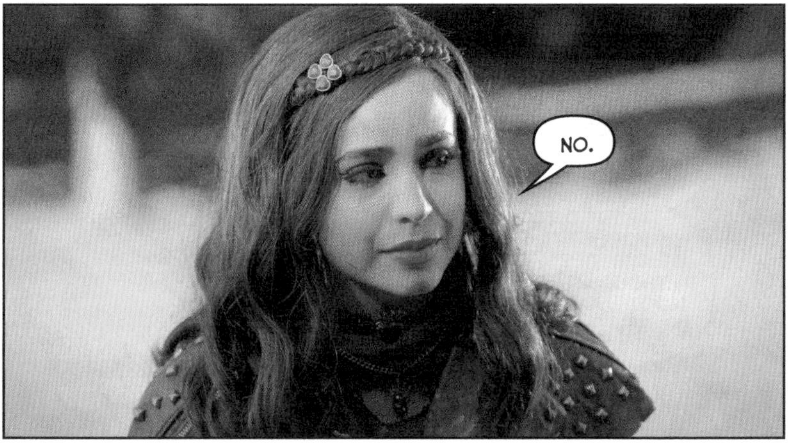
NO.

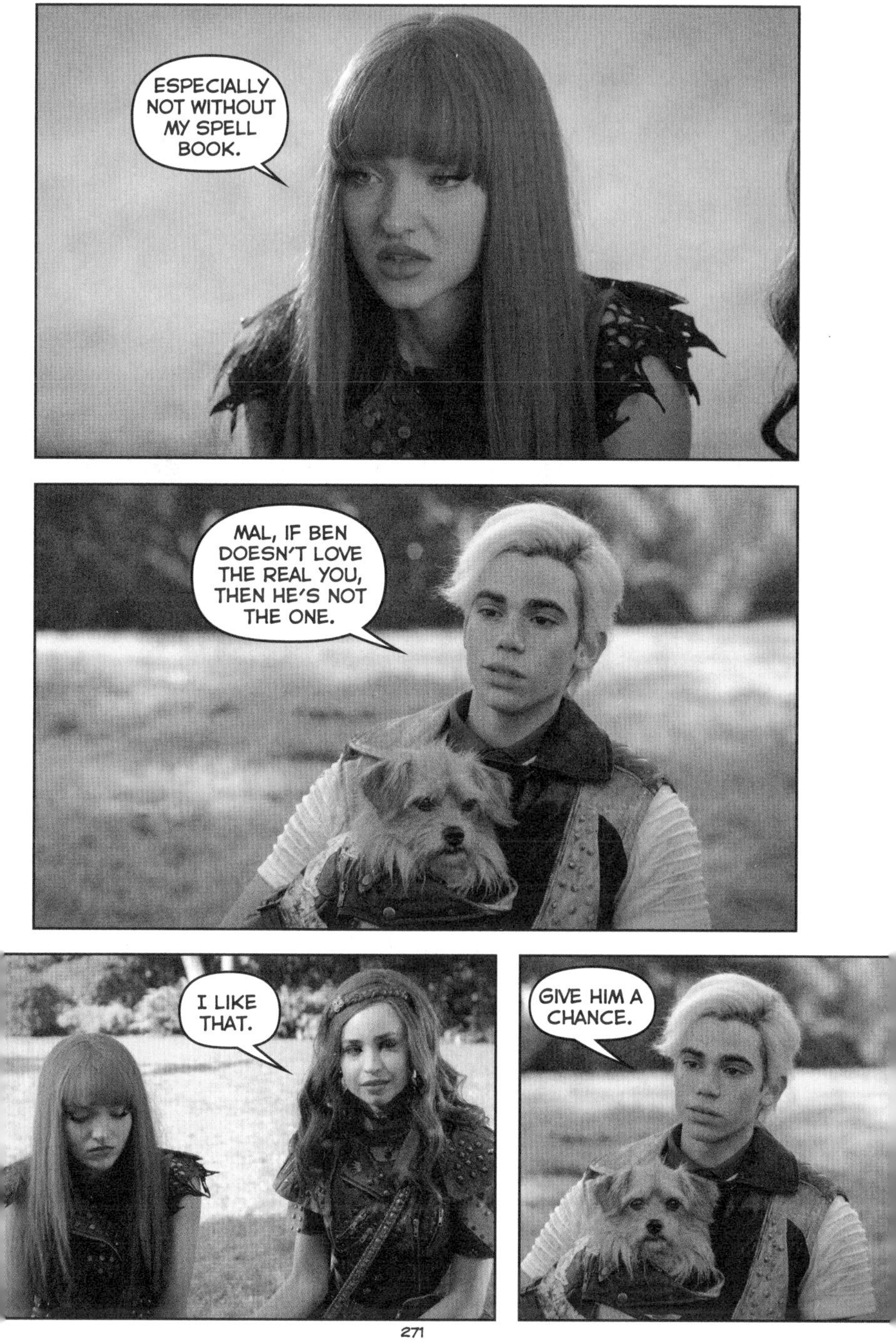
ESPECIALLY NOT WITHOUT MY SPELL BOOK.
MAL, IF BEN DOESN'T LOVE THE REAL YOU, THEN HE'S NOT THE ONE.
I LIKE THAT.
GIVE HIM A CHANCE.

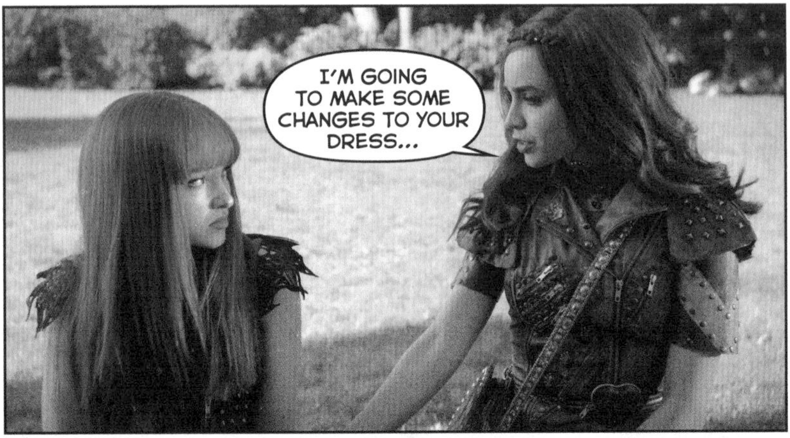
I'M GOING TO MAKE SOME CHANGES TO YOUR DRESS...
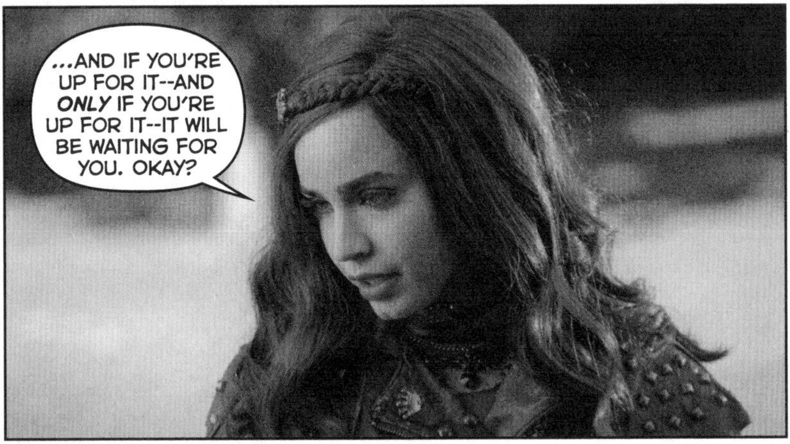
...AND IF YOU'RE UP FOR IT--AND *ONLY* IF YOU'RE UP FOR IT--IT WILL BE WAITING FOR YOU. OKAY?
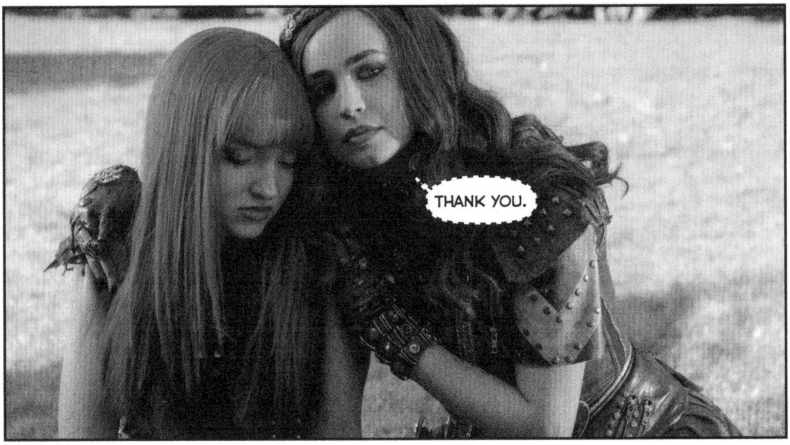
THANK YOU.

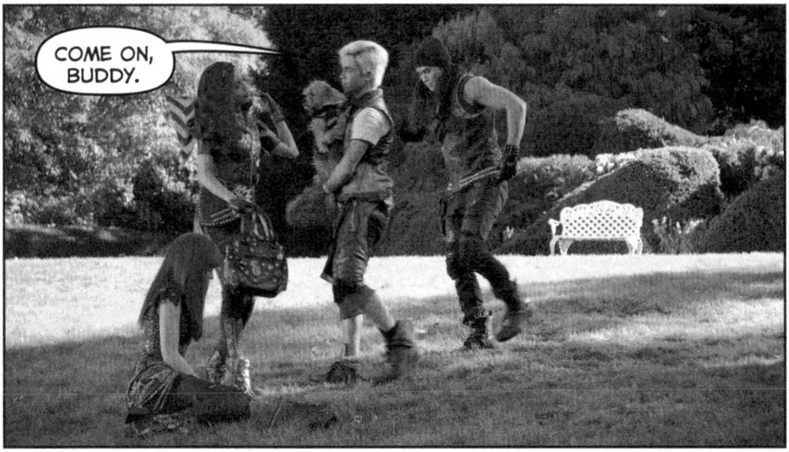
COME ON,
BUDDY.

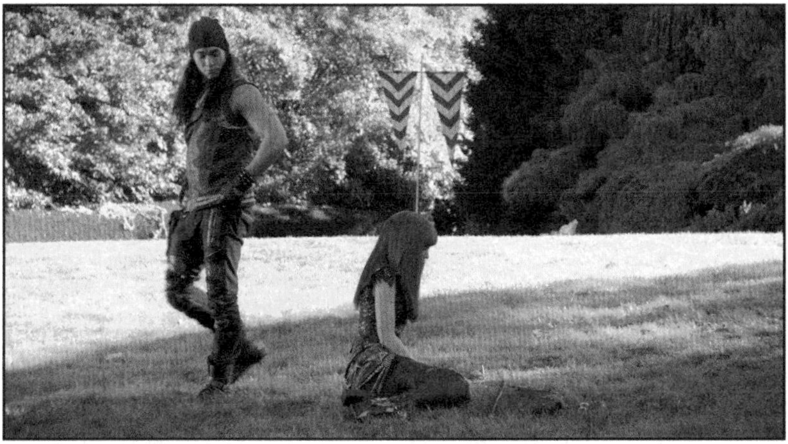

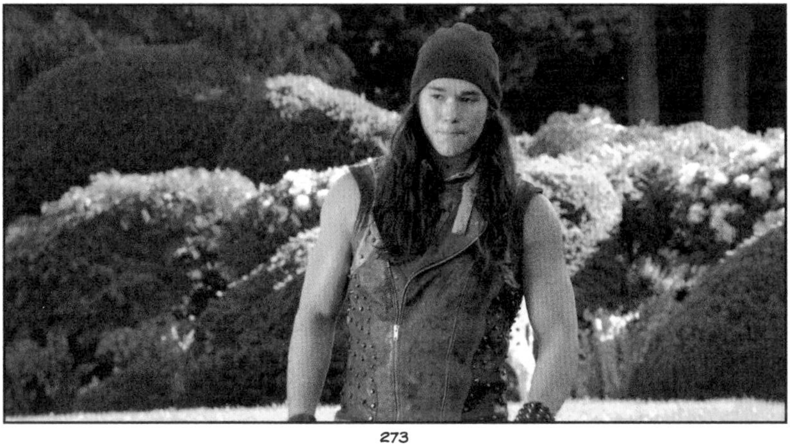

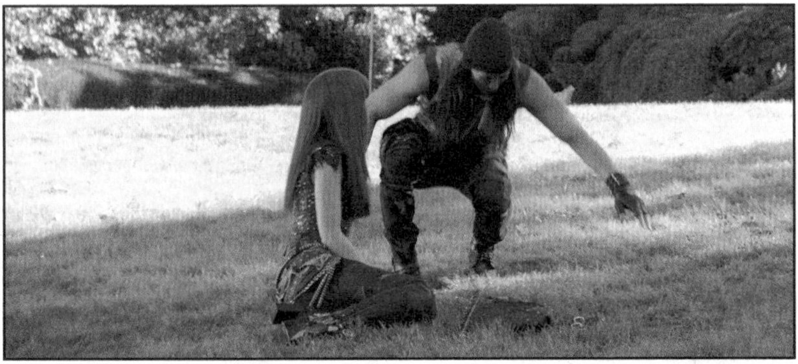

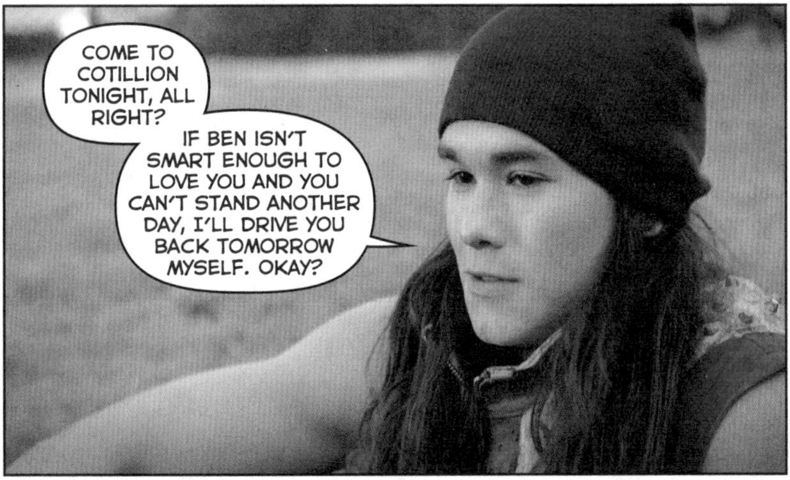
COME TO COTILLION TONIGHT, ALL RIGHT?
IF BEN ISN'T SMART ENOUGH TO LOVE YOU AND YOU CAN'T STAND ANOTHER DAY, I'LL DRIVE YOU BACK TOMORROW MYSELF. OKAY?

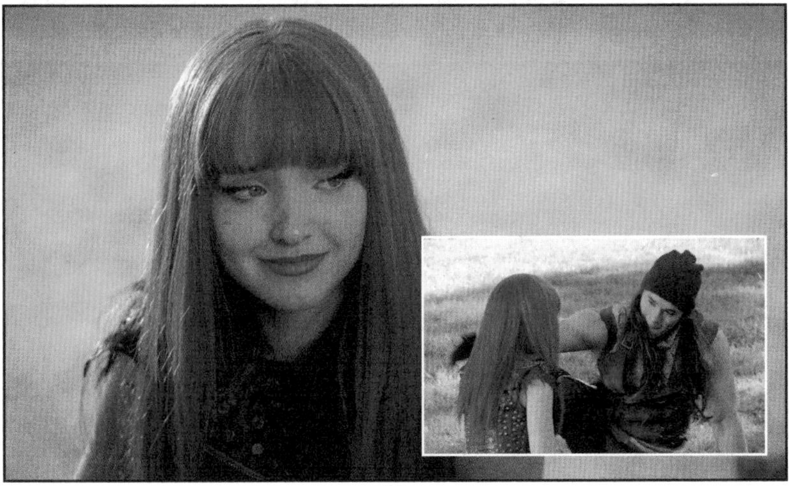

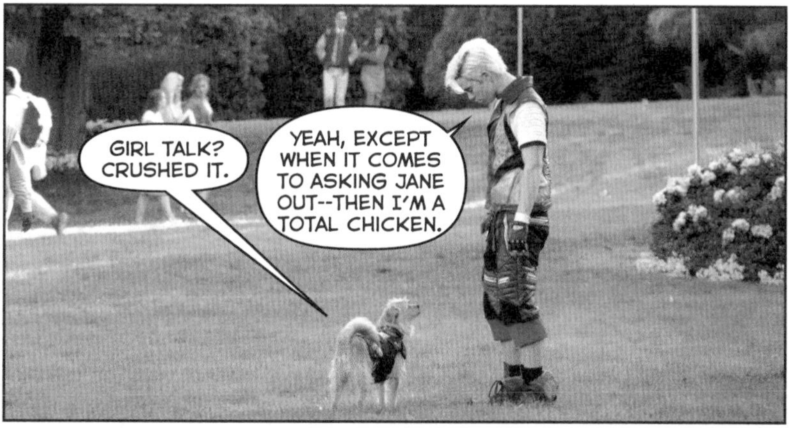
GIRL TALK? CRUSHED IT.
YEAH, EXCEPT WHEN IT COMES TO ASKING JANE OUT--THEN I'M A TOTAL CHICKEN.

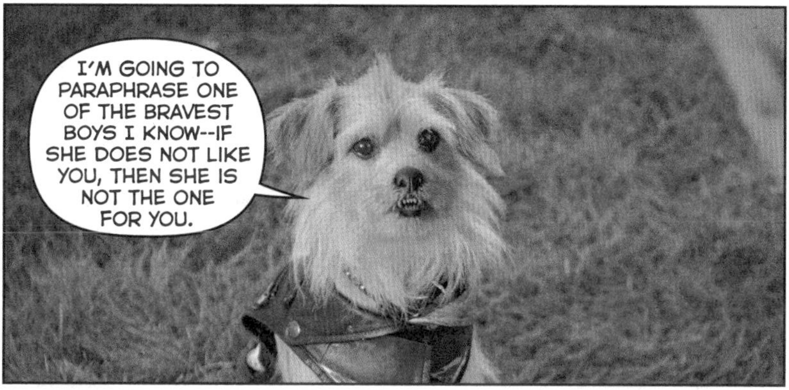
I'M GOING TO PARAPHRASE ONE OF THE BRAVEST BOYS I KNOW--IF SHE DOES NOT LIKE YOU, THEN SHE IS NOT THE ONE FOR YOU.

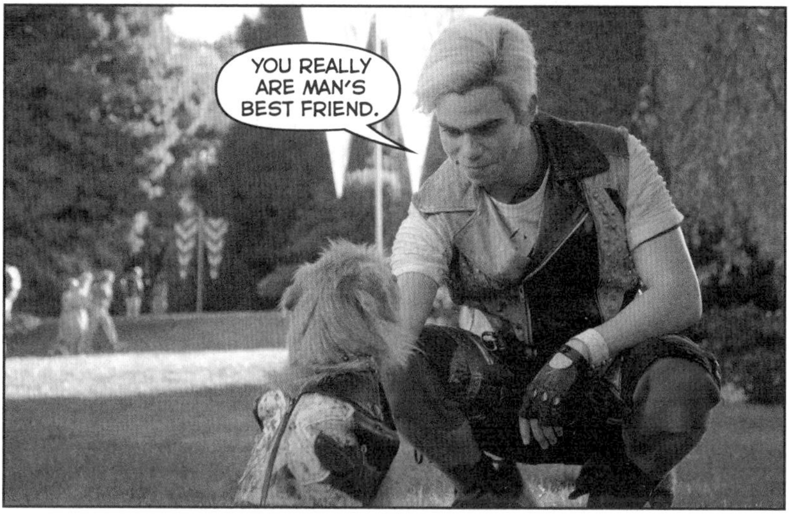
YOU REALLY ARE MAN'S BEST FRIEND.

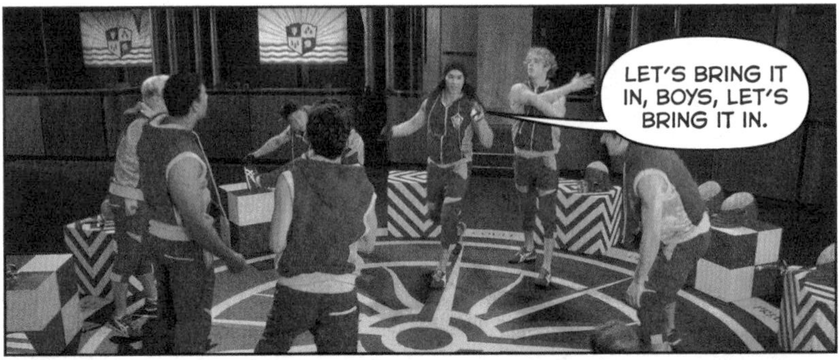
LET'S BRING IT IN, BOYS, LET'S BRING IT IN.

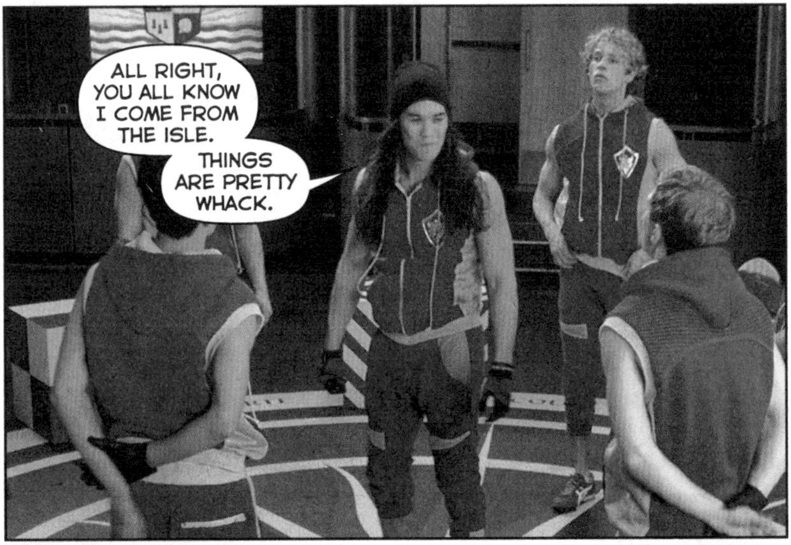
ALL RIGHT, YOU ALL KNOW I COME FROM THE ISLE.
THINGS ARE PRETTY WHACK.

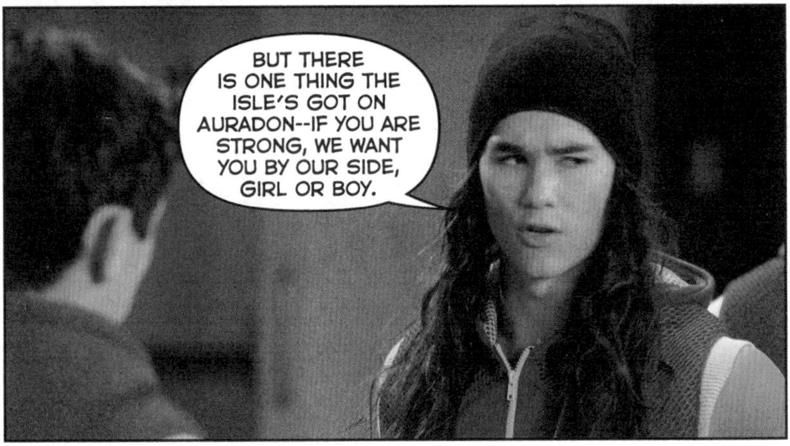
BUT THERE IS ONE THING THE ISLE'S GOT ON AURADON--IF YOU ARE STRONG, WE WANT YOU BY OUR SIDE, GIRL OR BOY.

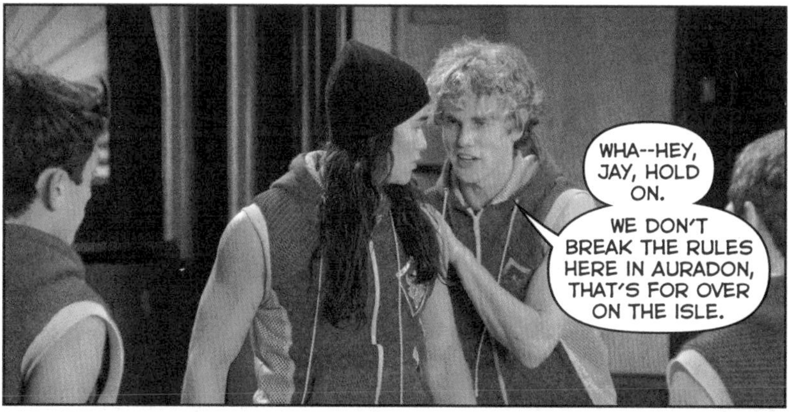
WHA--HEY, JAY, HOLD ON.
WE DON'T BREAK THE RULES HERE IN AURADON, THAT'S FOR OVER ON THE ISLE.

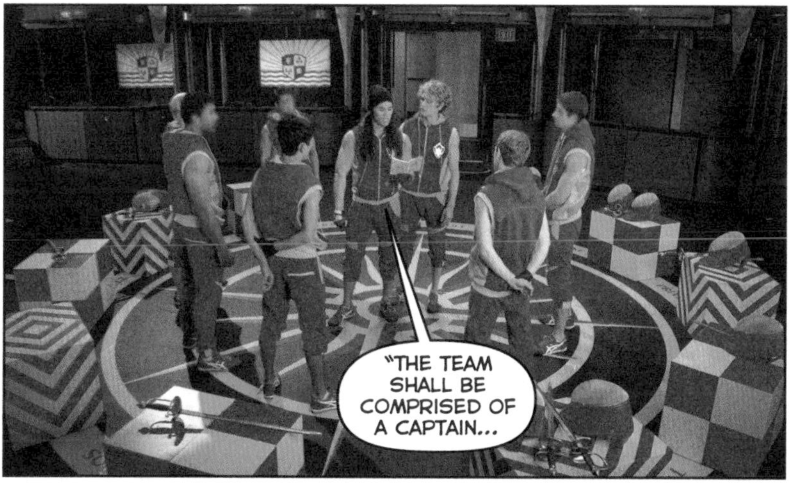
"THE TEAM SHALL BE COMPRISED OF A CAPTAIN...

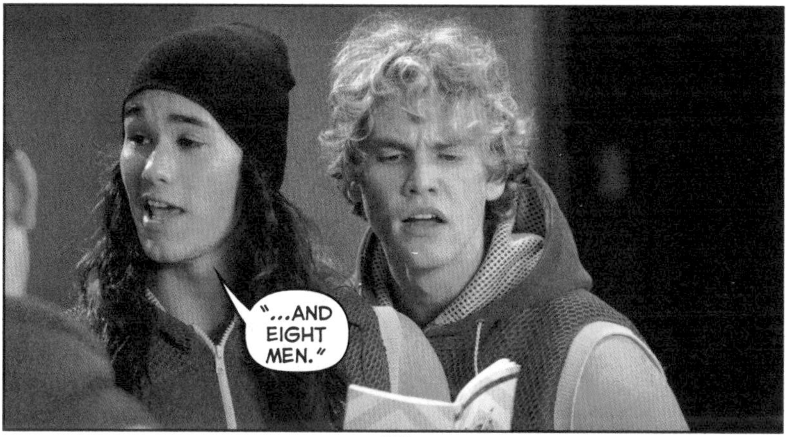
"...AND EIGHT MEN."

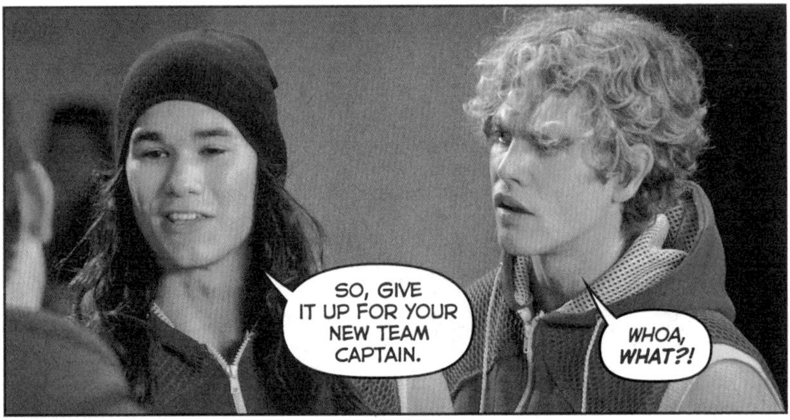
SO, GIVE IT UP FOR YOUR NEW TEAM CAPTAIN.
WHOA, WHAT?!

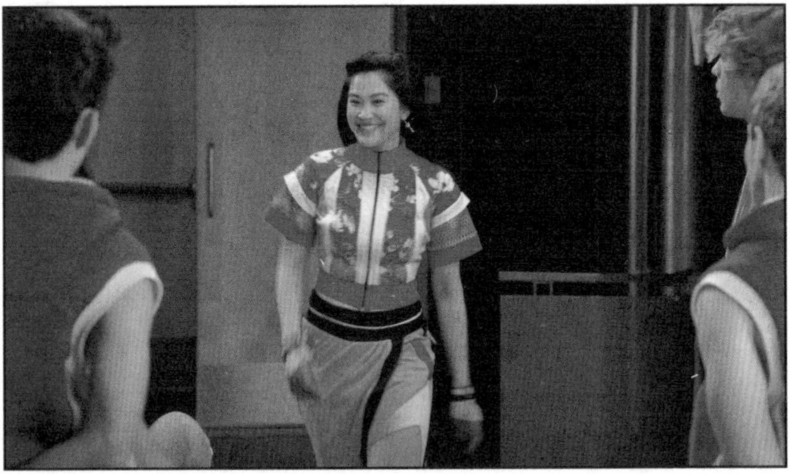

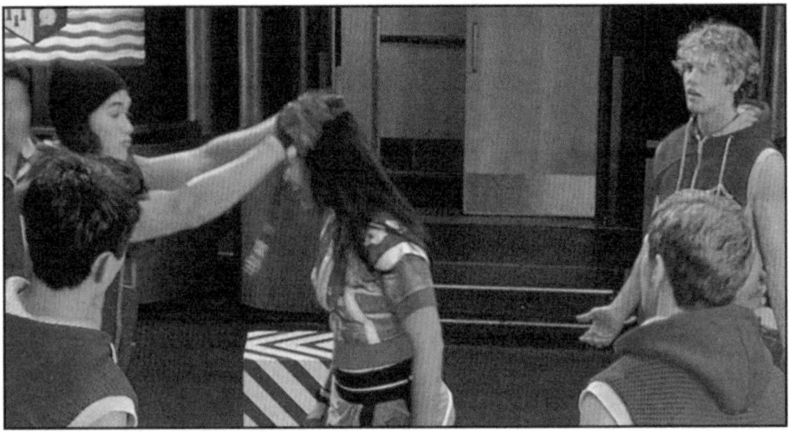

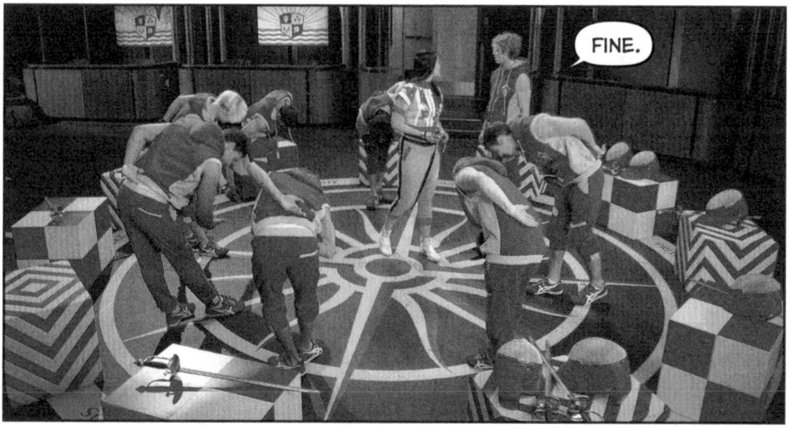
FINE.

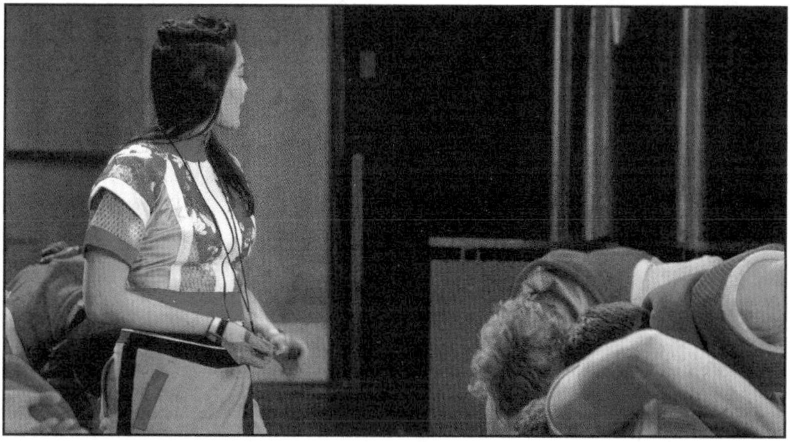

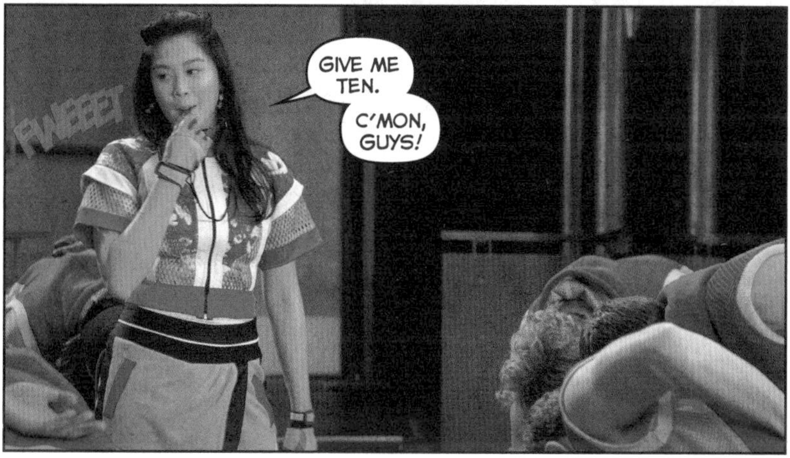
PWEEET
GIVE ME TEN.
C'MON, GUYS!

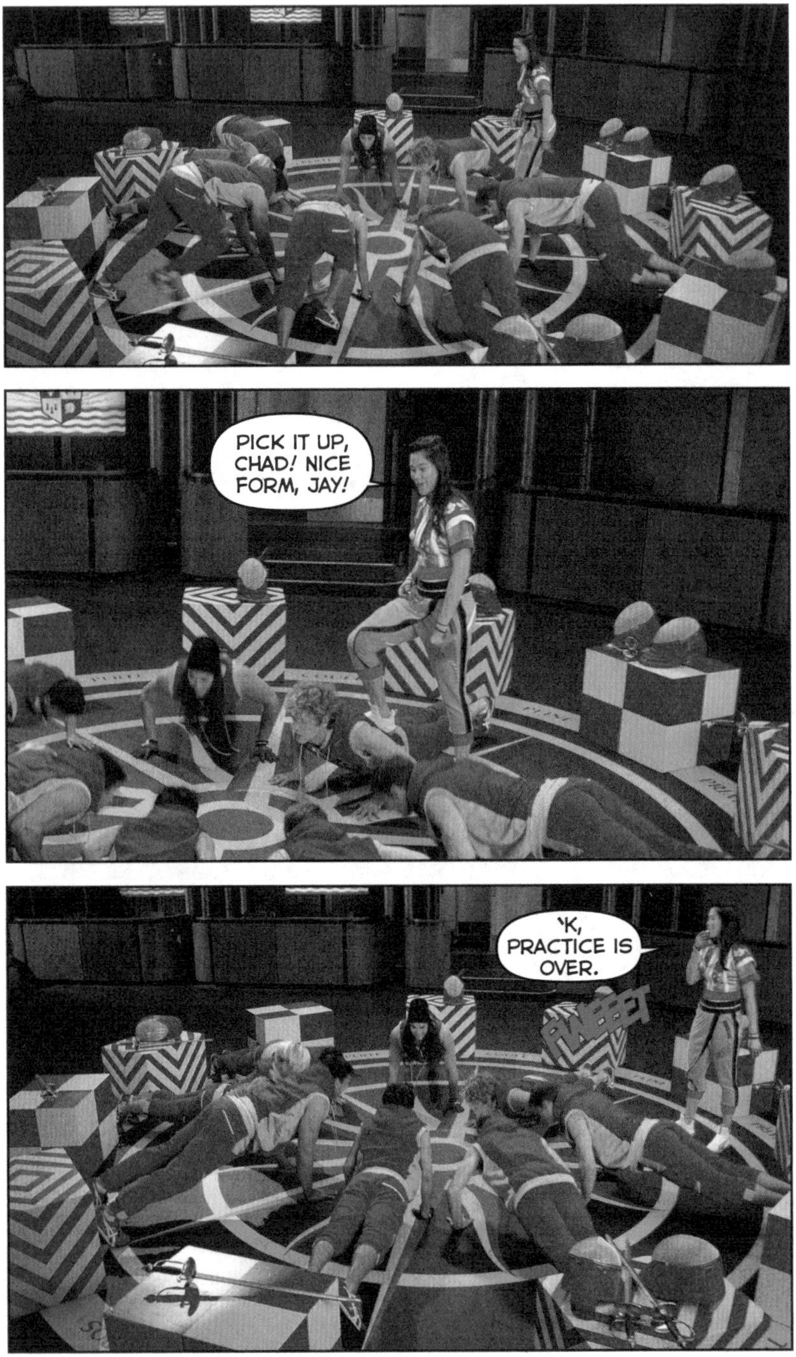
PICK IT UP, CHAD! NICE FORM, JAY!
'K, PRACTICE IS OVER.
FWEEET

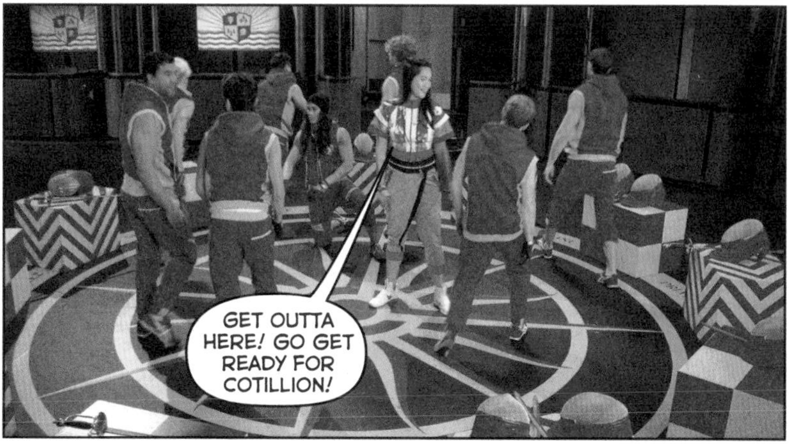
GET OUTTA HERE! GO GET READY FOR COTILLION!

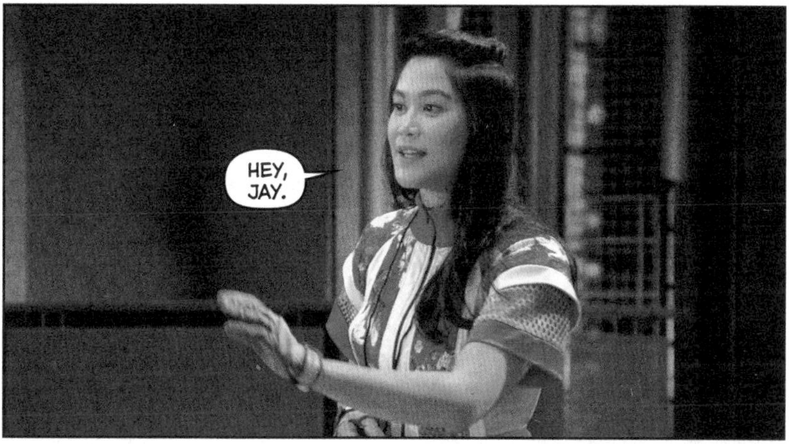
HEY, JAY.

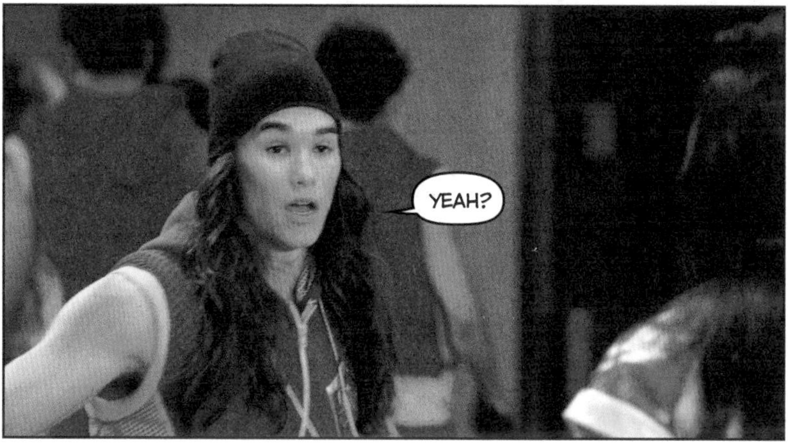
YEAH?

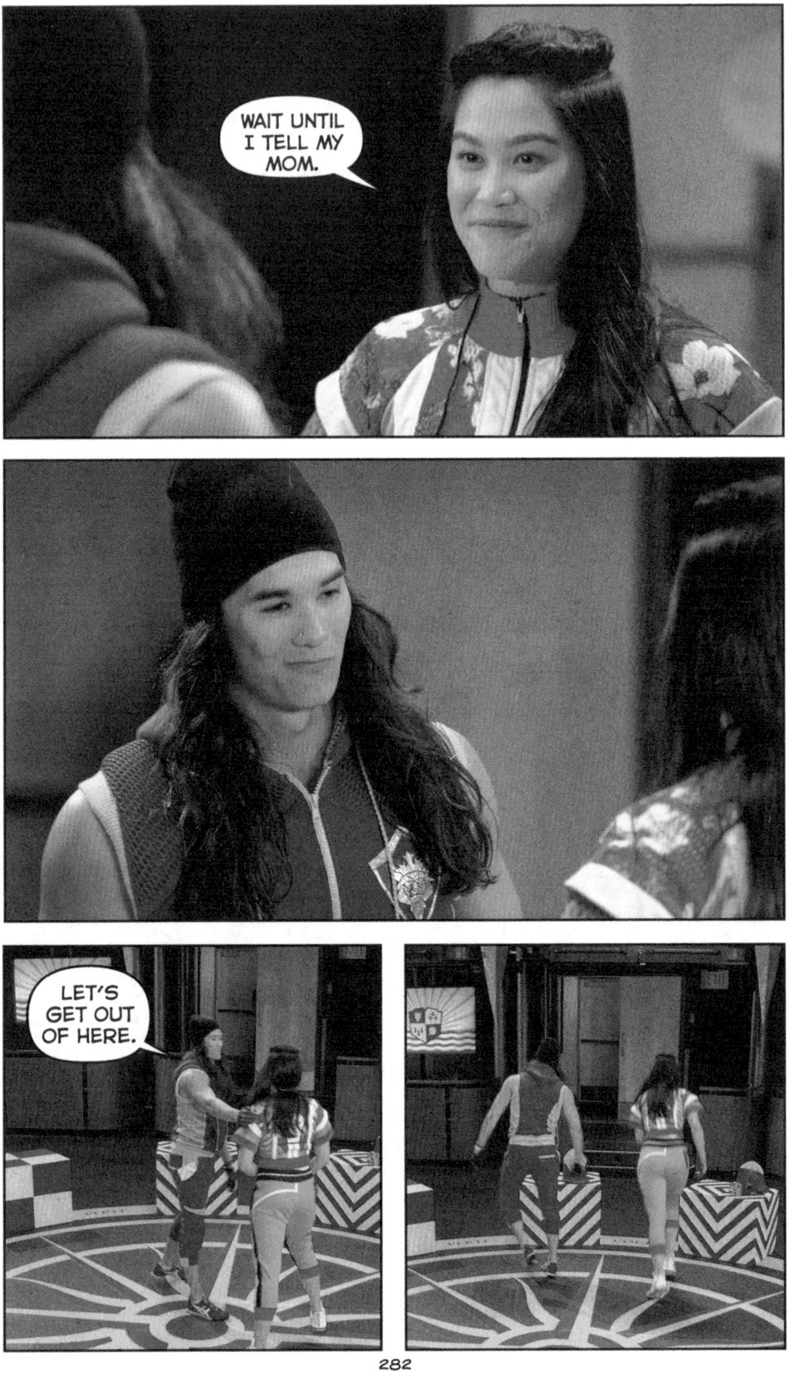
WAIT UNTIL I TELL MY MOM.
LET'S GET OUT OF HERE.

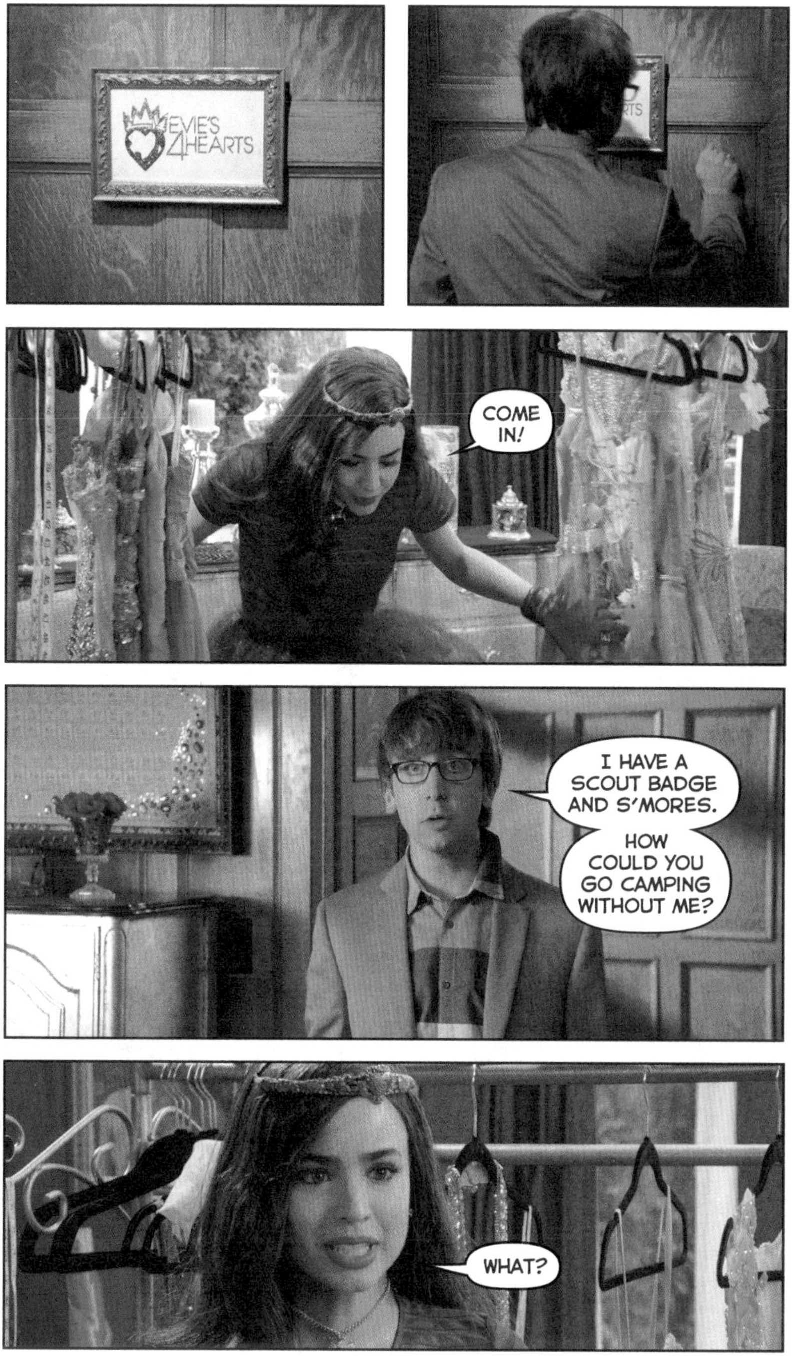
EVIE'S 4HEARTS
COME IN!
I HAVE A SCOUT BADGE AND S'MORES.
HOW COULD YOU GO CAMPING WITHOUT ME?
WHAT?

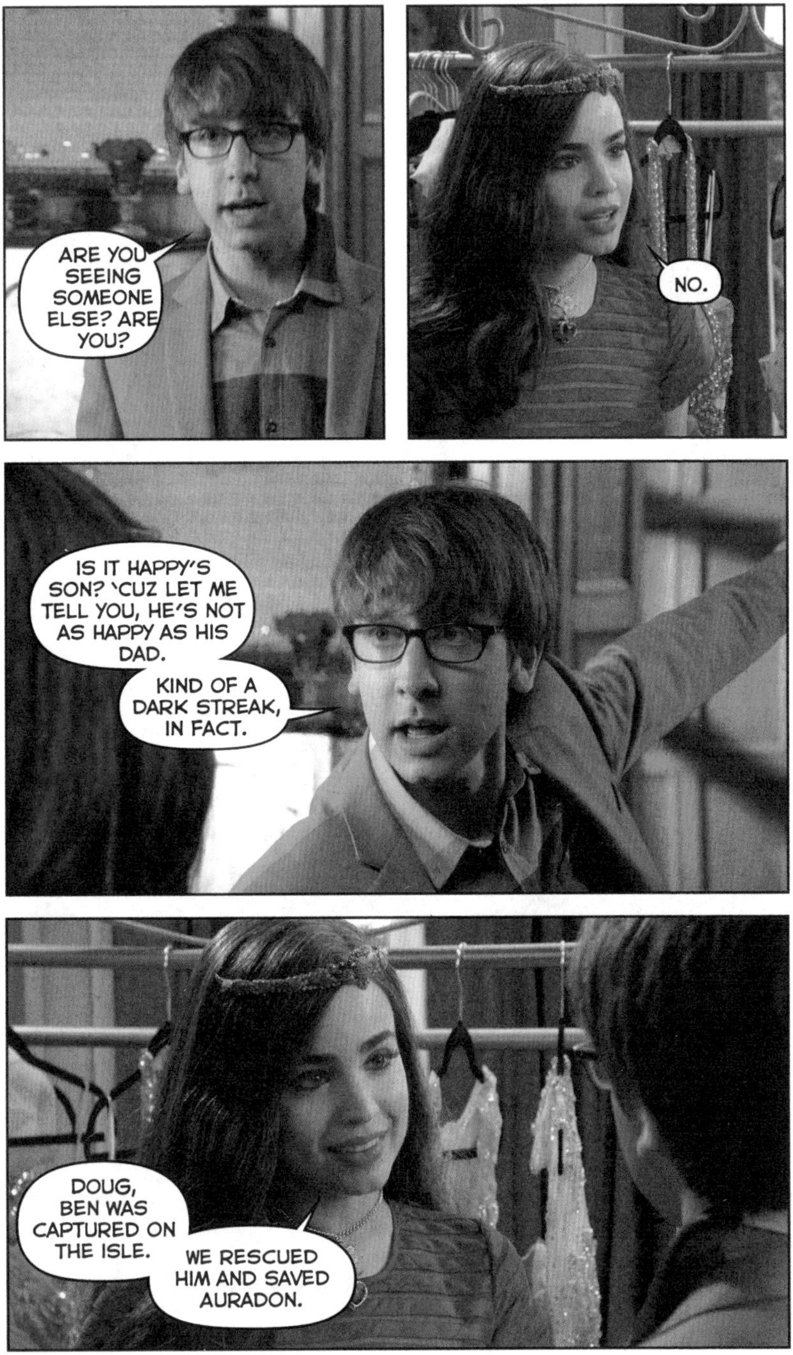
ARE YOU SEEING SOMEONE ELSE? ARE YOU?
NO.
IS IT HAPPY'S SON? 'CUZ LET ME TELL YOU, HE'S NOT AS HAPPY AS HIS DAD.
KIND OF A DARK STREAK, IN FACT.
DOUG, BEN WAS CAPTURED ON THE ISLE.
WE RESCUED HIM AND SAVED AURADON.

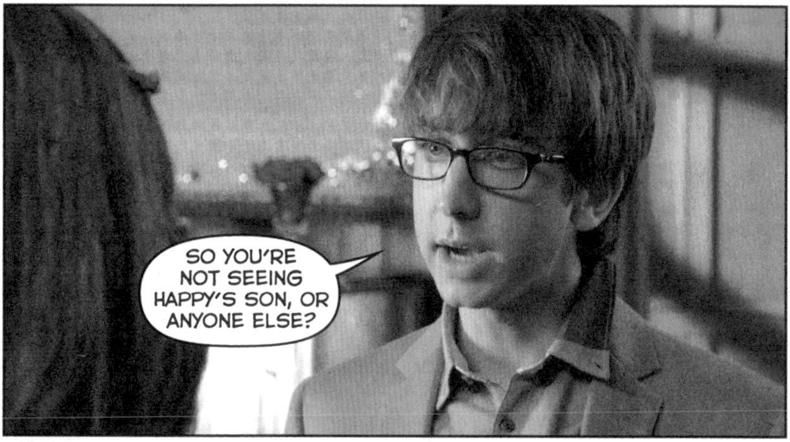
SO YOU'RE NOT SEEING HAPPY'S SON, OR ANYONE ELSE?

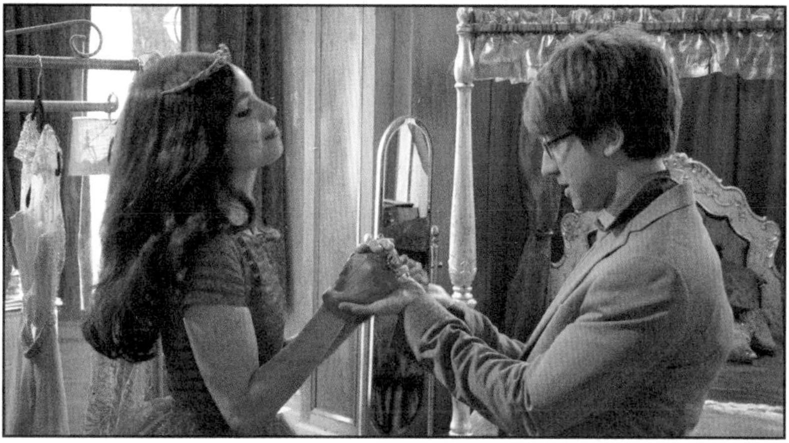

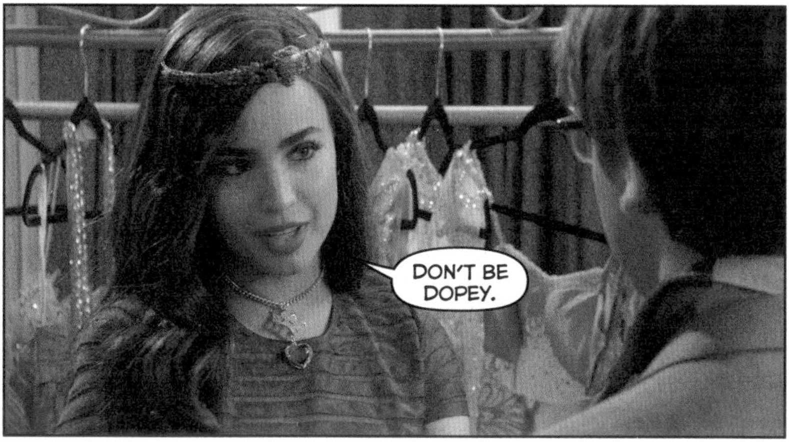
DON'T BE DOPEY.

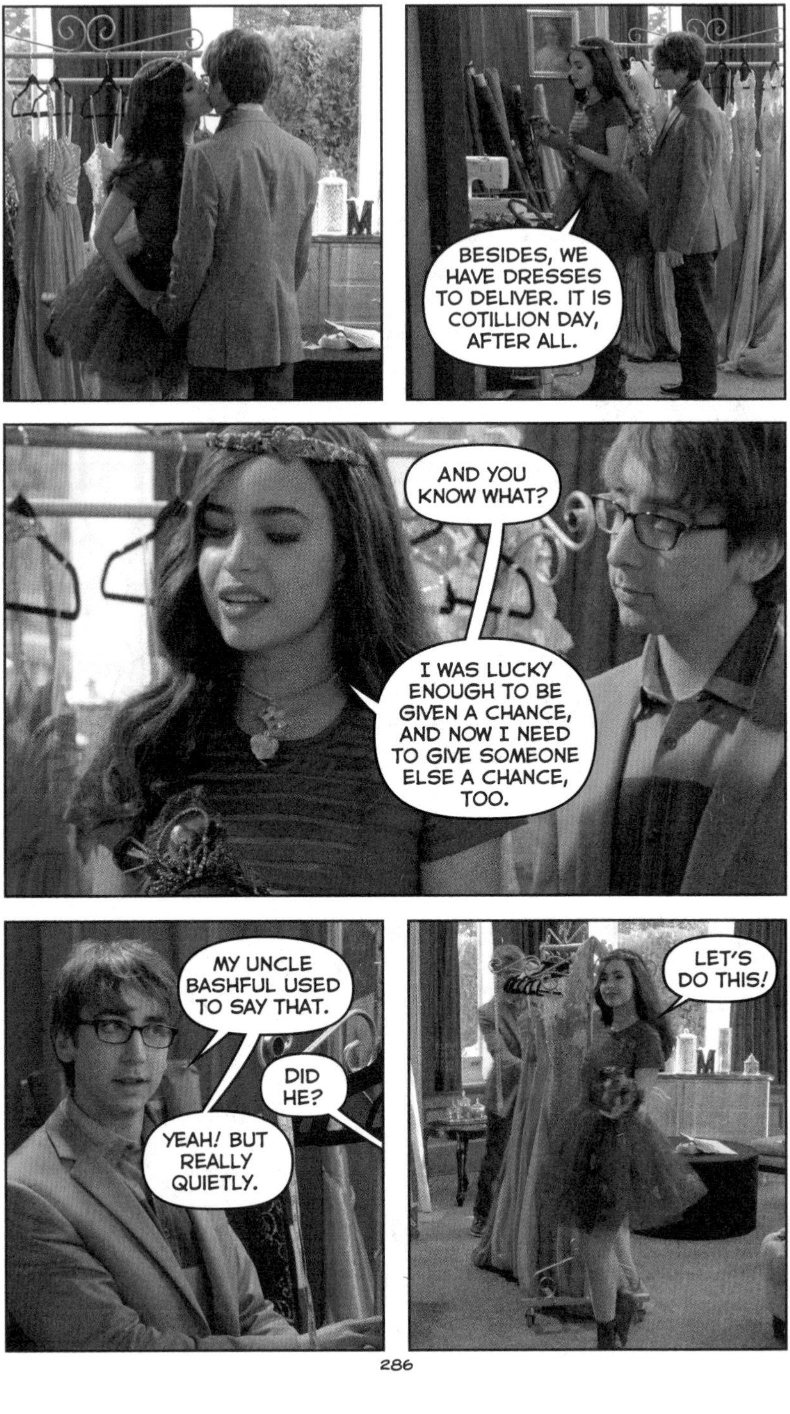
BESIDES, WE HAVE DRESSES TO DELIVER. IT IS COTILLION DAY, AFTER ALL.
AND YOU KNOW WHAT?
I WAS LUCKY ENOUGH TO BE GIVEN A CHANCE, AND NOW I NEED TO GIVE SOMEONE ELSE A CHANCE, TOO.
MY UNCLE BASHFUL USED TO SAY THAT.
DID HE?
YEAH! BUT REALLY QUIETLY.
LET'S DO THIS!

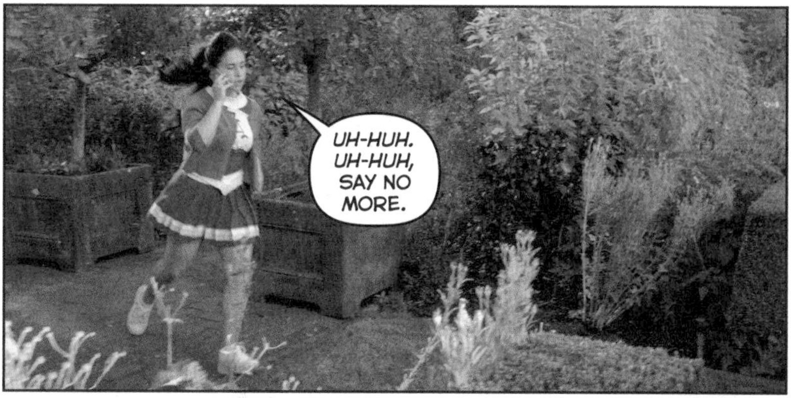
UH-HUH.
UH-HUH,
SAY NO
MORE.

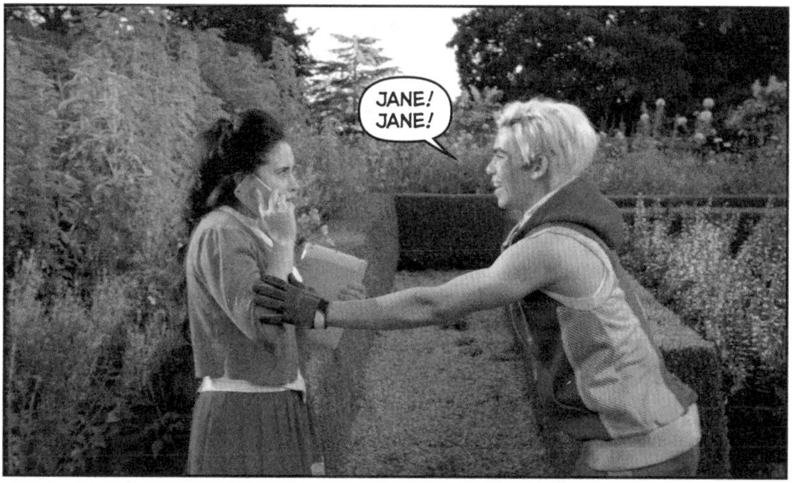
JANE!
JANE!

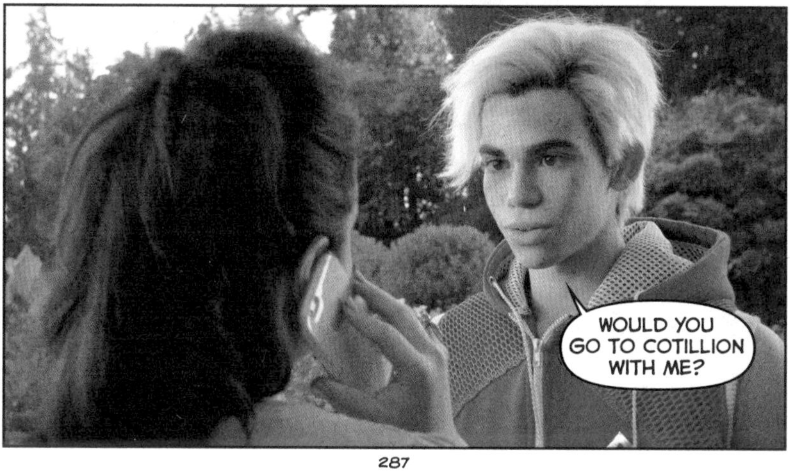
WOULD YOU
GO TO COTILLION
WITH ME?

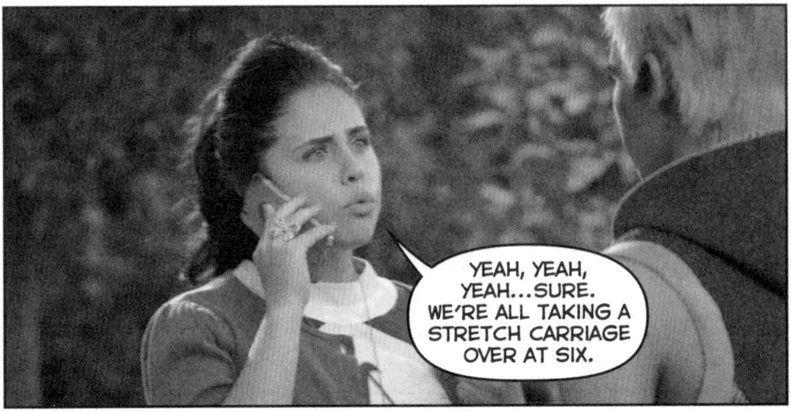
YEAH, YEAH, YEAH...SURE. WE'RE ALL TAKING A STRETCH CARRIAGE OVER AT SIX.

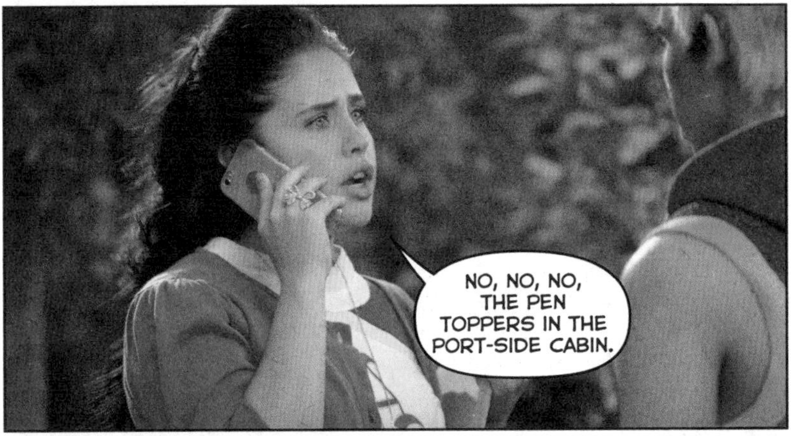
NO, NO, NO, THE PEN TOPPERS IN THE PORT-SIDE CABIN.

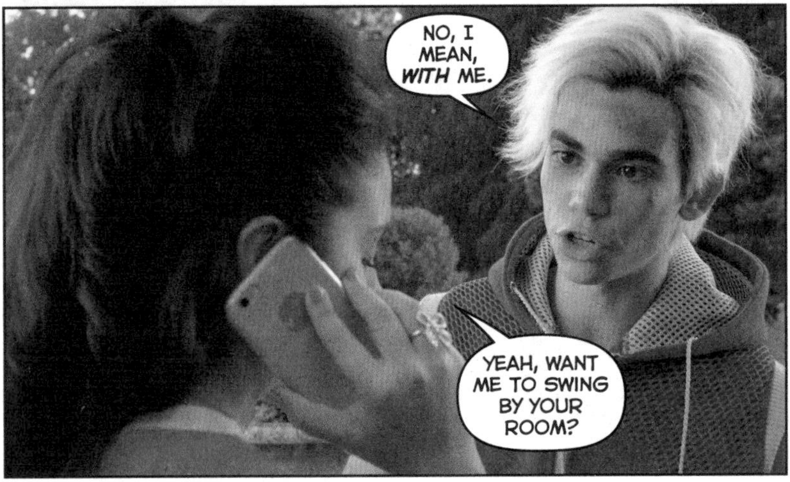
NO, I MEAN, *WITH* ME.
YEAH, WANT ME TO SWING BY YOUR ROOM?

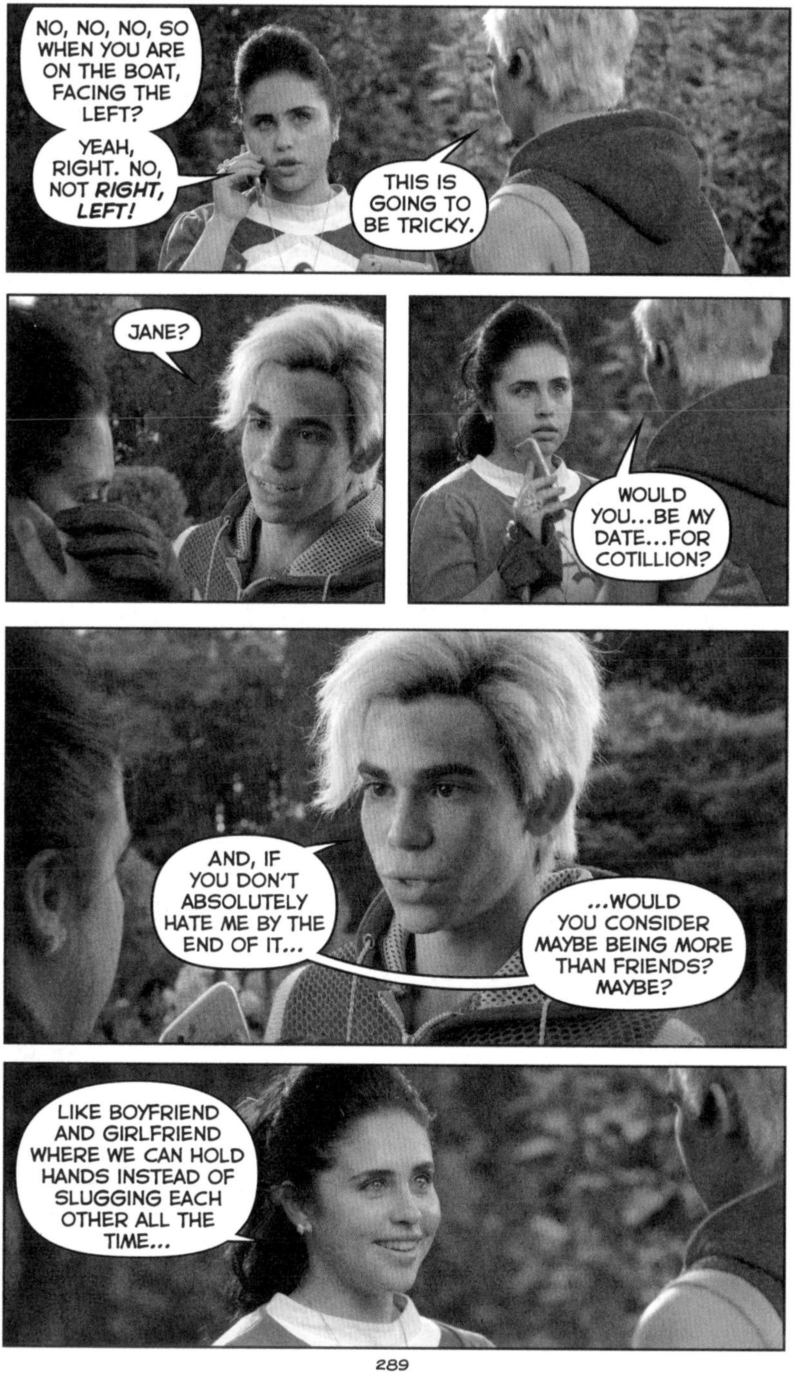
NO, NO, NO, SO WHEN YOU ARE ON THE BOAT, FACING THE LEFT?
YEAH, RIGHT. NO, NOT *RIGHT*, *LEFT!*
THIS IS GOING TO BE TRICKY.
JANE?
WOULD YOU...BE MY DATE...FOR COTILLION?
AND, IF YOU DON'T ABSOLUTELY HATE ME BY THE END OF IT...
...WOULD YOU CONSIDER MAYBE BEING MORE THAN FRIENDS? MAYBE?
LIKE BOYFRIEND AND GIRLFRIEND WHERE WE CAN HOLD HANDS INSTEAD OF SLUGGING EACH OTHER ALL THE TIME...

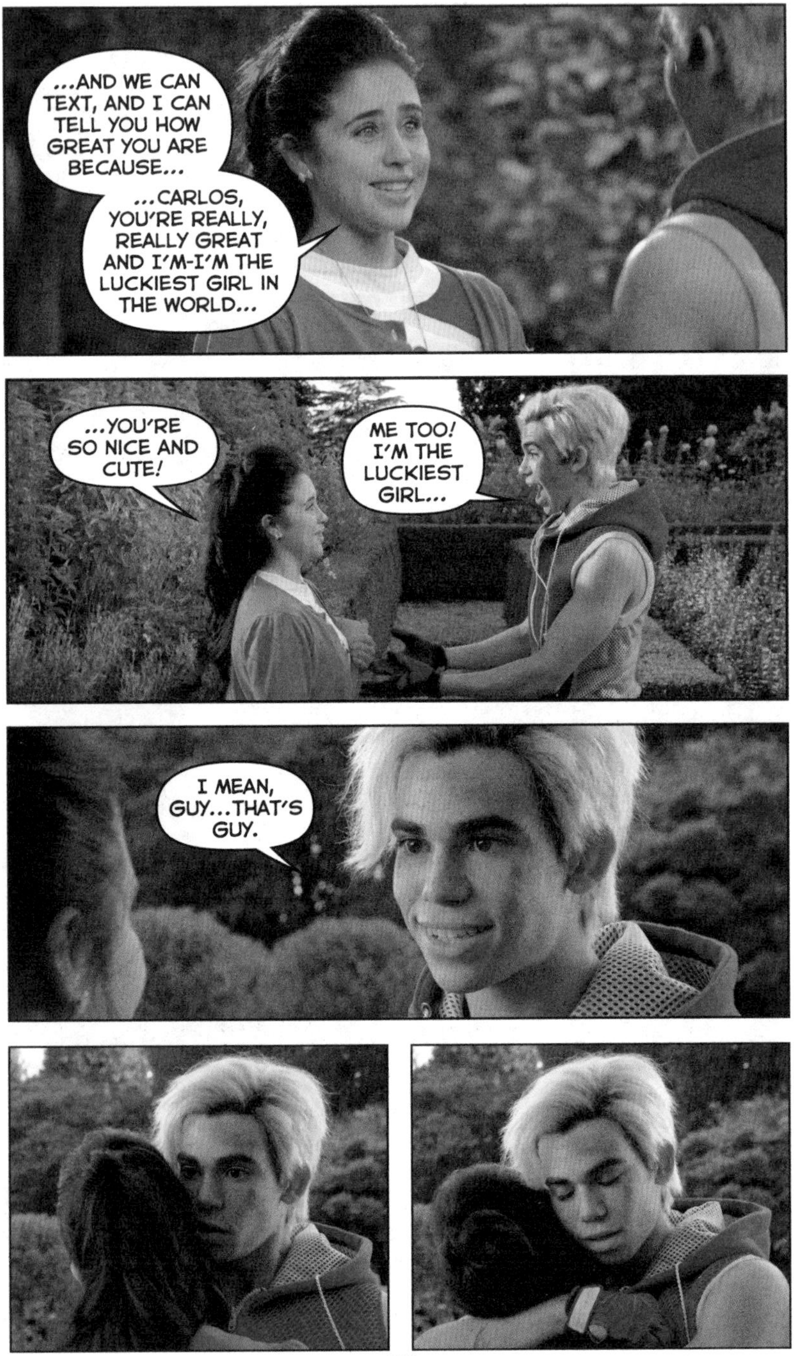
...AND WE CAN TEXT, AND I CAN TELL YOU HOW GREAT YOU ARE BECAUSE...
...CARLOS, YOU'RE REALLY, REALLY GREAT AND I'M-I'M THE LUCKIEST GIRL IN THE WORLD...
...YOU'RE SO NICE AND CUTE!
ME TOO! I'M THE LUCKIEST GIRL...
I MEAN, GUY...THAT'S GUY.

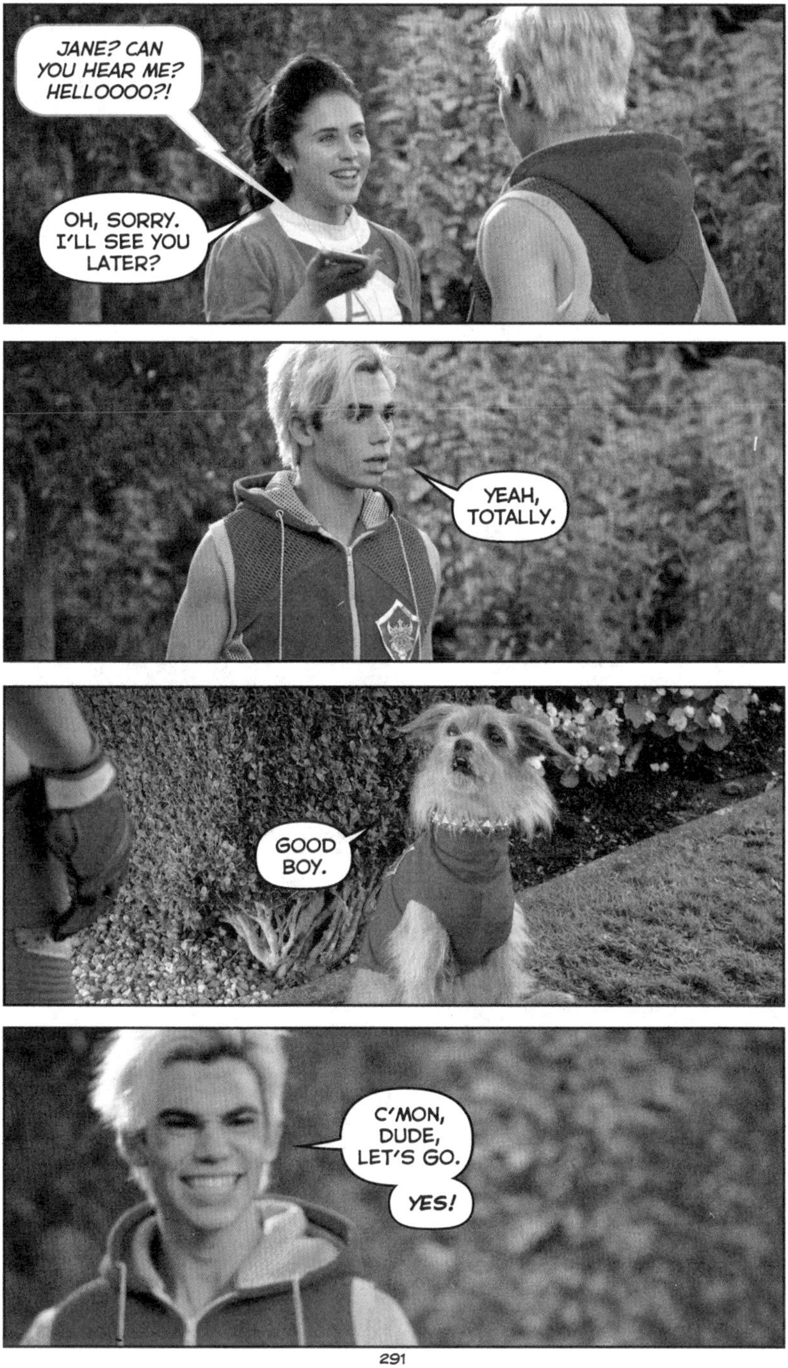
JANE? CAN YOU HEAR ME? HELLOOOO?!
OH, SORRY. I'LL SEE YOU LATER?
YEAH, TOTALLY.
GOOD BOY.
C'MON, DUDE, LET'S GO.
YES!

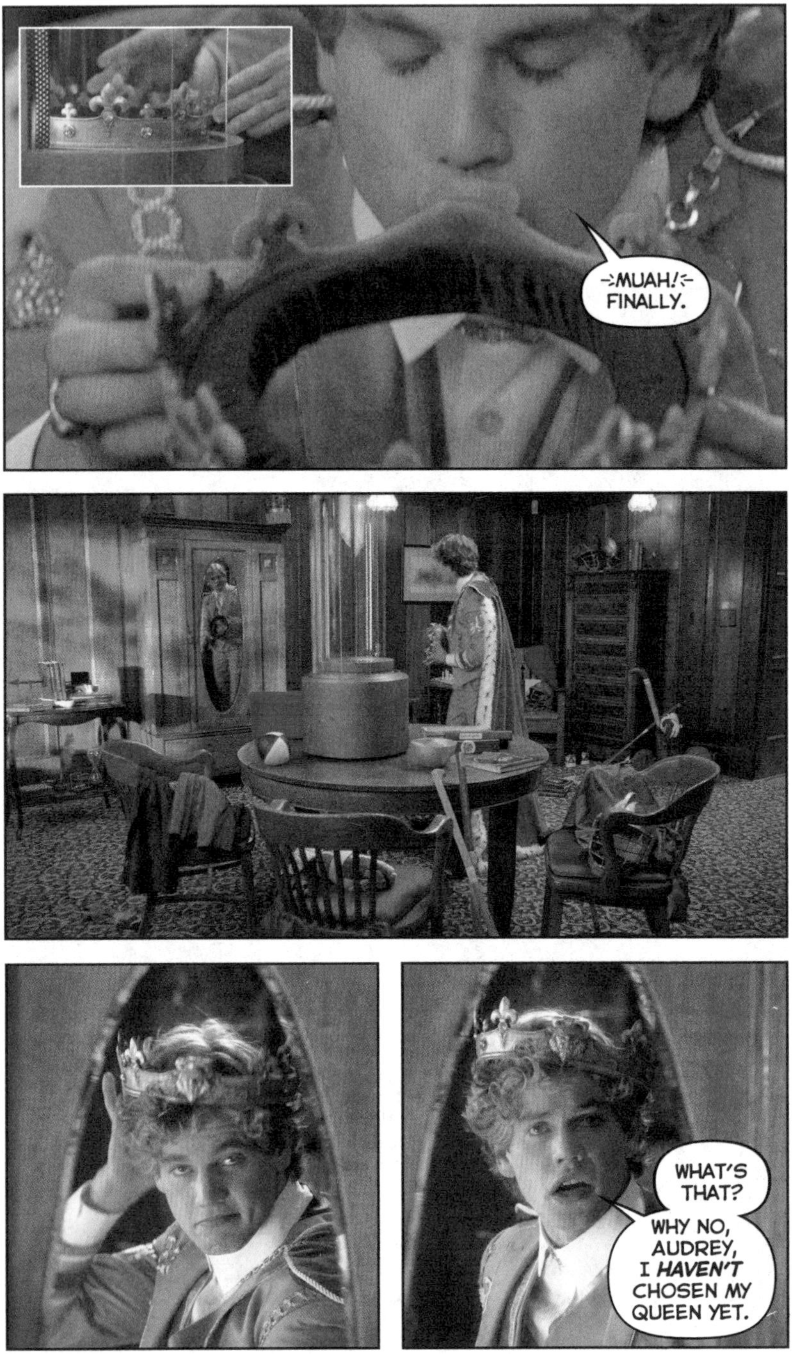
-MUAH!- FINALLY.
WHAT'S THAT?
WHY NO, AUDREY, I *HAVEN'T* CHOSEN MY QUEEN YET.

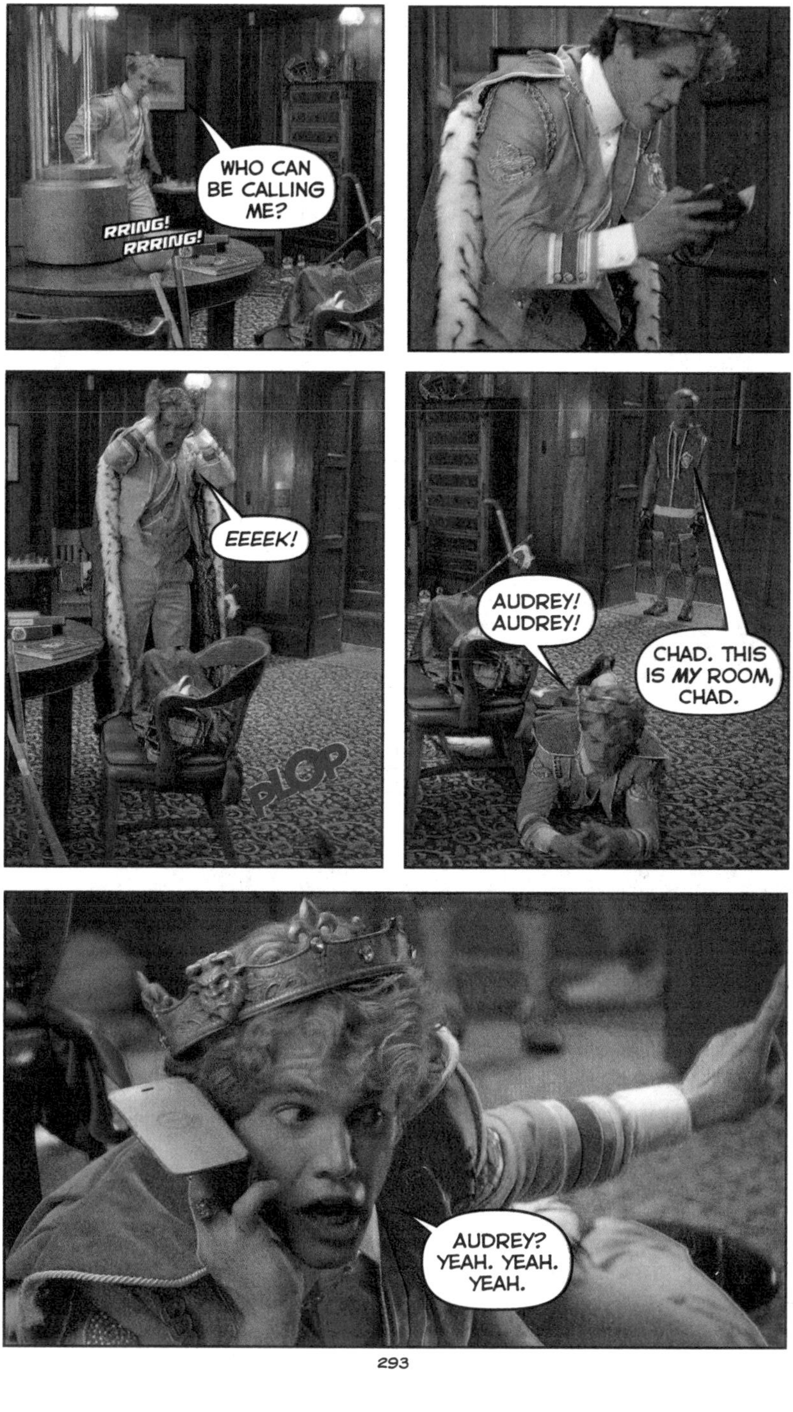

WHO CAN BE CALLING ME?
RRING!
RRRING!
EEEEK!
PLOP
AUDREY! AUDREY!
CHAD. THIS IS *MY* ROOM, CHAD.
AUDREY? YEAH. YEAH. YEAH.

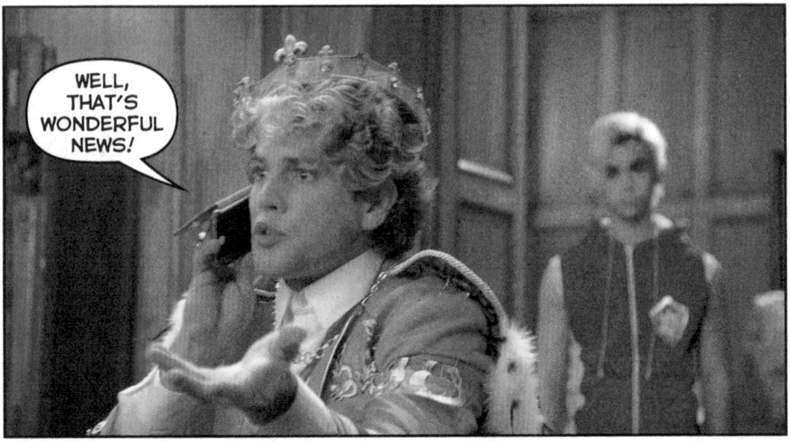
WELL, THAT'S WONDERFUL NEWS!

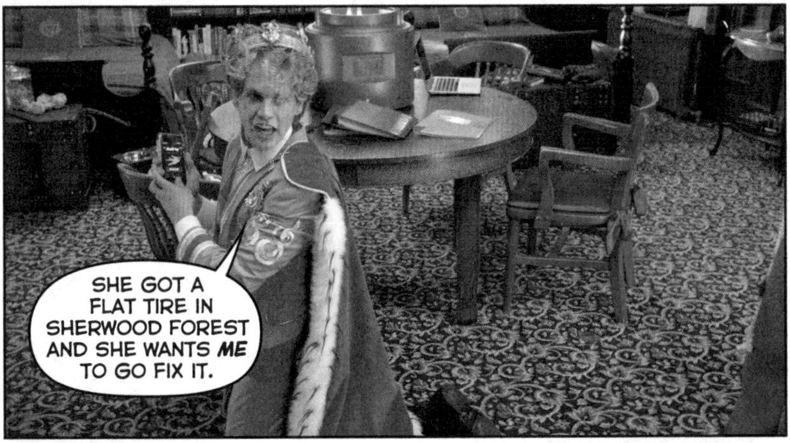
SHE GOT A FLAT TIRE IN SHERWOOD FOREST AND SHE WANTS *ME* TO GO FIX IT.

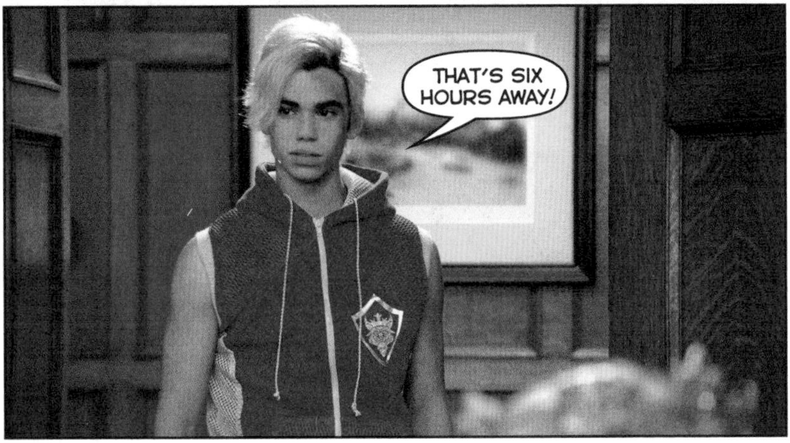
THAT'S SIX HOURS AWAY!

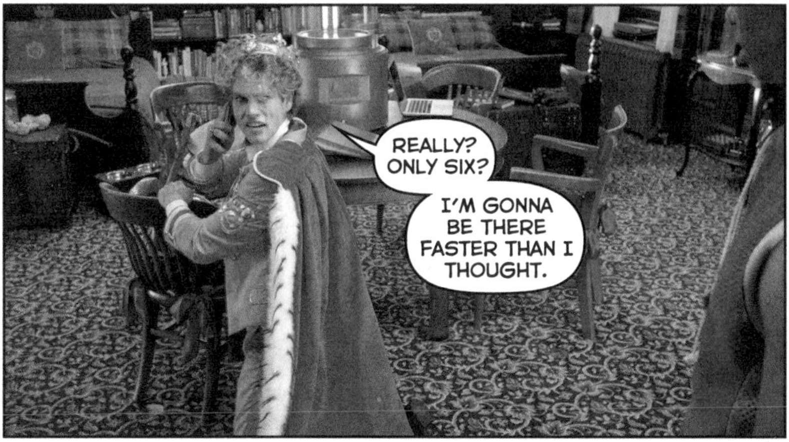
REALLY? ONLY SIX?
I'M GONNA BE THERE FASTER THAN I THOUGHT.

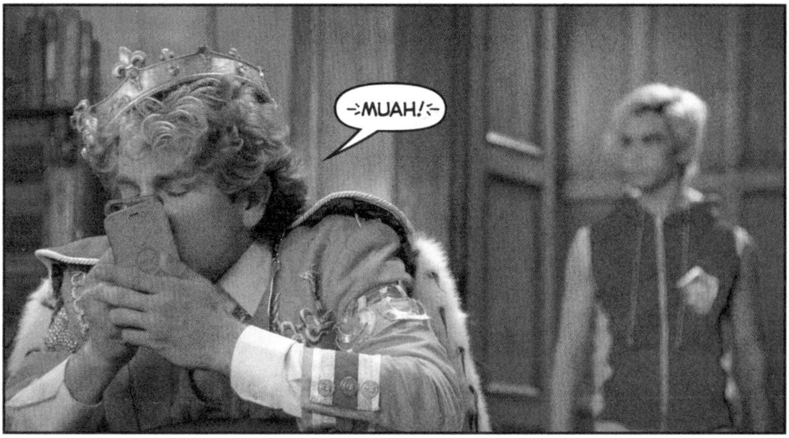
MUAH!

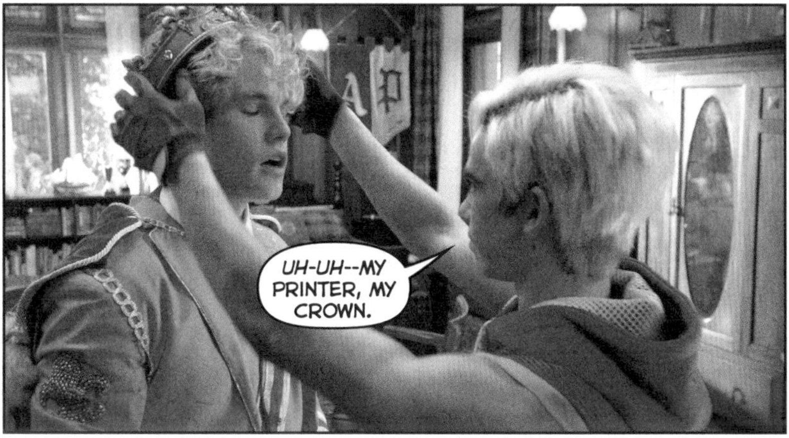
UH-UH--MY PRINTER, MY CROWN.

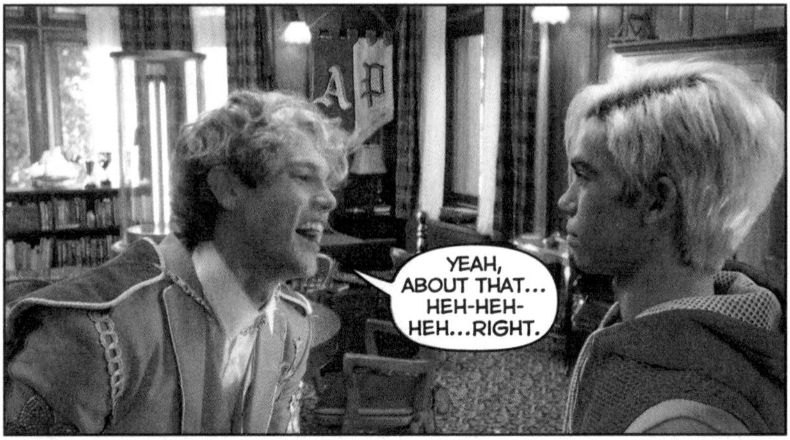
YEAH, ABOUT THAT... HEH-HEH-HEH...RIGHT.

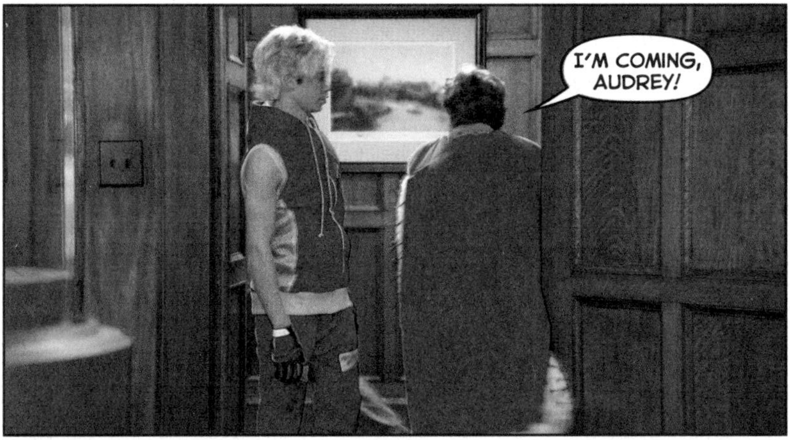
I'M COMING, AUDREY!

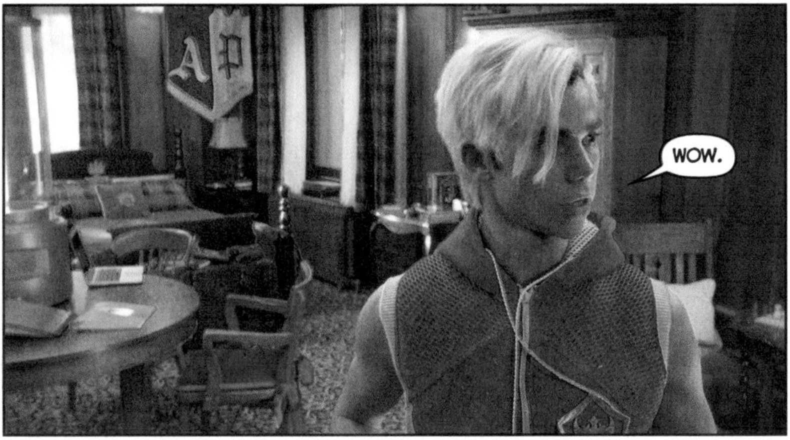
WOW.

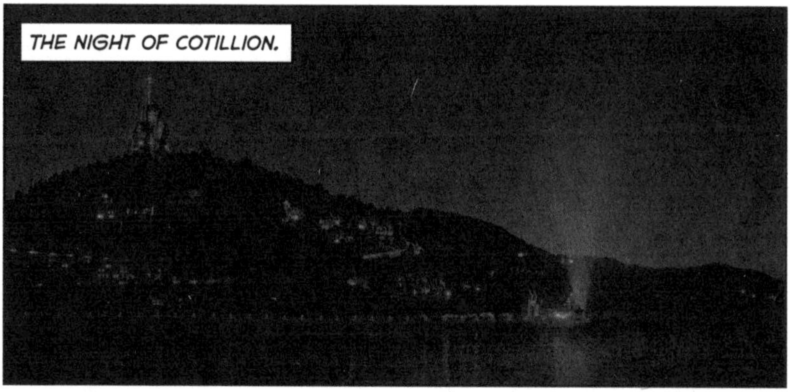
THE NIGHT OF COTILLION.

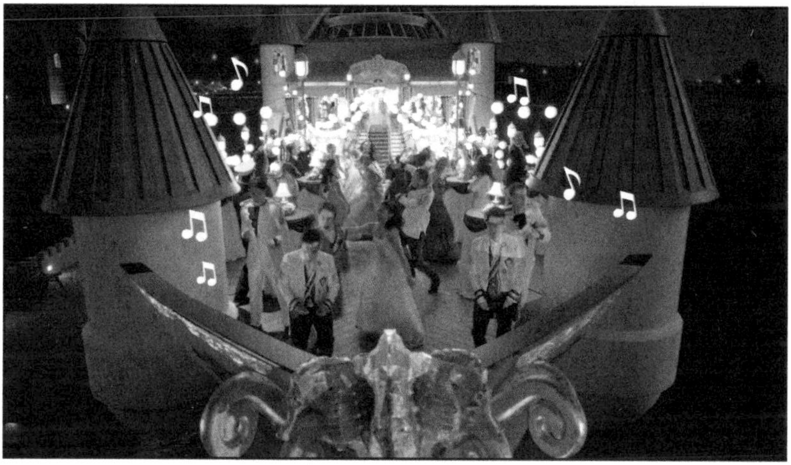

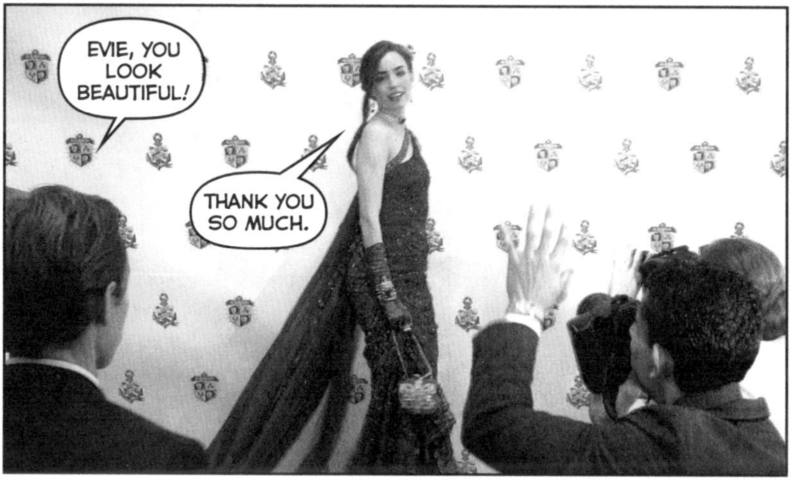
EVIE, YOU LOOK BEAUTIFUL!
THANK YOU SO MUCH.

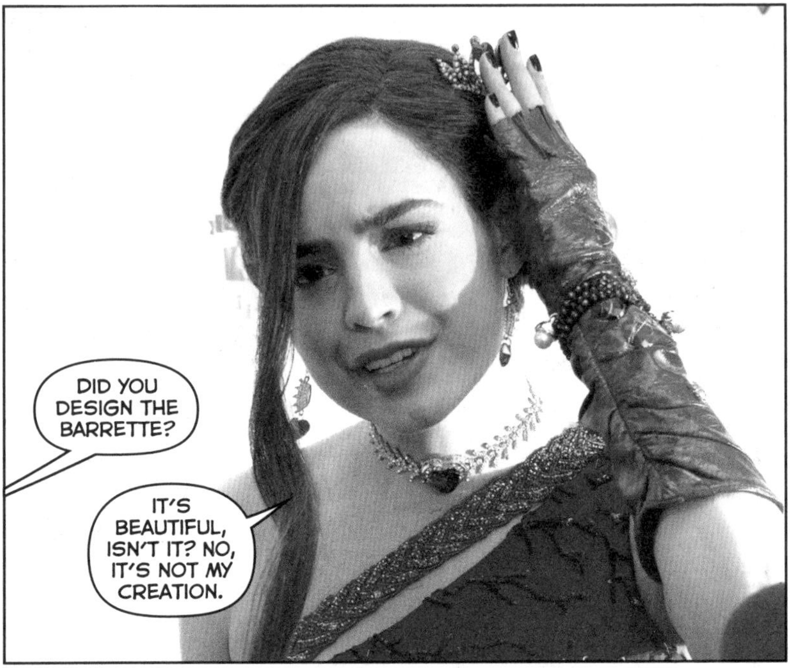
DID YOU DESIGN THE BARRETTE?
IT'S BEAUTIFUL, ISN'T IT? NO, IT'S NOT MY CREATION.

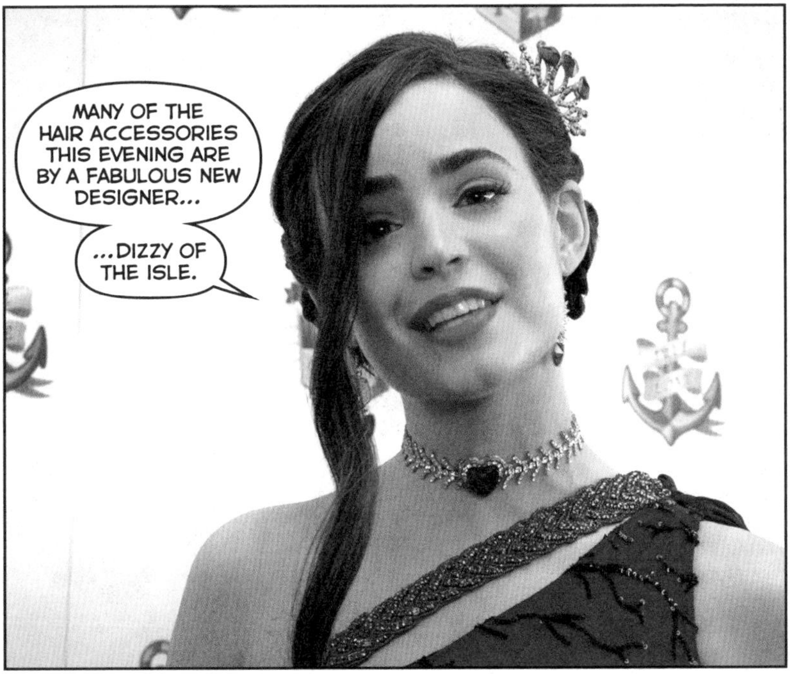
MANY OF THE HAIR ACCESSORIES THIS EVENING ARE BY A FABULOUS NEW DESIGNER...
...DIZZY OF THE ISLE.

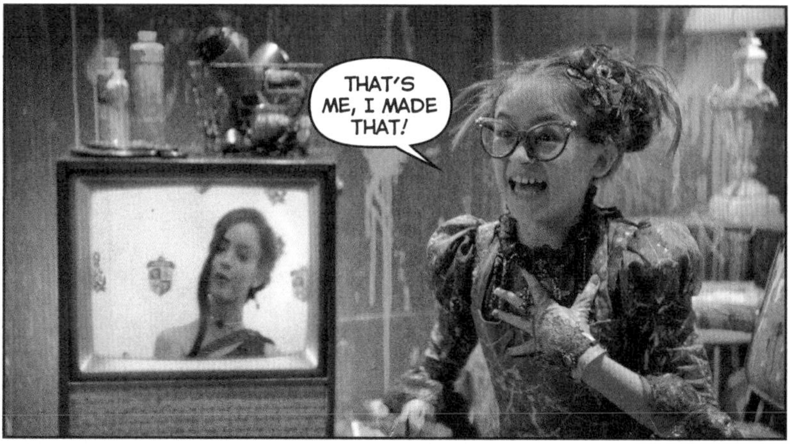
THAT'S ME, I MADE THAT!

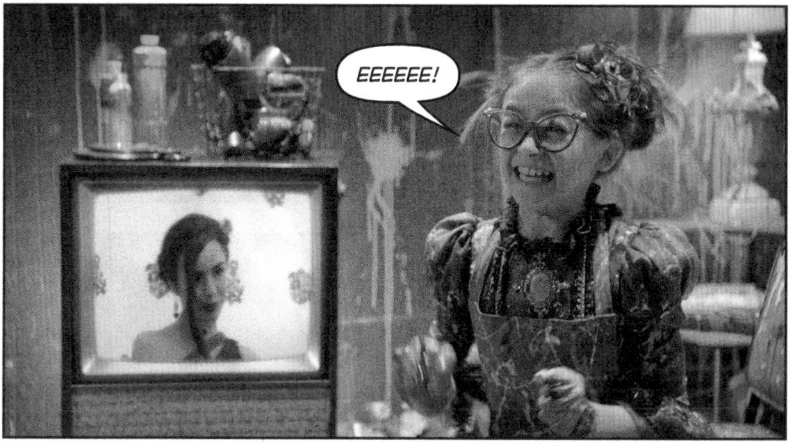
EEEEEE!

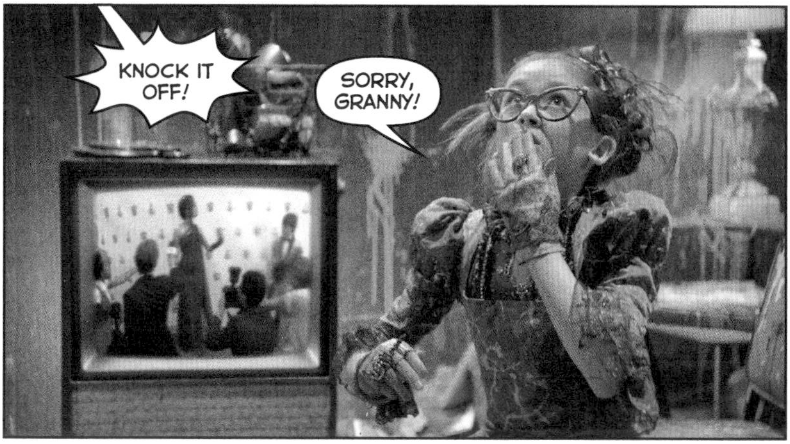
KNOCK IT OFF!
SORRY, GRANNY!

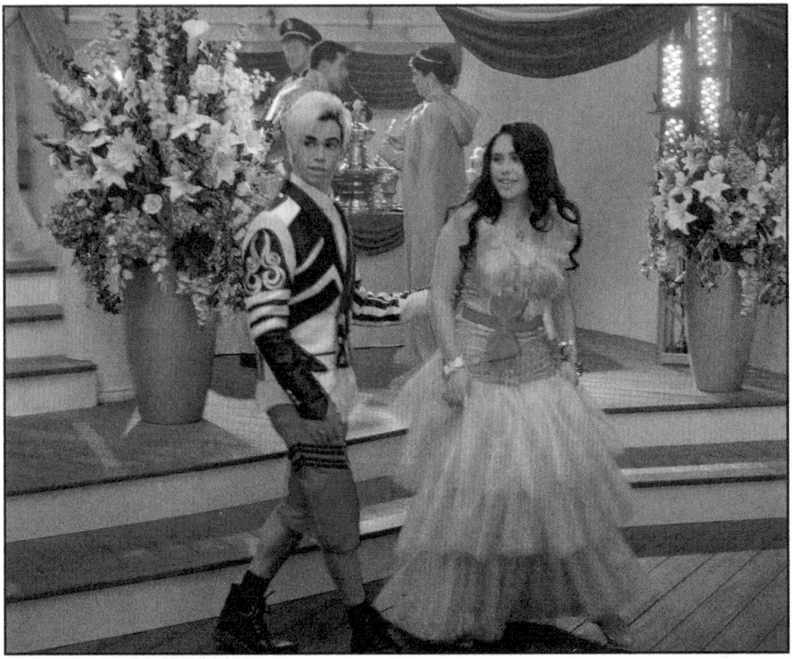

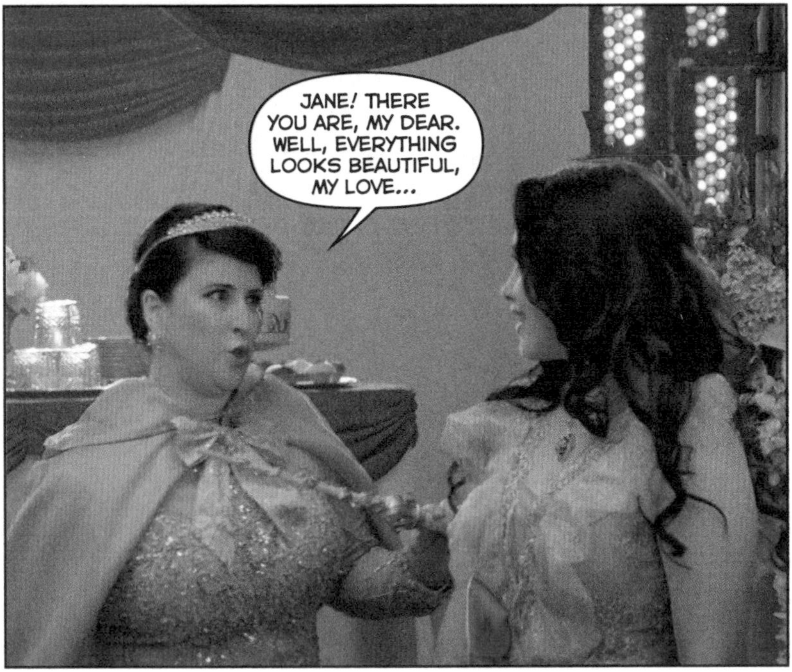
JANE! THERE YOU ARE, MY DEAR. WELL, EVERYTHING LOOKS BEAUTIFUL, MY LOVE...

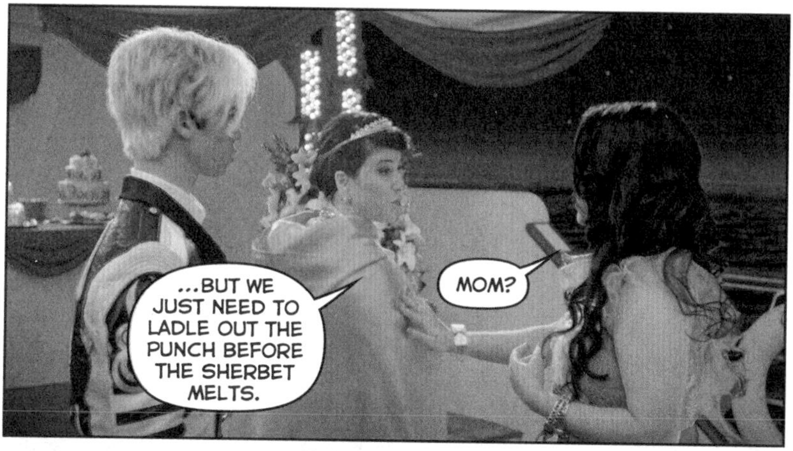
...BUT WE JUST NEED TO LADLE OUT THE PUNCH BEFORE THE SHERBET MELTS.
MOM?

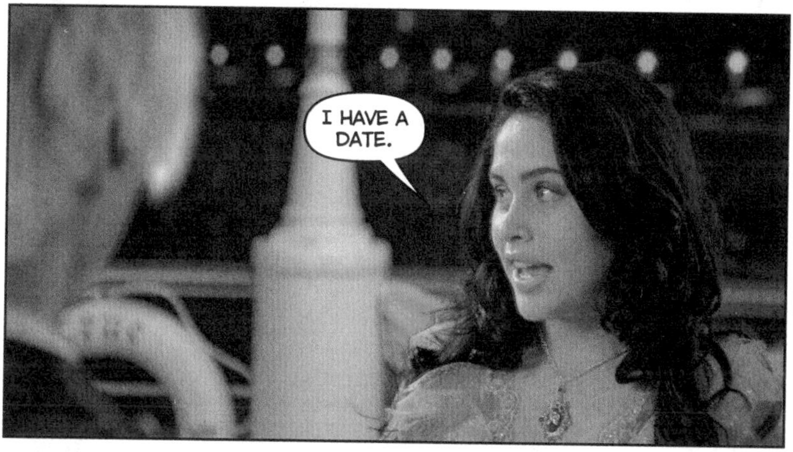
I HAVE A DATE.

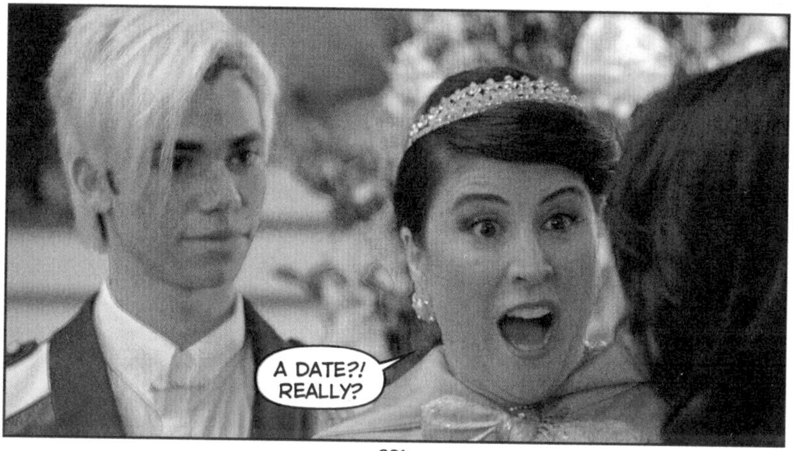
A DATE?! REALLY?

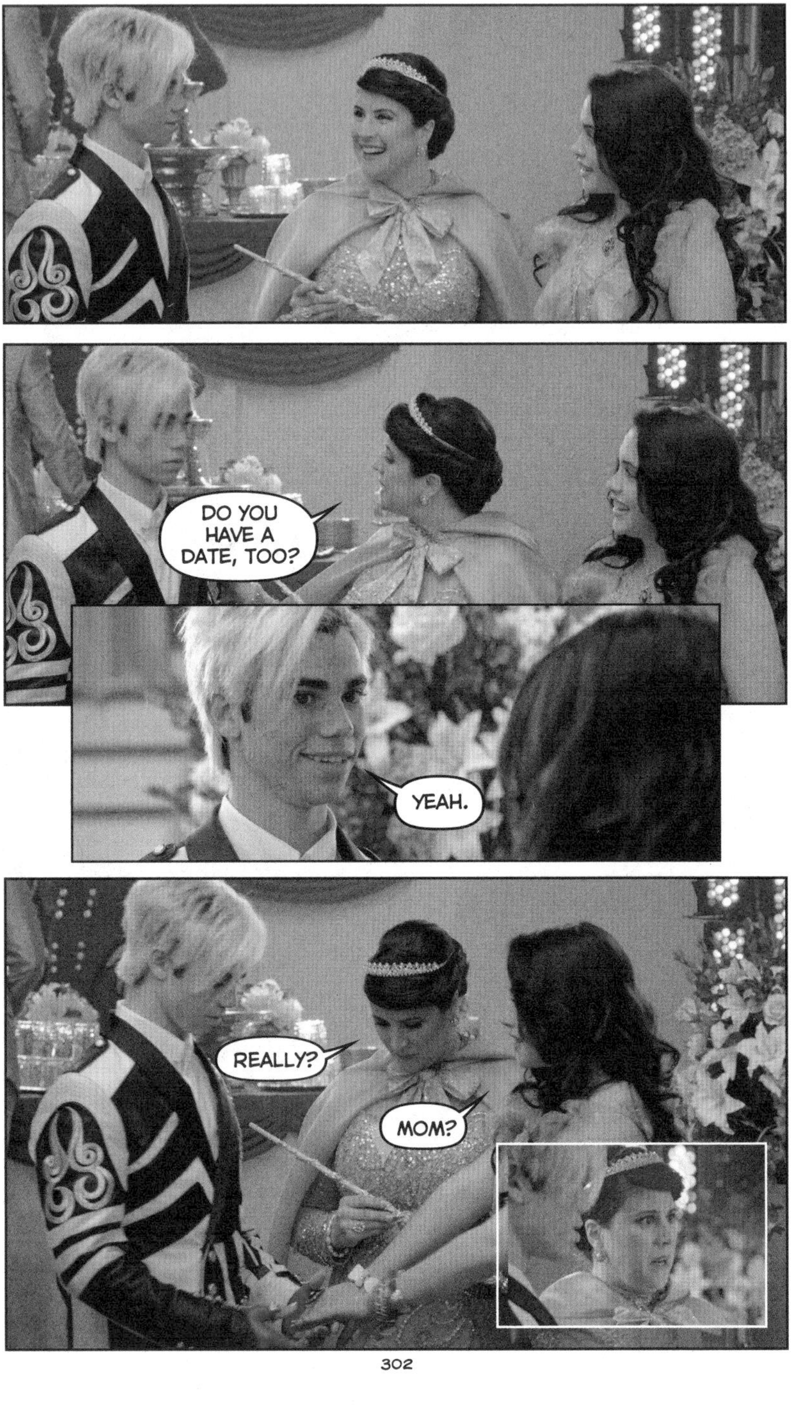
DO YOU HAVE A DATE, TOO?
YEAH.
REALLY?
MOM?

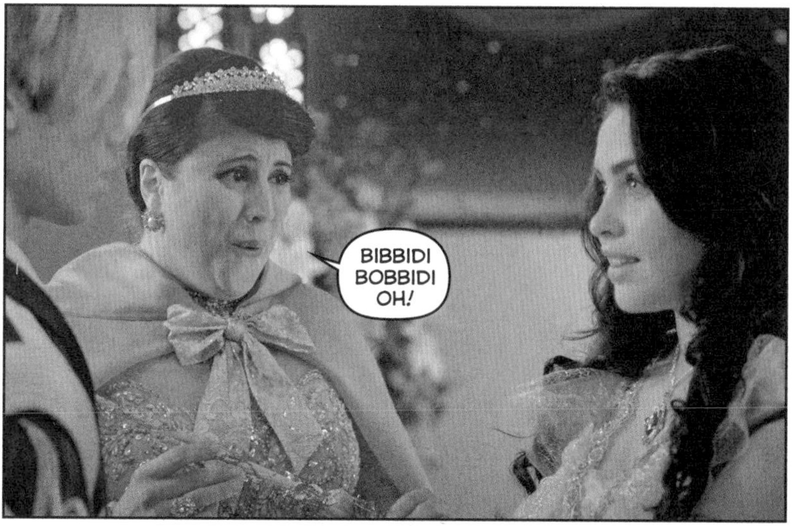
BIBBIDI
BOBBIDI
OH!

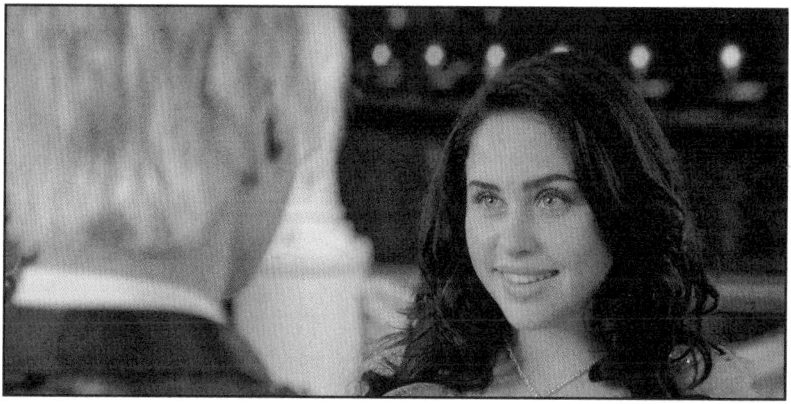

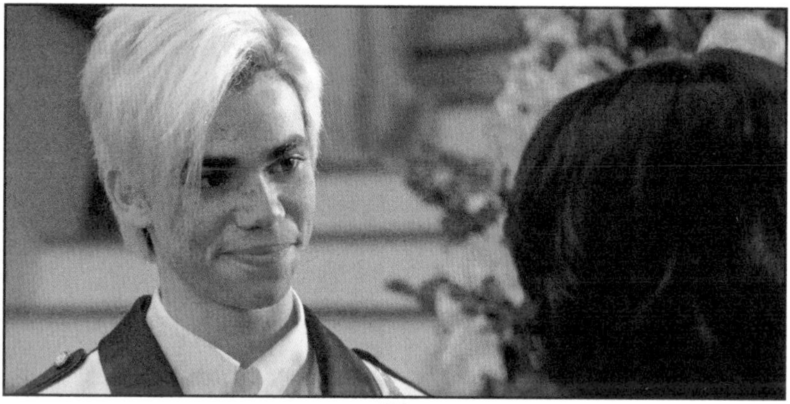

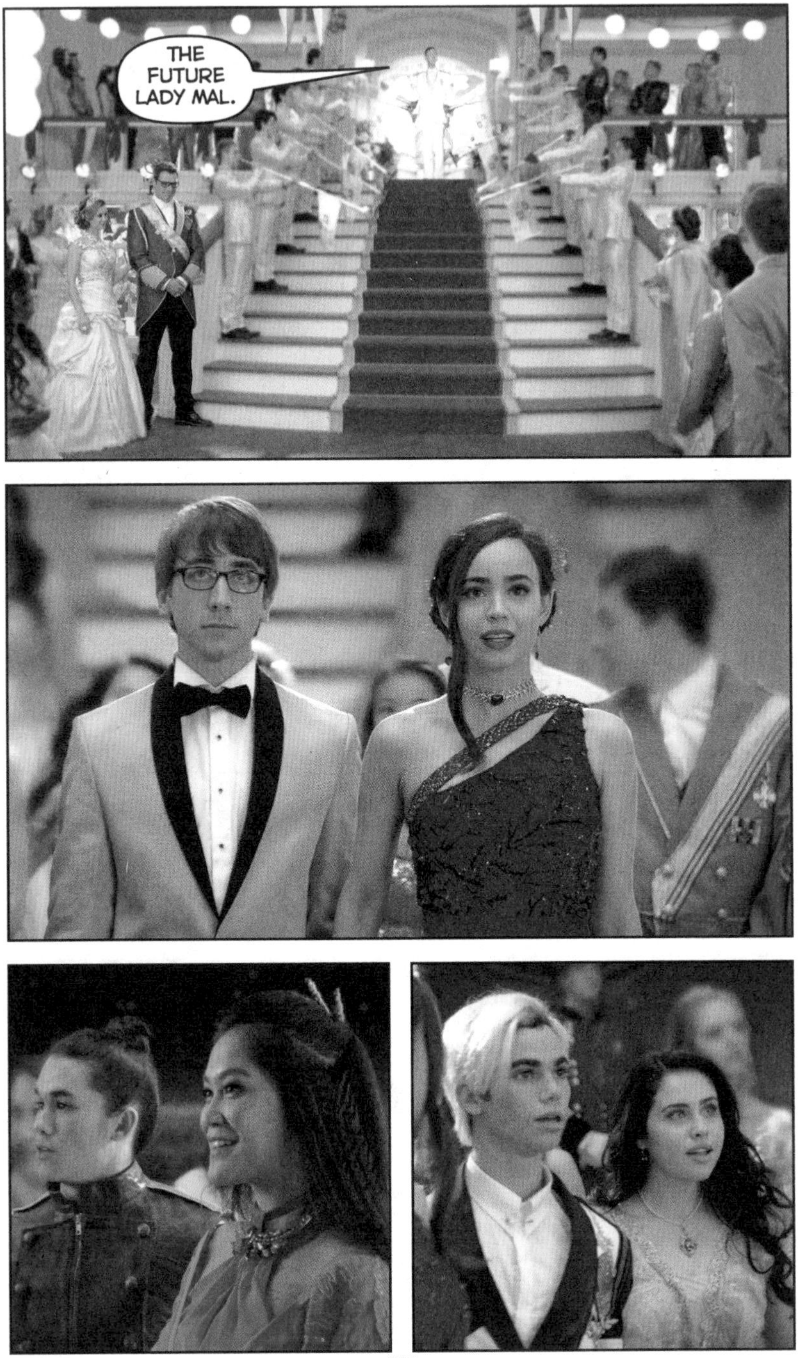
THE
FUTURE
LADY MAL.

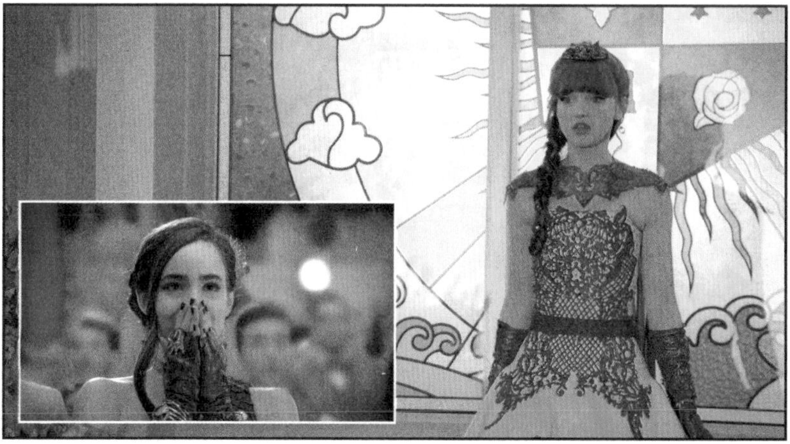

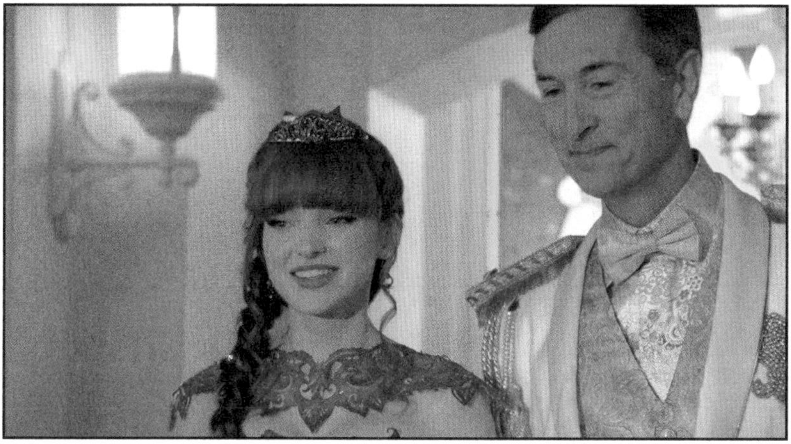

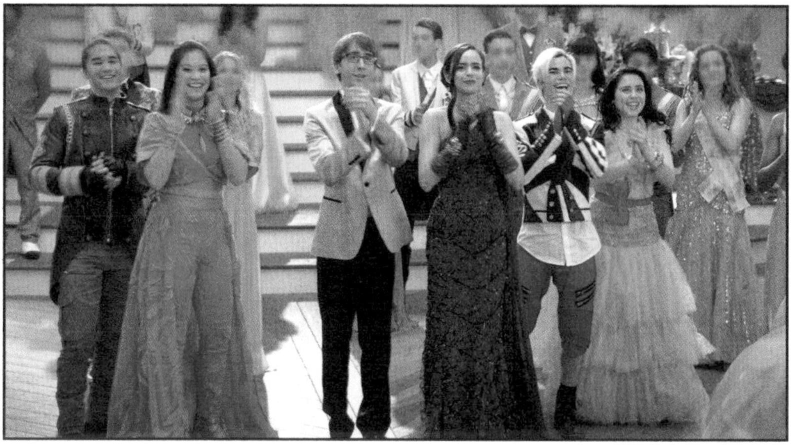

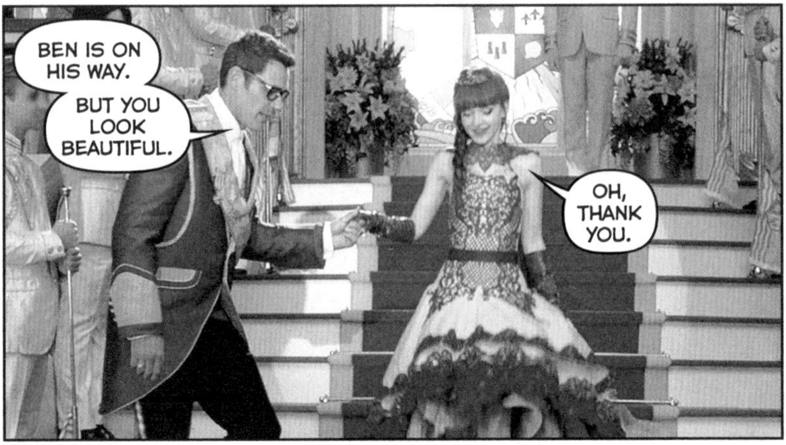
BEN IS ON HIS WAY.
BUT YOU LOOK BEAUTIFUL.
OH, THANK YOU.

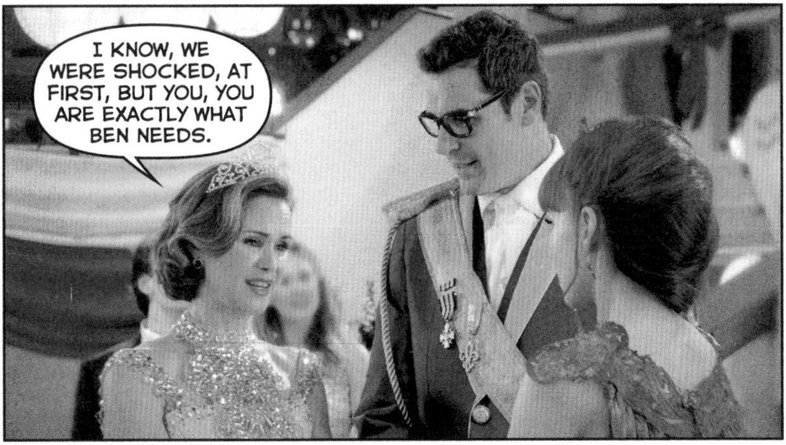
I KNOW, WE WERE SHOCKED, AT FIRST, BUT YOU, YOU ARE EXACTLY WHAT BEN NEEDS.

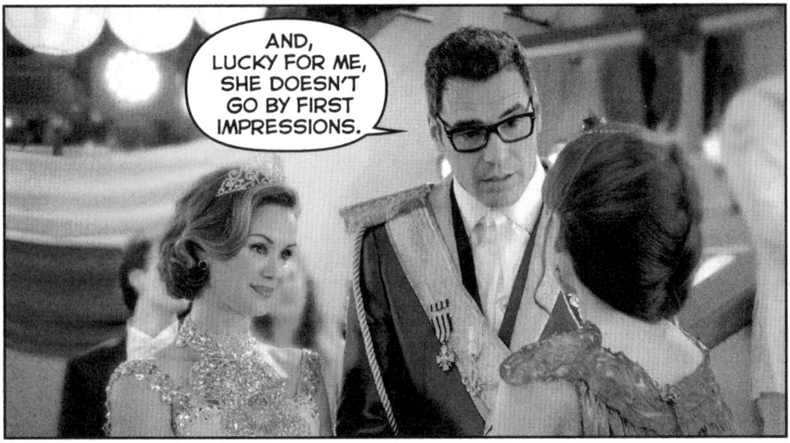
AND, LUCKY FOR ME, SHE DOESN'T GO BY FIRST IMPRESSIONS.

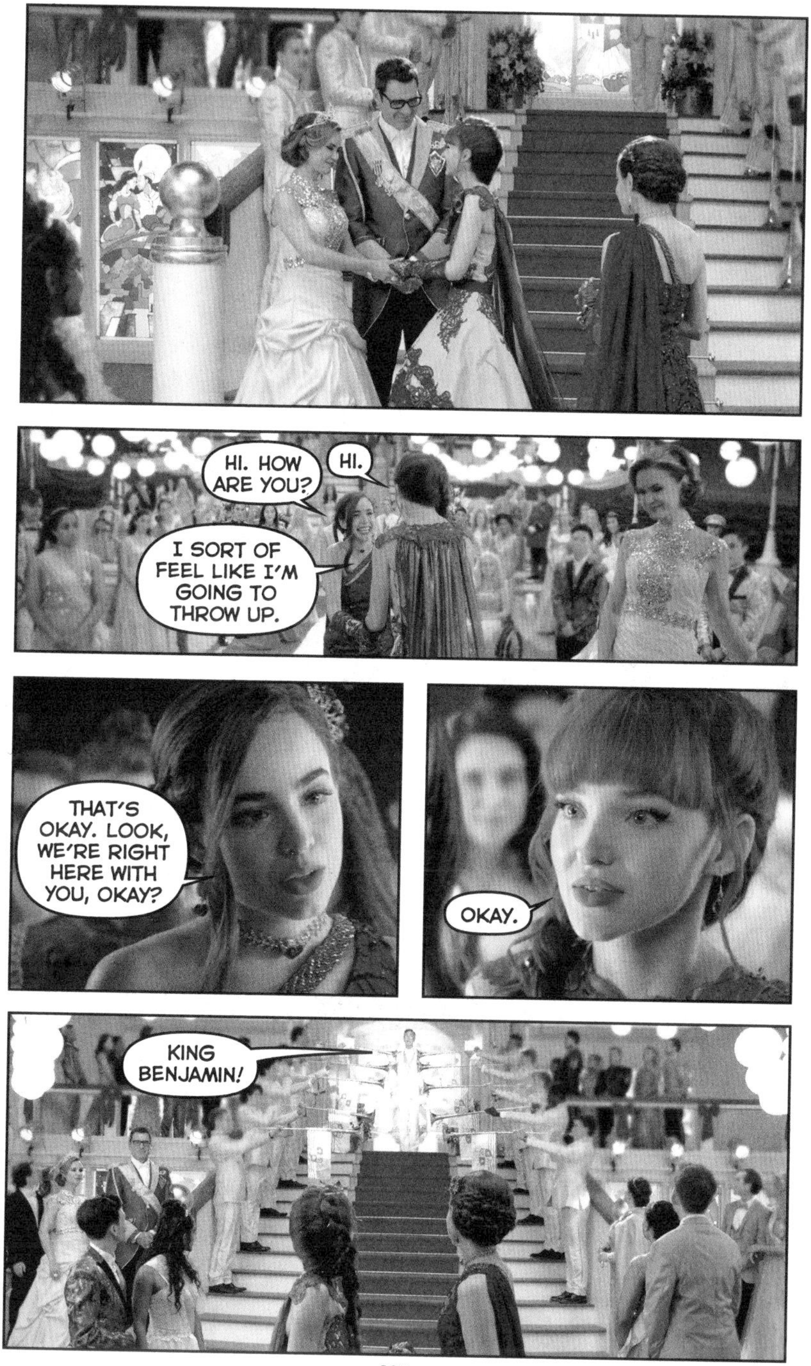
HI. HOW ARE YOU?
HI.
I SORT OF FEEL LIKE I'M GOING TO THROW UP.
THAT'S OKAY. LOOK, WE'RE RIGHT HERE WITH YOU, OKAY?
OKAY.
KING BENJAMIN!

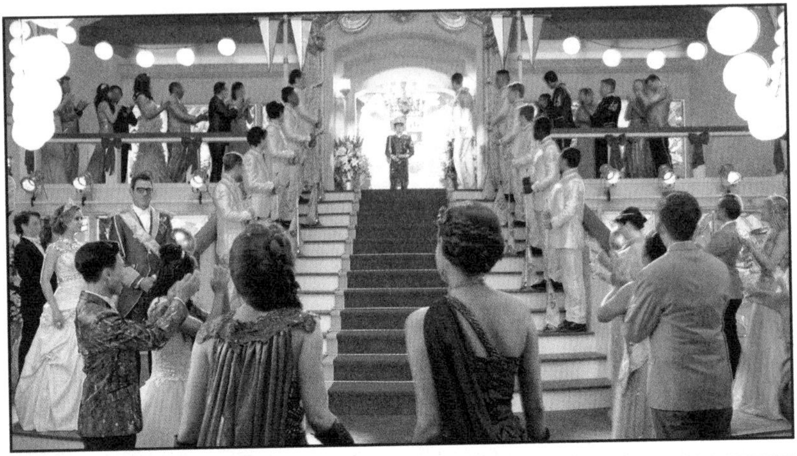

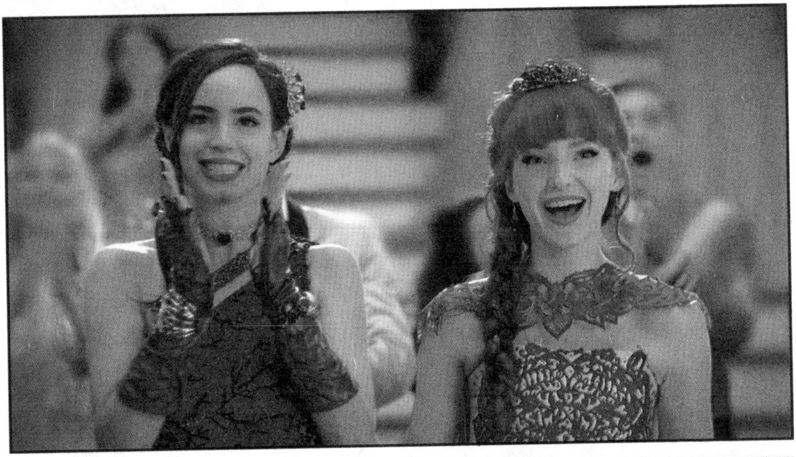

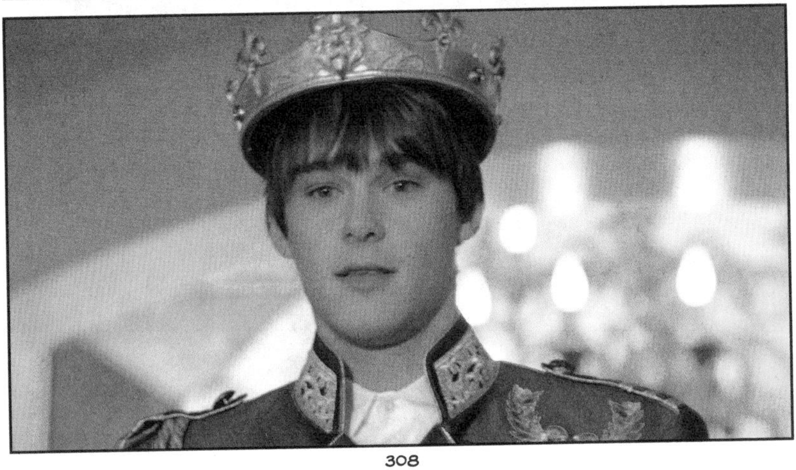

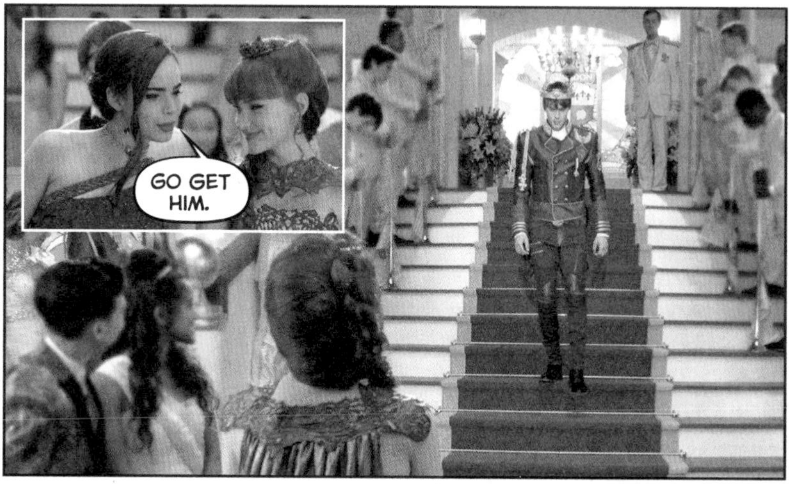
GO GET HIM.

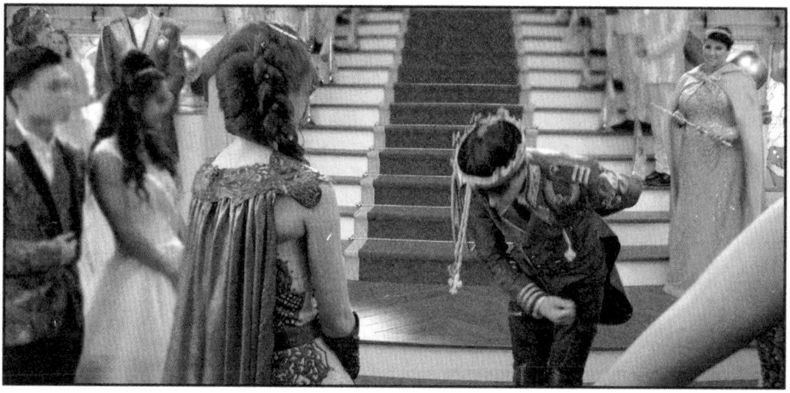

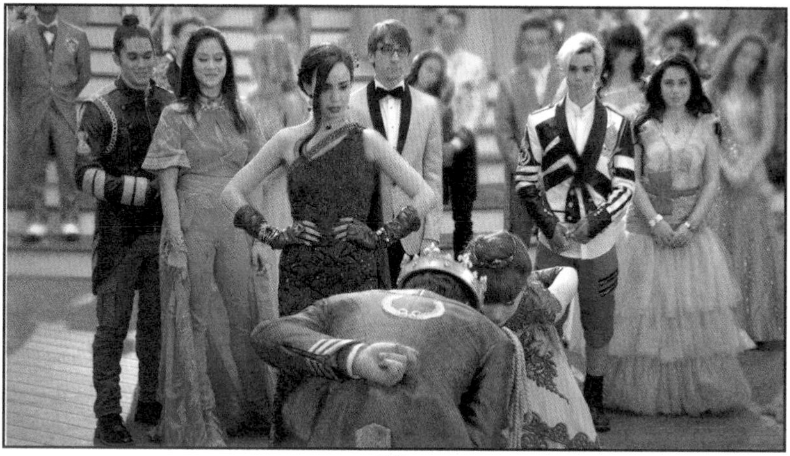

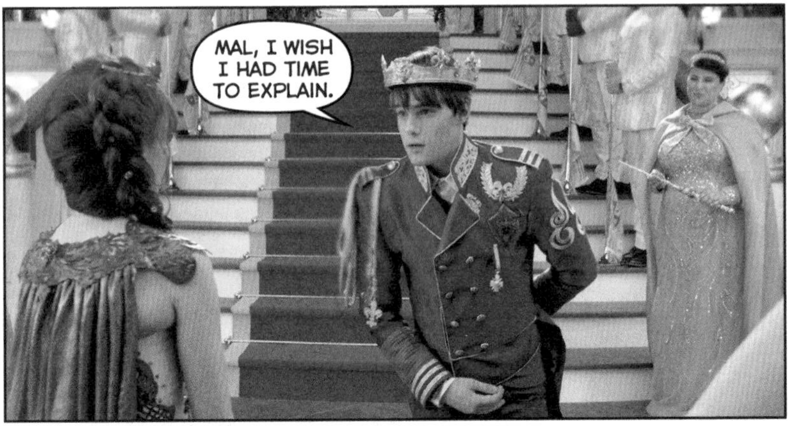
MAL, I WISH I HAD TIME TO EXPLAIN.

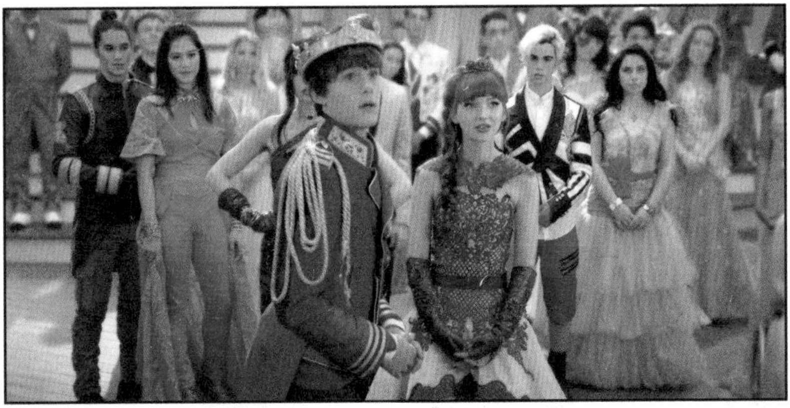

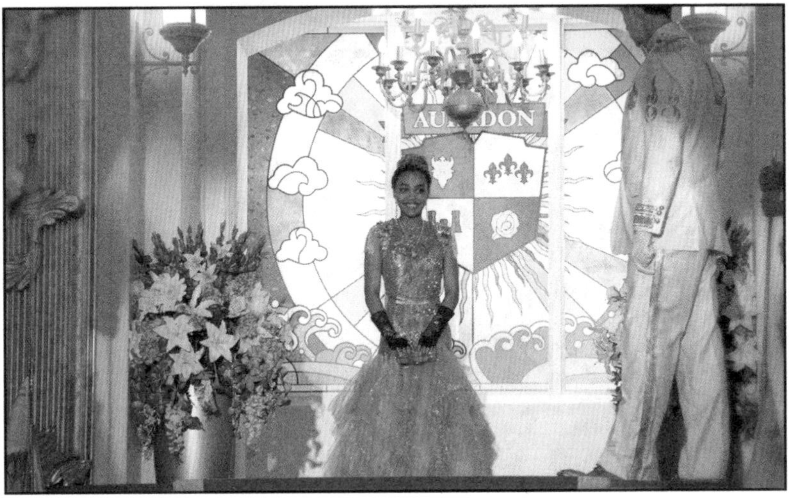
AURADON

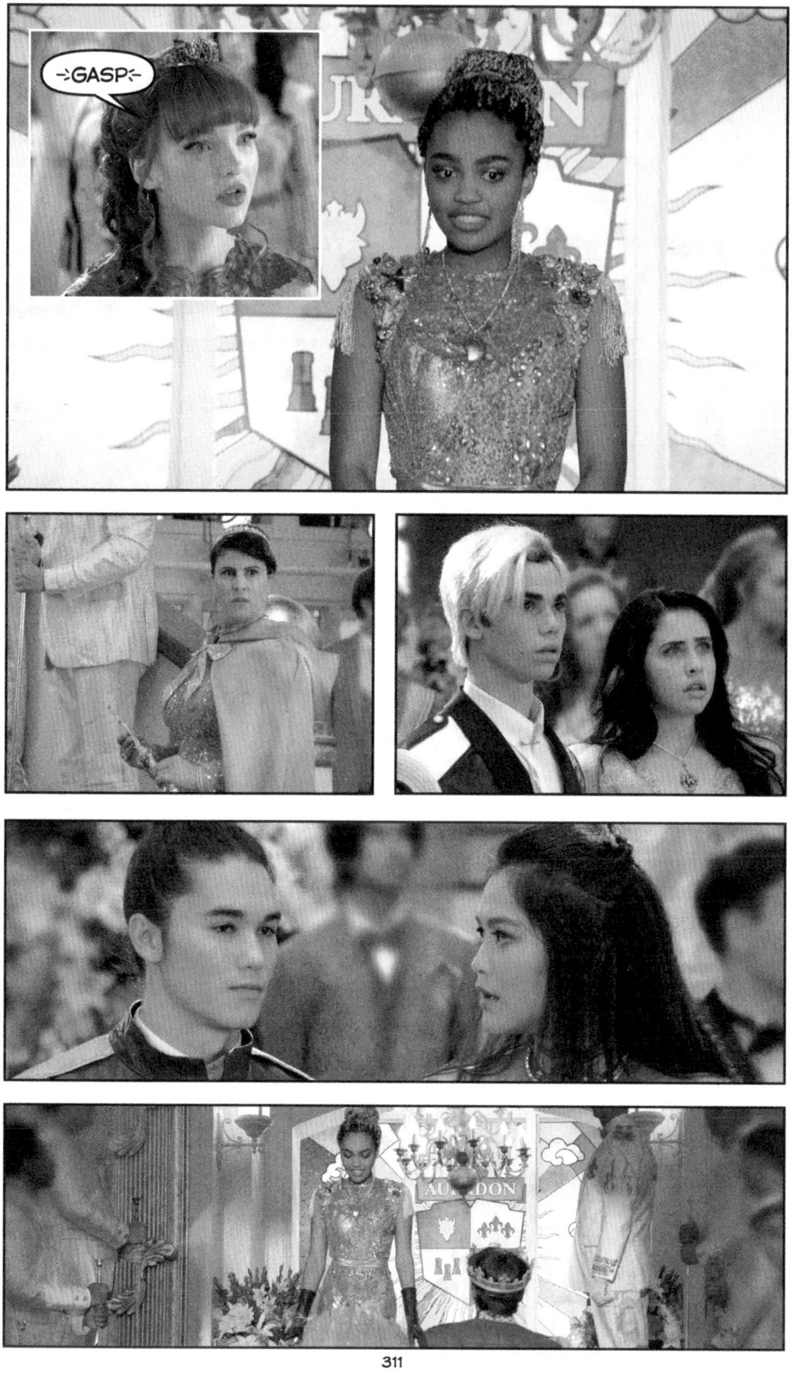
GASP

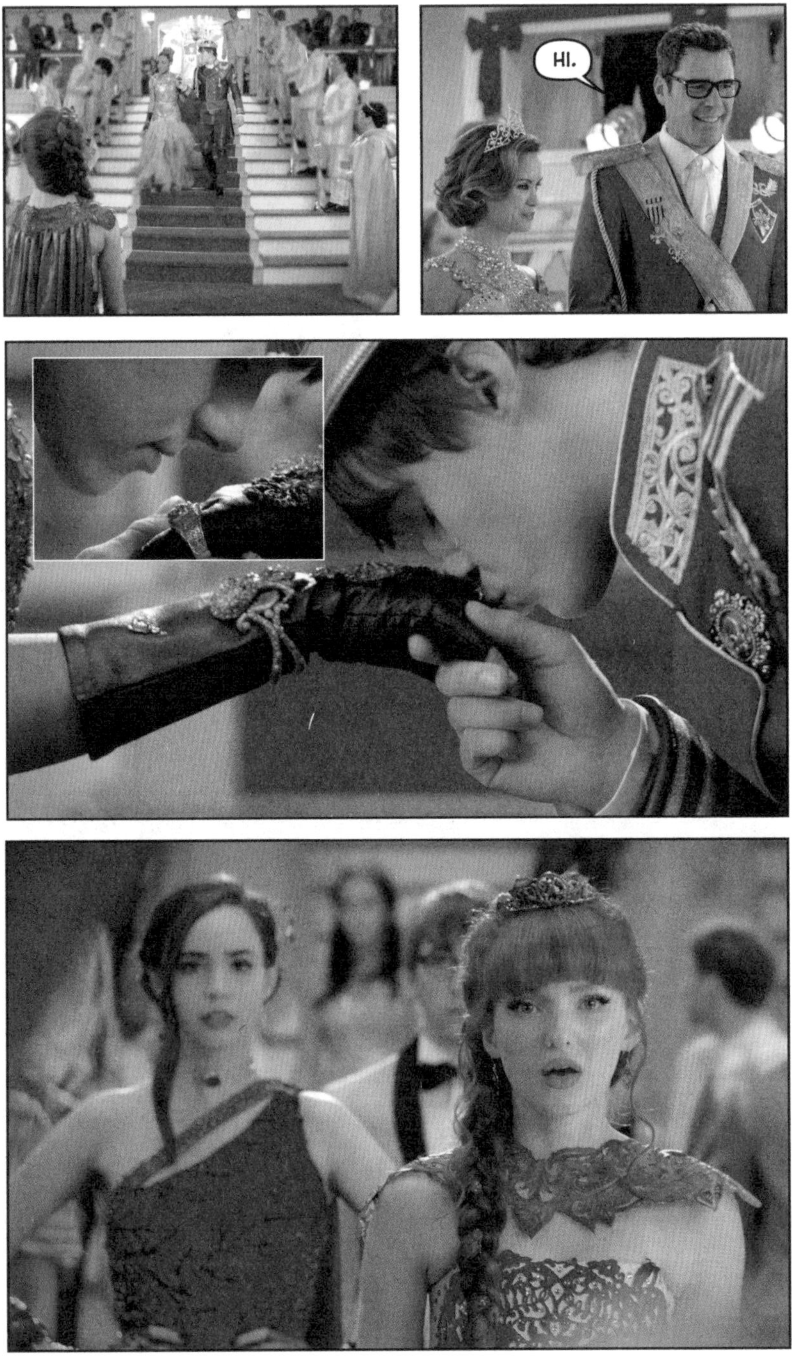
HI.

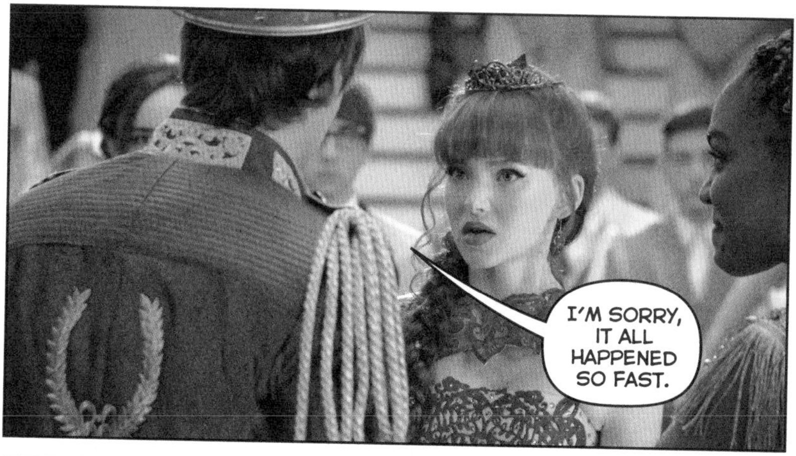
I'M SORRY, IT ALL HAPPENED SO FAST.

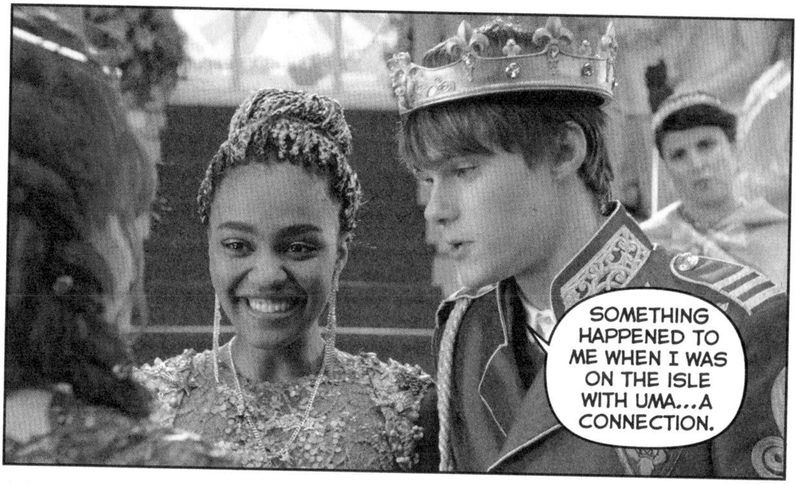
SOMETHING HAPPENED TO ME WHEN I WAS ON THE ISLE WITH UMA...A CONNECTION.

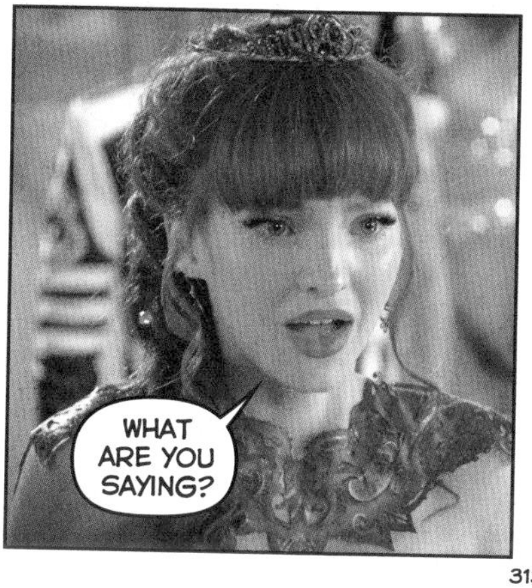
WHAT ARE YOU SAYING?

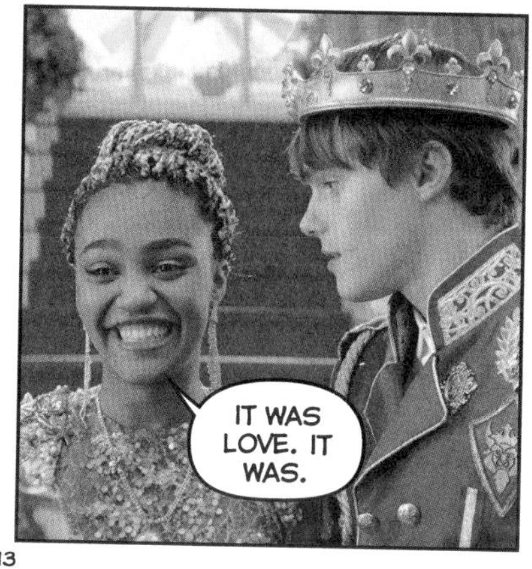
IT WAS LOVE. IT WAS.

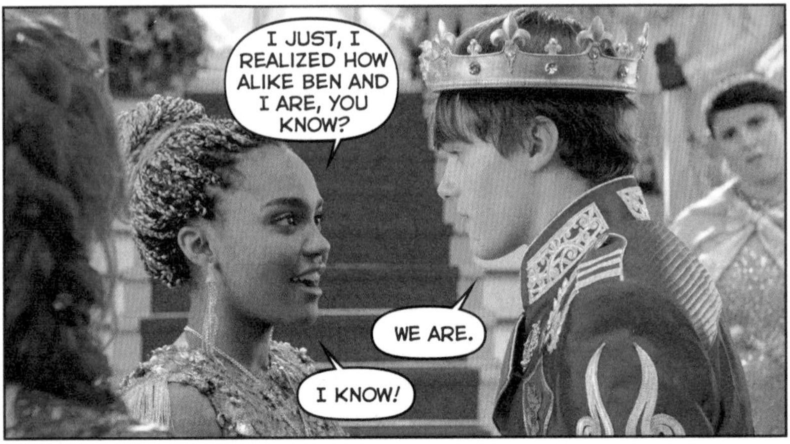
I JUST, I REALIZED HOW ALIKE BEN AND I ARE, YOU KNOW?
WE ARE.
I KNOW!

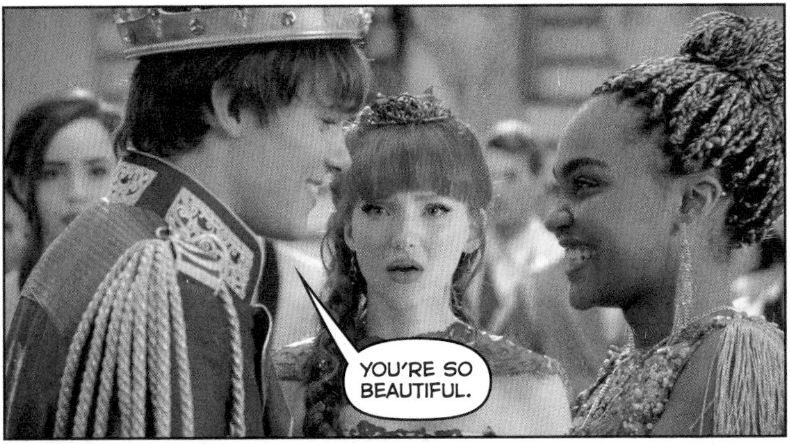
YOU'RE SO BEAUTIFUL.

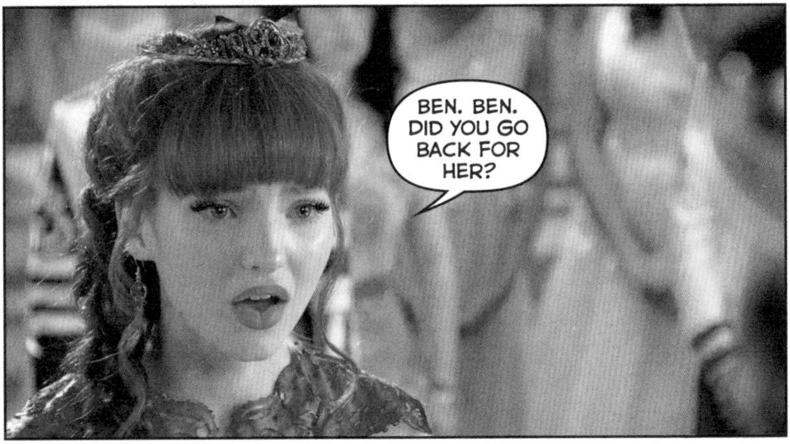
BEN. BEN. DID YOU GO BACK FOR HER?

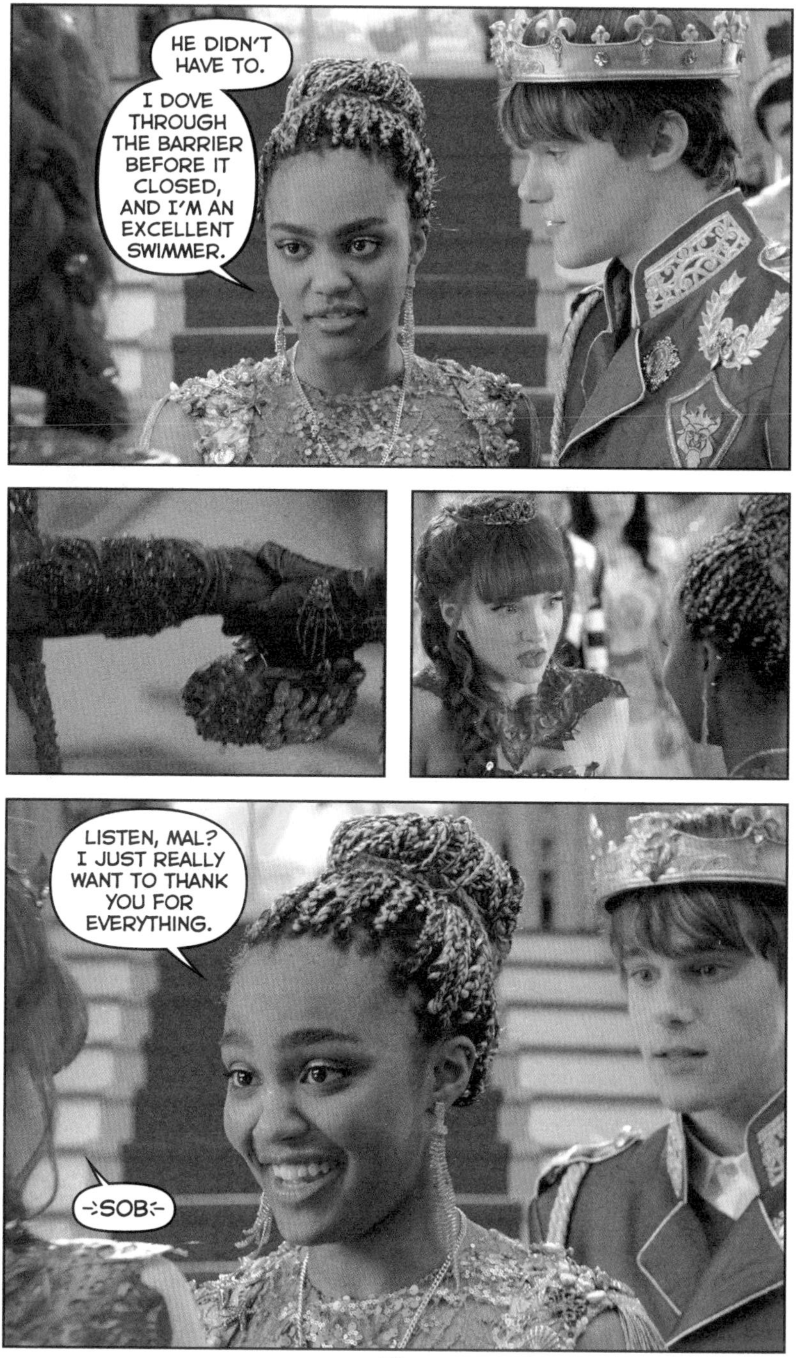
HE DIDN'T HAVE TO.
I DOVE THROUGH THE BARRIER BEFORE IT CLOSED, AND I'M AN EXCELLENT SWIMMER.
LISTEN, MAL? I JUST REALLY WANT TO THANK YOU FOR EVERYTHING.
-SOB-

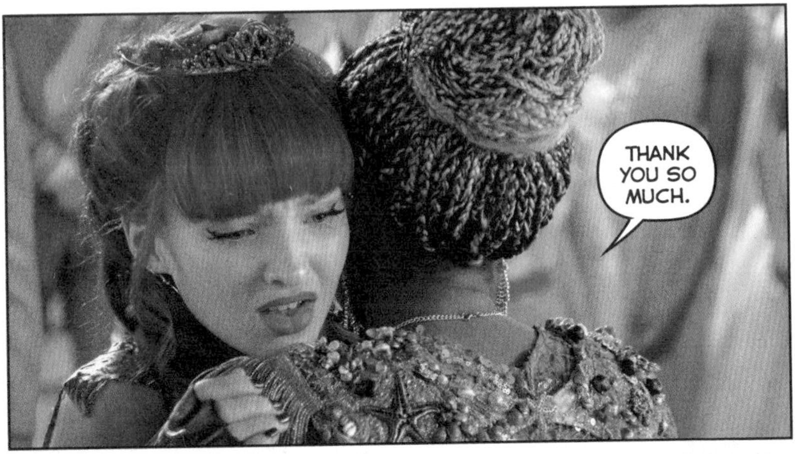
THANK YOU SO MUCH.

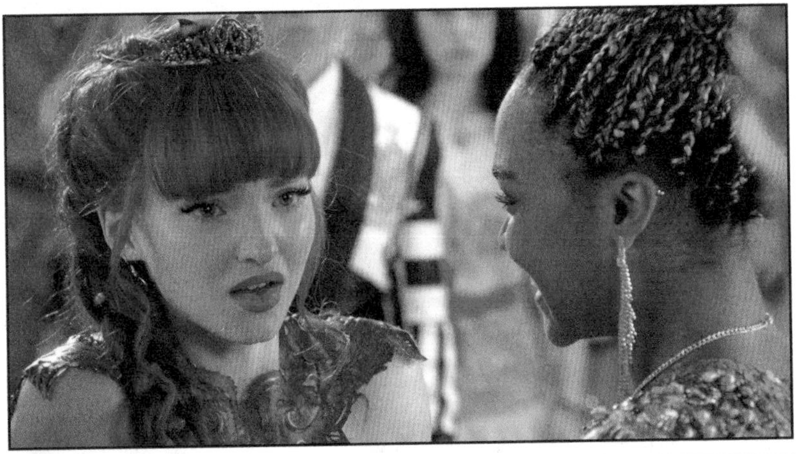

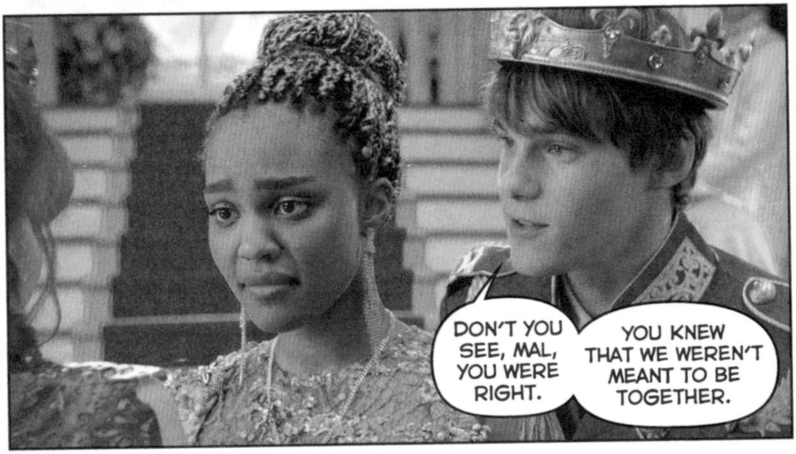
DON'T YOU SEE, MAL, YOU WERE RIGHT.
YOU KNEW THAT WE WEREN'T MEANT TO BE TOGETHER.

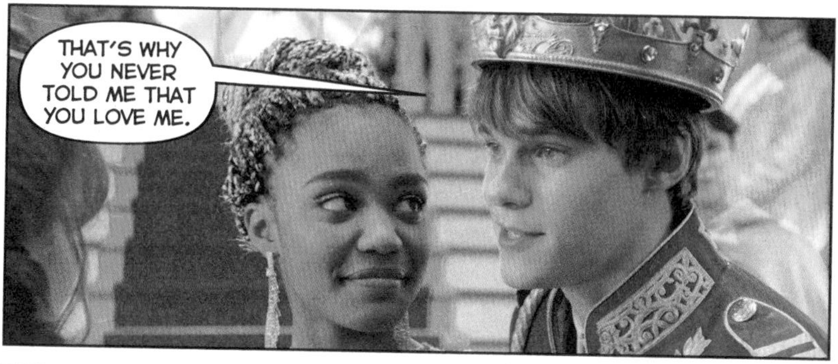
THAT'S WHY YOU NEVER TOLD ME THAT YOU LOVE ME.

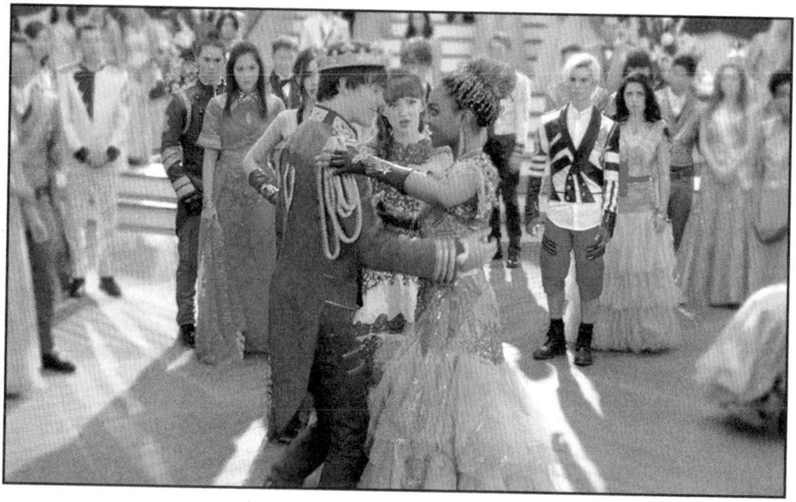

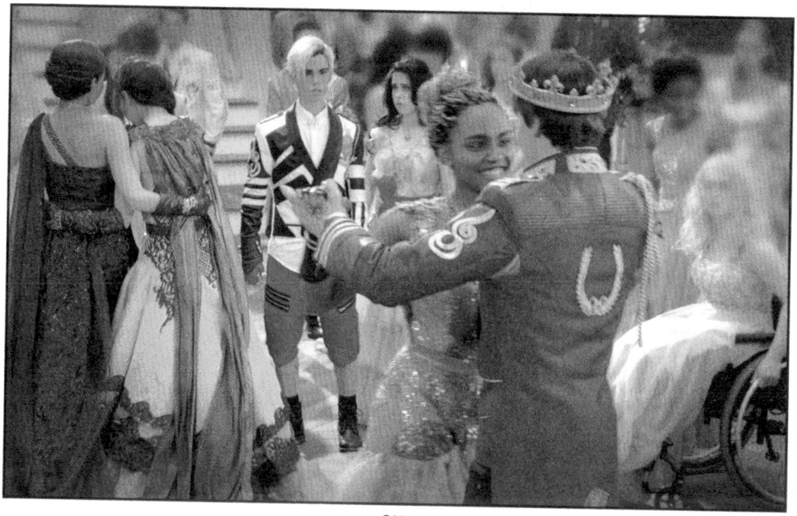

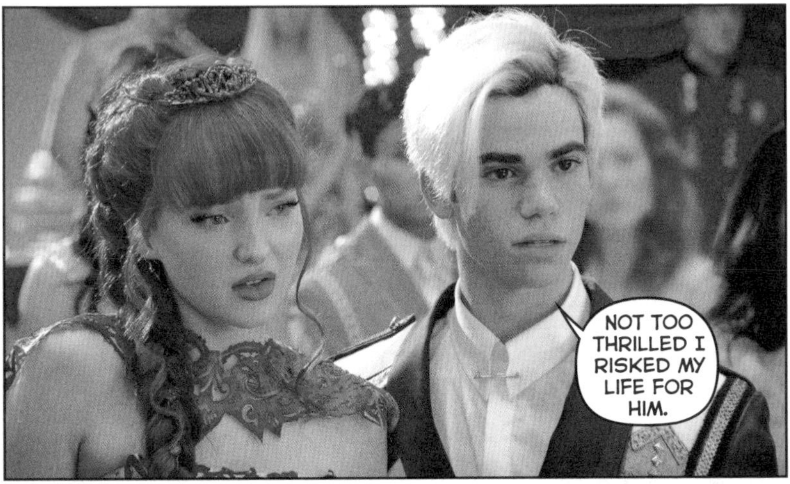
NOT TOO THRILLED I RISKED MY LIFE FOR HIM.

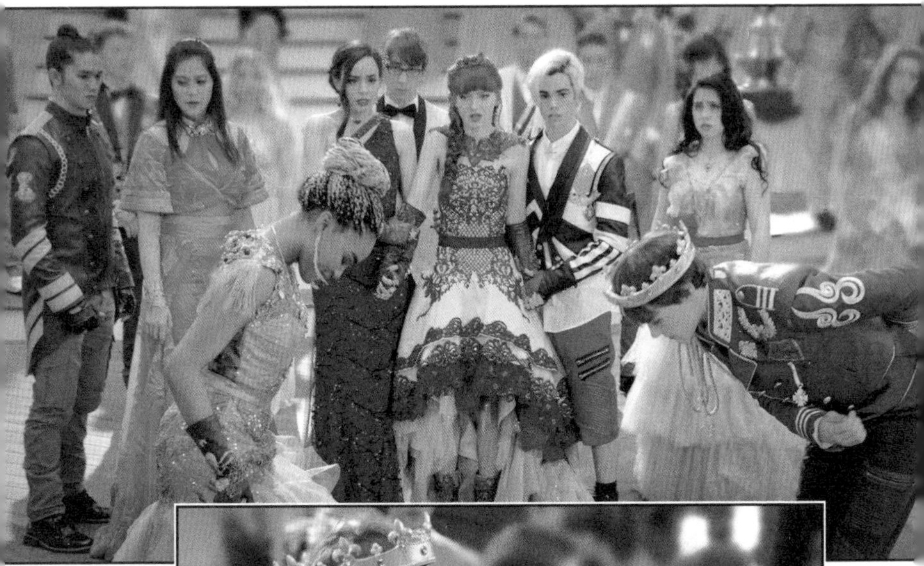

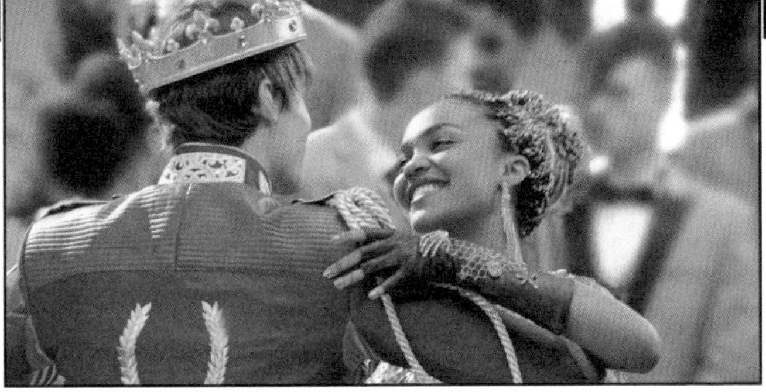

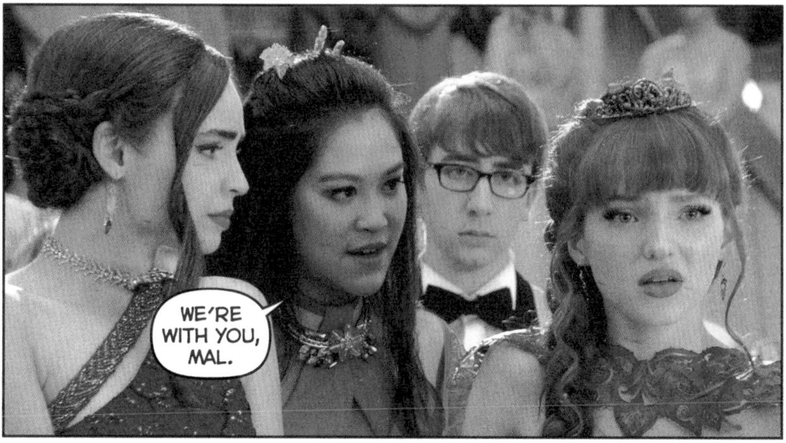
WE'RE WITH YOU, MAL.

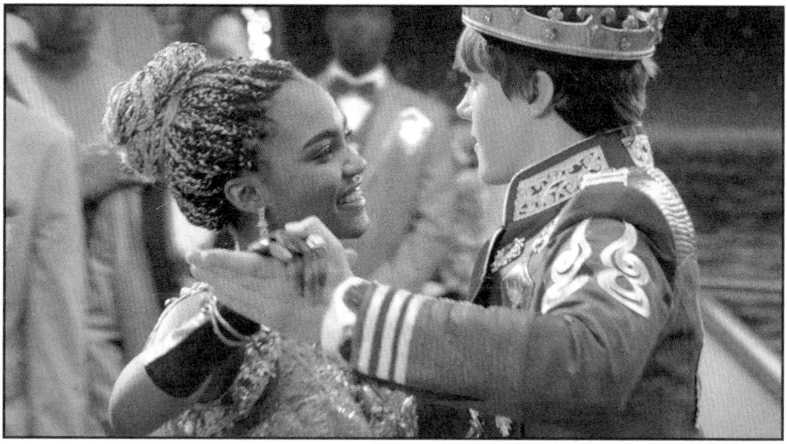

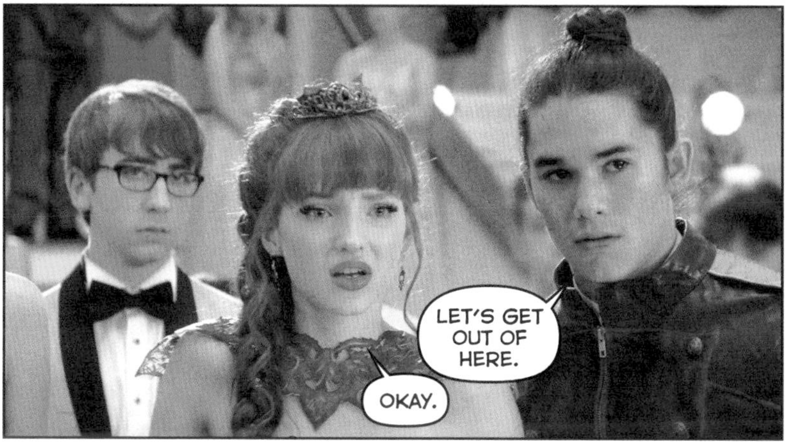
LET'S GET OUT OF HERE.
OKAY.

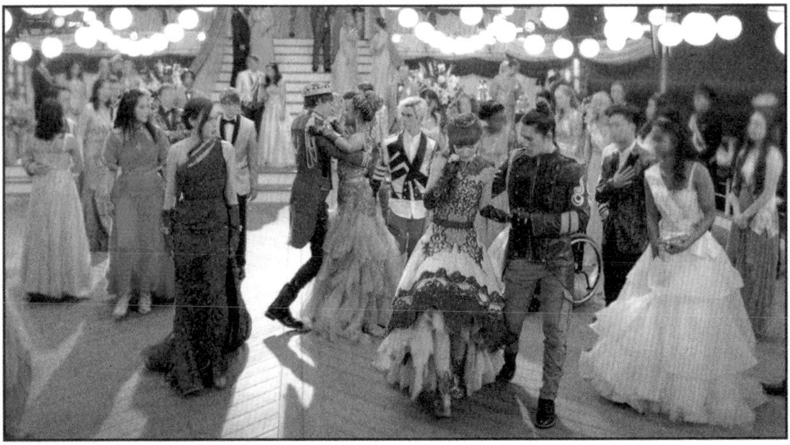

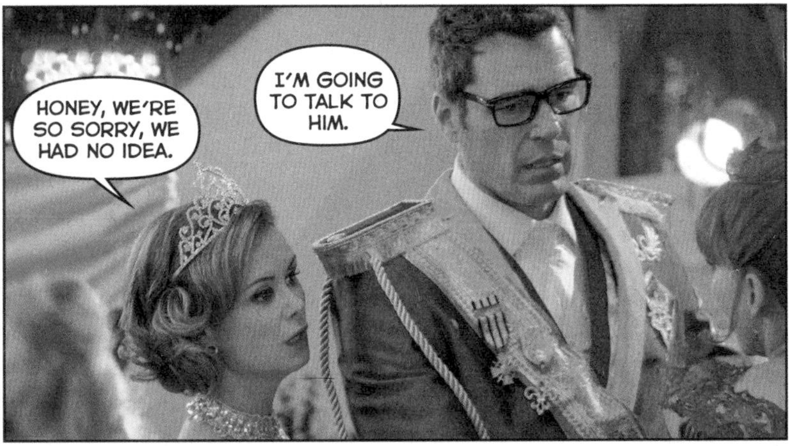
HONEY, WE'RE SO SORRY, WE HAD NO IDEA.
I'M GOING TO TALK TO HIM.

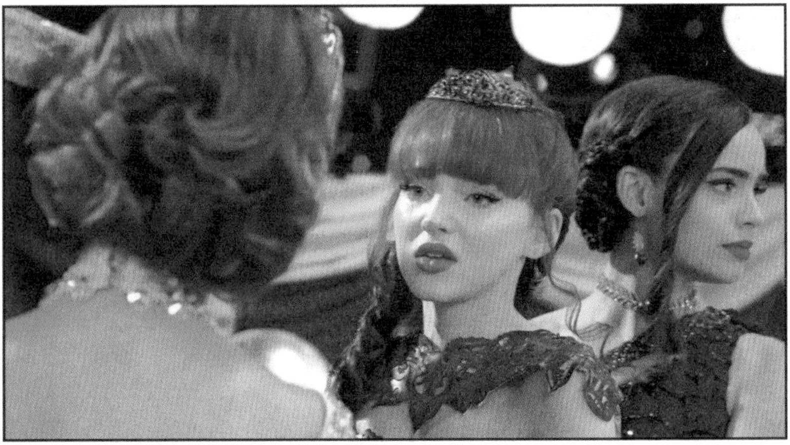

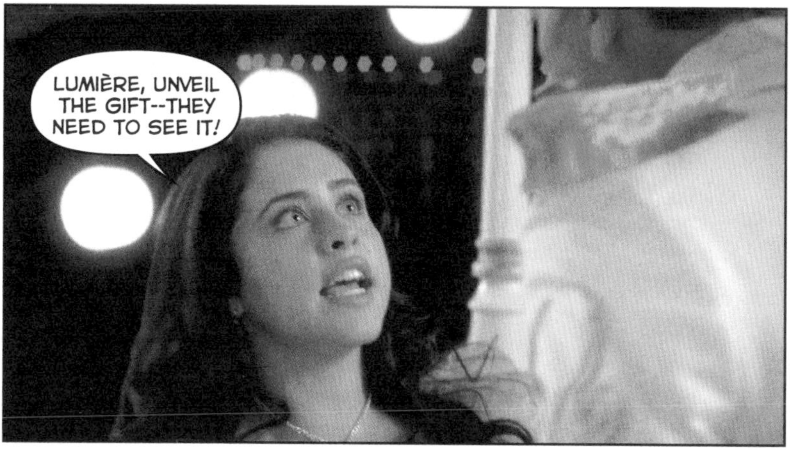
LUMIÈRE, UNVEIL THE GIFT--THEY NEED TO SEE IT!

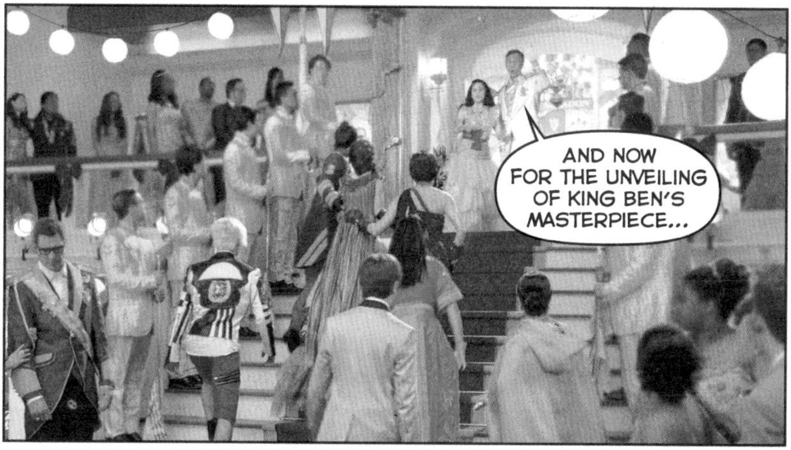
AND NOW FOR THE UNVEILING OF KING BEN'S MASTERPIECE...

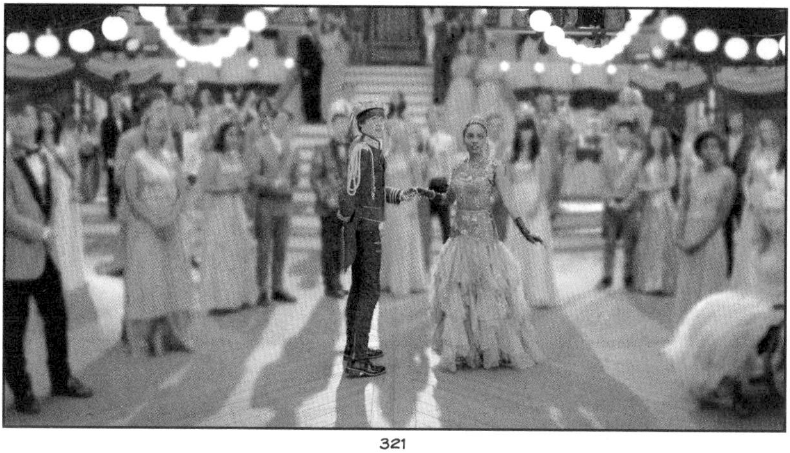

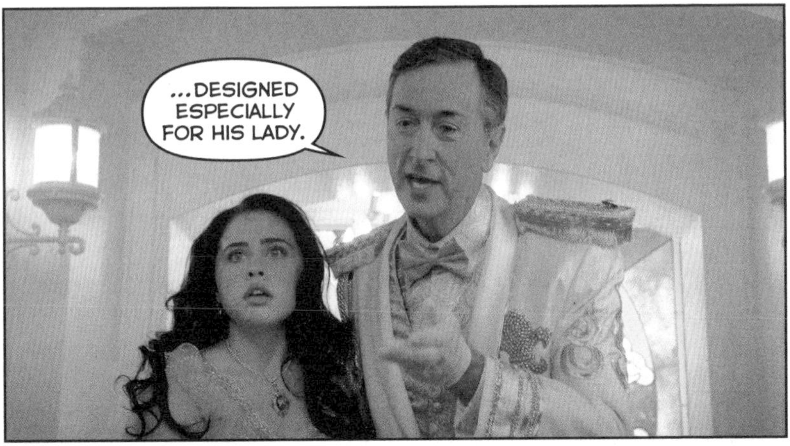
...DESIGNED ESPECIALLY FOR HIS LADY.

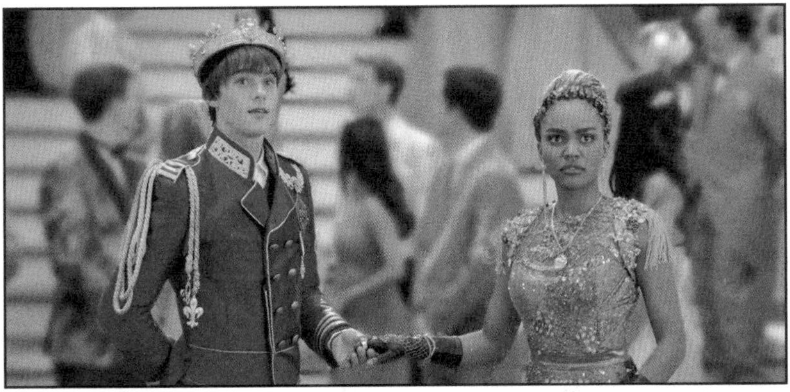

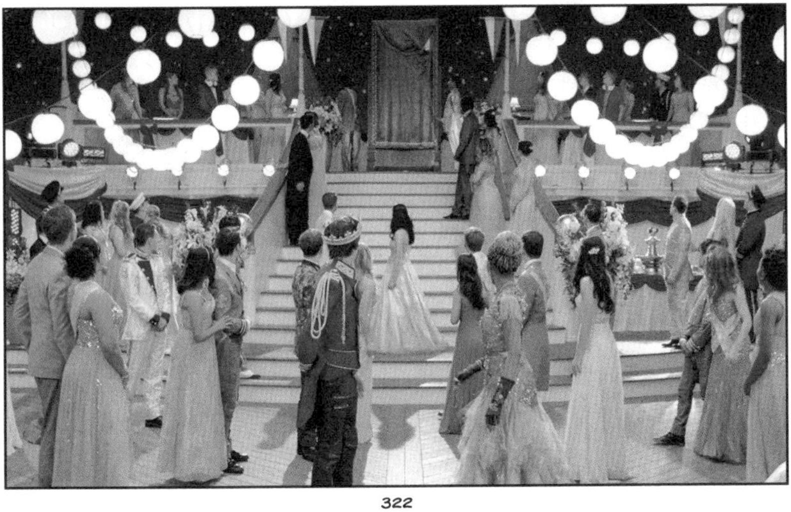

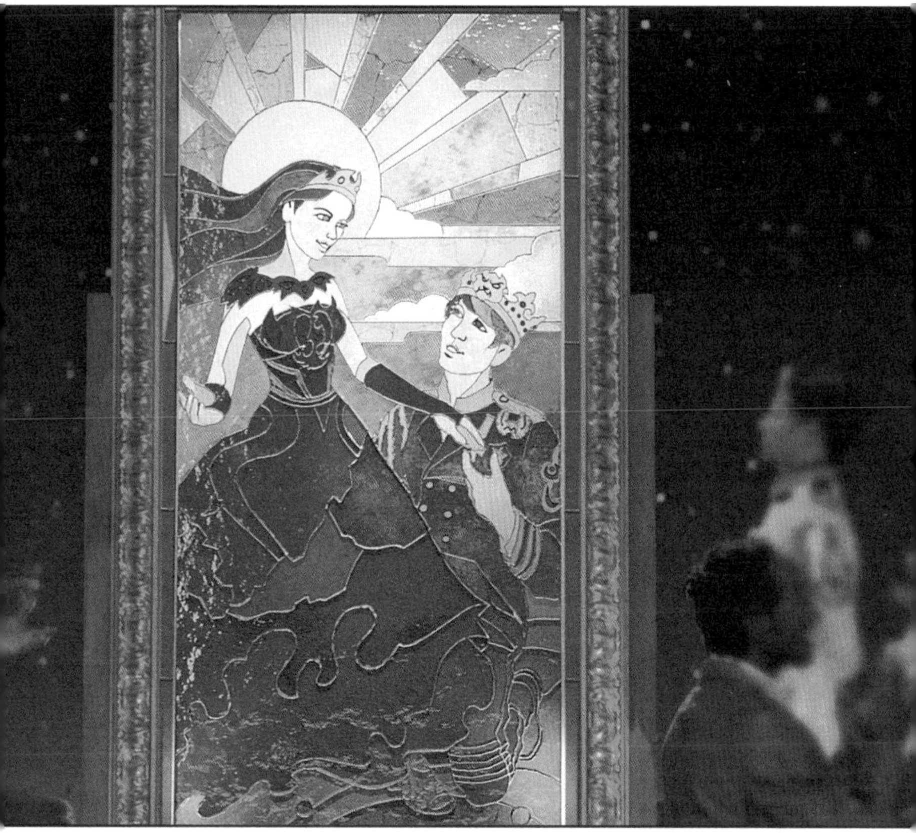

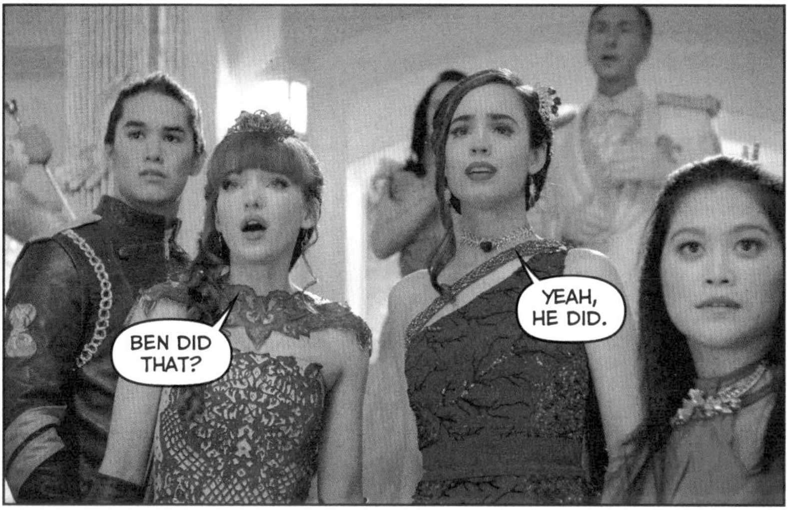
BEN DID THAT?
YEAH, HE DID.

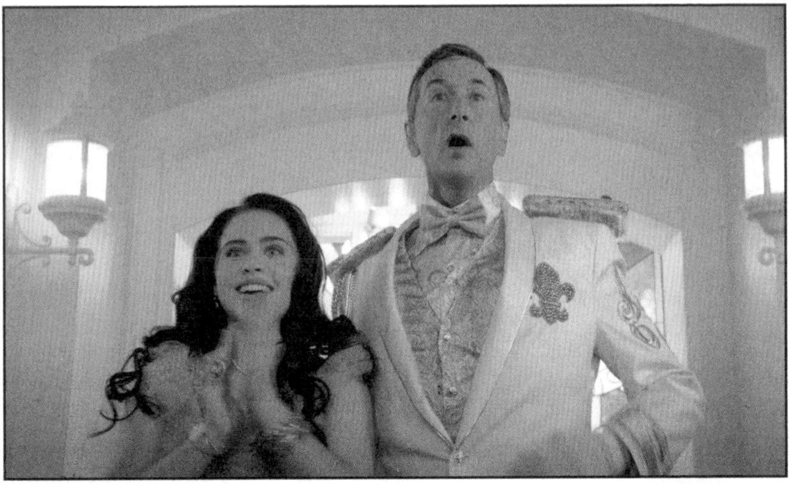

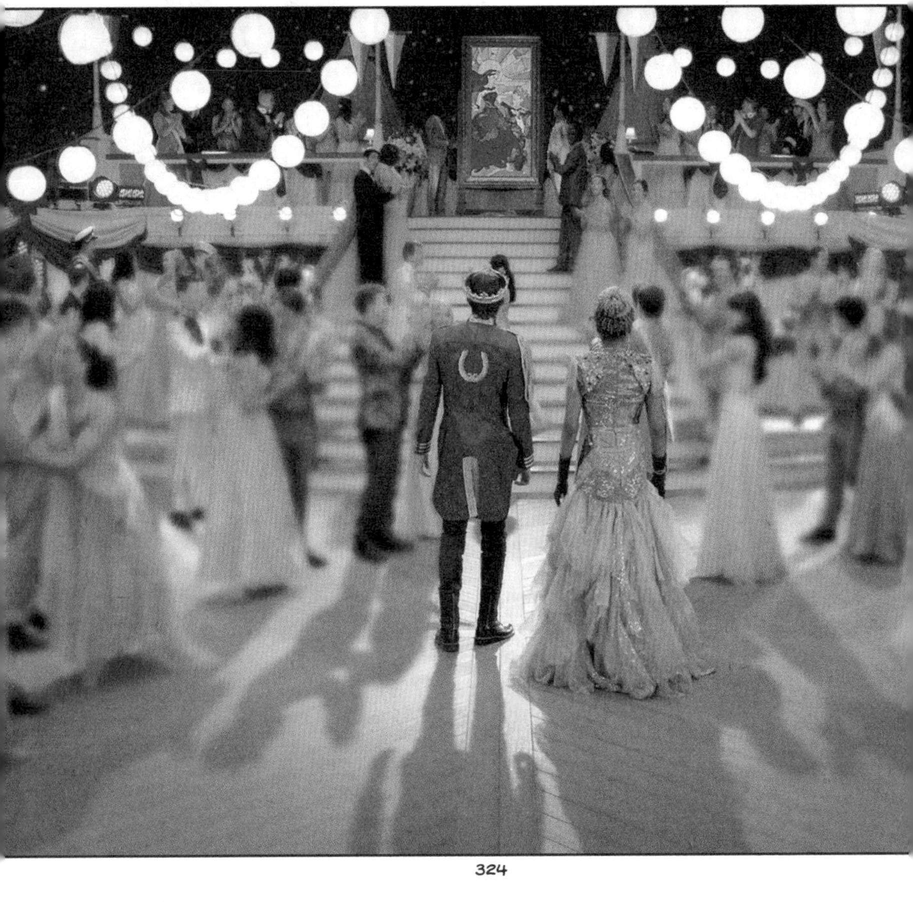

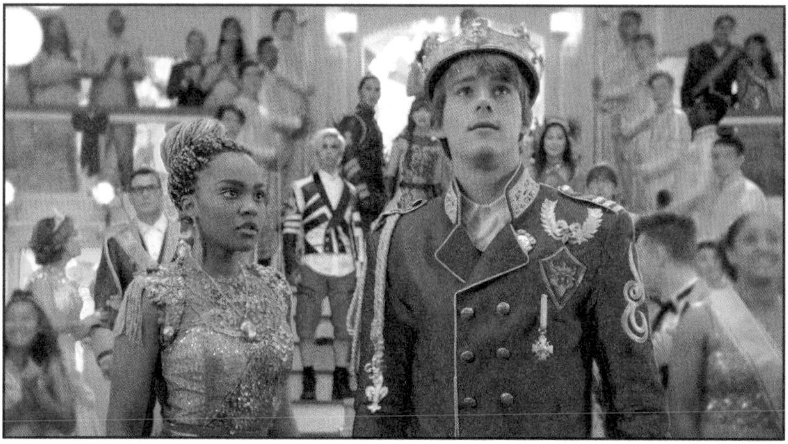

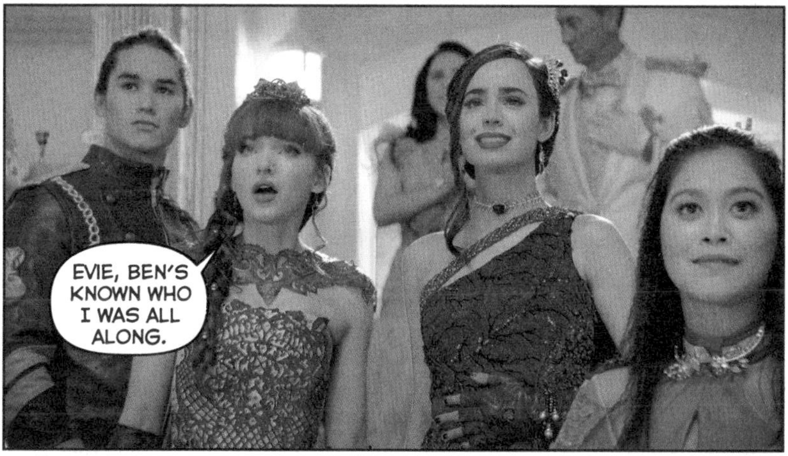
EVIE, BEN'S KNOWN WHO I WAS ALL ALONG.

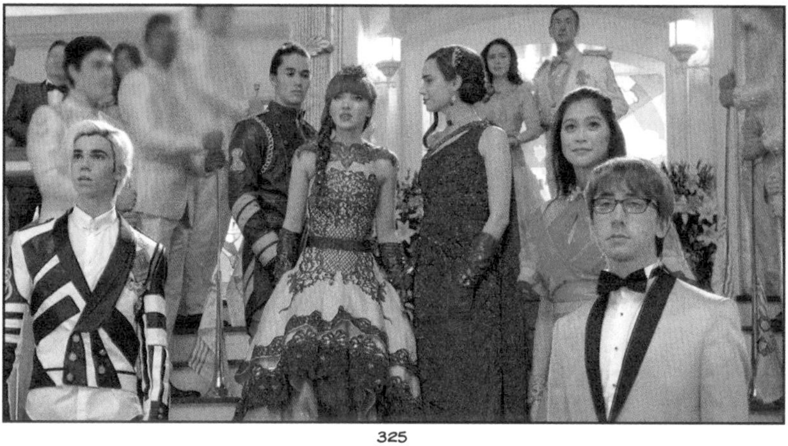

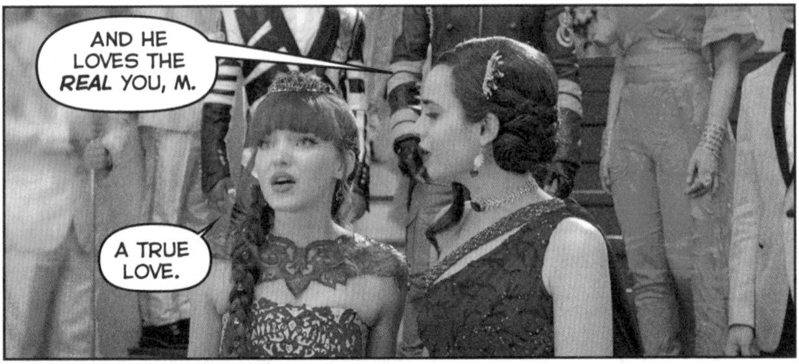
AND HE LOVES THE REAL YOU, M.
A TRUE LOVE.

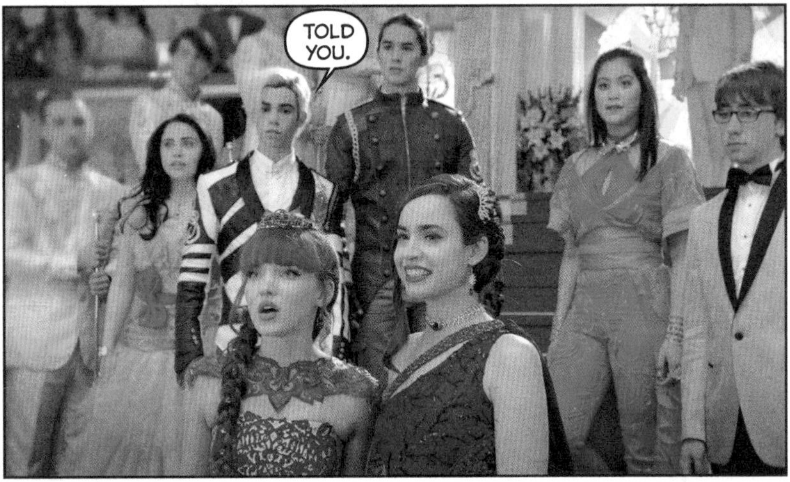
TOLD YOU.

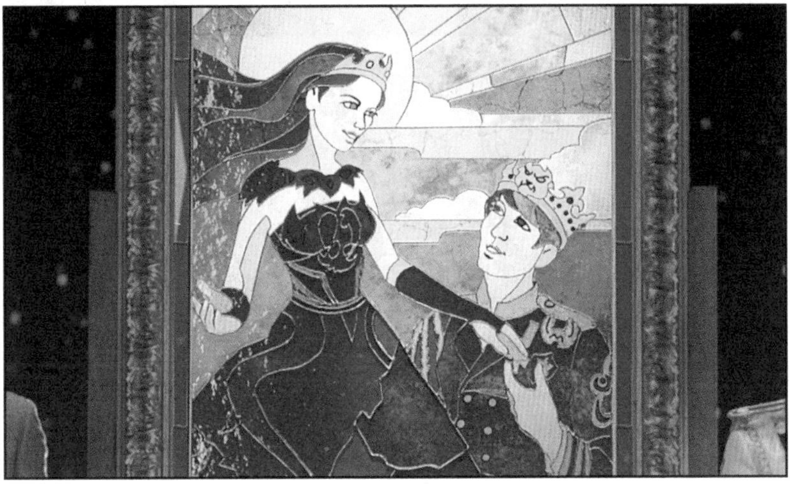

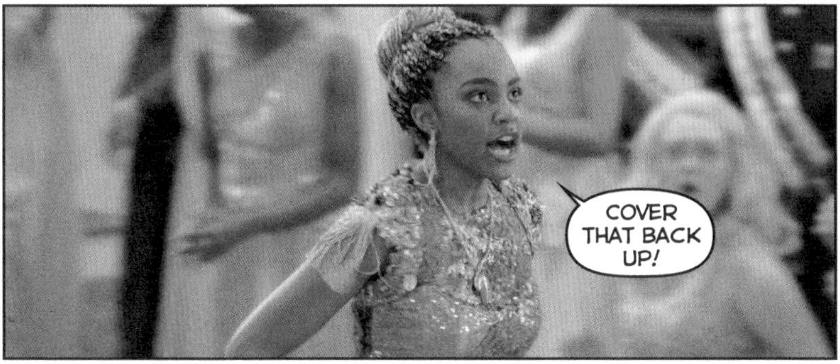
COVER THAT BACK UP!

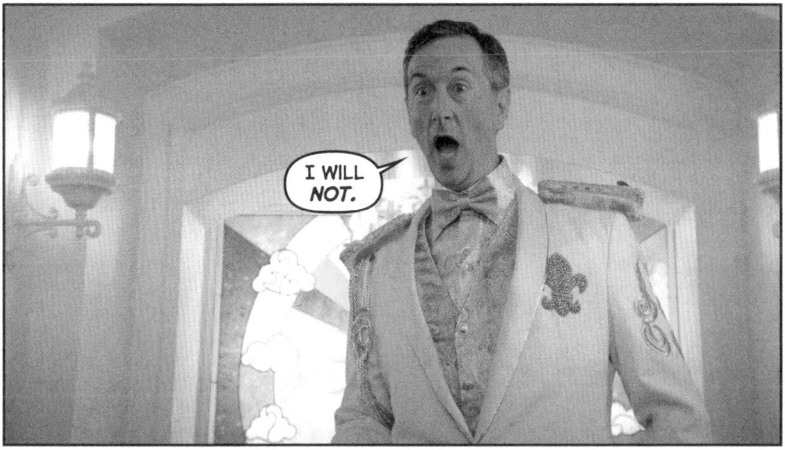
I WILL *NOT.*

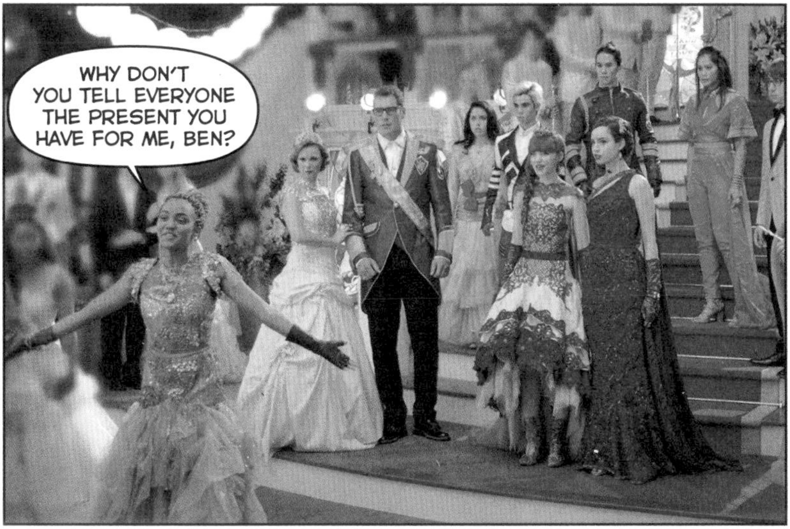
WHY DON'T YOU TELL EVERYONE THE PRESENT YOU HAVE FOR ME, BEN?

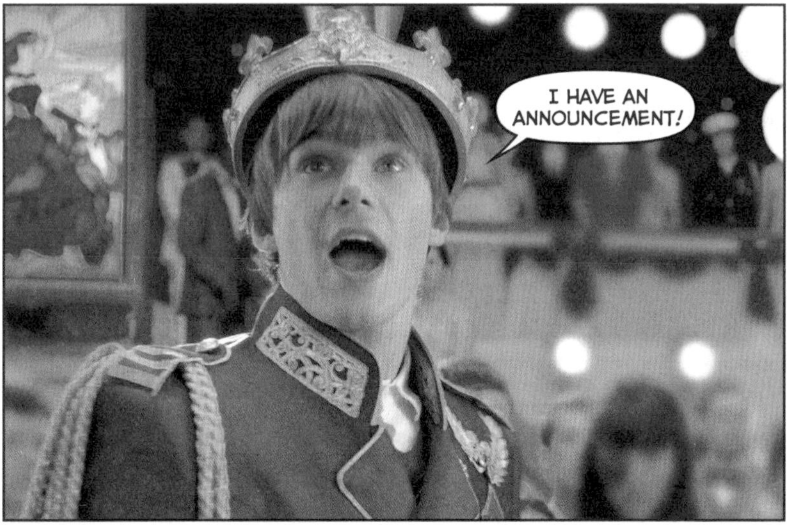
I HAVE AN ANNOUNCEMENT!

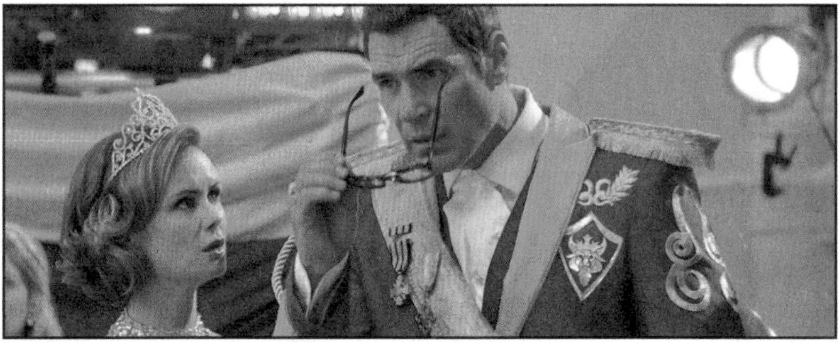

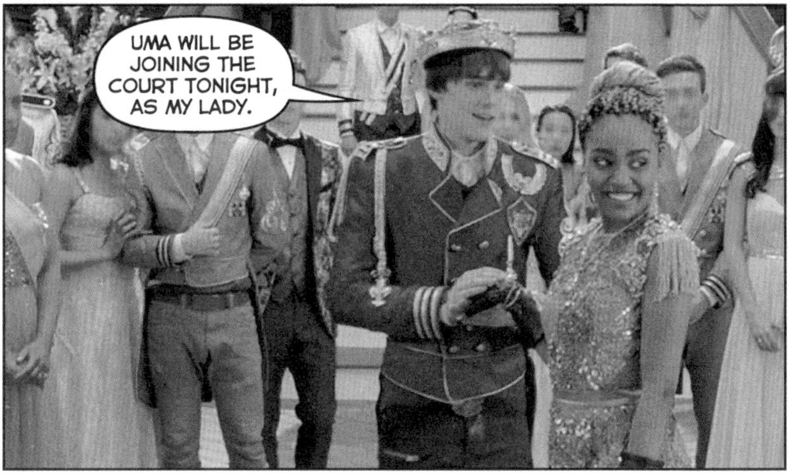
UMA WILL BE JOINING THE COURT TONIGHT, AS MY LADY.

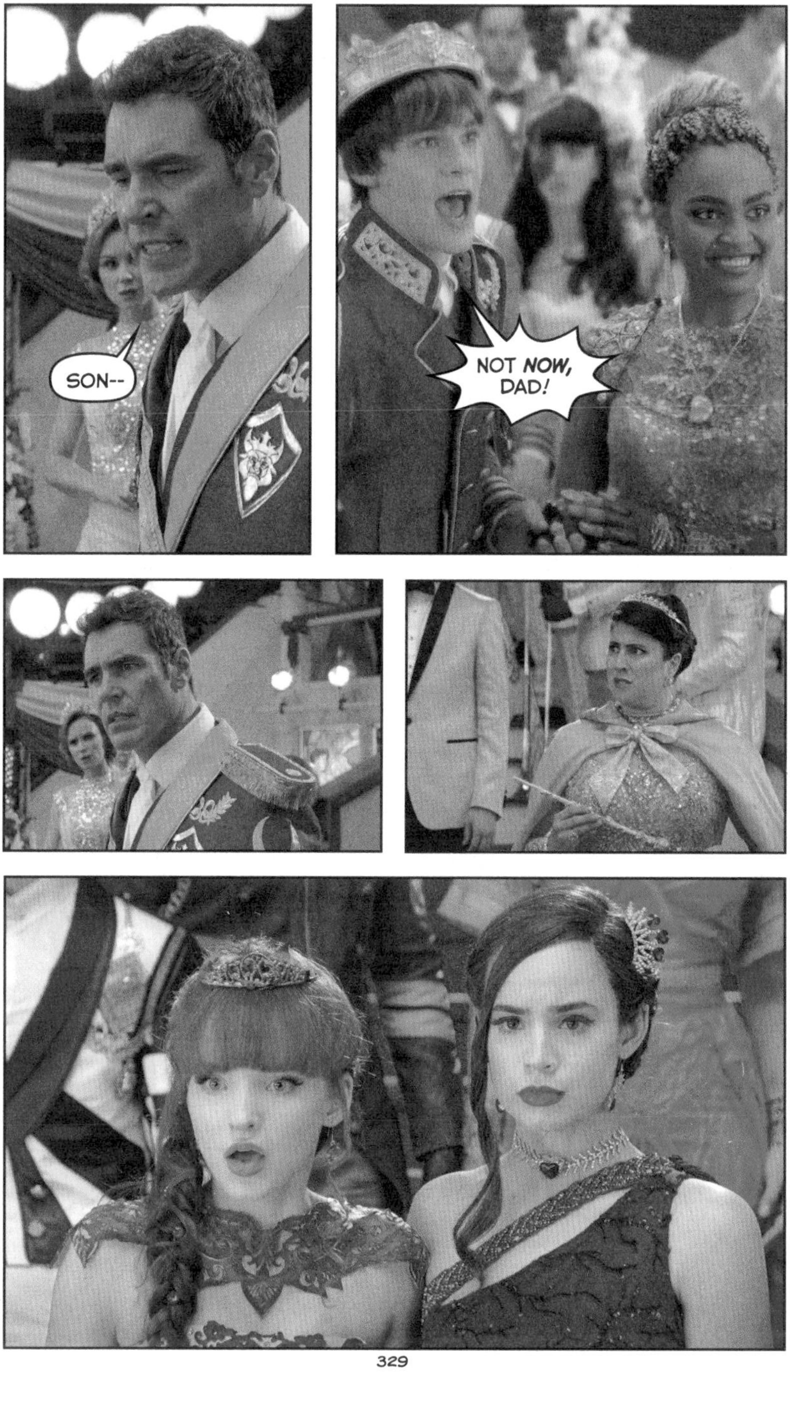
SON--
NOT *NOW,*
DAD!

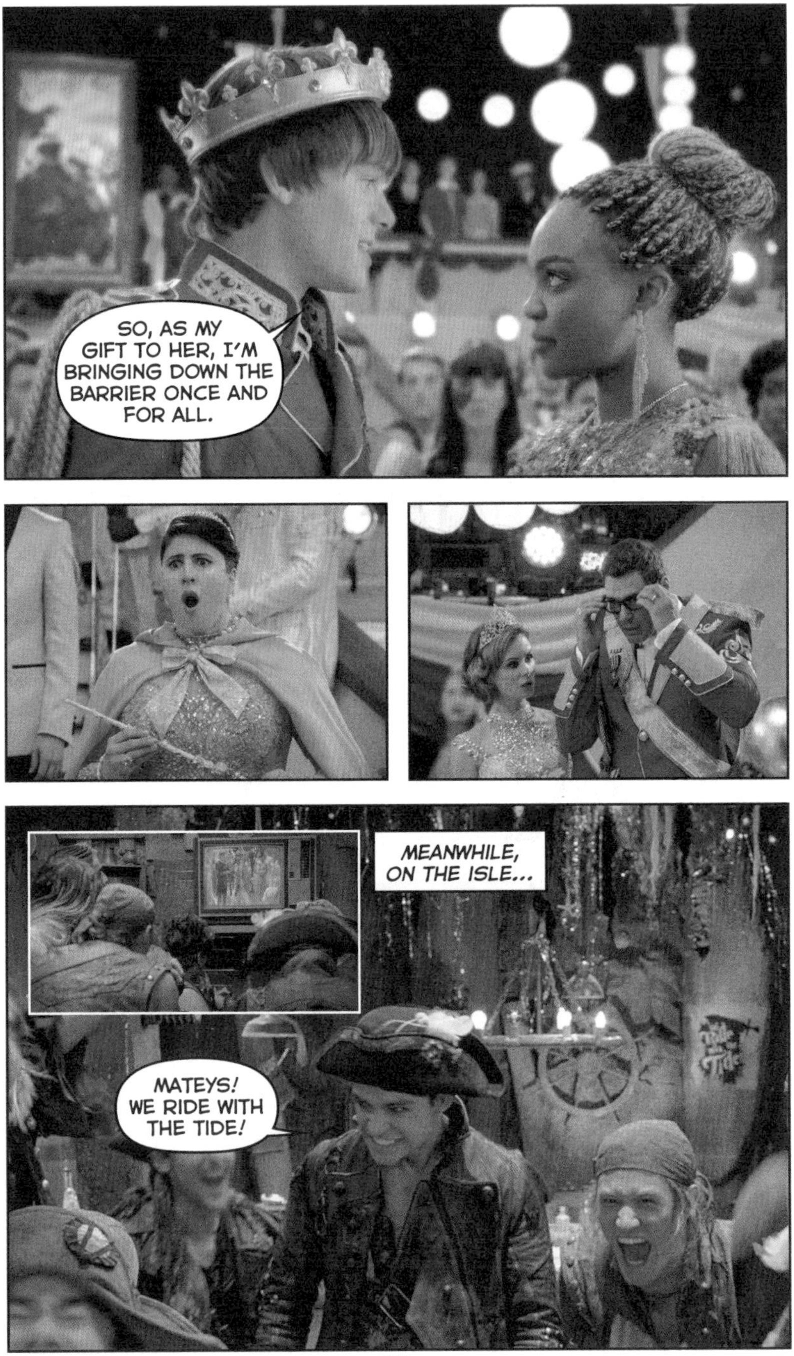
SO, AS MY GIFT TO HER, I'M BRINGING DOWN THE BARRIER ONCE AND FOR ALL.
MEANWHILE, ON THE ISLE...
MATEYS! WE RIDE WITH THE TIDE!

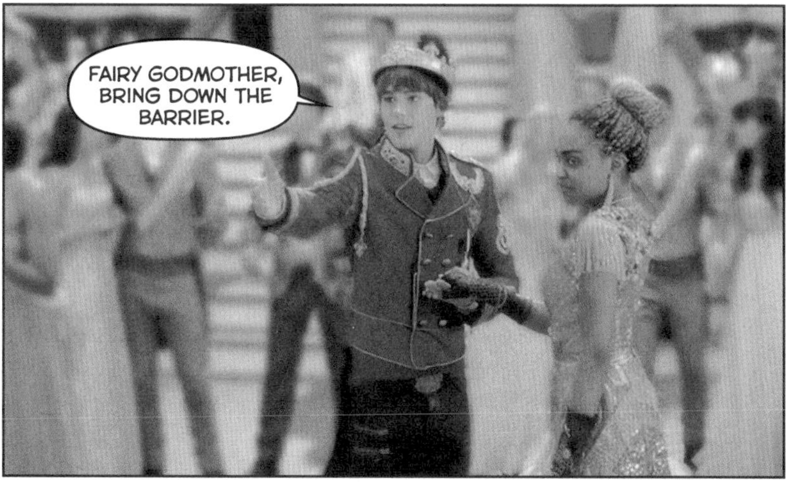
FAIRY GODMOTHER, BRING DOWN THE BARRIER.

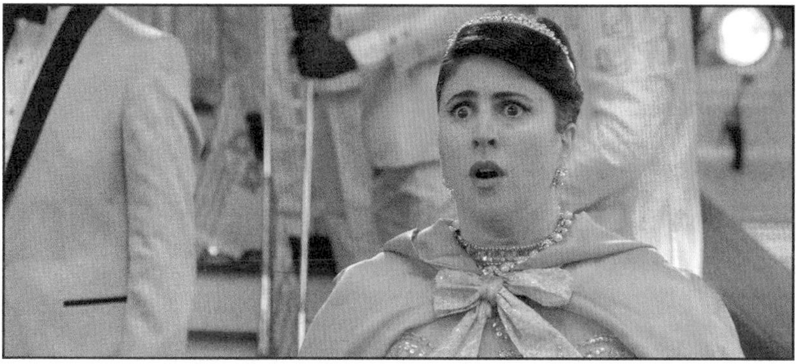

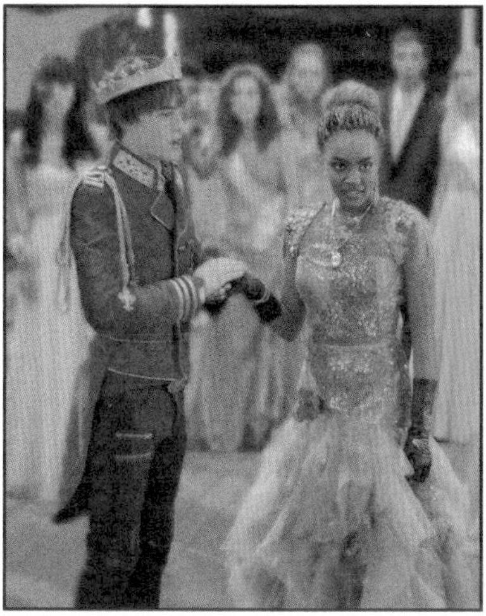

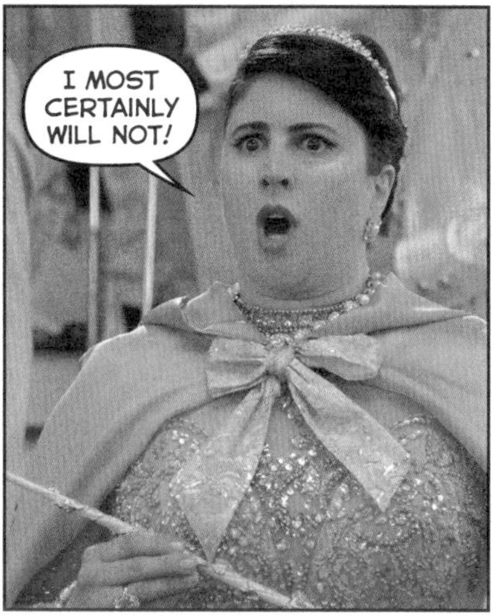
I MOST CERTAINLY WILL NOT!

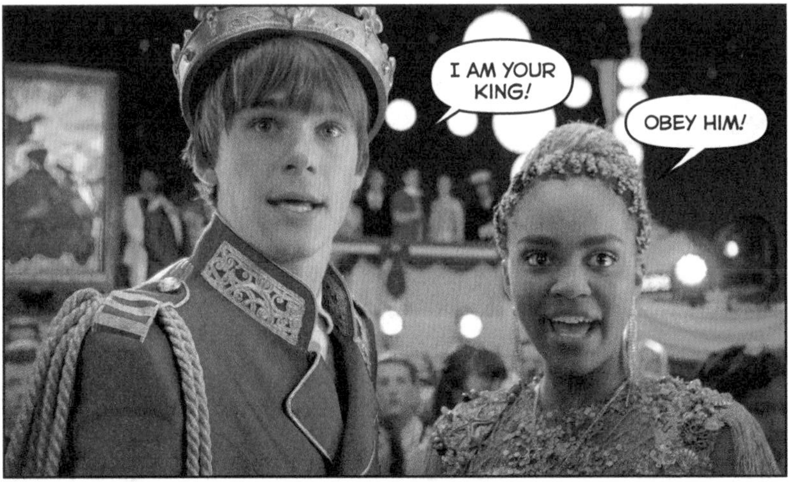
I AM YOUR KING!
OBEY HIM!

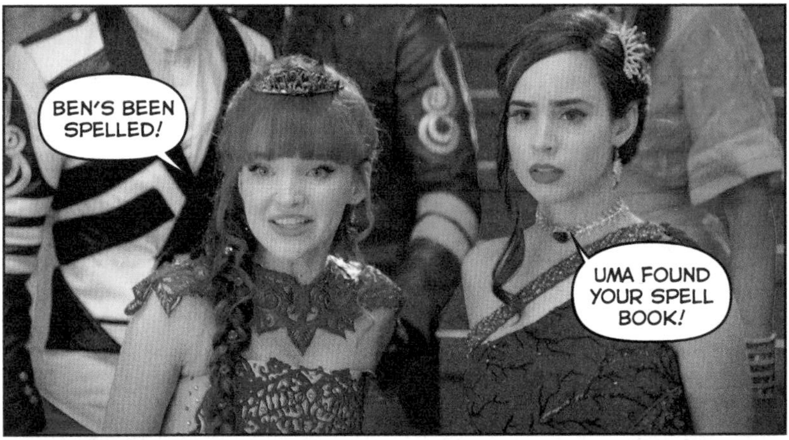
BEN'S BEEN SPELLED!
UMA FOUND YOUR SPELL BOOK!

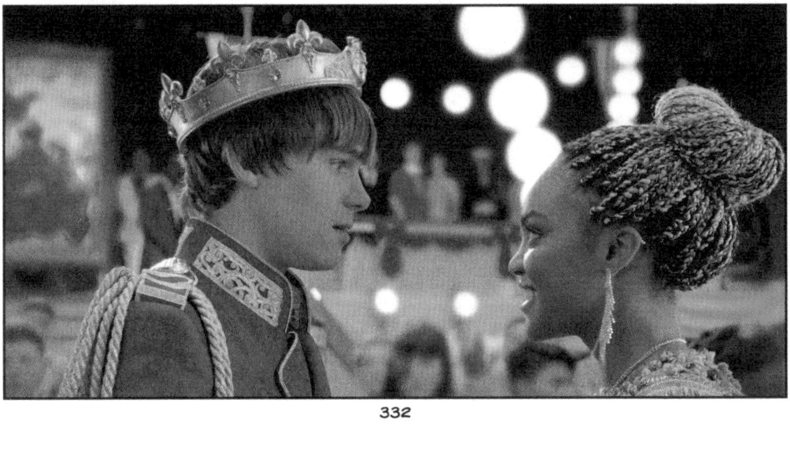

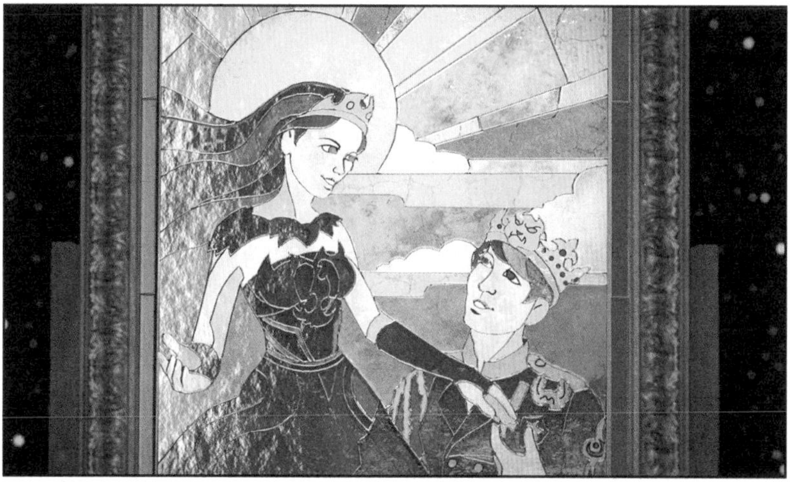

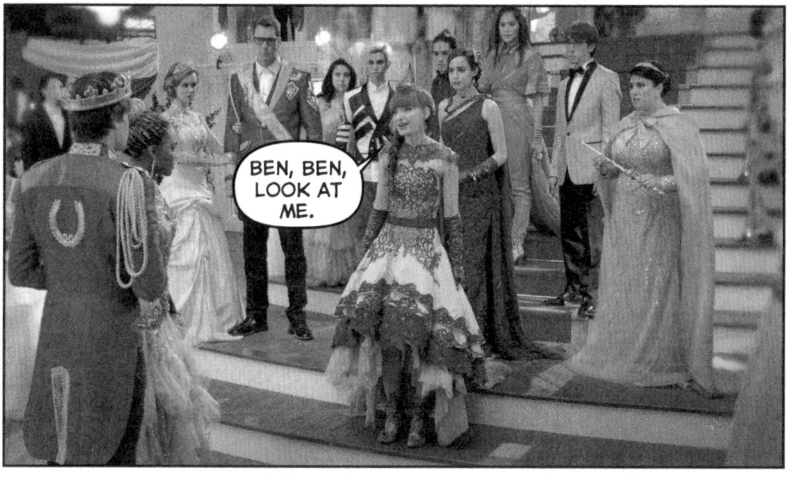
BEN, BEN, LOOK AT ME.

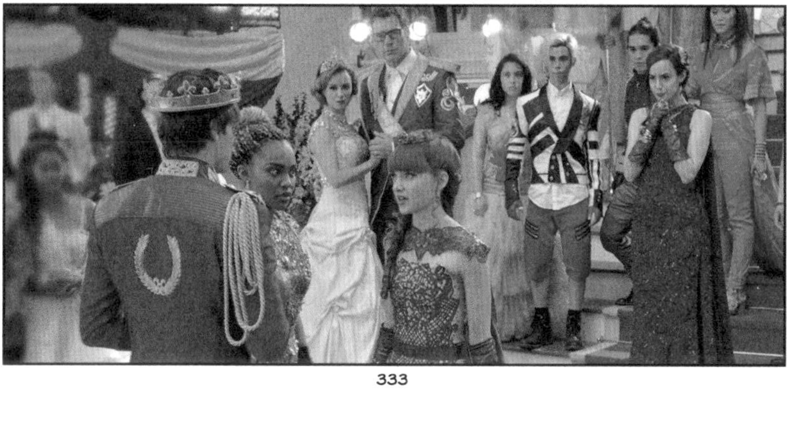

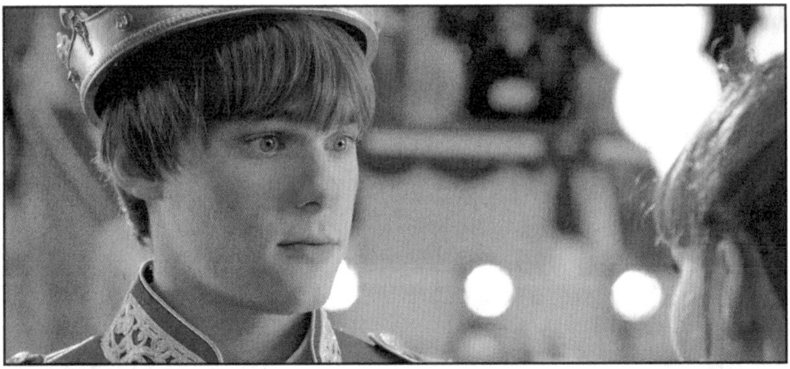

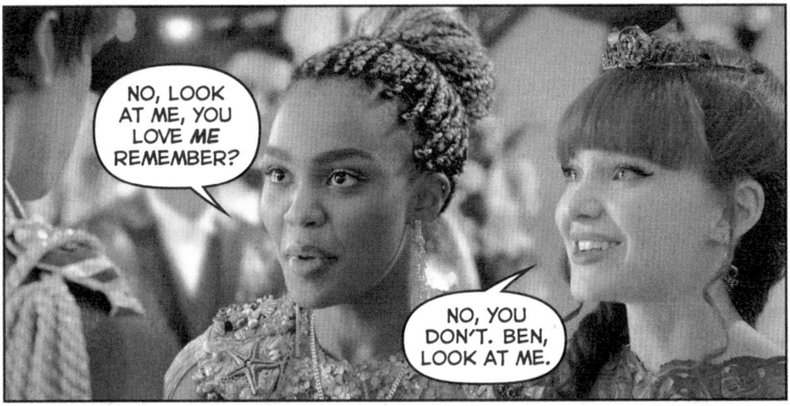
NO, LOOK AT ME, YOU LOVE *ME* REMEMBER?
NO, YOU DON'T. BEN, LOOK AT ME.

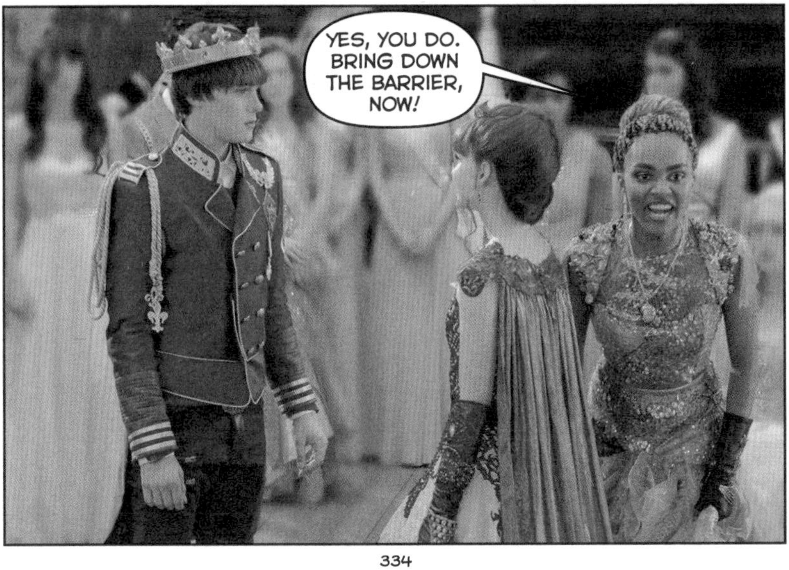
YES, YOU DO. BRING DOWN THE BARRIER, NOW!

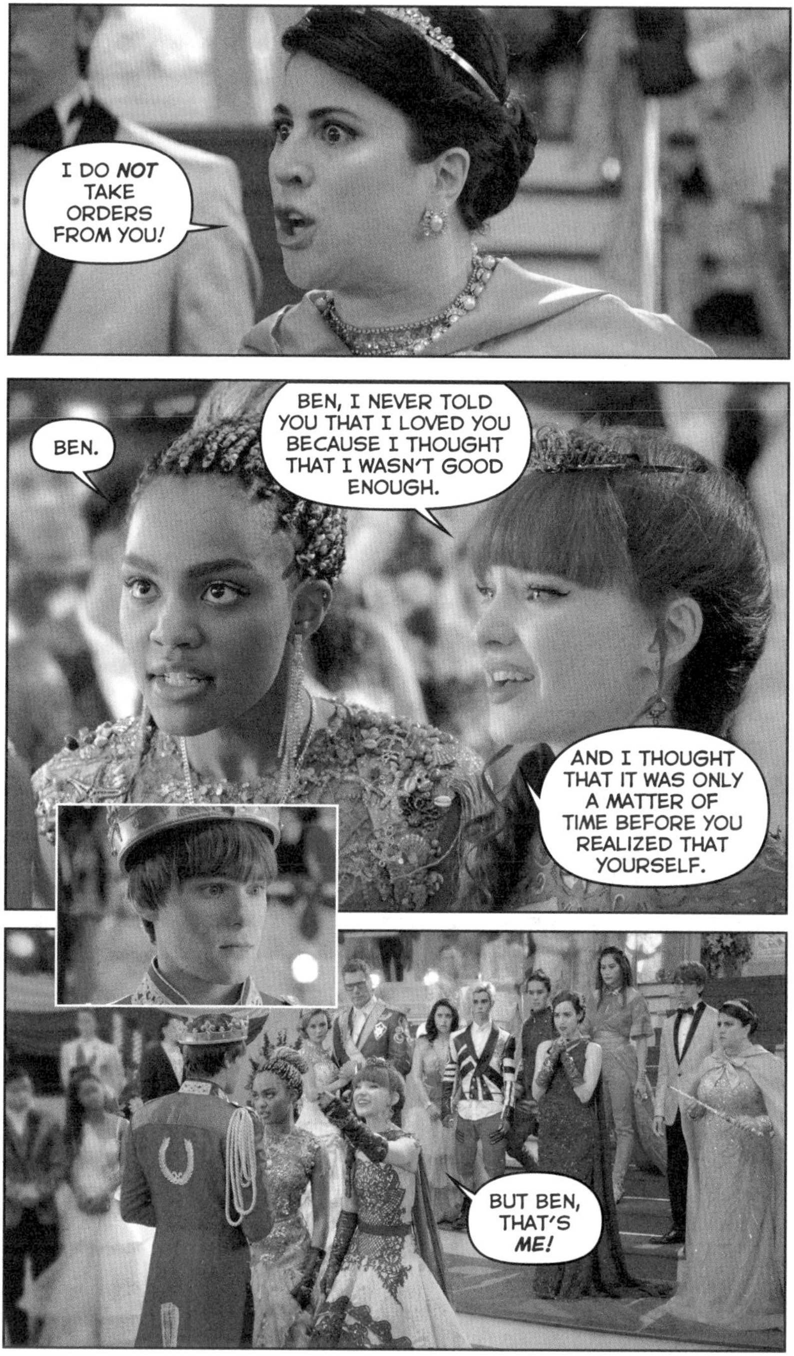
I DO **NOT** TAKE ORDERS FROM YOU!
BEN.
BEN, I NEVER TOLD YOU THAT I LOVED YOU BECAUSE I THOUGHT THAT I WASN'T GOOD ENOUGH.
AND I THOUGHT THAT IT WAS ONLY A MATTER OF TIME BEFORE YOU REALIZED THAT YOURSELF.
BUT BEN, THAT'S ***ME!***

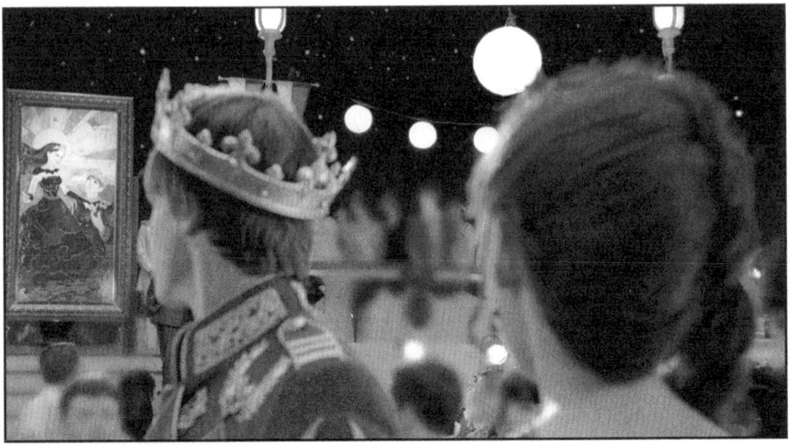

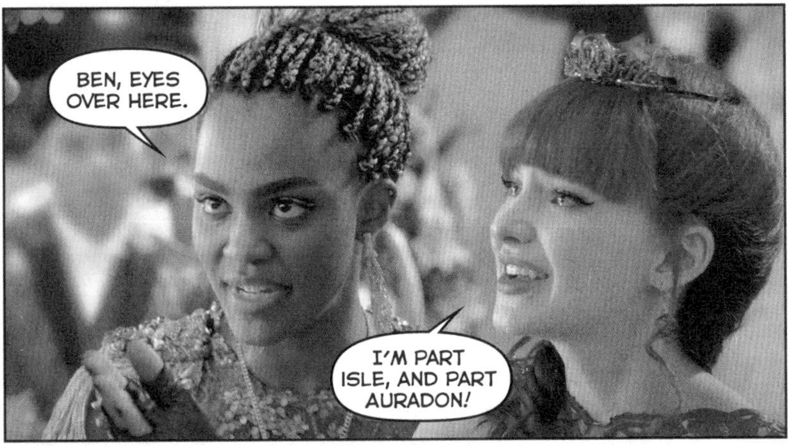
BEN, EYES OVER HERE.
I'M PART ISLE, AND PART AURADON!

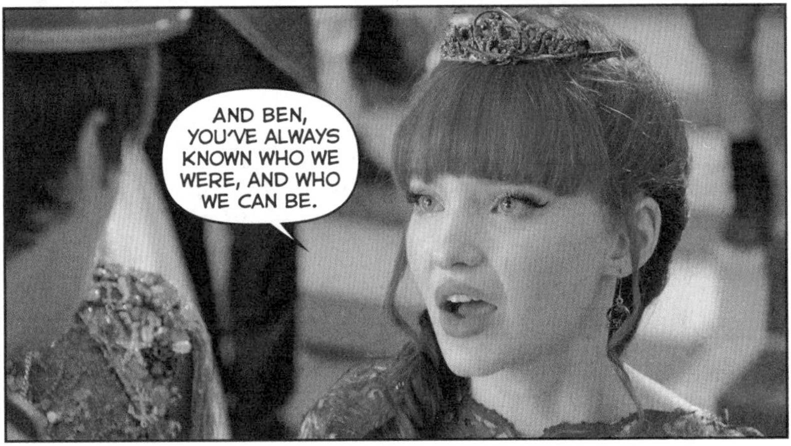
AND BEN, YOU'VE ALWAYS KNOWN WHO WE WERE, AND WHO WE CAN BE.

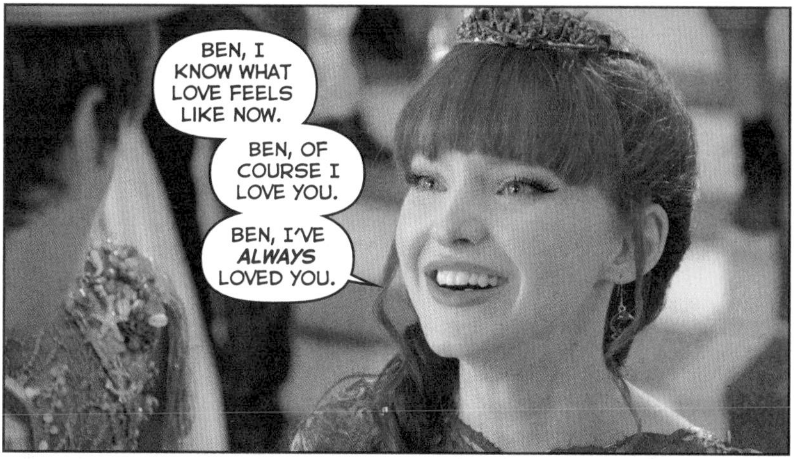
BEN, I KNOW WHAT LOVE FEELS LIKE NOW.
BEN, OF COURSE I LOVE YOU.
BEN, I'VE *ALWAYS* LOVED YOU.

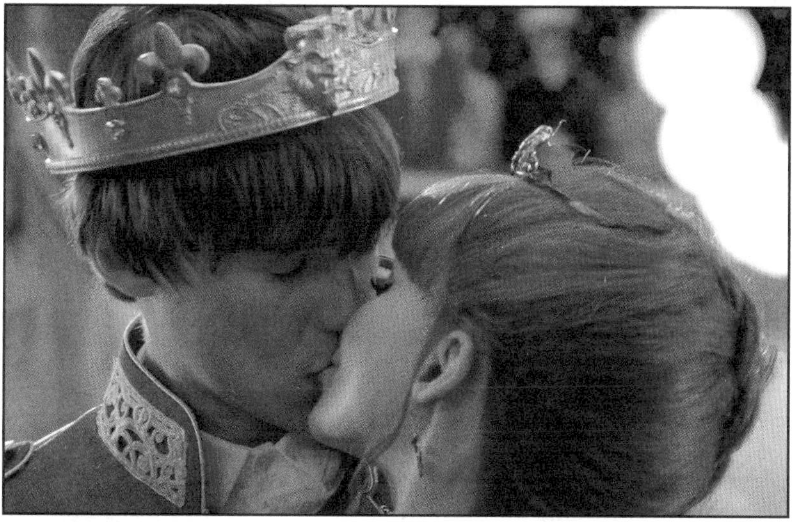

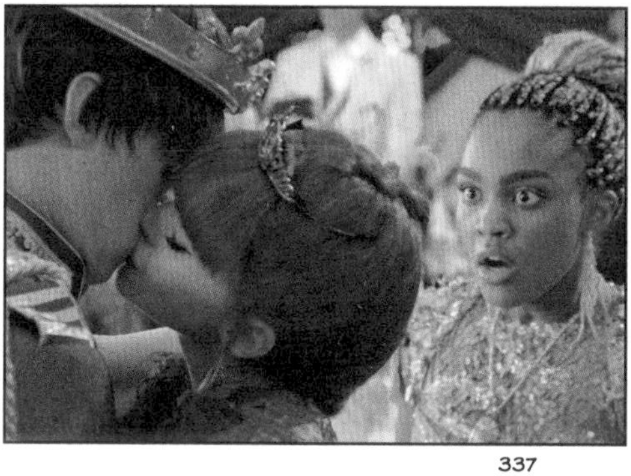

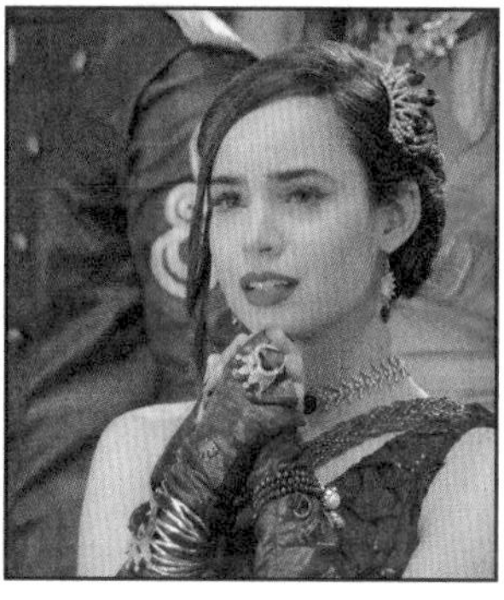

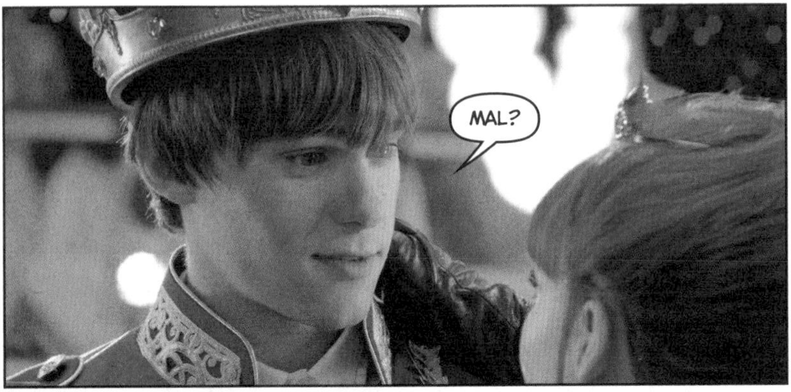
MAL?

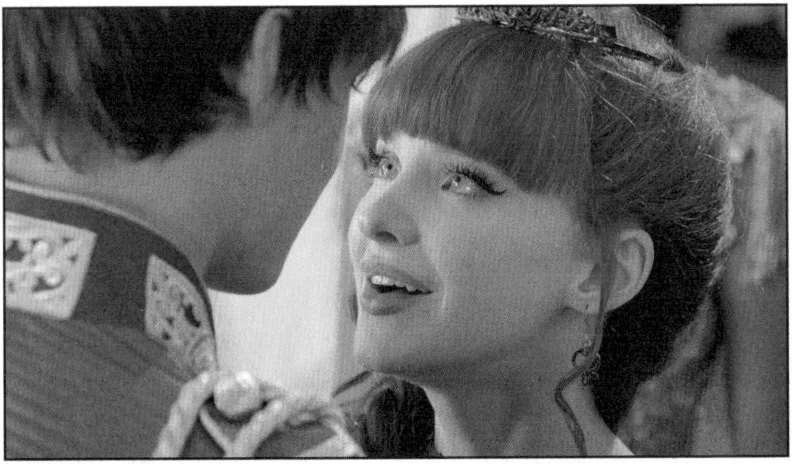

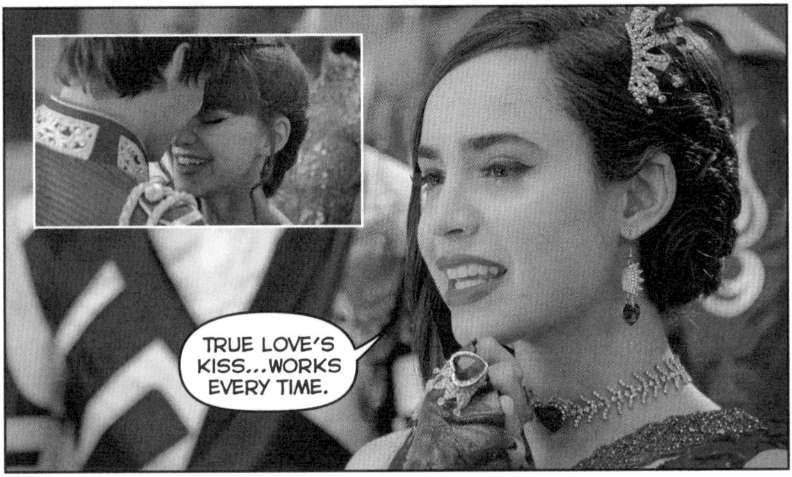
TRUE LOVE'S
KISS...WORKS
EVERY TIME.

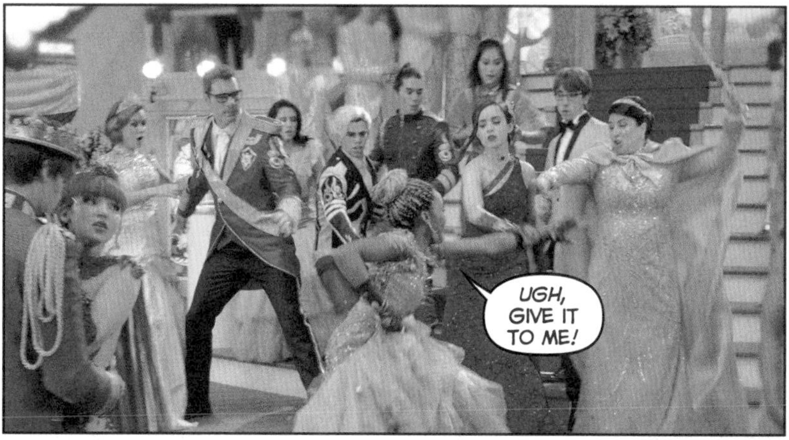
UGH, GIVE IT TO ME!

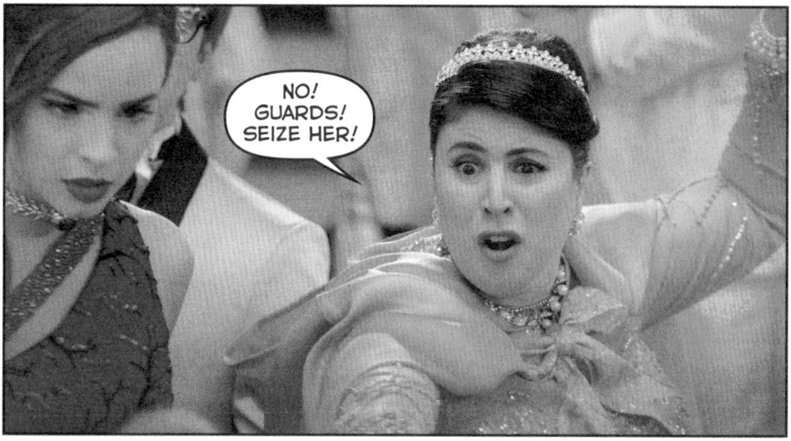
NO! GUARDS! SEIZE HER!

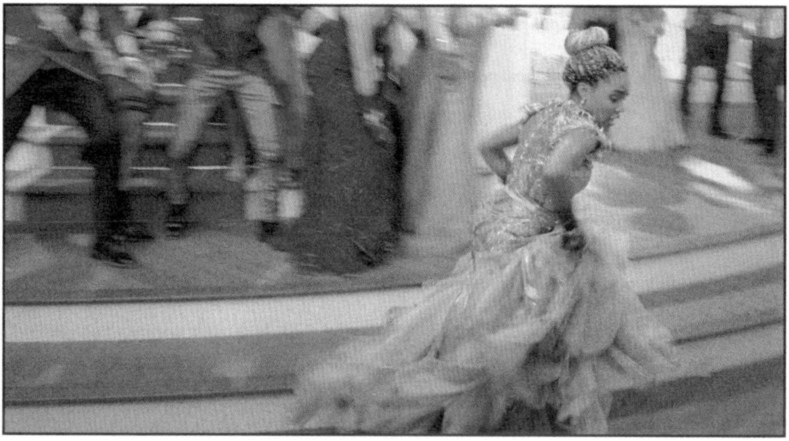

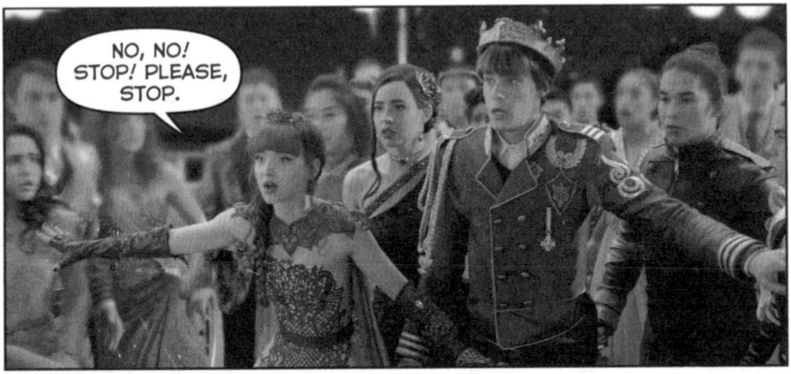
NO, NO! STOP! PLEASE, STOP.

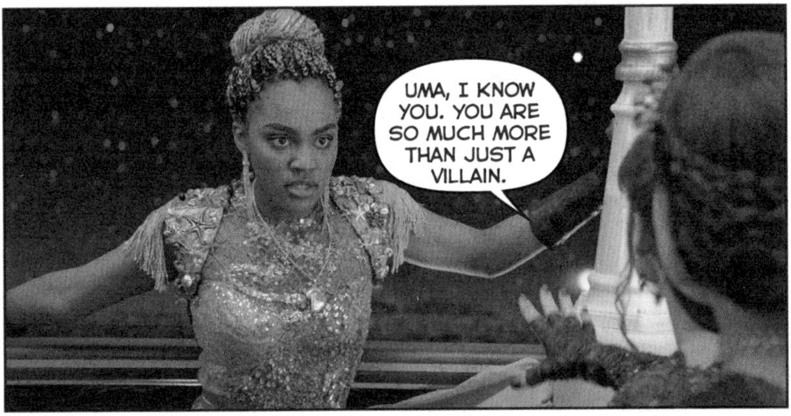
UMA, I KNOW YOU. YOU ARE SO MUCH MORE THAN JUST A VILLAIN.

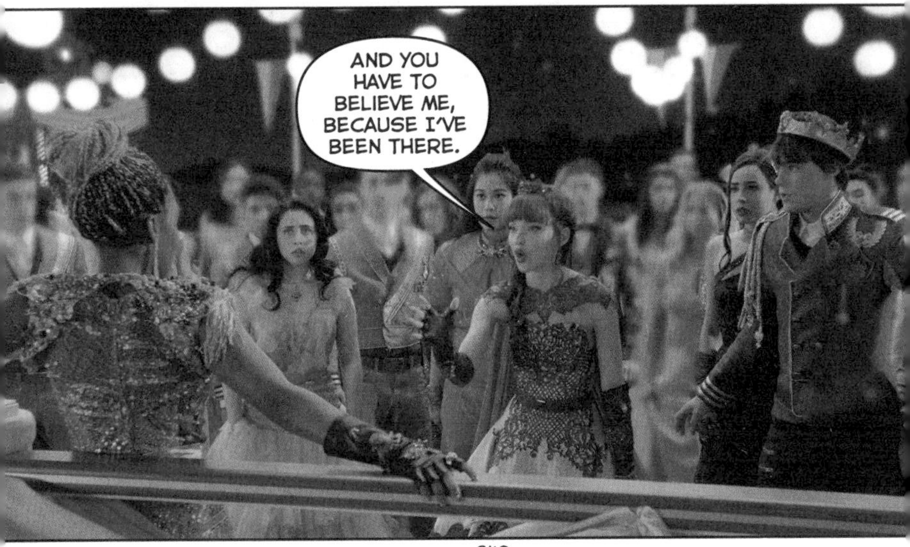
AND YOU HAVE TO BELIEVE ME, BECAUSE I'VE BEEN THERE.

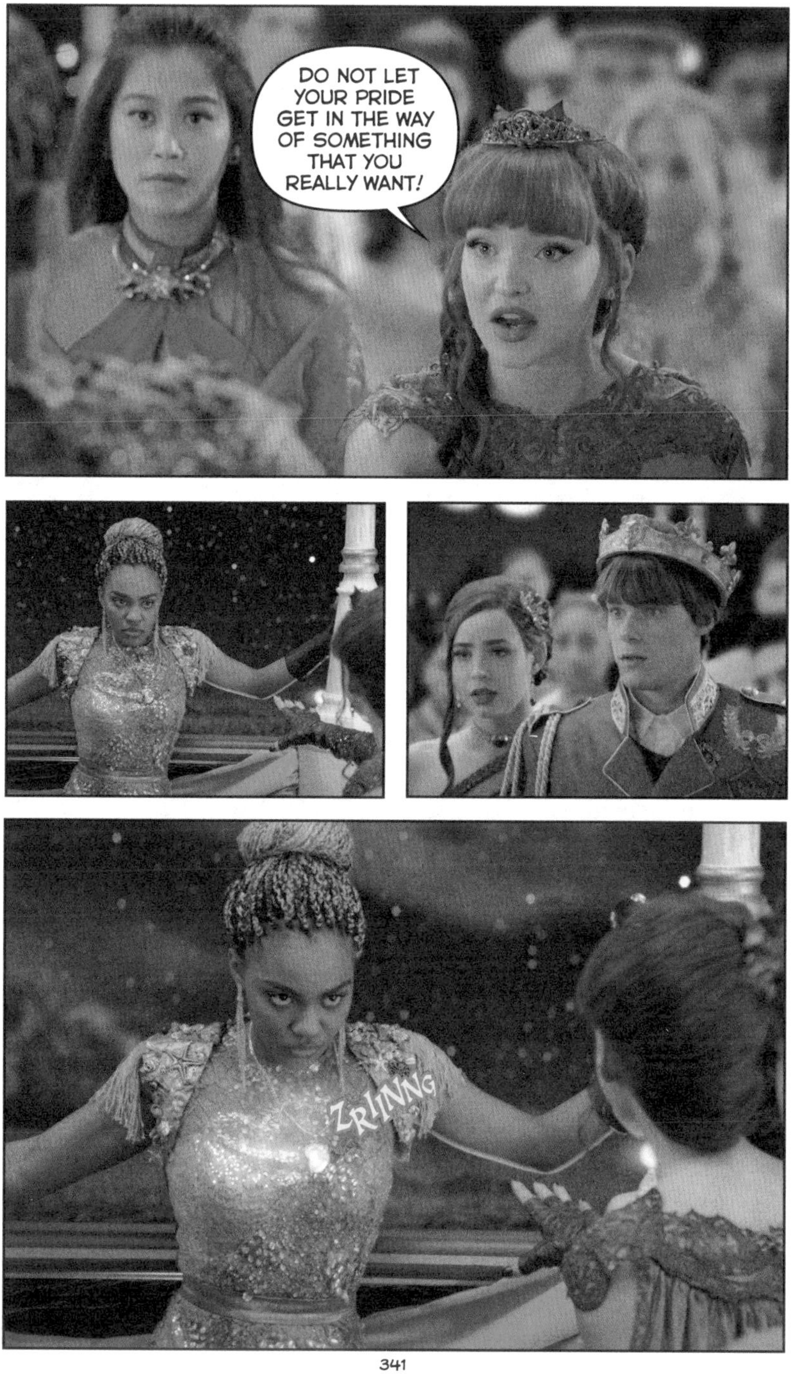
DO NOT LET YOUR PRIDE GET IN THE WAY OF SOMETHING THAT YOU REALLY WANT!
ZRIING

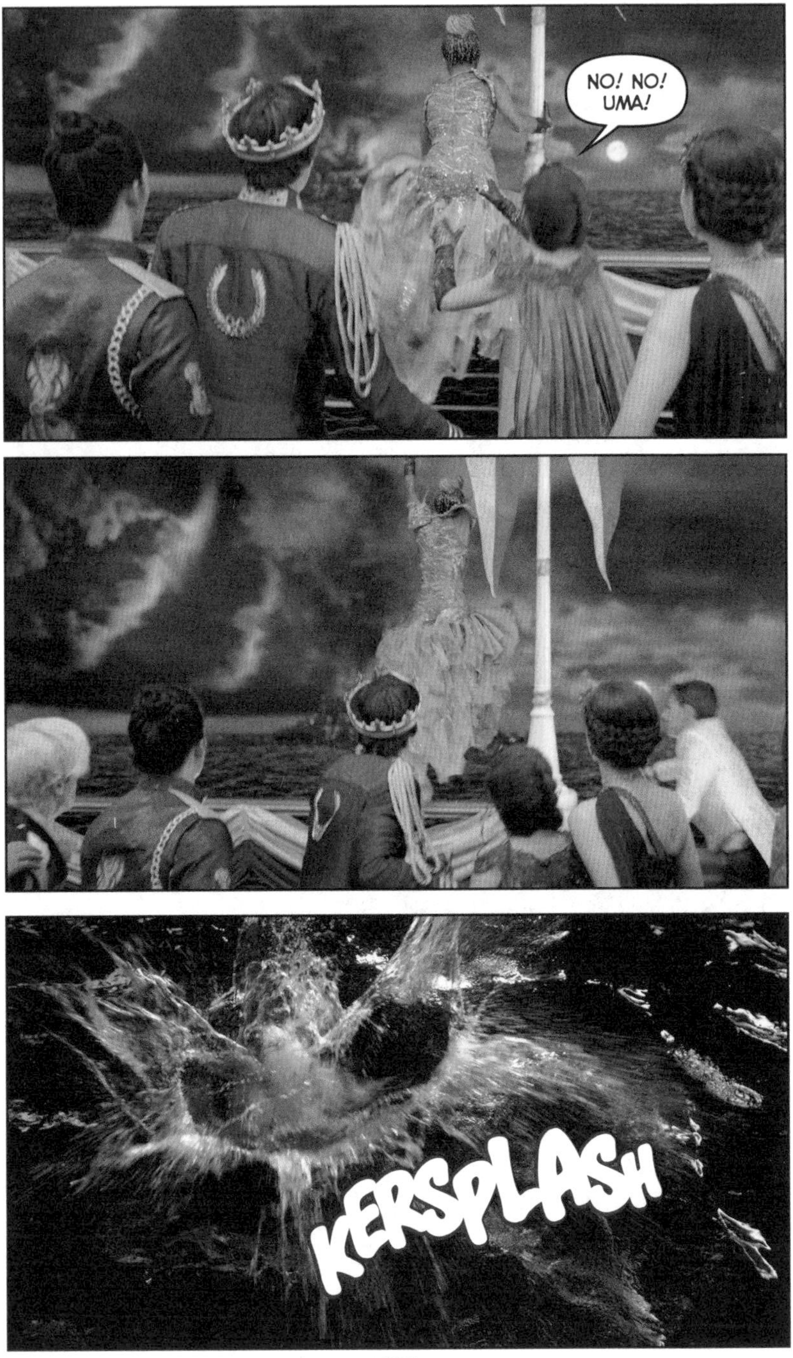
NO! NO! UMA!
KERSPLASH

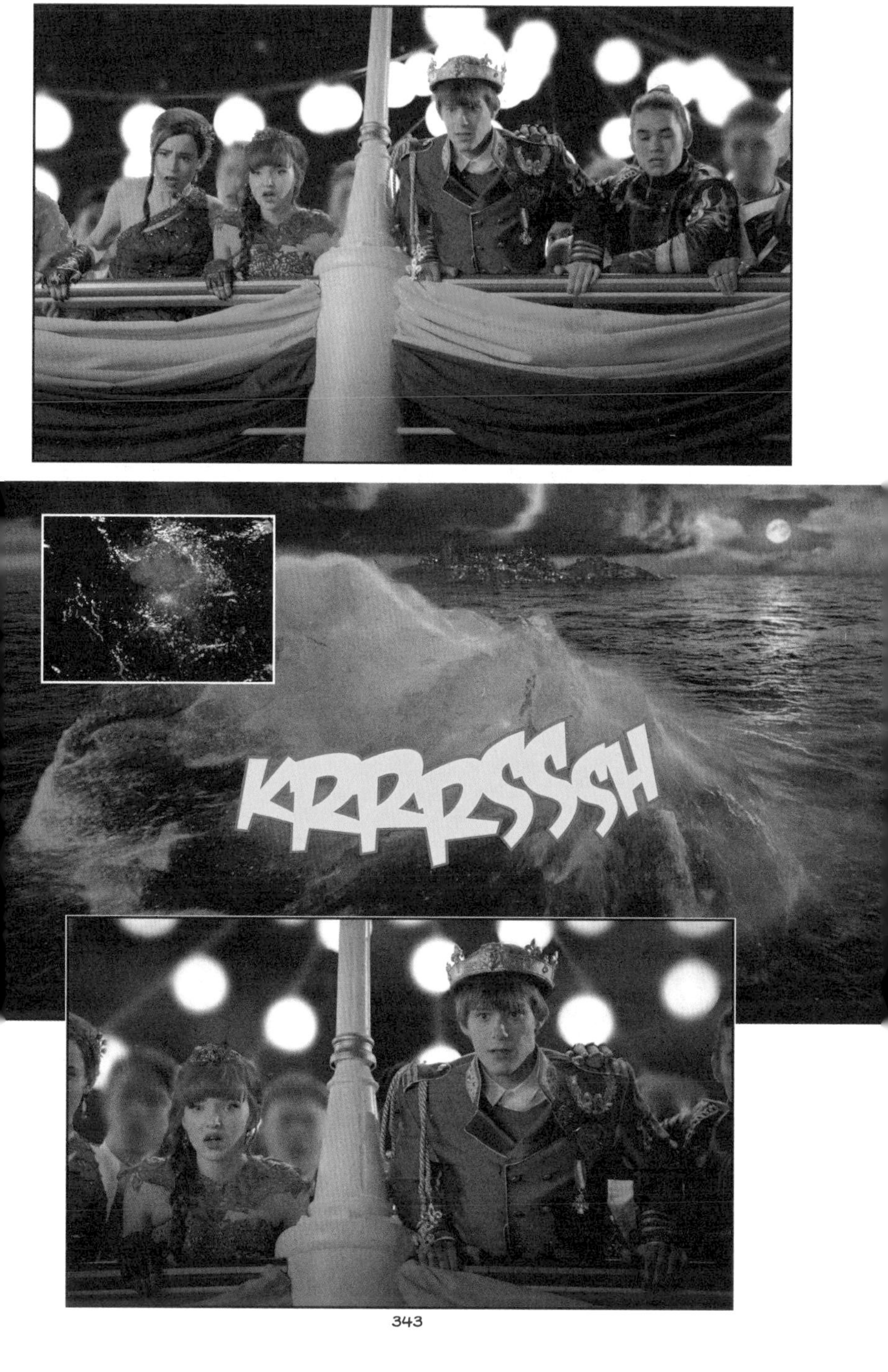
KRRRSSSH

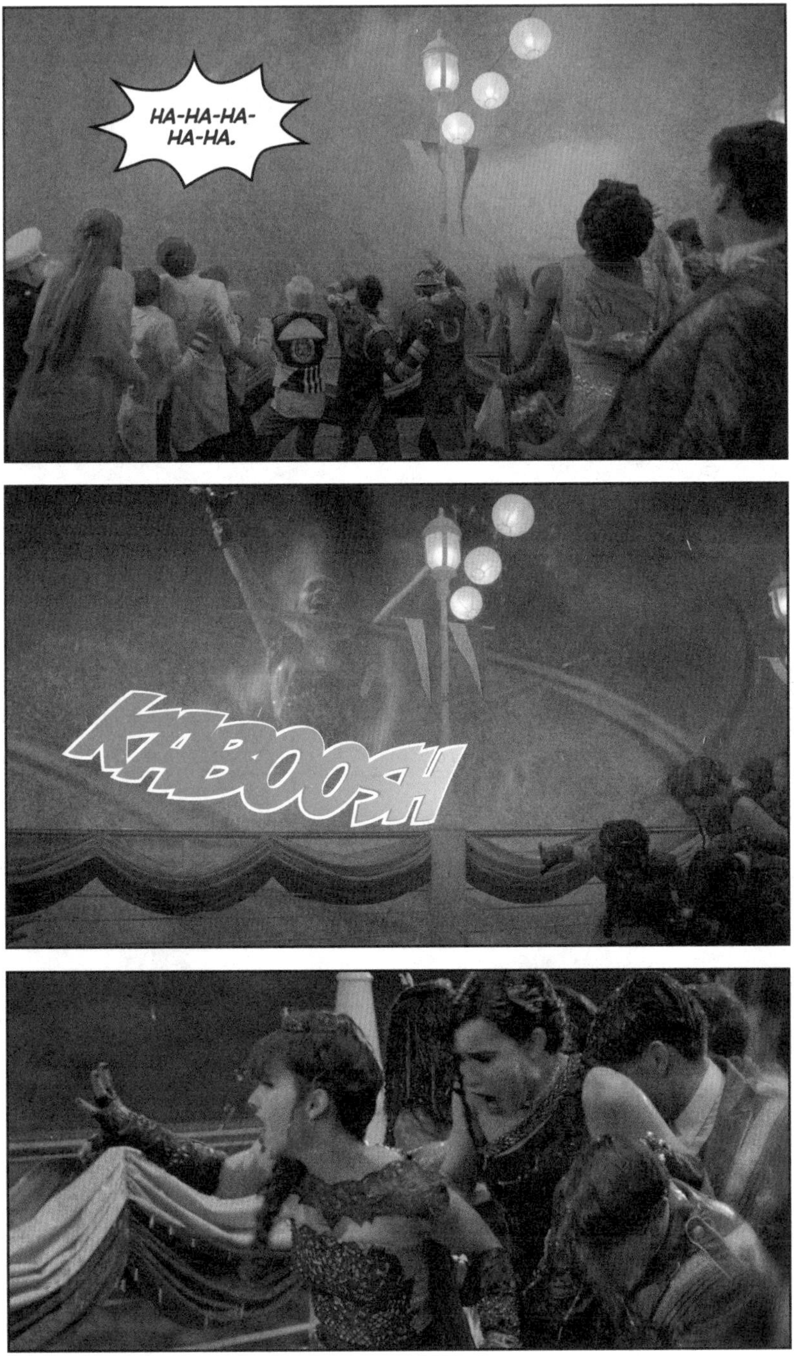
HA-HA-HA-
HA-HA.
KABOOSH

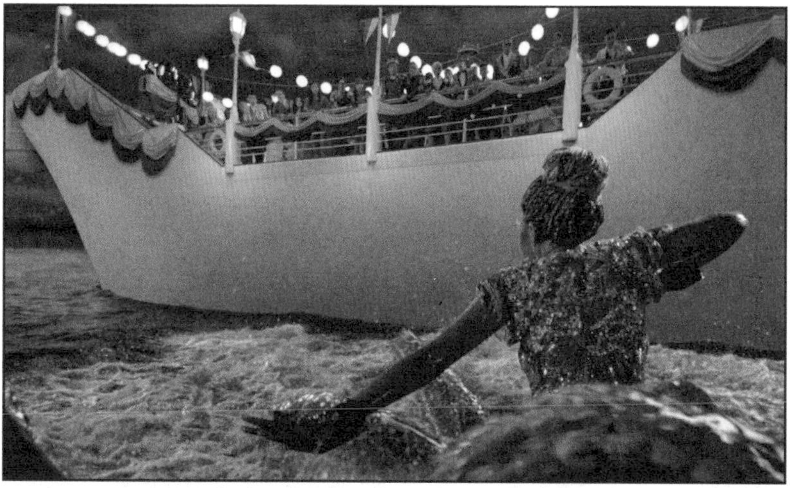

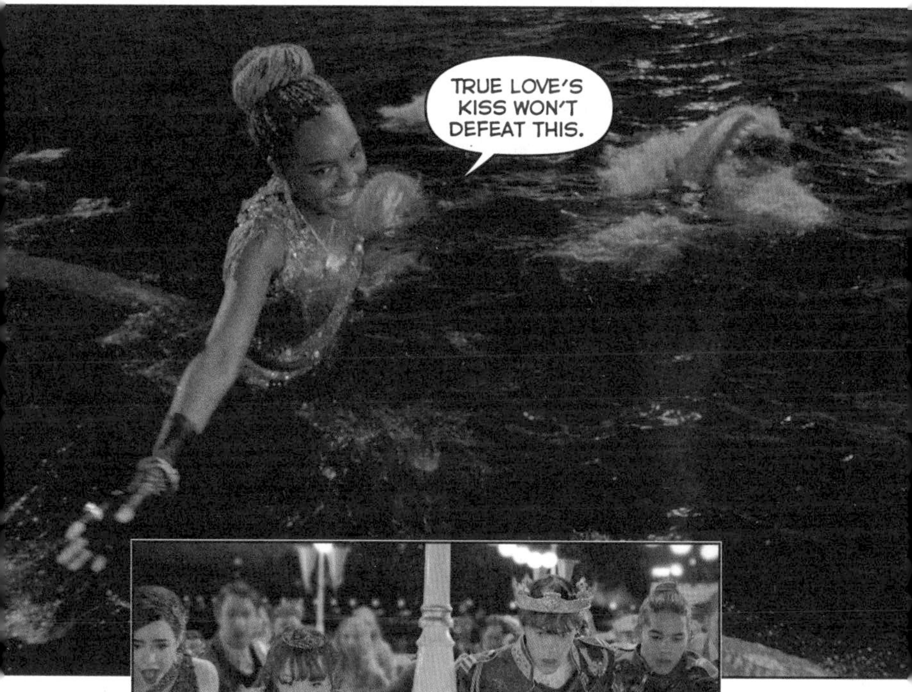
TRUE LOVE'S
KISS WON'T
DEFEAT THIS.

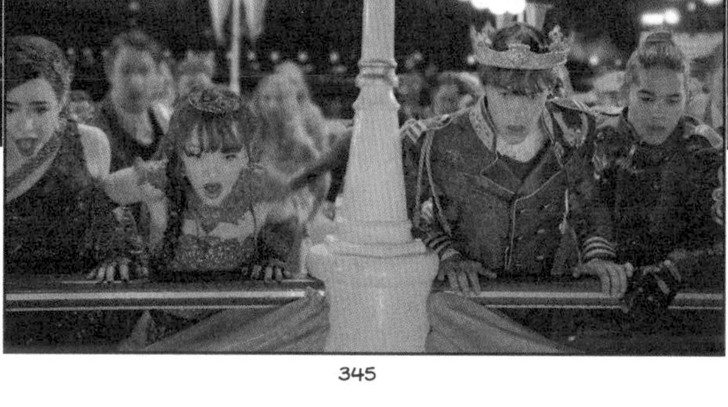

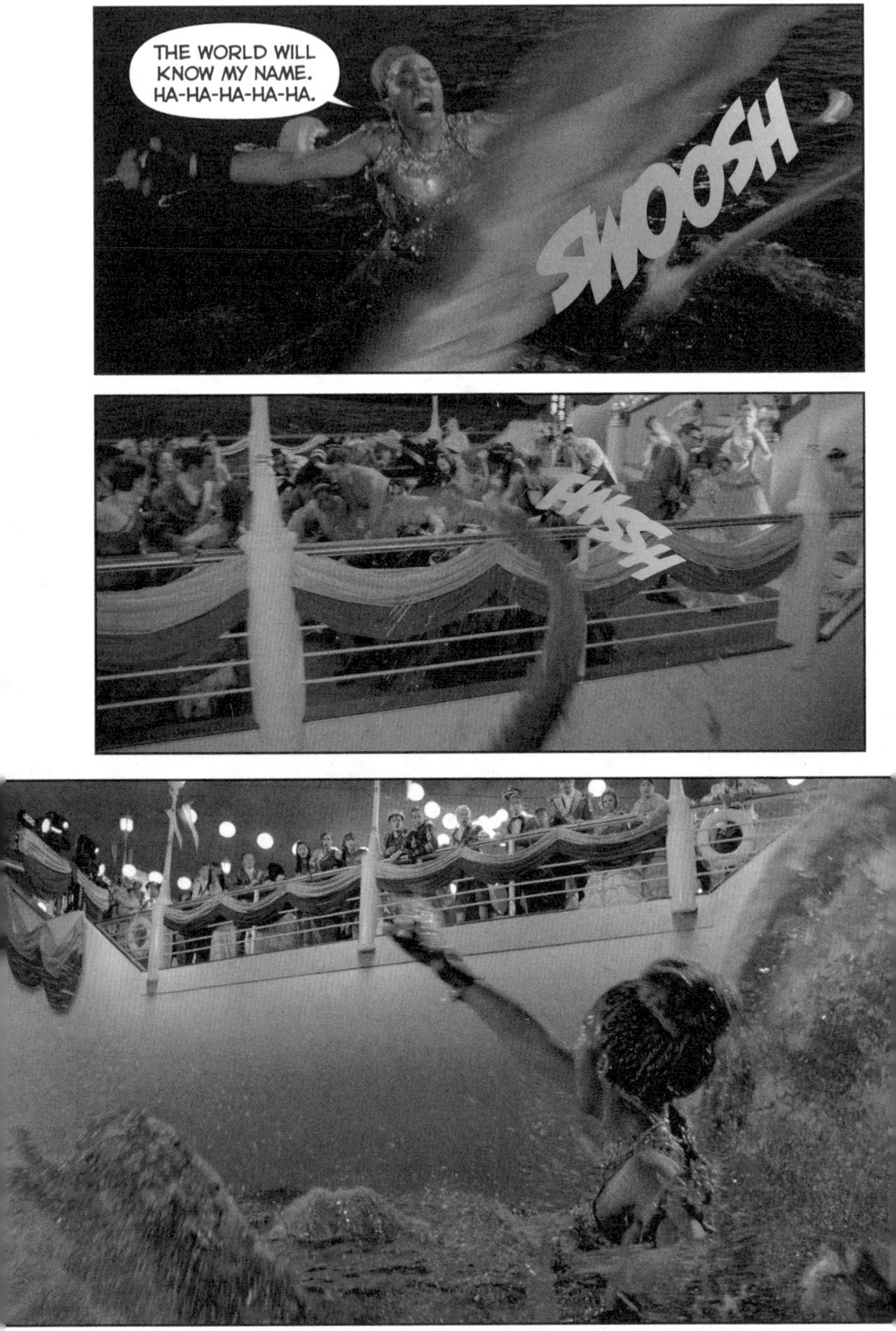
THE WORLD WILL KNOW MY NAME. HA-HA-HA-HA-HA.
SWOOSH
FWSSH

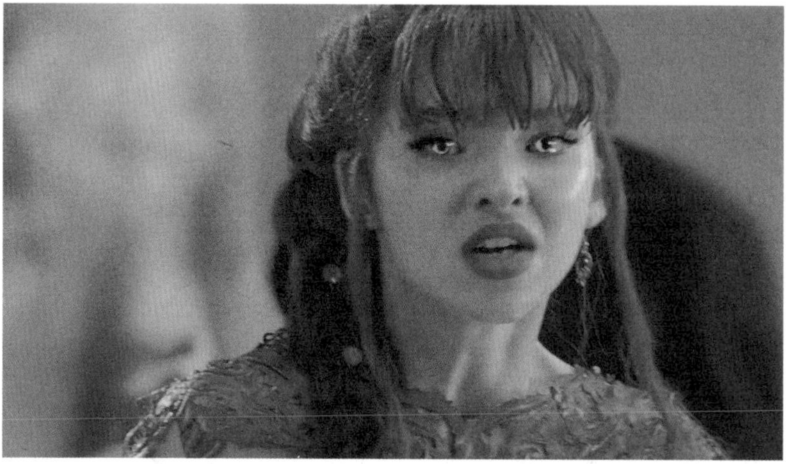

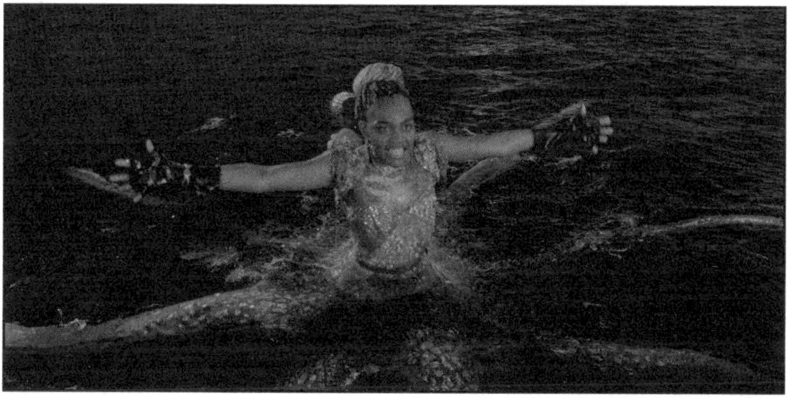

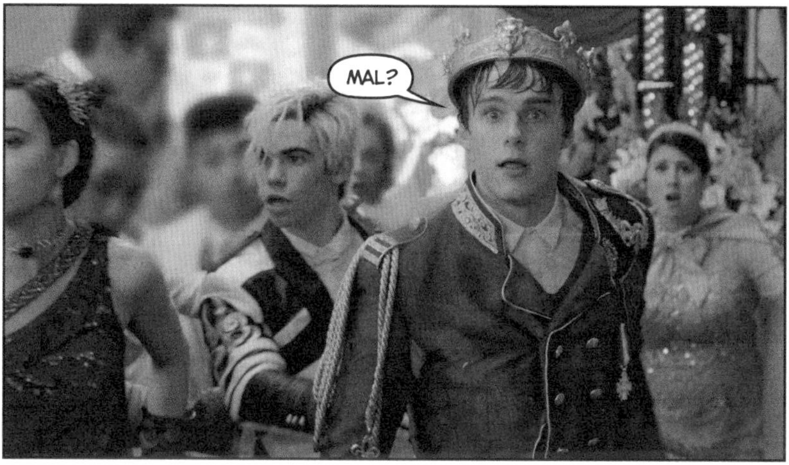
MAL?

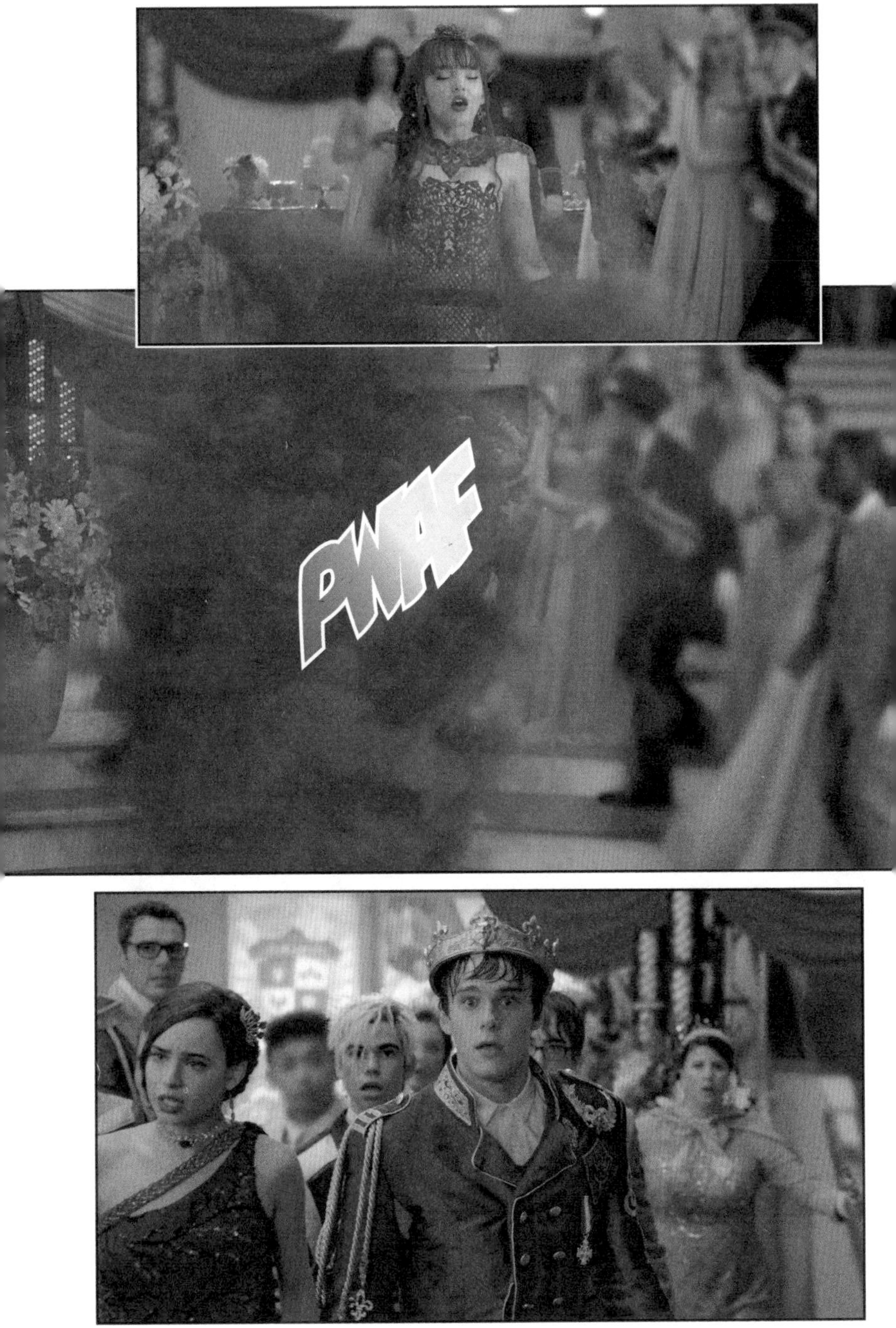
PWAF

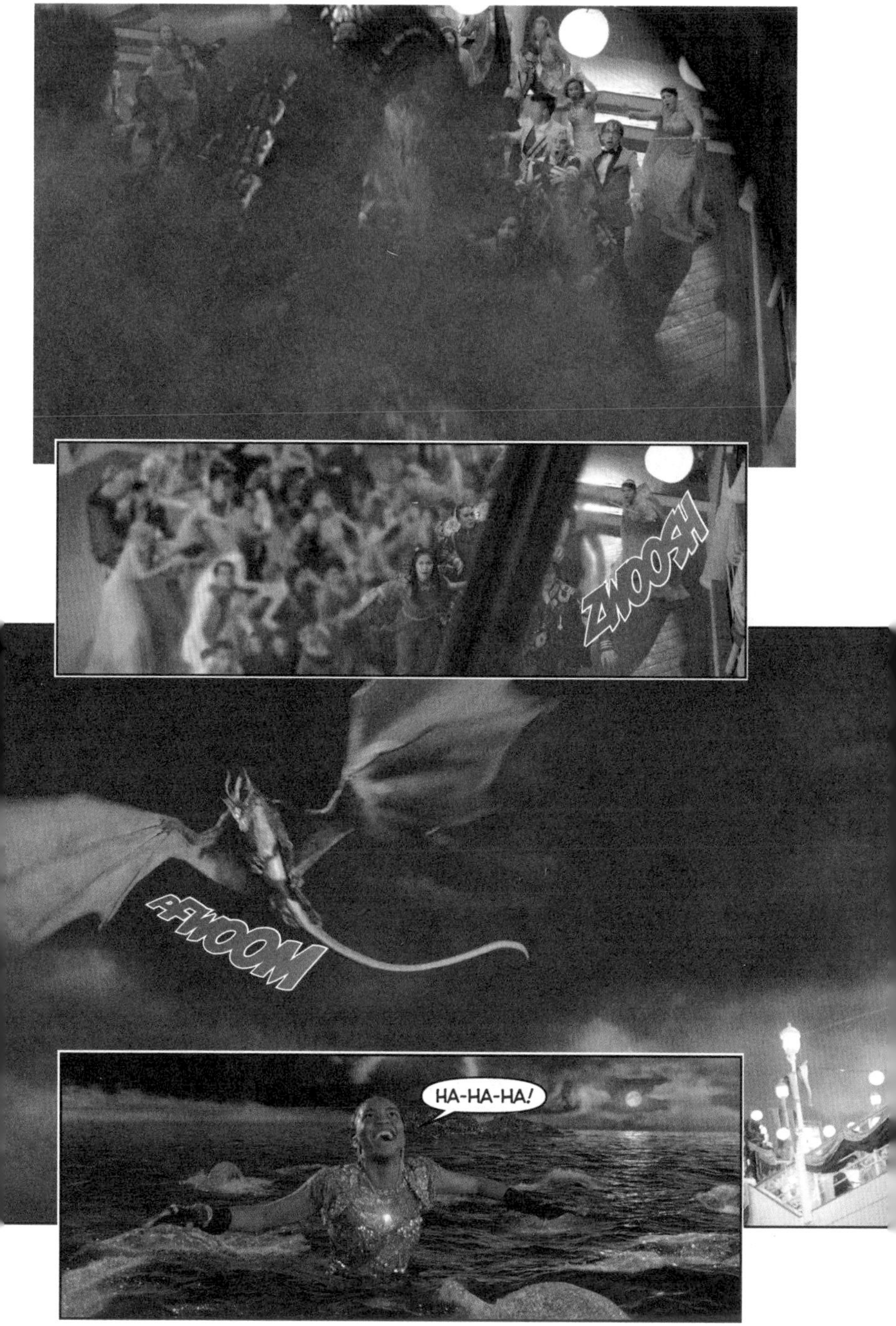
ZWOOSH
FFWOOM
HA-HA-HA!

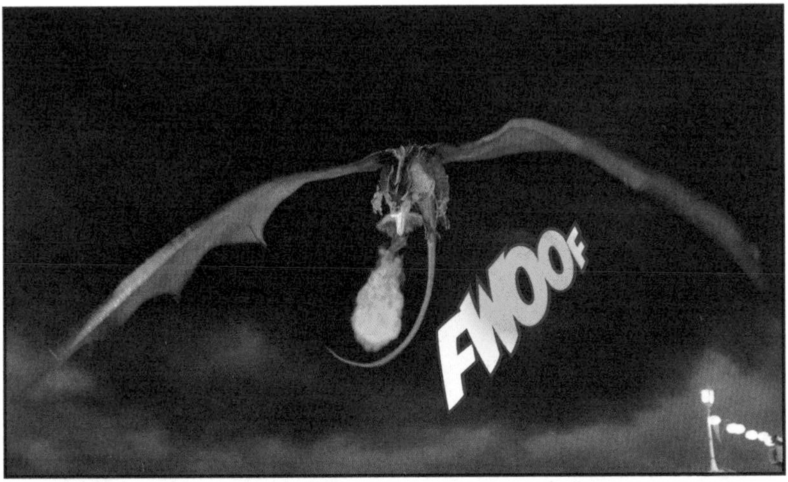
FWOOF

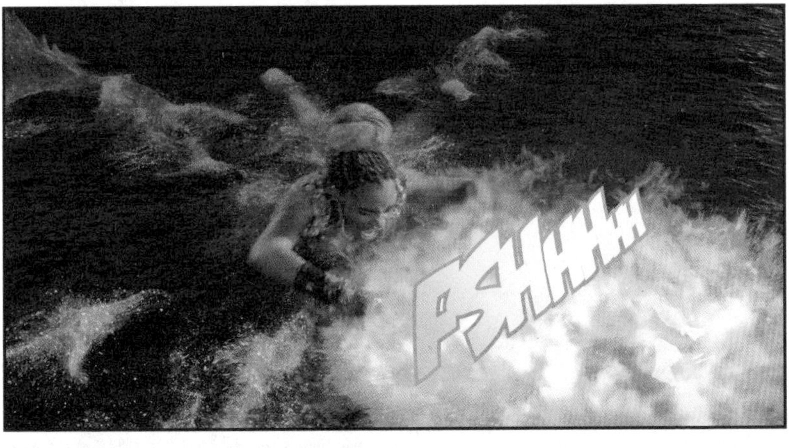
PSHHHHH

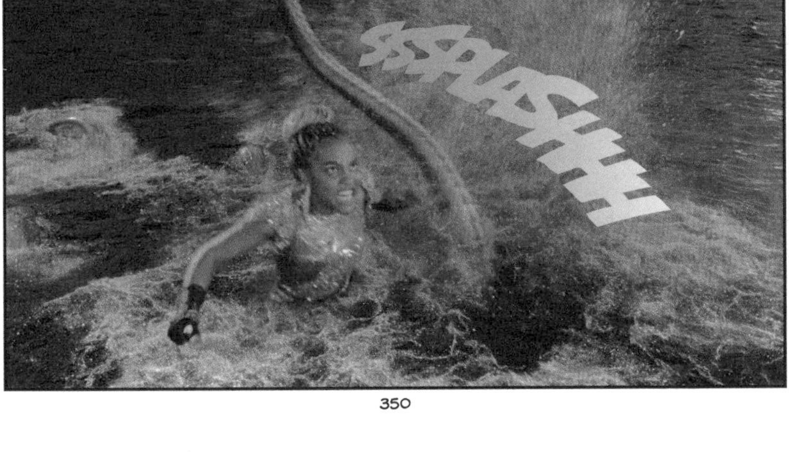
SSSPLASHHH

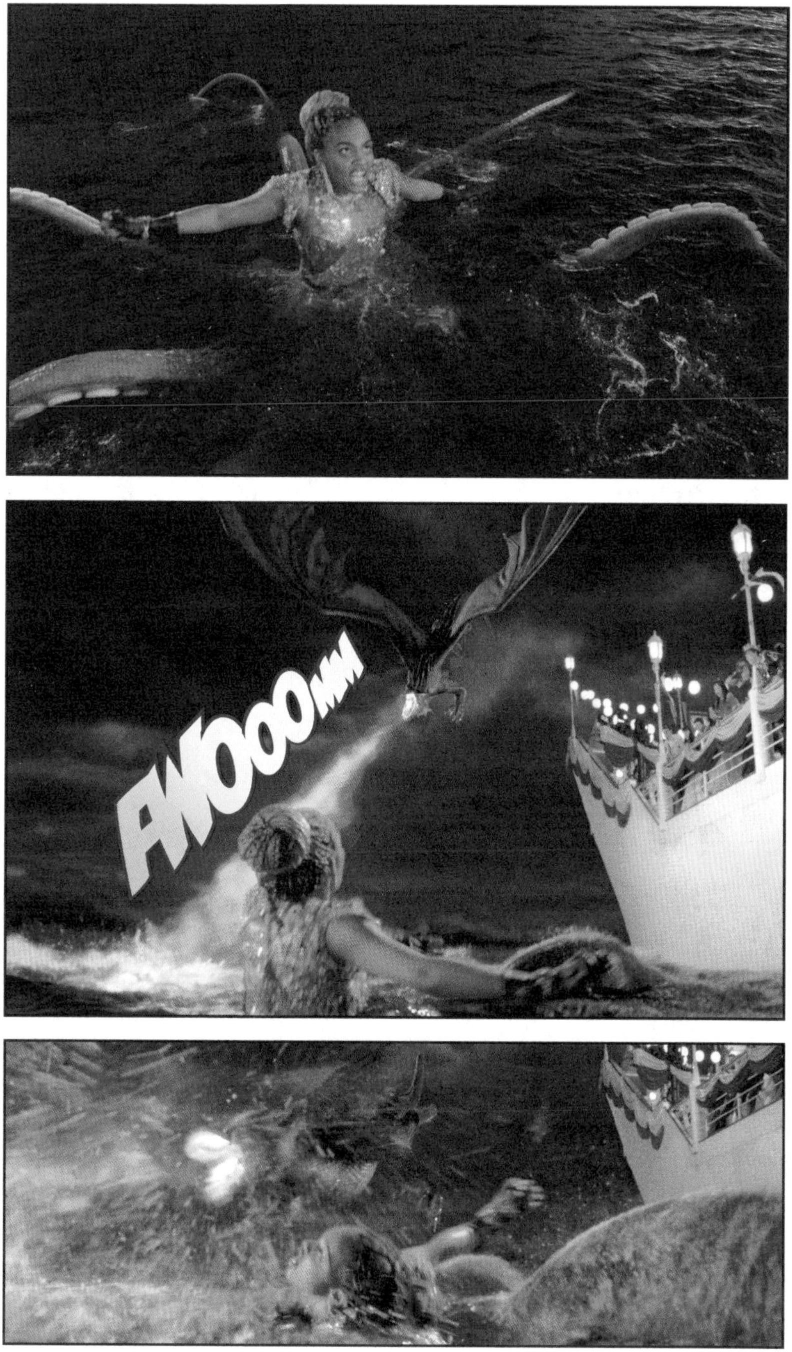
FWOOOMM

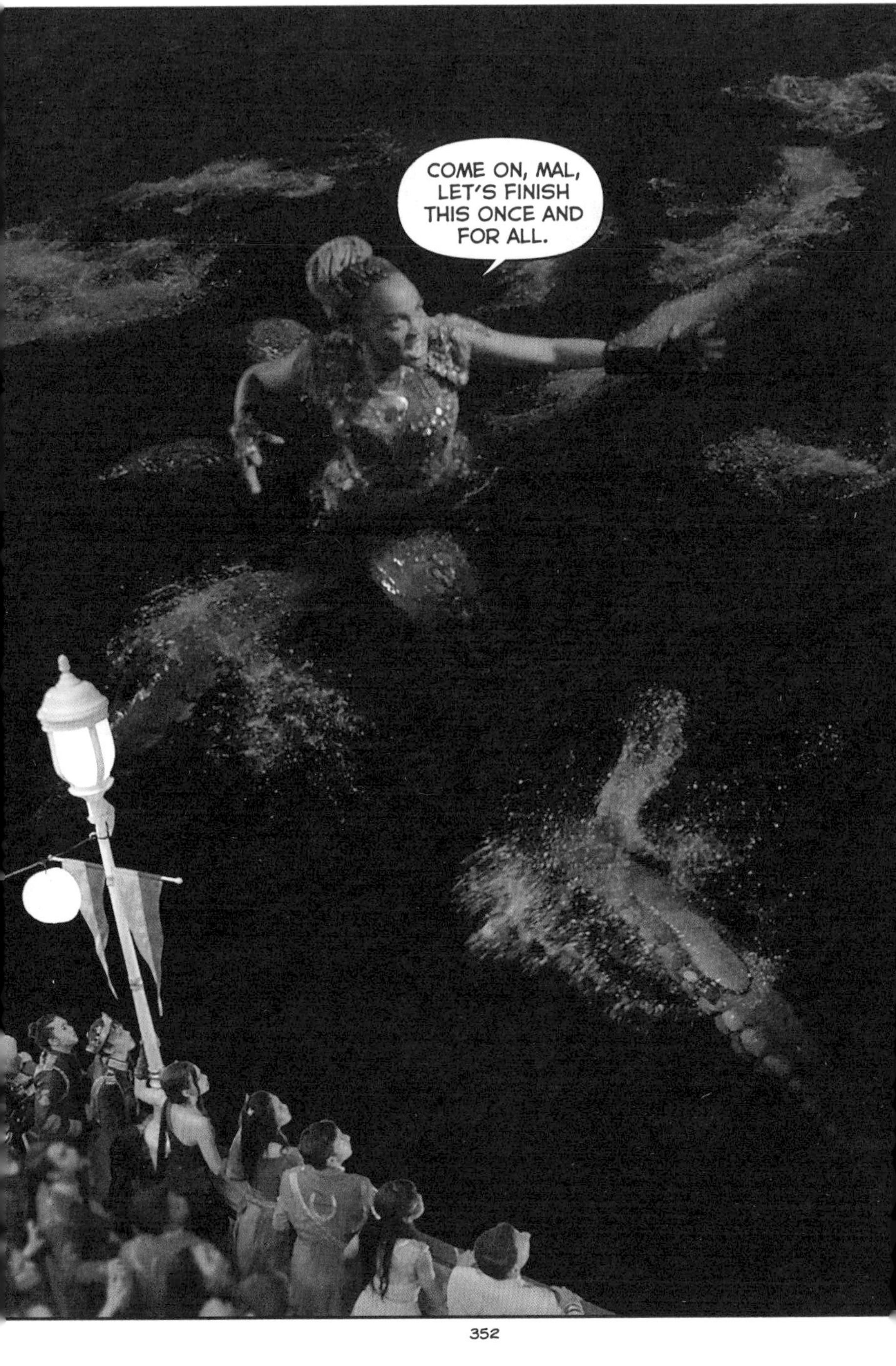
COME ON, MAL, LET'S FINISH THIS ONCE AND FOR ALL.

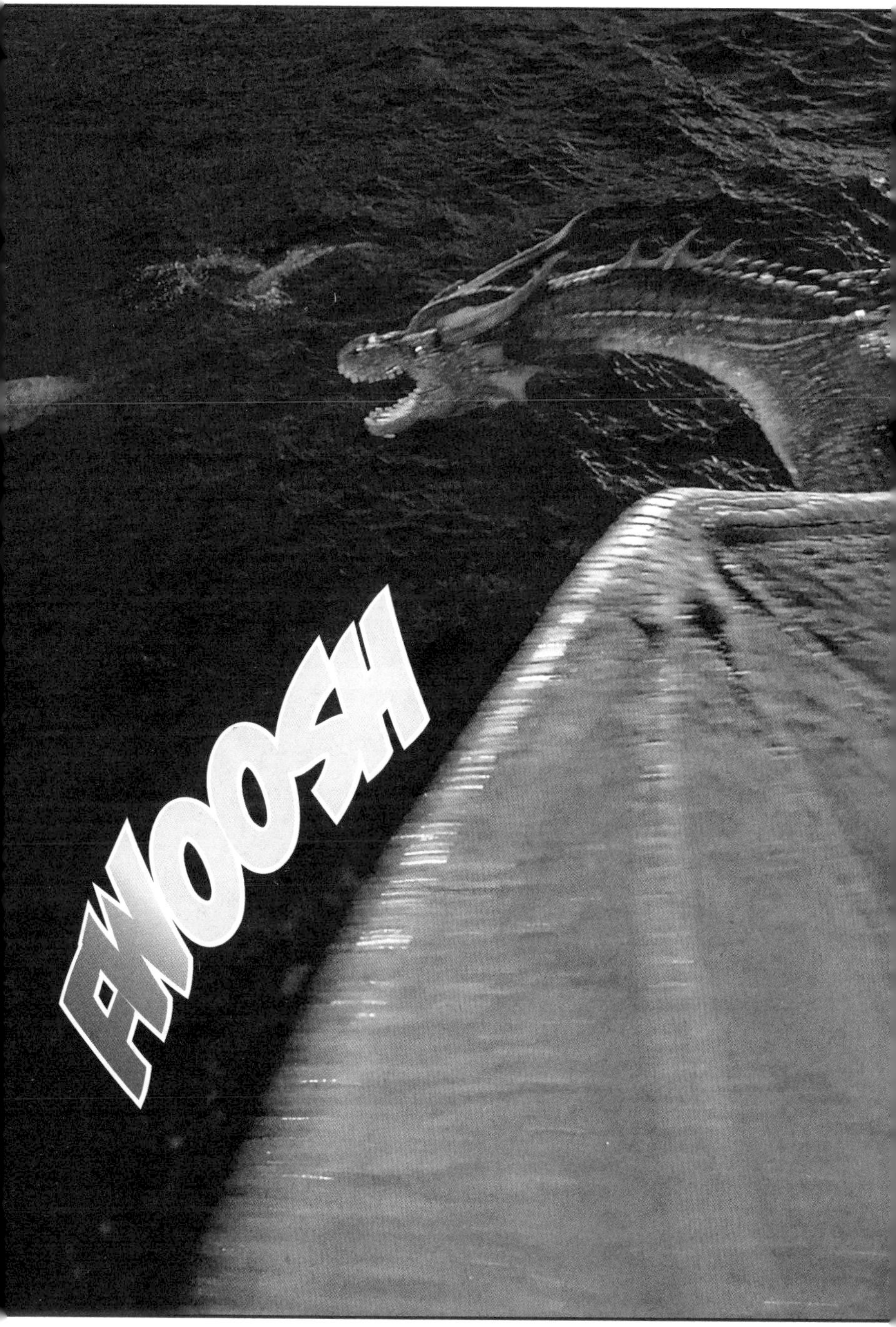
WHOOSH

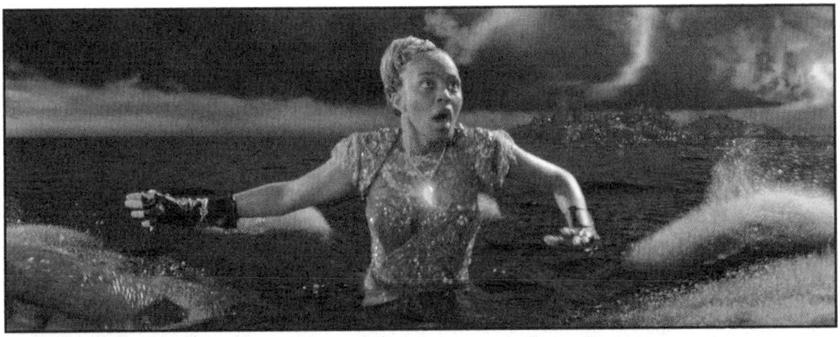

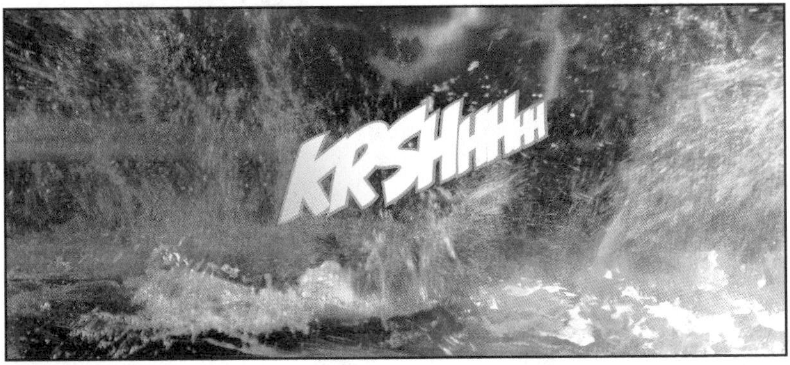
KRSHHHHH

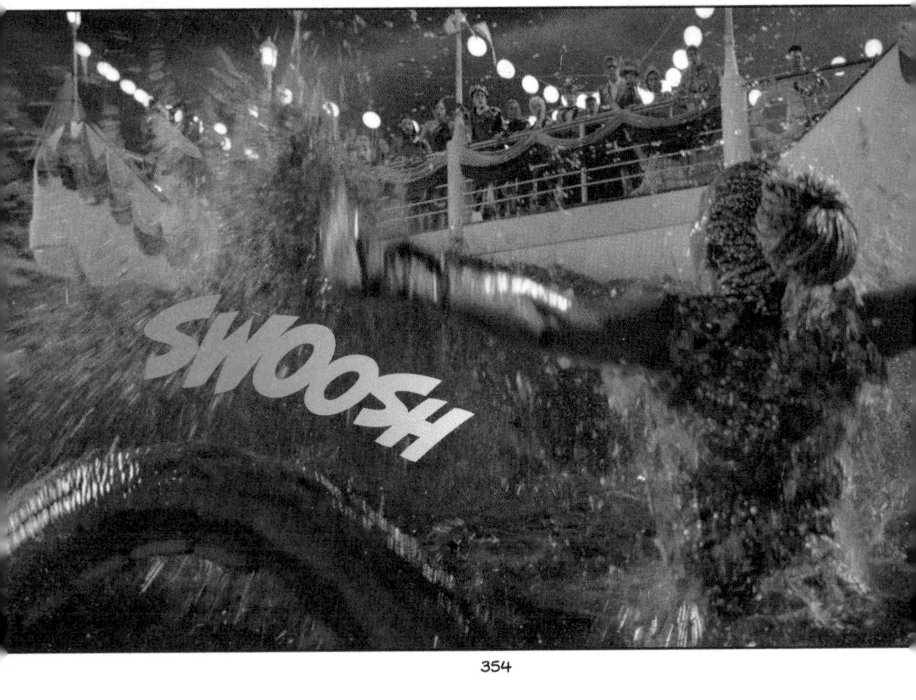
SWOOSH

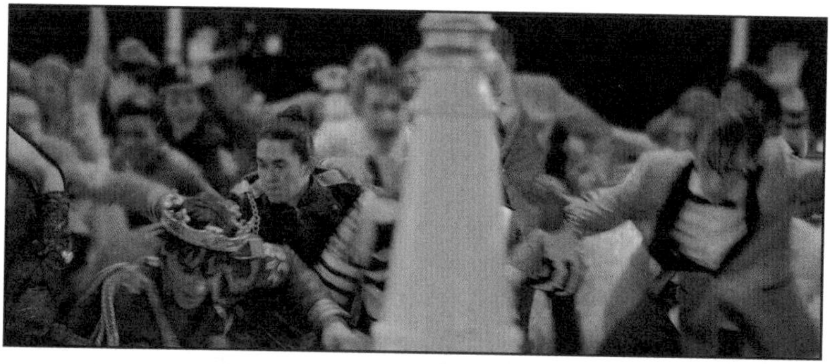

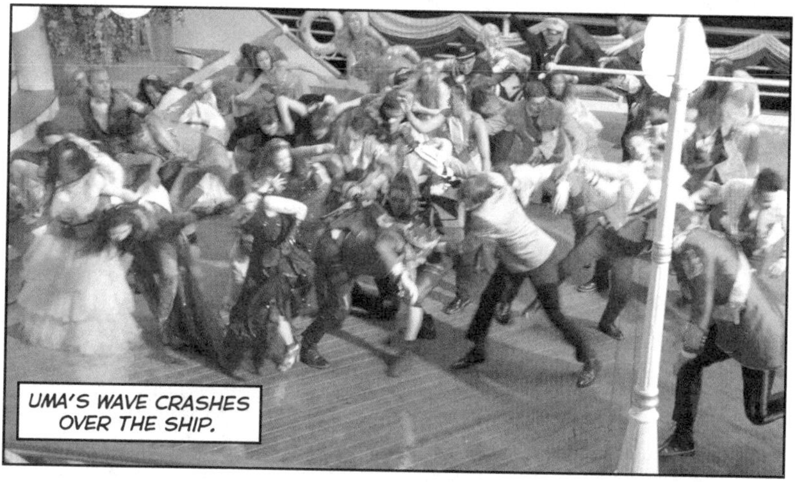
UMA'S WAVE CRASHES OVER THE SHIP.

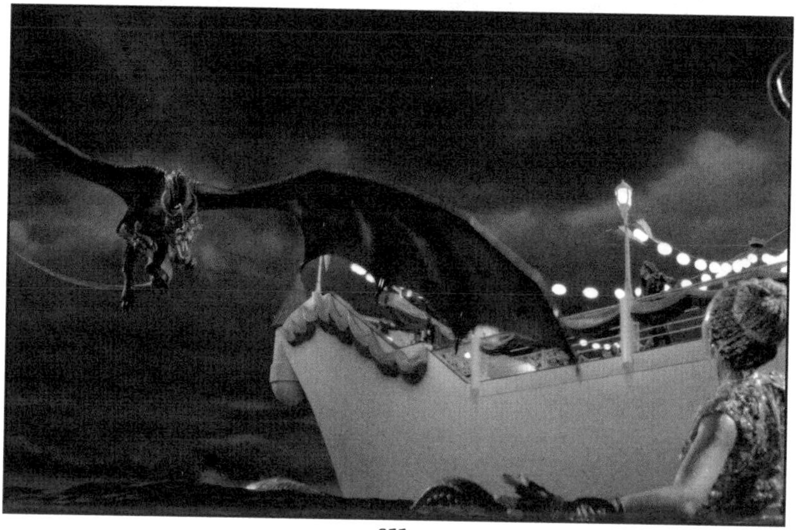

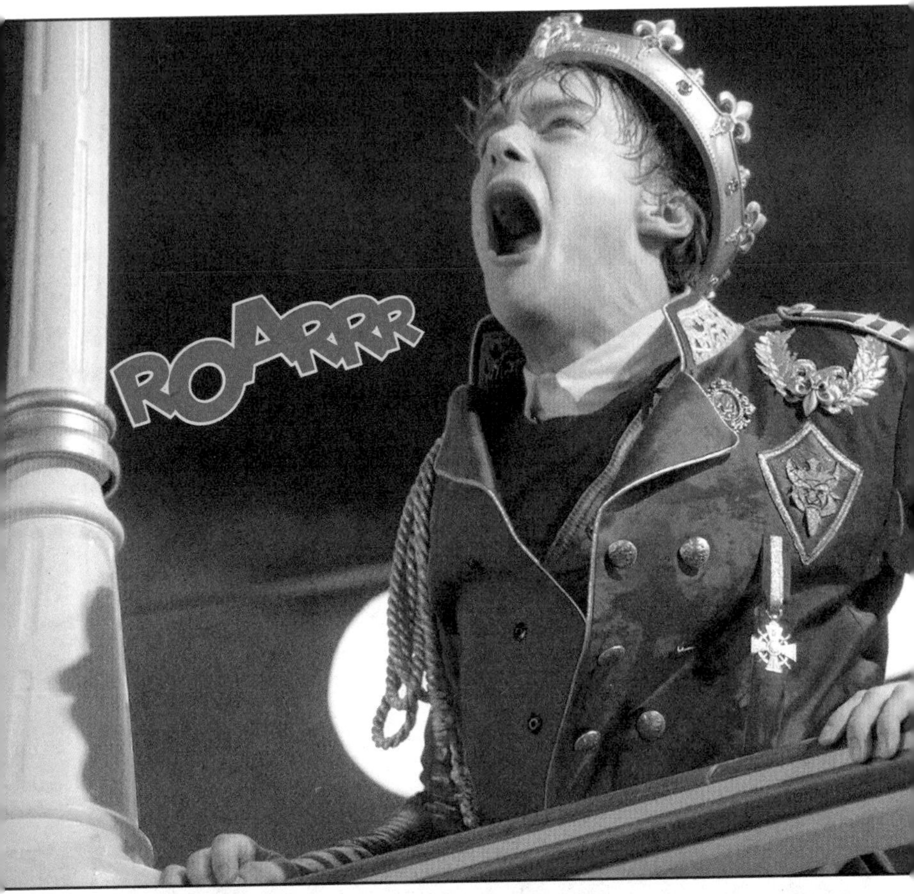
ROARRR

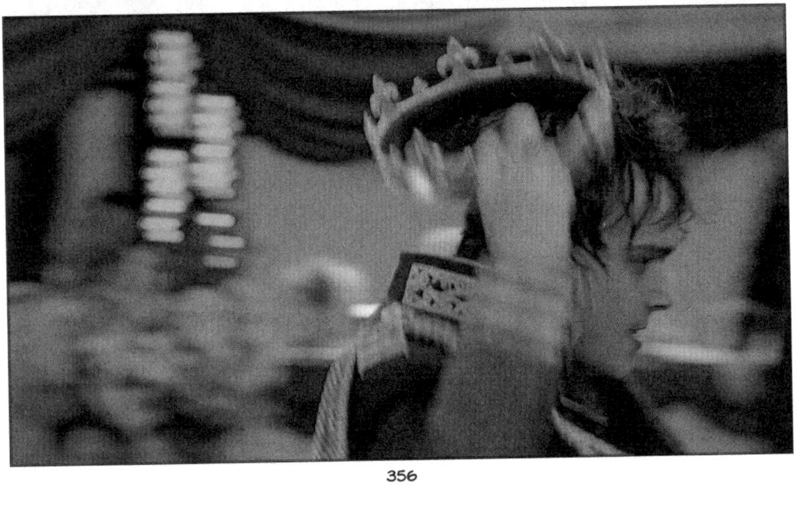

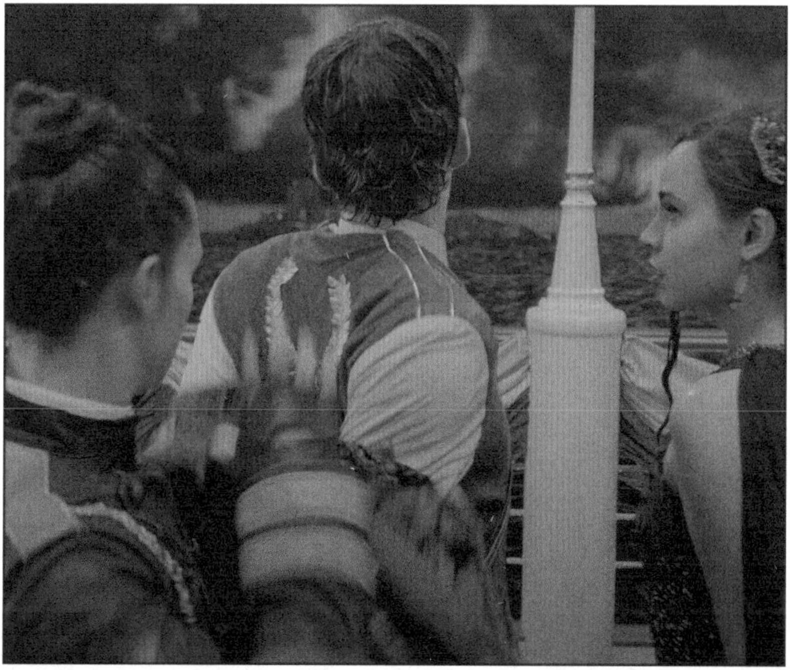

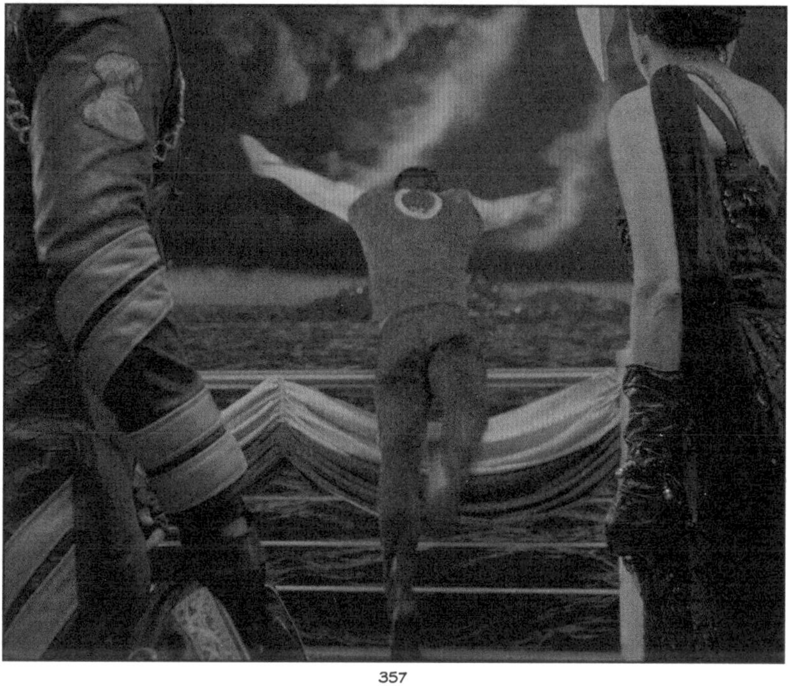

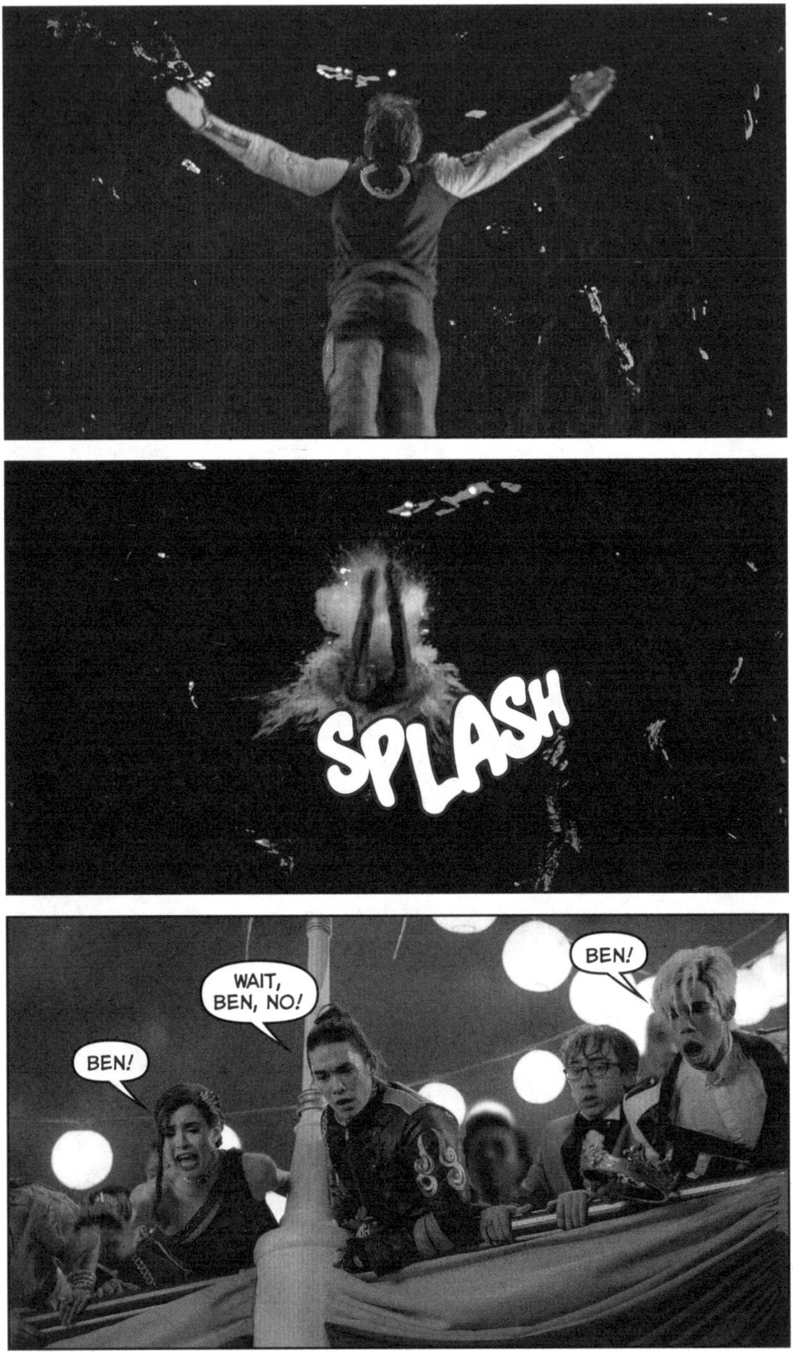
SPLASH
BEN!
WAIT, BEN, NO!
BEN!

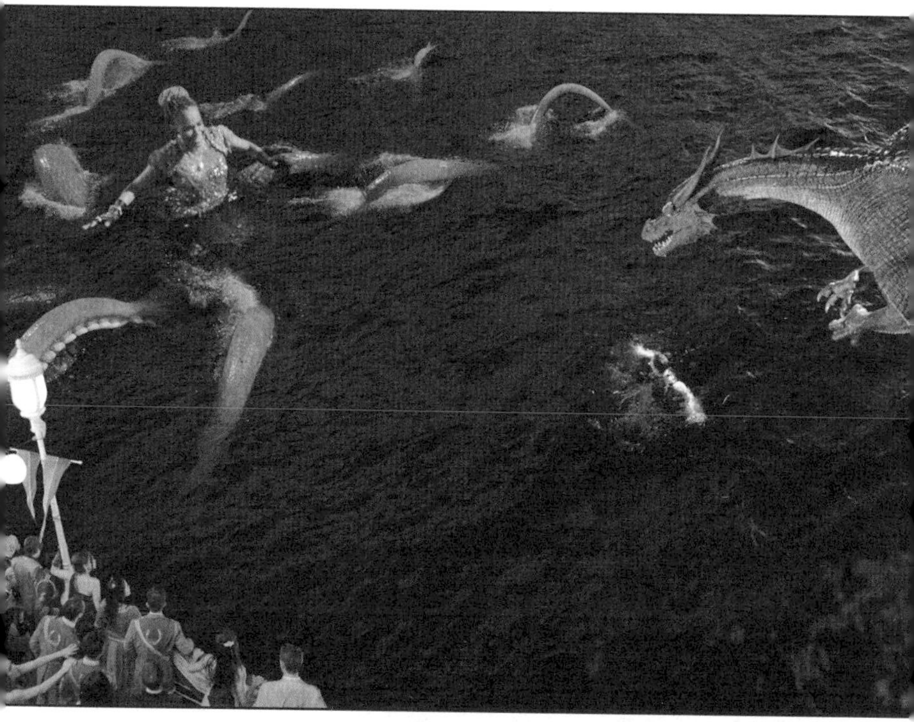

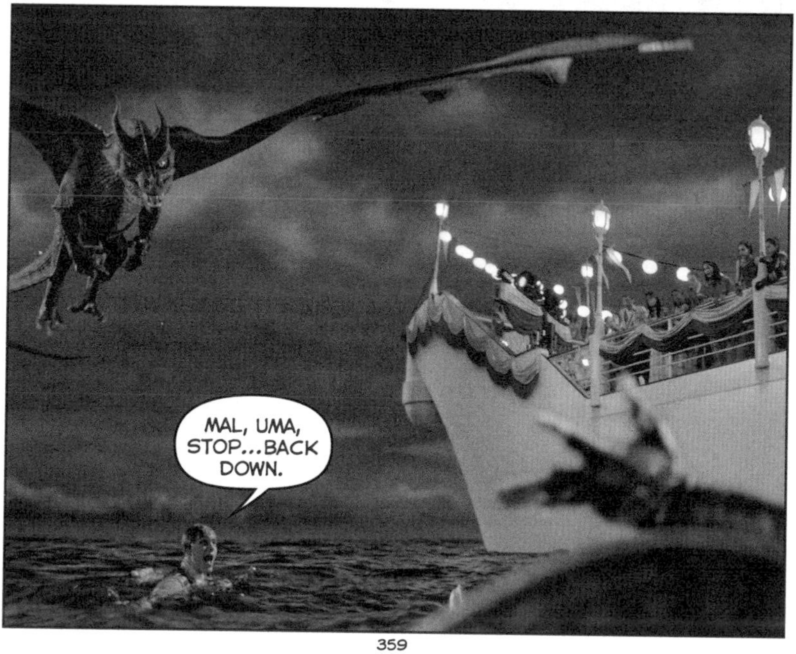
MAL, UMA, STOP...BACK DOWN.

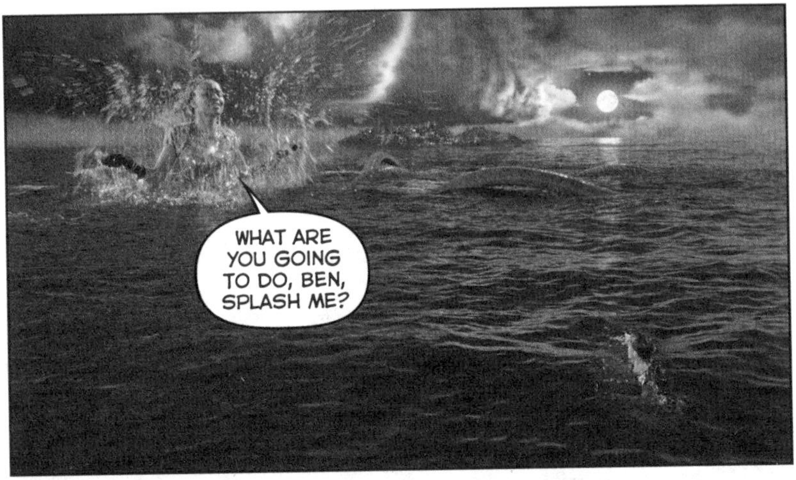
WHAT ARE YOU GOING TO DO, BEN, SPLASH ME?

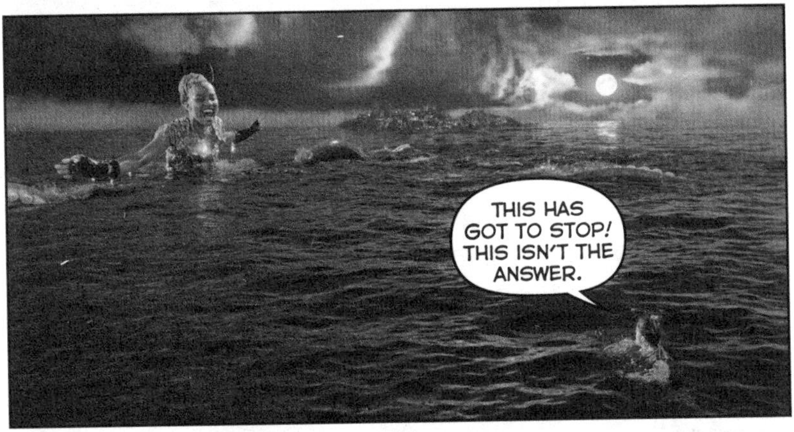
THIS HAS GOT TO STOP! THIS ISN'T THE ANSWER.

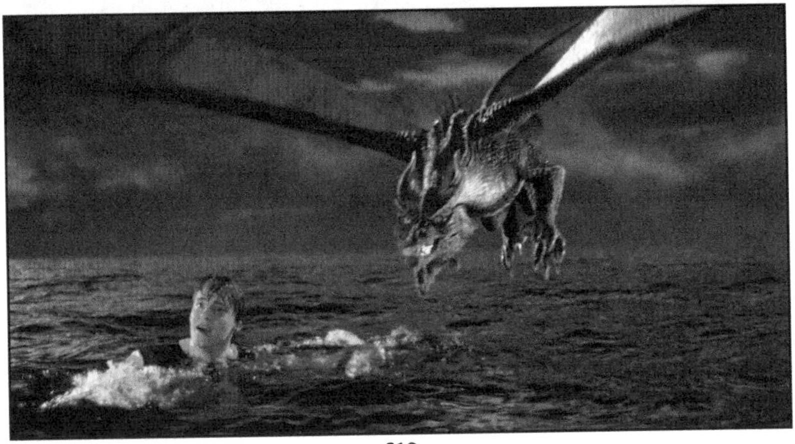

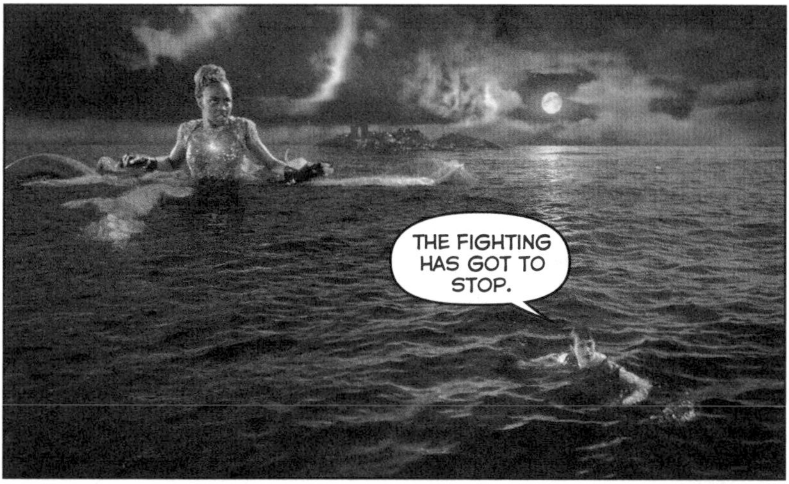
THE FIGHTING HAS GOT TO STOP.

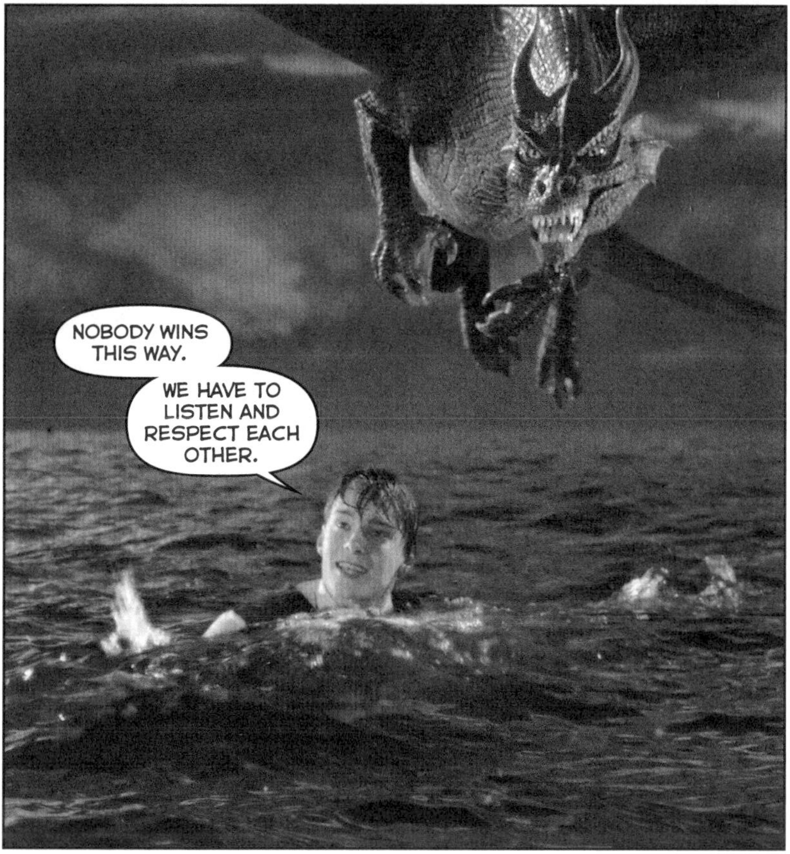
NOBODY WINS THIS WAY.
WE HAVE TO LISTEN AND RESPECT EACH OTHER.

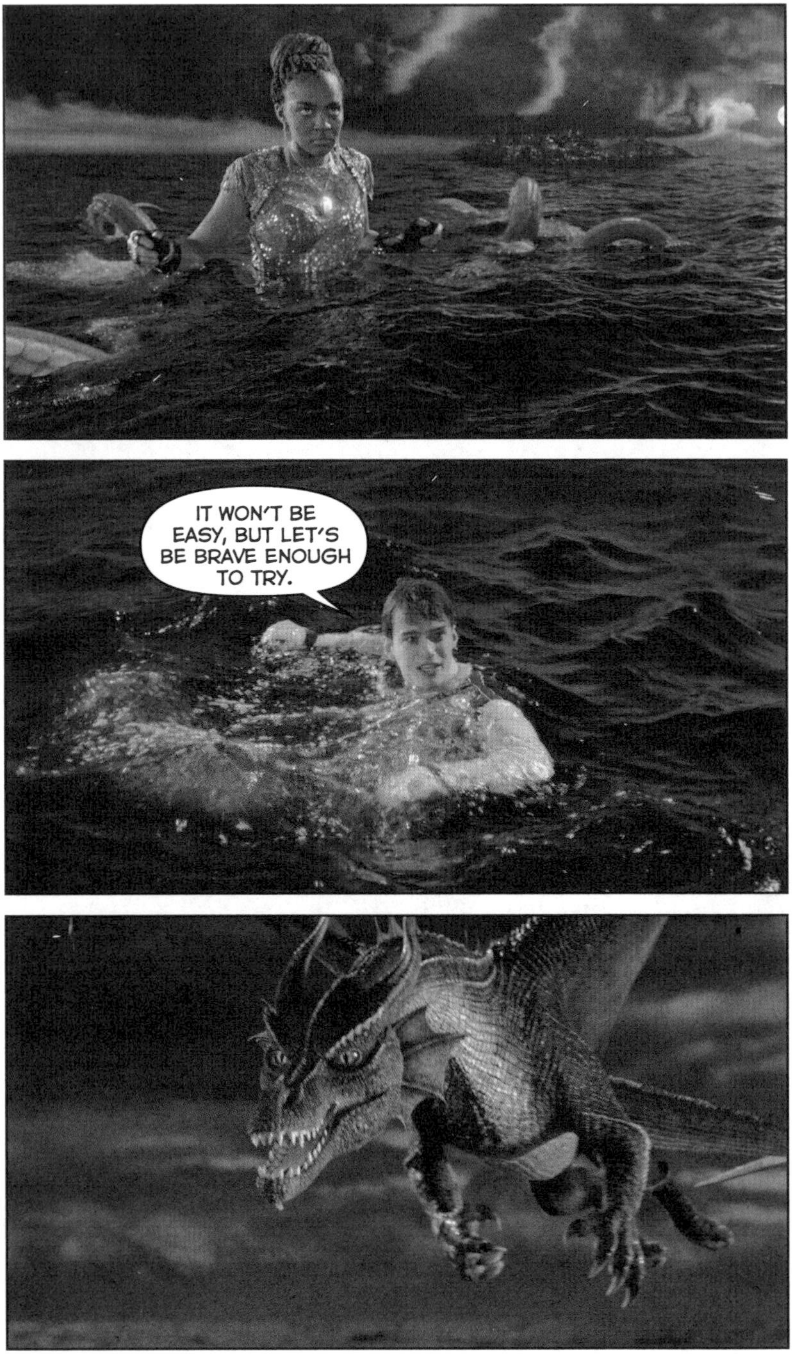
IT WON'T BE EASY, BUT LET'S BE BRAVE ENOUGH TO TRY.

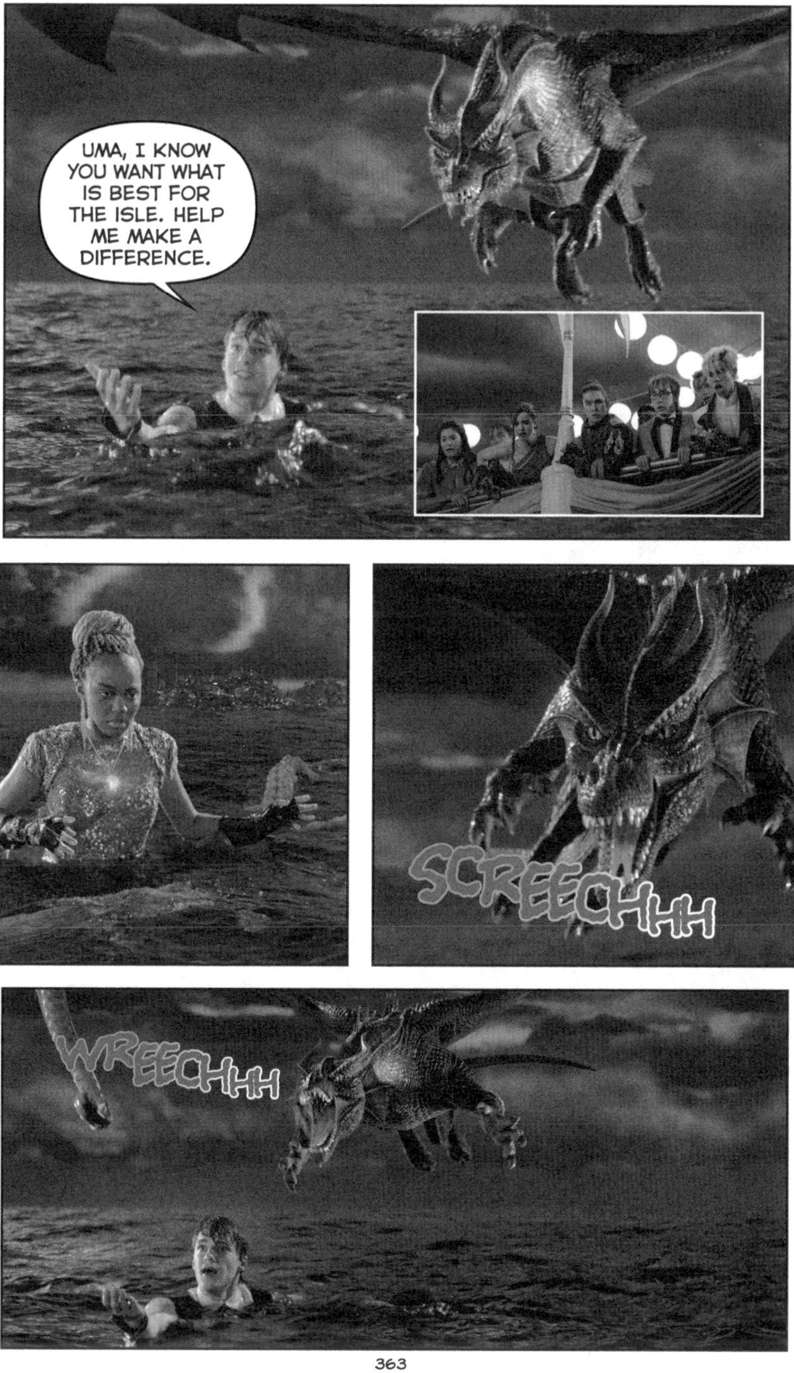

UMA, I KNOW YOU WANT WHAT IS BEST FOR THE ISLE. HELP ME MAKE A DIFFERENCE.
SCREEECHHH
WREEECHHH

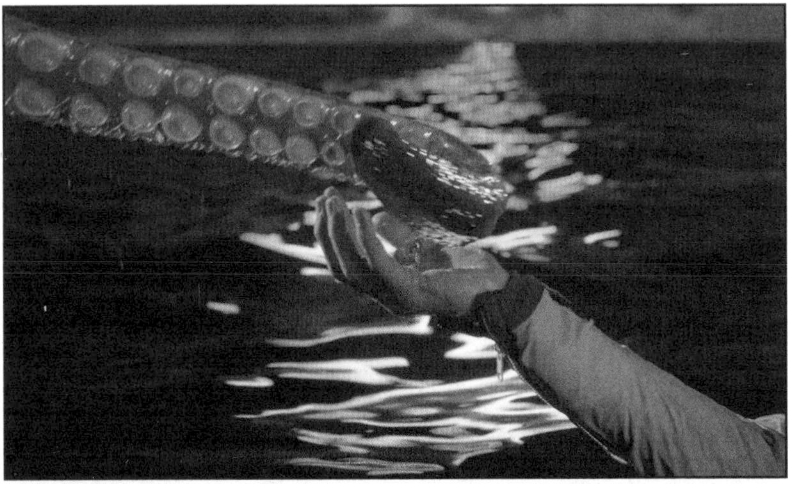

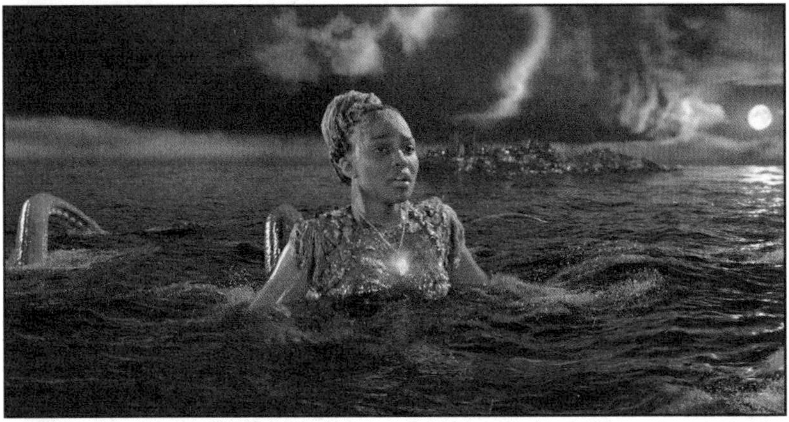

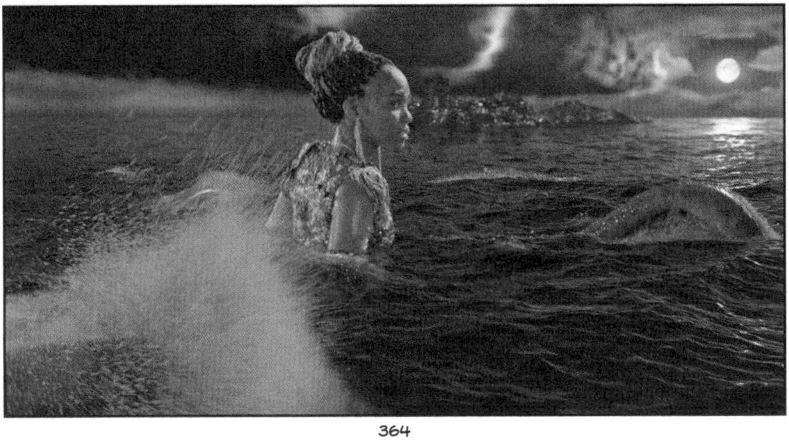

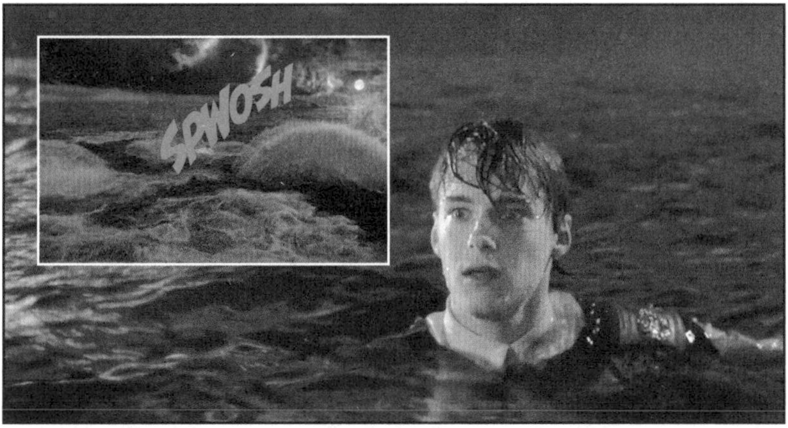
SPWOSH

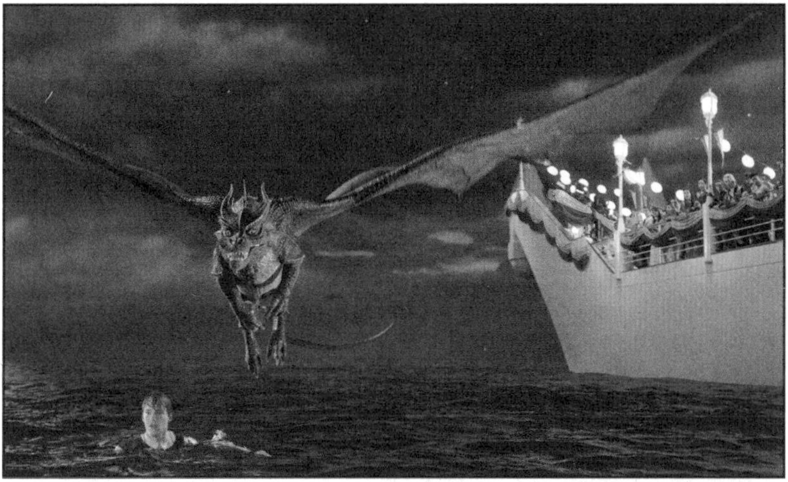

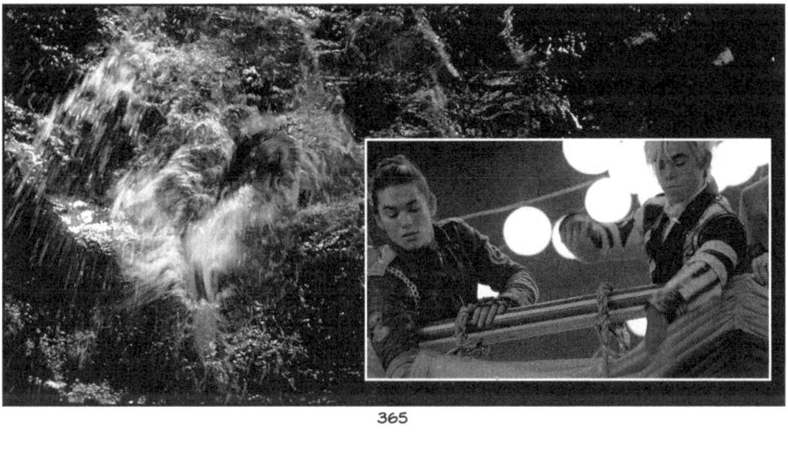

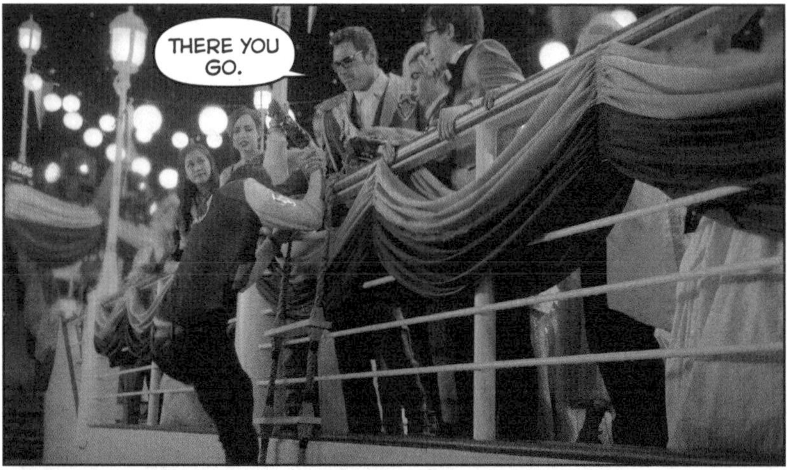
THERE YOU GO.

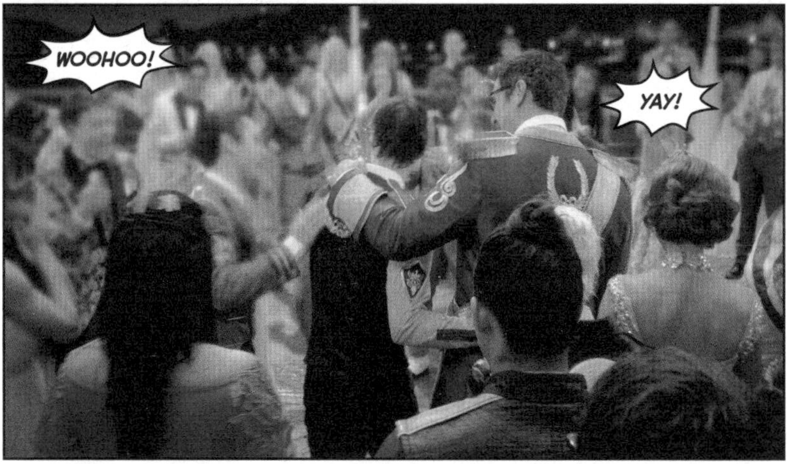
WOOHOO!
YAY!

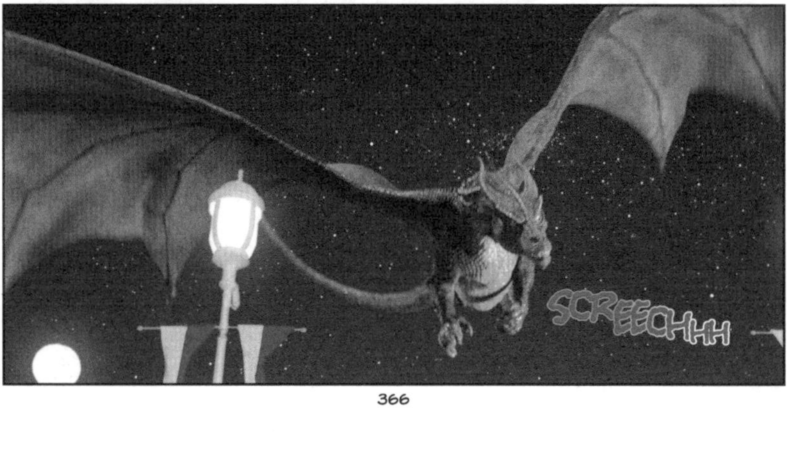
SCREECHHH

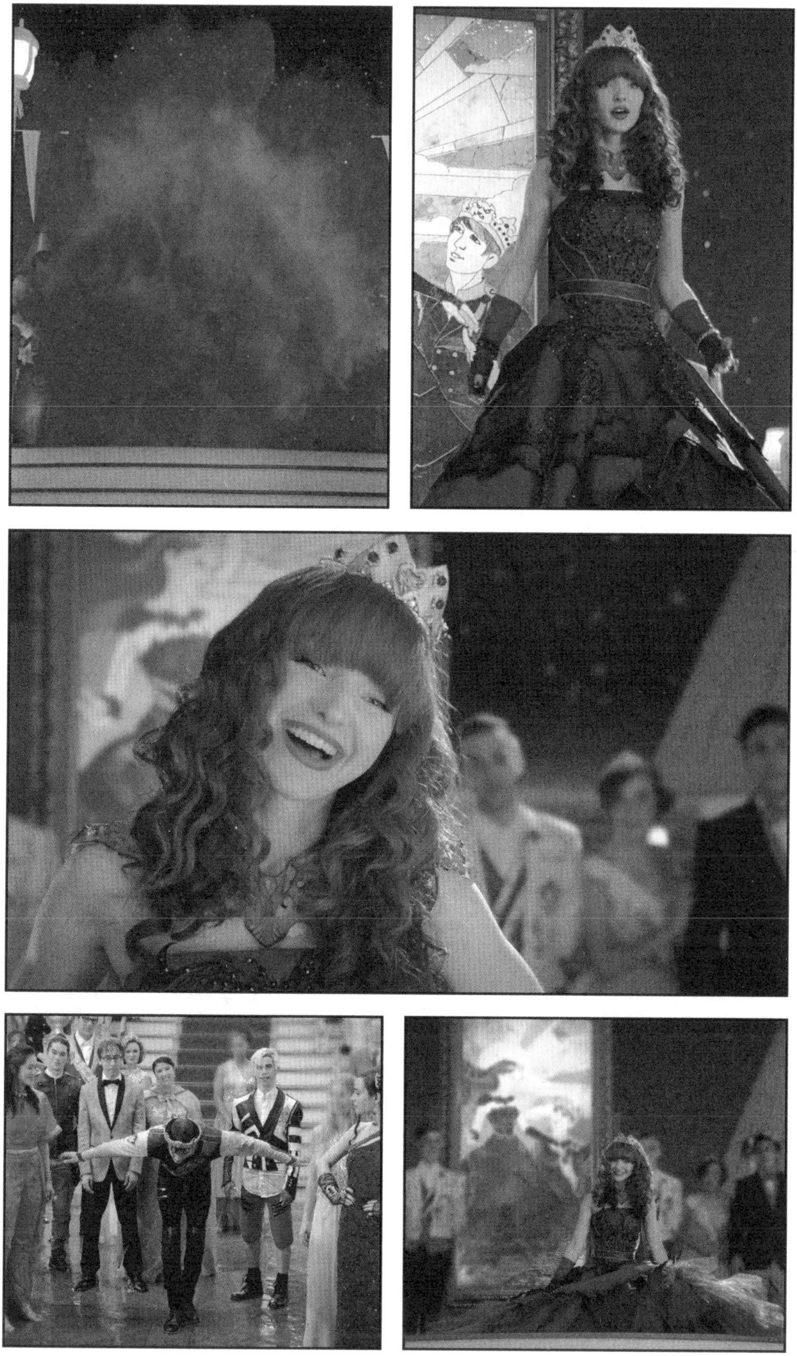

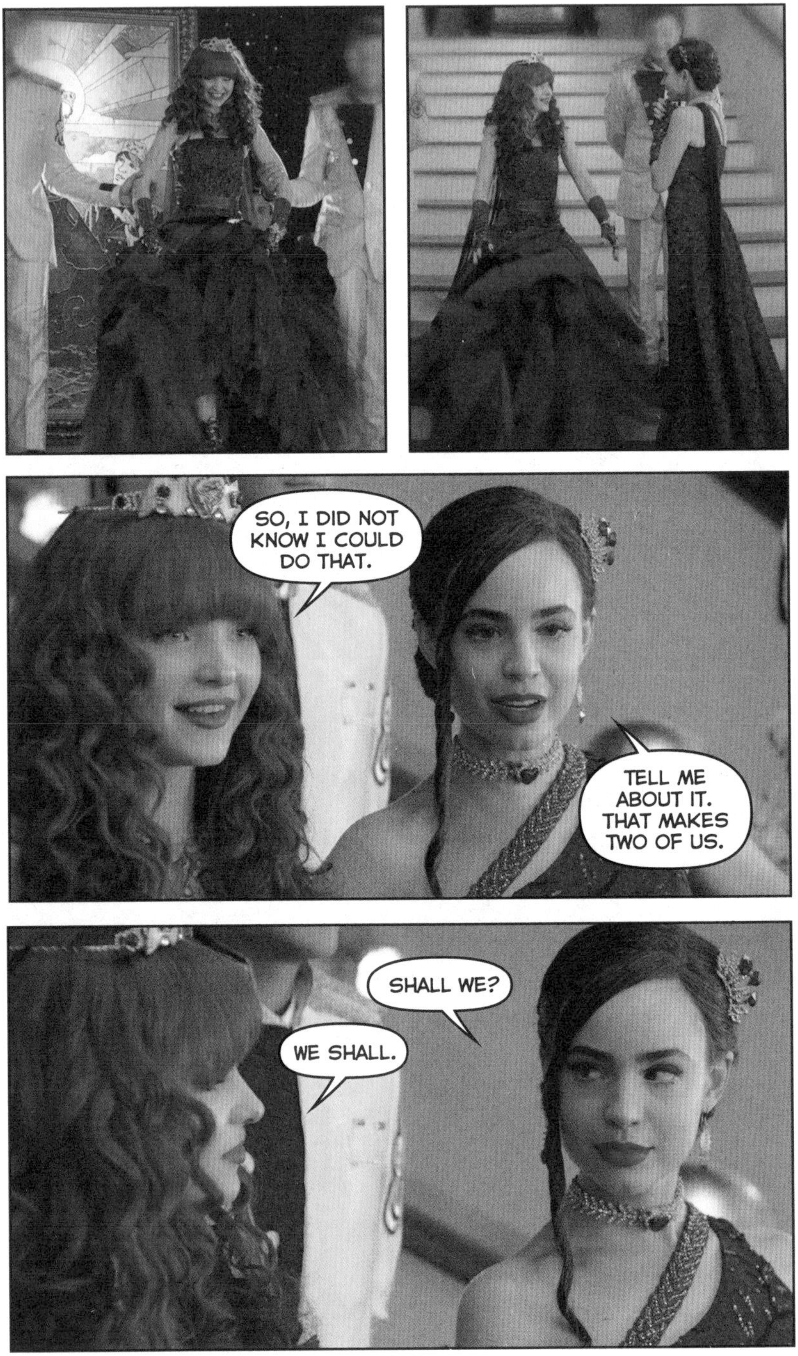
SO, I DID NOT KNOW I COULD DO THAT.
TELL ME ABOUT IT. THAT MAKES TWO OF US.
SHALL WE?
WE SHALL.

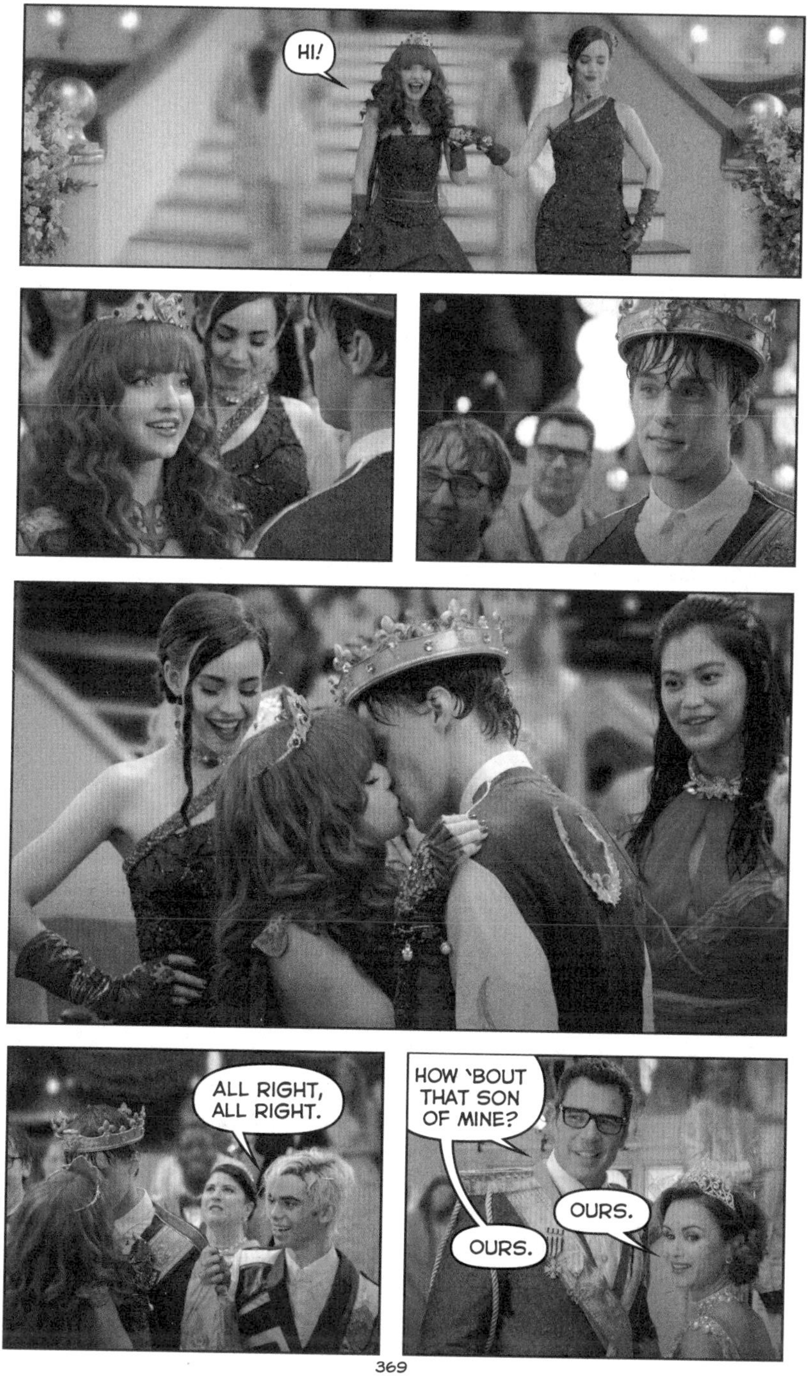
HI!
ALL RIGHT, ALL RIGHT.
HOW 'BOUT THAT SON OF MINE?
OURS.
OURS.

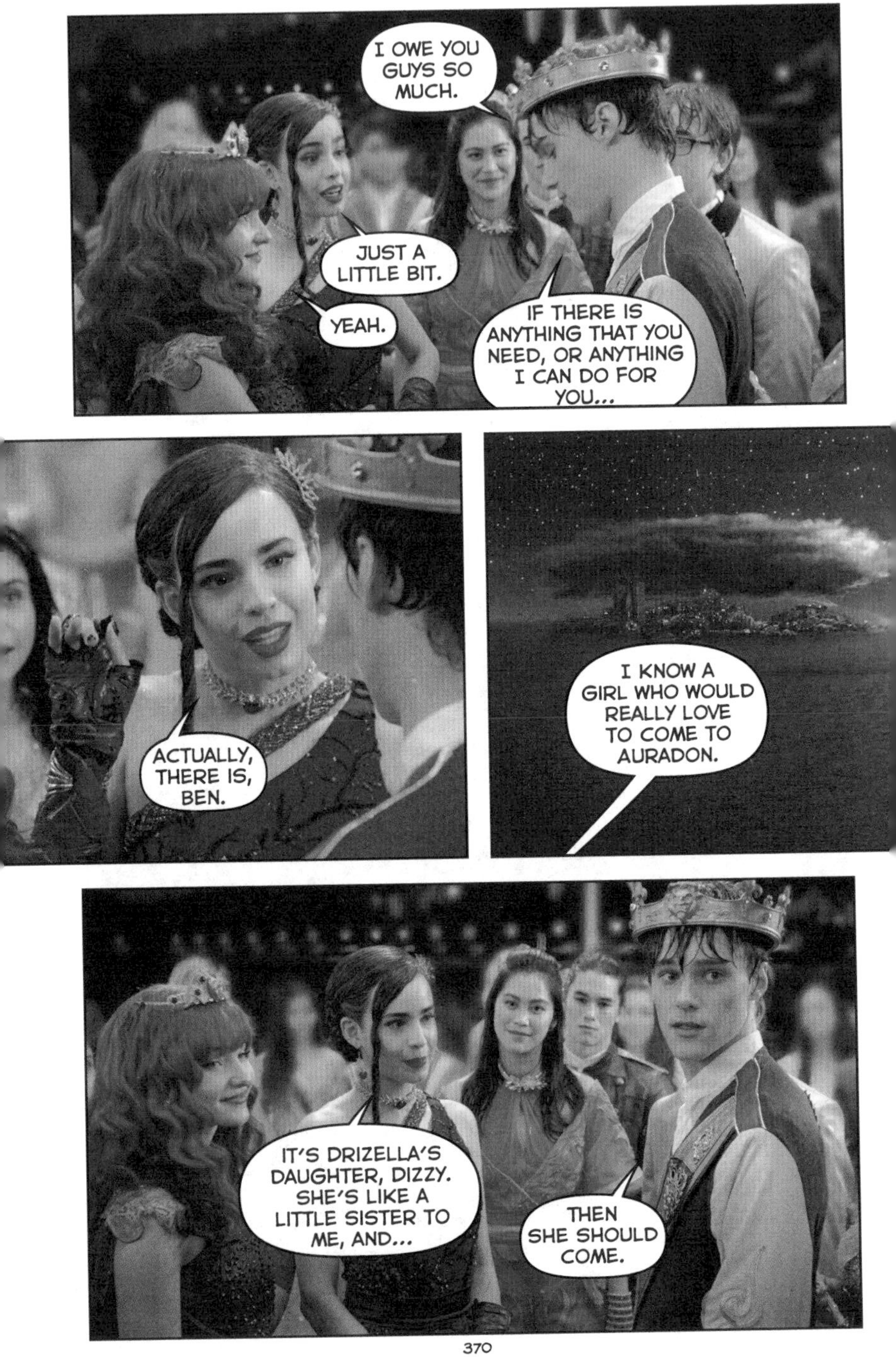
I OWE YOU GUYS SO MUCH.
JUST A LITTLE BIT.
YEAH.
IF THERE IS ANYTHING THAT YOU NEED, OR ANYTHING I CAN DO FOR YOU...
ACTUALLY, THERE IS, BEN.
I KNOW A GIRL WHO WOULD REALLY LOVE TO COME TO AURADON.
IT'S DRIZELLA'S DAUGHTER, DIZZY. SHE'S LIKE A LITTLE SISTER TO ME, AND...
THEN SHE SHOULD COME.

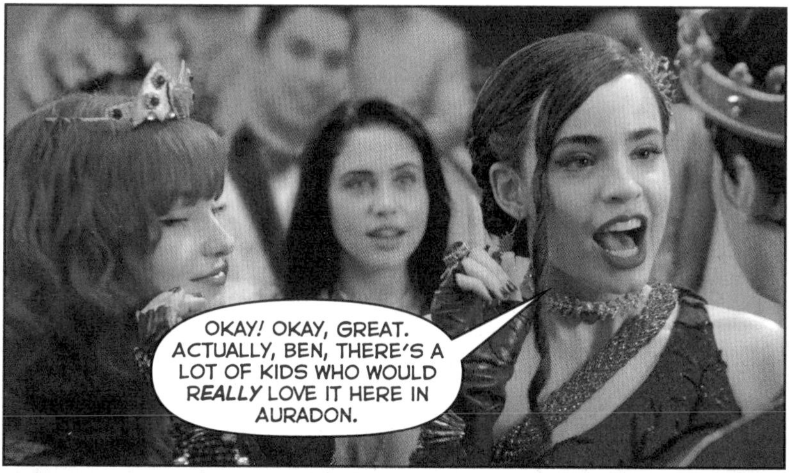
OKAY! OKAY, GREAT. ACTUALLY, BEN, THERE'S A LOT OF KIDS WHO WOULD *REALLY* LOVE IT HERE IN AURADON.

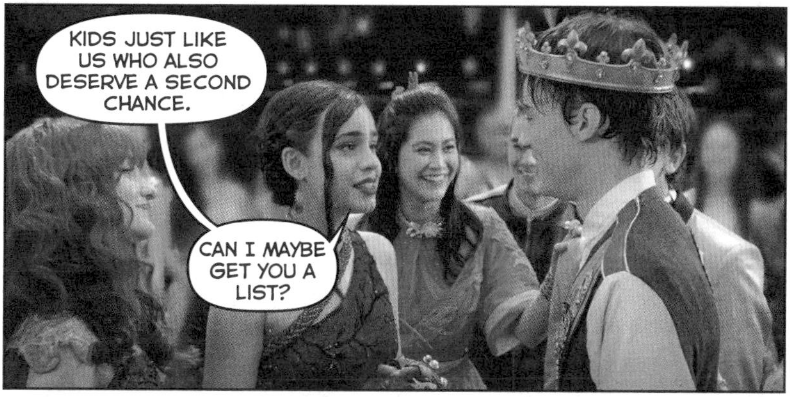
KIDS JUST LIKE US WHO ALSO DESERVE A SECOND CHANCE.
CAN I MAYBE GET YOU A LIST?

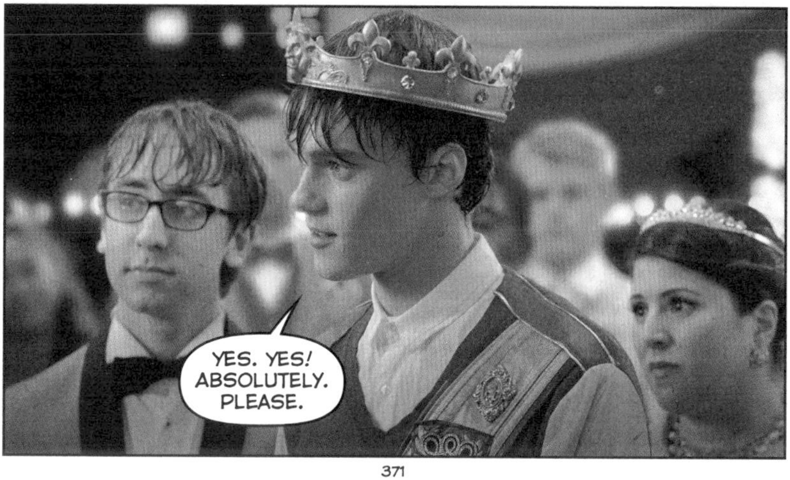
YES. YES! ABSOLUTELY. PLEASE.

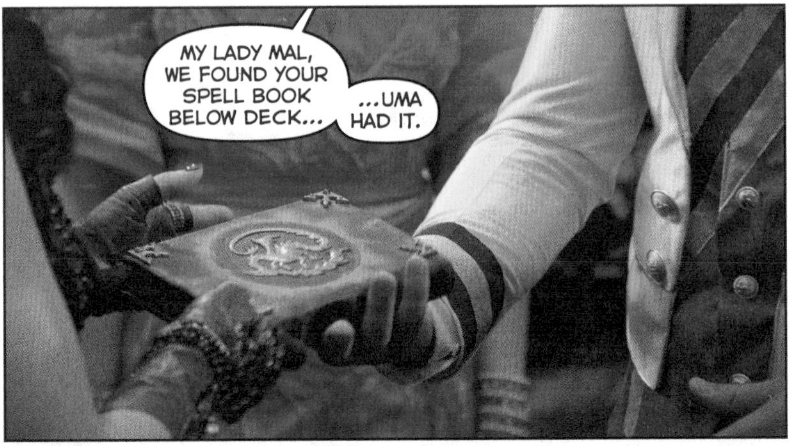
MY LADY MAL, WE FOUND YOUR SPELL BOOK BELOW DECK...
...UMA HAD IT.

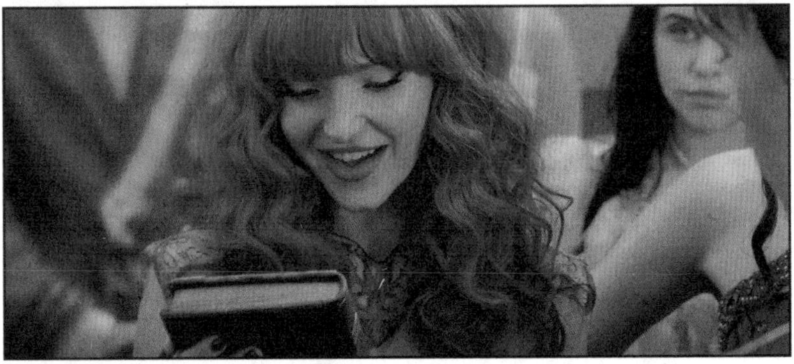

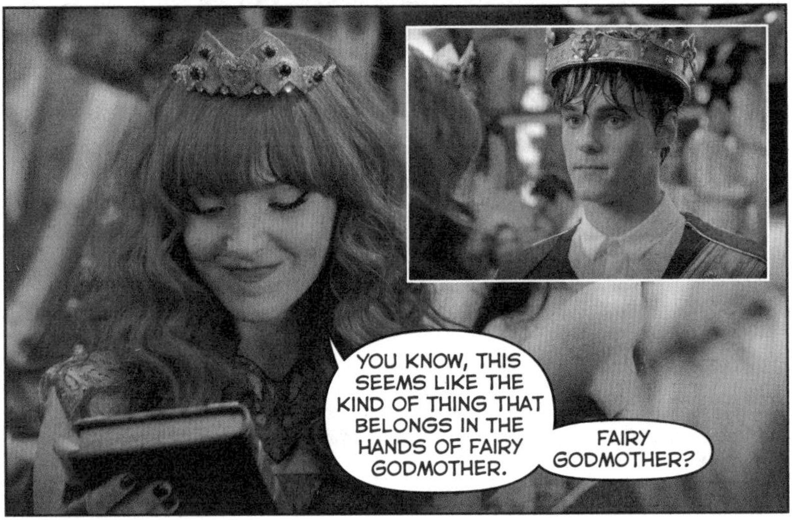
YOU KNOW, THIS SEEMS LIKE THE KIND OF THING THAT BELONGS IN THE HANDS OF FAIRY GODMOTHER.
FAIRY GODMOTHER?

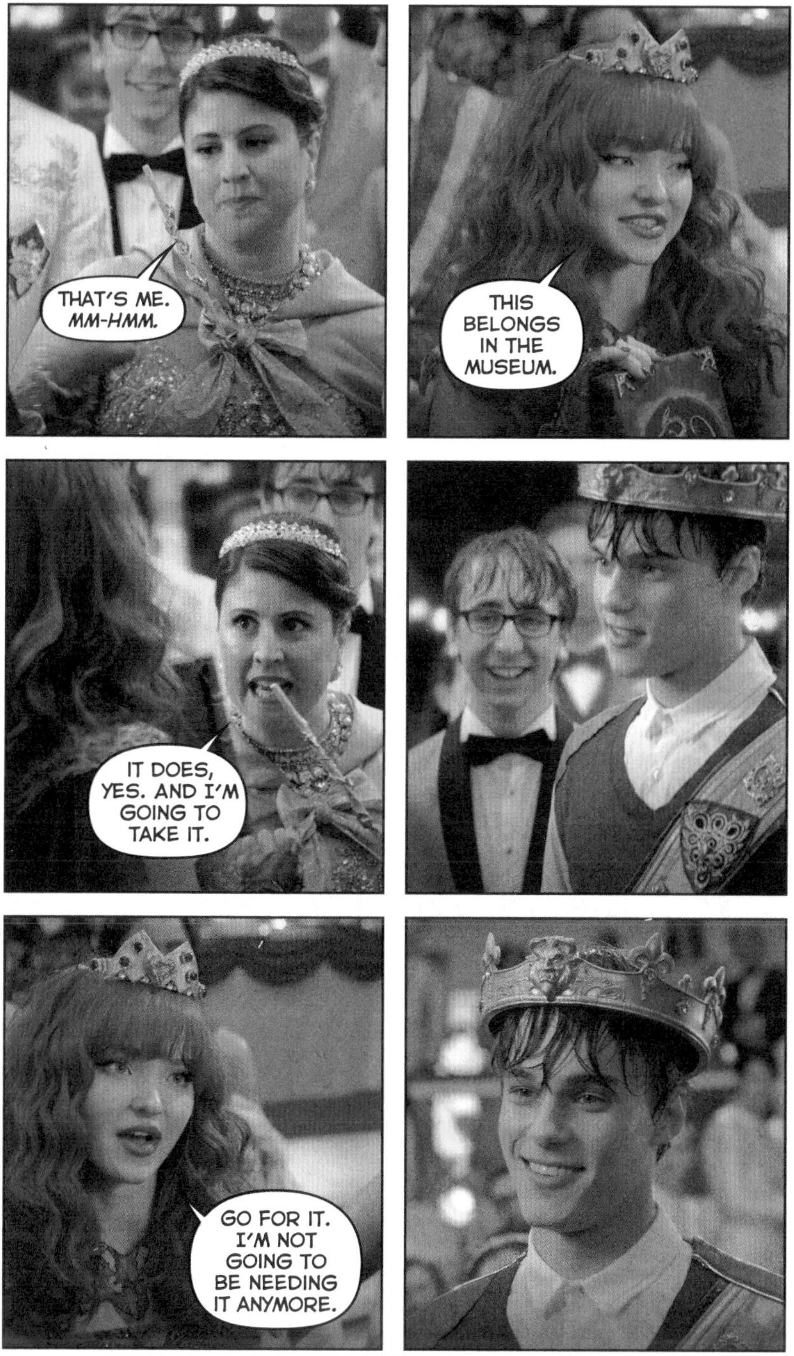
THAT'S ME. MM-HMM.
THIS BELONGS IN THE MUSEUM.
IT DOES, YES. AND I'M GOING TO TAKE IT.
GO FOR IT. I'M NOT GOING TO BE NEEDING IT ANYMORE.

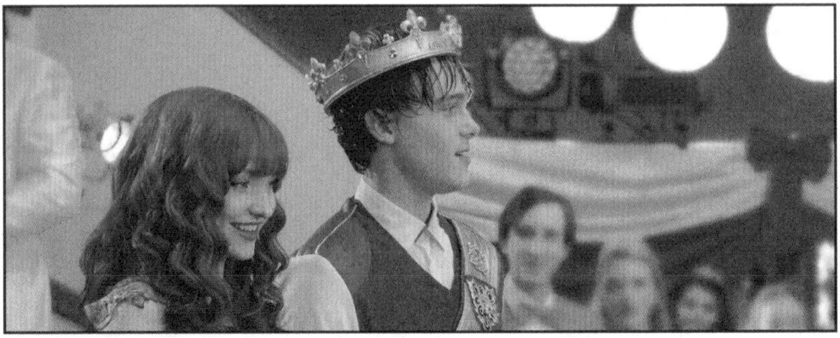
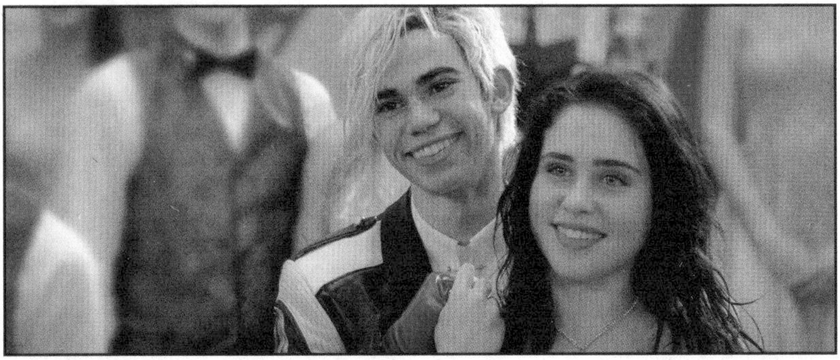
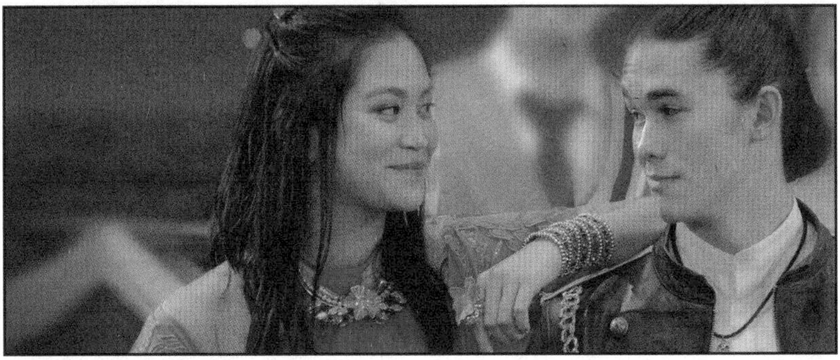
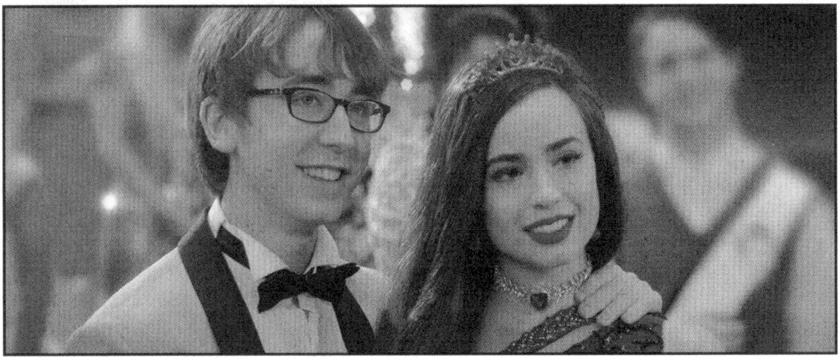

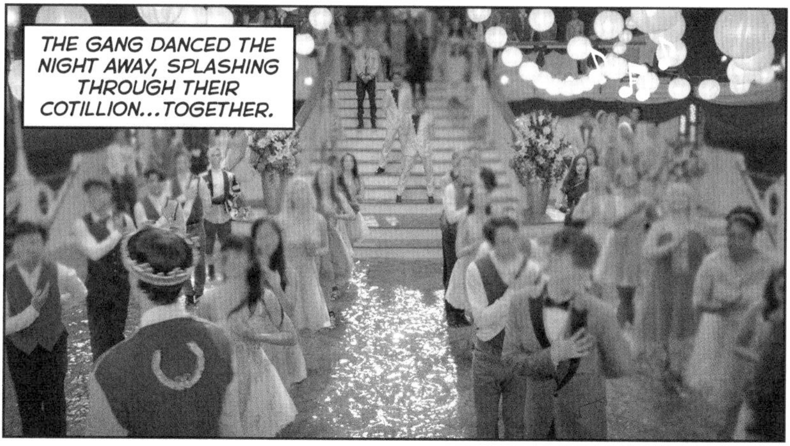
THE GANG DANCED THE NIGHT AWAY, SPLASHING THROUGH THEIR COTILLION...TOGETHER.

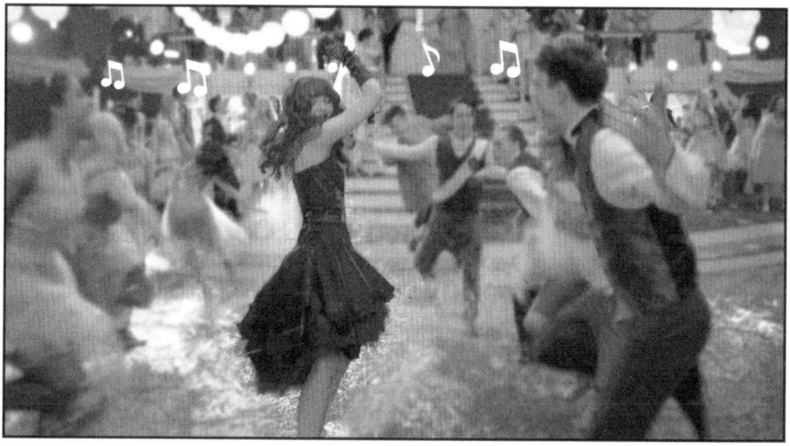

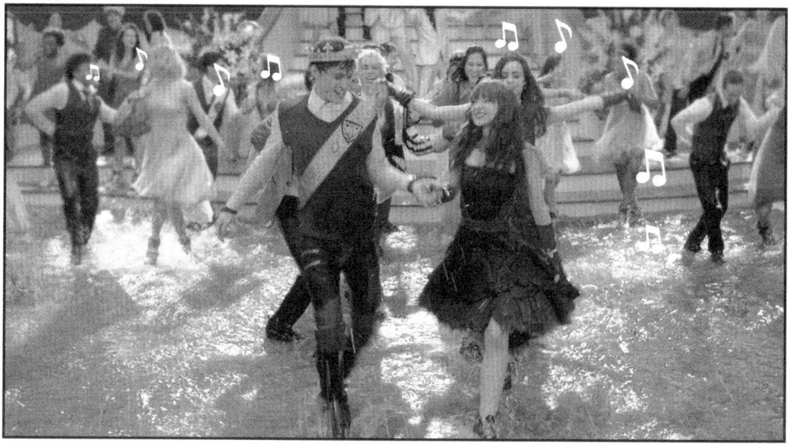

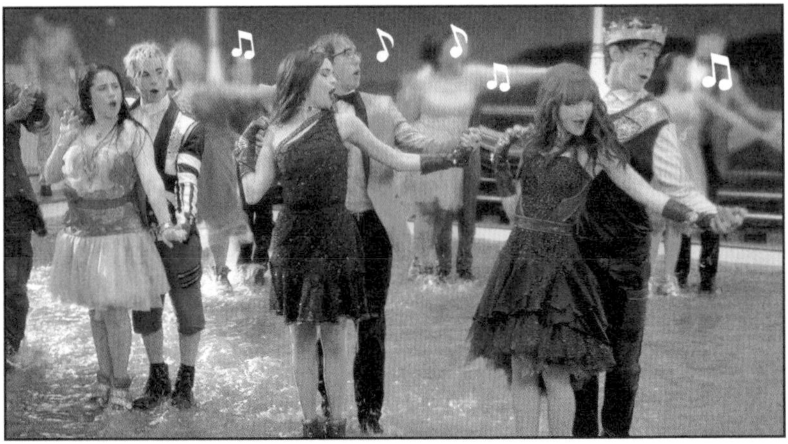

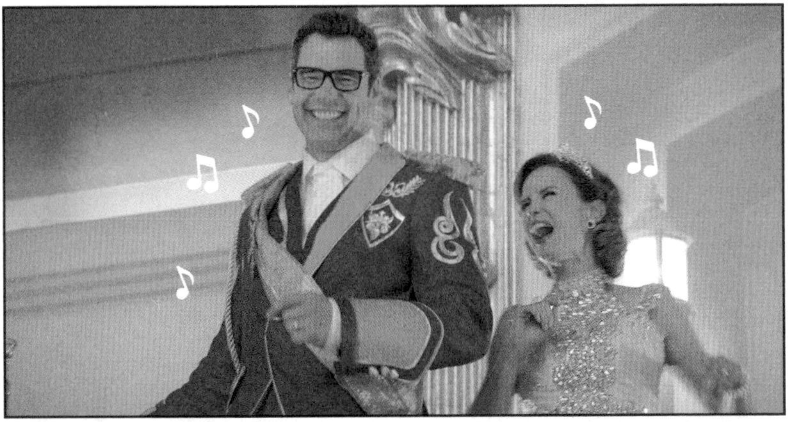

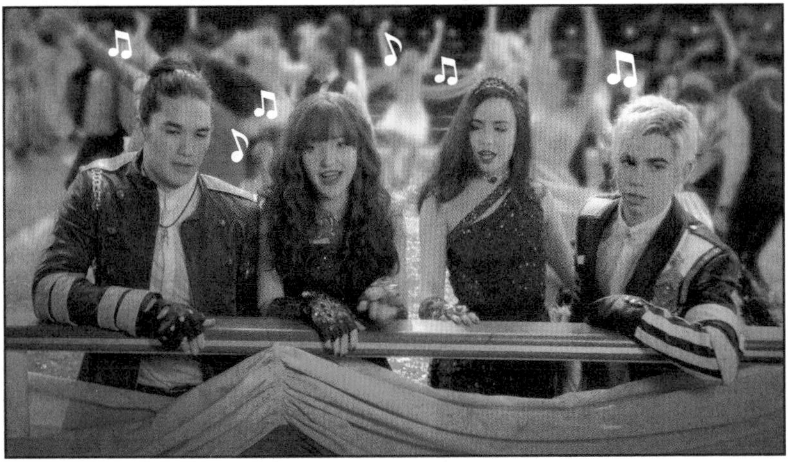

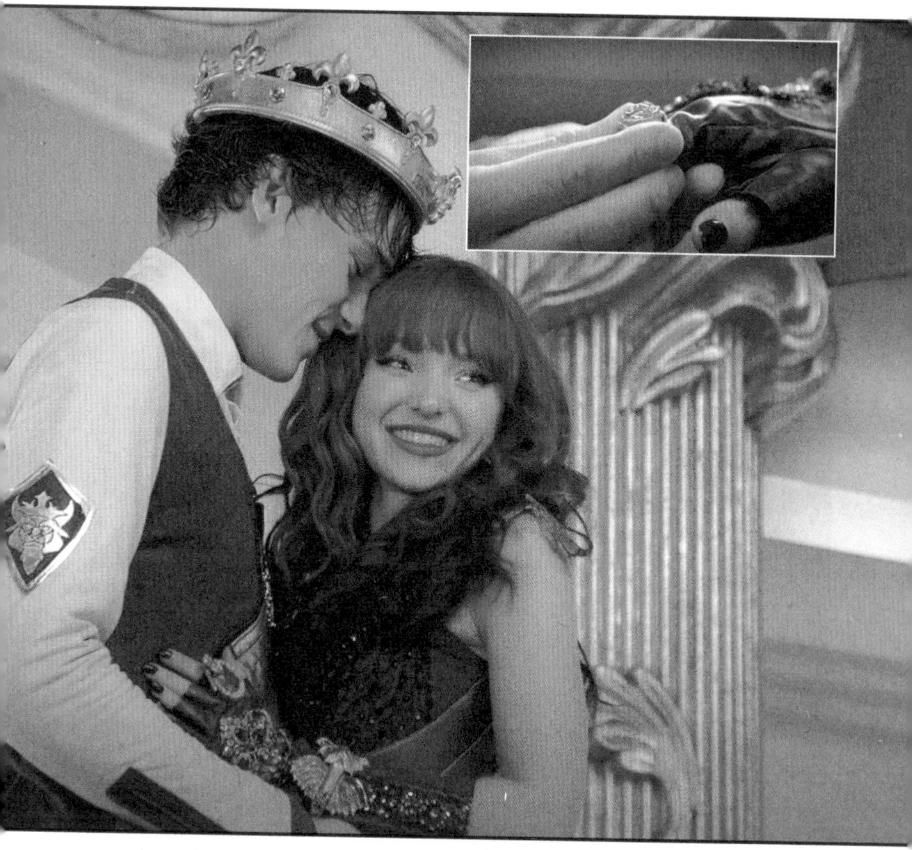

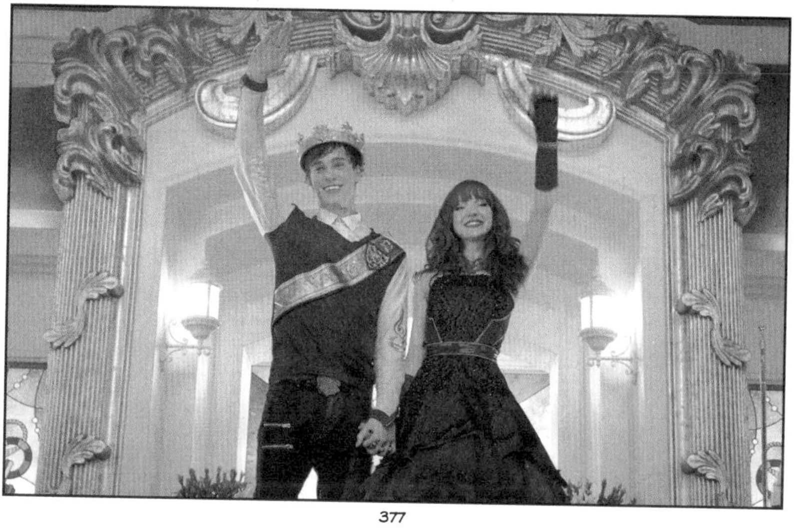

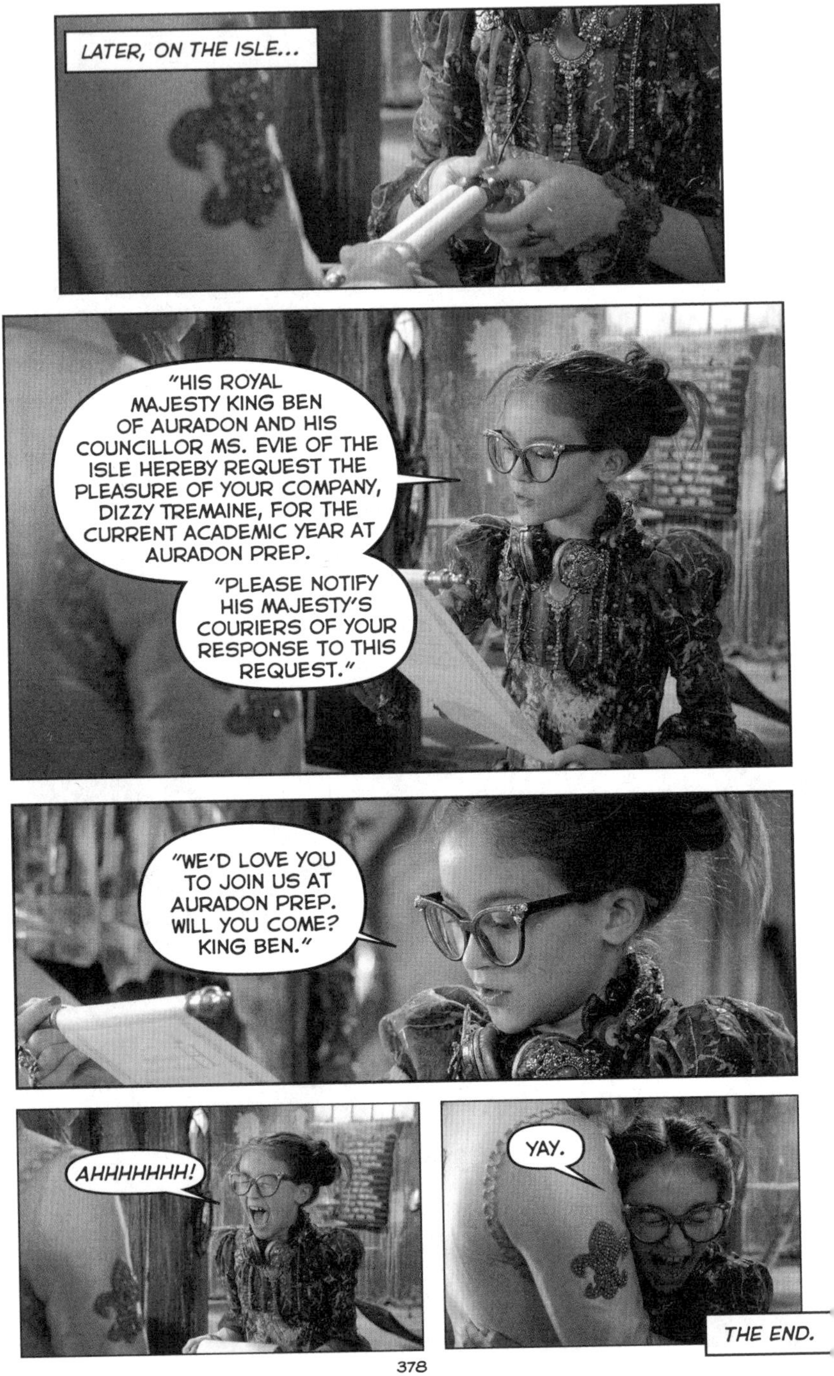
LATER, ON THE ISLE...
"HIS ROYAL MAJESTY KING BEN OF AURADON AND HIS COUNCILLOR MS. EVIE OF THE ISLE HEREBY REQUEST THE PLEASURE OF YOUR COMPANY, DIZZY TREMAINE, FOR THE CURRENT ACADEMIC YEAR AT AURADON PREP.
"PLEASE NOTIFY HIS MAJESTY'S COURIERS OF YOUR RESPONSE TO THIS REQUEST."
"WE'D LOVE YOU TO JOIN US AT AURADON PREP. WILL YOU COME? KING BEN."
AHHHHHHH!
YAY.
THE END.

Directed by
KENNY ORTEGA

Written by
SARA PARRIOTT
&
JOSANN McGIBBON

Executive Producer
KENNY ORTEGA

Executive Producer
WENDY JAPHET

Executive Producers
SARA PARRIOTT
&
JOSANN McGIBBON

Produced by
SHAWN WILLIAMSON